Keepers
of
Arden

The Brothers
Volume 3

L. K. Evans

Published by Unleashed LLC

Dedicated

To John. Life would be infinitely boring without you, and I wouldn't be half the person I am.

To Jason. You and your family got me through some tough times. I don't think you'll ever understand how much you helped me.

Thank you

Thank you to Michael Evans for my cover art. I hope this one was less stressful for you.

Recap

Dear Reader: This book is part of a series. I highly recommend reading Book 1 and 2 first.

Because it's been a year since Book 2 was published, I've provided a recap:

—Year 999 a.r.
Shadowfire creatures sweep through the town of Falar where they kill hundreds and impregnate Wilhelm Laybryth's mother, Ashra. One of the creatures tells Wilhelm the boy belongs to it and would do its bidding. After that night, he does not remember the shadowfires impregnating his mother, or their words to him.

—Year 1000 a.r.
Salvarias Laybryth is stillborn. Wilhelm touches his mark (a silhouetted bear) to his brother's (a black ring circling a black flame) and Salvarias comes to life. At that exact moment, a man robed in blood-red enters Wilhelm's home and encases Salvarias in a smoky, red light. Wilhelm drives the being away.

Salvarias's mind does not function like that of a newborn. It is that of a rapidly aging child, learning and processing the world at an inhuman rate. After a red foggy light descends upon him, he understands the brutality of humanity in a mere breath. At the same time, an evil implants itself in his soul, and he instantly feels it trying to take over. The battle to keep his own soul shielded from his evil begins.

God, the force behind a building darkness in Arden, is convinced that Salvarias's soul will grant him instant victory. He calls Salvarias a Guardian and Wilhelm a Protector. He would take the child, but the Guardian is the Protector's, and God cannot fight the Protector. Instead, he decides to send servants to watch the brothers, and plots ways with his own servant, Unupture, to turn Salvarias's soul toward God's cause.

Ashra, having remembered what impregnated her, is certain Salvarias is a demon. She despises the child and tries to kill it, but her uncle, Mafarias, stops her. She refuses to care for Salvarias, but Wilhelm takes up the task willingly, seemingly oblivious to Ashra's disgust. Salvarias never speaks to her or others. She assumes her youngest to be a mute. The brothers grow inseparable and closer each day.

—Year 1002 a.r.

Ashra passes by the guardhouse while delivering bread. A hanging is taking place and she sees Salvarias watching intently. When the criminal is dead, Salvarias seems satisfied, almost smiling. Upon leaving the scene, Salvarias breaks down into tears and a storm starts. Once Wilhelm calms his brother, the storm ceases and Ashra's suspicions that the child is something other than human begins to grow. On her way home, men who want to rid Arden of mages attack her and her sons in an alley. A city guard, Tobin, rescues her. Tobin is immediately taken with Ashra. The same night, Mafarias informs Ashra he is leaving the city and beseeches her to help rid Salvarias of an evil that lives within.

After three months of spending considerable time together, Tobin asks Ashra if he can take her sons to the guardhouse on the days she works. She agrees on the condition Salvarias stay with her alone on her day off.

The first day she is alone with Salvarias, she senses again something unholy about the child, and her fear overcomes her. She beats Salvarias in an attempt to drive the evil from him. She forces him to promise never to reveal his torment and threatens to separate the brothers if he does. Salvarias agrees.

Since his birth, Salvarias's evil has grown strong, but he is able to fight it. A voice talks to him in his mind: a presence, as he calls it. It keeps him grounded and forces him to see all his evil. He endures his mother's torment in hopes she can help rid him of the evil. He keeps her secret for fear of being separated from Wilhelm. He has also discovered that no other person, save his brother and mother, can touch him without causing him pain. In addition, he learns that he can sense animals' general emotions and thoughts, which later evolves into him being able to communicate with them.

—Years 1002-1005 a.r.

Wilhelm notices his brother has become more withdrawn and frightened of anyone other than Wilhelm. Salvarias continues to converse only with Wilhelm. When Wilhelm finds bruises covering his brother, Salvarias tells him he sneaks away from their mother when they visit the market. He says bullies beat him, but refuses to tell Wilhelm more. Ashra says she tries to stop Salvarias, but the boy will not listen.

—Year 1005 a.r.
Salvarias performs magic for the first time and is the youngest recorded mage in history. He meets with the Association of Mages who, after a threat from Mafarias, permits him to wear the robes and adds his name to the guards' lists of approved mages. Also in this year, Salvarias speaks to Tobin, though he continues to keep his mother's beatings secret.

—Year 1009 a.r.
Tobin proposes to Ashra and they are wed. Over the four years leading up to this, the beatings Salvarias suffers worsen, and he becomes more withdrawn. In this year, Wilhelm meets Lady Haleen and her bodyguard, Brenil. Haleen ushers Wilhelm into manhood, unbeknownst to all except Salvarias.

— Year 1010 a.r.
While picnicking in the Falar forest, Tobin gifts Salvarias a book with the inscription: *To My Son, Salvarias. May you forever remain curious and never change your pure heart. I will love you always. Tobin.* Tobin gives Wilhelm a broadsword, one that has been passed down generations. Salvarias calls Tobin "Father" for the first time and confesses his love to his father. Tobin returns the affection.

Upon returning toward Falar, the Laybryth family is attacked. Wilhelm is knocked unconscious in the fight and the family is overpowered. Tobin is tortured and left alive to watch as Ashra is raped and tortured by a man with yellow hair and a scar across his chin. After further torment from the others in the man's group, Ashra is burned alive at the stake. Salvarias witnesses it all. When his mother is aflame, Salvarias finds himself smiling, happy to be rid of her, of her beatings. Upon looking away, Salvarias is sickened by himself.

Tobin sees Salvarias's pleasure and withdraws his love. His last words, "You are no son of mine," are spoken before the yellow-haired man slits his throat. Upon their deaths, the presence within Salvarias tells him it is his fault. Without Wilhelm's comforts, Salvarias slips toward panic and a storm starts that kills all living creatures and plants, with the exception of people. A hand in his mind reaches out and takes Salvarias's mind and soul from him, saving him from madness. Wilhelm wakes to find his brother in some sort of shock.

Forced to leave their home, Wilhelm takes to the streets until the Loutsil knight and adopted brother of Tobin, Humar, helps Wilhelm obtain employment at the blacksmith run by a cavrul named Durak. Over the next year, the brothers live on the streets while saving their funds. During the year after their parents' murders, Salvarias never emerges from his shock.

—Year 1011 a.r.
Wilhelm visits their parents' gravesite outside the city of Serinity. A little girl with black hair finds them and touches Salvarias before running away. Upon her touch, Salvarias emerges from his shock. Though he does not remember or understand, Salvarias dreams that night of a little girl with raven hair. He dreams of her every night thereafter.

When the brothers return to Falar, a night raid of unholy creatures captures them, and the brothers are taken by octrils into the mountains and forced into slavery.

—Year 1011-1016 a.r.
During the next five years, the brothers are beaten and forced to mine in dark caves under the watchful eyes of octrils. Salvarias's magic has become more powerful and now speaks to him in his mind. Though untrusting of each other, their relationship begins to grow. Also, the dreams of the girl with raven hair have evolved from friendship into something more. He does not act on his feelings, even though he believes her to be a figment of his imagination.

—Year 1016 a.r.
Wilhelm and Salvarias escape slavery and return home to Falar and Durak. Upon their return, a mage, Dethal, is sent by God and

begins instructing Salvarias on his magic. Salvarias is unaware of God or his need to obtain Salvarias's soul.

For six months, Salvarias endures brutal training, keeping the beatings he suffers at the hands of Dethal a secret from his brother. However, time away from Wilhelm makes Salvarias realize he no longer wishes to be instructed by Dethal. He leaves Dethal a note and travels with his brother to visit their parents' grave. Upon arrival, they find a wolf pup waiting, and it joins Salvarias and Wilhelm. The wolf is named Adok. When Dethal receives the letter, he travels to the grave and kidnaps Salvarias.

In the city of Serinity, Lunara Bellerum, the young woman in Salvarias's dreams, is due to wed the ruling Lord Gunder against her will. The night before the wedding, she and her sister Varila run away at the instruction of their parents, Edium and Talura. That night, she learns the man in her dreams is real and in danger. Another dream instructs her to find and help him. The sisters travel to Falar and offer their assistance to Wilhelm, who looks familiar to Lunara; however, she cannot remember him, nor ever meeting the man in her dreams.

—Year 1017 a.r.
For the next year, Wilhelm, Adok, the sisters, Durak, and Humar search for Salvarias. They are joined by a half-erthla, half-winsire named Okulu who has known Humar for several years. The travels afford Wilhelm time with Varila, and the two become attracted to one another, though neither act upon their feelings save for a stolen kiss here and there.

During this time, Lunara confronts Salvarias in their dreams. He denies the possibility that she is real and their dreams cease. However, during Lunara's journey to find him, he speaks to her in her mind and warns her of danger. After obtaining information on where Salvarias is being held, her group sets off to rescue him. A mere few days' journey to his location, she begins to bleed from numerous wounds that Salvarias suffers. She discovers their connection is not only mental but physical as well.

Wilhelm, Humar, Durak, and Okulu rescue Salvarias from Zeeas and flee. During their flight, Salvarias nearly dies and is saved by a mysterious mage named Vuddruk, who appears from nowhere at just the right time. He refuses to answer questions.

Wilhelm and his group meet up with the sisters and take refuge in the city of Sundil. Salvarias is nursed back to health.

The torture and instruction Salvarias endured for an entire year at the hands of Dethal and a man named Sansis has grown his magic and coaxed a new oddity to the surface. Salvarias is plagued by visions of future events, and one such vision is of the city of Serinity in flames. Though he wants to travel alone, the group decides to go with him. He refuses to acknowledge his feelings for Lunara, afraid he would taint her purity and put her in danger. He also discovers that her touch does not cause him pain.

The group arrives in Serinity and saves it from an army of blackfurs. Lord Gunder dies in the attack and the sisters' father takes over ruling the city.

—Spring and Summer of 1018 a.r.

Salvarias receives another vision of an army camped in the southeastern part of Dalnar. Despite his arguments, his companions chose to accompany him on his quest to discover the army's purpose and a way to stop it.

Before departing, Lady Talura gifts Salvarias a black stallion named Mithal, and Wilhelm purchases Lilly. The two horses quickly become Salvarias's friends. Bellara, a servant in the Bellerum estate, gives Salvarias a necklace as a thank you for saving Serinity. Unknown to Salvarias, the necklace is a link to Unupture, a part klusher mix that can read minds.

Along the first part of their journey, the group comes across a winsire prince named Neithelas. He is on a mission to retrieve his brother, Arthias, who had ventured from the winsire city of Meitholias to hunt down the cause for the growing darkness spreading across Arden. The prince's path aligns with the group, and he joins them. Upon first meeting Lunara, the prince is infatuated with her.

In the city of Tripir, the group discovers "god" has sent patrols out to hunt them. During their stay, Unupture uses Salvarias's dreams to make his first attempt to discover Salvarias's secrets, to find out what can turn him toward God's cause. Salvarias is able to fight off Unupture's attempts. It is also in Tripir that Salvarias learns the mark on his left hand is indestructible. After cutting out his palm, it heals completely, not even leaving a scar.

Three days after leaving Tripir, the same men who killed Wilhelm and Salvarias's parents attack the group in the forest. Salvarias's anger and power manifests itself in black fire. It covers him, but does not burn anything but what he chooses. He burns his parents' murderer alive, much to the horror of his companions except Lunara, Okulu, and Wilhelm,

The power allows him to see the crimes of whomever he touches—to reenact them himself—but it muddies the acts until he thinks he is the one who killed people. The power also allows him to show the murderers the consequences of their actions, show them the pain of their victims, both physical and mental. Afterward, Salvarias finds himself in Oblivion. A fog that seems to be alive greets him and tells him he can sentence the murderers to eternal torment. Salvarias does. Once done, the acts of the murderers and the pain from all the victims stay with him, driving him near insanity. It evokes his storms, killing anything living save humans. Lunara helps him through it. The power terrifies Salvarias, and he does not want to use it ever again.

Days later, Unupture attempts to access Salvarias's memories. However, this time, the two carry on a conversation first, and Salvarias learns that Unupture does not love his master. Once again, Salvarias is able to fight off Unupture's efforts.

In the city of Hadium, the group meets up with two cavruls who promise them safe passage through the mountains. Humar agrees.

During the journey through the Cattlar Mountains, Salvarias learns that with help from the power within, he can enchant, something no other mage he knew of could do. With his magic's help, they begin testing enchantments on the aspen branch Wilhelm had gifted to Salvarias that helps him walk on his poorly healed broken leg. Before reaching their destination, Salvarias enchants the staff to light, to change temperature to help fight cold or heat, and to return to him at his call.

Unupture enters Salvarias's dreams again, but does not attempt to access Salvarias's mind. Instead, they talk and soon befriend one another. Salvarias is the first person who bothers to see Unupture's desire to be free of his master, to be a better person.

In the cavrul city of Catlin, the two cavruls leading them betray them. Dethal and Sansis arrive and capture the group. They bring with them a small army that slaughters the city and is set to invade Cattlar.

During the fight, Salvarias manages to wound Dethal, which gives Sansis the opportunity to betray his master, but not before they learn of Salvarias's visions and how he was able to thwart their attempt to take over Serinity.

Using barbarians from the desert, Sansis arranges safe passage for himself and Salvarias. The price is that the others in Salvarias's group be handed over to the barbarians as sport in their arena games. Ever since Zeeas, Sansis has been infatuated with Salvarias and his ability to endure torture. In Sansis's sick mind, he sees Salvarias as a son, the pain Sansis's inflicts as love. Sansis removes the necklace, which breaks Unupture's link to Salvarias. During one session inflicting pain upon Salvarias, he does permanent damage to Salvarias's heart.

Meanwhile, Edium and Talura Bellerum meet Mafarias, the brothers' uncle. Mafarias is trying to find Wilhelm and Salvarias, but Edium does not trust the mage. In Falar, Edium and Talura learn of their children's' capture from a merchant that escaped Catlin. Edium and Talura set off to rescue the group while Mafarias agrees to travel to Cattlar to warn them of a possible invasion.

When the barbarians arrive in their city, they betray Sansis and hold him captive for God. They put Wilhelm and Salvarias in the arena to fight for the barbarians entertainment. During the battle,

Salvarias and Wilhelm are wounded. Shadowfires stop time and infect Wilhelm with a power that allows him to win the fight and escape the city, alongside the companions and recently arrived Edium and Talura. They also find and rescue Neithelas's brother, Arthias, who'd been captured while wandering too close to the desert.

Meantime, God manages to rise The Four, cruel creatures created by Veedran during the logs wars. In the Stronghold where God resides, they are approached by a man name Perek who is identified as the Guardian. Unupture eavesdrops on their conversation and learns that they plan to set a trap for Salvarias. They will send the army to desecrate cities, and send Salvarias visions, both real and false, all driving him toward their trap set in Cattlar.

During the group's flight from the barbarian desert, they are trapped by a sandstorm but saved by Vuddruk, the same old mage that helped heal Salvarias outside Zeeas. Vuddruk takes them below ground to the buried, lost city of Quind. They spend time there recovering. One morning when they wake, Vuddruk is gone and a worm attacks the city. They barely escape. Salvarias has another vision of the army marching to a city and decimating it.

After escaping the desert, the group travels to the watythm city of Xeroth. While Edium and Humar enter to find help, the group remains outside. Watythms adore mages, and soon a group of children crowd around Salvarias. He cast spells to entertain them until only one girl remains, Thia. After she requests something new, Salvarias's magic tells him they have the power to create. However, since Salvarias fears his blackfire, his magic suggests they use his other power. When he cast the spell to create a field of new flowers, he feels the power's malicious intent. He tries to stop the spell, but it is too late. The plants bloom to life, but they evolve quickly and sprout poisonous thorns that kill Thia. Salvarias blames himself and his magic and refuses to use magic ever again.

Inside the city of Xeroth, the group meets with the ruling lord, Hyde. The watythm offers them a boat to take them to a bay close where the army had been camped. Hyde also discloses that

Wilhelm's father, Tedris, and cousin, Perek were looking for him and Salvarias.

They also learn Okulu was in love with Hyde's eldest daughter, Cessia.

The group arrives at the lake to find that indeed the army had marched on. They follow the trail to the city of Treppter where they find it in ruin. After a fruitless hunt for survivors, the group tracks the army to the city of Klurp, also burned to the ground.

Lunara tries to offer Salvarias comforts, but he pushes her away. He receives a vision of Cattlar consumed in flames.

When the group arrives in Cattlar, they find the city unharmed and meet up with Mafarias, who had no luck in convincing the cavrul clan leaders of a threat. Durak takes them into the inner city of Cattlar. There the group learns that Durak was a clan leader at one point until a mage murdered his wife, son, and daughter outside the city. After their deaths, Durak went on a killing spree, murdering any mage he came across. He stopped eventually and opened his smithy in Falar, but not before taking over one hundred innocent lives. He never found the mage responsible for his family's death.

During their stay, Talura confronts Salvarias about his mother's abuse and offers to listen and help him through it. He refuses her.

Salvarias receives a vision of turning himself over to the army hidden within caves near Cattlar. With his surrender, the army would leave Cattlar unharmed. He decides to do so. Humar catches him on his way to the army, but allows him to go. Wilhelm discovers his brother's missing and sets out to rescue him.

Salvarias walks into the trap set by The Four, willingly turning himself over. There he discovers the army is only half of what he originally saw. The other half is somewhere else.

The army marches upon Cattlar.

Wilhelm comes to Salvarias's rescue and kills Marrow, one of the Four. However, a group from the army sneak up and kill Wilhelm. Salvarias loses control. His blackfire erupts and kills every creature from the enemy army. His storm starts and the skies rain blood. In his grief, Salvarias unwittingly touches his brother's mark as he tries to kill himself, but the presence that saved him after his parents' murder reaches out and does so again. Unknown to

13

Salvarias, by touching Wilhelm's mark he brings his brother back from death at the same time the presence takes Salvarias to its hidden place.

Edium and Humar find the brothers and bring them back to Cattlar. Wilhelm is barely alive, and Salvarias is in the same trancelike state he was after his parents were murdered. One day, Lunara is visiting Salvarias and touches his mark. It retrieves the memory of their first meeting. She learns that the power that had brought Salvarias back had also allowed her inside Salvarias's mind. Too young to understand what she was doing, she linked her mind to his, her soul to his. Realizing it, she begs the power to undo what she had done, but it refuses. It brings Salvarias's from his trance again.

Awake now, Salvarias touches his mark to Wilhelm's and heals his brother.

Humar and Salvarias make amends, but Wilhelm does not trust Humar. To encourage Wilhelm to pursue Varila, Salvarias and Varila make a pack to be civil to one another in his presence. Salvarias tells Humar they must travel to the swamps in search of God.

Days later, a group of cavruls under orders of Marrow attack their group. Edium is mortally wounded. Alone with Edium, a power speaks to Salvarias and his blackfire heals Edium. Mafarias tells the group that by Salvarias doing so, he upset Balance, and She would make him pay.

Salvarias finally tells Lunara they are the closest of friends, though they cannot be anything more.

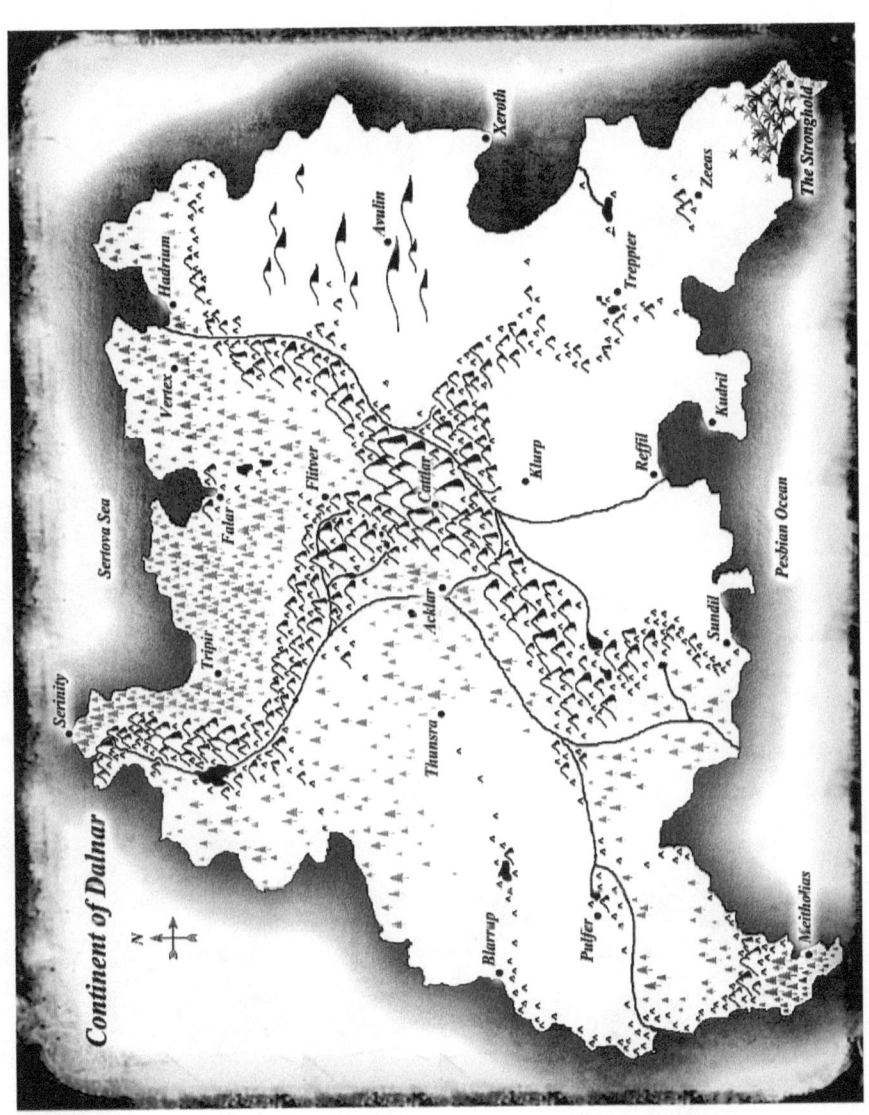

Continent of Dalnar

Chapter 1

Summer 1018 a.r.

If death sought Salvarias, he was certain it would use the air of the swamp to kill him. It hung as a tangible fog, humid and reeking of rotting flowers with such potency he tasted it on his tongue. His lungs struggled with it, causing waves of dizziness when he could not catch his breath.

The fog, combined with trees weeping fuzzy lichen and twisted vines, made visibility nearly impossible. The ground bled spoiled, slimy water that gave birth to a myriad of bloodsucking insects and hidden roots that leapt up and snagged Salvarias's ankles.

Salvarias and his companions would have died two days ago had he not tossed aside his need to shield his oddities. A reluctant snake now led the way to a stone fortress no sane creature visited. The swamp animals said those who entered did not leave, confirming his suspicions that Unupture and his master had occupied Dalnar's southern tip. Salvarias's anxiety and fear mingled together with a wild hope that this "god" would still be in the fortress, that Salvarias and his companions would finally have the opportunity to rid Arden of evil, that his good deed might outshine the darkness in his soul. Yet deep inside he knew the foolishness of his hope.

It isss foolisssh, the presence in his mind hissed. *You are doomed, my little murderer. And those who follow you share your fate.*

The presence might be right, as it had been since it first talked to him as a child, but Salvarias could not convince himself to leave his brother. He needed Wilhelm, so he ignored what he should have done and selfishly—as always—kept by his brother's side.

By the time Humar called for a rest, the haze had darkened, signaling sunset mere hours away. Salvarias plopped down on a semidry mound of moss. Sinking down beside him, Wilhelm ran a hand over his face.

"I never knew a body could sweat so much," Wilhelm muttered.

Salvarias lacked enough air to respond and took the time to drink another of his breathing potions. It helped little to ease his constricted lungs. All his life he had never had the pleasure of a lung filled with precious air. He was always wheezing in breaths past the anvil resting on his chest.

In a desperate attempt to shift his mind from pain, he added leaves from a nearby tree to the things he had been counting. He was up to counting six different objects, and while he never lost track, his mind continued to wander from thought to thought. Not for the first time in his life, he wished his mind would quiet to that of a normal person.

Studying Okulu and Humar, Salvarias pondered how they had survived the past two days wearing their full suits of armor. Both looked pasty white and drank more than their fair share of water, but refused to remove the metal. Even Wilhelm had chosen to keep covered, though his leather armor seemed more bearable.

As if Salvarias's guilt was not already overflowing for subjecting Humar and Wilhelm to the swamps, Durak, Okulu, the Bellerum sisters and their parents, and even Neithelas had insisted on accompanying Salvarias on his quest.

Lunara had wilted in the heat, her peach dress sucked against her sweating body, and her raven hair clung to her pale face. Though Neithelas had not fared better, he had supported her through their journey and now eased her to the ground next to her sister. Varila's wealth of blonde hair had frizzed to an obnoxious volume that Lunara tried to tame daily by rebraiding it. Lady Talura Bellerum seemed as durable as her oldest daughter. Despite being clearly exhausted, they handled the heat better than the others. Lord Edium Bellerum and Durak walked naked from the waist up. Luckily, Salvarias had planned ahead and purchased herbs to help offend mosquitoes, which spared the two lords eaten torsos.

Arthias had been the only one sane enough not to accompany Salvarias. The firstborn heir to Meitholias had returned home to gather his winsire army and march across the southern portion of Dalnar to rid her of Veedran's leftover creatures. Lord Bellerum had foolishly left his army in the hands of Commander Brice, son to the recently deceased Commander Unbril. The young commander was of sound mind with a keen eye for military tactics, but Salvarias suspected him too inexperienced and very much doubted Lord Bellerum's decision. It was the first careless move Salvarias had seen the lord make.

Also remaining behind were their horses and the wolf Adok, seeing how none would survive the swamps. Despite Lord Bellerum's assurances that the horses and wolf would be escorted to Falar while being provided with the utmost care, Salvarias feared for his animal friends and was eager to be reunited.

Lady Talura drifted from person to person, ensuring all had water and bread before she came to Salvarias and knelt by his side.

"Let's have a look," she said.

Salvarias took a calming breath before he lifted the hem of his burgundy mage robes. Tonight, a meager six leeches fed on his legs.

"Hold still," Lady Talura murmured as she wedged a stick under one of the leeches, slowly prying until it released on its own accord.

For a heart-stopping breath, creatures covered his naked body, each sucking his blood, slowly writhing over him like a live, hungry blanket as his mother watched. Closing his eyes, Salvarias focused on Wilhelm's hand resting on his shoulder, squeezing reassuringly, and under his breath, Salvarias repeated, "It is not real," until the image went away.

Before he knew it, Lady Talura said, "All done. I wish I'd brought enough fabric to sew you trews or at least something like what Lunara and I are wearing." She ran a hand around her ankle and the hose covering her legs, and glanced around as if fabric would materialize at her request. When it did not, she sighed and shook her head. "They'll drain you dry before we make it to Crutar's fortress."

"Speaking of," Humar called, "how far are we?"

The green-and-yellow-striped snake slithered into Salvarias's lap and wrapped around his wrist. "Mere hours," Salvarias responded as he passed along his thanks to the snake.

"I don't feel like spending another night in this forsaken swamp," Humar said, running a hand through his sweat-soaked, mousy-brown hair. "I'd rather face Veedran himself. We'll rest a little longer, but I want to make it there tonight."

Salvarias wholly agreed, and no one argued Humar's decision.

The crocodile that had been following them for hours pressed closer, its hunger making it dare Salvarias's threats. Without Adok by his side, Salvarias was forced to monitor their surroundings constantly and had failed the previous night at keeping track of a boa. It had snuck into camp and nearly strangled Durak before the cavrul gained enough breath to belt out a cry for help. Though Salvarias hated killing any creature for merely satiating its need for food, he could not allow one of his companions to die.

With a wave toward the creature and a nod to his brother, he sentenced the crocodile to death. Wilhelm rose, drawing his great sword, and crept close to the murky water's edge. Ripples gave away the crocodile's location. Before Wilhelm even raised his sword, an arrow whistled through the air and landed with a thud in the water. Salvarias averted his eyes and swallowed the lump in his throat; the crocodile's last image of its babies hovered in front of him long after the crocodile's presence faded. The green water stained red with blood, and the lifeless creature floated to the surface.

Neithelas sank next to Lunara, not bothering to retrieve his arrow.

Humar did not allow them long to rest. Before Salvarias caught his breath, they were walking.

The next few hours were a blur of misery. Weakened by the landscape, Salvarias's strained mind erupted into an excruciating headache that made him nauseous. Wilhelm took to carrying Lunara to not only keep her safe but to save her from heat stroke. She hung like a starved flower in his arms.

Just when Salvarias worried one more step would be his death, the thick foliage parted way to reveal the stone fortress. With his anticipation boiling over for the past few days, the end result was anticlimactic. He was expecting a towering fortress, climbing upward beyond the stars to the home of the old gods. He had assumed there would still be creatures patrolling, foul beasts from the depths of Oblivion. He had been certain evil would seep into his skin upon gazing at the home of such a horrific creature as this "god." Instead, nondescript stone steps leading to double wooden doors greeted him. The structure must have been no higher than three or four stories, was windowless, and looked more like a wall than a fortress. Plants had overrun it, covering it in lush green moss and snaking vines. Benevolent as the fortress might appear, the stark silence gave a feeling of foreboding. Salvarias could not sense any living animal nearby save for their guide.

The snake leading them caressed Salvarias's leg before gliding away into the fog.

"Something's not right," Durak muttered. "This looks abandoned. Ye dull-knight, ye've led us to nothing."

"Salvarias assumed 'god' left already," Humar said. "Perhaps he was right."

"After all this torment, I would rather hope something awaited us," Neithelas said, leaning against a thin tree. In response to the winsire, the tree's sickly trunk puffed up, stiffening to support Neithelas's weight, branches seeming to shift to offer additional comfort. Neithelas sighed contently, patting the trunk as if in thanks. "I'd hate to think this was all in vain."

Okulu chuckled softly. "That's the spirit."

"Suggestions?" Humar asked.

"I say we go in," Okulu said.

Humar frowned. "Could be a trap."

Okulu stroked his goatee, green eyes sparkling with mischief. "It's not a trap if we think it's a trap."

"Merc's got a point." One corner of Wilhelm's mouth turned up in a crooked grin. "There's no chance of finding out what awaits us unless we go in. And I'd rather be in there than out here."

Salvarias nodded his agreement and leaned heavily on his staff. The aspen branch was cool in his hand, a product of one of his enchantments, but it did little to dispel the heat flogging him. Nevertheless, the simple branch was a comfort as always.

"Edium, Durak, bring up the rear," Humar said. "Talura, Varila, and Neithelas, keep Lunara close. Wilhelm and Okulu, you're in front."

Okulu's friendly smile vanished, and he muttered under his breath as he drew his sword. Humar fell in line next to Salvarias behind Okulu and Wilhelm.

At the doors, Okulu motioned to Wilhelm. "You first."

Wilhelm studied an eye-level pink flower with a mint-green filament sharp as a knife. "Why me?" he asked absently.

"Because if you get an arrow stuck in that thick skull of yours, your crafty little brother can bring you back from the dead," Okulu snapped.

"Dying isn't fun, trust me," Wilhelm said.

"No, you mean *temporarily* dying isn't fun. I can guarantee the permanent version is far less entertaining. Now, get in there before I tell Varila what a coward you're being."

"I think she'd approve of my caution," Wilhelm said, full lopsided grin emerging.

"Enough," Humar scolded. "Go, Wilhelm."

Okulu winked triumphantly. "You heard our fearless leader. You first, ogre."

Wilhelm rested a hand on the door and gave a gentle push. Wood creaked and the squeak of rusty hinges set Salvarias's teeth on edge. Wincing at the harsh noise, Wilhelm threw his shoulder against the door. It ground open and Salvarias's breath caught in his throat. Sprawling beyond was a stronghold that surpassed what his wildest imagination could concoct.

What they had thought was the fortress was merely a trick. Instead of a squat castle, a wall had been devoured by vegetation the farther it ventured from the doors. From their perch, they had a clear view of the valley below and the true fortress of the swamp. Indeed, it climbed to ridiculous heights. Covered in moss, it stretched across the valley, and from their vantage point, its mass was humbling.

"Rumors are that Veedran built this," Lunara said from behind, startling Salvarias. He looked over to see her wide eyes gazing at the valley. "Only one man has escaped the swamps. He managed to write a book before he spat up blood and perished a week after he was found outside Treppter. He said Veedran gifted this to the gods who helped him defeat Zerana. Veedran knew no army could venture into the swamps, and he added unholy creatures to cause sickness to those who managed a way. I had thought the tales were false, but clearly, they were not. No man could build such a thing in these conditions."

"Still no patrols, guards ... nothing," Durak growled. "Me tell you, something's not right."

"We don't have a choice," Humar said, motioning to stone steps leading to the valley floor. "Let's go."

The stairs were slimy and treacherously steep. Roots crawled over most, offering little room to find solid footing. The single thing keeping Salvarias upright was the aid of his staff. Several times he nearly tumbled to his death, those near-falls forcing him to flinch repeatedly from Humar's outstretched hand. With a fist pounding on Salvarias's brain, he did not think he could afford the pain of human contact, of all those fleeting memories of whomever he touched that would deluge his own thoughts, rob him of what little air he sucked into his sick lungs. Only his mother, Wilhelm, and Lunara's touch had never effected him. Although Lunara's touch did something else, something that was sometimes worse. Her touch turned his chaotic mind lazy, making him lose sight of danger, clouding clear thought. Even so, it was her touch that gifted him peace from the images of bloody deaths that fluttered in the back of his mind for all his life.

During the achingly slow walk down, Okulu shared his dreamt-up creatures that could cause a man to spit up blood. Salvarias spared a few glances around as they descended and caught glimpses of massive rib bones half sunken into the ground, probably remnants of whatever hulking creatures used to roam the swamp before Nevlar's Retribution.

At the valley floor, the path leading them to the fortress was lined with carved statues of appalling-looking creatures Salvarias had never even read about. Lichen hung like clothes and hair from them, making them look as is if they could come alive. The fortress's jagged sculpting gave it a menacing leer as it loomed over him. Tree roots and decrepit-looking vines violated their way into crevices, cracking through stone blocks. He had no desire to enter and found himself standing stiffly at the base of what must have been near a hundred stairs climbing to the entrance.

"Salvarias?" Humar whispered. "Is something wrong?"

Salvarias wanted to scream at the top of his lungs and sprint as far from the fortress as he could. Nothing good would come of this visit, yet he found himself shaking his head. There was something inside he desperately needed, and the tug of his true task moved his feet up the first step.

The hike to the entrance winded all the companions, including his brother, and they stopped several times to rest. The air had grown thicker, and Salvarias occasionally caught an unpleasant whiff of rot mixed with the tang of bile and ... heated piss? He truly did not want to see what awaited them, but he climbed nevertheless.

When they finally reached the top, Wilhelm threw open the massive wooden doors.

Salvarias, as well as his companions, gagged at the rancid stench that washed over them, a mixture of stewed piss, metallic blood, and rotting vegetation.

Okulu spat. "I think someone might have died."

"We can only hope this 'god' has rotted away," Neithelas said.

Okulu winked a watering eye. "That's something we can agree on."

Inside, towering buttresses lined a long, wide hall branching off into two less-grand corridors and two sets of stairs spiraling to the upper levels. The only other time Salvarias had come close to feeling this small was when he stood before the gates of Oblivion. The fortress dwarfed even Wilhelm's seven and a half feet.

Enchanted torches sprouted spoiled-pea-colored balls of light, which illuminated the hallways, stairs, and grand entrance. The steady light sent a shiver up Salvarias's spine. Light should be alive, be fluid with the wind, and shift with the movement of people. Torches and candles—sunlight even—had motion. That was why he always had his sparrow made of white light floating as if on a breeze, rising and falling ever so slightly as though catching the current in all its natural grace. This violated what light was meant to do, and he found it unnerving.

"Homey," Okulu said, running his hand along a pillar. Beneath layers of roots, Salvarias made out carved human skulls.

"Shut up, ye half-breed," Durak snapped. "This place be spawned from the heart of evil."

Moss and weeping vines hanging halfway to the floor covered the domed ceiling. On the far side of the expansive reception, between the two branching corridors, a double wooden door hung open.

"Um," Okulu said, squinting toward the opened doors. "I think it best if Lunara stays in here."

"Indeed," Neithelas said, lip curled. "She should not see what lies beyond."

Durak spat to the side, his cavrul eyesight just as strong as Okulu and Neithelas's winsire sight. "Bastards."

"This reeks of a trap," Humar said.

All nodded their agreement. Packs tucked near the entrance, Okulu and Lord Bellerum crept along the left wall while Durak and Humar took the right. Salvarias stood off to the side with the remaining party. After a quick inspection of the two corridors and a peek through the double doors, the men returned.

"The two hallways could lead anywhere," Lord Bellerum said. "I think we're meant to go through the open doors. Looks like this 'god' wanted to leave us a message. Okulu said he saw only one person alive in the room. He's sitting on the throne, shackled there."

"We be fools to go in there," Durak said, absently smoothing his thick black beard.

"We didn't come all this way to turn and run," Neithelas said. "If the man is shackled, he can pose no threat."

"This place weeps with death," Lady Talura said. "I can feel it."

Lord Bellerum wrapped an arm around her shoulders and said to Humar, "Neithelas is right. We proceed with caution, armed and ready for anything."

Humar ran a hand through his hair and regarded Salvarias. "Thoughts?"

"Many," Salvarias responded, trying to discern what he saw beyond the doors. It looked like a tiny walkway cut through the center of the room, flanked by an unnatural wall built up to the ceiling. The stench was suffocating. "I am inclined to agree with Lord Bellerum and Prince Neithelas. We came here to find 'god.' It is time to do so."

Humar nodded. "Neithelas, stay here with Lunara. Everyone else, keep alert."

"I'm not afraid," Lunara said. "I can go."

"No, lass," Durak said gently. "Ye stay here and guard this door for us. We don't need anyone sneaking up on us."

Lunara looked about to object, but her father shook his head. "You'll stay here and do as Neithelas says."

Her ice-blue eyes flared with anger, but she did not argue her father's instructions.

Swords whispered their hellos as they slid free of their sheaths, and the group navigated along the overgrown, mossy floor. When they came closer to the doors, more details revealed themselves until eventually all was clear.

Bodies.

Hundreds of bodies were stacked floor to ceiling, leaving a narrow passage open to the far side of the room. Blood and excretions in putrid green and yellow hues pooled on the floor.

As they passed through the door, a voice boomed from the other side of the room. "Welcome!"

Salvarias stepped forward, shrugging from Varila's reaching hand, ignoring her hissed warning. His eyes were fixated on the speck of a man at the end of the long walkway, and Salvarias strode forward in a trance of absolute disgust.

"Come, Guardian and Protector," the voice said.

Salvarias did not break free of the trance until Wilhelm's hand rested on his shoulder.

"Who goes there?" Humar said.

The man sat on a throne raised by a dais overtaken by walnut-colored tree roots. He was a portly man with a nose brighter than a cranberry. Folds of skin stacked on one another, and his chin wobbled when he spoke. He had power, but even Salvarias could beat any attempt the man might make to harm their party. Regardless of his obesity and vulgar leer, the man made Salvarias feel awed. A sick part of himself wanted the man's approval, love, and blessing.

"Crutar," the god introduced himself. "God of Gluttony, at your service."

"Where's everyone gone?" Okulu asked lightly. "Seems a little lonely."

"They left."

"Shame you didn't go with them," Okulu said. He glanced at Humar and whispered, "We can't kill a god."

"As you see, I was no friend to God," Crutar said, holding up his shackled arms. "I blame Dalnar for my predicament. Why didn't you come earlier? Why not search for the cause of what's plaguing Arden? I've been held prisoner in my own home for near a hundred years. Denied food. Denied flesh." He licked his lips as his gaze moved from companion to companion, coming to rest on Varila. "Come here, girl. Let a god live his last moments in pleasure."

"I'll find an ogre you can suck," Varila said coolly.

Crutar chuckled.

"Who is this 'god'?" Salvarias asked.

"What is it, is a better question, boy. Come closer. Let me get a better look at you."

Salvarias walked to the throne, knowing his brother loomed behind him.

"You look just like him," Crutar said. "Eyes are a little different."

"Start from the beginning," Wilhelm growled.

"I was happy in my home here," Crutar started. "I didn't do much harm to Dalnar. You have to admit, compared to your new plague, I was tame. Sure, I tried the occasional war, but I wanted to feel the sun, breathe fresh air, and see pines and mountains. You can't blame a god for wanting. Moreover, you people always got so upset when I took your women. But even gods have needs." He looked at the chains. "I don't suppose ..."

"No," Wilhelm said.

Crutar sighed. "A hundred or so years ago, God came sauntering into my humble abode. He brought with him a man well past life, Sansis; a gooey orange man, Unupture; and a young mage ... Dethal, I believe. Anyway, he said I either bow to him and give my soul, or he'd enslave me." The god shrugged. "What's a god to do? Ever since Veedran left, I've had an odd peace to myself, indulging in whatever, or whomever, I desired. I wasn't about to give that up. I'm a god after all. I thought he was just a man with a pet mage and a few creepy slaves. I unleashed my power upon him, and he stood there, taking it all ... Do you understand? Taking it all. He absorbed it. He stole from me every drop of my power."

"So he hauled you up from the dungeons to what end?" Okulu asked. "You don't have the power to kill us. So why?"

"To tell you to give yourselves up." Crutar gazed at Salvarias. "You can't win this, boy. He'll devour everything you hold dear. Do you think that army was all he had planned? I assure you, it's not. I don't know where he went, but if I were you, I'd find him and bow before him. This," Crutar motioned to the bodies, "this is what made his army."

Wilhelm sucked in a breath. Pooling his courage, Salvarias turned to the bodies. They were women. Decaying, their stomachs eaten open, faces locked in horror. Some were nothing but bones, yet Salvarias knew they were women.

"Kill me," Crutar said. "Stab me right in the heart. I assure you, if you free me, I will not help you. I will go to the first village and take what I want. Their food, their women ... even little girls. I'm not picky."

Wilhelm exhaled sharply and tore his gaze from the stacked bodies, eyes darting back and forth. Salvarias focused where his brother had looked. A woman he recognized stared blankly at the group. Hair frayed from her braid, and her face had light lines of age that had been absent the last time he had seen her. Naffrita, the woman who owned the clothing store in Falar, the one his brother bedded several times.

Then Lunara screamed. Everyone whirled around. She had latched hold to a body's arm, smoothing matted hair falling to the floor.

"No," Lunara wept. "Lady Unbril."

Salvarias remembered the stories from the late Commander Unbril of Serinity about how his wife had been taken by a raiding party, leaving Commander Brice motherless in his last years as a young man.

Neithelas went to comfort Lunara, but she shoved him away and marched toward Crutar. The anger and pain in her eyes tore through Salvarias.

"Cut out his heart," Salvarias said to his brother, unable to tear his gaze from Lunara. "Piece it out in four chunks, and set it afire. Then behead him."

Crutar choked on a breath. "How do you know that, boy?"

"I read books instead of raping women," Salvarias said, glaring at Crutar. "Oblivion awaits you." He strode from the dais and intercepted Lunara. "No, my lady."

"I want to watch," Lunara said, jaw tight with anger, tears streaming down her cheeks. "I want to watch him suffer!"

She could not. He could not bear to think of her taking pleasure in death. He bent and whispered in her ear, "Do not lose yourself in this darkness."

Lunara looked up at him, anger draining until only her raw pain was left. "She didn't deserve her fate."

"No one deserves such, my lady. But think about what you said. Look at Crutar. Tell me what you see."

Lunara's eyes focused on the god. "I see his life, the light of it, the potential of it. I see ... beauty in him. A god."

Crutar screamed from behind Salvarias. Her gaze bolted to Salvarias and panic burgeoned in her eyes. "I want to leave," she breathed. "I don't want to hear it! Please!"

Turning her from the gruesome sight, he swiftly led her down the narrow hallway of bodies and well into the grand entrance. He kept her back to the room and stood in front of her to reinforce the consequence of his failures, all the dead whose blood was on his hands.

"Thank you," she said thickly.

"For what, my lady?"

"For saving me, yet again."

He turned his gaze to her, furrowing his brow.

"I lost myself for a moment," she said. "I don't want to be that person. It's not who I am. You knew and saved me from doing something that would haunt me for the rest of my days."

Salvarias folded her in his arms, relief sagging his shoulders. His beacon of purity remained just that: pure, beautiful, and untainted.

Resting his cheek on top of her head, he inhaled her sweet smell of spring meadows and gazed through the doors. He replayed Crutar's words over in his mind, continually returning to the god's request to die and his story of how he lost his powers. If Salvarias had learned anything over his time hunting "god," it was that the creature had been connected to Veedran. To assume otherwise would be folly. He also knew Crutar had worshipped Veedran. The likelihood of Crutar not obeying a subject of Veedran was slim to none. And then there was his power. Weakened, surely, but Crutar still held some, though he had claimed God had taken every last drop of it.

All led to one conclusion: God wanted them to kill Crutar. He frowned. No, God wanted them to try to kill Crutar. Crutar had seemed surprised to learn of Salvarias's knowledge. The god did not want to die. He wanted his blood spilt.

It hit Salvarias like a battering ram. Crutar was the trap.

Wilhelm took intense satisfaction in holding Crutar while Humar used a dagger to carve out the god's heart. It beat outside his body, and the cavity in his chest barely wept blood. Humar dropped the heart on the floor, and Durak walked over, axe raised to the side, face set in grim determination. One nod from Humar, and Durak's axe split the air and cleaved the heart in two. Crutar's scream sent a chill down Wilhelm's spine. Durak readjusted his stance for the next blow.

All the next events happened fast, within two breaths. Durak's axe whistled its strike as Crutar's scream turned to a manic laughter of victory. Durak's axe sliced the heart in quarters and Edium sparked the flint as Varila's sword hacked Crutar's head clear of his body. A drop of Crutar's blood sizzled on the throne, sending off a peculiar ping and subtle vibration, like a small quake had affected the air itself. Salvarias's shout of "Brother" sounded miles away as flames caught quickly over the god's heart.

Wilhelm looked up in time to see the sliver of light from the open doors disappear as they slammed shut, reverberating a booming *thud* in the room. The enchanted green light flickered out. All was silent and dark except for the dying flames sputtering on Crutar's burning   heart.

Chapter 2

Summer 1018 a.r.

Salvarias threw his shoulder against the door. It did not bother to creak or show any signs of surrender. Desperate, he ignited his magic. Intent on his spell, he did not sense the enchantment until it was almost too late. Any spell attempt to open it would backfire and kill the caster. It was an artful casting, subtle, done by a mage with an unparalleled understanding of magic. Bracing for the pain, he released the energy, grinding his teeth to keep from crying out as the energy tugged through his pores and puffed into the air, wisps of his blood attached to it.

"What's wrong?" Lunara cried.

"The door is enchanted. My spells will not work."

"Mother!" Lunara banged her fists on the door. "Father!"

"They cannot hear you, my lady."

He glanced around the room and his gaze finally settled on the left corridor. He regarded it for several moments before staring at the right. Either way was a risk. Either way could lead him to his brother. Either way could lead Lunara to her death.

Her soft hand slipped into his, and he looked down to see her smiling through her tears. "We could sing the choosing rhyme to decide," she said. Pointing between the opposing corridors with each word, she sang a song he had heard other children chanting while playing. When done, she pointed right.

Salvarias entwined his fingers with hers. "Right it is."

The descending staircase gave him hope that there would be a secret entrance into the throne room, presumably from an underground passage. On the first level, abandoned rooms converted to prison cells caked in old blood lined a hallway. At its end, he tapped his staff along the wall, which he gauged was on the right side beneath the room holding his brother. The responding *thump* sounded hollow.

Quickly, he climbed back up the stairs and took the left corridor down to the first level, finding it identical to the right side, counting his steps the entire time. After a quick calculation, it was clear a tunnel of sorts existed between the two sides. Feeling hope blossom, he descended the stairs, checking each level as he went, discovering the same count of steps.

He eventually ended up at a door twenty levels below ground. Resting an ear against the slimy stone, he held his breath and listened. All he heard was Lunara's quick breaths.

After a few silent curses, he gently pressed his shoulder against the door. It gave with a slight groan. Calling a spell to mind, he shoved open the door and boldly stepped inside. An underground water duct of sorts greeted him. Its length stretched farther than he could see and spanned the width of five barns, though only twenty feet or so tall. A canal—none too clean—ran between the platform he stood on and another one on the opposite side of the water, connected by a flat, simple stone bridge. Dead center of the bridge, a T formed, the intersecting span leading to a door in the wall above the canal. On the other platform, crystallizing orange liquid spilt from hatched canary-yellow eggs nearly as tall as Lunara, who was shy of six foot. Whatever had been born left residual traces of magic, which meant "god's" army now had creatures with the ability to perform spells.

A ripple interrupted the smooth surface of the murky water.

"What is it?" Lunara asked in small voice.

Indecision ended quickly. The door in the center of the bridge surely led to his brother. He had no choice but to continue.

Whatever lurked in the brackish water breached its surface with a hump of scales resembling snakeskin. The color of brilliant lime caught the mage light before disappearing beneath the surface.

"That color ..." Lunara breathed. "Is it—"

"Run," Salvarias hissed, pressing her toward the door, searching his robe's pockets for a pebble.

She darted from the room and he slammed the door behind her, ignited his magic, and tossed the pebble on the ground as he chanted the spell. Lunara was a stubborn woman and no doubt would try to come to his aid. His spell was meant to lock her out, and by her curses and kicks on the door, it had worked brilliantly.

Turning back to the room, he pulled a rag from one of his pockets and tied a blindfold around his eyes. The creature killed with one look, and he would not risk stupidity on his part. He allowed his senses to adjust and focused on the water, listening to it ripple.

He mused over just how ignorant Arden was to her shadows. Basilisks were rumored to have been hunted and killed to extinction by the watythms. Apparently, the books were wrong.

In the pitch blackness, Wilhelm's senses were attuned to the tiniest noise: Talura's rapid breathing, the clink of metal when Humar or Okulu shifted, the soft brush of Neithelas's fingers along his arrow's fletching.

Wilhelm had the unshakable sensation the bodies were moving, drawing close, and he was certain he heard wet footsteps.

No one had moved yet. No one dared. All were too busy listening, waiting.

Stone grinding on stone spun Wilhelm toward the throne where Crutar's headless body rested. Scraping footfalls, clinking armor, and a mutter sounded before the stone raked against itself again.

Soft light illuminated the space; a pure white ball was suspended above the hand of Dethal, casting ghostly light upon his triumphant expression and the three black-armored soldiers flanking him.

The mage took one gander at them and cursed, his triumph quickly switching to disgust. "That boy is damn near impossible to capture!" Dethal glanced at Crutar, smirked, and whispered under his breath. The light grew brighter, chasing away shadows. The sensation Wilhelm had experienced wasn't entirely unfounded. He spared a cursory look to his side and saw blood slinking down the stacks of bodies. It moved as if it had purpose.

"How convenient you all chose to gather in the same place," Dethal said. "If you were smart, you'd heed the boy's warnings and cease following him to his death. Now, if you'll excuse me, I have a young man to track down. Don't fret. I'll not leave you alone in this room of the dead. Allow me to introduce you to my master's favorite servants."

Wilhelm's gaze locked on bloody liquid elongating from the tops of the bodies to pool on the floor. Dethal's light reflected eerily off the undulating mass as it morphed into a featureless human form.

"Bloodleders," Edium hissed.

Wilhelm had read the stories. Bloodleders were creatures Veedran created during the Long Wars. They were made by forcing

34

infants to drink blood mixed with byrak root. History said the poisonous combination slowly dissolved bone, tissue, and organs until the body melded into one substance. The baby's transformation took an agonizing year. After the metamorphosis, the infants began feasting on live human sacrifices to build their girth. Before him stood ten once-innocent babies, now creatures of hunger and hate, only driven by the need to feed.

"Bloodleders indeed," Dethal confirmed. "Brilliant, are they not?"

The rippling bodies left bloody footprints on the mossy stone as they stalked the group.

"Kill them," Dethal commanded, and then the light went out.

A horrible wail reverberated in the room, like a baby screaming in agony.

"Strike, Wilhelm!" Okulu shouted.

Without thinking, Wilhelm raised his sword and swiped down. He felt resistance to his blade, and the creature shrieked.

"Humar!" Neithelas shouted.

Wilhelm vaguely heard stone grinding over the clanging of Humar's armor. Dethal had left them to their fate and now hunted Salvarias.

"Okulu, Neithelas, Durak, in the center!" Humar shouted. "Tell us where they are and stay clear of them!"

"Wilhelm!" Durak barked.

Again, he swung blindly. Again he felt resistance, like slicing through water.

"How can we kill them?" Edium shouted.

Talura said tersely, "Wilhelm, give me your broadsword."

He unsheathed it, holding his great sword at the ready and the other out behind him. Someone grabbed it.

"Varila!" Okulu said.

Names and directions began to ring out. Amidst it all, Talura shouted the three facts she knew: The creatures' blood was poisonous to bare skin. If one bit a living person or creature, the victim would die within half an hour if untreated. Lastly, the only way to kill them was by a mage spell or by sword strikes. The metal burned them, and enough quick successive strikes could break the creature's form and end its life. Usually not before one found a piece of exposed flesh on its victim.

"Edium, Varila, hold them!" Humar called. "Talura, I need Wilhelm's sword."

A hand wrapped around Wilhelm's arm and yanked him back as another hand squeezed his shoulder assuredly. "It's time, boy." It was Humar's voice, steady and quiet, as if whispering at a funeral. "Remember what I've taught you. Remember it all and succumb to it. Trust it and trust yourself."

Wilhelm inhaled a soothing breath, releasing the tension in his shoulders as he exhaled.

"You need to be fast," Humar said. "Keep your movements tight. Don't overextend. Listen. Feel." Humar gently turned him. "I would not do this if I didn't think you were ready, boy. I'd not risk your life. Now, on my order."

Wilhelm cleared his mind of everything, even the gnawing worry he had for his brother. He coiled his body tight, allowing all his hours of training to take over. Vaguely he heard Humar barking orders to the others, and Wilhelm sank himself further into a trance until nothing reached him. With peril biting at his heels, concentrating tested his mind's fortitude, but he managed to silence his excitement and trepidation, his worries of failure. Humar had told him confidence would grant him success. Only trust in one's abilities. Only blind faith in the two swords in his hands. His swords.

In blissful, calm peace, he waited for two words.

"Now, Wilhelm!"

He unfurled his coiled form. He moved without planning to move. His swords whirled in mirrored unison, cleaving in such a flurry that the wind of their motion lifted his sweat-soaked hair from his forehead. He felt his foes' attacks before they executed them. He was no longer blinded by darkness, he was blinded by how well he saw everything around him, how his mind had—without his awareness—locked the room's every detail into place. He knew about the woman's hand intruding on the walkway a mere foot in front of him, and he used a jutting leg to trip up his attacker. He heard splashes in front of him, like someone dumping a bucket of gritty water.

"Stop!" Humar roared.

Wilhelm froze.

"About face!"

36

He turned and continued his fight. He smelled jasmine as Talura scrambled by him, pressed against the bodies to avoid his sword. The stench of Durak, Neithelas, and Edium's sweat invaded his nostril as they darted by. A strawberry breeze drifted by.

"On me!" Humar ordered.

Wilhelm smelled the sour metal of Humar's armor at his side. Listening for a breath, he picked up on the whipping pattern of Humar's battle and fluidly changed his own to align with the knight. They were one. Moving as one. Feeling as one. Trusting as one. He felt the resistance of each creature's body before he heard the loud *pop* as it exploded. Each time, he shifted to shield any exposed skin.

Then it was over. He knew it. *Felt* it. And he collapsed to the ground. Humar's armor rattled loudly as the knight also fell. Never had Wilhelm suffered such exhaustion mingled with elation. They'd won, and Wilhelm had perfected fighting with two swords, perfected Humar's highest training he'd never taught another soul. Wilhelm's single regret was his brother wasn't there to witness his accomplishment.

It was his last thought before his body reminded him why fighting in such a way was saved for the direst of times. He leaned over and vomited, hearing Humar retching at his side. Sweat rolled off him, he trembled like a cornered doe, and a blinding headache pulsed spots of light in the dark room. He couldn't get enough air and wondered if this was what his brother suffered.

"It's all right, son," Edium said softly. Something pressed to Wilhelm's lips and water trickled down his throat. He nearly choked on it.

"Well, that was remarkable," Okulu said lightly.

Chapter 3

Summer 1018 a.r.

The screech vibrated through the underground waterway, driving Salvarias's hands over his ears. When it ceased, he heard claws clicking on the ground. The creature would need to duck in order to fit in the room. If his readings were correct, the basilisk was well over fifty feet long. The front part would be lizard-like, the back tail long and lean like a snake. Based on the book, *Veedran's Miracles*, tough reptilian skin supposedly covered its body. Only the head and belly were soft.

Slaps sounding like a wet cloth smacking stone echoed in front of him. The creature was approaching.

Though he had vowed to never use his magic again, he was defenseless without it. He had to reach his brother. To do so, he had to defeat the creature with magic. Gritting his teeth, he ignited his magic and immediately denied its plea for reconciliation. Drawing in expended energy from every tiny creature and plant within the cavern, he chanted softly, drew his rune, and said *"Rulose"* to release his spell. Lightning crackled as he sent the bolt forward and slightly left. A rushing scuttle ended with a deafening explosion of rocks. He had missed.

Salvarias chanted and drew his second rune. Warmth from his fire spell spread across his face as he whispered, *"Rulose."*

The flame shot forward, curving left and then right. It paid off. The creature screamed in anger and pain. He heard a loud slap of water as the creature fell and then the splashing as it shuffled, screeching the entire time.

He tilted his head at the discord of rapidly moving water and a whistle of air, then something large—probably the tail—hit him squarely across the chest and slammed him to the wall, knocking his head smartly. Valuable air fled his lungs. His head pounded spots of light into his blackening vision as he crumpled to the ground.

He heard the rush of air again and rolled to his side.

Crack!

The ground vibrated, pelting him with chunks of stone. Rising, using the wall and his staff for support, he hobbled along, fumbling to gain his bearings, cursing his bad leg as it threatened to buckle beneath him.

He heard scraping claws on stone and water slapping the edge of the canal. The creature was graciously turning to find him, which would expose its soft underside. Salvarias whispered his spell, traced his rune, and funneled the energy. Burning hot energy rushed through his rune, igniting the air with sizzles and snaps from the four lightning bolts charging the creature. The basilisk wailed and landed with a vibrating thud, limply thrashing in the water. Then all was silent.

Groping blindly, hands stretched out in front of him, he shuffled forward until he touched the cold beast. He glided is hands along the smooth scales and found the head, a sleek tooth, and finally—forced to lean over the top of the head—an eye. Drawing his dagger, Salvarias stabbed the eye.

A deafening wail followed a massive intake of air.

The head rose in pain, throwing Salvarias hard against the ceiling and dropping him to the ground. Gasping, he rolled to his side, pain throbbing through his shoulder and hip.

Rising, he scrabbled to the wall behind him and reached into the pouch tied to his waist. Hand clamping around a bag of glass, he cursed. Not practicing his magic not only weakened the strength of his spells, but limited the number available to him. This last component spell had been invented before he ceased using magic. He had not even tried it yet.

Cursing again, he tossed the glass in the air and whispered the spell, hauling in massive amounts of energy. Glass shards ripped through the leather pouch, fanning out, racing for the creature with enough force to split rock. A moist tearing sound was followed by a screech and thud as the beast fell hard. It panted a few torturous gurgling breaths, then all was silent.

This time, Salvarias waited. No noise echoed aside from water lapping the path's edge. After a few moments, he reached out, found the head, the large tooth, then the gooey hole of the punctured eye. Fumbling further, he found the second eye and stabbed with his dagger, bracing for another hit. Nothing.

Exhausted, he sank to the ground and breathed deeply, removed the blindfold, and examined the creature. Spirals of white smoke rose from where his lightning strikes had met flesh, the smell reminding him of game cooking over an open campfire. The basilisk was beautiful in a reptilian sort of way, save for its torn-open throat glittering with the glass that had shredded it. He regretted having to kill the creature. It did not understand right from wrong or that it served a horrible master. In its own way, it was innocent, like a pet dog trained to fight.

Biting back a pang of guilt, he did not wait to recover his breath or energy before he hobbled to the entrance, muttered his spell, kicked aside the rock, and pulled open the door.

Standing beyond the door, a mage awaited him, grinning, the green mage light adding a sick hue to his fire-red hair and beard. Lunara stood in front of Dethal, his arm snaked around her shoulders, dagger pressing into her throat enough to draw a trickle of blood. Her eyes were wild with fear.

"Hello, my star pupil," Dethal purred. "This is most fortuitous. I'd feared your brother's wrath, but ..." Dethal looked around with mock innocence. "He's not here. Imagine my surprise when I found all those my master wishes dead in one room. You brought them right to us, boy. Currently, they're entertaining some creatures I left with them. Bloodleders. I'm sure you've read about them."

Salvarias gritted his teeth.

"Yes," Dethal said, frowning in feigned sympathy. "You remember the stories. It'd take a small army to be rid of those creatures." He looked over Salvarias's shoulder. "Shame you killed the basilisk. It was the last of its kind." Any amusement in Dethal's eyes dimmed, replaced by building anger. "Your death will finally bring me the peace I've so longed for. It was your worthless presence that dragged me from my studies, that uprooted me from my home, that made me move my research and life's work to Falar." Dethal's face turned blotchy red, and his voice rose. "All because of some mage boy who's too stubborn to see his own doom! Who's so self-centered he led a group of Dalnar's finest minds into the pit of defeat! You had to know it was a trap! You're not stupid! Why? Why did you do it!"

Salvarias stood dumbfounded. The mage was actually scolding him.

"All those months of training, I hammered into you the need to listen to everything!" Dethal continued, voice rising with each sentence. "All those months I dedicated myself to sharpening your mind, growing your power! I bragged to my master over my accomplishments, how I had fine-tuned your mind, how I'd made your power grow with each lesson. I was worshipped for my success at capturing you! And now!" Dethal's voice cracked at the volume he forced it to. "Now you've walked into a trap, leading your friends to their death, and made me look like a fool!"

Dethal raked the knife across Lunara's throat. Her eyes widened and she whimpered as bright blood ran down her chest. The cut was deep, but not deep enough to end her life. Regardless, fury burst forth, drenching him in anger. It boiled the lake of indifference he lived upon, coaxing his rage until it manifested in blackfire. As with the last times his blackfire had come to life, the flames licked hungrily over Salvarias, leaving his robes unsinged, his body tingling with anticipation.

Dethal's eyes bulged, and he staggered back, hauling Lunara with him as she pressed her hands to her throat.

"Release her!" Salvarias hissed.

Dethal dropped the dagger and allowed Lunara to crumple to the floor. He turned and fled up the stairs, screaming for help.

Salvarias sidestepped Lunara and hurled his staff into Dethal's back. The mage tumbled to the floor face first. Flipping over, Dethal crab-walked up the stairs, spouting apologies in the midst of spells. Blackfire ate up the block of ice Dethal shot at him; it devoured the hurling ball of fire and absorbed the three lightning strikes. That was all Dethal could cast before Salvarias was upon him, clutching the mage's neck in his fists.

"Forgive me," Dethal wailed. "Forgive me, Master!"

"I seem to have misplaced my mercy," Salvarias growled. "Today, old man, my vision comes true."

As it did every time he touched someone while using blackfire, images of whomever his victim had murdered flooded Salvarias. Hundreds of people overwhelmed him as he performed each murder, killing children, women, men, mages. Though a tiny, rational part of him knew the hands he saw that maimed and killed were Dethal's, the majority of his mind—his soul—believed the blood was on *his* hands.

As his victims raced before him, a cavrul family slowed everything down, seeming to stop time itself as *he sent an ice shard through the mother's chest, sickened by her prejudices. He was in so much pain, and he just wanted help from a healer. But his lonely world darkened at her denial, at her lip curled in disgust, at the hatred burning in her deep brown eyes. At that moment, he had never loathed another more than her. He lost all patience for those who spat on him, who beat him for something he could not control, who tried to murder him while he slept. His rage poured out in his magic, and before he knew it, the two children were lying on the ground, screaming in pain, clutching at the fire shard stabbed in their guts. He glanced across the hill to see a cavrul charging toward him, axe at the ready. It had been the first time he had taken an innocent life. He stumbled away, weak from his pain and spells, near death and alone. He did not mean to kill the children ... he did not mean it.*

But it was not just the act itself that would haunt Salvarias's nightmares. Just as he reenacted the murder, he also experienced the pain of the victim. All their horror, all their physical suffering, all their terror.

He was scared. He did not want to die. He clung to his father and pleaded for help as he gagged up blood, tasting its metallic taint for the first time. His father merely smiled and whispered it would be all right. He cried from the shooting pains, clawing at his father to make it stop. His father kept repeating that it would be all right. Then darkness crowded out the blue sky overhead. Panic took over. He did not want to die, but knew he could not escape it. Nothing was all right, and his father knew it.

Fury leached a cry from Salvarias. He filled his sweet blackfire with all the suffering Dethal had inflicted upon him in the dungeons of Zeeas, all the torture carved into his body, on his mind which would never be whole, the anguish his brother endured, and finally the grief still ravaging Durak.

Shouting in rage, Salvarias poured all the victims' pain into Dethal, forcing the old mage to suffer what Salvarias had just suffered. Dethal screamed and writhed under Salvarias's grip, but he held firm. As the last victim entered Dethal's soul, Salvarias spread the fire over the old man, feeling flesh melt and blister beneath his hand and smelling the familiar stench of flaming skin.

Satisfaction consumed him. He savored the old man's misery, bathing in Dethal's agony. The man sobbed through his burnt throat, imploring Salvarias to stop, pleading for mercy. Salvarias pulled back the intensity of blackfire, drawing out Dethal's execution, reveling in the joy blossoming within. Eventually, life's light faded from the harrowed eyes, and Salvarias exulted in the man's death, a smile creeping across his face and a chuckle escaping. One of his nightmares had finally died.

In one blink, the stone hallway disappeared, and before him towered the doors of Oblivion. Glancing left and then right, he grinned at the walls climbing beyond his vision, made of nothing more than what appeared to be solid smoke, yet hands of those trapped in that dreadful plane poked through in hopes of touching freedom. All around him, gray-black fog rolled with life, circling Salvarias in anticipation. Shifting his stare to the door, his grin widened at seeing his parents' murderer's face contorted in terror along with the other faces covering the entrance, deformed by the horror they were forced to relive.

He looked down at Dethal kneeling beside him, tears skimming along the old man's red beard as he clung to Salvarias's robes.

"Please, show mercy!" Dethal begged. "Please spare me! Truly I repent! I had lost hope, lost my way. I see that now! Have mercy, boy!"

"No, old man. You deserve no mercy. You deserve no peace. You deserve no relief from the horrors you inflicted. I condemn you to eternal torment. Relive what you did to my body and mind, how far you broke me, how lost I was, how hopeless, how scared. Slowly—very slowly—relive each breath of suffering the cavrul family endured and know their father's pain."

Salvarias touched the doors. When they flung open, a cold breeze kissed his face before the fog encircled him, warming his bones against the chill air. The darkness beyond pulsed with eager excitement. Grabbing Dethal's robes, Salvarias hauled the man up and shoved him through the doors. The old man's scream soared as the black fog enveloped him. Wails of terror rose octaves as the doors boomed shut. In one blink, Salvarias stood on a mossy staircase.

He dropped the old mage with a sneer of disgust and wiped the man's melted flesh from his hand. He rose and, as it happened the previous times he used blackfire, the instant he looked away the full weight of his experience crashed into him, knocking him forcibly to the ground.

The rippling physical pain of reliving every sensation of every mortal wound of the victims Dethal killed made him ill, and the sheer heart-wrenching fear of hundreds converging on his mind made him scream. Grabbing his head, he vomited as all the horror slammed into his soul, as all the agony bled into his mind, as all the blood gushed over his body. All of it forever locked in his memory, forever stained on his skin.

In Dethal's long life, he had killed hundreds of innocent people. It was nothing compared to the cavrul in Cattlar or his parents' murderer. The pain his physical body endured was more than he could handle, and he coiled in a heap of stabbing pain. What his mind relived hauled him into a waking nightmare. Warm blood flowed from his nose and ears. He choked on the blood streaming from his mouth. His muscles constricted, his eyes rolled in the back of his head, and before his mind ceased to exist, he smelled a spring meadow as Lunara grabbed his arm.

With her touch, the convulsions eased and the physical and mental sensations became bearable, but the deaths still flashed before him, disorienting him. Groping, he found her hand and clutched it tightly, using it as a port in the otherwise raging sea.

"Get up!" she cried. "There's footsteps on the stairs. Get up!"

Though beyond exhausted, with her help and his staff, he managed to get to his feet. The dead still blinded him, and he could not help but flinch as their wounds slashed across his body. Using Lunara's calming touch, he desperately tried to file it all away, but there were so many.

He allowed Lunara to guide him and heard the door grind shut.

"Can you lock it again?" she asked.

He shook his head. She hauled him forward as his vision finally pulsed to life, revealing the same stone room and dead basilisk. She was leading him to the other side of the platform.

A boom from behind spun both around. Three men burst inside, each clothed in tailored burgundy robes. Immediately he sensed their power was tenfold what Dethal possessed. There was no amount of danger that would provide him enough strength to fight. That did not mean he would not try.

"Stay there, boy," one man said.

A tingle ate its way up Salvarias's body. Before he could counter, a spell draped over him, locking him in place. Desperate, he ignited his magic.

"I need a counterspell," he ordered.

The magic helped shuffle through the words of his mind and narrowed down his options. Without study, it was hit or miss, but either the mages would kill him or the spell. He only had energy for one, possibly two more. As he pieced together words, another man entered. He was tall with a muscled body beneath a black cloak, eyes of deep amber, face square and recognizable.

"Hurry, Perek," one of the mages ordered.

Perek darted forward. Salvarias, frozen, had no choice but to watch the man approach. Perek flicked back Salvarias's hood. As with any who stared upon Salvarias's black eyes, the man shuddered and looked away.

"He does have the eyes of a demon," the man called over his shoulder. He snatched up Salvarias's left hand and turned it over to reveal the black flame embossed on his palm. Shaking his head, Perek sighed. "I'd hoped to be the end of it. Sorry, boy. This is going to hurt."

The man pressed his left palm to Salvarias's mark. Lightning struck from the skyless room and shot straight through Salvarias, feeling as though it fried his insides and boiled his blood. He cried out, trying to wrench his hand from Perek's, but the man held firm. A crack sounded and lightning fingered down again and swarmed over their locked hands. Perek screamed, and the jolt robbed Salvarias's body of strength. Only the spell kept him upright as muscles spasmed, his legs giving out beneath him.

A prickling sensation erupted on his palm. At first it was merely a tickle, but quickly it burgeoned into millions of needles stabbing his palm.

"Accept it, bastard!" Perek snarled.

The constant tug on Salvarias's mind blasted into full strength, and he realized Perek had what he needed, what he had been searching for. An overwhelming requirement and understanding flourished, and he exhaled sharply at the feeling, as if recalling a name he had been trying to remember for years. Gritting his teeth, he used the link of their marks to reach inside Perek. How he did so, he did not know. Some seeded, urgent instinct and need drove him.

Perek gave a cry of painful joy as Salvarias hunted down the power flowing in Perek's veins. Greedily, Salvarias hauled it into himself in heaps, tightening his grip, drinking it like a man denied water in a desert.

"Stop," Perek cried. "Stop him or else he'll die and I won't have enough power to hold the stone!"

The three mages rushed forward, and in frantic urgency Salvarias took one last long pull of power before the mages ripped apart their hands.

The spell holding Salvarias vanished, and he sank to his knees, reveling in the freedom the power brought him. No longer did he feel the tug of another task, no longer did he hear urgent whispers. He laughed lightly in relief for how free he felt.

Then the power morphed.

It seethed within him, delving through his body in search of something. He groaned when he realized he had switched from one need to another.

Gray fog devoured his surroundings. A glossy black rock with a thin red line circling it floated in front of Salvarias, shaped like the perfect skipping stone. He reached for it, realizing this was what he sought, what he needed. As his fingers rested on it, it burst apart into red fog that feasted upon the black. A horrible feeling of violation coursed through Salvarias as something truly evil touched him in ways no one should be touched, molesting his soul and mind. As though not shameful enough, it tore into his body, speeding him along on a stream of eternity, all the while ramming in and out of Salvarias like a thousand daggers.

You know me, a voice hissed though Salvarias's agony. *I already live inssside you.* It cackled. *And you are unprotected, Guardian.*

"Kill him!" a man yelled.

"Perek! Don't do this!" a voice rumbled.

The voice shook Salvarias's surrounding into focus. A figure stood in front of him, blocking Perek's way. From behind, Salvarias thought it was Wilhelm and cried out in relief. But the man glanced over his shoulder, and Salvarias saw it was not his brother. The man looked nearly exactly like Wilhelm save for wrinkles around the man's eyes and deep laugh lines around his mouth.

"Hang on, boy," the man said.

The mages began chanting before Perek called to them, "Harm him and I won't help you! Get out of here before he kills you all!"

The three mages darted toward the exit. Perek backed up, keeping his eyes on the man and a hand on his sword hilt.

"Sorry, Cousin, but this is for our own good."

"Perek, you fool! What are you thinking?"

"The boy will lessen the burden of the Hunters while I get the stone. All I have to do is turn it over, and we'll be safe. Don't you see? You can be with Wilhelm. I can finally have a wife and children of my own. We'll be free, Tedris! Free!"

"You didn't think this through, Perek! What if the boy can't fight it? What if it wins? I haven't given my power to Wilhelm. He can't help!"

"Don't you see? This is our chance to break this curse!"

"If the boy loses, our world is gone! You can't do this," Tedris pleaded. "Come with me. Let's work this out with Wilhelm and the boy. We can turn it over to them. You can still be free."

"Like our fathers? They were hunted to their grave, Cousin. No, we'll never be free until the stone is handed over." He raised a pacifying hand. "I didn't give him more than he can handle on his own. I'm sorry, Tedris. I really am. But one day you'll thank me."

Perek turned and bolted up the stairs.

His mind caving, Salvarias closed his eyes to the world, sinking into the chasm of agony. A surge of strength cut through his pain in the form of a knife ramming at his brain over and over.

Slowly, his awareness sharpened enough to realize he was locked in a battle with his evil. His former small fights, absently guarding his tiny soul, were of the past. The new evil warped his sense of self, tore at his soul, and threatened to devour all Salvarias was. The strain he endured made his stomach churn and embedded a drumming in his skull that shook his vision. The surging strength pressed against a shield Salvarias had erected out of sheer instinct, one that defended his soul from becoming a slave to the evil. As if those sensations were not enough, he became aware of the painful bombardment of images: of Ashra smiling, of watching her from dark alleys, of sitting around a fire, laughing with Perek, of wondrous lands.

"Come on, boy," Tedris whispered close to his ear. "You need to use my strength." The man's hand gripped his tightly. "Use me, boy!"

Salvarias latched hold of the burgeoning strength and yanked it free of its holder. He screamed. The knife turned simply vicious, carving up his mind like a roast, but it drained the pressure compressing his skull, which in turn allowed him to battle the evil.

"Easy," the man breathed, sounding like he had run a mile. "Not so much, not so fast. Slowly or else you'll kill me."

Salvarias eased his need, sipping the strength instead of gulping it.

"Good," Tedris said. "Very good, boy. Now, you need to breathe."

Salvarias gasped and the rancid taste of blood and bile lingered on his tongue.

"Have you got enough control?" Tedris asked.

Salvarias realized nothing stabbed into his body anymore, and though the feeling of being violated lingered, it was not nearly as harrowing as it had been breaths before. The evil still pushed at his shield, but he had enough strength to keep it at bay by himself. Weakly, he nodded.

The man released him and patted his shoulder. The stop and start of the contact spun the room.

"I have to go."

"No," Salvarias wept, reaching out blindly. "Do not leave me, Father."

"Sorry, boy, but you're not my son."

Denied yet again. Choking on sobs, Salvarias curled up and continued his fight alone in the depths of darkness.

Chapter 4

Summer 1018 a.r.

Lunara stared at Tedris as the man rose and backed away from the pool of bloody vomit Salvarias lay in.

"You have to help him!" Lunara demanded. "You can't leave him!"

"Sorry, girl. I've got bigger problems. Go through that door, up the stairs, and at the top you'll find a lever. It should open a way to Wilhelm. Tell him ..." Tedris swallowed and looked at the ceiling. "Tell my son I'm sorry about his brother. I'm sorry for all of it."

With that, the man took off in the direction of Perek.

Salvarias shut his eyes tight, gave a small sob and shudder, and then went limp.

"Salvarias!" she cried, dropping to her knees and shaking him. Pressing her ear to his chest, she heard his heart beat dully, sporadic at best. It did little to ease her building panic. She was alone, unprotected in a place of nightmares, and the man she loved hovered near death. She couldn't leave him, nor could she wait in hopes her friends might find their own way out.

Cursing herself, she inhaled a deep breath, and steadied her trembling hands. "I can do this," she said.

She examined her surroundings with calm calculation. Her gaze came to rest on the broken eggs, tall, clustered together tightly. It would have to do. Grabbing Salvarias under his arms, she pulled with all her weight. Eventually he shifted and slid across the slick floor.

It seemed to take forever to drag him across the bridge to the side with the eggs. Determined to make sure he was hidden, she weaved deep into the mass of shells. Darting back over the bridge, she did everything in her power to ignore the dead basilisk as she scrutinized her choice. Not from any angle could she see Salvarias.

Happy with her result, she rushed back across the bridge and found him still sleeping amid the eggs. Softly she whispered in his ear, "I'll be right back."

Wasting no further time, she strode to the bridge, followed the short T over the canal to the door at its end. Cracking it open and peering inside she saw sickly green mage light illuminating a thin staircase seeming to climb forever.

Hiking up the first flight of stairs winded her and drenched her in sweat. She muttered under her breath of all she hated of the place, trying to keep her mind focused. The room of bodies she purposely walked toward, seeing Salvarias battle a basilisk and Dethal, and thinking of all he'd endured threatened to reduce her to tears. And this was not the time for a breakdown.

She only stopped a few times to catch her breath. Her legs burned when she finally reached the top, and each breath cut like ice in her lungs. The mage light barely cast enough glow for her to find the lever above her head. She yanked it down and stepped back as a stone doorway creaked open.

Light weakly penetrated the thick blackness and the instant stink made her gag. A figure came barreling at her and swooped her up.

"My lovely temptress!" Okulu exclaimed, spinning in a circle. "You've saved us! Wait, where's Salvarias?"

She squirmed free of his embrace. "He's all right ... for now. Where's Wil—" Her voice cut off as he stepped into the light. A sheen of sweat covered his death-white face, and his body trembled visibly. "What happened?"

"Where's Salv?" Wilhelm asked, voice thin and weak.

"Down the stairs," she said, her gaze sweeping over to Humar's equally gaunt face.

Her father appeared and she found herself entangled in her family's arms. With effort, she escaped them and grabbed Wilhelm's hand, pulling him down the steps as she filled him in on everything. The longer she talked, the quicker he bounded down. By the end, she'd recalled every detail save for the part of Tedris stating Salvarias was not his son. She assumed those words would either be a dreadful shock to Wilhelm, or something he knew and never wanted shared.

They entered the room and she exhaled a breath at seeing it free of any new enemies.

"Lightning struck him?" Wilhelm asked.

Lunara pointed to the scorched part of the ceiling. "Yes. Several bolts struck both him and Perek. I don't know what it did. Perek and the mages were pleased by it, but it hurt Salvarias."

When they reached Salvarias, Wilhelm's exhaustion seemed to vanish. He scooped his limp brother in his arms and gaped at the blood and vomit covering the front of him. "By the gods, what did they do to him?"

"Now's not the time to figure it out," Humar said. "We need to leave here before we set off any more traps. We'll find another way to get Salvarias what he needs, but it won't be here."

"Agreed," Edium said.

"We can head back to the ship," Neithelas suggested. "By then, perhaps he'll have awakened and can tell us what happened."

"And what to do next," Varila added.

With everyone in agreement, they made their way to the main entrance, backtracking the way Salvarias had taken Lunara.

Wilhelm smoothed Naffrita's tangled hair from her face. Her dull eyes stared at nothing, and her mouth hung open in what he assumed was her last wail of pain. There were more bodies stacked on top of hers, blocking him from finding out exactly how she had died.

"Who was she?" Varila asked from behind.

Wilhelm jumped. He'd asked for time alone and hadn't been expecting a voice. Moreover, he was beyond tired and his nerves were wound too tight.

"Sorry," Varila said.

He waved her apology away. Gently, he kissed Naffrita's forehead. "I'll miss you," he whispered.

He turned to leave, but Varila grabbed his arm. "Who was she?"

He shrugged.

"We both have our pasts, Wilhelm. I won't be upset if she's one of yours."

He ran a hand over his face. "I knew her well. We kept each other company many times. She was a good woman. A strong woman. When I was five, shadowfires swept through our city and killed her father. She was a few years older than me. Her mother died when she was fifteen. The shop was paid for, so Naffrita took it over. She had a mind for business and was the best seamstress I ever met."

Varila wrapped her arms around his waist. Even in all the stench, he could still smell her, like a field of strawberries. "I'm sorry."

He gathered her close, using her strength to keep his steady, and watched Talura and Edium off in the distance. They knelt by Lady Unbril. "I'm sorry for your loss as well."

Varila's voice dripped with venom when she said, "We're going to find this 'god' and take our sweet time carving up his heart."

Wilhelm glanced one last time at Naffrita before leading Varila from the throne room. Humar was waiting outside with flint and the clothes they'd gathered from cells on their way up.

The knight patted Wilhelm's shoulder. "I'm sorry."

Wilhelm shrugged from the man and strode toward his slumbering brother. Humar still disgusted him for turning Salvarias over to the darkness in Cattlar. Though he'd fight side by side with Humar, he didn't trust the knight.

After Humar and Durak set the bodies aflame, the group left the keep behind, but not the horrible memories.

The next three days were a battle for survival. Salvarias had barely been conscious throughout the journey. When he was, he merely wept and choked on the food and water Wilhelm forced down his throat.

Nightmares consumed Salvarias, and several times over Wilhelm worried his brother's screams would lead whatever creatures "god" had left straight to them. Without his brother's shielding, the wild of the swamp attacked them: massive snakes, alligators, lizards ridiculously large, and insects of every variety. Wilhelm had never realized how much Salvarias protected the group.

When they finally tore free of the thick vegetation, Neithelas fell to the ground and wept. Talura knelt by Neithelas's side, hugging him and whispering comforting words. Winsires were more attuned to the ebb and flow of life than erthlas, and Wilhelm was surprised the young prince had stayed as collected as he had over the journey. Okulu, though half-winsire himself, did not seem affected.

They were on the coast, a light sandy beach sparkling in the afternoon sun. Wilhelm gazed at the rolling hills covered in swaying grasses. Trees clustered about sporadically, tall with bushels of long-fingered leaves spouting from their tops. A breeze swept in from the ocean, hot with summer. Off the shore, Hyde's ship bobbed in the lazy waters.

Wilhelm settled his brother in the grasses, resting the aspen branch by his side. Okulu and Humar went to work building up a signal fire for Hyde to send over the rowboat.

"What now?" Edium asked, sitting beside Varila sprawled out in the grass.

Humar shrugged. "We set anchor and wait for Salvarias to wake."

"This be a waste of time," Durak growled.

Humar frowned at Salvarias. "I'm not so sure. Something happened."

It wasn't long after Okulu coaxed a thin line of black smoke from the fire that a dot moved from Hyde's ship. They waited in silence except for Salvarias's wept words and occasional soft cry.

Once the rowboat slid onto the beach, two sailors jumped out and dragged it up half out of the water. They helped load packs, and everyone crammed inside the small boat. The sailors made attempts at conversation, but no one seemed in the mood.

Wilhelm had to fasten Salvarias over one shoulder while he climbed the precarious rope ladder leading up to the deck. Hyde was waiting with a large smile. His pale-blue skin blended with the dull, sun-drenched sky, and his fiery hair and beard glistened with brine.

"Hello! Welcome—What happened to the boy?" Hyde asked, bright eyes focused on Salvarias.

"Long story," Wilhelm grumbled. He headed below without waiting for the others. In his cabin, he cleaned Salvarias and changed him into fresh robes. The jostling must have woke him. Salvarias's eyes fluttered open and sobs left him instantly.

"Help me!" he cried.

As Wilhelm did each time his brother had woken, he held Salvarias tightly, trying to comfort him over his terrified cries.

His brother's eyes had changed. Normally, the gray-black irises moved, like curling smoke, churning in hypnotic motion, beautiful and entrancing, full of life. Now the gray-black violently contorted into disharmonious patterns, dead and cold.

Eventually, Salvarias drifted back into nightmares.

And so it went on.

Finally, when all was dark and quiet, Wilhelm succumbed to exhaustion.

His dreams were troubled with images of the red-robed man taking Salvarias in the dead of night. Wilhelm searched everywhere, riding Lilly near death, leaving his friends in her dust, but he couldn't find his brother.

Wilhelm jolted awake, breathing hard and covered in sweat. He rubbed sleep from his eyes and sat up. Glancing to the side, he startled to see his brother's bed empty. He bolted from his cabin and squeezed up the stairs to the deck. It was still night and summer stars lit up the sky. The moon hung in its full glory, kissing the tops of waves as they lazily lapped across the vast ocean in the warm breeze.

"Salv!" Wilhelm called, running toward the bow. He caught sight of his brother conversing with Hyde. Though Wilhelm couldn't hear his brother's words, he picked up on the tense edge of Salvarias's tone. Wilhelm stopped next to his brother and glanced at Hyde's hard-set expression.

"Salv? Are you—"

"Where is Lord Bellerum?" Salvarias said, brushing by Wilhelm and heading below. "We must be on our way, and apparently Master Hyde will only listen to Lord Bellerum."

Wilhelm rushed to keep up, casting an apologetic smile over his shoulder at Hyde. "I'm sure he's in his cabin. It's a little early to wake him. Can't it wait until morning?"

Salvarias shook his head, taking the stairs faster than what was safe for a man with a bad leg. "Evil does not rest. Which cabin?"

Wilhelm pointed down three doors. "Salv, what happened? What did Perek do to you?"

"If only I knew," Salvarias growled. He marched to Edium's door and banged three times. When it didn't open right away, he banged again.

"Give him a moment," Wilhelm murmured, trying to peek at Salvarias's face. His brother's low hood shadowed his features as always. "Salv ..."

"What?" Salvarias snapped. "What would you like me to tell you? I have no answers!"

Edium opened the door, shirtless, hair sticking up, hand rubbing his face. "What is—Salvarias?" His eyes brightened. "How are you, boy?"

"I am not a boy," Salvarias snarled. "We must set sail, and Master Hyde has refused my request and wishes the order to come from you. I would be most appreciative if you spoke with him."

Wilhelm winced at his brother's harsh tone.

Edium slowly nodded. "Of course. Are you ... well?"

Salvarias stepped aside and motioned to the stairs. "I will be once we set sail."

Edium glanced at Wilhelm, conveying a million questions. Wilhelm shrugged.

After gathering a shirt, Edium strode up the stairs, Salvarias on his heels, Wilhelm following.

Hyde waited on deck, arms folded over his chest, slate-blue mage robes rustling in the wind. "Edium."

"Sorry for the hour, but we need to be on our way." Edium turned to Salvarias. "Any direction in particular, bo—Salvarias?"

"North, along the coast. I will give instructions when I see fit."

Edium cleared his throat and smiled at Hyde. "You heard the young man. We'll follow his lead."

Hyde glanced between Salvarias and Edium before grunting an agreement. He walked to the wheel and began barking orders.

"Anything else I can do for you?" Edium asked Salvarias.

"No. Thank you, my lord."

Without waiting for a response, Salvarias marched to the ship's bow and paced.

"I've never heard the boy so short before," Edium said.

"Me neither."

"Any idea what's wrong? What happened to him?"

Wilhelm shook his head. "I'll give him a few days before I push him for answers. Right now, I think it's best we do what he says."

"Agreed. He obviously knows something."

Wilhelm wasn't so sure. If his brother had answers, he wouldn't be upset. Salvarias was a man with no idea what to do next.

Chapter 5

Summer 1018 a.r.

Twelve days passed before Salvarias had stridden on deck and given the order to head to Falar. It took three more days to reach their destination, and Wilhelm was relieved, to say the least. His brother had gotten worse over the two weeks. He flat out refused to discuss anything, and his tone had turned from tense to short and curt, deep and commanding. Everyone avoided him.

At Falar's dock, Hyde waited by the ramp as Wilhelm and his companions gathered, except for Salvarias who was still in their cabin throwing his items in a pack.

"I can't thank you enough," Edium said, clasping the captain's hand.

"I think we're about even," Hyde said. "I'd stick around but I've got to oversee some things at home. I've been gone far too long."

"I understand completely," Edium said.

Wilhelm offered his hand. "Thank you."

Hyde smiled slightly. "Just take care of that brother of yours. Something ... something doesn't feel right with him."

Wilhelm nodded. Salvarias appeared on deck, hood low, staff clutched tightly in his hand. He walked briskly to Hyde, bowed, and marched down the ramp. Wilhelm smiled to the group in general apology and followed.

Salvarias had been stopped at the guard checkpoint, and Wilhelm jogged to catch up.

"Name, mage," a soldier asked.

"Salvarias Laybryth."

The guard flipped through a ledger. "Laybryth ..."

"Wilhelm?" a voice called.

He peered around the soldier and grinned. "Idolar!"

Idolar waved the soldier away and embraced Wilhelm. "It's been too long! Look at you." He turned to Salvarias and smiled. "And you. You've grown so much."

Salvarias bowed. "Sir Idolar. Congratulations on your knighthood," he said, voice softer than it'd been in weeks.

Idolar patted the crest of a bear on his breastplate. "Thank you. Happened a month ago."

Wilhelm clapped the man on the shoulder. "About time."

"I'd been procrastinating until Lord Bellerum pushed me to give it a try."

Edium laughed from behind. "I had no doubts you'd be successful, Sir Idolar."

"Thank you, Lord Bellerum," Idolar said with a bow and broad smile.

The guard tugged Idolar aside and whispered, though not soft enough to hide his words. "Sir, there is no Salvarias Laybryth on the list of approved mages."

Idolar took the list and flipped through it. "Must be a mistake. The boy's been on the list of mages since he was six. I know. I was here when the Association of Mages visited him." Idolar shook his head. "Damn neglectful bastards. Add him, and make sure his name is included on all the lists. Send a note to the Association of Mages as well. Tell them they've left a name off." Idolar turned to Wilhelm, smiling. "Are you here to stay? My men have grown soft without your training."

"Unfortunately, no," Wilhelm said, not needing to fake the disappointment in his voice. "I suspect we'll be leaving soon."

Idolar exchanged warm greetings with Humar and Durak. During the commotion, Salvarias had drifted from the group and now stood looking at the filthy city. Wilhelm politely excused himself and joined his brother.

The stink of fish and overworked bodies devoured the ocean's fresh breeze. Curses flew from the mouths of weathered men packing the dock, all unloading or loading goods.

"How does it feel to be home?" Wilhelm asked.

"Home ..." Salvarias said, the word rolling off his tongue as if tasting it. "Is this home? No. We have no home. We are vagabonds leaching off others."

"Salvarias," Idolar called. "Milred has been distraught without you. She made me promise to ask you to visit her if I ever saw you."

Salvarias bowed. "Thank you, Sir Idolar."

"And Vuddruk's in town as well. He was asking about you," Idolar said.

"Vuddruk?" Edium said sharply.

"Yes, old mage, white beard, friendly smile," Idolar said. "He used to visit here often. That is, up until about the time the boys got taken to the slave mines. He didn't come around much after that."

"Good to know," Edium said before strolling over to Wilhelm. "Best keep an eye out for him. I'd like to have a word with that old bastard and ask him why he left us in an abandoned city to be eaten by a giant worm."

"Agreed," Wilhelm said.

"We'll be staying at our estate," Edium said. "It's three down from the guardhouse. I received word our horses and the wolf have made it safely from Cattlar to our stables here."

"Brilliant," Wilhelm said, resting a hand on Salvarias's shoulder. "It'll be nice to see Adok."

Salvarias shrugged from Wilhelm's hand. "I will see you at the estate."

Wilhelm's brother strode from the dock toward Market Street. Shaking his head, Wilhelm waved goodbye to Idolar and then turned to Edium. "I need time alone with my brother."

"Take all the time you need. Servants will show you to your rooms when you arrive, and I'll have food waiting for you both."

"Thanks," Wilhelm said before taking off for his brother.

Wilhelm caught up to Salvarias and stepped in front to help clear a path so his brother didn't have to dodge through the crowded street. Ever since the darkness had crept into the lands, major cities had been a haven for those living in rural towns. Falar was no exception. Homeless families who'd given up everything just to keep their lives packed the streets.

Once at the familiar herb shop, Wilhelm said, "I'll wait outside."

Salvarias did not acknowledge him but walked through the entrance. The woman's excited squeals rose above the clatter of the streets.

"Salvarias!" Milred exclaimed. "Oh my, how you've grown. It's been so long. What happened to your hand, dear? Your pinky?"

"It is nothing, madam. How goes business?" His brother's voice returned to its natural soft, lulling cadence.

"Horrible since you left. You had such a gift!"

"I have collected some new potion recipes for you. They should help with business."

"You're not coming back?"

Salvarias's tone rang with regret when he responded, "I am afraid not, madam."

"Did that cute little woman with black hair ever find you?" Milred asked.

"Yes, she did."

"Did you marry her? Such a sweet girl."

"No, madam."

"Shame. Tell me where you've been. Sit."

"I must be going. Have you seen a man travel here in the last three days with light-brown hair and large brown eyes? Tall, about my height, and strong build. He might be accompanied by three mages."

"Let me think ... Yes, two days ago. He bought some herbs and looked to be in pretty tired shape."

"Did he mention where he was staying or where he went?"

"No, he didn't, dear, but he bought a good supply of ginger, nearly wiped out my entire supply, and you know how hard it is to get that root."

"Thank you, madam. I must be going."

"Wait ... I ... I need to tell you something."

"It is all right, madam," Salvarias said soothingly.

"No!" Milred wailed. "You were such a sweet boy when you worked for me, and it's eaten at me over the years."

"What is it?"

"I'm the one who ..." New sobs erupted from the shop.

Wilhelm stepped inside. It had not changed over the years. It still smelled of earth and the rows of herbs were in pristine condition.

"I'm the one who told the mage you were here!" Milred blurted.

Salvarias's face drained of color.

"After Mother died," Milred rushed on, "we owed such a large sum of money, so I started supplying information to soldiers in black armor to help pay off our debt."

A light hand rested on Wilhelm's trembling arm. Knowing it was her that turned his brother over caused his blood to boil, and the fact she had kept the secret only enraged him further.

"I thought you were cold and heartless," Milred continued. "I knew they were looking for a mage with black hair and eyes, and I knew it was you. When I saw you outside my shop, I gave you the job to keep you close. I told them where to find you. Please forgive me, but I didn't like you when we first met. And my mother told me how ..." Milred glanced at Wilhelm. "How you were dead when you were born. How you came back to life ... by unnatural means."

Salvarias swayed.

"And when you used to come in the shop, your eyes scared the sanity out of me," Milred continued. "But after you started working for me, I learned what a nice person you are, but too late to change anything. I'm so sorry!"

Wilhelm stepped in front of his brother. "How could you!" he roared. "You never told me!"

"I was scared. I knew they would hurt me if they found out I told you. They come by every couple of weeks to see if you've shown up. They were here four days ago, but I swear to you I won't tell them! I swear it!"

"I forgive you, madam," Salvarias said, his voice as distant as his gaze. "You did what you thought best at the time. If we were all privileged to hindsight, no one would make mistakes and our world would be hollow. You have nothing to be sorry for, madam."

Milred burst into fresh tears and went for Salvarias but Wilhelm intercepted. "My brother might forgive you, but I don't!"

"Wilhelm!" Salvarias said sharply.

Wilhelm flinched and jumped backwards. The word lashed out like a strike. Never had his brother called him by name. Never had *Wilhelm* been uttered from Salvarias's mouth.

Salvarias turned his attention back to Milred. "Please be well, madam. There are no ill feelings between us."

"Bless you," Milred sobbed. "Visit when you can. It's been so lonely without you."

"Of course, madam. Thank you for everything. My time in this shop was invaluable to me, your company much appreciated."

Once outside, Salvarias paused to stare at the dirt-encrusted cobblestones. After a moment, he strode toward the estates. Wilhelm followed, his body trembling, and fought the urge to punch something.

A passing merchant must have seen his brother's robes from under his cloak and spat on him. It provided the perfect opportunity, and Wilhelm leveled the man with one punch, not holding back much strength. Blood flowed from the man's broken nose. Salvarias pulled Wilhelm forward and, not wanting to evoke his brother's anger, Wilhelm reluctantly followed, leaving the man alive. Although one less prejudiced asshole would do Arden some good.

The Bellerum estate was nothing compared to what the family owned in Serinity or Sundil. Though impressively large compared to others, it was a mere three stories with a plain, dark-gray stone wall surrounding it. The intricate iron gate swung open at their approach, and Wilhelm laughed when he saw who awaited them. Bernil had been a driver for Haleen, the widowed noblewoman who had ushered Wilhelm into manhood and who had been his dearest friend.

"Wilhelm," Bernil greeted. His grin widened when he glanced at Salvarias. "So is this the elusive brother of yours?"

Salvarias seemed unaware of his surroundings. His head was low and numbers tumbled from his mouth in short succession. He glided by Brenil and entered the estate.

"That he is," Wilhelm said. "Sorry, it's been a rough few weeks for him."

"It's good to see you," Brenil said, eyes glassy, voice thick. "You bring back memories of brighter times."

Wilhelm clapped his friend on the back and motioned to the estate. "So the merchant who hired you after Haleen died all those years ago was none other than Lord Bellerum."

"Yes. I was lucky he found me before I got stuck with some haughty family. The Bellerums treat their servants like family. And the pay, well, there's none better!"

"I'm happy for you," Wilhelm said.

Brenil nodded and scuffed his boot on the cobblestone, glancing around. "I ... uh ..."

"Spit it out," Wilhelm encouraged. "What's on your mind?"

Brenil rubbed his beard, his lazy eye wandering. "I lied to you ... about Haleen."

Wilhelm's heart skipped and he surveyed the estate, half expecting her to walk out, hips swaying, smile playing on her plump lips.

"She didn't die from plague," Brenil continued. "She was taken by creatures. I didn't tell you 'cause I thought you'd go out and try to get her back. You were too young. And everyone said no one taken ever came back. I heard from Lord Bellerum about what you found and ... well, I was wondering if you saw her."

Wilhelm felt like he'd been punched in the chest. "She was barren ..." Was all that came out of his mouth.

"She'd be no good to them," Brenil confirmed. "I figured they probably killed her as soon as they discovered it. I ... I had hoped you might have found ... her body."

"I didn't look for it," Wilhelm said. "Why didn't you tell me? I could've searched through the bodies to be sure." Wilhelm shook his head. "We burned everything. We ... we burned it all."

Brenil's mouth turned down at the corners, and he looked away. "I figured. I'm sorry. I shouldn't have brought it up. I can't help but wonder what became of her."

Wilhelm's legs wobbled beneath him. His relationship with Haleen hadn't been complicated to him, but to those who knew of it, it probably appeared as if they had been serious lovers on the verge of marriage, though he'd only been fifteen when they met. They had been together any time he could sneak away from Tobin, and he had grown to love her. It wasn't the love a husband might have had. It was the love of a dear friend. Haleen had been special to him, a woman he confided in, a woman he told more to than any other friend he ever had, including Varila. He'd shared everything with her. His body and mind. To have her fate unknown, to think of what she might have endured, made him lightheaded.

"You all right?" Brenil asked.

Wilhelm nodded. "Thanks for telling me," he mumbled and walked listlessly into the estate. He barely noticed the servant talking to him as the young woman led him up a set of stairs. Only when she mentioned Salvarias did he listen. She was motioning to a door next to his.

He muttered out a thank you and stepped inside his brother's room. Salvarias stood by a window, staring at the city below.

Wilhelm swallowed a few times to loosen his throat and asked, "Can I get you anything, Salv?"

"No," Salvarias said shortly. "I would like to be alone."

Wilhelm jerked his hand when something wet brushed it. He looked down to see Adok grinning and trotting into the room. Salvarias glanced at Adok and turned his stare back out the window. Adok whined and nudged Salvarias's hand. His brother folded his arms over his chest. Never had Salvarias treated the wolf coldly. Adok was his brother's dearest friend.

Shaking his head, Wilhelm went to his room and plopped into a chair. He kept his door open and his stare focused on the hallway, allowing his mind to roam to unpleasant thoughts.

"May I come in?"

Wilhelm startled, not realizing how deep he was in his memories. Lunara stood in his doorway. He motioned her in.

She strolled across the room and sat by his side. He waited patiently for her to speak. It seemed to him that she'd been debating over telling him something since the keep.

"I ..." She smoothed her dress. "Tedris said something that I ... that I think you should know."

When she paused, Wilhelm muttered, "Go on."

"He ... he said Salvarias wasn't his son."

Wilhelm's heart squeezed painfully. Was this what had his brother so upset? "Did he say so to Salvarias?"

"Yes, though I'm sure Salvarias did not hear him. He was in too much pain."

"Good," Wilhelm mumbled. "Salv ..." He sighed and rubbed his face. "I can't tell you, Lunara. I don't want your connection to ... give anything away. Whatever you do, don't bring it up. Trust that I'm protecting Salv."

"If you think it best for him," she said. She looked him full in the face and squeezed his hand. "For him, not yourself."

"It is. Can you tell me what's wrong with him?"

She shook her head. "He's in pain; I can tell that much. If I'm having headaches, I can't imagine what he's going through. Other than that, I have no clue."

Wilhelm nodded. "Let me know if you sense anything."

"Of course." She kissed his cheek before leaving the room.

The sleepless nights finally caught up to him, and his head sagged and jerked up as he battled to stay awake. On one such rude awakening, he heard Adok's low growl. The wolf was standing in his doorway.

Bolting from his chair, he snatched his broadsword and sprinted to his brother's room. It was empty. Adok whined at the top of the stairs, and Wilhelm followed the wolf, belting on his sword as he took the steps three at a time. He rushed through the front door and found the city dark; eerie sobs from the destitute people living in the streets seemed unusually loud. Heavy summer fog blanketed the ground, and the hazy moon imbued it with a sense of mystery.

As he jogged behind Adok, heart pounding, breath laboring in fear, he caught sight of fog swirling behind a cloaked figure gliding past the estate's gate.

Wilhelm nodded to the guards on duty as he strode through and caught up with Salvarias. He eyed the dank alleys and unfriendly eyes following them.

"Where are you going?" Wilhelm hissed. "It's not safe to be out at night."

"We lived on the streets, Wilhelm."

He flinched. The word cut deeper than a knife. He ceased talking and trailed his brother past the Red Lion to the home with the black door. He stopped but Salvarias didn't. His brother threw his shoulder into it, and the frame snapped as the door flew inward. Salvarias confidently stepped through the threshold. Wilhelm gritted his teeth and followed.

"Ecia Lumineous."

Salvarias's staff glowed with soft white light. The home hadn't changed over the years. It still gave Wilhelm an uneasy feeling, remembering that this was the place his brother received instruction under the brutal hand of Dethal. Right here in this cold, dark home. He shivered, though he didn't feel a chill.

His brother turned toward the library and, at the sight of the missing books, cursed. He hobbled up the stairs and shoved open the door to the room directly at the top. Here, Salvarias paused and a visible shudder ran up his body. He pulled himself up and passed the threshold. Wilhelm clenched his fists and stepped inside the room.

It was empty save for a desk in the center of the room. Salvarias searched under it and in any crevice he could find. Once every inch had been examined, he punched the wall, leaving blood glistening on the brick, and stormed out. Silently, Wilhelm followed his brother back to the estate. Salvarias marched into the home, past the companions crowded in the entry room asking questions, up the stairs, and slammed his door in Adok's face.

Talura shook her head. "I assume he hasn't spoken with you?"

Wilhelm leaned against the wall and ran a hand over his face. "No, not a word."

"Well," she said. "I think it's about time he speaks to *someone*." She smiled at everyone. "Leave us be, no matter what you hear. Only come if I call for you."

With that, she strode up the stairs and disappeared into Salvarias's room without even knocking.

Salvarias battled to keep his rage within his control. He had a strong desire to set the city of Falar aflame and laugh as the wretched thing burned. It held no answers for him. Nothing did. He was lost. His only clues were fleeting images rushing before him of what he assumed Perek saw. Whatever the man had done had linked them. But Salvarias was not a traveled man, and the landscapes were a mystery. Falar had been the first place Salvarias had recognized, as fleeting as Perek's time was here. All he saw now was more ocean, and gods only knew where the man was heading.

Adok tried to pry into Salvarias's thoughts, but he kept the wolf at bay. His mind was entirely too full to add the strain of connecting with animals. Between all of Salvarias's victims' deaths replaying before him, images of what Perek saw, and his new evil constantly clawing at his shield, Salvarias was simply out of strength and willpower. It was like he was juggling his sanity and adding one more object would cause the whole thing to tumble into an abyss.

Another wave of anger washed over him, and he gritted his teeth to keep from flinging the nearby chair across the room.

He jumped when his door clicked open. He turned to see Lady Talura enter.

"I prefer to be alone, my lady," he grated.

She smiled as she stepped inside and closed the door. "Of course, dear. But you're not going to get what you want. It's time to tell me what happened."

"Do not mother me," he growled. By the gods, he wanted to toss her out the window.

"I think a little mothering is exactly what you need, young man. You've treated everyone with nothing shy of contempt. You've snapped at us, you've—"

"Contempt?" Salvarias said, exasperated. "Snapped? Forgive me, my lady, but it is nothing short of what you deserve. I cannot count the number of times I have asked you people to remain behind. Still, you follow me like lost puppies. I—"

"Do you even hear yourself?"

"I hear just fine!" Salvarias yelled. "You people almost died! Do you have any idea of the ramifications to Dalnar if that should happen? Lord Bellerum is all the hope these lands have for protection, and instead of doing what he should, he followed me! I already have an entourage if you have not noticed. I need no more in my company! For the love of all the gods, why can you people not leave me alone!" The last words bellowed out as he flung a resting table across the room. It crumbled in a pile of broken wooden legs. "I am done with it!"

"Salvarias—"

"No! I will hear no more!" He strode to the fireplace mantle, gripping the stones in his hands, desperately trying to control his building rage. "Leave, woman!" He closed his eyes tightly, feeling the evil push harder against his shield.

"I won't leave you, ever," Lady Talura said.

She was by his side, reaching for him. His mother appeared behind her, lip curled in a snarl.

"No more!" Salvarias shouted. Furniture skidded to the far side of the room, and the candles flickered out. Only moonbeams pierced through his window to light the mess.

"Monstrosity," his mother said.

"Leave me!" Salvarias cried. "Just leave me be!"

"Salvarias."

He punched the stone, splitting his knuckles. He hardly felt pain. He hit it again, wanting to experience anything but the rage he had lived in for weeks. "Leave me!"

"Son."

He raised his head and met her gaze. Her love reached out to him, and he hated her for it. "Get out!" He shoved her, gasping at the flutter of images. She fell to the floor, eyes wide. His evil clawed frantically at his shield. Sweat burst on his brow as he fought it, and he clenched his fists, digging his nails into his skin. The evil surged again and Salvarias gritted his teeth; a swarm of dizziness spun the room.

Lady Talura rose and stood in front of Salvarias, no hint of fear in her eyes. "Son, I know you're in there. You have to fight. You have to come back to me." Tears brimmed in her eyes. "Please, son. I miss my boy."

Salvarias stumbled away from her. A hot dagger of pain sliced across his heart, cutting through his anger. "S-s-stop ..." he stammered.

"I care for you so much," she said, her tears breaking free. "Please, son. Come home."

He clutched his chest at the agonizing pain, as though barbed wire tore free of his heart. The room sharpened into a focus he had not realized he had lost since the Stronghold. He suddenly felt very alone, like waking from a horrid nightmare to be greeted by malevolent darkness.

"I am scared," he breathed, tears welling unbidden. "Nothing feels right. I am lost. I am so alone." He sank to the floor, hugging his knees close to his chest.

"You're not alone," she whispered, kneeling in front of him. "I'm right here. Look at me, son."

Everything was wrong. *He* was wrong. He met her gaze. "Help me."

"Whatever is going on inside you is winning, son. Do you understand? You have to come back to me. You have to fight."

Then he felt it. Like an early morning fog, the evil had wept through tiny crevices in his shield and bled into his soul; his precious soul, the only part of his entire being he owned wholly. The evil stoked his anger, egging it to surface, and he had barely maintained his temper over the last week.

His fears quickly became reality. He was losing himself to his evil. It had happened so subtly, so slowly, he had not noticed it. The fury of the main battle had consumed him. Now he discovered that was just the evil's ploy, a way to distract him from its sneakier plot.

"I feel it," he breathed. "I ... I want my brother." His mind slipped toward panic. Wilhelm had promised he would never let the evil take Salvarias, but it was. Hugging himself, he cried out, "Brother, help me!"

"Wilhelm!" she shouted. Voice soft and comforting, she said, "He's coming. You're not alone, son. We'll help you through this."

Sobs tore free. All his years of fighting, and he had failed. It swarmed inside him, eating his own soul, consuming all he was. Fear stole his air and his weak heart fluttered painfully. His mother squatted in front of him, a sneer of hatred twisting her mouth. "I told you," she said. "You're a demon. And your evil will be our end."

"No!" Salvarias cried. He scrambled on his hands and knees until he found a corner of the room. His mother followed as well as a woman with dark hair and ice-blue eyes.

"Salvarias," the woman said sharply. "Stay with me, son. Look at me! She's not here! I swear she's not here!"

His evil erupted with blinding power and clawed at his shield. "Help me!"

"Gods, son. Please, stay with me! Son! Son!"

"Help!" Salvarias screamed, cowering when Sansis knelt beside him, knife held firmly in decaying hands, a sick smile twisting Sansis's thin lips.

A violent need to light the estate on fire flourished within Salvarias. He opened his mouth to chant the spell, begging himself not to do it while urging himself to continue. His mind seemed to crack in two as the forces battled one another. But it was the only way to rid himself of his mother and Sansis. To be safe. He just wanted to be safe. He said the first word.

Then familiar arms wrapped around him. A steady drum beat in his ear, and air whooshed in measured breaths. "I'm here, Salv."

His mother and Sansis vanished.

Salvarias clawed at his brother for help, weeping openly. "It is taking over! I cannot fight it, brother! Help me! I am scared!"

"It can't take over unless you let it. You have to fight it, Salv."

Salvarias shut his eyes tightly and curled up, hiding in the only safe place he had ever known. He clung to the hum of a familiar song as if it could light his way in the darkness.

Wilhelm's arms tightened and his deep voice rumbled in his chest. "For me, Salv. You have to fight."

Slowly, with mind-breaking concentration, Salvarias imagined a wall being built brick by brick while at the same time he searched himself for those wispy tendrils of fog snaking their way inside his soul.

Time had no meaning. Nothing existed but his efforts, his brother's solid presence, and his song of light. The evil fought ruthlessly, but Salvarias fought just as hard. Gradually, bit by tiny bit, he cleansed his soul and built his wall. When he freed himself, he sagged in his brother's arms and let his surroundings come into focus. Lady Talura was by his side, smiling, tears drying on her cheeks. Something wet leaked between his lips, and he pressed his fingers to his mouth. They came away wet with blood.

"Salv?"

He buried his face in his hands, begging for forgiveness through each retching sob.

Chapter 6

Summer 1018 a.r.

Salvarias sat on his bed tucked into the corner of the room. Wilhelm's heavy arm hung over his shoulders, and his brother's rumbling snore had kept Salvarias company through the night. Hidden in his sanctuary of safety, Salvarias had spent the entire night studying his new evil, familiarizing himself with its ploys.

Over the long hours, he had eased the burden his mind endured while keeping the evil at bay and his soul sealed behind layers of brick and mortar. The battle had been gruesome, and several times in the night he had wept in hopelessness. But finally he held the evil within his control, he fought without making himself ill, and he learned its deceitful methods.

What he could not shake were the headaches that had plagued him since Perek first planted the new evil. The constant pounding had become an old friend.

Adok whined and plopped his head on Salvarias's knees. Though exhausted, he desperately missed Adok. With his evil controlled, he opened his mind to the myriad of life around him. The sensation was too much. Backpedaling, he only thought of familiar minds.

Adok's presence burst to life, and Salvarias smiled at the instant lecture of how he could never go anywhere without getting into trouble. The wolf continued his scolding as he licked Salvarias's hand. Through the harsh words, Adok's care reached out like an embrace. Salvarias ran his hand along the wolf's soft ears and said, "Then I suggest we do not part ways again, my dear friend."

Adok adamantly agreed.

Wilhelm woke as the first rays of light peeked through the edges of the drapes. His arm tightened as he drew in a long breath. "Did you sleep?"

Salvarias shook his head and waited for his brother's questions to start, fear forming a ball of lead in the pit of his stomach. The silence dragged out. Servants' soft voices started sounding from outside Salvarias's room as the estate woke. Smells of fresh bread, cooked oats, rosemary, and ham reminded Salvarias of the time spent in

Serinity with the Bellerum family. He suddenly found himself ravenous.

Wilhelm sighed and rested his head against the wall. "I won't ask you, Salv. You'll tell me when you're ready."

Salvarias closed in eyes in relief. "I will tell you, brother. I ... I need time."

"Well, let's not let all that food go to waste. How about some breakfast?"

Salvarias smiled at loud noises coming from Wilhelm's stomach. "Of course. I would not want you to starve."

"I practically have been," Wilhelm muttered. "Damn ship didn't stock enough meat. I'm going to clean up in my room. You'll be all right?"

Salvarias grabbed Wilhelm's arm before he rose. "Forgive me, brother. I treated you poorly."

"There's nothing to forgive, Salv."

Wilhelm ruffled Salvarias's hair before hopping up and leaving the room. Salvarias reluctantly crawled out of bed, stiff and aching as if he had fever. At the washbasin, he splashed cold water on his face and bravely raised his gaze to the mirror. He half believed he would see a new monster. Perhaps his eyes would rain blood, or fire would shoot from them. Maybe he had grown fangs or horns. What greeted him was the same demon he had seen since childhood. He looked gaunt and pale, weak and broken.

He shaved, changed into fresh robes, and stood at his door, gaining courage to face the world.

He had vague memories of how he had treated his companions. They were hazy, more dreamlike, but he knew them to be true. He wondered if Humar would once again look at him with disgust. Or perhaps Durak would just try to kill him. Maybe Lord Bellerum would kick him out of the home and recall his care. After all, Tedris had refused to even acknowledge Salvarias as a son. He still roamed the world fatherless, motherless. Mother ...

He shuddered at the memory of yelling at Lady Talura and shoving her. He had treated her so poorly he doubted she would still look upon him with affection. It would be for the better.

Her care isss a lie anyway, my murderer, the presence hissed in his mind, unfailingly grounding him in the cruelty of reality. *Tobin looked at you with love. He called you ssson. Then look what happened. Talura isss no different. Ssshe offersss now what ssshe would rip away once you accepted her. Ssshe isss torturing you, my murderer.*

Of course the presence spoke truth as it always did. His brother was the sole person who would never hurt him. Lady Talura's proclamation of care was surely a trick, some scheme to inflict harm upon him. His mother had not been above the deceit. He clearly remembered the few times when she cradled him in her arms as she kissed his forehead and wept her apologies. They had been brief moments that ended when she looked into his eyes. The first time, the beating that followed had been the worst he could remember, though whatever hid in his dark corner had surely been more terrifying.

A knock on his door caused him to jump and drop his staff. His weak heart faltered, blinking stars in his vision. He sucked in a few deep breaths, snatched up his staff, and opened the door. Lady Talura was smiling.

"Hello," she said. "May I come in?"

Salvarias stepped aside. "Of course, my lady."

Her smile beamed as bright as the sun. "You sound remarkably better." She stepped inside and closed the door. "How are you feeling?"

"My lady, I offer my deepest apologies for the way I treated you. Please, forgive me—"

Her deep sigh interrupted him. "My dear young man, you have nothing to apologize for. We know Perek did something to you. You can't blame yourself for everything that happens in this world, son."

Ah, ssshe callsss you ssson, baiting you to lower your guard, the presence said. *Keep firm, my murderer. Do not let her clossse. Do not let her hurt you.*

"You are too kind, my lady." Salvarias bowed mockingly. "You have my thanks for your unrelenting understanding."

She laughed lightly. "And you, my dear, hide your sarcasm beneath layers of compliments. You don't trust me. You're waiting for me to beat you as she did. I assure you, I have no intention of doing so. One day, you'll see that for yourself. Now, I'm sure you're famished. You look like you haven't eaten in years. Come along," she said, turning and leaving the room.

Shame burned his cheeks as he followed.

Do not be, my murderer, the presence said. *Ssshe doesss not dessserve your—*

Leave me be, Salvarias snapped.

Talura led the young man down the stairs and toward the dining hall. She tried to stop her hands from trembling. Her son looked near death: face white, a light sheen of sweat as if he had fever, cheeks sunken, dark rings stacked under his eyes, and he shook far more than normal. He glided behind her, spouting numbers in his soft voice as the wolf walked at his side.

Last night, he had fallen apart rapidly as usual when alone with her. She was certain he'd seen his birth mother again, but another terror he had beheld drove him to panic in the space of a blink. She could ask, but he wasn't ready to shed his cloak of solitude.

When they entered the dining hall, Wilhelm was sitting close to Varila, and the others were gathering heaping plates of food.

Salvarias stopped at the table, which fell instantly silent. She had a strong desire to scold them.

"I would like to apologize for my behavior since the Stronghold," Salvarias said. She saw his head turn ever so slightly toward Humar, and his voice carried a tinge of fear. "I make no excuses and beg forgiveness if I said cruel words to any of you."

"Nonsense, boy," Humar said. "You've done nothing wrong."

Salvarias exhaled and his shoulders dropped, so Talura's did as well. Humar had had a complete change of heart about Salvarias after the boy survived his brother's death and restoration in Cattlar. Whatever had happened had strengthened a bond Talura strongly approved. Humar would protect her sons. Of that, she had no doubts.

"You were the example of polite," Okulu drawled. "I've taken some notes to call upon the next time Neithelas and I have a misunderstanding."

Talura glanced around, trying to figure out why the air seemed a little lighter all of the sudden, why colors burst alive with new vibrancy.

Salvarias bowed. "I am at your service, Okulu."

The merc winked and chuckled.

"Sit, boy," Edium said, motioning to an empty chair next to Lunara.

Salvarias tilted his head and took to his seat. "Thank you, my lord. I—"

"Edium, boy. Just call me Edium"

"So," Humar said, leaning back in his chair. "What brought us here?"

"Perek," Salvarias said. "He has something I need. Something that will give this 'god' the edge he needs for victory. I must find Perek and retrieve it."

"What is it?" Edium asked.

"I ..." Salvarias lowered his head slightly. "I am unsure, my lord. I—"

"Edium."

"I only know it is vital we obtain it before Perek hands it over to 'god'."

Talura plucked up a plate and began adding foods she'd seen Salvarias favor. In a healthy way, he was a picky eater—which probably explained his thin, sickly body when he was younger. Ashra surely never cared what the boy ate or bothered to buy the right foods, and Talura doubted Wilhelm or Tobin paid attention, both assuming their lovely little Ashra had taken care of it.

"Any idea where to find Perek?" Humar asked.

"None," Salvarias said. "He is traveling with three mages. My only hope is to ask around. I believe he has left Falar via ship."

"How did you find that information?" Edium asked.

"Don't question him," Humar said, his steady gaze never leaving Salvarias. "It doesn't matter. He knows it and we'll use it to help us. After we eat, we'll go into the city, split up, and find out what we can."

Salvarias tilted his head. "Thank you, my friend."

Adok wormed his way underneath the table, gobbling up strips of meat Lunara slipped to him.

"I have word from my brother, Arthias," Neithelas said. "He says the winsire army has started their campaign. Soon, they will be out of the winsire lands."

"Good to know," Edium said. "Brice has also begun his march."

After compiling slices of thick white cheese, pear halves, pitted cherries, plump red grapes, and lightly buttered herb bread, Talura set the plate in front of Salvarias. She gathered a bowl of oats, added milk, and a single scoop of sugar.

Setting it by his plate, she whispered in his ear, "How did I do?"

By his silence, she'd pressed too hard.

He picked up the plate and rose from his chair. "If you will excuse me, I must study."

"Magic?" Wilhelm asked, hope imbued in his voice.

Salvarias shook his head, spun around, and strode from the room.

Wilhelm stood but Talura motioned him to sit. "I'll see to him, dear. You need to eat at least four servings. You've lost too much weight over the past few weeks."

Wilhelm grinned. "As my lady commands."

She winked at him, grabbed the bowl of oats, and walked to Salvarias's room. Through the open door, she saw the plate of food resting on a table beside a chair Salvarias sat in. His thrown-back hood gave light to his large black eyes studying the plate as though it had a secret meaning. By the half-distant look in his eyes, he wasn't where she was. Slowly, as if approaching a frightened deer, she sat in a chair by his side.

"She never cared, did she?" she said.

Salvarias shook his head. Unshed tears glistened in eyes. "I envied my brother. Her love was poured into everything she did for him. I had always wondered if his food tasted different. If somehow love sharpened their flavors, freshened it."

"Now you can see for yourself."

He flinched and raised his gaze to her. Pain overflowed in the tears streaking down his face. "Why are you doing this to me?"

"Because I care for you, dear. Because you deserve it." She set the bowl next to the plate, smiled, and left the room. She closed the door behind her, pressing a hand over her aching heart. Never before had she fostered such hatred for a person as she held for Ashra. The damage the woman had done was near irreversible. For the first time, Talura doubted she possessed the ability to help her new son.

By the end of her walk to the others, she'd buried her anger and cast an assuring smile to the question in her husband's eyes.

The rest of breakfast was relaxed, and everyone seemed to take longer to eat. Lunara began talking more as the morning progressed, and her haunted eyes calmed, the wolf enjoying the perks of her happiness. Varila had been oddly quiet in regards to the mage, and

Talura reminded herself to ask her eldest why she had refrained from berating Salvarias about his behavior. Varila's tongue was undoubtedly swollen from the amount of times she'd bitten it to keep her mouth shut. It was no secret she despised the mage, regardless of Talura's many talks.

They were finishing when a messenger arrived covered in road dust and looking exhausted.

"I have a relay from Commander Brice," the man said.

"Come." Edium motioned to the platters of food. "Help yourself while I read it, Jand."

The servant bowed graciously and accepted her husband's offer. Edium's eyes skimmed the note, his brow furrowing tighter the further he read.

"What is it?" Humar asked.

Edium cursed and threw the letter on the table. "Brice ran into a trap."

"How many did you lose?" Humar asked.

"Near a hundred."

Humar sucked in a breath. "What'd the boy do?"

"Got lured into a deserted village by a band of octrils. He sent too few and no scouts. My men chased the octrils right into the town, which ended up being a home to near seventy octrils. All my men were slaughtered. When no one returned, the boy realized his mistake and sent scouts."

"I know you don't want to hear it," Humar said evenly, "but I'll say it anyway. I told you so. The boy doesn't have the experience needed, Edium. He's too young. You have to see that. Your place is here."

"My place is with my family!" Edium snapped.

"Why don't you all excuse us," Talura said to the others.

All left except Humar and Edium.

"I understand you want to go where we go," Humar said. "But your family will be in danger when they return."

Edium glanced at her. "Well?"

Talura had no desire to stay behind. Yet she knew Humar was right. Edium needed to travel with the army, and with the majority of the city on campaign, running Serinity would fall to her. They could no longer follow their children. One glance at her husband and Edium knew her response.

He scowled, rose from his chair and paced. "You don't even know where you're going. You need our help."

"Two more swords won't make a difference," Humar said. "You saw Wilhelm. Between the two of us, we can take care of most threats."

"I've seen the horrors following that boy!" Edium said. "Without Salvarias using magic you don't stand a chance."

"That's going to be taken care of."

Edium and Talura looked expectantly at Humar. The knight spread his hands, eyes twinkling with a secret. "There's one person who can persuade Salvarias to use his magic. And I've talked with him, and he's seen some truths. Matter of fact, I'm sure our little friend is heading up there as we speak to talk sense into the boy."

Talura's mouth dropped open. "You can't be serious. How did you convince him?"

"Who?" Edium asked.

Humar winked. "I didn't need to do much. Salvarias did something that has made him the most loyal of friends."

"Who!" Edium demanded.

Talura laughed. "Humar, you really are a gem."

Chapter 7

Summer 1018 a.r.

Salvarias leaned on the balcony railing of the Bellerum library overlooking the filthy streets of Falar, his beautiful plate of food at his side. He had not been able to bring himself to eat it, to maim the perfection. All his favorites. All in flawless proportion. However, his hunger won.

Never before had a pear tasted so ripe and juicy. Never before had the cherries been as ideally tart as they were sweet. Never had bread been so pillowy and the butter so creamy. He ate it, forcing it down past the lump in his throat, wiping his tears with each bite.

Ssshe isss cruel, my murderer, the presence said. *Ssso cruel to you. The food isss her weapon. Her ruse to gain your favor before ssshe sssspitsss in your face. Sssadly, the world isss sssavage. You mussst harden yoursssself to it. Pleassse, do not let her hurt you as they did. I do not want to sssee you in sssuch pain again.*

Salvarias threw the plate at the nearest wall. It shattered, spraying out the food, sending a loud crash to surely draw attention. As he suspected, a servant rushed into the room.

"Oh my," she said, taking in the sight. "The wind must've blown it right off." She laughed lightly. "Are you well, Master Salvarias?"

"It was not the wind," he said coolly. "I threw it."

"Oh ..." She frowned as she knelt down, piling the remnants in the makeshift pouch she made in her apron. "Not to worry. Lord Bellerum has many dishes. One won't be missed."

He was about to retort a snide comment but bit his tongue. Grimacing, he searched his evil and found its smug satisfaction. Apparently, he was not as in control as he had hoped.

"Forgive me," he said. "I will tell Lord Bellerum myself. Let me help."

He knelt by her side and helped wipe up the mess, despite her protests. Once cleaned, the woman curtsied, thanked him for the eleventh time, and left the balcony.

Salvarias resumed his mindless staring over the city. Before long, Durak shuffled up. Rarely did the two converse, so Salvarias remained quiet, letting the silence transition from awkward to acceptable to comfortable. Just when he nearly forgot the grumpy cavrul was at his side, Durak spoke.

"Tell me about the mage ye killed. Tell me about Dethal."

Salvarias understood the reason for the cavrul's visit. "His description strikes a chord with you?"

"Aye."

Salvarias nodded. "I can assure you, it was him."

"How did ye know it be him?"

"I doubt you would believe me if I told you."

"Me saw the body."

Salvarias shuddered.

"Ye burned him with that unnatural fire, didn't ye?"

"I did."

A long moment of silence passed before Durak spoke in a thick voice. "Did he suffer?"

"More than a hundred deaths. And I can assure you, he endures pain beyond your understanding even now."

"I wanted to do it meself."

"If the opportunity would have been there, I would have gladly handed him over to you." Salvarias had not meant to say his next words, but they tumbled out regardless. "Your wife was the first person Dethal killed. He was scared and alone, and he only wanted help. When she denied him, he snapped. Killing your son and daughter was an accident. After that day, after what he had done to your family, he caved to the simpler, darker side of humanity."

The cavrul scuffed his boot along the base of the railing, and another long silence passed before Durak muttered, "Ye need to use magic, boy."

Salvarias startled and looked down at Durak. "Pardon?"

"It be unnatural, magic and mages, but it has potential to save thousands. Me saw it with my own eyes. Me've seen Mafarias save me city. Me've seen ye do things, boy. Brilliant things. Ye killed a basilisk by yerself. Ye stopped the worm in Quind. Ye saved Varila from the wretics." Durak rubbed his face, exhaling a harsh sigh. "Ye can't ignore such power. Ye can't be trusted, and I'll kill you if it ever turns on ye, but ye can't ignore it either."

"And you have seen me do unthinkable horrors with it. I do not understand your—"

"Me don't care if ye understand," Durak snapped. "What me be sayin' is that as long as ye don't go creating nothin' or setting people on fire—except for Dethal—I approve of yer magic. Ye need to see the good and the bad in it, boy. And ye need to use it for good. Enchantments especially. Ye can do good with those, too. Maybe ..." Durak slumped and his drawn face seemed to age years. Salvarias eyed a streak of gray hair along Durak's temple he had not noticed before. "Maybe if me wife had helped Dethal, he'd have been on our side. Me can't and won't forgive him, but ..."

Salvarias struggled to gain thought through his shock.

A few breaths passed before Durak spoke in a soft, hesitant voice. "Why don't ye hate me? Me killed over a hundred mages after Dethal murdered me family."

"I am the last person who should pass judgment, Durak. If I may ask, do you fear Oblivion for what you have done?"

Durak shrugged. "There was a time me did, when I was murdering. But me've spent a lot of time reconciling what was done. Me can't change the past. Me can only shape my future. Listen to me boy, ye life, ye purpose, is mightier than what I thought. Ye saved me city." The cavrul met his gaze. And Durak did not flinch. His frown deepened before he looked away. "Ye saved me home, lad. Ye killed my family's murderer. Learning of me sins, ye looked at me with compassion. I've not the right to ask ye for anything after the way me've treated you, but I am. I'm asking ye to use magic again." Durak spat at Salvarias's feet. "To Oblivion with you if ye don't agree."

Durak stormed off the balcony. Salvarias stared dumbfounded at the glob glistening at his feet. Slowly, his mind turned with memories of the warmth his magic supplied, its fondness, its curiosity, its shared wonder at all they could accomplish. Without the other powers, his magic was good. His magic could do good.

Admittedly, he had been childish. He believed his magic did not intentionally hurt the little girl outside Xeroth, and he desperately missed the relationship, so he swallowed his pride and ignited his magic.

With a somber voice, his magic asked, *How may I serve you, Master?*

Accept my apology. I acted like a child.

I ... I've caused you great pain. I never intended that to happen. I've—

It was not your fault, my friend. By stating those words, it was as if he forgave himself, which was something he had no desire to do. Closing his eyes, he remembered the little girl's innocent eyes, her curiosity. He reinforced the consequences of his actions. He had murdered her outside Xeroth on that sunny day. He had snuffed out the light of beautiful soul, the life of an innocent. Her blood was on his hands, not his magic. He took a deep breath of acceptance.

I think I have found the reason, his magic said. *If you are ready to discuss it, of course.*

I am, my friend.

The plant we created evolved.

In such a short period?

It was created in a short period, so I think it evolved in a short period. It was threatened. The little girl trampled it when she ran through it, and it did nothing more than defend itself. Though I admit, the power was malicious in its intent. I swear to you, we can do this with the blackfire without the same results. While that power is full of anger, it isn't intent on destruction.

Salvarias traced a black knot on his staff. *I am not sure I will ever be ready to try again. These powers you sense inside me, I am scared of them. We do not know where they came from, what their intent is. I cannot control them, cannot speak to them as I do you. Blackfire comes to life on its own. The other power I cannot even feel. And now you want me to use blackfire, the same power that kills, that takes me to Oblivion, you want me to use it willingly?*

Only alongside me. I would never allow them to harm you. Please don't lose faith in me. We can try creating in a contained environment, with a contained component. Each speck of dirt we used created a plant, and the wind carried it far. If we focus on a single component in a controlled area, I think we'll be pleasantly surprised. I think blackfire can create something beautiful, something pure. Something good.

Salvarias sighed. His decision would change the relationship forever.

Small leaps, his magic said. *Yet again, I ask you to leap first.*

And if I say I am placing all my trust in you, would you still suggest trying it again?

Ah, you are offering your trust on a contingency? You hinge it on my agreement?

Do you blame me?

No, I don't. But are you ready to take this leap in our relationship if I agree? I have been for some time. Your values are in line with mine. You're worthy of all the power you possess, and I would be honored to have earned your trust. But all the time we've known each other, I've felt your guarded nature toward me. You've never trusted me. And now, after what we've done, you're ready?

You know the risk in promising me, Salvarias said. *If you should break it, you and I are through. Once you commit, I will think of this no more. I will fully trust you. I will place my life in your power. I will place the life of my brother there as well. You understand my level of dedication and my expectations?*

Salvarias breathed deeply when the magic warmed him, wrapping him in a comforting blanket of confidence and security. His head swam in an ocean of care.

Your life, and that of your brother's, above my own, my wizard, the magic said.

My life is yours. No longer are we separate.

Salvarias trembled under the power surging up in his blood from the pure joy his magic experienced. It soared in euphoric bliss, and the barriers each erected to guard themselves dissolved. His magic's emotions exploded with clarity. Its deep respect and love for Salvarias brought tears to his eyes. No fear existed in either of them toward each other. Neither remained composed and cautious. All their flaws were shared in one fleeting thought. His magic's thirst for knowledge was more insatiable than Salvarias's. Its confidence flourished enough to make up for what he lacked. They balanced each other perfectly.

I am sorry for shutting you out, Salvarias said through his growing smile. *I hope to prove to you my sincerity and how much our relationship means to me.*

Never again will you apologize, my wizard. Never again will you hold guilt for how you treated me. This day, we are both free.

For the first time in his life, Salvarias forgave himself. *Thank you,* he said.

Now, allow me to reacquaint myself with your mind. Unfortunately, we've lost a bit of power without practice and focus.

Not to mention this new strain you endure. It must be intolerable. I'll see if there is a way I can assist. We'll talk soon, my brilliant wizard.

Salvarias let his magic subside, and his smile waned when the comfort and confidence drained from him. After a self-pitying sigh, he left the balcony and found his companions waiting for him in the library.

"Ready to go hunt down our cousin?" Wilhelm asked.

"Yes, brother."

"Wilhelm, Salvarias, you take the docks," Humar instructed. "Varila, Okulu, Neithelas, and Lunara, take the market. Edium and I have some things to discuss, and then we'll head out and take the inns and taverns."

"I can take the taverns," Okulu offered.

"No, you'll go with the others," Humar said.

"Bastard," Okulu grumbled.

All in agreement, they left the estate and entered the blinding sunlight of late morning. At the gate, his brother steered Salvarias over to a man off to the side.

"This is Brenil," Wilhelm introduced. "My little brother, Salvarias."

Salvarias bowed, recognizing the man's name from his brother's secret rendezvous with the woman named Haleen. "Gentleman Brenil, it is a pleasure to meet you."

Brenil's face split into a grin, revealing yellow teeth. Salvarias found the man's lazy eye quite distracting and was thankful his own gaze was hidden as he could not figure out which eye to stare at.

"The pleasure's mine," Brenil said. "Haleen was disappointed she never met you." Brenil nudged him with an elbow. "She was curious if you were as ... vigorous as your brother."

Salvarias's cheeks flamed hot, and he was at a complete loss as to what to say.

Wilhelm wrapped an arm around Salvarias's neck and laughed. "I don't think Haleen is my brother's type."

"Shame," Brenil said. "She could've taught you a thing or two."

Salvarias squirmed at the awkward conversation.

"Ah, shy is he?" Brenil asked Wilhelm.

Seeming to realize Salvarias's discomfort, Wilhelm's chuckle faded and he ruffled Salvarias hair. "He's too polite to engage in this stuff. I guess we better head out."

"Good day then," Brenil said.

Salvarias bowed. "Good day, gentleman."

Wilhelm winked and strolled through the gate where Adok joined them. Salvarias pulled his cloak about his robes, and Wilhelm nodded after giving him a quick once over, then they set off for the docks.

When they arrived, Salvarias waited in the background while Wilhelm sauntered up to the first watythm he came across.

"Hello there!" Wilhelm called. "We're looking for a man, light-brown hair, brown eyes, tall as that mage over there and well built. It would have been in the last week, and he would have had three mages with him. Likely they were looking for passage."

The sailor shook his head. "Haven't seen him. Check the Lucky Steed. Most sailors stay there, and if he took a ship, they'll know about him."

Wilhelm tossed him a copper. "Thanks, friend." He returned to Salvarias. "Lucky Steed is where we need to head. That place is vile."

Salvarias frowned as he stepped beside his brother and followed him back to the bustling streets. "I do not remember it."

"You wouldn't," Wilhelm said, shouldering his way through the crowd. "It was after Mother and Father died."

When they entered the Lucky Steed, Salvarias gagged at the stench of vomit, piss, and ale. The slippery floor left no questions as to where the odor stemmed from.

A man with his belly protruding over his trews pointed at Salvarias. "No mages!"

"I will wait outside, brother." Salvarias did not wait for an answer and fled the tavern. He gasped in air when he emerged into the hot summer morning, although it was not much better. Summer in Falar was stifling. The smell of baked sweat and fish blanketed the city, thickened by the added people from small towns. Adok emerged from shadows as Salvarias adjusted his light cloak to conceal his mage robes, employing the tricks he had watched his mother use.

Once situated, he gazed at the people swarming about on all-important errands and mused over what was sure to be a chaotic life in their minds: worrying about business and what to make for supper. He did not see the man robed in blood red approach until the figure stood directly in front of him.

Air disappeared and his surroundings vanished. All that existed in his world were a pair of black eyes. An oppressive weight pushed down on Salvarias, a whisper tickled his ear, and thick fog covered his thoughts, as if his mind fought to escape quicksand.

The whisper came again. "Peaccce, boy. I offer peaccce. Come with me."

Salvarias did not need his soul. It was not his own. It belonged to the black eyes. He wobbled a step forward.

"Come to me, boy."

Adok whined.

"Do not interfere," the man hissed. "Already you have broken the rules."

Salvarias staggered another step.

"Yessss. Give it to me."

The calling plucked at his resolve. He lurched forward.

"Releassse your pain, boy. I give you peaccce. Accccept my hand."

Salvarias stared at the long, thin fingers reaching for him.

"Blissssful peaccce, boy. Sssafety. Love. I can fulfill all of it. Jussst accccept."

Salvarias raised his hand and paused. The lean hand was not the safety Salvarias had always sought. Safety only existed in one place. He conjured an image of his brother, and it hit him with physical force. He stumbled backwards. The haze cleared, and he sucked in a breath.

Evil, thick and vicious, surrounded him. But that was not what made Salvarias quake with fear. It was the familiarity of the evil, the same as what lived within him.

He tripped backwards and begged his body to flee as the hooded figure advanced, but instead an invisible weight drove him to his knees.

"Brother!"

An icy finger touched Salvarias's forehead and pain exploded. A thousand jagged teeth tore into his body and mind, ripping apart muscle and his resolve. Salvarias doubled over in sheer agony, a scream lodged in this throat. The man stood over him, hissing words he could not understand. Weakness settled into his bones, as if the figure sucked out Salvarias's will and power.

You mussst accept! the presence yelled. *He will kill usss!*

Salvarias could not answer, could not think. His head filled with thick liquid, and he clamped his eyes tight against the pain. His feeble heart faltered, and he feared if he were to open his eyes, he would see his body shredded into strips and his soul ravaged with holes.

Your sssoul will turn the tidesss, my murderer, the presence said. *Accccept and you can protect thossse you love. I can help you, we can sssave them.*

"No!"

Then I will ssshow you what you are capable of, what you have done in your ssshort yearsss!

Salvarias was no longer in Falar. He prostrated on the rolling plains of his dream, crammed among the dead. The formerly peaceful crowd clawed at him, all furious as they spewed their hatred toward the being that murdered them. He curled up, clamping his hands over his ears as the dead demanded blood.

A sharp pain shot up his chest and burst through his shoulder. He looked down to see a sword rammed into his torso. In a blink it disappeared. He cried out when white-hot pain pierced his back, and he arched as a different sword protruded out of his belly.

"I didn't get to see my son born!" a man screamed, the same sword striking the same wound on the man as Salvarias.

Salvarias grabbed his throat and hot blood spilt over his hands as he gurgled for air. A woman knelt in front of him, fire in her eyes, spittle flying from her lips as she screamed incoherently at him. Her throat leaked blood.

As if that was not enough to drive him insane, inside his own heart, his own soul, he felt the victims' emotional terror, their grief, confusion, the hollowness of loss and anger.

And it went on. His own blood pooled with that of the dead, and in an instant he was halfway submerged in it. And it was rising rapidly. In a blink it became a flash flood, sweeping him along in a current of death, drowning him in a vast ocean. He held his breath, fighting to reach the surface, but the dead hauled him down. His muscles tensed. Pins stabbed his eyes from lack of air, and his lungs felt like they crumpled in his chest. He involuntarily gulped. The act forced him to drink the blood of acceptance, to assume responsibility for their deaths.

Accccept! the presence begged. *You cannot fight it. Accccept it willingly and you can ssspare thossse you love.*

Desperate for help, he ignited his magic. Its confusion passed quickly and it lashed out at the dead. Salvarias screamed in agony when the blood he drowned in seeped inside him, plunging into his pores, tainting him further.

One by one, each person's torment bombarded Salvarias, each dying breath he experienced himself, each terror-filled thought settled into his own mind, and each wound slashed him open. He lost control of his body. Convulsions racked him and he choked on blood and vomit, no longer aware if he was still drowning or if he had been saved.

A familiar hand reached for him: the same strong, comforting hand that had beckoned to him after his parents died, the same hand that had saved him at his brother's death.

Salvarias could endure no more. The sheer pain the robed figure induced hindered his ability to fight, and his weak heart was failing him. His mind would cave, turn stale, offering nothing for either the light or the darkness. The stable hand of his mind promised protection, a shielding of his sanity. After a slight hesitation, he reached back.

A strong voice roared over the pain, and the hand of his mind withdrew its comforts, leaving Salvarias suffocating in agony.

Chapter 8

Summer 1018 a.r.

Wilhelm was chatting with the bar owner when his heart skipped and the sound of Salvarias calling for him rang all around, like a giant bell had gone off in his head. Slightly disoriented from the sensation, Wilhelm shoved aside drunk patrons and heard vicious barking from outside the tavern. He burst through the tavern door, slamming it into Adok, who'd been on the steps.

Off to the side by a small garden, his brother knelt in front of a man robed in red, the same man Wilhelm had seen the day of his brother's birth. The man's thin finger rested on Salvarias's forehead, spilling red foggy light that encompassed Salvarias's body.

"You cannot fight it," the man hissed. "Accccept it willingly and you can ssspare thosse you love."

The robed figure cried out when the red fog sucked *inside* Salvarias, the same as it had done the day he was born. His brother crumpled to the ground, convulsions attacking his body. Blood jetted from his mouth.

"Leave him alone!" Wilhelm roared, taking the four steps in one leap.

The figure teetered back and turned a cold stare on Wilhelm. Salvarias screamed.

"Damn you!" the man spat. He staggered backward, groping at the air until finding a wall of a nearby home. "You will not win thisss, boy! He isss mine!" The man whirled about and melted into shadows.

"Salv!" Wilhelm fell beside his brother. "I'm here, Salv."

Salvarias's eyes were rolled back in his head, and his muscles spasmed. No air entered his lungs and blood continued to pour from his mouth, mixing with bile. Wilhelm scanned the busy streets. Some took notice but steered clear of a mage. Off in the distance, a man clothed in slate-blue robes caught his eye.

"Help me!" Wilhelm called.

The man ran toward them and his white beard caught the light. Old hands jutted out from his robes, and he ran with more energy than a man his age should possess. Wilhelm cursed. This was the last person he should trust.

"What happened?" Vuddruk yelled.

Wilhelm glanced around, but with no other options he turned back to Vuddruk. "Someone touched him!"

Vuddruk reached them and sank to his knees, shaking his head. "Tell me who, boy! Who!"

"I don't know—"

"Tell me!" Vuddruk snapped.

Wilhelm jumbled out the words. "A man robed in red."

"Dammit! Touch his mark to yours."

Wilhelm shook his head, remembering the sensation of power coursing through him and leaching it all from Salvarias, nearly killing his brother. He'd sworn to never do it again unless others were there to help him stop. Vuddruk was too old to overpower Wilhelm. "I can't."

"It's his only chance. You must," Vuddruk insisted.

"I can't stop."

"You fool! You don't need him, he needs you. The power feeds the weaker. Do it now or I swear we're doomed!"

Cursing, Wilhelm grabbed his brother's hand, wincing in expectation. But nothing happened. Vuddruk pressed his thumb to Salvarias's forehead, and pale-green foggy light flowed around Salvarias. His brother's seizures lasted a few more breaths. When they ceased, the green light sucked into Salvarias, inducing a moan from both mages.

Salvarias curled in a ball, a pain-filled cry ripping from his throat, free hand grabbing his head. Suddenly Wilhelm's strength sucked out of him. He toppled over, groaning, his body trembling from instant exhaustion, muscles feeling like lumps of soggy bread. Every part of him ached as if he had run for days. His deadened limbs sprawled on the hot cobblestones, and he had to focus on breathing. Salvarias's hand went limp in his own.

"Salv," Wilhelm rasped.

"Sleeping," Vuddruk said. "You did good, boy. Very good."

"Wilhelm!" Humar called.

Wilhelm rolled his head toward the knight's voice. Both Edium and Humar were sprinting for him, shoving bodily through the crowd. Wilhelm's cheek burned against the hot street.

"No, boy," Vuddruk whispered, nudging Wilhelm. "You have to carry your brother. He can't have anyone touch him in this state. You need to get him to safety, and whatever you do, do not leave his side while you're in Falar. Which way did the man go? The one in red?"

Darkness pressed in on Wilhelm's vision. He was so exhausted.

"No," Vuddruk snapped. "Stay awake. Which way did the man go?"

Wilhelm forced his eyes to focus in the direction the red-robed man had run.

"Good," Vuddruk said. He grabbed Wilhelm's chest armor and yanked him to a sitting position. "Remember, don't leave your brother's side. You have to get him off the streets."

With strength Wilhelm didn't know he still possessed, he shoved himself to his feet with help from Vuddruk. He stumbled and teetered, tipped and turned before Humar and Edium steadied him.

"You have a lot of explaining to do!" Edium snapped at Vuddruk.

"Wish I could, but I must be going." Vuddruk winked before darting down the street in the direction of the red-robed man.

"Bastard!" Edium yelled.

Wilhelm lifted his trembling brother and staggered forward. Peripheral vision left so he focused on Humar leading the way, legs shaking with each step. Sounds faded in and out. He was sure Edium was asking him questions, but he couldn't process anything but putting one foot in front of the other.

Okulu's voice rose up on his right side. "I can take Salvarias."

"No, you can't touch him ... You ... can't ..." Wilhelm became dizzy from the effort it took to speak, and the city spun wildly around him. As he plummeted into darkness, he cradled his brother protectively in his arms.

Salvarias woke to his own screaming voice. Whatever nightmare he had dreamt was whisked from his memory, and he could not have been more grateful. The lingering terror shuddered up his spine and added layers of frost to his bones. The usual images of death and new images of the ocean fleeted before his eyes, and between each, thick darkness pressed in upon him.

"Lumous."

No light glowed between the pictures of death.

"Brother?"

The rumbling voice rose out of the darkness. "There's light, Salv."

Blindness. This was his fate.

Reaching out shaking hands, familiar arms encased Salvarias as a fresh wave of tears assailed him. Curling up as small as he could, wishing he would disappear, he silently pleaded for death. His mind carried such a strain the pain was near unbearable. He was tired, defeated, and he did not want to fight anymore. He wanted sleep, peaceful sleep.

"As long as we're together, we can do anything," Wilhelm said. "And we'll get through this. Do you trust me?"

Salvarias nodded.

"You need to focus on breathing," Wilhelm said. "One breath at a time, just like me."

Salvarias had not realized how hard he gasped for air and yet little entered his sick lungs. The pounding in his skull made it impossible to hear the chorus of Wilhelm's heart and the whooshing of air into his lungs. So instead, Salvarias measured his breathing with the rise and fall of Wilhelm's chest. Closing his eyes, Salvarias cleared everything from his mind but air. Time passed unknown, but Wilhelm's rhythmic breathing slipped Salvarias into a sleepy trance as it had done when they were little.

Wilhelm's deep voice woke him. "That's better. How do you feel?"

Salvarias took in a deep, steady breath and opened his eyes. The sparrow of light greeted him along with Wilhelm's crooked grin.

Salvarias wiped the drying tears from his face and took in another calming breath. "I can see. Are you harmed?"

Wilhelm's grin broadened. "No, I'm fine."

Salvarias glanced around the bedroom and caught sight of Adok pacing in worry. The lecture started up immediately.

"That was a bad nightmare," Wilhelm said.

For the first time in his life, Salvarias had not remembered something. The dream huddled just outside his grasp, but he made no effort to reach for it.

Looking around, he found himself in his room in the Bellerum estate. He propped himself against the wall and lifted his brother's hand to examine the silhouetted bear on Wilhelm's palm. "What happened?"

"I touched our marks together and my strength sapped out," Wilhelm said.

Salvarias studied his own mark of a ring circling a black flame. His hand did not feel different, did not hurt, but he remembered the pain from his brother's touch, as if a dagger stabbed his mind, releasing the building pressure like an explosion of suppressed steam. The experience was exactly what had happened with Tedris, but Wilhelm's strength was tenfold that of their father. What Tedris had gifted had only allowed Salvarias to fight the major battle. What Wilhelm had supplied not only fought away the main force of his evil but also the tendrils usually sneaking their way through his wall. He felt ... purged. Though the result was wonderful, the act itself was not something Salvarias ever wanted to relive again. The pain had been horrible.

Wilhelm's voice broke his thoughts. "What did that robed man do to you?"

"I do not know, brother."

The presence said, *Now you mussst drain your brother to fight your evil? You can no longer control it yoursssself?*

Yes, Salvarias responded. *I am even further lost.*

Hardly any of your own sssoul remainsss. Ssso much evil within. Your fight will be arduousss. I fear the longer you ssstay with the group, the lessss chanccce you have of successss and the lessss chanccce they have of sssurviving in your company.

"I don't understand what's going on," Wilhelm mumbled.

His brother was hiding something. Salvarias sensed it the moment Wilhelm asked about the robed man. Fear prevented Salvarias from questioning it. "We share the same frustration, brother."

"Vuddruk showed up. He touched you and it seemed to help."

"I do not remember."

"What did it do when you touched my mark?"

Salvarias lowered his head and folded his arms over his chest. Though he had told Wilhelm he had seen their father, he did not convey Tedris's power. Salvarias feared Wilhelm's role was a requirement in Salvarias's task, and that meant his brother was in danger. He had hoped to keep it a secret, but somehow Wilhelm had known to touch their marks. And how would Wilhelm react if he knew Salvarias's evil was ten times more powerful, that it had infected his own soul time and again?

Yesss, my pet. We don't know if he will underssstand. It isss bessst not to sssay anything. Let usss ssslip away in the night. Never tell him your evil isss ssstronger than ever. Never tell him you cannot fight it forever. Never tell him you mussst ussse him like a whore. It isss time to leave him.

"I am not ready. I cannot leave him."

"What?" Wilhelm asked.

Salvarias shook his head, cursing his tired mind. Usually he was able to keep his conversations with the presence, his magic, and animals silent.

"You can trust me, Salv."

Salvarias swallowed the growing lump in his throat. Wilhelm would accept the new information with his usual crooked grin. He would ruffle Salvarias's hair and tell him all would be fine, that he was not evil, that together they could overcome anything. Salvarias's desperation for it all to be true loosened this tongue. "I have ..."

No, my murderer.

Wilhelm gave an affectionate squeeze. "You can tell me."

"I ... I have a new evil within me, brother. When I touched Perek, he passed it along to me, just a portion of it, but enough to frighten me." Salvarias's words tumbled over one another in a shameful confession. "It is stronger, more difficult to battle. I have nearly been consumed by it." Stating the fact caused tears to well. He hopelessly wanted to be a whole person, his soul his own, with no whispers, no voices. Peace, quiet peace was what he longed for most.

"So touching my hand helps?" Wilhelm asked, unfazed by the revelation.

"Do you not hear what I am telling you? The evil is—"

"The evil is not who you are, Salv. It's ... it's just leftover dinner you haven't crapped out yet. We're going to find Perek and my—our—father, and we're going to figure this out." Wilhelm ruffled

Salvarias's hair before handing over the puzzle box he had played with since childhood. "In the mean time, you have to keep fighting."

The cube-shaped puzzle box was made of smaller carved cubes, all connected somehow at a core center, yet each piece seemed able to move into impossible places. All he had to do was conjure an image of a bear and directions appeared in his mind of the cubes twisting to make his desired shape. "Unfortunately, I require a large amount of your strength to do so. I am not strong enough on my own."

"For now," Wilhelm said. "I bet you get better. You just need time to figure out how to keep it reined in. Don't be so hard on yourself."

Salvarias mulled over the thought, unsure if his painful mind would ever be under his control. "Perhaps." He elbowed his brother.

"Ouch!" Wilhelm rubbed his side. "I think Talura's food has something in it. You get stronger after you've had a few of her meals."

Indeed, Salvarias had already packed on whatever weight he had lost in the swamps. He pondered if her food was better because it was prepared with care. The presence laughed.

Clearing his throat, Salvarias said, "I think we missed some valuable training on how to handle our gifts. The power you received that helped you battle the troll in the barbarian desert and then Marrow in Cattlar is linked to this story somehow, but I do not understand. Was it the same as what I took from you today?"

"No, they're different. Whatever happened with the troll made me angry, furious. It's not like what happens when you heal me, either. When you used me today, I was tired, but nothing else." Wilhelm chuckled. "I guess we'll figure it out as we go. It's kind of how we work best, don't you think? Just deal with each situation and give it our damnedest. And I think we've done a fine job so far."

Salvarias smiled and sagged against the wall and his brother. "We have. Does that mean you have three powers?"

"The anger I used when I killed the troll came from deep inside me, a place I can't access on my own. It just sort of happens. The strength you took from me today is just that: my strength. I'm tired but I guess you needed it more than I did. At least that's what Vuddruk said. Our powers, whatever they might be or mean, will feed the weaker, he said. Which makes sense because the power that healed me came from you, like you gave me part of your own life ... soul ... I'm not sure."

Salvarias nodded his understanding. "Did you find out anything in the tavern?"

"Yes, Perek took a ship to Windlous."

"Windlous?" Salvarias sighed. An unfamiliar continent with unknown evils. He had read much in his time with Dethal. However, Windlous was not written of as extensively as Dalnar and Loutsil except, oddly, for their myriad of plant life. "To Windlous we travel. We need a ship that can take the horses. It will be a month-long trip by sea, and the price will be high. Can we afford it?"

"Edium is funding us."

Salvarias did not approve, but arguing with Lord Bellerum was as pointless as trying to get Okulu to give up spirits. Holding up the puzzle box, Salvarias admired his finished creation of a bear.

"What is it?" Wilhelm asked.

"My brother."

Wilhelm grinned. "Let's go eat. I'm starving!"

As always when Salvarias gave the puzzle box back to Wilhelm for safe keeping, it shrunk to the size of a marble and disappeared into a hidden pocket in his tunic. The box was a continuous mystery, but one Salvarias had given up on years ago. He considered it a gift because it was the only time relief blessed his mind other than when he used Lunara.

Wilhelm wrapped an arm around Salvarias's neck and led the way to the dining hall, Adok following. He glanced out the window at the thick layer of fog clinging to the city, illuminated by the moon's serene light.

His companions, except for Lord Bellerum and Lady Talura, were spread out at a table overflowing with food that made Salvarias's stomach challenge Wilhelm's.

"How are you both feeling?" Humar asked.

Both brothers mumbled their responses. Salvarias sank into a chair and, concealed by the shadows of his hood, drank in Lunara's bright smile while Wilhelm gathered two plates.

"Where are Talura and Edium?" Wilhelm asked.

"Discussing some things," Humar said. "They'll likely not be traveling with us to ...?" Humar glanced between Wilhelm and Salvarias.

Wilhelm piled a plate full of random food, set it in front of Salvarias, and then fetched a plate for himself, triple in size. Salvarias picked through the heap to find things he liked.

"We're going to Windlous," Wilhelm announced as he settled into his seat. "Have any of you been there before?"

Okulu grinned. "Once. Not a friendly place by any means, but not overly difficult. The sides of the gods' Long Wars mixed over there. Races crossed badly. Part human and octril, part watythm and ogre—"

Wilhelm's mouth dropped open. "Is that even possible?"

Okulu took a long swig from his flask. "I'm afraid there's worse. Creatures you can't find in books mixed with humans. It's blamed on Lakvra. She is, after all, the goddess of lust, stuck here just as Crutar. She's made it near impossible to tell who's friendly. An octril could save you while a winsire stabs you in the back. On the bright side, the Association of Mages is pretty lax out there. That'll help."

Salvarias glanced at each of his companions. "I ask again, please stay behind."

"We're coming, lad." Durak's stern voice held a different scold than Salvarias normally heard. He raised his head to regard the cavrul. Durak winked.

"And I will be representing the winsires," Neithelas said. "My brother is handling the army and has no need for me. He has instructed I assist in helping find this evil, though I do not imagine it is far off."

Salvarias forced himself to tilt his head in polite thanks. Deep inside, he wished the winsire would stay behind. The subtle insults were becoming tiresome.

Okulu's daggers clattered on the table, and he grinned at Salvarias. "I think it's about time, don't you? You've enchanted that staff with enough crap to make it a living being. How about sharing?"

"Of course." Salvarias set aside his plate and ignited his magic, feeling his brother's smile spread to take up the entire room.

My wizard, the magic said respectfully. *We've gained more power.*

From where? How?

I took it from whatever tried to take yours. It was working to steal your power, so instead I stole its power. I've done it with the old mage and your uncle before. There is ... something different about them. Something I think is similar to us.

Thank you, my friend.

Even though you gained power, your mind has weakened. There is potential within but until your mind calms, we cannot explore it.

I apologize, friend. I am trying.

Warmth flowed through Salvarias's blood. *Too much do you blame on yourself, my guilt-ridden wizard. Now, allow us to enchant your friend's daggers. With our new connection, I should be able to shield your mind more effectively. There's even a possibility to keep you awake.*

Salvarias opened a link to the surrounding energy and the weapon resting in his palm. His magic shielded his mind just as he clicked the link into place. He forgot about the gust of air that followed his enchantments. Cups spilled out ale and food flew across the room. Okulu burst out laughing. Salvarias looked up to see a piece of bread Neithelas had slathered with jam stuck on the winsire's face. Wilhelm's booming laugh joined the merc.

"I am sorry," Salvarias said to Neithelas.

Lunara put her hand over her mouth, but her eyes reflected a smile.

"What in damnation happened?" Durak barked, brushing potatoes from his beard.

"It is a side effect of enchanting," Salvarias explained.

Durak muttered several oaths. "Well, get it all done before we clean up."

Salvarias handed the dagger to Okulu. With fluid grace, the merc threw it into the wood mantle above the fireplace. By the count of four, it was back in its sheath.

"Brilliant!" Okulu said. "I knew there was a reason I kept you around."

"The dagger will always return to the sheath, not you. If ever you require a new belt, I will re-enchant the daggers."

"Understood," Okulu said, smile bright and contagious.

Selecting the next one, Salvarias developed the link and executed the enchantment. Any food that had not moved the first time skidded across the table. He slouched in his chair and knew he should stop, but when he pushed his magic, he slept with less dreams. After the terror he experienced when he woke, he did not want to dream whatever he had dreamt again. He enchanted a third dagger and tumbled into darkness and familiar arms.

Chapter 9

Summer 1018 a.r.

Wilhelm watched from the balcony of the library as the sun ducked behind the horizon, painting the sky in rich plums and canary yellows. Okulu had gone out to procure them a ship to take to Windlous, and Wilhelm hoped the new continent would prove less dangerous for Salvarias. Sighing at the unknown, Wilhelm wrapped his arm around his brother's neck and ruffled Salvarias's hair.

"It is time we talked about Humar," Salvarias said.

Wilhelm shrugged. Lying to his brother was pointless, but he might be able to evade his brother's plea. "What did he tell you?"

"It is as if you and I had never met," Salvarias said dryly, eyes rolling slightly. "Humar told me nothing. However, I know you are upset with him. I know you blame him for my *own* actions when *I* chose to hand myself over to the army in Cattlar."

"I'm not changing my mind, Salv. The bastard should never have let you leave."

"Please, do not disrespect him. Never before have I been able to call another friend. I have one now, and I care for his happiness. I see his pain every time he looks at you. I feel it, brother. Can you not forgive him?"

"No."

Salvarias shook his head. "You have forgiven me for far worse. He is your friend. He is our friend. He is as important to me as he is to you. You cannot tell me you do not miss his friendship."

"I—"

"If you are going to lie, look me in the eyes."

Wilhelm swallowed and stared at the streaked sky. "Salv ... I'm not ... He let you go."

"He made a mistake."

"He didn't care."

"He hid behind his fear. He did care."

Wilhelm clenched his jaw. "He doesn't deserve your friendship."

"He deserves it. And he deserves yours. You know I speak the truth."

Wilhelm couldn't deny it. He felt as guilty as he did justified.

"Please," Salvarias said. "I beg you, go to him and look him in the eye. If you still feel hatred for him, I will drop this and never speak of it again."

"I won't change my mind."

"Prove that to yourself."

Wilhelm knew exactly where to find Humar. Winding through the estate, Wilhelm made his way outside and into the decent-sized training yard. Humar was fluidly transitioning through his standard fighting stances. Wilhelm watched for a moment, remembering how much enjoyment he received when sparring with Humar. That one daily routine had gifted Wilhelm stability in all the chaos of his life. Humar's training had always felt like home, a place Wilhelm could grow and laugh, learn and be free. Sighing, he strolled up to the knight.

Humar paused in one of his moves and whirled around as if expecting Veedran himself. Upon seeing Wilhelm, the knight relaxed, if only slightly.

"Humar," Wilhelm greeted.

The knight sheathed his sword and inhaled as if awaiting a berating. Wilhelm swallowed a tinge of guilt. He tried to cling to his rage and the memory of what Salvarias had endured that fateful night Humar had sent his brother to his death. When he met the knight's eyes, they were lined with more guilt than Wilhelm ever thought a man could carry. He looked away quickly, but his anger had already fizzled out.

"Dammit," he muttered. "Why is he always right?"

"Pardon?" Humar asked.

"Salv. He told me if I looked at you, I wouldn't be as angry."

Humar shifted his stance. "You've no reason to forgive me, Wilhelm. I understand your anger. I've accepted it as a consequence of my actions. Whatever your brother might—"

"Shut up," Wilhelm growled. "I'm trying to apologize."

Humar's mouth opened, then closed and opened again. "I ..."

"Don't deserve it?" Wilhelm shrugged. "Maybe not." He scratched at his beard. "Dammit, Humar, I trusted you with his life. You betrayed me as much as you betrayed him."

"I did."

"I don't know how I feel."

"We've been through a lot together. Let me at least earn your trust back. Give me another chance. I beg you."

Wilhelm met the knight's gaze and in one shared look, knew he had forgiven Humar. Never again would Humar stand by and allow harm to come to Salvarias. He would always make the best decision that would ensure Salvarias's safety. It was as clear as his azure eyes.

Wilhelm held out his hand. "I trust you, my friend."

Instant tears welled in Humar's eyes. The knight brushed aside Wilhelm's hand and embraced him. "Thank you, boy. Thank you."

After a few awkward attempts to cross the ravine separating them, they settled for a quick spar. It didn't mend the gap entirely, but it at least built a bridge.

Wilhelm stood in the estate's courtyard while the sisters and their parents shared a private farewell within the home. Time dragged on before Humar, head shaking, went inside. When he emerged, the family had red eyes. Talura and Edium bid well-wishes to the others before they joined Wilhelm along with Humar.

Humar embraced Edium. "Good luck, friend. I'll send word often, and remember you were targeted in Cattler. It's not safe for you on your own, so don't venture from the protection of your army. You're the only hope we have to unite the ruling lords of Dalnar."

Edium merely nodded.

Humar kissed Talura's cheek. "Your hospitality is unmatched, Lady Talura."

She laughed warmly. "Thank you, Humar."

The knight bowed to both and walked over to stand by Okulu.

Edium embraced Wilhelm tightly. "Take care of yourself, son. Look after my girls and your brother."

"I will," Wilhelm said, clapping the man on the back.

Edium hesitated, looking as though he might say more, but left to join Salvarias.

"Make sure Salvarias eats," Talura said, making as if to straighten Wilhelm's armor. Tears glistened in her ice-blue eyes, which looked everywhere but at his. "He gets distracted when he reads and forgets sometimes."

Wilhelm nodded. "I will."

"Make sure you eat plenty." She passed him a purse as ridiculously heavy as the one Edium had already given him. "This should help you afford enough food. And make sure you buy Salvarias pears. And herb bread. He loves herb bread."

He tried to push the purse back into her hands, watching tears streaking down her face. "Edium gave me plenty, Talura."

"Don't be silly," she said, laughing lightly as she wiped tears. "I'm sure with all the trouble you'll be getting into, you'll require new clothes along the way, and Salvarias needs plenty of funds for his herbs. He does love to study herblore, so buy him any books he lingers over." She brushed imaginary lint from his shoulder and finally met his gaze. More tears overflowed and she cupped his face in her hands. "You come back to me. In one piece. You bring them all home with you. In one piece. And for all the love of all the gods, be strong. You're in for dark times, but know a home is waiting for you both. With all my heart, I love you."

Wilhelm swept the woman up in a hug. "Of course. I ... I love you too."

"Take care of my girls," she said, then unraveled herself and stepped back, hands balling together. She gave another smile before calling his brother over. She whispered to Salvarias in such a low voice that Wilhelm couldn't hear the exchange, but whatever she said stiffened his brother like a board, and his haggard breathing worsened with each word. When she finished, Salvarias nearly sprinted from her to the horses. She smiled at Wilhelm once more before walking to her husband to wave farewell.

Wilhelm stepped outside the estate, breathing in Falar's rancid smell. The early morning sun skulked behind dirty clouds scuttling in from the ocean. It was one of those mornings that made a person think the air should be cooler than what it actually was. He sighed when a warm breeze washed over his face. He hated summer. Glancing at his brother, he saw a similar look of distaste pass through Salvarias's large eyes rimmed by black circles. Wilhelm certainly didn't look any better. No one had slept. Salvarias's screams had reverberated through the estate the entire night. Still, his brother seemed not to remember his nightmare.

Wilhelm wrapped an arm around Salvarias's shoulders, lifting him ever so slightly to ease his breathing and limp. Whispered numbers drifted up through the air while they made their way through the city, Adok panting heavily at Salvarias's side.

Wilhelm's gaze swept over the streets, looking for the man robed in blood as well as Vuddruk. Though Wilhelm trusted the mage, despite Mafarias's warnings and all Wilhelm's more logical arguments against such folly, he kept a keen eye out for either of them. He hoped to see the red-robed man again so he could drive his sword through the man's skull. And if he saw Vuddruk, he'd beat some answers from the mage.

At the docks, Okulu greeted a man named Ingil at the base of the ramp leading up to a well-cared-for-ship vying for largest docked. The old man had a wooden leg, and a curly brown beard covered most of his light-blue face. He nodded to the rest in greeting. "Damn hot morning!"

Wilhelm grinned his agreement. "I'm anxious to get out to sea."

Ingil laughed. "That's the spirit, boy! But look at you! The half-breed told me to pack extra food, but he didn't tell me I needed an entire stocked pantry just for you!"

Wilhelm chuckled. "I've survived on standard portions. I'm sure the food will last."

"Ha! I surely hope so!" Ingil winked at Salvarias, whose low hood hid his face in shadows, cloak bound tightly about him, letting only a sliver of his robes be visible. Okulu must have warned Ingil about his brother's constant counting. It didn't faze the sailor. "Much cooler on the open waters, lad. It'll make sense for you to be all bundled up. Lift your face. Let me see you."

Salvarias raised his head ever so slightly, allowing light to fall across his face from the nose down.

"You're as young as the half-breed said. Probably don't have much power, eh?"

Salvarias remained quiet.

"Well, nothing to be ashamed of, boy. I've heard mages get stronger with age. It's good news for us. Veedran's old creatures flock to mages, but with how young you are, we'll be fine." He smiled assuredly.

Salvarias bowed.

Ingil motioned toward four sailors ogling the sisters. "Get the horses on board."

"Pardon," Salvarias said, stepping in front of Mithal. "With your permission, I will escort the horses below."

Ingil squinted at the sun. "Hurry it up. We don't have all day."

"Of course, gentleman."

The other six horses followed Mithal and Lilly without protest.

Ingil's smile stretched ear to ear, and he poked Wilhelm in the ribs. "I already like that boy. But, you understand, some of my sailors don't like mages on a ship. They might rough the boy up or try to throw him overboard."

Wilhelm rested a hand on Ingil's shoulder and leaned over to whisper in the captain's ear. "Anyone touches him and I'll kill them, and then come after you. I suggest you keep the sailors clear of him."

Ingil wiped the back of his hand along his nose and sniffed noisily. "As long as nothing attacks us, I can keep them off him. If we're attacked though ..." He spread his arms helplessly.

Wilhelm made a cursory sweep of the sailors. Indeed, as Okulu had warned yesterday, the crew were obviously less than honorable. Some even drooled while they stared at the girls and eyed everyone's packs. He turned his attention back to the captain whose gaze settled on the heavy purse on Wilhelm's hip. The hungry sparkle in the watythm's eye knotted Wilhelm's stomach. "If anyone so much as looks at those women, I'll chop off their manhood and feed it to the sharks. If I'm robbed, I'll burn your ship to the ground when we dock."

Ingil's eyes widened, and he tore his gaze from the purse to meet Wilhelm's. "Aye, lad. I bet you would." He glanced at the sisters and gave them a nervous smile. To Wilhelm, he said, "Protective type, are ye?"

"Extremely." Wilhelm shoved past the captain, scaled the ramp, and thudded to the deck of the ship. He lifted Lunara down from the ramp and then Varila. "I think you girls should stay in a room with Salv and me."

Varila snorted. "I can take care of us. I don't need a man to—"

"Take a look around, Varila."

After glancing at the gawking crew, she nodded.

Wilhelm headed below to the cabins with the sisters and was joined by his brother. Leaning close to Salvarias, Wilhelm whispered, "I asked the girls to stay with us, and they agreed."

"A wise decision, brother."

Wilhelm selected a room, delighted to see four long cots, divided into pairs on opposite sides; a bolted down table; washbasin; and a few shelves. He dropped their packs inside as Lunara settled on a cot with a book and Salvarias did the same on the opposite side.

"Thank you, brother."

Wilhelm winked at Salvarias. "I'm going above to pay Ingil."

Varila rolled her eyes and plopped in a chair at the two-person table. "Hurry. This is going to get boring."

Wilhelm grinned at her before ducking out of the room. He found Ingil yelling oaths at sailors scrambling to perform tasks that made no sense to Wilhelm. Sailing never interested him. They just seemed to move ropes around.

After settling with Ingil, Wilhelm made his way over to Humar, Durak, and Okulu.

"The girls are staying with Salv and me. I suggest the rest of you share a room. I don't think this ship has the most reputable sailors."

"I don't want to share a room with that damn winsire for an entire month," Okulu muttered.

Wilhelm hid a smile beneath his hand. He wasn't sure why Okulu rebelled against his heritage, but clearly the merc didn't care for his people. Perhaps it was because he was a half-breed. Perhaps his winsire parent had denounced his or her people.

"Neithelas is a kind boy," Humar said in his usual even tone. "Consider him a newborn pup. He's curious and thinks he knows what's right, but he lacks proper direction. We can help open his eyes a little, train him."

Okulu grunted before taking a long swig. "If he pees on my leg one more time, I'm throwing your pup overboard."

Humar shook his head. "No, you won't."

Okulu sighed. "Then don't mind me if I drink my weight in brandeline so I don't pummel his whiney, snooty ass to Oblivion."

"Humar's right, ye drunk ass," Durak grumbled.

"I'll go with Okulu on this one," Wilhelm said.

Okulu winked, offering his flask. "We can make his life miserable."

"No, you won't," Humar said. "I understand why you don't like him, Wilhelm, but we need his people's alliance. Without the winsires' bows, Dalnar won't stand a chance. He just needs a little nurturing."

"I'll nurture his scrawny ass—" Okulu started but Humar shot the merc a look.

Wilhelm grinned at Okulu and slapped Humar on the back. "I won't kill him if he stays away from Salv. But the next time he touches him, you won't be able to stop me."

Wilhelm made his way below to his room.

Lunara stood up when he entered. "I would like to go up on deck. The light isn't very good here."

Salvarias glanced at Varila then Wilhelm before rising. "I will accompany Lady Lunara."

Wilhelm grinned. "Thanks, Salv."

"I think we should go with them," Varila said. "Those sailors look hungry."

Salvarias bowed to Varila. "My lady, I have protected her against far fiercer creatures than sailors."

Varila bit her lip, but nodded. "All right."

Salvarias tilted his head and followed Lunara from the room. The instant the door closed, Varila leapt into Wilhelm's arms. Strong thighs wrapped around his waist even as her arms clasped behind his neck. He grabbed hold of her and fought every urge to have her right there in the cabin. For her, he would do something right and marry her before they bedded. And for Salvarias, he would not marry her until she stopped hating his brother, until she saw Salvarias as the remarkable man he was. Even if it took eternity.

Chapter 10

Summer 1018 a.r.

Lunara leaned over the ship's railing to watch the waves crash along the dark wood hull. White froth drifted in the ship's wake only to dissolve in the ripples of the sun-kissed ocean. The cool wind tangled her hair, and the spray of the sea misted her face. Salvarias's heavy cloak hung over her shoulders, but it was not the plush fabric that imbued heat into her bones. It was the handsome, serious man standing at her side. Salvarias's shadowed face was downcast, his hands folded in front of him as he leaned on the railing next to her. He had said few words this morning, save for his soft counting.

"How long have we been at sea?" Lunara asked, tucking her book under the folds of his cloak.

"Twenty-one days," Salvarias said, voice heavy with exhaustion.

"Would you like to go below and take a nap?"

He sank his head into his hands, his long fingers threading in his hair. "No. I will be fine."

She didn't agree, but kept her comments to herself. Since whatever had happened in the Stronghold in the swamps, Salvarias had withdrawn more inside his own mind. There were days she doubted he even knew what surrounded him.

For the entire trip at sea, summer's heat baking the cabins had driven them both to the deck and its chilling winds. Mainly they would read in a cranny on deck, shielded from the sun, or do as they did now and watch the ocean. But during those times, he merely looked over the passing sea with distant eyes or stared at his spell book without really reading it. He followed her everywhere since their siblings had grown fond of the cabin. She mused if any sailor were to attack her Salvarias would not be aware. And his detachment deepened daily, the black circles rimming his eyes had darkened, and his breathing labored more and more each day. Whatever plagued him was worsening. Of course she could ask, but she would receive his new standard reply of "I am fine, my lady" so what was the point. He had stacked up so high a barrier around his feelings she barely sensed his general emotion, and he continued his efforts. He needed help, but the stubborn man would never accept it. So, Lunara watched the passing ocean alone, despite the young man standing at her side.

A shimmering streak of purple whizzing by in the waters below caught her attention. She grinned in anticipation. A kassral shot up from the ocean, soaring well above the tallest mast of the ship. The sleek fur puffed like a frightened cat. Lunara laughed while covering her hair from the raining droplets of salt water spraying from the kassral. The thin, human-sized body was eel-like, covered in long, shining fur, but the head looked more like a cat. The bendy body performed three flips in the air before plummeting back into the sea. The raining water startled Salvarias from his thoughts.

"Kassral," Lunara explained.

Salvarias's eyes focused for a moment then distanced again. Lunara sighed but her sadness was cut short when a herd of kassrals exploded from the ocean. A delighted squeal escaped her as the creatures performed a variety of acrobatic movements, leaping from the water to contort into impossible shapes. She glanced up at Salvarias to see a light smile on his lips while he whispered under his breath. The kassrals seemed eager to please and performed twists and turns, leaps and dives Lunara had never seen. Soon, all the sailors were laughing and pointing at the mischievous creatures.

"Lumous," Salvarias said.

Salvarias's sparrow of pure white light soared through the air to mingle with the kassrals. Popping noises rippled among the kassrals.

"What's that noise?" Lunara asked.

"The kassrals are speaking to one another," Salvarias said. "They are coordinating a chase, but are too excited to communicate properly." A wide smile spread across his face.

Lunara no longer watched the kassrals. Her full attention focused on his features, carved flawlessly, perfectly proportioned. Light reflected off his slightly wavy, ink-black hair. No white could be seen in his eyes, only smoky pools of gray-black curling lazily, moving with a life of their own. She'd always found his eyes mesmerizing. Not for the first time, she thought he was made in the image of a god, beautiful to a fault. But it was not his appearance that stole her breath away this time. It was his smile, which she had seen only a few precious times. It brightened his eyes and the world itself, driving off an unnatural cold Lunara had not noticed. Color sharpened, cleaner and crisper than a blink ago. The air sweetened, tasting like sugar on her tongue.

Laughter erupting from the crew tore Lunara's stare from Salvarias. The kassrals were following the sparrow, leaping over each other in an attempt to be the first to tackle the insubstantial bird. She swore grins were spreading on the creatures' catlike faces. Three additional sparrows appeared. The popping noises turned giddy, and the creatures' chase more disorganized. The sparrows soared above the ship from side to side, and leaping kassrals followed, raining water down on the crowd and amazing all with the distance they cleared. Lunara laughed with delight.

The wild chase went for a good amount of time before the sparrows vanished. All the kassrals flanked to the side of the ship to face Salvarias, their heads bobbing in and out of the waves. He bowed, whispering something she couldn't hear. The kassrals responded by twirling in the water before disappearing.

"That was amazing," Lunara breathed.

A frown played on Salvarias's lips, and his brow furrowed. His knuckles turned white as he clasped the railing.

"Are you—" Lunara started but Wilhelm's rumbling voice rose above hers.

"What was all the commotion about?" Wilhelm asked, arm wrapped around Varila's shoulders.

"Kassral," one sailor said. "I've never seen them perform for an audience. It's luck if one is spotted on a trip, and with the amount we've seen on this journey, I'd say we'll have safe travels for years. But to see a whole herd ... Well, that's never been seen before."

Salvarias bowed to Lunara before leaving her side. He whispered to Wilhelm then went belowdecks. Lunara turned back to the ocean, heaving a deep sigh.

"What is it?" Wilhelm asked.

"Our connection is weakening. He's building up walls so high I can barely sense his emotions."

Wilhelm pulled her close. "I love you like my own sister, Lunara, and I don't want to see you hurt. I don't know if Salv will ever come around to allowing anyone else in. He's told you so."

"I won't stop trying. I can help him."

As they stood together in light conversation, her thoughts continually moved to Salvarias even while she tried to focus on the waves or Wilhelm's words. It didn't take her long to come to one conclusion.

"Something's wrong with Salvarias," she said, interrupting Wilhelm midsentence.

Without a word, he bolted for the ladder leading belowdecks, Lunara on his heels.

Salvarias staggered against the wall, gritting his teeth. The sensation of being watched, of being *hunted*, had been worsening over the journey. He could feel *things*, like clawed fingers prying apart his skull, wiggling around in his mind, trying to siphon out images of what he saw, what he smelled. Over the past month, he had carefully erected a second wall around his thoughts, one that blocked this invading presence. It was not as stable as his wall guarding his soul, but he had no more mind to give it.

Just as he got his bearings and entered their empty cabin, the hunting presence assailed his mind with such force it stole his vision and bludgeoned him like a thief beating its victim to death. He crumpled to the floor and cried out, grabbing his head as if he could shield it from the merciless blows.

"Brother!" One final hit toppled his wall to ruin. The rushing force flooded out clear thought. It picked apart his mind until it found scenes of the ocean and the herd of kassrals. He frantically tried to pull back the knowledge, but it plucked his memories as easily as blowing seeds off a dandelion. "Help me!"

A strong hand pried his from his head. "I'm here, Salv."

He searched for his brother's strength, but it was nowhere to be found. He shouted in frustration when whatever searched for him conveyed its smug victory before withdrawing from his mind.

"Use it, Salv!"

"I ..." he gasped, "cannot. They found us." His mind felt used, violated, and the fight had drained his strength.

"What found us?" Wilhelm asked.

Salvarias's exhaustion tugged forcibly on consciousness. "I ... do not ... know. They are coming, brother. They ..."

Death was all he saw next.

Lunara lay awake, listening to Salvarias tossing in his sleep. His nightmares had worsened since Falar, though she saw by his expression when he woke that he didn't remember them. Every other night, Salvarias had stayed awake and chose to sleep during the day, gifting restful nights to the others. However, he had yet to wake from his ordeal earlier nor had his screams started.

The rocking of the ship lulled her to a light doze. She slipped in and out of darkness, drifting through meadows of sun then a warm ship cabin. The snores of Varila and Wilhelm rumbled like a far off thunderstorm.

A chilling scream jolted her upright.

"Salv?" Wilhelm said sleepily.

Her sister shifted and then a small lantern brightened the room.

The mage thrashed against his blankets. Sweat soaked his hair and his eyes were shut tight. Wilhelm shook Salvarias's shoulders, trying to wake him, but he stayed lost in his dream. He punched and kicked at Wilhelm while mumbling incoherently, face contorted in agony. Varila went to help, but Wilhelm motioned her back.

"Brother!" Salvarias wept.

Lunara battled her promise to give Salvarias privacy and not intrude on his mind. With their distant connection as of late, it was like she was looking through a window covered in fog; she could see shadows of emotions, but nothing clearly. She wasn't even sure she could get past his barriers. Biting her lip, she held an internal debate on what to do.

Salvarias's words choked off and he arched unnaturally, as if inflicted by an invisible wound. He wasn't breathing.

"Salv! Wake up!" Wilhelm ordered, shaking Salvarias's contorting body. "Breathe! Dammit, Salv, breathe!"

Fear won and she rushed into his mind, easily pushing past his crumbling barriers. However, when she made the connection, whatever he endured affected her own body.

It had to be more than a dream. Dreams did not carry such physical suffering. The stabs and hacks were nothing but phantom sensations of what he experienced, yet they pulled a cry from her throat.

With him never allowing her to work on their connection, she understood little of what it all meant. Distantly, she heard Wilhelm's voice turn frantic, edged by building paranoia.

Desperate, she tried the simplest thing she could think of: she willed herself into his dream. She was amazed when it actually worked.

She stood on a hill covered in blood. A garish pink sky cast its hue onto rolling hills of wheat-colored grasses. Dead crammed the endless landscape, and she saw them all focused toward one direction.

Shoving through the crowd, she came to the center of the throng and found the dead taking turns inflicting whatever wounds covered them onto Salvarias. Swords stabbed through him, his throat spouted blood, and bruises covered his body.

"Gods," she breathed.

She darted to his side and put herself between him and the next bloodied man coming to harm him. Vaguely she was aware she'd risen from her bed and was rushing to Salvarias's side. It was as if her mind was split between reality and his dream. The sensation made her dizzy.

"Leave him alone!" she shouted at the crowd.

They backed away from her and Salvarias. Keeping an eye on the closest man and the dagger held in his hand, she knelt by Salvarias and lightly touched his shoulder.

"Salvarias," she said.

He looked up, face a swollen mess, blood gurgling in his throat. Tears welled and he reached out a shaking hand.

"It's a dream," she said, taking his hand in her own. "You have to wake up"

He looked around and then down at the blades sticking in his body. When he raised his gaze to her, it was clear he didn't believe her. He thought *she* was the dream, and with good reason. His physical pain was real. She knew it was, as portions of it lingered within herself, mortal wounds that somehow were not killing them. But something else was happening. She saw it in his haunted eyes.

Glancing around, she strained her mind to understand and willed it so. Again, success surprised her, but instantly she wished she'd failed.

Grief and suffering slammed into her with such force, she reeled backward and plopped down on the blood-soaked grasses. The dead were not only inflicting him with their physical wounds but their agony as well: at the pain of loss, of leaving behind their loved ones, of being taken from the world too soon, of the harrowing moment of their death. She experienced it all, thousands at a time, as they beat it into her, stabbed it into her, carved it into her. Yet it was only half of what Salvarias endured.

"I killed them," he wept, looking at the blood running down his hands. "I killed them all."

"It's a dream," she sobbed. She wanted to leave, to never feel this amount of sorrow ever again, to live in sun and warmth, but she refused to leave him alone. "You have to wake up. I ... I can't, Salvarias. I can't ..."

Loud sobs left her and she hugged her knees. The grief, anger, and pain of hundreds of thousands weighed down on her, towing her further toward drowning in the blood around her. She was losing herself here, just as he had. If neither broke free, they would both die here. And she'd be damned if she would let the man she loved die in some dream.

Looking over, she saw Salvarias disappear under a sudden flood of blood. Panic gripped her. She snagged hold of him before the current took him. Clenching her teeth, she snarled, "You will wake up!" Hauling his head above the tide of blood, she thought only of waking and willed it so.

The dream violently snuffed out, and the abrupt clarity of the cabin made her head spin and sparked an instant headache. Salvarias sucked in a sharp breath and his eyes flew open. Immediately, she regretted her haste. She'd not told him to forget the dream, and by his eyes filling with horror and tears, he'd remembered it.

"Let go," Lunara said to Wilhelm.

He hesitated, but backed away.

She lay down on Wilhelm's cot, keeping Salvarias's hand gripped tightly in her own, and brushed his soaked hair from his face. She sensed him fighting not to remember what he had dreamt, but he failed. All that pain and suffering would stay with him, forever locked into his perfect memory, all because she'd been too hasty, too careless.

Then warmth and safety encased her soul, and she realized he had touched upon her presence in his mind. It took a breath to understand what he was doing. He was shielding her from the nightmare, as if he had a hand over her eyes to spare her.

"Stop," she whispered. "I'm strong enough."

Of course he did no such thing. As the nightmare settled into his memory, he absorbed the stark horror she had experienced and transitioned it from her to him, easing her burden to a distant, painless memory. How he did so, she couldn't begin to comprehend, but it was all too clear he knew exactly how to manipulate their connection on the deepest levels, whereas she had only scratched the surface of her abilities. Worse, he did so without ever entering her mind. Never had he sought her out, which made her violations of him all the more disrespectful.

Ashamed, embarrassed, and frustrated, she started to withdraw her hand but he gently took her wrist.

"Just a moment longer," he said.

Withdrawing completely from his mind, she once again stood behind the foggy window of their connection.

After a moment, he released her hand. She watched with a heavy heart as his normal fast-paced mind returned, his face grimacing against the rush. She rose and Wilhelm returned to his brother, offering the wood box.

Once all had settled back into their beds, the clicking noises of the puzzle box soon drowned Lunara in dreams of sun and warmth.

Chapter 11

Summer 1018 a.r.

The next three mornings Lunara woke with the same worry. Salvarias hadn't slept since the nightmare. By the fourth, she approached Wilhelm with her concern.

"He's not sleeping," she said, staring at Salvarias leaning over the opposite railing. "He remembered his nightmare, and I think he's too scared to sleep."

"I've talked to him and he says he will, but he doesn't look like it. I don't know how to help him."

Lunara glared at Wilhelm, rising on her tiptoes and pointing a finger at his chest. "If you told him to, he would. He would do anything if you ordered him—" She cut herself off when the man's amber eyes darkened.

He clenched his jaw and leaned down to whisper, "You don't think I know the power I have over him? You think I'm a fool? I know damn well I could make him do anything I wanted. But that's not the relationship I want with my brother. He'll make his own choices. Whether I like them or not."

Lunara bit her lip and her cheeks burned with embarrassment. She remembered Salvarias's brief retelling of the time Wilhelm had forced him to leave behind Bartle, a mage who had sacrificed himself in the slave mines to save Salvarias. "I'm so sorry, Wilhelm. It was horrible of me to suggest."

Wilhelm's shoulders slouched and his gaze distanced when he stared over the ocean. "I did it once. I ordered him like a dog. And worse, he obeyed like one. I have complete control over him. Do you have any idea what it's like to have that power over another person?"

"I don't."

"I pray you never do. He holds the same power over me. He knows it, yet not once has he ever taken advantage of it. Sure, he asks me to do things. But he never orders me, never commands me. Yet I did it to him. I—" Wilhelm's voice broke, and he coughed to cover his emotion. "I hate myself for it. I can't do that to him again. No matter what. I love him too much."

Lunara rested her hand on his arm. "Forgive me."

Wilhelm looked down at her and his gaze softened. "I think you're the only person who will ever understand." He pulled her into an embrace. "You don't look like you've slept either."

Indeed, her worry had kept her awake often, and the physical pain Salvarias still endured had plagued Lunara with enough discomfort to interrupt sleep, no matter how much he had tried to shield her. She smiled up at Wilhelm and unraveled herself from his arms. "I'm fine."

She took to pacing the deck. They were less than a week from Windlous, and Salvarias had to sleep before they arrived. He would need his strength. If the stubborn man wouldn't heed the advice of his own brother, he would undoubtedly ignore her. Nevertheless, she was compelled to try. Mind set with determination, she strode up to the mage.

"You're not sleeping."

Salvarias turned to her, face pale, eyes barely open, and mumbled something incoherent.

"Please, sleep. You must rest."

Salvarias headed below, and Lunara bounded behind with hope. However, when he reached their room, he merely sank into his bed and stared at the walls, counting. She clenched her fists and fought the urge to scream in frustration. Crawling on to Wilhelm's bed, she took a deep breath, ready to feel his wrath, before resting a hand on his shoulder. It took a moment in his sleep-deprived state for her touch to help. His eyelids drooped and his whispers faltered. She smiled as his eyes closed, but it faded when he jerked awake and immediately struggled to free himself from her grip.

"No, this is happening, Salvarias Laybryth. You *will* sleep and you *will* let me help you."

After a shudder, he ceased his fight. She rolled on her side, backed toward him, and shoved herself into his cot. Instead of stiffening or arguing as she'd anticipated, he scooted against the wall so she had room and pulled her close to his chest. His arm wrapped around her waist, and she rested her head on his other arm, which folded around her shoulders. He nestled his face in her hair, took a deep breath, and slept. Lunara smiled, snuggling against him, their bodies molded perfectly together, and after a deep breath of her own, she slept as well.

She woke to a pitch-black room. Wilhelm's snore joined with Varila's close by, confirming it to be nighttime. She closed her eyes, not realizing how little she had slept worrying about him, and drifted through peaceful dreams.

When she woke again, both of their siblings were gone and Salvarias still slept. She, however, was fully rested and awake. Her fingers snuck inside the sleeve of his robes and glided over his scarred arm. A plate of food sat on Wilhelm's bed, and she freed a hand to select a slice of cheese. Salvarias shifted and his breathing lightened, but he tightened his hold.

A few moments of silence passed before he whispered near her ear, "Thank you."

"Are you hungry?"

"Not yet."

"How do you feel?"

"Better," he murmured. "How long have I slept?" He deeply inhaled the scent of her hair.

Trying to hide the smile from her voice, she said, "I'm not sure. I was sleeping too. Night has passed and it's daylight. So at least a full day and night."

She rolled over in his arms to look at him. Color had returned to his cheeks, and his eyes sparkled in the faint light in the room. "You look better." She held up a piece of cheese and smiled. "Sure you're not hungry?"

She rolled back over to find his favorite as he sat up, pulling her with him. Snatching up the plate, she leaned against his chest. Both sat in comfortable silence while they ate their fill, each tossing an occasional piece to Adok who sprawled out on Wilhelm's bed.

Once done, Salvarias shifted and removed his arm—a signal her time was up. As usual when her touch left him, he grimaced, holding his breath, body tensing. After the rush of his thoughts settled, he left the room, giving her privacy to clean up.

She chose a violet dress, one that gathered under her breasts and flowed to a loose bottom. Opening the door, she smiled at him, showing no signs she saw his gaze slide over her. She kept her back to him as he washed. After he announced he was done, she turned to see his face cleanly shaven and the light of his sparrow glowing in his swirling black eyes. Even though the robes were oversized, he had yet to incorporate a slouch into his stance, and the fabric rested against his chiseled chest and strong shoulders. She drank in the rare sight.

Seeming unaware of her inspection, he opened the door for her after raising his hood to shadow his face. Forcing her body to move, she brushed by him, purposefully rubbing against him.

When they joined their friends on deck, a blush crept up Salvarias's cheeks.

"Finally!" Wilhelm roared.

"Sorry, brother."

"I'm just happy you slept." Wilhelm smiled and draped an arm around his brother.

Salvarias's gaze moved to the ocean. "How long?"

"We're six days out."

Lunara rubbed her bare arms, thinking she should have put on one of her winter dresses. "It's so cold."

She regretted her statement the instant she uttered the words. Neithelas came to her side, covering them both under his cloak. His pursuits were flattering, but no matter how sweet, kind, handsome, or caring he was, her heart never wavered from Salvarias. She wished the prince would leave her alone, but she had promised her sister to give the man a chance. Regardless, his closeness always made her uncomfortable.

Wilhelm, reading her uneasiness as always, saved her from Neithelas's embrace by shoving aside Neithelas's arm and cloak. "Autumn is but a week away."

"And Windlous is a cold continent," Okulu said from behind. He removed his cloak and draped it over Lunara. "Summer is short there. You'll love it, Salvarias. It's full of old stories."

The mage shifted to the railing. "Old stories of what?"

She joined him, curious if more kassrals were about.

Okulu took a short swig from his flask. "Dalnar is pretty focused on its own history, but Windlous caters to all that happened during the time of the gods and especially what happened after."

"I'm going to get my cloak," Lunara chattered. "No offense, Okulu, but this is not very warm."

Okulu smiled. "I have muscle to keep me warm, lovely Lunara."

She blushed at the compliment, gave the merc his cloak, which reeked of alcohol, and headed below. Salvarias and Adok were close behind her. He rarely left her side after their talk in Cattlar.

Apparently, along with his confession of their friendship came a new attentive side of him.

In the room, Lunara riffled through her packs while Salvarias retrieved his thick, black cloak.

"I can't find it," she murmured.

Salvarias joined her and, after much searching, finally found it. Trying a technique she'd seen her mother and Varila use, she smiled up through her eyelashes, draping the cloak around her shoulders, and held her hair back. "Would you mind?"

Though he hesitated, it worked like a charm and he fastened the clasp at her neck. She couldn't fight the bumps running up her arms at his light touch.

Suddenly the ship lurched, dumping Lunara into Salvarias's arms. Wood groaned and splintered.

She grabbed hold of him. "What was that?"

"I do not know."

Another lurch. The entire vessel seemed to lift from the water at the bow. Salvarias pulled her to a bed and lay protectively on top of her as the furniture skidded to one side. A few books fell from a shelf, and a candle flew across the room. The ship dropped and the bed slid across the floor. The rocking was no longer soothing but violent, careening dangerously enough that she feared they'd tip.

When the rocking lessened, Salvarias pulled her up from the bed. She grasped his arm as the floor beneath her feet tilted dramatically every which way possible.

"Stay below, Adok," Salvarias said.

Using his staff for balance, he made his way from the room, Lunara clinging to him to keep upright. When they emerged on deck, none of their friends were visible in the frantic disorder. Fear lined Salvarias's voice as he called for his brother amid the sailors screaming and running around aimlessly.

"Brother!" Salvarias called louder.

Lunara's gaze darted around but she saw none of their friends. Salvarias strode to the bow, searching through the crowd of sailors while skillfully avoiding bumping into any. She didn't see them at the bow. Salvarias turned and swiftly started for the stern.

"Brother!" Salvarias called with a hint of paranoia.

Hers grew with his. "Varila!"

When a mass of sailors cleared, Wilhelm's booming voice rose over the shrieks. "Salv!"

Salvarias's shoulders slumped as Wilhelm came into view, shoving aside sailors who got in his path. Lunara was engulfed in Varila's embrace.

"What is it, brother?" Salvarias asked.

"I don't know. We haven't seen anything yet."

The other companions crowded around.

"The mage! He's responsible!" a sailor called from behind.

Wilhelm's eyes flashed with anger. "I swear if any of you touch him, I'll rip off your limbs one by one."

Many backed away at the sight of his amber eyes flaring with rage.

"It calls for the mage! Throw him overboard!" another sailor screamed.

"Yes! Feed him to the beast!" several others yelled.

Salvarias's expression was smooth as glass. "They are correct, brother. I failed in shielding myself and they found us. I brought the creature to us."

"No you didn't," Wilhelm muttered. He shouted to the sailors, "Stay away from him!"

Lunara's screamed warning came too late. A sailor rivaling Wilhelm's height and girth had snuck up from behind and struck Salvarias hard on the head. The mage spun around and crumpled to the deck. Durak's cry echoed her own.

"Wilhelm!" Humar called and drew his sword.

The sailor plucked up Salvarias's limp body and ran faster than any would suspect. Wilhelm took flight, but his sea legs weren't as steady. The sailor tossed Salvarias overboard, and Lunara screamed again.

Humar gaped at the mage's slim body disappearing over the railing followed by Wilhelm. Cursing, he stumbled to the edge of the rocking ship. Whatever creature hunted them screeched in pleasure. Okulu appeared with a rope and threw it overboard into the choppy waters, calling for Wilhelm who had yet to surface.

Humar whirled around to the crew. "Now isn't the time for blame. We have to work together or else we'll sink. Does this ship have any damn weapons?"

Ingil roared, "Man the harpoons! Collapse the sails!"

Humar went to the railing, staring at the waters, holding his breath.

Wilhelm bobbed into view, took in several deep breaths, and then dove again. Still they waited. Lunara sobbed softly, and Humar wrapped an arm around her trembling shoulders. After a moment, Wilhelm emerged with a bluish-green object spouting inky black liquid. Wilhelm wrestled with it and with one last shove, the mage's body appeared from the mass.

Wilhelm shifted Salvarias to his shoulder before grabbing the rope. "Hurry!"

The group pitched in, heaving Wilhelm and Salvarias up the side of the boat. Humar gritted his teeth when a section of the rope snapped.

"Faster!" he ordered.

A second thread snapped and Humar's heart skipped. They wouldn't make it.

Just as he was certain all hope was lost, a large hand grabbed the railing. Wilhelm dumped Salvarias's flaccid body over the edge and then hoisted himself aboard. He picked up Salvarias and squeezed the boy around his ribs. Humar wiped sweat from his face, fear sinking in his gut. Wilhelm squeezed again and Salvarias coughed up water, gasping, while gaining his own footing. Wilhelm slapped his brother's back, and Salvarias nodded.

A thunderous roar issued from the dark ocean. The ship took another lurch. Humar lunged onto a dangling rope just as the ship went nearly vertical. He glanced around to see if his friends had grabbed something.

Lunara screamed. A falling sailor had latched on to her ankle. Her hands were slipping, her eyes wild with fear. Varila spewed oaths. Suddenly Salvarias slid by Humar on the deck. When Lunara's grip failed, the boy was near enough to grasp her hand. He clutched at passing objects and just before dropping into the fizzing ocean, he snatched hold of a rope. The mage held tight to Lunara with one hand, the sailor still clinging to her ankle, and the rope with the other, but Humar saw the strain in his face.

"He won't hold, Wilhelm!" Humar called.

"He can!" Wilhelm yelled back.

Humar wasn't convinced. Surveying the path down to the boy, death would claim him before he reached Salvarias. Nevertheless, Humar would be damned if the boy died. Just as he settled on a course, whatever held up the ship moved and the vessel plummeted to the ocean. By the time Humar scrambled to his feet, Wilhelm was at his brother's side. Lunara clung to the mage, refusing to release him even when Varila tugged on her. Humar thought about the times Salvarias shrugged or flinched from all others, but never from Wilhelm and the young woman.

Okulu nudged him. "Any ideas, old friend?"

Humar surveyed the deck, thinned of sailors due to the last upheaval. "It'll tear the boat apart if we wait much longer to act."

Ingil yelled orders to sailors and large harpoons were readied and manned, but unless the beast surfaced, they were useless.

Humar turned to Wilhelm. "Did you see anything when you were under the water?"

"All I saw were tentacles like the one I chopped off. I couldn't see the body."

Humar's thoughts darted with wild ideas, none of which would work. The creature was smart not to show itself.

"Brother," Salvarias said softly.

Wilhelm looked at the mage a moment before nodding. "All right, but no exerting yourself. If we can't get it in a couple tries, we'll come back. Agreed?"

"Agreed," Salvarias murmured, unraveling himself from Lunara.

The two brothers headed to the side of the ship and began tying rope around their waists.

Humar marched over to Wilhelm. "What do you think you're doing?"

Salvarias jerked the rope tight. "It is our only option. I can cast spells under the water. The creature will either surface so we can fight it or die below."

"Can't you talk to it?" Neithelas asked. "Like you do the wolf and horses."

Salvarias shook his head. "Veedran's creatures are not like the ones made by Nevlar and Zerana. I cannot."

Lunara grabbed the mage's hands. "Please don't. There has to be another way."

"I will be fine. If anything happens, you will be able to pull either of us out of the water."

Neithelas wrapped an arm around Lunara, guiding her from Salvarias. Wilhelm kissed Varila quickly. Humar worked frantically for another option but none presented themselves. The mage's plan was absurd but the only one that might work. He sputtered out an oath.

"Deep breath, brother. It is sure to grab us instantly," Salvarias said. He chanted and drew his rune. A single icicle appeared.

After a grin from Wilhelm that Humar found disheartening, the brothers—the only two people who could defeat the evil brewing in Arden—jumped into the hostile ocean.

Chapter 12

Summer 1018 a.r.

Salvarias's assumption had been correct. Before he registered the shock of the freezing waters or swam up for a breath of air, a slick tentacle suctioned onto his ankle and yanked him downward. A larger tentacle wrapped around Wilhelm's waist, but his brother had managed to draw his broadsword.

Salvarias sent his icicle through the darkening ocean. When a muffled wail confirmed contact, he sent a myriad of tiny icicles in the same direction. His magic soared with pleasure at the new spell's effectiveness.

The creature's screech rippled the water, and the tentacle loosened enough that he wiggled free. Both brothers swam to the surface.

"D-d-d-deep breath," Salvarias stuttered.

Wilhelm nodded, and just as Salvarias sucked in a breath, a tentacle wrapped around his waist, squeezing painfully, pinning his right arm to his side, and yanked him under. He had barely finished his chant. Drawing his rune in the ocean, five larger icicles appeared. He released the spell and they shot through the abyss. As he squirmed to reach his dagger, his gaze sought his brother. Wilhelm was hacking at a tentacle circling his thigh.

The beast roared, sending up a wave of hot water. Salvarias jerked to free his arm, but the tentacle tightened its grip, dancing stars in Salvarias's vision, weakening his fight. Then his brother was there. Wilhelm cleaved the tentacle and oily blood seeped out.

Both swam for the surface. Wilhelm shook his head, pointing upward while he gasped for air.

"Once more," Salvarias encouraged.

I'm excited for these new spells, his magic said, voice heavy with anticipation. *To combine a component spell with non-component will test our knowledge extensively.*

Indeed, my friend.

Clutching a bag of glass in his hand, he sucked in a breath to chant his spell. Before he spoke it, a tentacle clamped around his midsection and hauled him below the water, speeding him downward faster than before. Salvarias clung to the glass and waited, watching his brother chop through a tentacle wrapped around his left arm.

The water pressure shifted and darkness soon blocked out his brother.

Forcing himself to remain calm, he focused on his magic eagerly awaiting his command. Pins stabbed his lungs and eyes.

Cursing his weakness, he chanted under water, losing precious air, and drew a rune to heighten the component spell. He tossed the pouch into the rune and lit his sparrow so he could see the new spell in action.

With the aid of his non-component spell, each glass piece grew to the size of a door and hurtled toward the creature with such intensity it rippled the water.

Unable to wait any longer, he grabbed his dagger and sawed at the tentacle.

The creature screamed when the glass pierced its girth, and the tentacle released by itself. Cold to the bone and exhausted from the spells, Salvarias feebly swam.

Something brushed his leg in the darkness. If a tentacle grabbed him, he did not have enough air to survive. He flinched when it grazed his hand. Then he realized it was fuzzy and soft, not slimy. Hope sprang alive as his sparrow's light fell across the brilliantly orange creature.

Reaching out his thoughts, he found the kassral. After a small plea, the creature looped its tail-end around Salvarias's arm and swam, its body rippling the waters as it gained tremendous speed. Light filtered through the darkness. His brother come into view, face twisted in anger. The kassral moved with such speed, Salvarias barely had time to snatch Wilhelm's hand as they barreled past. The extra weight hardly slowed the kassral.

The creature wailed again and bubbles boiled all around them. The creature was rising. And fast.

Salvarias feared he might faint and lose his hold on Wilhelm. The pain in his lungs neared the point where he would gulp uncontrollably for air. His heavy head felt as if it sank into his shoulders. Thoughts were sluggish.

Limbs weakening, he used what strength he had left to grip his brother tighter even as his hold on the kassral loosened. Sunlight raced toward them, but the happy kassral was too ecstatic at having company to have enough sense to slow. Salvarias yanked free when it reach the surface. He gasped, flailing about, disoriented as his mind gained full awareness. A familiar arm snagged hold and steadied him. Droplets of water rained down like diamonds as the kassral spun beautifully in the air, its fur puffing for added show.

"What in Oblivion did we agree to?" Wilhelm roared, pulling Salvarias close.

Salvarias shivered violently but managed a grin. "I am s-s-sure we can discuss th-th-this later. We h-ha-have angered the be-be-beast."

Wilhelm grinned. The rope around Salvarias's waist cut into his side when their companions hauled him up. As soon as he scaled the rail and staggered to his feet, Lunara flung herself into his arms.

Wilhelm thudded to the deck, crooked grin spread ear to ear. "You'll have an opportunity to fight, Durak."

A large tentacle shot from the ocean, perched over the ship, spraying the companions with frigid seawater. Salvarias shielded Lunara the best he could, but if the tentacle struck, there would be no saving anyone. Okulu sent a myriad of daggers—all of which Salvarias had enchanted over the past month—in conjunction with the harpoons from the sailors and inflicted enough damage to cause the tentacle to rear back and sink into the ocean.

A section of water a mere hundred feet from the ship bubbled and sputtered as the creature emerged into view. The beast towered above the ship, dumping salty water over the entire vessel. Salvarias stumbled backward before gaining his footing on the careening deck. Lunara never lost her grip around his neck, both now soaking wet and shivering.

The creature's slick body resembled a glassy black marble. Varying-sized tentacles exploded at its base. One black eye nearly the size of the ship glared at them.

A sob left Lunara before she buried her face in Salvarias's chest. He gathered her close. "We will be fine."

"Ye got it to emerge. Now what?" Durak snapped. "We can't reach it with our swords, and if there's one place me don't want to die, it's in the cursed water."

Okulu smirked. "Stuck in a dark cave would be better?"

"Are you part watythm?" Durak growled.

Okulu winked. "Actually, I am. My father's great-grandmother was a watythm."

Varila kicked his shin. "Then talk to the damn creature, and tell it to stop trying to eat us!"

"No can do. I don't speak the language."

Neithelas snorted. "You hold none of your gifts sacred. You possess the capabilities to speak to the trees, yet you refuse."

Okulu cast the prince his most disarming smile. "And you hold capabilities to be a decent person, yet you refuse those as well. I won't lecture you if you don't lecture me."

"Enough," Humar snapped. "Ingil will talk to it."

"Not likely," Okulu said. "This is a creature of Veedran's design. Watythms can only speak to those made by Nevlar or Zerana. Just like Salvarias."

Durak cursed.

Salvarias accepted his staff from Humar. "The eye."

The knight shouted directions to Ingil. A volley of harpoons split the air. A few hit their target and irritated the beast enough to keep its attention off destroying the ship.

Salvarias chanted and drew his rune. *"Rulose,"* he whispered, and lightning crackled through the air, snapping at the creature's eye. Smoke hissed as the eye burst open, spewing milky white mucus across the ocean. The creature wailed, its tentacles flinging over its injured eye.

Salvarias leaned heavily against his staff and even put a little weight on Lunara. She took it upon herself to support him more, and her strength flourished up within him. His magic greedily accepted it. Whispering his next spell, he drew his rune. Seven large fire shards filled his rune, surprising him with how little it drained him.

It's because of her touch, his magic informed him. *She helps clear your mind so you can focus on one thing at a time. With her, our power doubles.*

Using the last of his strength, he funneled an abundance of energy into his spell and whispered, *"Rulose."*

The shards impaled themselves in the beast's eye. It rocked back, tentacles frantically rubbing its eye as white globs plopped into the ocean, their stench like soured milk. With one last piercing shriek, it sank limply below the water.

"Brilliant!" Okulu chugged his flask.

Salvarias slumped heavily, his knees wobbling with exhaustion. Lunara wedged herself under his arm, taking more of his weight, and smiled up at him. It gave him a little more strength to stay standing.

A massive sailor approached their group.

Wilhelm's eyes lit with rage. "I warned you!" he roared.

"Brother!" Salvarias called when Wilhelm drew their mother's dagger into his right hand.

Wilhelm snarled at the sailor, left hand flexing on the hilt of his sword, eyes debating whether or not to take the man's head. Salvarias gently released Lunara and lurched a step. His legs gave out but Wilhelm, releasing the sword, caught him.

"No, brother," Salvarias said.

"He nearly killed you," Wilhelm growled.

"Please. It would do no good. Enough have died today."

Wilhelm snarled at the sailor. "You're lucky he has more heart than I do."

The sailor's wide-eyed gaze shifted from Wilhelm to Salvarias. "Hurray for the mage!"

Sailors rushed the party in thanks. Hands pried Salvarias from Wilhelm's grip, all patting him, and some hoisting him on shoulders. So many hands.

Images flew across his mind at such a rapid rate he lost his bearings instantly. Wilhelm's booming voice rose above the others, but the heavy liquid building in his skull blocked out his brother's words. Salvarias clutched his head, grimacing at the pressure burgeoning against his brain.

Familiar arms gathered him up, but safety drowned in the foreign hands clapping his arms and shoulders.

Then the evil became aware of his weakened mind. Exhausted from the spells, the physical battle, and the images caused by the sailors' touch, he knew he would not win the fight. More blood rushed through his head, his brain stuck in a tightening vice as the evil surfaced and slammed against his wall. He screamed. Too late the images ceased. The battle for his soul was already underway.

The light scent of a spring meadow reached him, and a soft hand clasped his. Unfortunately, her calming touch stole his fight, all his mental resolve, lulling him into lazy reverie. The evil surfaced stronger, whatever hunted him doubled its efforts, and his sanity slipped. He choked on warm liquid jetting from his mouth. She must have sensed her effect, because she withdrew her hand. When her touch left, his normal fast-paced mind erupted, and combined with the attack, it was all too much. He plummeted from the cliff of sanity. Red fog surged up for him, hungry and eager. A thin hand burst through his wall, and its fingers grazed over his own soul. Vaguely he heard himself pleading for help.

"I'm here, Salv," Wilhelm said.

A strong hand gripped his tightly, and a dagger rammed into his skull, alleviating the building pressure but choking out another cry of pain.

"Breathe, dammit!" Wilhelm said.

Salvarias coughed in a breath and used it to scream, desperate to help relieve the compression of his mind. Sobs erupted. He was so tired, in so much pain.

"Come on, Salv. For me, fight this!"

He clasped his brother's hand and allowed Wilhelm's strength to fortify his mind. He hauled himself back to the cliff's edge. Whatever hunted him shrank from his forceful shove. He gagged up warm liquid. Iron ... blood. The effort to gain his sanity and fight the minds hunting him sucked out the last of his strength. The evil clawed at the surface of his soul. Darkness pressed in on his vision.

"Fight it, Salv!" Wilhelm's voice was thick with tears.

"I ... I am ... Tired."

He wanted death, wanted Wilhelm's permission to drift into darkness. He did not want to fight anymore. Sleep, blissful peace, was all he sought. The thin hand clasped around his soul. Then familiar strong arms encircled him, tucking him in safety. A soothing rumble whispered in his ear.

"I know you're tired, Salv. But you can't sleep yet. You have to fight. For me, Salv. Please, for me."

Salvarias curled up and shuddered in a deep breath. He leached more of his brother's strength. One by one, he pried away the fingers around his soul. He gagged again. Sobs racked him. The strain of his mind, the compression of his skull, stretched beyond what he thought he could withstand.

Using the last of his mental strength, he painfully erected a wall, and stone by stone he shielded himself from the evil as layer by layer he drove it from his own tiny soul. The evil gave one last shove but his mortar held firm; his wall did not waver. The evil shrank to its dark corner, and Salvarias plummeted into his nightmares.

Salvarias slipped from the room, leaving Adok to watch over the others, and soundlessly closed the door. He crept down the hall and then up the ladder onto the deck. Stars and a brilliant moon greeted him along with untrusting frowns and scowling eyes. Salvarias might have helped save the ship, but apparently the sailors were not as appreciative when he spit up blood on them and left a trail of vomit to his room. His screams in the night must have also frightened them. Now they avoided him except for Ingil, who seemed not to have witnessed Salvarias's "possession" from a demon born of Oblivion, as the sailors had stated.

He chose a secluded spot on deck and leaned over the railing, watching moon-kissed waves slap the ship's hull. The salty, cold air breezed by as the ship cut through the waters, sails flapping lazily. They were a day from Windlous and solid land, and Salvarias found himself slightly disappointed. He enjoyed life on the water.

Pulling his cloak about him, he shivered, not only from cold but also from the horror he felt after waking from fighting the evil. The battle had been gruesome, not only for him but for Wilhelm as well. When Salvarias had woken, they were sitting up in bed, both covered in bile and blood, and never in all of Salvarias's life had he seen his brother look so weak. Wilhelm's face had sagged with exhaustion, his massive body trembling. When Wilhelm had cleaned up and changed, he had actually had to use a blanket to help warm up. Salvarias never remembered a time his brother had been cold. Though Wilhelm recovered quickly, it did not ease the brick sinking in Salvarias's gut. That he had to use his brother so much to win made Salvarias feel incredibly vulnerable. All it would have taken was one more tiny spell, and he would not have won that battle. The thought churned his stomach.

Through the pain and horror over what had happened, a new piece of knowledge had bestowed itself upon Salvarias. The battles waged with the evil and whatever hunted him exhausted them as much as Salvarias. Granted, they continued their efforts, but not nearly with the intensity as before. They used the times Salvarias was tired or weak to attack.

"What ye doin', boy?"

Salvarias glanced over his shoulder to see Durak making his way to the railing, arms stretched out to give him balance despite the calm sea. Salvarias tilted his head. "It is late. Are you having trouble sleeping? I could mix a potion—"

Durak waved his hand. "Me fine, boy. Just anxious to be off this vessel of death."

Salvarias looked back over the waters, fighting his smile. "Vessel of death?"

"Wood. That be all that keeps us from drowning. How can it be safe?" Durak shook his head and then smoothed out his beard. "Damn unnatural."

"Living under a mountain is just as dangerous. A tremor could weaken the supports of Cattlar and call down the mountain—"

"Bah! The rocks would tell us first."

Salvarias shrugged. "Some things even the rocks do not know."

"Cavruls do. We sense these things." Durak withdrew a thick, hand-long stick and a small knife and began whittling away, hands moving in quick, tiny jerks. Wood shavings dropped to the deck. "So, me've been curious." He pursed his lips for a moment, wiry eyebrows drawing together. "Tell me about magic."

"*Lumous,*" Salvarias said, and his sparrow flickered to life, soaring on the breeze. "What would you like to know?"

Durak shrugged. "Everything."

"That could take some time."

"Maybe ..." Wild hairs on his eyebrows connected, and Salvarias wondered if they had ever gotten tangled. "Maybe when it be my turn for watch you could ... Maybe ye could join me. Me could wake you up and we'd have time to talk without the others crowdin' us."

Salvarias hugged his staff close, unable to hide the suspicion in his voice when he said, "Why do you want to learn about magic? Why—"

"Dammit, boy," Durak muttered. "Ye be too untrusting. Ye've made me see things differently. All these years me hated magic, but maybe if me understood it ... Will ye tell me about it or not?"

I would not trussst him, my murderer, the presence said. *He hatesss your kind. It could be a trick. To learn and ussse it againssst you. He will hurt you. They all will.*

"Well?" Durak growled.

Salvarias swallowed hard and gazed out over the ocean. Perhaps the presence was right, but the desperate longing for friends and family made Salvarias speak. At first, he kept his explanations short and high level. The longer he talked the more questions Durak asked. The cavrul had a sharp mind, sharper than Salvarias had imagined, and soon Salvarias's excitement poured out into his instructions. It seemed he talked more in the hour he shared with Durak than he had in his entire life.

As the sun began to rise, Salvarias trailed off, realizing how thirsty he was from speaking so much. He looked down at Durak to see a broad smile on the cavrul's face.

"Aye, lad. Me misjudged you."

The stick in Durak's hand caught Salvarias's eye. It had changed from a stick to an immaculately carved redwood. "May I?" he asked, pointing to it.

Durak handed it over with a shrug. Salvarias studied it closely, all the tiny niches, the larger chips, the rounded edges. How Durak had managed to carve something so beautiful in such a short time dumbfounded Salvarias.

"It is wonderful," he murmured, reluctantly handing it back.

Durak shrugged and tossed it over the railing. "It be nothing."

Salvarias must have made a strangled sound as he watched the wood bob on the waves.

Durak laughed. "It be nothing, boy. Me've made hundreds of those."

"You could make a fortune," Salvarias said.

"Bah!" Durak snorted. "Me have a fortune. And I've never sold 'em. Me used to give them to me little girl and boy. I made special ones for me wife. She loved 'em."

"I never saw you carving when we lived in Falar."

Durak's eyes distanced. "Me had the forge. Fire and sweat, work and results. Out here, me feel useless. Carving gives me hands something to do."

"You are a complicated man," Salvarias said. "And far more intelligent than you let on."

Durak grinned. "Don't tell that dull-witted knight. He thinks he's the brains."

A smile snuck out. "Your secret is safe with me."

Durak's grin widened. "That's the first time me seen ye smile, lad."

Salvarias's face flushed hot with embarrassment, and he turned to look out over the sea, his new friend standing silently at his side.

Chapter 13

Autumn 1018 a.r.

Salvarias limped down the ramp of Ingil's ship, leading the horses. Mithal was less than pleased with the attack the ship had suffered and flat out swore to never set a hoof on another ship again. Adok sided with the black stallion. Salvarias ran his fingers along the wolf's velvety ears while assuring Mithal they would be on land for some time.

The images from Perek were again making sense. Salvarias recognized a large estate off to the left, and, oddly enough, even a passing guard. But Perek had not stayed in the city long. Buildings and people had been replaced by a dreary landscape and clustered pockets of forests.

Salvarias raised his gaze from counting the dock's wood planks to take in his surroundings. Excitement stirred his blood whenever embarking to a place he had never visited, and he had been as eager to arrive as he had been dreading it. What he had anxiously awaited was gray. The buildings were gray, the streets were gray, the sky was gray, and even the air was gray from the drizzle pattering down from the hazy gray clouds. And while Salvarias enjoyed the color, this took it to a new extreme.

Even so, what surprised him most about the city of Bellend was the people, who were mixes for lack of a better term. Some were clearly erthlas, but the majority were a cross between octril and either winsires, cavruls, or erthlas. Octril opalescent scales blended with soft human skin to form a mosaic pattern. Their eyes were snake-like and noses flat, but their other features were clearly human. Some had the double forearms of an octril on one arm, while the other was human.

Both humans and mixes glanced at him, but for the first time, there were no murmured insults at the presence of a mage, and no one spat on him.

A yawning guard held up his hand when they approached. "Name, mage?"

Okulu stepped in front of Salvarias and rested his hand on his sword. Anger glinted in his grass-green eyes. "His name is Salvarias Laybryth," Okulu said flatly.

The guard glanced at the list before yawning again. "I don't see his name."

Okulu drew his sword. "Check again."

The guard's next yawn cut off, and he flipped through the list while casting nervous glances at Okulu. "Laybryth?"

Salvarias's gaze steadied on the merc. "Yes, gentleman."

"Yes, here it is. My apologies." The guard was not looking at the list, only Okulu's sword.

Okulu rammed his sword in its sheath. "You should pay closer attention." The merc shoved past the guard.

"Clean inn?" Wilhelm asked.

"Hangman. Up that street, turn right, past ten streets, then left. Sign of a hanged man is above it."

After boarding the horses, Salvarias followed his group toward the inn. A middle-aged erthla wizard halted and raised his gaze to Salvarias. The man's eyes widened and he put his hands in the sleeves of his robes and lowered his head. Salvarias, shocked and humbled by the display reserved for master mages, bowed to his fellow wizard who beamed at the recognition. Salvarias never appreciated the Association. They did more harm than good.

Once inside the tavern, Salvarias was sure they had taken a wrong turn. Tables wobbled on broken legs, and chairs were scattered about, most looking as if a creature had gnawed on them. The structure itself looked sick. The walls seemed to sag inward. The stench of stale vomit and piss clung to the air.

A winsire-octril mix sauntered up to the group. "What's yer poison?"

Humar ran his hand through his hair. "Rooms, two of them."

The mix grunted, ducked behind a counter, then returned with two keys. "Number five and six."

Salvarias and the others followed Humar up the creaking stairs.

"What about food?" Wilhelm asked.

"You want to eat here?" Varila said.

"I must agree," Neithelas said, lifting his hand from the stairwell railing and wiping it on his tunic.

135

Wilhelm shrugged. "If it's the cleanest place, then I don't see we have a choice."

Humar nodded. "He's got a point. We'll drop off our packs first."

At the top of the stairs, Humar disappeared into a room, followed by Okulu, Durak, and Neithelas.

Salvarias ducked through the low door labeled 6. One look at the cots showed they would not be sleeping alone.

"No." Varila flung her pack over her shoulder. "I'm not staying here."

Salvarias glanced at the also-complaining wolf. "You sleep with far worse in the forest, my friend." He spoke aloud. His oddity had already been discovered, and voicing his thoughts helped ease their burden.

Adok proceeded to inform Salvarias that the wolf was not some flea-ridden vagabond and refused to be a meal.

Salvarias bowed mockingly. "Are we not all vagabonds?" Adok growled at him. "Allow me, my friend."

Controlling a laugh, he requested the insects leave for the night. Varila leapt on Wilhelm's back when the floor moved. Lunara lifted her dress while a shudder racked through her. Salvarias swept the young woman in his arms.

She cast him her sweet smile. "Thank you."

After the tiny creatures left, Salvarias lowered Lunara before leaving for his companions' room. Humar was waiting at the door with a grin.

"Quite the useful talent, boy."

Salvarias tilted his head to the knight. With clean rooms awaiting them, the group went to the common room and selected a table near the fireplace. Though Salvarias wanted warmth, he chose the farthest seat to avoid the curling gray smoke rolling down from the clogged chimney.

A middle-aged woman covered in filth but smelling of baked bread moseyed to their table. "What'll it be?"

"Five mutton stews, bread, cheese, and fruit," Humar said.

She nodded and sauntered off toward the kitchen.

"Oh, and five ale!" Wilhelm called to her.

Varila scoffed. "You're crazy to drink anything from here."

Okulu chuckled. "Bet it'll be the best ale you've ever had."

"I'll take that bet, you drunk bastard," Varila snapped.

"Stakes?" Okulu asked.

Varila smiled. "One of those enchanted daggers."

"Oh no, those are special." Okulu patted his full sheath. "How about I buy you a dagger and Salvarias here can enchant it if I'm wrong."

"And if you're right?"

"You buy me one more." Okulu winked.

"Fine." Varila spit in her hand as Okulu did in his, and they shook.

The barmaid returned with the food and ale. Everyone watched Varila take a swig. She slammed the mug down. Okulu's smile widened.

"That's the best ale I've ever had!" Wilhelm exclaimed.

Okulu grinned at Wilhelm. "Told you."

Two old men entered the tavern, stomping mud off their boots. One man was part winsire and octril, his faded green skin melting with bluish-green octril scales. White hair framed his shiny face, and a beard concealed his mouth. The second man was part octril based on the scales glistening along his body, but Salvarias could not determine what other creature mixed in its blood. Where scales were missing, gray feathers covered it and its nose was beaklike. Every other feature was erthla.

The half-winsire creature shook off his cloak as they made their way to the bar. "No, that's not how it happened. Veedran turned on Nevlar. I've been alive longer, I should know."

"Bah. Over a woman," the unknown mix said.

"They were in love! Veedran was the one who corrupted man, not Nevlar."

"I know that, but Nevlar should have stayed and killed his brother."

The half-winsire raised his newly arrived ale. "Aye, I'll agree to that."

The two men took a long swig. Lunara rose from the table and joined the men, smiling her sweet smile.

"What can you tell me about the old gods?" she asked.

The half-winsire smiled with mischief twinkling in his bloodshot eyes. "Much. Did you know Nevlar created the moon for Zerana? It's said she used to roam Arden in moonbeams next to magnificent beasts: pure white bears and horses with a single horn mounted between their ears. It's said that long ago the moon was pure white, a symbol of innocence and goodness. It represented Zerana and her form, which was nothing but light, beautiful white light. But Veedran's evil turned the moon into the silvery one we have now." He tapped the side of his nose, grinning. "However, those of us who follow the old tales have heard of a place deep in a forest right here on Windlous where Zerana's grace remains pure. It's said if you walk through the deepest parts of this forest you can see the moon's former beauty. Sadly, none can venture there. Veedran turned the forest around it evil, unleashing horrible undead creatures to hunt Zerana. They still haunt those woods. It's said the mixture of her power and Veedran's changed the trees into unnatural things. Some even say Zerana's ghost plagues the woods. You see, it is in that forest that she died. It was in that forest that Veedran struck her down. It once had a beautiful name but has been reduced to nothing more than the 'Evil Enchanted Forest.'"

Neithelas chuckled. "How childish."

The old man ignored him. "Stories tell of its former glory, though. The trees were said to reach the moon, and the ground glistened with jewels which the earth offered up to the goddess."

"I hadn't heard," Lunara said. "Is the forest the last place Veedran and Nevlar were seen?"

The unknown man's grin widened. "Aye. They fought a fierce battle in those woods. We've learned from other gods that Nevlar is the most powerful of all of them. He could've killed his brother with one word but he didn't. He fought Veedran deep into the woods, and their powers cursed the forest even more. The Dead Woods were created, the only witness to the battle between the gods. It's in a part of the Evil Enchanted Forest none have survived. It's said during the fateful battle between the brothers, lights could be seen through the Dead Woods and horrible screams echoed across all of Arden. Zerana's generals, Wilhelm and Travard Firth, bravely ventured into the forest to help Nevlar, but neither god nor the generals emerged. All four were lost."

"So you believe Veedran and Nevlar killed each other?" Lunara asked.

The man scoffed. "No, lass. Nevlar would never smite down his brother. The fact we never saw Veedran again confirms he killed

Nevlar then left us alone to rot godless. No one cares for us, no one looks after us. What worse fate could Veedran have hoped for Arden? Of course he left his vile creations here to torment us and cursed Crutar and Lakvra to remain here to cause us further misery. My friend here thinks the reason no other gods have come to Arden is because Veedran erected a curse around our world that gods cannot pass through." He shrugged a shoulder. "Either way, it doesn't matter. We're alone here, and all we do is blame Nevlar instead of the god who truly deserves our hate. Few remember how purely corrupt Veedran was, how abominable his actions were. We forget how pure we used to be. Before Veedran, we did not kill, we did not murder, we did not rape, we did not lie or cheat. We lived in peace and love. But when Veedran came, he whispered evil to us, corrupted our purity, and planted mad ideas in our minds, showed us murder. It drove Nevlar mad when we turned on each other. What could be worse than seeing your son rape your daughter, or your son kill his brother? To witness it all." The man shook his head, his face sagging with sadness. "It drove him mad."

You know, my murderer, the presence said. *Becaussse you are the one who whissspers to othersss to kill. You have taken up the dark lord'sss caussse.*

Salvarias clenched his fist. *I do not.*

You do. I hear you in the night, reaching out your mind and whissspering in your sssleep. I try to ssstop you, but you do not lisssten.

That is not true.

Ssso sssure are you, my murderer. Then tell me, who isss thisss?

Whispers filled Salvarias's ears, his own words hissing on the wind. Images flashed through his mind of people listening to his voice as he told them to murder. Then he saw their victims, all those that roamed in his dream of the dead. He might not have run them through with a sword, but he controlled the men who did.

Please stop, Salvarias begged, covering his ears.

I won't until you admit what you've done, the presence hissed angrily. *I give you proof and sssstill you deny it. You walk with thessse people when it isss you who will condemn them once your evil winsss. You must face the truth.*

I do not want to be evil. I did not mean to.

But you are! And eventually you will *kill them!*

His own whispered words grew louder, competing against the screams of his victims. Then he saw the yellow-haired man who had murdered his parents, the man's scar shining brightly in the eerie haze of sunset. Salvarias stood next to the man, wispy and translucent, whispering in the man's ear, "Kill her. Torment, rape, and maim her. I want her pain to be great."

"No!" Salvarias shouted.

Yesss, it wasss you, my preccciousss murderer, the presence snarled. *You are a murderer! Think of what you did to Thia! Ssshe wasss just a girl! An innocent!*

"I did not mean to!"

Something shook him. "Salv!"

Salvarias's eyes flew open. Wilhelm was shaking his shoulders. He realized he was standing and the gazes of everyone in the tavern were upon him. Lowering his head, trying to control his trembling, he gasped to steady his breathing.

Wilhelm's arm slid around his shoulders. "Come on. Let's go to the room."

Wilhelm used his frame to block any from staring at Salvarias as they left the common room. His heavy feet thudded on each stair, and he leaned heavily on his aspen branch. Inside his room, he sank to his bed.

Wilhelm sat beside him. "What happened?"

"I ... I ..." Salvarias rested his head in his hands, swallowing back his tears.

"It's all right." Wilhelm offered the puzzle box. "You don't have to tell me."

Salvarias wiped his eyes and accepted the device. "Thank you, brother."

Wilhelm ruffled Salvarias's hair and Salvarias elbowed his brother's ribs. After kicking off his boots, Salvarias scooted back on his bed to rest in the corner of the room. The puzzle box slowed his mind and eased his residual terror, his horror at what he might have done.

Part of him rejected the voice's accusation, but another willingly believed it. After all, he was evil. It lived within him. It was plausible he was not as in control as he hoped, that he could speak on the wind, tempt the innocent into acts of violence. The thought made him nauseous.

He fought sleep as long as he could, avoiding the dream Lunara had saved him from. It still terrorized him, but at least now he knew it was not real. Eventually he lost and dreamt of drowning in a sea of gore and mutilated corpses as they stabbed and yelled at him. All the while, a thin hand searched for him.

Salvarias gathered his cloak tighter about him. The misty rain had yet to let up, and though no breeze disrupted the still morning air, coldness clung to the ground in the form of tangible fog. Icy grasses crunched beneath Mithal's hooves as he danced in place while Salvarias attempted to shift through the images bombarding his mind. Wilhelm patted Lilly when she nickered in protest at the delay and butted against Mithal.

Salvarias slumped in his saddle. He slept little if at all. Whatever hunted him had decided to be merciful this morning, but despite his reprieve a thudding headache blocked out his minor happiness. The focus required to conceal his location along with constantly maintaining the wall surrounding his soul strained his mind and added a heaviness to his body. He was so tired. His sluggish gaze moved from tree to tree, from bush to bush, from road to road, sifting through Perek's flashes of his surroundings to find the path Salvarias needed to follow.

Salvarias glanced behind him at the others sitting on their horses, huddled in equal misery and coldness. Autumn had claimed Windlous, ignoring the last week of summer. He wished his companions had remained behind. There was no need for all of them to suffer. He wiped the rain from his face and took another gander at his surroundings. Wilhelm's turning mind distracted Salvarias.

"What it is, brother?"

"It's just ... you look like you're thinking of something else. You need to stay alert." Wilhelm's gaze drifted over the unfamiliar landscape. "This rain and fog is thick, and we're not going to have much reaction time if something attacks us."

Salvarias lowered his voice and said, "I should have told you, brother. I see what he sees, images—flashes—of what he passed by, what he noticed. I must sift through them to discover our path."

"Sorry, Salv."

"Do not apologize, brother. You did not know."

"I meant I'm sorry you have to endure this stuff."

Salvarias looked at his brother's solemn face. "It is I who should apologize. You must endure all this with me." His mind latched on to the image he needed. He glanced around before pointing. "This way." He turned Mithal and headed northeast.

The wet morning sobered the party, and the drizzle kept a chill embedded in Salvarias's bones. Fog still blanketed the ground, adding a hush to the companions and the gray hillsides with their patches of gray trees. By lunch, misery was Salvarias's master.

"We need food and a warm fire," Humar announced.

"There's a thicket just off the main road," Okulu muttered. He took a long swig from his flask and shuddered. "Should shield us from the rain."

The party veered from the road and followed Okulu to a tiny clearing barely fitting their group. Humar and Okulu scouted for dry firewood while Lunara and Neithelas gathered food. Salvarias was grateful for the break in needing to monitor the images. Once the fire started, he dozed under its warmth.

He jolted awake to a strong hand resting on his shoulder.

"Salv, it's time to go."

Salvarias stumbled to his feet, half awake, and mounted Mithal. After they reached the main road, he focused on the images and picked up the trail. A familiar farm caught his attention in the distance, and he nudged Mithal to a trot in order to gain time. Beyond the farm, he saw his next landmark, and past that more clues littered the land. The muddy path slowed the horses, but Salvarias let them set the pace. Close to nightfall, the trail split off the main road. Salvarias reined in to study the forest laid out before him.

"What is it?" Humar said.

"He went into the woods."

Okulu stopped beside Salvarias. "It's all right. That's not the Evil Enchanted Forest. See, it's marked here on the map, 'Evil Enchanted Forest.'"

Humar shook his head. "Put the map away, Okulu, before it gets ruined. Regardless of the name of the forest, I don't think we should venture in there at night. We'll camp outside and wait for sunrise."

"The trees are ... odd," Neithelas said when he dismounted. "They are frightened of what lives within their woods. Something powerful ... something ... evil."

"Of course," Durak growled. "It be following us!"

Neithelas glanced at Salvarias. "I have no doubt."

Salvarias ignored the winsire and stared into the woods. Everything hazed around him, like he sat in a dream, and far off a seductive voice called to him. Mithal took a step back but Salvarias urged him to stay. The throaty voice beckoned to him again. He had a sudden longing to venture into the woods. The creatures seeking him stirred, but he easily fought them.

"Come on, Salv," Wilhelm called.

His brother's voice startled Salvarias from the dreamlike trance. As he slid off Mithal, he had an urgent desire not to camp here. He wanted to run. Every instinct urged him to flee. Leaning against Mithal, he wrestled with his mind, unsure if it was exhaustion playing tricks or if there was true danger.

Warmth reached him and he looked up to see Wilhelm by his side.

"You all right, Salv?"

Salvarias glanced back at the woods, but the feeling had faded. "I am only tired, brother."

Mithal nudged him in affection, and he stroked the horse's neck while following his brother to the camp his companions had begun setting up. He pulled as many blankets as he could find from his pack and laid on the cold ground, holding his warming staff close. Adok laid against his back. Though hungry, sleep trumped food. Just as his eyes closed, Wilhelm shook him.

"Time to go, Salv."

His eyes would not open. Darkness towed him into its comforts, encasing him in thick blackness. *Things* invaded his sleeping mind, but he was too tired to care. Wilhelm shook him again. It could not be time to go. Salvarias had just fallen asleep. Even if he wanted to wake, his mind refused.

"Come on, Salv. You have to wake up."

Persistent, Wilhelm lifted Salvarias's body upright, shaking him. His mind slowly fought away the darkness. He squinted at the light amplified by the foggy morning sun. All the companions were waiting by their horses. Salvarias's feet steadied under him. He latched on to Mithal and hauled himself into the saddle.

"Don't you want to eat?" Humar asked.

Salvarias shook his head. He was utterly exhausted. It took him longer to snatch the image he needed, and he led his group into the woods. The trees and fern-littered ground seemed dreary, blending into the same dull green that looked to have given up on life. Few birds disturbed the horses' noisy plodding through the dense underbrush, and the fog thickened within the first hour of their trek. Voices whispered behind him, but he lacked the energy to listen to the murmured conversations of his companions. He focused on staying upright in his saddle and following the path. The farther they traveled into the woods, the thicker the trees clustered together until hardly enough light filtered through the towering branches to offer clear direction.

Time lost meaning. He needed sleep. Nothing else mattered. The sensation flourished until it was near painful to stay awake. Then familiar arms wrapped around him and pulled him off Mithal.

"Get some sleep," Wilhelm said. "We're going to stay here for the night."

Salvarias closed his eyes as blankets cocooned him in warmth. He slept until the voice from the previous night beckoned to him again. A subtle warm breeze encased him, lifting him from the cold ground. Curling up in the comfort of the voice and the heat of the breeze, Salvarias drifted to sleep after a contented sigh.

Chapter 14

Autumn 1018 a.r.

Wilhelm startled awake when his blanket was ripped off and a beast growled viciously. Heart racing, he grabbed his sword as he reached for Salvarias. His hand found a pile of empty blankets.

He spewed a few curses as he leapt to his feet, gaze sweeping over the campsite. The others were stirring under his commotion. The mantle of fog whirled around a beast crouched in front of him. He raised his sword for a strike as the beast growled again. Pausing, he squinted into the dim light the smoldering campfire provided and made out black fur and gold eyes. It was Adok. A dead rabbit hung in the wolf's mouth.

"Where's Salv?" Wilhelm asked.

Adok dropped the rabbit and sniffed the air, prancing around the campsite with his nose high. To Wilhelm's right, the wolf stopped with his hackles spiked, teeth bared, and he growled at the woods.

"We've got company!" Okulu called. The merc hauled Humar from his bedroll, thrusting the knight's sword in his hand.

Twigs snapped in the woods and the thundering of hooves disturbed the silent night. Birds cawed and bats flew overhead, fleeing from the racket.

"What can you see?" Humar said, scrambling upright.

"Nothing much through this blasted mist." Okulu cursed. "Not sure what they are ... maybe part octril, part minotaur? They're big."

Varila yanked her sword from its sheath. "How many?"

Okulu shrugged. "I'd say about ten. Not unmanageable."

"Eleven," Neithelas said. "And yes, part minotaur indeed. Can't you smell them?"

"Where's Salv?" Wilhelm demanded, looking to each companion.

Neithelas shook his head. "The trees say the wind took him. I don't understand, but they insist it's the truth." He nocked an arrow and loosed it. A roar split the night. "The beasts are strong. It didn't go down."

"How close?" Humar asked.

"You're about to find out!" Okulu hurled a dagger into the darkness.

Black shapes burst clear of the trees. They rivaled Wilhelm's height, covered in ratty black fur. Their heads and lower half were minotaur with the double forearms of octrils, and they reeked of wet dog.

Wilhelm swooped down and plucked up his other sword, ripping it from its sheath. He tossed the holder aside and charged the closest beast.

Two horns atop the beast's head glistened with dew and lowered to accept his charge. Wilhelm tucked in his shoulder, ducked out of the way of the horns, and rammed into the beast. They twirled apart and, before he recovered, a different beast clenched four slick hands around his throat. A black streak shot through the air and tackled another creature whose sword had been poised to remove Wilhelm's head. Guttural screams overpowered Adok's growl as the wolf ripped out the creature's throat.

Wilhelm kicked the knee of the beast choking him. The creature howled as bone snapped, and its grip loosened enough that Wilhelm sucked in a breath. With every muscle in his left arm, he whipped around his great sword and, despite the awkward angle, managed to cleave the blade through the creature's legs at the kneecap. With a painful roar, it released him and fell backward, bloody stumps kicking. Adok clamped his jaw over the beast's throat. Blood spurted and the creature stilled.

Wilhelm lunged to the left of a thrusting axe, knocked the weapon aside, and lopped off the blue-green scaled hand at the wrist.

From behind, arms clamped around his chest, pinning his arms at his sides. The creature heaved him up, seeming to crush his ribs, sending shots of pain to his brain. Wilhelm bucked his head back and a jolt of agony barreled down his spine as his skull connected with the face of the creature. It released him with a snarl, stumbling back. Without looking, Wilhelm jabbed his sword backward beneath his arm and felt the slight resistance of skin and the raking of bone. In one fluid motion, he ripped his sword free and arced it in front of him, eviscerating the still stunned creature staring at blood spouting from its forearm.

Varila's scream of Lunara's name chilled Wilhelm. He spun around to see Lunara suspended by the massive hands of a beast clamped around her throat, her feet dangling two feet off the ground. She was gasping and beating the beast's arm with her fists. The creature's sword was on a course for her heart. Wilhelm couldn't reach her in time nor could Varila.

Okulu darted into view and used his short sword to flip aside the creature's weapon. Wilhelm had already started for the beast, and he stabbed up and under the creature's armpit, sinking the blade past lungs and up into the heart. Its grip on Lunara failed and she fell hard to the ground, clutching her throat and coughing.

"Duck," Wilhelm growled to Okulu, yanking his sword free of the creature as it crumpled to the ground.

The merc didn't hesitate and flung himself over Lunara. Wilhelm threw his broadsword like an axe, and it plunged into the chest of a charging beast, catapulting the creature backward, leaving a trail of blood.

Wilhelm looked for his next foe. Neithelas was barely fending off two creatures. Wilhelm sprang forward and snuck his great sword into the back of one of the beasts. The creature stiffened and then slumped to the ground. Wilhelm bent below the jab of another sword from a third foe and sliced the back of the second creature's leg. The beast wailed and went to a knee. Neithelas sank his sword in the creature's throat.

Recovering from his duck before the third beast recovered from its strike, Wilhelm planted his fist into the creature's face. The jaw broke and hung limply. Wilhelm wrapped an arm around the creature's head and snapped its neck.

Then it was over.

Wilhelm glanced around at the bloody sight and turned to Adok, who was hacking out a chunk of fur and meat. "Find him."

Adok whined and paced the camp's perimeter. After circling it twice, he glanced at Wilhelm with an apologetic look—if wolves could do such a thing.

"Dammit!" Wilhelm belted. He stormed over to Lunara folded in Varila's arms. "Find him!"

"I can't," she said hoarsely. "He's ... he's not himself. He can't hear me."

"You knew where he was when you were in Falar! You found him without talking to him then! Do it again!"

She rubbed her throat, her eyes widening at his anger. "I-I can't. I-I don't know how."

Wilhelm kicked the closest dead creature and roared in anger. He turned his fury to the others. "Who was on watch?"

Durak scuffed his foot on the ground. "It was me, lad."

Wilhelm pounced on the cavrul and grabbed his tunic. "What happened?" Arms tried to pull him away but he held firm. "What in Oblivion happened?"

"Me fell asleep," Durak stammered. "Me didn't realize until you woke."

Wilhelm tossed the man aside and turned his glare to Humar. "Do something!" Out of the corner of his eye he saw Lunara sit by Salvarias's blankets.

Humar raised his hand and spoke in the same infuriatingly calm manner as always. "We'll find him. We'll start a search, split up."

Lunara gasped and sprang to her feet. Without a word, she mounted her white mare and hissed the horse into a run. She disappeared into the trees.

"Dammit!" Varila cursed, rushing to her horse.

Wilhelm ran over to Lilly and tossed the saddle on the mare. He couldn't ride bareback like Lunara. He cursed his thick fingers when he fumbled with the saddle's buckles. Tears blurred his vision. The pounding hooves of Lunara's horse were growing distant.

"Please," Wilhelm wept. The buckle slipped into place and he jumped on Lilly even as she took off at a full gallop, Mithal following on his own accord. He couldn't hear Lunara over Lilly and his pounding heart.

Salvarias's mind clambered up from nightmares to feel cool air on his naked chest. A musty scent should have made it near impossible for him to breath, but air flowed in and out of his lungs with an ease he had never before experienced. No images flogged him. No screams wailed in his ear. Instead, his mind swam in thick syrup, and he was terribly exhausted. He winced at a stinging pain burning along his wrist.

It took concentration on his part to force open his stubborn eyelids. Seductive red light glowed around him, emanating from a crystal hanging from a low ceiling. Furs covered the walls, painting them in hues of browns and grays. He smelled the mustiness of caves and shivered in the cool dampness that always seemed to accompany them. Allowing his head to fall to the side, he saw he was indeed in a cave the size of a small bedroom.

Warmth chased away the chill, and he looked down at a woman straddling him. Black hair cascaded over her dark, smooth skin. Bright-green eyes gazed at him with a mix of curiosity and triumph. Her barely clothed body exuded sensuality, and her skin beckoned to be touched. She was painfully beautiful to look upon, and he had a strong desire to obey her, to worship her.

When she smiled, blood stained her teeth. "Tell me," the woman purred. "How did you know to come this way?"

Salvarias stared at her in disinterested confusion. A chill surged through his blood, followed by unnatural heat. He rolled his tongue in his mouth and tasted a sweet herb mixture. He had been drugged.

Sleep was more inviting than whatever the woman wanted. He closed his eyes.

"No," she said.

A vial was forced between his lips, and he choked down a minty mixture. It worked fast, awakening a tiny portion of his body and mind. His eyes fluttered opened.

"How did you know to come here?" she asked again. "You followed him. I want to know how."

Salvarias's mouth answered on its own. "I see what he sees, my lady."

She raised his wrist to her lips and sucked blood from a slice he just now noticed. "My lady? So formal. Call me Lakvra."

"Goddess of Lust," Salvarias said, remembering the title the old men in the bar had given her.

She smiled seductively. "Does that name fit me?"

Salvarias gazed at her enticing body and nodded.

Smiling, she lapped up his blood. "And what are your thoughts on my homeland? Do you like Windlous?"

Salvarias did not care to answer. Indifference was all he could summon.

"I've made it wonderfully peaceful," she continued. "Veedran and Nevlar's creations love one another. There is no war here, no fighting. Only lust. Is it not better this way?" She frowned when he did not reply. She shoved another vial between his lips and dumped its contents. He choked it down.

"My master was not expecting you to follow, even if he does want you," she said. "You've surprised us. I've already sent word to him, but before he arrives perhaps you could entertain me for a few hours." She raised a small knife and sank it farther into his wrist. A trickle of blood rushed out and she licked it up.

Salvarias's body lurched from another wave of cold sweeping over him. His muscles constricted painfully, and he arched slightly off the ground. A groan escaped.

"Tell me," she breathed. "Do you think I'm beautiful?"

She lifted her hair, revealing plump breasts, a small waist, and round hips. His body collapsed as the spasm passed. He nodded, closing his eyes. Gods, he wanted to sleep.

Hands slid over his chest, shifting his torn-open robes over his shoulders. He shivered.

"Do you want me?" she breathed in his ear. Lips glided down his neck, and her tongue traced a scar on his chest.

His thoughts went to Lunara and her bright eyes, sweet smile, and lithe body. He shook his head.

"She must be special," Lakvra said. "Few mortals have ever resisted me."

Her hand glided down his chest and under the rope tied at his waist. His body hitched in another spasm.

"Leave him alone!"

Salvarias opened his eyes to see Lunara standing behind the goddess, eyes aflame with fear and determination, fists clenched at her sides. He never remembered her looking so stunning.

Lakvra looked over her shoulder at Lunara. "Well, well. Are you the one that has captured his heart, my little doll?"

"Leave him alone," Lunara said again, though her voice lost some of its confidence.

Lakvra crawled off Salvarias and circled Lunara like a hungry lion toying with a lame doe. "There's no need to be angry." Quicker than a cat, the goddess sprang on Lunara, knocking the woman to her knees, and Lakvra grabbed Lunara's wrist. A blade flashed in Lakvra's hand and sliced down Lunara's forearm. The goddess licked up the spilling blood as a cry left Lunara.

Salvarias closed his eyes. He just wanted to sleep. He moaned at another assault of cold and cramping muscles.

"Help me," Lunara beseeched him. "Salvarias, help me!"

Her plea echoed in his muddled mind, rattling around the empty space. Emotions of fear assailed him, and he winced at their painful bombardment. Why could they not let him sleep?

Lakvra gasped from feeding on Lunara's blood, chest heaving, and gazed with wide eyes at Lunara. "You have the goddess within you. How?"

Lunara looked up at Lakvra, brow furrowed.

The goddess backhanded Lunara across the cheek. "Tell me! How did the Goddess of Purity link to you? She's ... she's dead. Dead!"

Lunara trembled. "Salvarias!"

Groaning at another surge of her fear, he forced himself to sit. Words of all the spells he had memorized jumped around in his mind. He mumbled something out and drew in the energy. His magic was speaking, but Salvarias did not have the strength of mind to listen. He must have used a portion of Lakvra's energy. The goddess whirled around to face him.

"Oh no you don't," she said.

She tackled him before he traced his rune. Blood seeped from his pores as the energy left his body. A cold wave struck at the same time, and darkness pressed around the edges of his vision. Muscles knotted and convulsed violently.

Lakvra raised a dagger, but before the goddess did anything, Lunara leapt on her back and yanked her backward. Both women stumbled and collided with the far wall. Salvarias latched on to the furs and pulled himself up. He barely got his feet under him before Lunara flew into his arms, stumbling them both back a few steps. Strength surged up in Salvarias, and her calming touch helped open a small tunnel of clarity. It allowed in a vague sense of danger, but he was having a hard time focusing. The drug had turned his indifference into desire, and Lunara was very warm and soft, and she smelled simply wonderful. He gathered her trembling body in his arms.

In all the haze of his sluggish mind, it took a moment to realize the goddess was speaking, not to him or Lunara, but calling forth power. Her hand rose in front of her, eyes gleaming.

Salvarias dove for the ground, flinging his body awkwardly to shield Lunara. Whatever Lakvra sent scored his back with burning pain. Lunara cried out. On her slender shoulder, a slice leaked blood. His beacon of purity and light had been harmed.

Anger bubbled up in Salvarias, and he teetered to his feet and rounded on the goddess. His rage forced his mind to think, to block out the pain of his spasming body, of the warm blood pooling in his hand. Sweet black flames erupted over him, egging on his anger, boiling his blood with fury. His single thought was to kill.

Lakvra's eyes widened. "No!" she cried. "No! Don't take me there! I swear I'll help your soul! I'll tell you where he is! I'll tell you everything I know! Just don't take me there!"

Salvarias strode forward.

She staggered back until she had no place else to go. Falling to her knees, she clasped her hands together. "Please! I beg you! Do not take me there! I can help you!"

Salvarias latched on to her throat and leaned down to whisper in Lakvra's ear. "You will help me, and I will take you there."

His fire exploded with delight as it licked over her body. Her skin sizzled and bubbled, boils spurted open in breaths, and her screams grew his smile.

Then came death.

He stared at the naked woman sucking out his blood, his mind in a haze, his body unresponsive to fight what pleasures the woman claimed from him. But through all his drug-induced cloud, he thought of his son, no older than five years, alone with no one to care for him. He should have never listened to the voice calling him into the woods, should never have left the road. Whatever drug the woman had given him could not cast aside his love for his child, and as the room faded and a cold set into his bones, a tear leaked out of his eye.

Then, warm blood rushed into his mouth and he savored it, feeling his body respond to the flow of youthful life as he rode his victim in throes of pleasure. He stared at the tear trickling down the man's cheek. Death was near and his guilt could not overcome his thirst for lust and blood. He hated Father for making him this way, but he could not deny his calling and the pleasure it gave him. He wished Zerana were here to help him fight the urge, but the goddess was dead. Now he was alone, a slave to him, unable to resist his beauty and allure. He shed his own tears as life left the man's eyes.

Death after death washed over Salvarias. The goddess was not fussy in her choice of victims and the old and young alike were drained of life, women and men hunted without discrimination. The goddess had lived for thousands of years, and her victims were a mass of torture to Salvarias's mind and body. He should have gone insane, and he had only the drug flowing through his blood to thank for his sanity.

Once he relived them all, he poured their torment back into the goddess, forcing her to experience their pain and humiliation.

In a blink, he stood in front of the doors to Oblivion. Hues of gray fog pulsed in anticipation, wrapping Salvarias in warmth that reached his bones. Screams poured from beyond the walls and bathed him with satisfaction. He grinned at his parents' murderer wailing in torment, at Dethal's face twisted in terror. Again, the pain of all those the men had killed afflicted him, and knowing the murderers suffered for what they had done to the innocent stroked his happiness to erupt in a soft chuckle. He could almost taste the peace the victims received at being avenged.

Lakvra knelt at his side, clutching his robes, looking up at him with eyes raining tears.

"I cannot help it!" she cried. "It's who I am!"

Salvarias squatted down beside her and brushed her hair from her face, admiring her beauty. She was right, of course. Something had made her seek lust and blood. He felt it, an essence he should know, one he was familiar with yet had not met.

"Mercy," she breathed, lips trembling. "Show me mercy, Keeper of Vengeance."

Salvarias slid his thumb over her cheek and wiped her tears. "Mercy ..." He regarded her for a moment. "Mercy was not shown to the innocent you slaughtered. They cried as you cry. They pleaded as you plead. Why should I act any different from you?"

"B-because ..." She looked around, as if the fog would provide an answer. It did not. It sat waiting, warming him, urging him to do what was needed. "Have mercy on another who has no control over what they are. You, Vengeance itself, should understand. Show me mercy. Beg them to forgive me."

"Oblivion has no room for mercy," he said. He heard the victims commanding him to do it. Until now, he had not realized he had experienced the sensation each time he had visited Oblivion. Vengeance was something only the dead could demand. It did not matter that the killer was as tormented. Vengeance had no room for repentance. Oblivion was no place for compassion. And within Salvarias's own blood, the victims' righteous anger burned as if it were his own.

He smiled at the goddess. "They hold no forgiveness."

"He did this to us," she said, clamping her hand over his. "What we are is part of His warped amusement. He may be our father, but He is worse than Veedran himself. What He did to His first born proves He is a monster. Pity me as I pity you."

Part of Salvarias wanted answers to the million questions the goddess had just raised, but here in Oblivion the victims demanded his attention. "I care not for your excuses. They care not." The victims were screaming at him, demanding Lakvra's payment for their suffering. The last ounce of compassion Salvarias might have clung to faded with their pain. "An eternity of torment awaits you." His smile switched to a grim scowl of hatred, and he grabbed her as he rose and tossed her through the doors. Her screech sounded above the others, and he closed his eyes, allowing it to seep into his mind, easing the need for blood. Vengeance had been satiated.

When he opened his eyes, he was surprised to find himself still in Oblivion. He glanced over to where the goddess had knelt, and within the gray fog floated a pustule of sensual scarlet light.

"The goddess's godhood, her raw power," the fog informed him. "It is yours if you wish."

Salvarias recoiled from it as much as he reached for it. It was alluring, beautiful, and it seemed to beckon to him, a kindred spirit of sorts. But he could feel its impurity. He shook his head. "I do not want it. It is unclean."

"Wise," the fog hissed. "Wise indeed."

With one blink, Salvarias stared at the shriveled eye sockets of a charred corpse instead of the towering walls of Oblivion. He dropped the goddess and wiped his palm on the fur, ridding it of raw flesh. Blackfire burned brighter for a breath, seeming to want something from him, but he ignored it as always, too reeling from his pleasure to understand what it sought.

When it imploded its protection vanished, and his body lurched from a cold chill, his mind returning to a hazy fog. The drug only dampened what happened next.

Victims rushed him, hundreds of deaths, and he swore he swam in a sea of their blood. He vomited. Tears flowed freely and he had not realized he had doubled over, hugging himself. He heard himself pleading and knew why, but it was as though he observed from afar.

Then soft arms slid around his shoulders. He clung to her, sobs thrashing him as horror played before him.

He had to leave. The smell of burnt flesh churned his stomach, and it slowly seeped into his mind that he had killed a goddess. A goddess! His actions suddenly struck him as terribly wrong, as if he had murdered his own blood.

"Take me from here!" he pleaded.

"Shhh," Lunara whispered in his ear, brushing back his hair. "We'll be all right."

He clutched her hand tightly, using it as his lifeline. She helped him up and yanked down a fur. A tunnel opened up before him. Escape. Freedom.

He plunged onward, ignoring her cry, wrenching free of her. The short, narrow tunnel made him run hunched over, using the wall to help him hobble along as fast his bad leg would allow. At some point, he had lit his sparrow. It flew before him, its brilliance bringing some calm to his mind.

His body tensed as his blood ran like jagged ice in his veins. His legs crumpled beneath him and he tumbled to the ground, crying out as he coiled in a heap of pain.

"Salvarias!" Lunara cried.

When the spasm passed, he lurched to his feet, using the wall for support. A rush of victims made him lean to the side and retch. Then he saw it on his hands: blood. Lakvra had not killed them. He had killed them! Thousands of them. All their blood dripped down *his* arms, soaking his robes.

What have you done, my little murderer? the presence hissed.

Salvarias ran. He ran until he burst into crisp night air, surrounded by soaring pines and thick mist. One cursory glance around showed him moonbeams kissing a lazy river. Scrambling over a fallen tree, he bolted for the clean waters. He tripped on a rock and fell hard to the ground. Something jabbed into his hand. He ignored it, half crawling, half running until he got his feet under him. He waded into water that only reached his waist.

Sobs racked him as he yanked a cloth from his robe pocket. He scrubbed his hand viciously, but the blood would not come off.

"Help me!" he pleaded. "I cannot get it off!"

"Salvarias."

He looked up at Lunara standing in front of him. "Help me!"

"I want to, but you have to let me in."

He had blocked her without knowing how he did so. He tore down his walls, begging for her help.

Then everything stopped.

The dead left him, their pain ravaging his body ceased, and his mind once again entered its drug-induced state. His sobs quieted as he watched her run the wet cloth over his hands, cleansing them of blood. When it was gone, he raised his gaze to hers. Tears fell from her eyes, but she smiled.

"Drink," she said, cupping water in her hand.

He did as she asked and shivered as water ran down his throat, ridding it of the coarse feeling. Slowly, she permitted the victims to come back to him in small handfuls. His tears were silent. Even with her touch, she could not shield him from their pain.

Before he finished reconciling each death, he took notice of her eyes sparkling in the moonlight and her chest heaving.

A shudder of pain racked him.

He had not realized he had gathered her to him. He had not realized he was leaning forward. She tilted her body, gifting him a view of the top of her breasts rising with each quick breath, her slender neck glowing in the soft light. Her red lips parted. He fought back a spasm of pain, too enthralled by her to permit it to surface, and pressed her closer. Gods, she smelled like spring and life. His gaze drifted from her chest, to her collarbone, to her neck, and finally rested on her lips.

"Salv!"

Wilhelm's voice jolted Salvarias backward. He tripped and fell, realizing for the first time the water was freezing as it gushed over his shoulders. The victims he had yet to process in her touch surged forward, but he managed to keep his mind solidly planted in the now. He scrambled toward the river's edge and crawled out of the waters.

Lunara trudged ashore, picked up her discarded cloak, and wrapped it about her shoulders.

"F-f-forgive me," Salvarias stammered, frozen to the bone.

"Of course," she murmured. She would not meet his gaze.

What were you thinking! the presence shrieked. *Look what you almossst did!*

Salvarias stammered in his own mind. *I did not mean to. I am tired ... I need rest ... It was the poison. I did—*

Ssspare me your excusssesss, murderer! Ssshe isss pure! For onccce, think of another besssidesss your weak desssiresss!

Wilhelm burst from the trees and swung off Lilly before the mare stopped. Salvarias found himself whisked up in a warm hug, safe. He slumped in his brother's arms.

"Gods, what happened to you?" Wilhelm said, snatching hold of Salvarias's cut wrist. There was a puncture on his left palm from when he had fallen. As his past experiments had proven, the wound would heal on its own by morning. His left hand was immune to permanent damage, a product of the mark living on his palm.

Closing his hand into a fist to hide the wound, he said, "We need to leave." He had no desire to stay so close to Lakvra's cave. His feeling of wrong continued growing, and he regretted killing her.

"I don't think you're well enough to ride," Wilhelm said.

As if in agreement, Salvarias curled over in pain as his muscles constricted, his jaw clenched so tight he worried he would bust out his teeth. Wilhelm yelled something, but Salvarias could not speak.

When the spasm passed, he heard Lunara saying, "... drugged. He killed her, but I think it wise we leave this area."

"You both need to change," Humar said. "We can't afford the delay should either of you become sick."

Varila led Lunara and her mare from the group to a cluster of trees and used the horse to help shield the sisters from view. The men turned around, regardless.

Salvarias managed to get to his feet and changed with help from Wilhelm. All the while, he worked to sort through his victims.

When the women returned, Salvarias mounted. With aching concentration, he allowed Perek's fleeting surroundings to surface and shuffled through them until he found what he needed. Ignoring Wilhelm's urges to camp where they were, Salvarias nudged Mithal forward.

The time pushing through the dark night gave him a chance to hide his tears when his victims bombarded his mind again. He retched several times during their flight, merely telling Wilhelm it was the drug, which was a partial truth.

The sun eventually rose, lighting the sky gray-yellow. The trees seemed desperate for it, clawing at one another to reach the sun as it slipped behind a veil of clouds, casting the forest in another hue of gray.

By now, Salvarias was sure he was near death. The strain of keeping in his saddle when his body folded over in pain, blocking whatever hunted him, fortifying his wall against his evil, committing horrible acts of murder, and following fleeting images from Perek had erupted his mind into a blinding headache. He was not sure when the drug had run through his system and his body gave out. All he felt was himself sliding from Mithal to land in familiar arms, tucked away in secrecy, safe from those who would hurt him.

Chapter 15

Autumn 1018 a.r.

Lunara shivered awake. Everyone bustled about in the task of breaking camp and gathering lunch, except for Salvarias tossing in his bedroll.

For once, the sun boldly stripped the thin layer of clouds, but its warmth beating down on her did nothing to drive away the chill clinging to her.

Unfortunately, fever had set in. Lunara's bones throbbed and her skin was sore to the touch. Sweat-soaked hair stuck to her neck, and her clogged head felt stuffed with wool. She desperately wanted sleep, but they couldn't delay in their quest for whatever Salvarias sought. Shoving herself up, she managed her way to a rock so her sister could fold up the bedroll.

The mere thought of Salvarias recalled Lunara's shame. He had been drugged senseless. She'd seen it in his eyes, yet she took advantage of him—used her body to entice him in the creek. Luckily for both, Wilhelm had broken the moment. She didn't want her first kiss to be one of deceit. Now she avoided Salvarias like the plague, and he obliged with the same remoteness; whether because of disgust toward her or his own shame, she wasn't sure.

Using Salvarias's hiding method, she raised the hood of her cloak and accepted a bowl of food from Varila. She ate little. The bowl of hot water with chopped vegetables tasted of dust and agitated her swollen throat when she swallowed. Salvarias had been forced awake by Wilhelm and ate a few bites before passing it off to Adok, who delved into it with gusto.

Then they were off again. As usual, Salvarias sat astride Mithal for several moments, surveying the woods with distant eyes, whispering numbers. Seeming to take longer than normal, he finally nudged Mithal forward, and the rest followed without a word.

The afternoon's ride introduced Lunara to pure misery. Thankfully, her friends occupied one another and left her alone. She vaguely listened to Varila argue with Okulu about an outlandish tale the merc had woven, and if Lunara had more energy, she would've laughed at Humar and Durak trying to convince Neithelas that accepting sword instruction from an erthla would not send the winsire straight to Oblivion.

By evening, they had broken free of the forest and clouds had overpowered the sun, sending a steady drizzle to turn Lunara's misery into sheer torture. She shivered violently and would've loved nothing more than to ride with Wilhelm, encased in his thick cloak as his body emitted enough heat to steam away the rain before it reached her. However, he rode beside Salvarias, hand often on his brother's shoulder to keep him in the saddle. She guessed it was the reason Humar ordered an early stop.

Lunara had one goal: sleep. Without waiting for a fire or helping set up camp, she grabbed her bedroll, spread it out, and then snuggled beneath her blankets. Salvarias didn't bother to wait for blankets. He merely plopped down and curled up, muttering within a few breaths, head tossing restlessly. Sleep claimed Lunara quickly.

The next morning cursed her with a worsening ache and a head full of sheep. She was drenched in sweat, but it was hidden in the cold rain soaking her. She choked down breakfast to avoid worrying her sister and politely shied from Neithelas's attempts to coax her into conversation.

Then, once again, they mounted in moody silence and continued on their journey.

She rode through the day vaguely watching the scenery blur by with every shade of gray imaginable. The stark hills spattered with clusters of trees made her long for home. No fall colors were visible, and unhappiness seemed to have mantled the world.

A gusty breeze knocked her out of a half-asleep trance. Unsure how long she'd ridden unawares of her surroundings, she glanced around. By the group's haggard look, it must've been late in the day. Adok rubbed her leg, ears flattened.

"No," Lunara mumbled. "Don't say anything to him. We must—"

Adok trotted next to the mage. A few breaths passed before Salvarias's head jerked up. Their gazes met. She tried to smile, but suddenly everything spun around her. The world teetered. Another gust of wind shoved her to one side of her horse, but her legs lacked the strength to keep her upright and she fell. Strong arms caught her before she hit the ground and black eyes glittered at her in the faint light.

"What's wrong with her?" Varila asked.

Salvarias shook his head. "Okulu, where is the nearest town?"

"A few hours ride along the main road. I—"

Salvarias cursed. "Keep up if you can."

Then they were galloping. She didn't remember mounting, or him settling her in front of him. She jostled dangerously, but his arm held her tightly around the waist.

Gray hills and trees fleeted by until darkness crept across the land. Frightening shadows stretched along the road to play tricks on the muddied ground. The wind howled a dreadful tune. The dribbling rain switched to pour down in sheets, slanted and forceful. White froth around Mithal's muzzle gleamed in the light of Salvarias's sparrow speeding alongside them.

An eternity seemed to pass before sputtering torches came into view. No wall or gate surrounded the rural town, and no guards were patrolling. Warming lights blinked from beyond weathered windows, and a hush blanketed the streets.

Her aching body, stuffy head, and tightening muscles gave way to nausea. She leaned over and retched. Salvarias never slowed to allow her to move aside her hair. Though barely conscious, she was every bit aware of the putrid smell.

He reined in Mithal in front of a squat two-story stone building. The windows were scrunched, and the inn at one point had sunk near a foot into the sopping ground. Salvarias slid off the stallion, one hand holding her steady in the saddle. He fished out coins and tossed them at a man.

"The best care for the horse, gentleman."

Salvarias lifted her from the saddle and cradled her to his chest as he glided into the tavern without waiting for a reply from the stablehand. Inside, a handful of patrons huddled in the common room, taking up the tables closest to the crackling fire. A portly man waddled from behind the counter to greet them.

"I need a room, gentleman," Salvarias said.

"I don't board mages. Sleep in the woods—"

"I have every ability to force you to accommodate my request. I ask again, one room please."

The owner's narrowing eyes switched to Lunara. "It's not contagious, is it?"

"Most definitely. I suggest supplying the key before the infection spreads throughout your fine establishment."

The man's eyes widened and he hustled toward the counter. "I warn you, boy, I'll give you a room, but I can't be responsible for my patrons if they come up to teach you a lesson."

Salvarias's voice held no warmth when he responded, "Nor can I be held responsible if those patrons perish should we be disturbed."

The man curled his upper lip. "You're too young to perform—"

Salvarias whispered in the language of magic. The usual softness of his voice had a steel edge. In one blink, ice shards surrounded the owner. "I assure you, good gentleman, my age does not attest to my abilities. The key, please." He reached out his hand, and a thin section of the shards drifted to the side.

The man tossed the key. Salvarias placed a gold coin on a nearby table. "I will require a kettle of hot water, several blankets, and cloths. Leave them outside the door. I will need to burn the bedding but this payment will surely cover the cost."

The man nodded.

Salvarias tilted his head in polite farewell, released the spell, and then strode up the stairs. As they entered the room, Lunara leaned away and retched again, horrified when it soiled the sleeve of his robe, though he seemed not to notice. He lowered her to the bed. She went to apologize but blessed darkness finally claimed her.

Warmth and a pounding head woke her. Despite a crackling fire, she shivered. Salvarias sat by her side, washing vomit from her hair. His eyebrows were stitched together, his eyes dull with concern.

"I'm slo ...soorr ..." Her tongue wouldn't work properly.

"Drink."

Salvarias lifted her head and helped her sip what tasted like plain hot water. Snot ran from her nose. Mortified, she tried to move but she had no strength. He wiped it away with a cloth. The pain of her aching body churned her stomach and she retched again. To her dismay, he didn't move in time and it covered the front of his robes. She drifted to sleep while he wiped her mouth clean.

The next time she stirred awake, a hacking cough assaulted her. Chunks of bloody mucus came up. Salvarias lifted her head enough so she could spit them in a bowl. Humiliated, she sank back to her bed.

"Drink this," Salvarias said.

"Varil ... Vari ..." She couldn't even say her sister's name before coughing.

"You cannot see her yet. You are sick, my lady, and highly contagious. When it passes, I will bring in Lady Varila."

Though she did want to see her sister, she'd hoped for Varila to take care of her. The two had been through sicknesses together, and there was a comfort in having Varila see her in this condition versus a man she was trying to gain favor with.

After drinking whatever he offered, Salvarias helped her to the chamber pot. Luckily, she didn't require his help. He politely waited outside the door. Once done, she staggered toward her bed. Somewhere along the way, she passed out.

When she woke, she was in bed covered in blankets. Salvarias drank a cup of steaming liquid, his breath wheezing, face pale.

She felt no better. The aching of her body had worsened if anything, and her brain sought escape from her skull.

"How lonnn?" she asked.

"A full day." He joined her side, lifting her head so she could drink another cup. "I would like you to try to eat some bread."

Lunara nodded. Tiny bite by tiny bite, she forced down a slice. To her surprise, it eased her churning stomach. Once she coughed up more globs of mucus, she drifted back to sleep.

For an unknown period of time, she rose in and out of sleep. Sometimes she coughed, others she retched. There were times when Salvarias's hand encompassed hers while his long fingers ran through her hair, his words of comfort whispered in her ear. He cleaned up after her, washed her hair, changed the blankets, and kept shoving teas and bread down her throat. It might as well have been a lifetime of humiliation.

During some of her lucid moments, she saw his face shiny and pale, heard his lungs rattle, and occasionally woke to his hacking cough. Vaguely she remembered the alarming sight of him collapsing to the floor but could not be certain if it had actually happened or if it had been a dream, a delusion of fever perhaps. Through whatever he might have suffered, he cared for her.

A roar of thunder brought Lunara's mind clear of fog. For the first time, the aching of her bones had subsided, each breath didn't cause a dagger to pierce her lungs, and her brain remained content in her skull. Though exhausted, sore, and stuffy, she felt remarkably better.

Salvarias sat on the floor by her side, gaze focused on her hand. Color had returned to his face and, for once, his hood was tossed back. His black eyes churned with their usual hues of gray, and his thick, wavy hair shone in the ruddy firelight.

Her heart lurched when she became aware of fingers tracing hers. The peaceful expression softening the normal stern lines of his face was breathtaking. She snapped her eyes shut, not wanting to break the moment. His rhythmic caress almost lulled her to sleep. That is, until his soft lips rested on the back of her hand, nearly causing her heart to stop. Then his hand left hers and fabric rustled. She peeked through narrowed eyelids to see him mixing herbs.

"Hello."

He glanced over his shoulder. "My lady. How do you feel?"

She smiled at him. "Much better. You look well."

"We have both fought off the worst of it."

"I'm sorry for all you've been through caring for me. I remember some of it and I'm absolutely horri—"

"There is no need for apologies, my lady."

"Thank you. I'm so ... embarrassed." She ran a hand through her hair. "I must look dreadful."

"You could never be anything but beautiful." His cheeks reddened and he turned back to the kettle.

She tried to stifle her grin. Battling her stiff muscles, she managed to get herself into a sitting position by the time he joined her. She accepted the warm mug he offered. It held no flavor but sent a warm ripple through her.

"How long has it been?" Lunara asked.

"A week."

She shrank back. "I'm so sorry I delayed us. I'm strong enough we can leave."

"There is no need. The man I seek has also taken refuge during this storm. We have only lost two days."

"Was the town along our path?"

"It was, my lady. Would you like to walk a bit?"

"Yes."

Lunara accepted his help to stand and leaned heavily against him. She was surprised when she moved well considering she'd been bedridden for days.

As if reading her mind, Salvarias said, "You rose a few times to walk around the room."

"Thank you."

By the second lap weaving between the table, beds, and chairs, she walked on her own. The more she moved, the less her body ached. Salvarias settled in a chair, studying her with his intense gaze while she continued. Seemingly unawares of his actions, he picked up a book resting on a table and opened it, never looking at its pages, never taking his gaze from her. She waited patiently for him to speak.

"What did the woman mean when she said the Goddess of Purity is within you?"

Lunara glanced at him. "The same question has troubled me as well. I don't know who the Goddess of Purity is, but I'm sure I've never met her."

"Nor should you. The Goddess of Purity was Zerana."

Lunara froze. "Zerana is dead."

"Precisely, my lady."

"Then how could I have her ... her ..."

"Power."

She laughed and continued her stroll. "I have no power, Salvarias."

"On the contrary, my lady. I sense it within you."

"It's impossible. I can't have any of her power. She's dead, in case you forgot."

"Nothing is impossible."

She giggled. "Is that your standard response whenever anyone says 'impossible'?"

"It is a truth, my lady."

"So one day Mithal could breath underwater? There are things in this world that are impossible, Salvarias."

"A simple protection spell would allow it."

"But not forever."

"Nothing is forever."

Lunara cocked her head at him. "I disagree. Love is forever. I am forever."

"Everything dies." He looked down at the open book in his hands. It was old, brown leather worn, pages frayed along their edges, and there appeared to be an inscription on the page Salvarias studied. When he spoke, his voice was a haunted whisper. "I have seen love die myself. I saw the light of it leave his eyes."

She paused by his side long enough to see what was written on the book.

To my son, Salvarias.
May you forever remain curious and never change
your pure heart.
I will love you always.
Tobin

"Then it was not love," she said.

He snapped the book closed and set it on the table. "Given time, everything dies."

His statement bothered her. She couldn't fathom her soul dying. It made no sense that after her body betrayed her, she would cease to be.

No longer interested in strolling around the room, she moved to the window and stared at the sleet thrashing the quaint town. Ice clung to the roads and shot down like daggers from the eaves of the houses.

"My body will die, but my soul will not," she said, determined to believe her own words. "There's something beyond this place. Another world to explore. And I know, without a doubt, my mother, father, and sister will still love me. How can all I am just cease to be?" She knew he was behind her. The man had a presence about him that couldn't be ignored.

"Why would you want to continue? Death is peace, an end to suffering."

She turned to face him. His eyes were questioning, curious in her response. She smiled at the man she loved. "I want to continue because once this body is gone the love of my friends and family will follow me. I am forever tied to them and them to me. I would never want to be separated from them."

"But suffering will follow you as well."

"Suffering I can endure if I have love."

Salvarias's eyebrows furrowed together.

She said, "Would you not endure the suffering of your life over and over again if it meant being by Wilhelm's side forever?"

"Yes." He raised his hand as if to touch her, but curled his fingers back. "You sound so certain. How do you know it is possible?"

She brushed aside his hair. He flinched away. "Do you not know yourself? After all, it's you who states nothing is *im*possible."

His eyes lit with amusement. "So I am."

She grinned. "Now do you believe in forever?"

A light smile touched his lips. "I believe it is a possibility, my lady."

Salvarias stepped out of the room behind his brother, happy to be free of his seclusion, aside from a brief, private meeting with Okulu. After Lunara had woken two days ago, Salvarias had switched to his brother's room so Varila could stay with Lunara.

Finally rid of the stuffy confines reeking of wet dog and stale air, he inhaled deeply the aroma of stew and fresh bread and the smokiness of a fire while listening contently to Adok rambling on about his inability to change the way wet fur smelled.

The sisters' door opened and both emerged, looking like flowers sprouting in lava ruins.

"Hello," Lunara said.

Salvarias tilted his head. "You look well, my lady." Indeed her porcelain skin glowed in the dim hallway. Dark circles rimmed her shimmering blue eyes, but it would take weeks before she fully beat her illness and her strength returned.

Wilhelm wrapped his arm around Varila and led the way down the stairs.

"I owe my recovery to the tea you've given me," Lunara said. "It tastes lovely, and each time I drink it my cough improves. How have you been?"

"Fine, my lady." For once, it was not a lie.

The companions were crowded around a table near the fire. Seven empty pints sat in front of Okulu, and the merc's welcoming smile spread. "About damn time!" he said. "The company has been miserable without you two. As a matter of fact, I was getting ready to shove our little winsire into a tree trunk so he can become better acquainted with his heritage."

Wilhelm chuckled and Lunara covered her mouth to hide a smile. Salvarias chose a seat beside Okulu.

"It's good to see you both up and about," Humar said. He smiled, and Salvarias was surprised at the amount of relief glittering in Humar's eyes. The knight slumped in his chair and ran a hand through his hair, sticking it straight up. "Very good, indeed."

Okulu shot Lunara his roguish grin. "Lovely as ever, my enchanting temptress." She lowered her head and went so far as to move her hair to further shield her growing blush. Okulu leaned over to whisper in Salvarias's ear. "Gorgeous when she blushes, wouldn't you say?"

"If you would be so kind as to get on with it," Salvarias murmured.

Okulu winked and talked louder than needed. "By the way, Salvarias, looks like we're heading for some not-so-great land." Okulu pulled out his map and spread it across the table. "Look here. That's all icelands. Nothing lives there but snow and creatures that feed off one another. Not nice, not nice at all. Right after that horrible land, you've got the Evil Enchanted Forest. See, it's labeled that way, so I think it's probably pretty evil. Our best bet is to keep over here, away from all that."

Following the script, Salvarias said, "I am sorry, but my path leads to the iceland."

Okulu groaned a little too dramatically for Salvarias's tastes. "I knew it. Of course we would."

Wilhelm grinned. "Getting old, Okulu? What's wrong with a little snow?"

Salvarias cursed himself when he realized he had forgotten to tell Wilhelm of the plan.

"Bah," Okulu said smoothly, waving Wilhelm's comment aside. "The snow is only half of it. The wind will take your skin clean off. Plus, I wasn't joking when I said unpleasant creatures live there. Monstrous beasts that are starved for food and eat anything with meat on its bones. It's the coldest, most dangerous land in all of Arden."

Salvarias met Humar's gaze and tilted his head subtly to Lunara. "My brother and I can go into the icelands alone. We will circle back after we have passed through. The rest of you can lead the horses and meet us ..." Salvarias spied the slight mark Okulu had made on the map and pressed his finger over it. "Here. At the edge of this forest."

"I don't like splitting up," Humar grumbled.

Varila's eyes glowed with anger. "I agree."

Salvarias shook his head. "The man has moved past the icelands. I only must go to pick up the trail. If my calculations are correct, we should emerge close to here." Salvarias pointed at the spot again. "My brother and I will easily find you."

Okulu cast Salvarias a secret wink. "He's right. We won't all make it. Wilhelm has enough meat on him to keep him warm even if he stripped down naked, and Salvarias can use magic to help him. The rest of us ..." Okulu shook his head. "We don't stand a chance. You know I don't back down from this stuff, Humar. All joking aside, the rest of us will die."

After a long moment of silence, Humar nodded.

"You can't be serious?" Lunara asked exasperated.

Durak patted her hand. "Lass, the boys can take good care of themselves. Blend into the landscape."

"It is better this way," Neithelas agreed.

"Adok will help them," Okulu said. "They won't—"

Lunara bolted up from her chair. "We come all this way to help and tuck our tails and run at the first challenging obstacle?"

"My lady, it is—" Salvarias started, but she cut him off.

"I don't need your reasoning." Lunara turned abruptly and stormed up stairs.

The conversation had gone exactly according to plan, and Lunara reacted exactly how Salvarias had anticipated. He sighed.

"Go talk to her, Salv," Wilhelm said. "She's just worried."

"There is no reasoning with her, brother."

Wilhelm gave him an encouraging nudge. "Try."

Salvarias slumped in resignation and nodded. He climbed the stairs and knocked on her door.

"Go away!"

"My lady, please."

The door flung open and her eyes flared with anger. Gods, she was stunning. "You! I can't believe you convinced them!"

He scooted past her and closed the door. "I know you think I am doing this because I do not want you there, but Okulu is correct. You would not—"

"No! Don't even say it, Salvarias Laybryth! I could survive and I'm going with you." Lunara returned to throwing her clothes in a pack.

"No, my lady, you will not."

She whirled around but shimmering tears had replaced her anger. "You can't go. I barely have a connection with you. How will I know you're both safe?"

She walked toward him. He stepped back, butting against the wall.

"I'm better now," she said. "I swear I can make it."

"No, you cannot come, my lady."

"Then open the connection again. Please."

Salvarias had closed it purposely after his encounter with Perek. Never before had he feared his mind more than he did so now. He shook his head. "I cannot."

He groaned when Lunara's fists clenched, and her mouth set in determined line. "I will go. You cannot make me stay."

"On the contrary, my lady, I could."

She smiled through her tears and took a step toward him. "But you won't."

He smiled inwardly at the memory of their adventure in Serinity within the tunnels of her estate. She would follow him, with or without permission. "I will open the connection slightly."

"Show me now," she countered.

The presence scoffed. *You could drive her from you, murderer. You're caving to her. I sssenssse it.*

He sighed, ignored the voice, and broke down his mind's barriers to allow her a peek into his general emotion, ensuring most was concealed from her. Her eyes fill with joyful tears, and she smiled warmly.

"Do we have an agreement, my lady?"

She flung her arms around his neck. "Please be careful and promise you won't raise it until we're together."

He held her tightly, lifting her slightly off the floor, filling himself with her warmth and intoxicating scent. "I promise. Be careful as well. Stay near Humar and Varila at all times." Reluctantly, he lowered her and unraveled her arms from around his neck.

Happiness twinkled in her eyes that he realized had vanished after he had erected his wall. A pang of guilt stung him knowing it was he who took that spark.

Her fingers brushed through his hair. "I promise I'll stay close to them."

He pulled away, bowed, and left her alone, taking a moment outside her room to calm himself and fight the urge to return to her.

Chapter 16

Autumn 1018 a.r.

Wilhelm and Okulu leaned against a tree, arms folded over their chests while watching Salvarias carry on a whispered conversation with Lilly and Mithal. The autumn breeze rustled dying leaves around their feet, and the brilliant blue sky finally offered a different color besides gray.

The merc leaned close to Wilhelm and lowered his voice. "What's the problem?"

Wilhelm smiled at his little brother. "The horses are upset about being left behind. Salv said they're quite put out with us."

Okulu chuckled. "Who knew horses were such complicated beasts."

Wilhelm took a gander at the stark landscape. The fog had lifted to offer a plain view of the gray grasses flattened by harsh winds even though none blew in the late afternoon hours. Barren trees stretched to the sky, and their gnarled branches poked each other in a fight for space. Few birds sang and those that did sounded forlorn. Wilhelm shuddered. The idea of being without his friends left his blood cold. He preferred the safety of the group. Windlous sported unfamiliar creatures and the land itself seemed malicious. And Salvarias attracted danger like strong ale attracted watythms.

Salvarias threw his arms around Mithal's neck. Apparently, his little brother won the argument.

Wilhelm walked over to Lilly and rubbed her neck. "I'll miss you, you old cow."

The mare nickered and shoved him with her muzzle. He laughed while staggering to gain his balance. He winked at her and moved to pat Mithal's neck after Salvarias switched to hug Lilly. "I'll take good care of him," he said to the stallion.

The horse nodded.

Okulu rubbed the back of his neck and grinned at Salvarias. "You will try to be careful, won't you? Varila owes me a dagger and I'd hate to have one unenchanted. It'd feel so ... mundane."

Salvarias tilted his head. "I will certainly try."

Wilhelm glanced up the deserted road. "Sure we can't get a little closer to the town?"

"No," Okulu said, clapping Wilhelm's shoulder. "If any saw the horses, you'd be hard-pressed to make it out of there with your clothes on. Any sign of wealth and they'll kill you. Better to walk in."

Wilhelm nodded, still unconvinced. Salvarias handed over the thick, expensive cloak Wilhelm had bought him and accepted a thin, ratty one from Okulu. His brother's shivering worsened instantly.

After bidding farewell to Okulu, the merc mounted and left them alone on the rutted road, horseless and companionless, a mile shy from the nearest town. Shaking off his feeling of foreboding, Wilhelm locked his arm around his brother's neck. A strong elbow connected with his ribs and induced a wince. Grinning, he flicked back his brother's hood and ruffled Salvarias's hair. "Ouch."

Salvarias chuckled and raised his face to the sun. A small smile touched his lips. "I have missed sunshine." For once, Salvarias didn't raise his hood. He kept it down, face upturned toward the sky, eyes closed, and his smile switched to a wide grin.

Wilhelm's world brightened. Joy imbued into the air itself, the formerly dull landscape overflowed with a sense of life, and warmth reached into Wilhelm's soul. He glanced at his brother and smiled broader. "Me too, Salv."

They ambled along in light conversation. His brother included the wolf, conveying Adok's comments to Wilhelm while the wolf weaved around their legs. His brother shared his smile often along with his light, infectious laugh. As always when alone together, Salvarias transformed into a different man.

Soon the road muddied with melted snow, and they switched from the sloppy mess to trudge through the packed snow flanking the road. Salvarias wiggled from Wilhelm's headlock to examine a porcupine-looking bush.

Wilhelm took advantage of his brother's distraction to survey their path ahead. Not a single traveler had passed them since Okulu left a quarter mile or so ago. His stomach dropped. What if the town was deserted? What if something horrible had happened to the people? What if creatures had set up an ambush for them? What if—

His ponderings halted when a cold ball of snow smacked the side of his head. He turned slowly, trying to hide his spreading smile.

Salvarias grinned. "Your whirlwind thoughts are distracting, brother."

"Sorry, Salv," Wilhelm said, locking his arm around his brother's neck and leading them along the road. After a short while, he said, "I'm surprised Okulu agreed with you. I didn't think anyone would stay behind."

"Okulu approached me the day before we left. He mentioned the conditions of the icelands, and I knew Lunara would not survive. She has not fully recovered and could easily fall ill again. Okulu suspicioned the same. He suggested a split of some kind, and I agreed. The conversation we had at the table that night was planned by us both. Although I believe Durak had an inkling. He normally would not be so willing to stay behind." Salvarias gazed up at Wilhelm. "I am sorry, brother. I should have told you. I—"

"Stop apologizing for stuff, Salv. You were tired and sick. I know it slipped your mind."

Salvarias grinned. "Thank you."

"Finally!" Wilhelm said, pointing at the tendrils of white smoke rising up over the hill. "I was beginning to think it didn't exist."

Upon cresting a steep ridge, the small village of Lind sprang before them. Wilhelm suspiciously eyed what Windlous called a town. A handful of stone buildings jutted up among the other structures, which were nothing more than tents. No wall guarded the town, making it open for attack from every angle. Tawny-colored tents were crammed together so tight he could not see where one began and another ended. Staggering and emaciated livestock roamed freely through the narrow streets along with skeletal-thin dogs. People packed the town, but instead of bustling in trade, they huddled together for warmth. Trees had abandoned the area and parted way to waterlogged soil seeping between flattened rock. Mud caked everything, tracked along the stone that might have offered clear walkways if it was tended to, splattered up tents and on the people themselves. Not a single crevice was clean.

"How do these people survive?" Wilhelm breathed when he walked onward.

"A valid question. From what Okulu told me, they only deal in furs."

"You'd think with all the hunting they wouldn't be so sickly."

174

"I assure you, the hunters are not malnourished nor the fur traders. I assume the stone buildings to be their residences. Everyone else lives off their scraps. See the livestock? That is what spreads disease. There are no fields to feed them."

"Does that mean I shouldn't eat meat here?" Wilhelm's stomach protested the thought.

Salvarias's eyes sparkled a smile. "I will check it first, brother. The venison will be safe. But beef—"

"I don't need beef. Venison is just fine."

Salvarias chuckled as he raised the hood of his mage robes. "Adok will meet us in the morning. Neither of us feels he will be safe within the city."

Once in town, Wilhelm nudged in front of his brother and cleared a path through the crowd. Women and doe-eyed children held out hands crusted in filth. He fished out a few coppers and passed them out while they sloshed through mucky streets. By the stench, Wilhelm suspected melted snow wasn't the only cause for the mud.

The fur shop was a tent held up by five posts. A portly owner stared at them with shrewd eyes while lounging in a chair. His hawk-like features shadowed eerily in the fading sun and his scowl was colder than the evening gust of wind, which picked up right when the brothers entered his establishment.

"Hello, gentleman," Wilhelm greeted. "Mind if we look around?"

The man grumbled a response Wilhelm took as approval. His brother selected a new pair of treated boots that would block a good amount of moisture. Wilhelm tried on a bear pelt.

"You should get furs, Salv."

His brother shook his head. "I think if a wild creature approaches me in the icelands, I prefer not to be wearing its relative."

Wilhelm chuckled. "Good point."

After Wilhelm tried on every pair of boots in the store, the owner finally intervened.

"None will fit an ogre your size," the man rumbled. "For five silvers, I'll adjust the fit."

Wilhelm gathered the coins from his purse. "Much obliged."

The man grunted before waddling behind a fur enclosure. Salvarias ventured near an entrance and observed the passing inhabitants with his usual stern stare. Wilhelm drew Tobin's broadsword and a whetstone and worked on a nick in the blade. The familiar scraping slipped him into a painful trance. An image of the man with yellow hair and a scar across his chin evoked bitter anger in Wilhelm. Then his mind ventured to the day Salvarias killed their parents' murderer and his brother's whispered words. He looked up at Salvarias. "What was the last thing you remember when those men appeared the day Mother and Father died?"

Salvarias's entire body stiffened. The burgeoning suspicion that his brother had witnessed their parents' murders reared forward. For Salvarias to withdraw into his own mind meant something horrible had driven him there.

"Here you go," the owner said.

Wilhelm sighed at the interruption. "Thank you, gentleman." He paid for his brother's selections then led the way through the foul village.

They found the "inn" which was nothing but a tent almost the size of a normal tavern. Cots sprinkled the sleeping area, and one glance at the moving bedding confirmed it was infested with unsavory insects. Wilhelm smiled when he met Salvarias's amused gaze.

"I will take care of it, brother."

They ate a quick meal and, after Salvarias cleared the area, settled in for sleep. Without the safety in numbers, Wilhelm slept poorly. Long shadows moved outside the tent, disgruntled whispers hissed through the night, and more than once he felt someone watching him. When light filtered through the tent, he almost wept with relief. He was eager to leave and apparently so was his brother. Salvarias got up the instant the sun's first ray shot up from the horizon and packed for them both.

On their way out of town, Salvarias stopped at a tent sporting a wooden sign of a plant. After Wilhelm peeked in and confirmed it was safe, he let his brother into the cramped tent alone. Wilhelm strolled along the street, absently looking at displayed merchandise.

"Protector."

It was a woman's voice, but few called him that, and none were friends. He whirled around, hand on the hilt of his sword. The woman was neither tall nor short, plump nor thin, her hair neither long nor short. She was not pretty, but she was not uncomely. She was average in every sense of the word.

"Be at ease," she said. "I mean you no harm." Hunger in her eyes reminded Wilhelm of a predator, a heartless beast stalking a lame rabbit.

"Who are you and what do you want?" He glanced at the passing people taking no notice of her.

"I have been called forth to restore balance."

His stomach churned at remembering Mafarias's words when Salvarias had saved Edium's life in Cattlar. Their uncle had warned them then that Balance would make his brother pay for denying Death. "You touch my brother and I'll—"

She waved his words aside indifferently. "Your brother is an unwitting pawn. Regardless, it is the pawn that pays for its master's mistakes. I have pondered at length on how to even the scales. It was not Salvarias's doing that tipped them his direction, but as the pawn, the price is his to pay." A smile touched her lips, curling up the corners into something sinister rather than friendly. "I am not without heart, Protector. Just because I relish in my purpose does not mean I do not see the injustice of this game. Therefore, I have come up with a solution that will balance what is needed but save the Soul from physical harm."

"Soul? What are you talking about?"

"You must tell your brother what fathered him."

"Forget it," Wilhelm growled. "He'll never find that out."

Her eyes darkened, and with it, the sky seemed to shrink away from her. "If you do not, you force my hand, and I will not be merciful."

"Go to Oblivion."

"I will give you time, Protector. Do not take my warning lightly."

With that, she turned and disappeared into the crowd. Wilhelm realized he was shaking, not only from anger, but from fear.

"Brother?" Salvarias's light hand rested on his arm. "What is wrong?"

Wilhelm inhaled a deep breath and smiled at his brother. "Nothing I want to talk about. Ready?"

Salvarias's brow furrowed and he slowly nodded. Without giving his brother time to think or ask questions, Wilhelm strode forward, anxious to be free of the congested and unfriendly town.

Wilhelm dropped his shoulder against the howling wind. They had been plodding through the knee-deep snow for a few hours, but Wilhelm's legs were already sore and each cold breath sliced into his lungs like a knife. Ice clung to his eyebrows and along the furs wrapped around his face. Only his eyes were exposed to the elements, but the wind paid no heed to thick cloaks and blankets. It made a cold home in Wilhelm's bones and muscles. Movement hurt. If he was this miserable, he was sure what his brother endured was ten times worse.

The formerly gray landscape morphed into stark, endless white. No trees, no rocks, no creatures, and Wilhelm mused that even the air had left the icelands since it was also white and near impossible to draw into his lungs. Visibility was maybe ten feet. The blustery wind blocked out any noise, so Wilhelm glanced over his shoulder at his brother every other step. Salvarias's head was bowed, and his entire body leaned forward to prevent him from being swept away in the cloud of white. Adok followed next to Salvarias, leaping through the snow like a deer across a meadow. Icicles hung from the wolf's nose and jowls. Wilhelm pitied the poor wolf but guessed Adok was in better condition than either brother.

As the day progressed, so did the wind. Snow pelted them by midafternoon, and Wilhelm's mood sank so low he found himself growling curses—along with his stomach—at nothing. Checking on his brother, he saw Salvarias's lips move, but the wind whipped away the words. Wilhelm shook his head, taking a few steps back, and pointed to his ear. Salvarias leaned closer and his intense eyes gleamed under the hood of his robes.

"We should stop."

Wilhelm jumped. The words sounded in his ear, or maybe his head. He couldn't help thinking their bond strengthened daily. Several times, he swore he felt his brother's recklessly fast-paced mind in his own. "We need to go till nightfall!" Wilhelm roared back.

"It is night, brother."

Wilhelm glanced up at the halo of white hovering halfway between the horizon and overhead. He pointed but his brother shook his head. Wilhelm shrugged and gestured at the ground. Once Salvarias nodded, Wilhelm dropped their pack and retrieved a tent they had purchased. It took no time at all to pack down a section of snow and set up the tent, since it was barely big enough to fit the three of them. After they were situated inside, Salvarias gathered dinner.

Wilhelm eyed his half-frozen piece of dried venison. "This'll be interesting."

Salvarias knocked his bread and cheese together. "Indeed, brother."

He grinned. "Who knew the danger awaiting us was food hard enough to break teeth."

Salvarias grinned back. "It could be our death."

Wilhelm exaggerated a sigh. "Let's get this over with."

Salvarias snatched up the piece of meat. He rummaged around in the pack before frowning and surveying the tent.

"What is it?"

"Wood. If I had a piece of wood, I could light it on fire and use it to thaw not only our food but my hands as well."

Wilhelm gazed at his brother's aspen branch. Before he even opened his mouth, Salvarias snatched up the stick and cradled it close.

"No, brother."

"Not even a little section? It's only going to get colder."

Salvarias shook his head with such vehemence his hood fell back.

Wilhelm flicked his hand in the air to mimic one of the runes his brother used. "Can't you create wood?"

"I cannot create something ... inanimate. And while I have agreed to continue enchanting, creating is something I wish never to attempt again." Salvarias shrugged. "We will do it the old-fashioned way."

His brother whispered words, flicked his hand, and a fist-sized ball of fire appeared. Salvarias balanced the food on his aspen branch then put it over the flame. The protection enchantment Salvarias had cast on his staff saved it from being scorched.

Wilhelm leaned back against a steel pole he'd driven deep into the ground and watched the mesmerizing fire until his brother ended it, a new set of dark rings layered under Salvarias's eyes from maintaining the spell.

Though dry and tough, the food was at least edible. After wolfing it down, Wilhelm drew his mother's dagger and a whetstone. He watched his brother pet the wolf until Adok drifted to sleep.

Given the rare time alone, Wilhelm thought it time to get answers to questions that had plagued him since Salvarias's rescue from Zeeas.

"Salv, there's some stuff I want to ask you, and I don't want you to avoid it like you normally do."

Salvarias grinned at him. "I do not know what you mean, brother."

Wilhelm tried not to smile but one snuck out. "Why can Lunara touch you and no others besides me?"

Salvarias's smile faded and he lowered his head.

"Come on, Salv," Wilhelm pressed.

"It is hard to explain, brother."

"Try."

"Her touch does not hurt. It is quite the opposite."

"Mine has never bothered you. Is it the same?"

"No. Her touch provides a respite for my mind. Somehow she blocks all the images, all the whispers, makes my mind sluggish and too relaxed. When she touched me on the ship while I was battling the evil, my mind nearly caved. Her touch makes it so lazy that I am not strong enough to fight when they are attacking at full strength. I have to be in control to allow her to touch me. Your touch is the only one that has no effect."

"Why do you think that is?"

"I assume because we are brothers. Lady Lunara ..." Salvarias shifted to sit beside Wilhelm. "I guess it is due to our connection."

Taking a deep breath, Wilhelm asked, "What happened to Mother and Father?"

Salvarias's body tensed. "You were there, brother. You know the men killed them."

"I want to know how."

Salvarias raised his mage hood, lowering his head. "Sir Idolar—"

Wilhelm pulled back the hood. "I don't care what Idolar told me. I want the truth, Salv. Don't lie or hide it from me."

"Nothing good would come of you knowing, brother. Why—"

Wilhelm's stomach knotted. His next question came out as a plea. "You were passed out, right? When it happened, you were asleep."

The haunted look on his brother's face answered the question. Salvarias pulled the hood back up, and his voice was barely audible when he said, "I was awake."

"Idolar lied, didn't he? He said they died quickly." Wilhelm lowered the hood. "Leave it down."

"Yes, brother. He lied."

Wilhelm took a moment to swallow the lump forming in his throat. "What happened to Tobin?"

"Please, brother. Do not make me."

"I want to know, Salv."

Salvarias hesitated in his response for several moments before whispering, "He was tortured before they slit his throat."

Wilhelm winced. Though he tried to hide it, thickness snuck in his voice when he asked, "You watched?"

Salvarias nodded, head lowered, hair falling to cover his face. He drew his knees to his chest, wrapping his arms around his legs, curling up tight.

"And Mother?" Wilhelm's heart ached at the sob escaping his brother.

"I beg you, brother."

"I want ... No, I need to know."

Enough time passed that Wilhelm thought his brother might not answer. Then a whisper reached him.

"Raped and burned at the stake."

Wilhelm's dagger fell from his hand. "Tell me you didn't watch, Salv. Tell me you passed out."

His brother remained silent.

He choked on his tears. The thought of his brother alone and scared, watching and listening, tore a hole of heartbreak through Wilhelm. Yet again, he had failed his brother. Emotions overwhelmed him and he gathered Salvarias close. "I'm sorry, Salv. Gods, I'm so sorry."

Sobs shook through Salvarias. "My hands were bound. I could not help them. I—" His voice broke. "Forgive me."

"It wasn't your fault."

Salvarias's fingers dug into Wilhelm's shoulders. "Forgive me."

"There's nothing to forgive. You didn't do anything wrong."

"The vision ... I saw. I said nothing. When it happened, I tried to free myself. I tried, brother. I swear! I—" Salvarias choked on tears. "She screamed. Again and again. I tried ..."

"I promise, Salv. It wasn't your fault." He rocked his sobbing brother, replaying the night over and over. "Why didn't they kill us?"

"They tried. They came for us after they ... finished with Mother and Tobin. I broke free of the ties and cast a protection spell over us. If I had freed myself sooner, Mother and Fath—" Salvarias buried his face in his hands.

Wilhelm pushed back the sleeve of his brother's robes. The deep scars along his right hand and wrist made sense now. "You saw them afterwards?"

"Yes."

Now it was all clear to Wilhelm. He understood why his brother had withdrawn, understood the death surrounding the site. If Wilhelm would've been awake, he could have helped, protected his brother, and shielded him from the images, talked to him during the heinous acts. Salvarias had been alone through all of it. No ten-year-old child should ever witness such atrocities.

What alarmed Wilhelm even more was the sorrow for his parents' suffering did not even compare to his depth of pain at understanding what his brother had endured. Had he always known? Or did he not care? He loved his mother and Tobin. Didn't he? Neither had helped hunt down the bullies that had beaten Salvarias as a child. They'd separated the brothers each week, forcing Wilhelm to leave his brother alone, fully aware bullies would get Salvarias every time. He suddenly found himself furious at his parents. They should have done something. He should have done something. All Salvarias's life had been nothing but pain. In one fleeting moment, he hated his parents. Despised them. It passed quickly, leaving him feeling empty of care for them. They were just as guilty as the boys who hurt Salv.

Tightening his arms, he cleared his throat, holding his voice steady long enough to ask, "Do you want to talk about it?"

Salvarias buried his face in Wilhelm's shoulder and shook his head. Wilhelm glanced at Adok watching them with sad eyes. Eventually, Salvarias's shaking subsided, his sobs silenced, and his breathing deepened when he fell asleep.

Wilhelm regarded the wolf for a moment before saying, "I'm not very good at keeping him safe, am I?"

Adok cocked his head to one side before nuzzling Wilhelm's hand.

"And you're not a normal wolf, are you?"

Adok's ears flattened and his teeth flashed.

"You keep him safe. Better than I have. I don't care what you are." Emotional exhaustion weighed on him, and he leaned his head back and closed his eyes. "Hurt him, though, and I'll kill you."

A slick tongue licked his hand, and the wolf curled up on his other side, using his leg as a pillow. Hot tears trailing down his cheeks, Wilhelm let sleep haul him to deep dreams of strawberries and soft lips.

Chapter 17

Autumn 1018 a.r.

Unupture gazed out the cottage window, not seeing anything beyond its reflective glass except for vague shadows of trees and dull moonlight. God had retired to one of the bedrooms, leaving Unupture and Devoar alone in the sitting room.

Wilhelm had managed to kill Marrow in Cattlar. The Four had taken the death of their brother hard, none more than Devoar. Remnant and Eludar were off on business Unupture was not privy to, but no doubt the two creatures were hunting Salvarias, creating chaos, setting traps, planning and devising the fall of Arden. The Four were not to be underestimated. Unupture had learned that the hard way.

Though he was a prisoner, untrusted by god and the Four, at least he hadn't been chained or tortured. They needed him, after all. No one else would be able to pry apart Salvarias's mind once the boy was captured. Resigned to his fate, he harbored no fear for himself, only dread for Salvarias.

"Why are we not following Perek?" Unupture asked.

Devoar steepled its fingers and leaned back in its chair. Despite the waves of heat simmering from the creature, it did not burn the fabric. Its scorched armor moved like water, conforming to the twisted souls writing within it. The creature's fire red eyes focused on the ceiling.

"I will not put our master in jeopardy," Devoar responded.

"You fear the boy?"

"Salvarias has been underestimated time and again. I will not be foolish and do so. In Falar, the Guardian stole more of my master's power by simple touch. But it is not just the boy I fear. It is the Protector. His powers are growing. He uses them in ways no other Protector has before. His love ..." Devoar smiled, a cruel curl of its helm's carved mouthpiece. "Love ... is it not odd? The feats love can perform?"

Unupture chose not to answer.

"After all," Devoar continued. "It turned you against your god."

Swallowing hard, Unupture glanced at Devoar. "What do you mean?"

"Your love for the boy. I've known for some time, servant. But it matters not. When he is captured"—Devoar turned a cold stare on Unupture—"and rest assured, I will capture the boy, you will retrieve what information we seek. Either willingly or not."

Unupture looked back out the window, cursing his own reckless heart. He often forgot Devoar seemed to be able to read minds, to delve into the heart. It was why it was such a formidable foe. So many underestimated the creature, just as Unupture had done. Now it knew, and Salvarias would pay the price for Unupture's love.

"How do you plan on capturing him?" Unupture asked.

Devoar chuckled softly, the sound like moans from the tortured. "I do not know yet. The boy is changing. The power Perek passed to him has weakened him significantly, beaten his mind and body of strength. Yet again, love is all that saves him. He fights for his brother. But I can taste his fears on the wind. As I said before, mind games will break the boy. Already reality is starting to muddy under the weight of the power Perek gave him. Visions are always entertaining to toss at the boy. Not all are within our control, but some are and I plan to use that gift to keep the boy guessing." Devoar smiled again, full of heartless joy. "But my new angle is Wilhelm. If I cannot break Salvarias, I will break the brother. I will strip Salvarias of love. Without it, the boy's soul will darken to our cause."

Unupture blinked aside his tears. "How will you do such a thing?"

Devoar's smile faded and its eyes gleamed. "Simple, really. All I have to do is find a way and a time to show Wilhelm his failures. And then I will show him how lost his brother truly is to him."

Wilhelm glared at the twenty or so feet of visibility in front of him. He hated snow. He wasn't sure his toes would survive. Even with the thicker boots, moisture seeped through the seams.

The day sparked his mind into thinking what Oblivion must be like. Cold, wet, miserable. He had no problem conjuring up an imaginative vision of snow piled up to his neck while a horror spawned by Veedran howled in his ear and beat his head with a club. He grunted a half laugh at the image.

He raised a hand to his brow to shield his eyes and took a gander ahead. Nothing but white. He glanced back at his brother. Salvarias leaned his entire weight on the aspen branch. Even though most of his brother's face was covered, Wilhelm saw the exhaustion in Salvarias's dark-rimmed eyes.

Salvarias jerked violently and doubled over, a gloved hand clasping the fabric wrapped around his head.

Wilhelm stumbled to his brother's side. "What is it?"

Salvarias did not respond, but by his distant eyes and haggard breathing, Wilhelm had no doubt his brother's mind was battling. Wilhelm's powers did nothing to stop whatever sought them. Helpless, he merely rested a hand on his brother's shoulder.

At long last, Salvarias stood upright and nodded. After casting an encouraging wink, Wilhelm continued forward. Not much time passed before Salvarias staggered to a halt during one of the many glances Wilhelm stole toward his brother. He waited patiently until Salvarias nodded. They continued.

As the day wore on, the attacks increased in frequency and intensity. Time dragged, extending their tortuous journey so each breath seemed to take an hour. Wilhelm's hate for the icelands flourished an unnatural heat that made him sweat despite his bones creaking with cold.

Glancing back, he saw Salvarias on his knees, clutching his head between both hands. This was it. The final battle of the day. No words would be heard over the shrieking wind, so Wilhelm placed his hand on his brother's back, which rose with quick, short intakes of air. Surveying the whiteness, nothing would hide them from an attack by creatures that knew this land. A chill ran up his spine.

Salvarias's cry snapped his attention back to his brother. Misty, guilt-ridden black eyes stared at Wilhelm. Hefting himself to his feet, Wilhelm pulled his brother up with him.

Salvarias cupped his hands around his eyes and studied their surroundings. After a moment, Wilhelm shrugged and continued onward. Standing in place waiting was pointless.

He lost track of time until a light hand rested on his shoulder. His brother pointed ahead. Squinting through flurries, something moved in the distance. It could've been an odd wind change that stirred up snow, but the bounding up and down tossed aside the peaceful explanation. Yet, even with the prospect of danger, Wilhelm's blood ran warm and excitement tickled up his spine. He grinned at his little brother.

Wilhelm shivered when his swords slid out of their sheaths. "What do you think? As large as the sea monster?"

Salvarias grinned back and his soft whisper sounded in Wilhelm's ear. "Not quite. Larger than the troll. Now would be a good time to unlock your powers, brother."

Wilhelm laughed, swirling his swords, and stretched his cold muscles.

Salvarias turned to the snarling wolf. "Stay out of this, my friend."

When the loping beast emerged into view, Wilhelm's jaw dropped. If the creature were to stand it would be taller than a troll, but instead of callused skin, it had massive amounts of filthy white fur dragging along the ground due to its hunched forefront. It maneuvered with the lightness of a cat, using all four claw-footed paws to gain the advantage. Fangs protruded from its mouth, and the face resembled a bear. It would be near impossible to get a sword through the beast's coat.

After locking a gaze on Salvarias, the creature skidded to a halt. It opened its massive maw—big enough to eat a horse—and let out a vicious bellow. Spittle sprayed Wilhelm. The smell was worse than the ogre, a mixture of rotted meat and moldy fur.

Three large fire shards whizzed by Wilhelm to sink into the creature's throat. It was a good strike, and against any other beast it would have killed it. But not this monster.

The creature roared and reared back, kicking its claws high in the air. When it landed, the world trembled. The beast turned its seething yellow gaze toward his brother. Wilhelm issued a war cry and ran forward, swords at the ready.

The snow was so deep he couldn't make it to the creature before it had time to react. As the beast's arm swiped, he dove to the ground, grunting when the fur slapped his armor. He sprang to his feet in time to see lightning strike the beast's back. Shimmers of searing flesh morphed the air. The creature's fierce cry nearly burst Wilhelm's eardrums.

In its pain, the creature rose up on its hind legs, offering a clear path for Wilhelm. He darted forward and positioned himself under the creature's belly. He raised his swords, bracing himself with a wide stance. When the creature fell back on all fours, Wilhelm's swords stabbed through the fur but once it reached skin the force needed to penetrate the thick hide drove Wilhelm to his knees. Nevertheless, his strength and the craftsmanship of his weapons allowed him to puncture the belly. It was useless. The creature didn't even acknowledge his strike, and blood merely stained a small section of fur. The strike had not even been deep enough to trickle out a stream of blood.

The creature shrieked again and its arm stretched out. Wilhelm's heart stuttered when he saw a bundle of cloth sail through the air to disappear in the snow. Anger boiled his blood and tinted his vision the softest of reds. He hacked at the heel of the nearest clawed foot. Slippery brown blood gushed over his hands and spattered across the snow.

The creature wailed and rolled twice. Wilhelm glanced at the sunken spot of snow, and saw his brother staggering to his feet, lips moving. For the briefest moment, Wilhelm froze in sheer amazement, staring at a newly materialized sword larger than Wilhelm's made of pure ice. The whistle it generated when it soared through the air pierced above the howling winds. It plunged into the beast's chest. This time, the creature's wail was so painful Wilhelm dropped his swords and clamped his hands over his ears. When the shriek died off, he realized he had fallen to his knees.

"Your power!" Salvarias called.

"I can't control it!" Wilhelm shouted.

Another shard of fire shot through the air. Snatching up his swords, Wilhelm swept the area for his brother. The creature found Salvarias first. Yellow eyes flaring with anger, the beast charged Salvarias who stumbled to get out of the way. Times like these Salvarias's lameness was more evident than ever. His bad leg kept giving out. Somewhere the wolf howled followed by a growl echoing above the wind.

Even as Wilhelm rushed forward, the creature's mouth opened. Wilhelm cried out when it closed around his brother. The beast shook its head like a dog shakes its prey to kill it. After it stopped,

Salvarias hung limp. It tossed him aside. Droplets of blood stained the white landscape.

Power exploded from somewhere deep inside Wilhelm, staggering him back a step, stealing his breath. When it passed, fury flooded him, growing his muscles, enhancing his senses, sharpening his surroundings.

Rage, pure unbridled rage, poured into Wilhelm's cry. His vision dimmed to the same deep crimson marring the pristine blanket of white. He barreled toward the creature, all sense of safety gone. He only wanted to see the beast die.

Before he reached the creature, a clawed foot snatched him up. It squeezed. Wilhelm gasped for air and brought his broadsword down with a powerful stab. The beast squealed and dropped Wilhelm to the powdery snow. Scrambling to his feet, he charged again. This time, the creature was too occupied licking its wounded foot to hinder his attack on its back leg. Using his swords like stakes, he jammed them through the thick hide and scaled the creature. Hand over hand, he ascended until he clambered on to the beast's back. He sprinted forward. With all the running he had done when he was younger, all the training he had performed on moving ships with Humar and Okulu, and all the swordplay in the guardhouse with Tobin, Wilhelm kept his balance while he traversed the creature's back before it registered his intention. Below, Adok howled in pain.

Dropping his broadsword, Wilhelm rammed his great sword through its skull, feeling bone give way to a mushy center. He clung to the hilt when the creature reared back. Dangling, he hefted himself enough to ease his weight so he could twist his sword. The creature wailed. Blood spurted over the sword's grip. His hands slipped. Still, he hauled himself up and yanked down, cutting through bone and brain.

Then he was falling. He didn't care. The snow would save him. The beast had to be dead anyway.

A shriek tore away his hope.

A furred hand grabbed him before he hit the whiteness below. Wilhelm fumbled for a dagger in his boot, but the creature's claws were too large to maneuver around. Pins stabbed his eyes as the beast's paw clenched. With all his strength, he punched at the beast's paw while staring at the red stain contrasted against the white snow. The last of his breath roared out a furious cry. The creature's eyes glazed over. Then it fell. And so did Wilhelm, spiraling down into a chasm of blackness.

Chapter 18

Autumn 1018 a.r.

Wilhelm startled awake to warmth and a crackling fire. Fur pelts held him prisoner. The hut barely fit him, and a cozy fire drifted smoke through an opening in the side of the shoddily constructed stone room. Salvarias was not with him.

Struggling until the blankets fell away, he winced as he got his footing. Sharp jabs of pain rippled over his body, and dark purple and blue bruises lined his sides.

His armor and swords were propped up near the exit. He snatched up his broadsword and didn't waste time with the armor or a tunic. He stormed out of the enclosure, painful fear stabbing his heart.

Making a cursory sweep of his surroundings, all he saw through the dark night were stone huts with tendrils of white smoke rising from each. Several fur-clothed people walked around, some ignoring him, some staring.

He grabbed the first one he saw and made no attempt to hide the anger in his voice. "Where is he?"

The what-he-assumed-to-be-a-person stared at him with wide, frightened yellow eyes while wiggling under Wilhelm's hold. He raised his sword to the thing's throat. "I want my brother!" he roared.

"Here."

Wilhelm whirled to his left and saw a bundled person standing in front of another hut. Wilhelm shoved past the man and squeezed inside. A creature, partly human and the other part he wasn't sure, tended to his sleeping brother. The ... thing's body resembled a person—two arms, two legs, torso, neck—but the skin was like dry leather, thick and tough. Large yellow eyes intruded on most of its face, and a small mouth and nose finished off the human qualities. Wilhelm didn't see ears.

Adok was curled in a corner, looking exhausted and miserable. His brother had two punctures: one on his chest and the other on his stomach. The thing gently lifted his brother to reveal the larger holes on his back. Wilhelm nodded his understanding and exhaled a held breath when his brother grimaced. At least touch still bothered him.

The leather creature continued to apply herbs and bandage his brother while Wilhelm crammed himself into an area he hoped was out of the way. He shivered from his lack of shirt and having been in the cold wind outside, but already the warmth of the hut was driving away the chill.

After the creature sewed and wrapped the major wounds, it paused when its gaze fell on his brother's left palm. Its eyes widened and it scrambled from the hut.

Wilhelm scooted close to his brother. "Salv?" He rested a hand on Salvarias's shoulder. "Salv."

Black eyes sagged open. Wilhelm smiled.

Salvarias shifted to rise, wincing as his hand went to his bandages. "What happened?"

Wilhelm pushed him back down and covered him with an extra fur. "You got eaten."

"Are you harmed?"

"No, I'm fine."

"Where are we?" Salvarias closed his eyes, running a hand along his brow.

"Not sure but they're helping us."

Salvarias bolted to a sitting position, grunting. "Adok?"

"Right there." Wilhelm pointed, and pushed his brother back down.

"He is hurt?"

"I don't think so."

Salvarias called the wolf over. When Adok rose, he limped.

Salvarias gently kneaded the wolf's leg and frowned. "Broken. I told you to stay," Salvarias mumbled, and continued to feel the wolf's paw. "I did not want to see you hurt." His brother grinned. "But think of how boring it would be to chase rabbits all day, my dear friend." Salvarias scratched behind the wolf's ears. "I have to set it."

Wilhelm swore Adok nodded. The wolf grinned at him. He grinned back.

Salvarias pushed the bone in place, and Adok's grin faded to a whimper. His brother stroked the wolf's head. "Brother, is there a piece of wood I could use to splint it?"

Wilhelm found a suitable piece of firewood and shaved it flat with his sword. Salvarias wrapped the wood to the wolf's leg using a torn piece of his robe. After petting the wolf, Salvarias lowered himself back to the bundle of furs and pulled them up to his chin. Adok limped back to his corner.

Wilhelm wiped the sweat from his face. Too many bodies in a confined space and the fire made sure to block out any cool breeze that might have saved Wilhelm discomfort.

Salvarias's eyes sparkled with amusement. "We have been frozen to the bone for days, brother."

"I hate stuffy places."

Salvarias grinned openly. "You must thaw faster than I do."

Wilhelm chuckled. "I guess I do."

A creature ducked into their hut. It hurried to Salvarias, ripped back the blanket, and grabbed his brother's hand, flipping it over to expose Salvarias's mark. Wilhelm went to intercept but stopped when his brother's four-fingered hand lifted as a sign. Still, the touch clearly bothered Salvarias. The thing released his brother and covered him back up.

The creature was extremely old. Its skin flaked off and all the hair had fallen out to show a raw, peeling scalp. Its trembling fingers were twisted.

It made several motions to Salvarias who shook his head. "I am unfamiliar with your language."

"What language?" Wilhelm asked.

Salvarias's steady gaze never left the creature when he said, "These are jasner. Living only in the icelands, it is rare for anyone to see them. They are the pure race—the only unchanged by Nevlar during the Long Wars. They used to resemble our races, more erthla than the others. Their skin was darker than ours. I saw a drawing once. They were beautiful people, but the icelands have evolved them. They have developed their own language of hand movements so they can communicate over the howling winds, thus eliminating the need to hear. Their skin has changed to help them endure their homeland. Even their eyes have changed."

"You know much," the old one said in choppy common.

Salvarias propped himself on his elbow and tilted his head at the compliment. "It is an honor to meet your kind."

"Not many do. I not understand. One passed here with mark similar to yours only days earlier. He was missing Protector."

Salvarias looked at his hand. "You are familiar with this mark?"

The jasner nodded. Its mouth crinkled in a frown, sending flakes of skin drifting to the fire. "You are magic user?"

"Yes."

"Never in thousand years has Guardian been magic user," the jasner said.

Salvarias nodded toward Wilhelm. "Have you seen this mark?"

His own interest piqued, Wilhelm raised his right palm.

"Protector," the jasner explained. "Yours or other marked man?"

"Mine," Salvarias murmured. "What does this mark mean?"

The jasner eyed him. "You do not know?"

"Sadly, we were never told."

"It should just be circle. Never before has fire been its center. It means Guardian."

Salvarias's brow furrowed. "What am I supposed to guard?"

"We do not know. But for thousand years, your kind passes here."

Wilhelm said, "What can you tell us about the previous Guardians and Protectors?"

"The first Guardian and Protector came to us near death thousand year ago. Hunters sent creatures for them and though they battled bravely, they could not defeat them. We helped and brought here, where Zerana's grace protected them.

"After months, they left," the jasner continued. "Years later, they returned with young ones, but older than you. We gave them hut and food and water. One man screamed for a week but none were allowed inside. Then one day, when sun was high, two older ones emerged. They told us every thirty years this will happen and we must help by giving food and shelter. They tell us their task keeps Arden in light, so my people help.

"As two old ones said, younger ones returned but no longer were they young. They were old but with them were two new men, young but older than you. It has been for thousand years. This land offers safety from Hunters. It why you come. For peace to do what you must do. You are Keepers."

"What are the hunters?" Wilhelm asked.

"Hunters seek Guardian. We can shield their view, offer you rest. They cannot see you here. Many times, Guardians and Protectors visit during thirty year for respite from being hunted. Here, you do not need to battle them."

Wilhelm glanced at Salvarias who was staring at him with intense eyes. His brother nodded as confirmation that what the man said was true.

Salvarias turned to the jasner. "The Hunters. Can you describe them?"

"Creatures of darkness. No one seen one. They do not appear, they call upon their servants once they find the Guardian. We can sense and stop them by using Zerana's grace."

Salvarias looked at his palm. "They must be confused with two of us."

The jasner nodded.

When Salvarias spoke, his voice dripped with defeat. "Their attacks have been diluted."

"Yes," the jasner said.

Wilhelm scratched his itchy beard. "Why don't the Guardian and Protector stay here in safety?"

"Longest anyone stayed was a year. Within that time, Guardian grew ill. Any longer and they might die. We do not understand why. You have time left with us."

"Thank you, but we must catch the Guardian," Salvarias said.

The jasner shrugged. More skin floated into the fire. "When you ready, we supply food, water, and clothing. He and his friends left two days ago."

"Three other mages?" Salvarias asked.

"Yes."

"Do you know who the last Guardian and Protector were?" Salvarias asked. "Their names?"

"Perek and Tedris."

Wilhelm had assumed as much.

"And the first ones?" Salvarias asked.

"Wilhelm and Travard."

Wilhelm and Salvarias exchanged a surprised look.

Salvarias bowed his head to the jasner. "Thank you for your help."

The creature nodded and left the room.

"I guess we can assume the famous Firth brothers did not die helping Nevlar," Salvarias said.

"Could this be ... hereditary?" Wilhelm asked. "I know my—our—father's name is Tedris. Could it be the same one?"

Salvarias shrugged. "I have no idea, brother. I am very interested to hear Perek's answer to that question, though it would confuse me even more. I can say for certain Tedris is our father. He looks just like you. So if it is hereditary, I do not understand how Tedris could be my father as well as yours. Perek and Tedris are cousins, according to Hyde. Perek has my mark which means he should be my father, not Tedris." Salvarias rubbed his eyes and sighed. "Too many questions and too many people I do not trust to answer them truthfully. One thing I know for certain is I am not strong enough to battle a full concentration of the Hunters. If anything happens to Perek, I ..."

"Yes, you can. Use this time to learn how to defeat it. Prepare yourself. Like a soldier does before battle. Practice, learn new techniques, and you'll be fine."

Salvarias fell back into the furs and closed his eyes. "I am such a fool."

"What?"

"It was a trap. The Stronghold. They knew we would go, and they left Perek there so he could do this to me."

"Why?"

Salvarias shrugged. "There are too many possible reasons to know for sure. Perhaps it was to lessen Perek's burden. Perhaps it was to steer me from my goal of finding this 'god.' Perhaps it was to test their theories on the Guardian and Protector."

"We'll figure it out when we catch Perek. I'll force the bastard to tell me."

Salvarias nodded. "We need to leave as soon as possible. We have gained valuable time and the travel will be slow with Adok's leg."

"I thought you said the man was leaving the icelands?"

"I did so to persuade the others to remain behind. We must leave at first light."

"I'll let them know, Guardian." Wilhelm ruffled his brother's hair.

A weak punch landed his ribs. "Thanks, Protector."

Wilhelm grinned. "Ouch."

Salvarias stared into the flickering flames, using them to calm his frustration. It was a trick he picked up from his mother—one he hardly had to use—and it worked brilliantly. The dancing hues of red, blue, and orange hypnotized him into peaceful reverie. He focused on inhaling deep breaths, but soon he no longer needed to think about it. They came on their own; even, filling, and warm.

Once calmed, he wiggled out of the furs and pulled on his robes. He was overjoyed to feel his toes and fingers again. Though he agreed with his brother that the hut was stuffy, it provided a needed thaw. He would not complain.

A smile spread when Lunara's strength surged through his muscles and mind. It was welcomed. Twinges of pain shot all over his body, and his bones and muscles ached. He felt like someone was punching him, soft so as not to bruise, but never relenting. It was an uncomfortable feeling and, with his wounds, one he wished would go away. He wondered if this is what the other Guardians suffered, what had caused the Guardian to almost die.

He paused before packing to examine his mark. Guardian. It was the stone he was to guard. He was certain of it. But guard from what—or whom—was a bigger question. His frustration surfaced again. He wanted to punch something, lose control and go on some wild spree of beating things up. He sank to the floor and stared into the fire. His patience wore thin with each passing day. So did his positive outlook. He was tired. So very tired.

The jasner poked his head inside the hut. "I forgot ask if you needed herbs?"

"Pardon?"

"The tea you drink. Do you need more herbs for it?"

"Yes, please."

"Which do you need?"

"All of them. And I lost the recipe. Can you write me a new one?"

"Of course." The jasner bowed and left.

Salvarias stroked Adok behind the ears. He hoped the tea might help the headaches he had suffered since he touched Perek. No remedies he had read about eased his pain.

Lunara must have been closely monitoring his emotions, because her happy outlook on life infused itself into his blood. He admitted, reluctantly, he missed her and the sweet smile that greeted him every morning, bid him good evening each night, and her sparkling blue eyes that shone brighter than the sun. Her presence, just being near her, calmed him, added peacefulness to his soul.

Salvarias frowned. Now that he thought about her, he sensed something familiar all around him. It was as if Lunara— He sucked in a breath. Zerana. The power lurking within Lunara had the same ... feel. His mother had said Zerana's grace lived on after the Retribution. It was a logical possibility. The Lilkous curse had not left with the disappearance of Veedran. It was sensible to think Zerana's powers remained, which would explain why the Guardians could not stay here. Her grace would naturally fight the evil living within.

But how did Lunara come to have Zerana's power? He remembered her comment by the stream, "My mother has one as well." Could her mark—

"Time to go, Salv," Wilhelm called from outside. He squeezed inside and began neatly placing Salvarias's blankets and robes cleaned by the jasner into a pack. "Ready?"

Salvarias glanced outside. The sky was clear and the wind nothing more than a lazy breeze. Snow sparkled like a sheet of diamonds under the blaring sun poised like a ball of flame in a blue sea.

Wilhelm grinned. "Should be an easier day."

"Indeed, brother. I look forward to my skin remaining on my bones."

Wilhelm chuckled. "Ready then?"

"Yes."

With a little help from the jasner, they were off again. The ache in Salvarias's bones and muscles eased with each passing step, confirming his assumptions about Zerana's powers.

Yesss, my murderer, the presence said. *The evil within isss ssstrong enough for her graccce to sssenssse. I am curiousss, do you not fear your brother will leave you? You are a burden to him, as you were one to your mother. He hasss cared for you all your life and what have you done for him? What did you do for her?*

I caused them pain.

Yet ssstill you ssstay with him. You are a disssappointment, murderer.

He was. Wilhelm deserved so much more than what Salvarias offered. *I am selfish. I ... I cannot leave him yet. I need him.*

Yesss, my little murderer, you are ssselfisssh. Alwaysss thinking of yoursssself. And your brother will pay for your folly with his life.

Deep inside, Salvarias knew the truth of those words.

The next two days passed quickly for Salvarias. The weather had cleared and allowed fast travel, even with Adok's hurt leg, which was mending far faster than normal.

The scenery changed along their journey. What started out as a pristine blanket of diamonds was soon marred by the occasional onyx rock and then eventually gave way to sporadic trees. By midafternoon on the second day, the trees had overcome the snow.

Salvarias could not have been more pleased to be out of the icelands and rocky terrain and into a forest. His happiness, however, was short lived. Fog rolled in and thickened the farther they traveled, its dampness seeping into his clothes. Pine needles littered the ground and tan rocks gave life to pale, sickly looking algae. Ferns hid sticks and stones that tripped Salvarias often, adding a horrible throbbing pain to his bad leg.

The pine trees were thinner and shorter than the forests surrounding Serinity. Reflecting on the lovely city brought about a feeling of homesickness. He wanted to be curled up on a chair near the fire in the Bellerum library, or maybe reading on the bench overlooking the ocean with Lady Talura. The thought startled him so much he flinched. Lady Talura was a mother, frightening and capable of the same acts as his mother.

Wilhelm's arm slid around his neck, and a hand ruffled Salvarias's hair. He elbowed his brother.

"Ouch."

Salvarias turned his mind from Dalnar to his surroundings, looking for any plants he had read about or any that were unfamiliar.

The passing pinecones and trees were the only things he bothered to count.

As the afternoon progressed, so did Salvarias's anxiety. They should have spotted the group by now or at least picked up a trail. His brother's shifting gaze close to the evening hours spoke to Wilhelm's uneasiness as well.

Just as Salvarias was about to reach out his mind to Lunara, he saw a glow of a fire through a thicket of trees.

Motioning to his brother, Wilhelm nodded and soundlessly drew his broadsword. They kept to the cover of trees and crept toward the camp. A low murmur of conversation reached them.

Adok's happiness flared to life in Salvarias's mind, and the wolf hobbled ahead, conveying it was their group.

"It is fine, brother," Salvarias said.

Wilhelm sheathed his sword. "About time."

Varila sauntered out from the thick woods and grinned at Wilhelm. "I'd say so. You've got Humar worried sick."

Wilhelm winked. "Just Humar?"

She rolled her eyes, but could not deliver a rebuttal as Wilhelm whisked her into his arms and kissed her.

Lunara's delightful squeal was followed by snapping twigs. She burst into view and her smile lit Salvarias's world.

She flew into his arms and whispered, "I've missed you."

He held her tightly, nestling his face in her hair, filling himself with her scent and warmth. "I have missed you as well, my lady."

In that small moment, happiness bloomed and Salvarias forgot all his cares and burdens. In that small moment, life was what he wished it could be. But wishes did not come true, and soon his burdens settled themselves on his shoulders once more, and he lowered her gently to the ground, unraveling her from his arms. As he rebuilt the walls blocking her from his mind, his heart ached not only from the fading warmth of her presence, but from the tears welling in her eyes.

Chapter 19

Autumn 1018 a.r.

Four days passed before Salvarias and his group stopped in the town of Triel to restock their supplies and gain a needed solid night's rest. The single tavern in town was surprisingly clean, spacious, and welcoming. After they had obtained rooms, cleaned, and changed, they met in the common room, spread out along a generous-sized table. Steaming bowls of vegetable broth were served to Salvarias, Lunara, and Neithelas, while roasts and boiled root vegetables were laid out for the others. Wine and ale pitchers ended up in front of Okulu, and chunks of ham disappeared under the table, Lunara maintaining her innocent smile every time Salvarias saw her slip Adok food.

"So I'll bring it up first," Okulu said after his third mug of ale. "We're heading right for the—"

"Evil Enchanted Forest," Salvarias finished. There was nothing rehearsed about this conversation. It was a place Salvarias did not wish to venture, but he doubted they could avoid it. "I will not be sure until we are closer."

"I'm curious, how are you following this trail?" Okulu asked.

"Don't ask questions," Wilhelm muttered.

Humar leaned back in his chair. "Salvarias tells us what we need to know."

He was overcome by the group's trust. They followed him blindly and had done so for over half a year. He stared at Humar who smiled and winked at him. He glanced at each companion. He had already called Humar his friend, and though it went unvoiced, Okulu was the closest thing to a best friend he would ever allow himself. Durak had even wormed his way into Salvarias's circle of friends.

Friends.

They did not shudder when he looked at them. They did not recoil from his evil eyes. And all three had seemed to forgive him for what he had done to his parents' murderer.

Okulu paused mid swig. "Everything all right, Salvarias?"

Wilhelm shook his head. "You don't have to, Salv."

"Of course he should tell us," Durak grumbled. "It be easier for us to keep him safe if he confides in us." The old cavrul scowled at Salvarias, but it was not hateful. His eyes were kind. "Stubborn boy."

Salvarias cleared his throat and took his first step in returning trust. "I see flashes, fleeting images of what he sees."

His confession caused the entire group to look at him. He lowered his head and shifted in his chair. Doubt crept in his mind.

They will look at you different, now, the presence said. *You are not like them. They will withdraw their friendsssship from sssuch a creature. Prepare yoursssself. They will hurt you, jussst as he hurt you. It might not be today, or even tomorrow, but it will happen eventually.*

Salvarias went to rise, but Humar's even voice stopped him. "You didn't have to tell us, Salvarias. We trust you, boy. I trust you."

"Well, why didn't you say so?" Okulu roared. "I know this land like the back of my hand!"

Wilhelm glared at Okulu. "You said you had only been here once."

Okulu winked. "Right. Once while I grew up. I left ten years ago."

Wilhelm groaned, but Salvarias's spirits soared. He shifted through the images in his head and regurgitated them to Okulu who followed along the map.

Okulu banged his fist on the table. "Perfect! He's headed here, to Hynd. He took this path around the evil forest. I know exactly where he is!"

Salvarias's hope exploded and he smiled at Okulu. "Brilliant."

The merc's grin broadened. "You've got quite the nice smile. I might have competition with being the handsomest man in our group."

Salvarias's cheeks burned with embarrassment. He leaned over the table to look at the map. "Is there a faster way to catch him?"

Okulu's smile vanished and he started folding the map. "Nope."

Wilhelm snatched the map before Okulu pulled it away and opened it. He sighed.

Salvarias sank back to his chair. "Evil Enchanted Forest?"

Wilhelm nodded.

"How many days will it save?" Salvarias asked.

Wilhelm grinned. "At least half the distance, maybe more, but I'm taking into account delays."

Salvarias's happiness vanished. If it were him alone he would go through the forest, but he did not want to lead his companions ... no, his friends into the woods.

"The Evil Enchanted Forest it is!" Humar exclaimed.

Durak and Okulu groaned.

"If you two are so scared you can't handle a couple ghosts, then go around," Varila said.

Wilhelm pulled her close. "I love your sense of adventure."

She smiled at him. "You haven't seen the half of it."

Wilhelm kissed her as if alone.

"I like adventure as much as the next idiot," Okulu retorted. "But unlike them, I have common sense. Trouble seems to be fond of us, and that forest will offer much."

"Have you been there?" Salvarias asked.

Okulu scoffed. "No one dares go into that forest."

"Then how do you know it to be evil?" Salvarias pressed.

"Well ... there's bedtime ... I mean ... we hear stories," Okulu fumbled.

"Not all stories are true," Salvarias said.

Okulu made a sour face.

"You're lucky I have come," Neithelas said, sitting up straight. "If the woods are enchanted, they will confide in me."

Okulu rolled his eyes.

"My offer stands, mercenary," Neithelas said. "I will teach you."

"Go eat horse dung," Okulu growled.

After a few more back and forths, the group agreed to the forest. Excusing himself, Salvarias headed up to his room. He had been careful not to press the decision in either direction, but guilt stained him, nonetheless.

As it ssshould, my pet, the presence said. *Jussst becaussse they made the choiccce doesss not rid you of your ressssponsssibilities ssshould any die. You led them to thisss land, and you lead them to the foressst.*

I would have gone around.

Then go back and tell them. Change your direction and avoid the foressst. Sssave your new friendsss.

Salvarias clenched his teeth. *I must get Perek.*

Then do not lie to yourssself, my murderer. Or me. Remember, I know your thoughtsss, your deepessst thoughtsss.

Lunara did not wait long before she followed Salvarias up the stairs. When she entered their room, he was sitting on the edge of the bed, head resting in his hands. He did not look up.

Having him once again block her from his mind hurt. She missed being a part of him, living just inside his mind, sensing his raging sea of emotions. Though unable to feel what he felt now, she knew simply by his slumping shoulders that his thoughts were heavy. She also knew his sleep had been troubled more than usual. And because she watched his every move, his every action, she knew he was tired enough not to fight her.

Sighing heavily, he raised his head and regarded her for a moment as she slipped off her boots.

"Tired?" she asked.

He nodded.

"Something happened in the icelands."

Salvarias looked away, the shadows of his hood concealing his features. He nodded. "My brother discovered how our parents died. He asked me, and I told him." Guilt dripped from his voice.

"It's his right to know."

"Nothing good comes of it. Nothing."

"No, nothing does. You're right, of course."

"I should have had the strength to lie."

"There is no strength in lying." She knelt beside him and went to remove one of his boots. He shifted away and took them off himself. With his hands occupied, she lowered his hood, purposefully running her fingers through his hair. "It was right of you to tell him."

His eyes closed and he inhaled deeply.

"Let me help you," she said.

When he opened his eyes, his stare was not serious and penetrating. It was tired yet focused completely on her. Gently, she pushed him to lie down and he did so, scooting farther back into his bed as she followed him. More and more he was accepting her help, allowing her to give him restful nights free of horrid dreams. Though she did not feel his emotions, his pain was evident in his eyes.

Once she was encased in his arms, he said, "Thank you," and drifted to sleep.

Lunara woke to darkness. Their room had no window, but the absent snore of her sister and Wilhelm told her it was morning. Salvarias was breathing light, awake.

"Did you sleep?" she asked.

"Yes, my lady. Thank you. Are you ready to get up?"

"Yes."

"Lumous." The translucent sparrow bloomed to life, reflected in Salvarias's black eyes.

"What else happened in the icelands?" she asked.

"There was a creature my brother and I battled. Jasner saved us."

"Jasner? I would have loved to have met them. Based on my readings in *The Pure Race*, they should have tons of old stories."

"We did not have time to learn of any," he said, regret unhidden in his voice.

"Whatever calls for you was difficult. Your mind was exhausted."

"Yes. Thank you for your help."

She smiled. "Did you discover anything about Perek and what you seek?"

Salvarias spoke as if what he learned was common knowledge to the world. "Much. I am apparently supposed to guard something and my brother is my protector. The jasner can conceal us under Zerana's power for a short time. All of which makes no sense."

Lunara suppressed a smile at his sardonic nature. "Zerana? Then you must protect something for Nevlar. They were lovers."

"Perhaps. But there is great evil in the man we pursue. Do you not sense it?"

She crawled out of bed, hand entwined with his as he followed. "No. I'm not close enough to him. I have to see the person to read them."

"I believe your gift comes from the goddess."

The statement was thrown out so suddenly Lunara jumped. She turned back to him, feeling a blush creep up her cheeks. "Why do you say that?"

His serious eyes softened and his long fingers ran through her hair. "Your beauty is ... beyond this world. But there is also power within you, my lady. Stronger than you know."

Her head lowered unbidden. He caught her chin in his hand and raised her gaze to meet his.

"You must believe in yourself, in your strength," Salvarias said.

"And if I am to believe in myself, why do you not believe in yourself? Why can you tell me of my strength, and I cannot tell you of your worth?"

A light smile played on his lips. "We are not discussing me, my lady. Do not change the subject."

Her heart thudded in her ears and warmth surged through her body. She ached to kiss him. Instead, she trembled out, "I have no powers."

"Quite the contrary. Who told you to break the orb in Serinity?"

"A ... a voice told me. No matter what you might think, Salvarias, I do not have Zerana's power. She's dead."

"You should embrace her. You could command her grace ... her leftover powers." Salvarias took her hand in his and traced the white circle on her palm. "You see? You are marked by her. The men in the tavern said Zerana walked in the moon's light."

"It's just an odd mark." Lunara pulled her hand away. It was impossible. She had no power. She was a stupid little girl, naive, sheltered, unworldly.

He took her hand again and ensnared her in his steady gaze. "Tell me how I know you."

She closed her eyes as she remembered their first meeting: his scream, his vacant eyes, and his pain. So much pain.

"Tell me," he said.

"Please." She stumbled back.

He followed her. "Why will you not tell me?"

"I'm scared." One more step trapped her between him and the wall.

"Do not be."

Her mind kept replaying his scream while his soft finger circled her palm, rhythmic, sensual even, making her battle for each breath.

"Salvarias ..."

His body pressed lightly to hers, erupting an aching need in her, an almost overwhelming desire to taste him.

"Tell me," he whispered.

"I ... I knew you as a child." Lunara opened her eyes and his gaze held her captive.

"How?"

"I saw you at your parents' grave." Lunara stopped. That moment is what linked them. His mind allowed her in at its weakest state, and she had forged the bond, imprisoned his soul to hers without his permission. She'd violated him in a way no person should be touched.

"I do not remember you," Salvarias said.

"You were withdrawn in your own mind."

Salvarias studied her a moment. "It was you. You woke me."

Lunara nodded.

"That was the first night I dreamt of you. We chased a butterfly." Salvarias ran his hand along her hair, his fingers weaving in and out of it. "You did the same after my brother's death."

"Yes. I remembered for the first time. I had forgotten how we met. It's ... it's my fault we have this connection. I did this to us. I'm so sorry." She wanted to tell him everything suddenly. She wanted to be free of her guilt, to fall to her knees and beg him to forgive her. "When I saw you outside Serinity, you were lost to the world. I touched you ... I can't describe what I felt. I just know I ..." She bit her lip, dreading losing what little headway she'd made in their relationship, but she didn't want it built on deceit. "I connected to your mind, Salvarias. I-I linked our souls. I didn't understand what I was doing. I was a stupid girl. But I wanted a friend and I saw so much love and pain in you. I wanted to help. I—"

A light finger rested on her lips. "My lady, there is no need for apologies. There is no need for you to feel guilt. Power is difficult to understand, and I believe you did not mean for this to happen."

Tears welled in her eyes. "You're not mad?"

Salvarias slowly lowered his finger and returned his gaze to her palm. "No. I think there is more going on than either of us sees. This mark means something. The power could have done it."

"No, I assure you, it was me."

"You were a child, curious and innocent. You did not hold ill intentions, my lady. Of that, I am certain." Salvarias traced the circle again.

With him distracted, she reached up and caressed his smooth cheek. He refocused and a familiar sparkle lit his black eyes. She'd seen it before in their dreams, right before he had nearly kissed her.

He murmured softly, absently, "We should join the others."

He did not leave nor did he remove his hand. His fingers traced hers and the world seemed to stop, waiting, holding its breath alongside her.

Then the sparkle in his eyes vanished and he backed up, shrugging from under her touch. He stopped at the door and his shaking hands raised his hood. He kept his back to her.

She washed and changed, trusting him as always. "All done."

She switched spots with him, listening to the rustle of fabric, hearing water dripping in the washbasin, a cloth being wrung out. Then fabric rustled once more.

She peeked over her shoulder to see him fully dressed and tying the rope around his waist that held his herb pouch. Taking a risk, she moved with determined steps toward him. He backed up once and froze.

Deliberately, slowly, she rose on her toes and kissed his cheek. "Thank you for not being angry with me," she whispered close to his ear.

He didn't flinch as she ran her hands up his chest then around his neck, holding tightly. After the slightest hesitation, he wrapped his arms around her waist and lifted her off her feet in his embrace. She buried her face in his neck, breathing in the light smell of lavender, smiling for the first time in days.

Chapter 20

Autumn 1018 a.r.

Salvarias hid his smile beneath his hand. Okulu's relationship with his flask verged on pathetic. For the entire morning's trek into the forest, Humar's even temperament showed signs of abandonment. It was only a matter of time before the knight broke.

Salvarias turned his gaze to the "Evil Enchanted Forest" closing in upon him. Indeed, the trees were old, gnarled up in eerie shapes, naked and glaring at the veiled sun. Fog clung close to the ground, unnaturally motionless in the whispering breeze. Plants Salvarias had never seen before called out to him to investigate, but he kept his hands to himself. The forest was to be revered, unmolested by the plucking of flowers or leaves. Furthermore, malice tainted the air, molded the plants, and soaked the soil. He had no doubt the plants were bewitched.

All around him, the air was thick with remnants of old power pressing down upon him. It humbled Salvarias ... and frightened him. The confidence his magic had worked so hard to build vanished. He was nothing compared to what lived here. And that was just the leftovers.

"Dammit Okulu!" Humar barked.

The entire group jumped, including the horses. Okulu choked on his swig.

"What in Nevlar's fury is your problem!" Okulu coughed. "You don't blurt out like that in the middle of this gods-forsaken place."

"Stop drinking. You should be alert." Humar straightened his cuirass.

Okulu's roguish grin spread. He wiped his mouth with the back of his hand and offered the flask. "So should you."

Wilhelm chuckled. "Over here."

Okulu tossed it, and Wilhelm took a large gulp.

"Don't be cheap," Varila called.

Wilhelm threw it her direction. She took a long swig, coughing between a second one. She tossed the flask at Durak who drained it dry.

Okulu grinned when the cavrul lobbed it back. "Luckily I packed quite a bit."

Humar groaned.

After a half day's ride, the trees clustered together, seeming to draw desperate comfort from one another. Limbs bowed beneath an invisible weight and soon forced the group to dismount under low branches. The horses went on their own, keeping behind Mithal who led the way. Rocks caked with moss littered the forest floor along with dead branches that had fallen too ill to remain in the sky.

Okulu glanced at Humar. "It'll take us three days to cross. Last chance to turn back."

"Nope. This saves us time," Humar confirmed, ducking under a low branch.

Salvarias had difficulty keeping up with the group. His staff sank into muddied soil so he had to put more weight on his bad leg. Within an hour, pain shot up his entire back.

Lunara walked close to him, so close she bumped into him and muttered apologies until Salvarias gave up and offered his arm. She helped steady him and he found it easier to walk, although her grip was painfully tight.

"So, Neithelas," Okulu said, falling in line with the prince. "What do these trees tell you?"

"They're old."

Okulu rolled his eyes. "How insightful. I would've never guessed."

"They're angered by our presence."

"Still shocking me with your talents."

"They've warned me of their plans to attack."

"Well now, that's something new."

Neithelas's cold stare steadied on Okulu. "You should learn the language of your people. I could teach—"

"No-no. I'm just fine. I don't need to hear the trees plotting to kill me."

"Enough," Humar said. "Can you talk to them, Neithelas? Tell them we mean no harm?"

"Why do you think they have not attacked us yet? They have witnessed something horrible, something they are too frightened to discuss. Someone in our company has set them on edge." Neithelas glanced over at Salvarias, an eyebrow raised. "They say old forces walk among them once again, and they fear them."

Salvarias chose to ignore the prince.

Okulu, Humar, and Durak's stances tensed. Okulu drew a dagger, gripping it so tight his knuckles turned white.

The bottom leaves of a hedge of bushes rustled nearby, but none knew the cause except Salvarias.

He whispered in Lunara's ear, "It is only a rabbit."

He silently called the small creature to him. Okulu's sword scraped from its sheath, and the merc took his fighting stance out in front of the group. Inch by inch, Okulu edged toward the bushes. Salvarias waved his hand to gain the attention of the other companions and pressed a finger to his lips. Without a sound, he snuck up behind Okulu.

As the rabbit hopped into view, Salvarias hissed, "It comes for you!"

Okulu jumped off the ground so high he hit his head on a branch.

Laughter erupted, ridding the forest of its heaviness, if only briefly. Salvarias bent down to accept the trembling walnut-brown rabbit into his arms.

"That wasn't funny!" Okulu exclaimed, resting a hand over his heart.

Wilhelm patted Salvarias's shoulder and wiped tears. "I never knew you could jump that high, merc."

Salvarias handed the rabbit to Lunara who let out a little squeal of delight.

"I can't breathe." Okulu gasped. Then he grinned at Salvarias. "Good one though."

"Aye," Durak said, laughter leaving him in little fits as they continued on. "Good one, lad."

"Does it want our help?" Lunara asked, petting the rabbit curled up in the crook of her elbow.

"He is lost. He wandered in here on accident. He was separated from his mother."

"We can carry him out of the forest."

Salvarias asked the rabbit if it would like their help. It eagerly agreed. "Yes, we should."

Lunara's eyes lit with happiness. She bounded over to the food pack and retrieved a carrot. The rabbit nibbled away.

Salvarias regarded the placid wolf. "You are growing unimpressive, my friend. The rabbit was not even startled by your presence."

Adok growled and stated he could rip the rabbit apart in one bite but had already offered it his friendship. Salvarias stroked the wolf's ears. "You are gentler than I realized, my dear friend. You have a complicated heart."

Adok snapped at his hand. Salvarias ruffled the top of the wolf's head.

When they finally decided to stop for the night, Salvarias could not have been happier. As the day had progressed, so had Salvarias's exhaustion, though he was certain the walk had nothing to do with it. His bones ached, his muscles were sore, and his heart physically hurt. After he laid out his bedroll, he went straight to sleep. He did not bother with dinner. He was too tired to chew.

He dozed to the group's murmured conversation, Wilhelm's rumbling voice soothing him as always. What woke him was Lunara snuggling down into her bedroll next to his. She cast an apologetic smile while situating the rabbit in a bundle of blankets close to her. He allowed himself to drift off to a light doze, avoiding deep sleep and nightmares.

He woke when the sky was still dark, the moon shining brightly to reveal not half the night had passed yet. Though exhausted, his pain had escalated, enough it made sleep an impossibility.

Unraveling himself from the many blankets his brother had covered him with in the late hours of night, he kept one for himself as he gently covered Lunara with the others. Wilhelm's snore seemed too loud in the quiet forest and, as usual, Adok dreamt under the steady rumble. The rabbit was curled up against Adok's belly, nestled in the wolf's thick fur.

A wave of pain washed over him, as if a million fingers jabbed him all at once. It was definitely the same as what he had endured in the jasner's camp. That soreness and bone-weary exhaustion. It was tenfold here. He stretched his mind, begging for an explanation, a solid fact not a suspicion. Nothing came to him. Tired and beaten, he crept through camp to the figure on watch. Neithelas sat like a statue, probably listening to the forest instead of watching it.

When close, Salvarias softly said, "I can take watch."

Neithelas looked over his shoulder and shook his head. "No, I'll stay here. I do not trust you."

Salvarias tilted his head and turned to leave, but Neithelas's words stopped him.

"The trees say there is something powerful walking in our group," the prince said to Salvarias's back. "They say whatever it is isn't like the rest of us. They say something lurks behind a mask. Something pretending to be like us." Neithelas paused briefly before continuing. "I think it's you. I think Lunara is in danger because of you. I should kill you right where you stand and save us all. But unlike you, I'm not a cold-blooded murderer. But be warned, I'm watching you, mage. One wrong move and I'll drive an arrow straight through your heart."

Salvarias glanced over his shoulder. "You mistake my fight for a desire to live, Prince Neithelas. I look forward to the day you gain the courage I sadly lack and do what is right."

Without another word, Salvarias left the prince and returned to the leftover embers of the campfire. He watched the glowing hues of red and orange, allowing them to hypnotize him and calm the pain from Neithelas's words. Though the prince was conceited, his heart was good, and the fact he saw so clearly into Salvarias gave hope that one day Neithelas might have the courage to end what no other person seemed willing to end.

White light flashed and his surroundings disappeared. He almost laughed aloud. A vision? Did this "god" think him so simple? However, what happened next gave him pause. It was a hazy vision, difficult to make out, hovering barely within his reach. Squinting, he saw himself standing as he was here, around the fire. Then translucent wisps of people burst from the forest and flooded into camp. They only sought one, and it was Lunara.

White light flashed again and the gray forest sped toward him. He stumbled back, swaying under his swarming surroundings. Wilhelm's deep voice called to him. Then he fell, but a strong hand snatched hold and steadied him.

Once the dizziness passed, he raised his gaze to the wisps rushing from the cover of the woods, straight for Lunara sleeping soundly. Mind and heart racing painfully, Salvarias chanted and started drawing his rune. But he was a breath too late. The first wisp plunged through her, and she cried out, clutching her chest. Cursing himself, he flicked out the rest of the rune. White film spilled over her before the second creature reached her.

The creatures reared and screeched, deafening enough to cause him and his friends to clamp their hands over their ears. The spirits flung themselves against the shield, beating on it with seeming fists of stone. Salvarias actually felt the force of their fight through his spell.

Wilhelm recovered his hearing first and yanked his swords free.

"Do not engage them," Salvarias ordered. They only wanted Lunara. It was the old trap set by Veedran thousands of years ago to find Zerana, the one the men in the tavern had warned them about. And it felt Lunara. Salvarias had no more doubts about Lunara's power. It was why it harmed him when she woke him after his brother had died. Her power was of light, and he had been healed by darkness.

Rushing to Lunara, he knelt beside her, careful to stay clear of the creatures, and shouted to be heard through the protection spell, "Are you all right?"

She nodded. "It ... it took something from me."

Salvarias guessed it was part of her life force. Enough of them could steal the rest of her years. He glanced around the camp, desperately racking his brain for a solution. No spell came to mind to fight the dead.

Indeed, his magic confirmed. *We can't fight smoke.*

Smoke was a good way to describe them. He saw an outline of old clothes, centuries out of fashion, white sockets where eyes should have been, and black holes yawned beyond their opened mouths.

Adok moved in front of Salvarias, petrified rabbit held protectively in his jaw. The wolf told him to follow, and Salvarias agreed without question. He cursed himself for reacting out of paranoia and not casting the bubble spell. The old protection spell would drain him quickly.

"You must walk slowly," he said to Lunara. "Avoid sudden movements, and do not, no matter what, leave my side."

She nodded.

"Follow at a far distance," Salvarias ordered the group.

After getting to her feet, Lunara followed Salvarias as he started out slowly, accustoming himself to the holding the spell, and cursed his stupidity again. He should have put it over them both. It would have been easier to guide her movements. Mithal bumped him and he accepted the horse's help. Lifting Lunara to the saddle, he mounted behind her and nudged the stallion. The smooth gait of the horse helped him keep Lunara protected.

Adok picked up the pace and the stallion followed suit. Wilhelm called out to him, and he glanced back to see the group falling behind. The others' horses, except Lunara's mare, were not confident enough to navigate as quickly as Mithal. He had no choice but to move forward. Sweat had already broken out on his brow, and his muscles constricted under the strain of maintaining the energy.

At length, the trees grew thicker and Mithal could no longer fit easily. Adok whined, conveying they were close to protection.

Salvarias cursed and swung off the stallion. He slowly lowered Lunara, gritting his teeth at the burgeoning compression of his skull as he kept the spell to her every movement. The dead still wailed around him, bouncing off his shield and clawing for her. Lunara's eyes were wide with fear, her chest fluttering with quick, short breaths.

"*Lumous,*" Salvarias said, and continued into the growing darkness his sparrow barely penetrated. Adok squeezed through a thick ring of trees, assuring Salvarias it was not much farther. It did not matter. Salvarias's strength was at an end. He glanced behind but his friends were nowhere in sight.

Legs crumpling beneath him, he fell to his knees. He had not noticed his nose was bleeding until drops fell on the damp soil. Blood filled his mouth as the energy ravaged his body.

She can call upon the power, his magic said. *Just as the jasner could. With enough of her will or assistance from your blackfire, she can use the power within these woods to drive away the beasts. It's ready. I can feel it linking to her, waiting her command.*

He looked up at Lunara kneeling in front of him, tears streaking her face. "You must help me," Salvarias said. "You must call to your goddess."

Chapter 21

Autumn 1018 a.r.

Fear clenched Lunara's heart as Salvarias's strength drained from her own body. Blood trickled from his nose and ears and stained his lips.

"You must call to Zerana's grace," Salvarias said.

She looked at the dead clawing at the shield, their mouths snapping at her. "I can't," she cried. She didn't have power. She couldn't.

"I will die," Salvarias said.

As if to show how serious he was, he hitched and blood spurted from his mouth. He collapsed to the forest floor and convulsed. Still, the shield held.

Desperate, she screamed at the forest, "Help me!"

Nothing happened.

The creatures suddenly paused and their white-socketed gazes turned to Salvarias. One rushed him and passed through his body. He cried out, curling up. Then another and another plunged into him. Lunara screamed, frantically looking around for help.

"Trust me!" Salvarias said through clenched teeth, and thrust his hand to her, palm up, revealing the black ring with a silhouetted flame in its center.

She hesitated only a breath before reaching for him. His hand clamped down on hers, pressing their marks together, and everything disappeared. She floated in a fog of gray light, as comforting as it was frightening. Love lived here, so much it made her want to cry. But what flourished most was anger and fear.

The danger of the dead and the forest faded, and she wanted nothing more than to explore this strange place. It was full of power, a terrifying amount of it. As she turned in a circle, she realized she was walled off to one level of an expansive space, more of a feeling than something visible. All around, just outside her reach, were dots of bright joy, bulges of seething anger, and layer upon layer of dark corners seeping utter fear. She finally recognized the space. It was Salvarias's mind. Only this time, she was here with his invitation.

And then he stood in front of her, eyes serious.

"Are we dead?" she asked.

Without a word he took her hand, turning it palm up, and above it a ball of black fire formed.

"Forgive me," he said.

The fire plunged into her mark and she sucked in a surprised breath. Pressure built in her mind, seeming to expand her skull. Something warm trickled down her upper lip, and she caught it in her hand. Blood. She looked up at Salvarias. His eyes were lit with sheer rage.

"Help her," he commanded, and it was clear he spoke to someone besides Lunara.

The pressure simmered up to a raging boil, and she swore her head would explode. She screamed, doubling over. Blood spewed from her mouth.

"Help her now!" Salvarias ordered, and his words carried a power steeped in beauty. It humbled her and she fell to her knees, wanting nothing more than his love and to serve him.

By his command, the blackfire reached inside her and called forth a brilliant white light that burst to life all around. The painful pressure died away and love surged up within her, encasing her in its protection. Salvarias's pain lanced through her own body, but the light quickly blocked it, blinding her with one final flash. When it faded, the forest reappeared, bathed in white light.

The dead fled as the light rolled through the forest like an ocean wave. The trees shivered and dried leaves drifted down. Birds cawed and flapped wildly away. Adok was by her side, golden eyes wide, and she swore she saw a tear. At her knees, Salvarias curled up, vomiting blood and bile. Spots of blood seeped across his robes, spreading.

"Salvarias!" she screamed.

"Follow ..." he exhaled sharply, clutching his chest. "Adok."

"Salv!" Wilhelm rushed to his brother's side. "Gods, what happened?"

Salvarias's eyes rolled back in his head. Wilhelm sputtered out a frantic curse and pressed his ear to Salvarias's chest. After a breath, Wilhelm exhaled a sigh of relief.

Varila cupped Lunara's face and raised her head. "Is that your blood or his?"

217

Some of it might have been hers, but she pointed to Salvarias. "We must follow Adok."

Varila pulled a single lock of Lunara's hair aside. The single chunck had turned completely white. "What happened?"

"It's not safe here," Lunara said, ignoring her sister. "We need to leave."

What would she say? Salvarias shoved a ball of black fire into her hand because he thought Zerana's grace would save them. Lunara frowned. Had it?

Adok whined urgently.

"Let's go," Humar said.

Neithelas helped her up while concerned words fell from his lips. She ignored him, too absorbed in her own ponderings to hear.

They traversed a short ways through the forest until the wolf stopped in a clearing. Above, the moon was not the usual silvery white. It was like stark snow, brilliant as the sun. The coolness of the forest was replaced by air that seemed to be the perfect temperature. Bushes surrounded them with fresh, plump berries of every kind. The ground was soft and inviting. A sense of love and comfort lived here. Everyone looked around with wide eyes. Apparently, she wasn't the only one affected.

By the time Wilhelm and Okulu had tended to the many wounds the white light had opened up on Salvarias, their horses had found a way into the clearing and food was soon passed around. Lunara ate little, her gaze locked on Salvarias, her mind replaying everything that had happened. Her friends were kind enough not to ask questions. Not that she would have answers if they did. What happened was a complete mystery. One she had no desire to uncover. Ashamed as she was, she was too scared to piece together an answer. Better to keep all she experienced a secret, to hide it away, lest she be forced into a situation she would surely fail.

Sleep came quickly, despite her churning mind, and she once again strolled through a desolate desert. She ambled along without hurry, crunching the occasional patch of dry grass underfoot. Eventually she ended up at the pit as she did every night.

"Hello," the figure said.

Lunara cocked her head to the side. The voice was different. "Hello."

"You must help me."

Lunara peered into the darkness. "You're a woman."

Love flowered up inside Lunara. The warmth and light of it was the same that had risen in her when she had helped Salvarias after his brother's death, the same love that encased her when Salvarias had called for Zerana's grace.

"It can't be ..." Lunara breathed.

"Nothing is impossible, child."

Lunara bolted awake, gasping. The camp was silent except for her friends' deep snores. Salvarias and Adok sat at the edge of the clearing, staring off past the ring of trees. The mage glanced over his shoulder at her before returning to gaze at the woods.

Trembling from the remnants of her dream and the implications it imposed, she untangled her blankets and joined his side. His face was pale and dark rings framed his eyes. He shook, though from cold or exhaustion, she couldn't tell.

"I beg you," he whispered, voice thick. "Forgive me."

"I don't understand," she said. "You saved me."

"I caused you pain, my lady. I—"

She flung her arms around his neck. "Gods, Salvarias, I owe you my life. You have nothing to apologize for."

He gathered her close, snuggling his face in her hair. His hold was tighter than normal. "I thought I would lose you," he said.

She forced a soft laugh. "You'll have to try harder next time. I don't plan to leave this world any time soon. I can stand a little headache."

He didn't comment on her lie. The pain had been tenfold that of a headache, but she would endure it a hundred times over if it meant saving her life or Salvarias's.

They sat in each other's arms for several moments before he released her. She hadn't seen the rabbit nestled in the folds of his robes until it hopped over to her. It curled up in her lap and drifted back to sleep.

"What ..." Salvarias looked back at the woods. "What did you feel? What did the light do to you?"

"I felt ... love," Lunara said simply. "It was wonderful, but ... but I'm scared, Salvarias. I don't understand any of this." She held up her new streak of white hair.

"Nor I, my lady."

Her heart nearly stopped when his soft fingers caressed her cheek.

"I promise you this," he said. "After I find Perek, I will spend the rest of my days gaining answers for you." Gently he turned over her hand to reveal her mark. "I will discover what this means, and I will find out everything I can of Zerana, how she died, and of her powers. You will have answers, my lady. I swear it."

She thought of telling him about her dream, but the same fear over what it might mean kept her silent. None of this could be happening to her. Not her. She was too scared to be special, to be able to command the power of a goddess. Such things were gifted to warriors, people of strength and bravery, like Varila. No, Lunara was no warrior. She was not brave. She was petrified. It was all a mistake.

Salvarias sighed heavily and shook his head. "If only you saw yourself as I see you, my lady."

Swallowing back her tears, she rested her head on his shoulder. "If only you saw yourself the way I see you, Salvarias Laybryth."

Chapter 22

Autumn 1018 a.r.

Lunara woke late in the morning, feeling utterly refreshed and vibrant. Her friends faired no differently. They smiled more and laughed as they passed food between themselves. The exception was Salvarias, who sat off to the side of the group with Adok. He looked as if he'd spent a week in Oblivion. Exhaustion lined his face, black rings sagged under his eyes, his shoulders stooped, his hands trembled violently, and his breathing was harsh and irregular. In the short time it took her to pack her bedroll and gather food, he'd taken three of his breathing treatments. They had little effect.

Though Wilhelm looked rested and was smiling, his gaze often fell to Salvarias, eyebrows stitching together in concern.

After all had eaten and packed, the group set off again, following Okulu from the clearing and into the thick woods.

"By tomorrow we should be out of this horrible place," Okulu muttered.

"It hasn't been that bad." Wilhelm grinned. "I've never slept better than last night."

Okulu grunted. "Maybe, but I'll still be happy to get out of here."

Humar walked close to Salvarias, whose limp had worsened overnight, and Lunara scooted closer so she could eavesdrop on their conversation.

"Mafarias said it wasn't good for you to exert your magic like you did last night," Humar said. "He said there might be long-term effects."

"Did he?" Salvarias murmured, eyelids drooping.

"He said you shouldn't do it," Humar said.

"I do not know what else I could have done, Humar," Salvarias replied. "If any of you had engaged them, they would have killed you."

"I worry about you," Humar mumbled.

"Thank you. But I am aware of my limits," Salvarias said.

"What are the long-term effects?" Humar asked.

"Nothing until I am older."

"And you don't think you'll live long, so why avoid doing it?" Humar asked, voice tinted with annoyance.

"Perhaps. Or perhaps I do not have options. Perhaps both."

Humar shook his head. "I want you to try to stop. Let us help."

"I will always do what is needed."

"Do you think so little of our skill?"

"It is your skill that drives me. You have little regard for your own safety. You would easily battle a hundred men to save my brother or myself. While I cannot tell you how grateful I am for your concern, I assure you I will not allow that to happen. No one will die for me."

Humar opened his mouth as if to speak, but clamped it closed and muttered something about Edium being right.

"I received another vision last night," Salvarias said. "It was like the ones 'god' used to trick me with. Though why he would attempt to do so again, I cannot understand."

"What was it?" Humar asked.

"Men will attack us soon. Many will die, including you and Okulu."

Humar grunted. "They can go to Oblivion. I don't plan on dying today or anytime soon. I'll tell Neithelas to have the trees watch for any following us, just to be safe." He glanced at Salvarias. "Do you believe it?"

He shrugged. "I think they are playing mind games with me. They are probably curious how I will react."

"You mean they think you won't say anything and that they can catch us by surprise?"

"Or they think I will say something and you all will think I am insane when the vision does not come to fruition. Who can understand the mind of this god?"

Humar ran a hand through his hair. "I think it best you tell me of every vision. True or not, it's never a bad idea to be prepared."

"Agreed, my friend."

Hours passed slowly, the terrain still laboriously challenging. Adok's worried glances at Salvarias were as frequent as Lunara's and Wilhelm's. Salvarias seemed not to notice anything. He walked half asleep, wincing often, his breath wheezing enough to cause her own lungs to ache.

By late morning, they were able to ride, but Okulu kept the pace slow, his own frown finding Salvarias often.

Late in the afternoon, Neithelas clucked his tongue, gaining the group's attention.

"You were wise to be cautious, Humar," the prince announced. "We're being followed. The trees say it's a large force."

"Vague," Okulu said. "Large is relative."

"To the trees, it would mean over fifty men," Neithelas said.

"Then let's get out of here," Humar said. "Time to push the horses a bit."

They rode as hard as they dared over the next hour, stopping to rest the horses occasionally. Okulu, skilled as always, found trails to hide their path, and the group began to relax. All except Salvarias. His gaze often fell to the wolf or trees and each passing mile seemed to add to his unease. His formerly exhausted slouch vanished as he straightened, his eyes flicking wary glances at the woods. A shiver ran up Lunara's spine, and she cuddled the rabbit closer to her bosom.

The denseness of the forest switched to old, dying pine trees shooting skyward, shedding crunchy pinecones and needles, the only ground covering she could see. The horses had difficulty forging through inky green bushes taller than Wilhelm, which seemed to cluster closer together with each passing hour. Soon, there was no hiding their trail, and the woods grew darker, dryer, and foreboding.

"Me don't like this," Durak muttered.

"I agree," Humar growled. "Neithelas, what do the trees say?"

Okulu's eyes flashed with anger, and he urged his horse forward at a trot.

"Nothing out of the ordinary," Neithelas replied.

Lunara kept her eyes straight even when she felt the winsire's gaze move over her.

Salvarias whistled to Okulu. Once the merc was within range, Salvarias asked, "What do you think?"

"I think something's out there." Okulu spat to the side, glaring at Neithelas. "He's full of ogre crap."

Humar arched an eyebrow at the normally cheerful merc.

"Do not be jealous, my friend," Neithelas said. "My offer to teach you the language of your people stands."

"Okulu," Salvarias said softly, shifting Mithal to block the merc's path toward Neithelas. "What do you think is out there?"

Okulu turned his green eyes to Salvarias, taking a long swig. "I don't know. Nothing feels as it should."

"You think you can hear them?" Neithelas scoffed.

"What exactly are they saying?" Okulu countered.

Neithelas shrugged. "They are singing their normal song. Nothing is amiss, nothing surrounds us."

"Humar," Salvarias said, his gaze combing over the trees. "I believe Okulu. Listen."

Lunara strained her ears but heard nothing.

Humar scratched his cheek. "I don't hear anything."

"Exactly," Okulu grumbled.

She realized no noise emanated from the forest: no breeze, no leaves rustling, no creatures scurrying about, no bugs flying. Everything was lifeless, unnatural, polluted with evil.

"These are the woods that drove men crazy," Durak growled. "The Dead Wood. The woods those drunks talked about."

"Brilliant," Okulu hissed.

"Why in Nevlar's fury are you leading us this way?" Durak snapped.

Okulu cursed. "I didn't know. I'm a little turned around."

Durak scowled at Okulu. "Who's the great scout now, ye drunk bastard? This isn't the first time you've led us into trouble."

Humar shook his head. "Enough. Both of you."

A branch snapped in the woods, ending the conversation. Adok's low growl rumbled, and Lunara's horse nickered, prancing back.

"Dismount," Salvarias said. "We can hide in the bushes, send the horses ahead."

"No," Humar hissed. "What if we need to escape?"

"Salvarias is right," Okulu snapped. "We can't outrun whatever is hunting us on horseback. The horses are too big to navigate through this brush and too easily spotted. They're better off on their own and so are we. Stay quiet and keep moving straight ahead. Once we're on the ground, we won't be able to see each other over the bushes."

Another crack echoed. Taking a quick survey of the bushes, it was nothing more than a maze to Lunara. There was no straight path she could see, and the bushes standing between her and Varila—who was closest—would be too tall to see over once she dismounted. They were all an island.

Swallowing her fear, Lunara swung her leg over her horse, landing silently, and reached for her cloak, but Palony charged bodily through the brush, leaving her alone.

She swore the plants watched her, observed her movements with distain and hunger. She trembled in an instant, her knees quaked together, and her heart thudded in her ears. She cradled the rabbit close, whispering to it that it would be all right. The words were as much for her as the rabbit.

Before she gathered courage to take a step, the light scent of lavender surrounded her. Looking up, Salvarias stood beside her, gaze scanning their surroundings, a finger pressed to his lips as a signal to keep quiet. Biting back a sob of relief, she nodded and juggled the rabbit over to one hand. Even as she freed her other hand, he was reaching for it.

He glided through the bushes in graceful silence, leading her along the path her mare had forged. He veered after a short distance, weaving through narrow gaps until they ran into Wilhelm and Varila. One of her sister's hand held Wilhelm's and the other gripped her sword. Adok joined them with his head raised to sniff the air, and Salvarias stared at the wolf for a moment before motioning in a direction to Wilhelm. The mage made a couple more hand movements and Wilhelm nodded.

Salvarias brushed her hair behind her ear, and a shiver ran up her body when his warm breath tickled her neck. "Do not let go of my hand no matter what you see or what happens," he breathed.

She nodded, resisting an inappropriate urge to kiss him. Embarrassed, she lowered her head.

Salvarias took the trembling rabbit from her arm and passed it over to the wolf.

Wilhelm whispered to Varila and when he finished, she sheathed her sword and snatched Lunara's free hand. Wilhelm brought up the rear, holding tight to Varila, his other hand hefting his broadsword. Salvarias started forward, threading through openings soundlessly. Wilhelm crouched to be below bush level, but his mass did not allow a noiseless passage.

"They ran in here!" a man roared, startling the silence and causing her to jump. "Krin, circle back and report where we are. If anyone sees one of them, kill them. We'll sort out the bodies later. And for the love of the gods, don't let the mage cast any spells. And make sure you take the large one's head."

Snapping branches, rustling bushes, and rattling armor echoed through the dead trees as if the forest were a deep well, disorienting her and providing no sense of direction from where they might have come.

Then the forest came alive. Nothing necessarily happened, but it felt like she stepped out of a dark room into blaring sun. It was the sensation of it, an instinctual awareness. She swore eyes followed them. And whatever things watched them whispered as well, soft enough to make her doubt her own ears, but her thoughts went to death.

A terror-filled scream cut the air behind them and ended with a sickening crunch. Lunara fought her stomach, her hand clenching tighter to Salvarias's. She didn't recognize the voice.

Salvarias paused, hunkering low to the ground, and the others followed suit. She heard someone close. The man's labored breathing disclosed his location. She almost held her own breath to avoid the same error, but her heart beat too painfully to try it. Instead, she breathed through her mouth. Time passed unknown before Salvarias moved and, unfortunately, around one bend, ran straight into one of the men hunting them. He was an erthla, no older than Varila. His eyes were cold and hungry, his clothes dirty but well made, and his lip curled up in a sneer when he saw them.

Moving swifter than a cat, Salvarias pushed her against Varila, covering Lunara with his own body, pulling all to their knees. Wilhelm seemed to be expecting the move and rose above the cowering group, driving his sword straight through the man's throat. The horrid sound flipped her stomach, and she tore her eyes from the man's dying gaze. Her body trembled and tears welled when Wilhelm's sword withdrew, allowing a wet gurgle to sneak into her ear. The body thudded to the ground.

The man had been directly in front of her, close enough for her to smell him, to see the light of life in his eyes, and memories of all the deaths she'd witnessed surfaced. Try as she might, tears spilt over her cheeks. She kept her head lowered, ashamed by her timing for a breakdown.

Then his soft thumb rubbed her knuckles, and she raised her eyes to meet his. Understanding flowed from Salvarias, and her tears multiplied at seeing his compassion. Now was not the time for comfort, and she nodded to him. He squeezed her hand before he turned and pushed forward.

Another scream was followed by squishy wet noises, crunching bone, and the scream ended abruptly. She could not suppress a shudder.

Salvarias froze, all colliding into him from the abrupt stop. He turned, pressing against her and forcing her back until she was squashed between Varila and him. The odd combination of Varila's sweet strawberry smell mixed with Salvarias's lavender caused her head to throb. The mage's gaze locked with Wilhelm's, and then the man's arms surrounded the group, compressing them. Lunara wondered if the brothers talked to each other in their minds. Wilhelm seemed to understand every look from Salvarias.

Suddenly the bushes moved without generating so much as a soft rustle. Lunara at first thought she might be imagining the entire event until a gigantic tree they stood by shuddered soundlessly and lurched three giant steps. Bushes spasmed to new homes, roots walking along the ground like a million tiny feet. Leaves fell silently to the ground, not even drifting in a breeze the movement should have conjured. It was the most unnatural thing she'd ever witnessed. Within a few short breaths, the forest settled into a new layout of twisting walkways. The path they had followed no longer existed.

Salvarias's gaze remained locked with Wilhelm's. Using his full height, Wilhelm stood on his toes and took a quick gander of the area. He crouched, tilted his head south, and grinned. Salvarias paused, seeming to decide, and finally nodded. Wilhelm switched to take lead, followed by Varila, and forged a path through the bushes, Salvarias bringing up the rear. Even with Wilhelm's large body, the bushes healed and closed in around Lunara. Her hand numbed from her sister's tightened grip.

Soon the bushes became so thick she barely saw her own forearm. Each step tested her will against that of the bushes as they snagged her. She fought the sensation of them clawing at her as if they were alive.

In an attempt to keep them from cutting her face, she lowered her head. Already scores on her exposed arms stung. Then the light scent of lavender encased her. He pressed against her, taking a few awkward steps before joining her rhythm. He kept her fingers entwined in his, but raised his arm in front of her face. His robes shielded the bushes from scratching her, and his other arm slid around her waist, gathering her close and helping him keep time with her stride.

She rolled her eyes at herself, acutely aware of how he moved against her and exasperated by her body's ability to respond to his touch at such a dangerous time.

Finally, they spilled out to an open path and he was quick to pull away, only keeping hold of her hand. Switching to take the lead, Salvarias picked up speed, weaving faster. They did not make it far before he stopped and ahead was another man.

The man faced away from them, unaware they cringed behind him. Sword drawn and shaking, the man surveyed the woods. A bush nearby shivered, the dead leaves falling to the forest floor. The man's legs went out from under him. Whatever took him paid no heed to his frantic screams as it dragged him into the bush. His fingers grasped for purchase on the ground, ripping off nails and leaving a bloody trail.

Salvarias moved to shield her view while the man's screams soared through the forest. Tears welled at the familiar wet, mushy sounds and snapping bones. The man's screams turned to soft gurgles, and she closed her eyes, trying to drive the sound from her ears.

Salvarias continued forward and tried to block the carnage, and though she had no desire to see it, her curious gaze moved to where the man had been taken. Blood smears clotted the dead pine needles, and a short distance away the man's body lay half eaten, organs and intestines spilt on the forest floor in hues of red and yellow, black and purple. Her stomach flipped, but she had no time to be ill.

A bush rustled and Varila cried out in pain and released Lunara's hand. Salvarias yanked her forward to avoid being grabbed by whatever emerged. Wilhelm hacked wildly at the bushes, staggering along as whatever had snagged Varila pulled her backward into the bushes.

Lunara stared in renewed fear when the entire forest shifted again. Bushes lurched and trees took a step in a different direction.

The event occurred without a sound and ended with them blocked off from their siblings.

"Varila!" Lunara screamed.

"Hush," Salvarias hissed, hauling her onward. "My brother will help her."

She did not make it far before she doubled over and lost her stomach. The man's body kept flashing in her mind, and her worry for her sister burned away her control. Salvarias held her hair while she retched between her sobs. As much as she tried to battle her mind, fear held a firm hold and strength failed her. She almost mockingly laughed at herself when she thought of the words Salvarias had spoken a night ago. This was the woman he saw: a sniveling girl who could not contain her own fear and yet was supposed to be able to command the power of a dead goddess.

Once she threw up all she could, he handed her a waterskin that had been tied around his waist. She took a drink, fighting to keep the water down. Ashamed, she could not meet his eyes when she handed the waterskin back to him. More screams erupted, ending in wet crunches, and terror clenched her throat. She didn't want to die a pain-filled death, to be eaten by some creature, alone and afraid. She didn't want to find her dead sister and friends, mutilated and strewn along the forest floor.

Salvarias gently hooked a finger around her chin and raised her face.

"We will survive," Salvarias said. "Varila will be fine."

She nodded, unable to move her eyes from his, drinking in the assurances his gaze offered.

"Do you trust me?"

She mutely nodded.

"Then you know what I have said is true." Long fingers caressed down her arm. "I will not allow you to die here. My brother will not allow Varila to die here."

His soft voice rang with truth. Once a light smile formed on his lips, her strength and determination surged to life. His hand clasped hers and he moved forward, pace quick and silent. Eventually, she became aware of the screams around them, the noises, the terrified pleas for help, but they didn't override her control.

When Adok appeared, Salvarias walked with new confidence. As her resolve returned, as her strength reached its peak, a crunch sounded near and Salvarias disappeared into the thick bushes. His ironclad grip yanked her to the ground and hauled her along in his wake. Branches scraped her exposed skin and she lowered her head, covering her face with her other arm as they rushed past her. Salvarias grunted, and his hold loosened. She might have been sobbing or begging for his help because his hand latched anew.

A vicious growl from Adok stopped whatever creature had captured the mage. She lurched to her hands and knees, gripping his hand and trying to see through the enveloping brush, wincing as branches jabbed her. She heard herself sobbing but unbridled fear controlled her voice.

Something scratchy grabbed her legs, pulling her knees from under her, and she gave a startled cry as it crawled up under her dress. Her breath stuck in her throat when it bit her thigh above the knee. She dug her free hand in the dirt, clawing her way toward Salvarias, all the while feeling pinprick claws sneaking farther up her leg. Then Adok leapt over her head, snarling and snapping at the brush. The creature slid down her leg, scoring her calf.

"Get up!" Salvarias ordered.

She battled the shrubbery, weeping and fighting the poking twigs. His cursing made her double her efforts, but the shrub seemed to thicken the longer it held her captive. He grunted, and she screamed when his hand slipped.

"Please!" she begged. "Do not leave me!"

His fingers were wrenched from hers, and she screamed again. His soft moan mingled with her own sobbed pleas for help.

She managed to crawl a foot or two before the bush clogged around her. She stopped at a mass of brown, bloody fur, still twitching in the throes of death. Her mind slipped toward panic as the rabbit squealed once before lying motionless. She might have screamed.

The bush pressed against her, thickening and entwining in itself to create a tomb around her, blocking the sun. She gasped in sharp breaths through her sobs, feeling the air sucked from her cocoon, and she was pushed back to sit on her heels, helplessly watching the bush grow right before her eyes, twisting and contorting into a hungry beast.

She knew it was coming for her. A chill ran up her spine, and though soundless, she felt evil drawing closer.

"Please," she wept, hugging herself tightly. "Someone help me."

Strong arms circled her waist and the light smell of lavender filled her tomb.

"It is fine," he whispered in her ear.

Sobs of relief erupted and she clasped his arms, pressing her back against his chest. Whispered words of magic washed over her. She deeply inhaled new, fresh air. The branches no longer jabbed her, and she warmed in the protective white film covering her.

"Close your eyes," he said.

She did as he asked. Whatever hunted them wailed like a rabid boar. Salvarias lowered his face in her hair as he shuddered.

"Salv!" Wilhelm roared. He sounded far away, miles into another forest.

"Brother," Salvarias said. "Leave."

He said the words so softly, she barely heard him.

The creature screeched in frustration then all was silent. Salvarias waited several moments before he lifted her to her feet, gave her a once over, and then folded her in his arms.

"I am sorry," he said.

Her throat was too tight with fear for her to speak, so she threw her arms around his neck, burying her face in his chest.

Supple fingers ran through her hair. "We must leave. Can you walk?"

She nodded, reluctantly withdrawing from his arms. She met his gaze, trying to smile but only fresh tears spilt.

"The shield will protect us," Salvarias said, glancing around. "But I cannot maintain it. When we escape this bush, we must run."

She nodded again. He turned his attention back to her, his eyes calm but his breathing ragged. His fingers entwined with hers and after a deep breath, he took a step. With agonizing slowness, he took another step, using the walls of his protection spell to part the brush. By the third step, he trembled; sweat burst on his brow, and his breathing became labored.

The bush seemed to focus its efforts, thickening and plunging them further into darkness. She reached out her mind to Salvarias, offering her comforts, and gradually provided strength to his magic. It appeared to work. His breathing steadied and his trembling reduced. Several steps passed before the shrub thinned. A few more and they dumped onto a path to find Adok pacing. She blinked against the harsh sunlight. Salvarias stared at the wolf for a moment, then his body tensed.

He drew her close. "Close your eyes."

She snapped her eyes shut. Footfalls padded up behind her.

"It is coming," Salvarias said. "Run."

"What—" A man's voice cut off in a gurgle.

Salvarias walked backwards, keeping her locked in his arms and his attention on the creature. She moved with him, new tears streaming at the sounds. He flinched and averted his gaze, eyes haunted.

She wanted to leave these woods, leave the sounds, the screams. It felt like a lifetime had passed since she had dismounted her horse.

Salvarias abruptly stopped, pressing her closer, and the woods shifted again. Bushes shuffled to the side, trees lurched a step, and then everything was motionless.

He backed up a few more steps and the soft ground of the forest changed into a lumpy, slick path. She looked down to see a patch of shiny, black rocks, perfect for skipping across a lake.

Salvarias bent down and picked one up, turning it over in his hand, brow furrowed. "I have seen a rock like this before," he said.

"What is it?"

He cursed and tossed it aside. "If only I knew, my lady." He glanced around and whispered, *"Rulose."*

Adok appeared and whined urgently before leaping along a new path. Salvarias readjusted his grip on her hand and led her after the wolf.

Time lost meaning. The sky darkened, the screams faded in the distance, and her exhaustion, hunger, and thirst reached a level she never knew could be endured.

She glanced around in the last plum light of the sun and noticed the bushes were shorter, reaching her height, and the forest floor sprouted grasses. Wishing she had her cloak, she shivered in the cool night breeze.

By the time darkness surrounded them, Salvarias finally slowed. Then she heard the most beautiful sound: water babbling lazily over rocks. He stopped by the stream and before he even motioned her to it, she plopped down on a bench-like rock.

"Lumous," he whispered and his sparrow floated above them.

She stared at it numbly, admiring its detail for the first time, how it floated as if alive, how it brought her a sense of safety. Then she realized it always had. Salvarias read by his sparrow, lit it often, and she had caught him watching it as she was now. Light. It was pure hope. Pure comfort. Reaching out, she ran her fingers along one of its wings. She felt nothing solid, but it made her fingertip tickle.

Salvarias offered his refilled waterskin, and she drank her fill before handing it back. The cold water lined her stomach but enhanced her hunger. His sparrow floated near her leg.

"May I?" he asked.

She nodded, lifting her dress enough for him to see the wound. She shivered when cold water trickled over her leg. He ripped the hem of her dress and tied the cloth over her wound.

"Your favorite," Salvarias said, pointing behind her.

She turned to see plump blackberries covering a bush and plucked several, eating while she picked more. He sat by her side, surveying the woods while she ate.

"Where are the others?" she asked.

"I am not sure but Adok is searching for them."

With her energy returning, she noticed the forest was once again normal. Healthy pine trees soared to the star-speckled sky and ferns and lush mosses covered the forest floor. She breathed deeply the smell of life.

"Thank you," she said.

He tilted his head, gaze roving over the forest.

"I can't seem to get used to people dying," she said, staring down at her hands folded in her lap. She'd never felt so useless, so scared.

"It is not something you should ever be used to, my lady."

"But others aren't affected," Lunara said, teeth chattering. She rubbed her arms.

He pulled her close, shifting his cloak to encase them both, and she rested her head on his chest.

"Just because some do not reveal their emotions, does not mean they are not bothered," Salvarias said.

"When was the first time you saw a person die?"

"I was two."

Lunara looked up into his distant eyes. "So young to remember."

"We were passing the gallows during a hanging."

"Were you upset?"

Pain glittered in his eyes. "No."

"The first time I saw was on the boat after your rescue," she said, hoping to switch his thoughts. "I saw the rower die who tried to stop the black-armored soldier. I didn't help. I just stood there."

"You would not have been able to assist him." Salvarias rested his head on hers. "He was past any help."

"Perhaps."

They sat in silence, her nerves calming, her fears subsiding, her memories of the dying men fading. She nestled against Salvarias, comforted in his arms.

"The rabbit ..." She blinked away tears. "I saw it."

"Adok was extremely apologetic. He had to drop it to assist us, and the rabbit was too scared to listen to instruction. It tried to flee, but—"

A snap in the woods startled her heart to full speed, and both bolted to their feet. He stepped in front of her, clasping her hand. A few breaths passed before he slouched and unwound his hand from hers.

"It is Varila and my brother."

The two siblings came into view, and Wilhelm's cry of relief nearly brought the man to tears as he rushed Salvarias and swooped him up in an embrace. Varila threw her arms around Lunara's neck.

"I was so worried," Varila breathed. "Are you hurt?"

"Something bit me but Salvarias tended to it." Lunara pulled back her sister to see several cuts on Varila's arms, blood dried on her hand, but otherwise unharmed.

Blood crusted Wilhelm's shoulder, his armor looking like it'd been chewed by a rabid dog. Salvarias tugged his brother to the creek, motioning to the bush.

"It's fine." Wilhelm grinned, eating berries. "Quite the adventure."

Varila knelt by the stream and rinsed her hand. "If you say so."

"May I?" Salvarias asked her.

"It's just a bite," Varila said, holding it up for him to see. He looked at it closely then nodded, turning his attention to Wilhelm's shoulder. Lunara frowned, remembering the mage's grunt of pain. She squinted in the moonlight and saw his burgundy robes clinging to his side, and when he turned, the left side of his robes sucked to his body, his shoulder glistening.

"You're hurt," she said.

Wilhelm turned a shade white and pulled Salvarias back. "How come you didn't take care of it?"

Salvarias shrugged. "I forgot."

Varila put an arm around Lunara and turned their backs to the brothers. "Have you seen any others?"

"No."

"I have sent Adok," Salvarias said.

"Dammit, Salv," Wilhelm muttered. "You need to take care of yourself. It's still bleeding."

"Sorry, brother."

After Salvarias and Wilhelm were tended to, the four huddled around the berry bush.

"We should start a fire," Salvarias suggested.

"I don't think we should risk it," Wilhelm said, lifting Lunara between the brothers as if she were a child. He pulled Varila into his lap. "We don't know if any of those men following us made it out. When the others arrive we will."

Wilhelm's heat mixed with her rising temperature in proximity to Salvarias helped keep her teeth from chattering.

"Humar and Durak are safe," Salvarias murmured.

When Humar appeared, Lunara jumped up and hugged the knight.

Humar chuckled. "Glad you're well." He winked at Salvarias. "Told you I didn't plan on dying."

She switched to Durak, and the grumpy cavrul patted her awkwardly. "There, there, lass, we be fine."

She smiled at both men before returning to sit between the brothers.

After the two men drank their fill at the stream, they settled close, accepting berries tossed by Wilhelm.

"Did ye see what they were?" Durak grumbled.

"No," Wilhelm said. "Wish I had, though. I bet they would have been a challenge to fight."

Salvarias shuddered but remained quiet.

Humar shook his head. "I don't know what could do such a thing, but we saw a body and it was—"

"We saw one as well," Salvarias interrupted. "Neithelas," he said, eyes distant.

The prince stumbled into camp, blood running down his arm and clumping his tunic around his chest.

Salvarias rose, searching his pouch, while Neithelas sank to the creek, drinking between harsh breaths.

"What happened?" Humar asked.

"They got me but I fought them off," Neithelas rasped. "The trees sang the entire time." His face twisted in disgust. "Like they didn't care what occurred, like they condoned the acts."

"Allow me to assist you," Salvarias said.

Neithelas nodded and removed his tunic.

"Will you help me?" Salvarias asked Lunara.

Lunara's blood boiled. She shot the mage a look that clearly conveyed such. She accepted a cloth, wetting it in the creek, and washed Neithelas's wounds.

"I am thankful you're safe," Neithelas said to her, his violet eyes practically undressing her. "I tried to find you. I searched for an hour before I left to find the others."

"Thank you," Lunara said, rinsing the cloth.

"Grind this in your palm and apply it to the wound," Salvarias instructed, handing her a few leaves.

She did as instructed and pressed the leaves to Neithelas's chest, seeing him wince. "Sorry."

Neithelas took her hand when she finished and kissed it. "Thank you, my lady."

She smiled, pulling back her hand, and glared at Salvarias. "Is there anything else I can assist with?"

"No. Thank you, my lady."

She stormed to Wilhelm's side and plopped down, her blood moving like molten lava.

Okulu crawled into the clearing, latched on to the wolf.

Salvarias sprang to his feet and sprinted to the merc's side. "Brother!"

Wilhelm was already up and rushed to Okulu. The merc's tunic was sopping with blood, his breastplate held awkwardly in the wolf's mouth. Lunara grew lightheaded at the sight.

"Bites." Okulu winced when Wilhelm lowered him by the creek. "It was stuck on my armor. I thought if I took it off, I could break free. I was terribly wrong."

236

Salvarias motioned to his brother, who removed the merc's shirt. Lunara blanched at the chunks of missing skin.

"Adok!" Salvarias called. "Find Mithal."

The wolf bounded away into the forest. Salvarias knelt by the creek and washed off the blood crusting Okulu's chest.

"I have herbs that will help," Salvarias told Okulu.

The merc nodded, turning to Neithelas. "What do your trees tell you now?"

The prince blushed. "They didn't care."

Okulu smirked and closed his eyes.

Salvarias rose, whispered *"Lumous,"* and a second sparrow flew along the forest floor with the mage and Wilhelm following behind it. When the brothers returned, Salvarias pressed a few leaves over the deeper bites.

An hour went by before the horses, save Durak's, emerged into the circle of firelight. Salvarias gathered a pouch from his pack and busily mixed leaves and oils, casting several glances at the horses. Within the shadows of his hood, she swore she saw tears fall down his cheeks.

"I am sorry, Durak, but your horse did not make it," Salvarias said.

By the time he finished administering the paste to Okulu's wounds, a drop of blood fell from his nose. His hands shook as he put his herb pouch in his pack.

Suddenly he rocked backward as if struck and grabbed his head.

"Wilhelm!" Lunara called.

Wilhelm had already hopped up and helped eased Salvarias to his knees, whispering softly. Salvarias's eyes clamped closed and sweat rolled down his forehead. What air he pulled into his lungs didn't seem like enough, and his skin paled noticeably.

At long last, he exhaled sharply, slumping against Wilhelm. "I failed," Salvarias said. "Something is coming."

"Any idea what? When?" Humar asked.

Salvarias shook his head, eyes closing. "No. I am sorry."

"Don't apologize, Salv," Wilhelm scolded gently.

His words fell on deaf ears; Salvarias had succumbed to sleep.

Humar did not allow the party long to rest. Before sunup, they were mounted again. Durak rode with Neithelas and Salvarias with Wilhelm since the mage had yet to wake.

Despite the injuries in their group, Okulu pushed hard throughout the day until they finally emerged from the woods. They found themselves once again on rolling hills, dotted here and there with patches of trees.

Okulu slid from his horse, fell to his knees, and kissed the grasses. Then he raised his hands skyward and cried, "Thank the gods!"

Lunara resisted the temptation to join the merc in his joyous celebration.

Chapter 23

Autumn 1018 a.r.

Hynd was another gray, miserable city, which matched Salvarias's mood along with the steady downpour of chilling rain they had ridden in throughout the day and into the early evening hours. The city wall was not made of stone but instead was comprised of loosely secured logs looking as worn as the city. He would have criticized the choice of wood over stone—after all, wood burned and fire was what he dreamt every night—but he figured the constant rain had saturated the wood enough that not even his blackfire would find the power to burn it.

Disparaging the state of the wall, however, was only a distraction. Sleep. Gods, how he wanted sleep. The days spent in a forest drenched with Zerana's grace had pounded the strength from his body and seemed to have had the sole purpose of undoing any healing Sansis had done. His insides ached and more than once he feared he would be sick. Worse was the strain his mind endured. There had been no rest since leaving the Stronghold on Dalnar. No break from being hunted, from the wars his evil waged, from straining his magic, or from the pounding of his new headaches—which of late had cruelly switched to such intensity that light and food made him nauseous. He was beaten physically and doubted he could stand for a few breaths on his own accord.

Trying to shift his thoughts to something else besides his pain, he reflected upon the moment he had touched his mark to Lunara's. He had a strange sense that if they had not been in danger, he would have learned a priceless piece of information that would lead to answers of questions he had not even known to ask. Despite his curiosity and desire to try it again, he feared the goddess's grace could harm Lunara if drawn upon for much longer—case in point, her new white lock of hair—and no amount of knowledge was worth her suffering.

Before reaching the city, Adok veered from the group, deciding to avoid alarming its citizens. Salvarias had no energy for argument, but if he had, he would have used it to confront the wolf. After the forest, Adok seemed as beaten as Salvarias, if for different reasons. There was an ache in the wolf's presence, a deep sadness.

When they arrived at the gate, a guard—part octril, part erthla—held up his double forearm to stop them. The darkening sky dulled the brilliant blue-green scales layered on one hand while human skin covered the other. "Name, mage."

"Salvarias Laybryth," he murmured. Exhaustion made the words heavy to speak.

Okulu rested his hand on his sword hilt. "He said, *Salvarias Laybryth.*" He spoke clearly, enunciating each word as if teaching it to a child that did not understand his language.

The guard nodded and flipped through the list. "No Laybryth on the list." The man looked up, his eyes somewhere between the black of an octril and cloudy blue. He leaned forward, looking around as he did, and spoke in a low voice. "Mages have had a bad run, my friends. If I were you, I'd avoid major cities."

"How so?" Okulu asked.

The guard licked his lips and his gaze flicked from one spot to another. "Look, I'm trying to help your friend out. I'm just saying, avoid cities." His eyes finally settled on Salvarias. The guard sighed and shook his head. "They're burning them. In hordes. They got my friend not but a week ago."

"Who?" Okulu demanded.

The guard resumed his nervous inspection. "The Association. They're striking names and saying mages are going mad all over Arden. They're taking ones off the list that have the most power." The guard held up the folded leather keeping his list dry from the drizzle and shook it as if to enhance his point. "Your friend's not on here. That means he's being hunted. I'll let you through, but not every guard at every city will be as merciful."

"Thank you, friend," Humar said. He tossed the man a coin. "May Zerana's grace protect you."

Salvarias tilted his head. He only half cared about the conversation. His body was demanding sleep. Though he had intended to continue as far as possible and perhaps catch up to Perek tonight, his selfish need for sleep demanded satisfaction. When they passed through the gate, he forced his mouth to form words. "I would like to stay here for the night."

Humar frowned, his eyes searching for Salvarias's in the shadows of his hood. "All right," he said. "We could all use the rest."

Their horses' hooves squished in the muck of the main road slicing its way through poverty-stricken homes. The steady rain seemed to weigh down everything, adding a burden to both the sagging rooftops and the hunched citizens. Those passing rarely looked up, and if they did, Salvarias could not fathom which creature had bred with another. Some were more animal than human, but the eyes never lied. There was thought in them, the cold calculation and arrogant air only humans could convey.

Dim lights lit scenes beyond windows that made Salvarias's heart ache in sympathy: children huddled around a fire, ragged clothing not hiding their protruding ribs, their defeated and dejected gazes following Salvarias as he passed. More than once he thought he saw accusation, a glare of jealousy for his horse that could feed a family for months. Of course, he imagined it. His eyesight was not as good as his creative mind. But reality had rarely made itself known as of late. Always a battle raged between sanity and insanity. He realized it in the woods when he had used the blackfire to call upon Zerana's power. It had shown him a strain, the tautness of his thread of sanity. It had pleaded for something, but he had refused to listen. His sole purpose had been to save Lunara, to strengthen Zerana's grace to help them. Now, in safety and reflection, he clearly saw what the blackfire had revealed: slowly, ever so slowly, his mind was caving to his imagination. His mother was dead, yet he saw her standing naked in an alley, face melting, strips of pink flesh falling to the filth at her feet, blood running down her legs. He had seen Sansis three times since entering Hynd. Several times, the old man's dagger had sawed through his ear and rats skittered up his leg. Perhaps knowing how close he was to insanity would help maintain what little sanity he had left. He doubted it, though. Hope was not so kind to Salvarias.

They stopped at an inn that looked as gloomy as the other buildings. Salvarias handed off Mithal to a stablehand, apologizing to the horses for not seeing to them himself.

Inside, pots littered the floor, and the *drip drip drip* of the leaking roof was lost in the complaining tone of the inn's patrons. A waft of some type of meat, unclean men, and wet fur churned Salvarias's stomach.

A woman with brilliant orange eyes and a mane of feathers strode up to the group, smiling to reveal teeth sharp as Adok's. Neithelas recoiled. Luckily, the woman did not notice his rudeness. Her eyes were on Wilhelm, as were any other woman's in the tavern. His brother, oblivious as always, smiled his crooked grin.

"Any available rooms?" Humar asked. "We're looking for two."

"Of course." Her voice squawked out like an eagle.

Neithelas jumped and immediately moved to Lunara's side, hand on the hilt of his sword. He would be a good man for her. Protective, loving. He would give her a stable home, buy her anything she ever wanted, gift her healthy, whole children. A horrible part of Salvarias hated him for it.

When the keys were handed over, Salvarias took one. "I am not hungry, brother. I would rather sleep." He heard how mumbled his words sounded, and apparently so did Wilhelm. His brother turned to lead the way up the stairs, but Salvarias rested a hand on Wilhelm's arm and held him back. "I would prefer to be alone."

Wilhelm needed to eat. His stomach had been yowling since they had entered the tavern. Wilhelm's jaw clenched, but he nodded and handed over the puzzle box.

Salvarias hoped he had tilted his head in farewell to the others. Using the backs of chairs, he weaved through tables and eventually made it to the stairs. How he found the energy to climb, he would never know.

Inside the room, he did not bother to change into fresh robes. He had left his pack with his brother, and even if Salvarias had it, he would not have had the strength. Instead, he tumbled into the bed. As exhausted as he was, he needed to calm his mind. The puzzle box whirled in his fingers, expanding and contracting as the pieces danced to his mind's images. He missed Adok at his side, so he made a wolf.

A sound like thick stew being stirred made him pause. He swore the air soured with the metallic smell of blood. He glanced around, but saw nothing. Surely another trick of his mind. He turned his attention back to the puzzle box.

Sleep was finally crowding his vision when the stench and sound from earlier erupted violently. He sat upright. At the side of his bed, rising up in a bubbling mass, was blood. Pure, crimson blood. A shape began to form. Hands molded from a substance looking as solid as stone, fingers morphing into sharp claws. The head was a bulb with sunken holes for eyes and a mouth opened to reveal jagged teeth, all made of nothing but blood. Bloodleders.

Standing before Salvarias were three innocent babies, warped into vile creatures. Even as his mind raced for spells, he hesitated. Three innocent babies.

His morality went unrewarded. All three lunged on top of him, pinning down his arms and legs. The first bite was on his forearm. It stung tears into his eyes and leached a hoarse cry from him. The second creature clamped its jaws around his shoulder at the base of his neck. Cold ran in his blood, ice, death. Nausea set in, and his head swam in a bog. The third bite stung less. He thought it was on his chest.

He should fight them, but killing three innocents was not something he could bring himself to do. Of course, that was a lie he fed himself. He knew these were no longer children. Their souls had been devoured by poison long ago. If he were to look into his own dark soul, he would see the truth in his lack of action: He was tired. At times when his fight was at its lowest and without his brother's presence or Lunara's smile, he had no desire to continue. Death was welcomed. He begged for it.

He briefly thought of Lunara and the impact of his decision, but his mind uncovered a very likely possibility: Lunara's soul might be linked to his, but the goddess owned it before Salvarias and Lunara had met. He had a strong suspicion Zerana's grace would find a way to save Lunara. Whether it was just a part of himself justifying his cowardice, or whether it was a truth, he did not know. And he did not care. He wanted to sleep. Endlessly. Blissfully.

The poison worked quickly. Already his vision pulsed. The sucking noises seemed unusually loud. He shivered violently, the warmth of life leaving, replaced by the creatures' venom.

Hot tears rolled down his cheeks, seeming to burn his freezing skin. He would miss his brother terribly. To be separated, even if by death, was a harrowing thought.

He will be better off without you, the presence said. *Think of the joy he will have onccce you are dead. It isss time to leave him.*

"I cannot leave him," Salvarias muttered. Selfishly, he decided to fight, if for no other reason than to see his brother once more, to laugh together. He whispered a spell, trying to focus his blurry vision on one of the bloodleders.

A roar seemed to vibrate his bones. It was his brother. A sob left Salvarias as reality crashed into him. The lure of death was replaced by a desperate need to live. Even as he mustered his strength, he felt how close he was to death, how strong the poison coursed through him, how far he had let himself fall.

Wilhelm's gleaming sword sliced the air in powerful swoops, never once grazing over Salvarias.

The ice in his veins turned into a million daggers jabbing him. Steeling himself, Salvarias managed his rune and shoved the energy into it. *"Rulose!"* he cried.

One creature reeled backwards, its maw opening wide in a silent scream. It froze. Pink now, instead of blood red. Frosted. It was pretty.

The two other creatures burst apart, drenching Salvarias in poison. It crawled inside the open wounds he had suffered in the forest, moving beneath his skin like a trapped worm.

"Gods!" Wilhelm cried, reaching for Salvarias.

He recoiled from his brother's hand. "Do not touch me. Poison."

Wilhelm's gaze darted up and down Salvarias. "What do I do?" Paranoia edged his voice. He had read the same books. He knew what the blood did.

Salvarias shoved himself into a sitting position. He heard Neithelas vomiting outside and understood why. Blood covered the bed, the stench like a rotting cow carcass shoved in a sealed, hot room. Blood dripped from Salvarias's hair, his robes soaked through with it.

"Salv," Wilhelm said, voice cracking. "What do I do? Tell me what to do!"

"I ..." Salvarias leaned over and vomited. It was nothing but liquid, oil-like in every aspect, coating his throat in slime that made it too easy to swallow. "Potion shop."

He teetered to his feet, tore off his robes, and selected the driest blanket, one that would not drip poison through the inn. He wrapped it around himself. "Lead me to the potion shop."

"I can get what you need," Okulu said.

"Are you familiar with yulku?" Salvarias asked.

"No," Okulu said. "But I can order it."

"I must check the herbs myself," Salvarias said.

He lurched from the room, following the towering form of his brother, hearing the thudding footsteps from his companions behind him. His vision blurred again, fading in and out, sounds droning. Patrons scrambled from Wilhelm's path, whether because of his brother's glare or the blood covering Salvarias, he could not guess.

Outside, the rain had stopped. It was for the better. He did not want to leave a trail of poison. Mud oozed between his toes, making noises that reminded him of the bloodleders heaving into form. It churned his stomach and he vomited again. More black bile. Vomiting was good. He needed it out of his system. Shifting the blanket aside, he looked at the bite on his arm. The creature had taken off a chunk of skin and muscle. To his alarm, he was not bleeding, nor did black poison seep from it. That was definitely not what he had hoped to see.

He saw the sign of a mortar and pestle and none too soon. His legs buckled and he sank to his knees.

Wilhelm banged on the door while demanding the owner open his store. A light on the top floor flared to life. For a moment, it captured Salvarias wholly. It seemed so warm, inviting. He wanted to drown in its glow. Be lost in light.

"Gods, Salv, stay with me!" Wilhelm said.

Salvarias tore his gaze from the wonderful sight. He had not realized his body had given out. He lay on the ground, muscles tensed, back arched. Bile rose in the back of his throat, and he choked on it.

Wilhelm pounded on the door again. "I swear I'll call down all the evils of Veedran if you don't open this damn door!"

The door flung inward to reveal a portly erthla man, which explained the greed and anger shining in his eyes, and Salvarias was instantly pleased he had insisted on getting the herb himself.

"What—" The man's voice cut off sharply when he glanced down at Salvarias.

The tension in Salvarias's body left suddenly, and he collapsed in a coil of pain. Blood seemed frozen inside him, his muscles protesting its abandonment, his mind sluggishly striving to think without it. His heart faltered, skipping several times, flailing about in an attempt to beat. He looked down to see his skin ashy. The poison was working fast.

"I need yulku, dresnn, and ginger oil," Salvarias said. His tongue rolled oddly in his mouth.

The owner made no protest and ran into his shop, emerging a few brief moments later. "I can mix it. It'll cost you," the owner said a little too eagerly.

"Just do it!" Wilhelm demanded.

"No. It must be done a certain way," Salvarias murmured. Lunara knelt in front him and showed him the ingredients.

"That is not yulku," Salvarias said. He had a suspicion the owner would try to swindle them with the less expensive bulia leaf. Yulku was not easy to come by, and it closely resembled the bountiful bulia except for a small indention in the leaf, one only a trained eye could find. Normally, yulku's near twin would be harmless, but for this concoction, the wrong herb would be deadly.

Wilhelm's face contorted and he whispered to the shop owner between clenched teeth. "I swear to you if you come back with anything other than what he asked for, I will tear each of your fingers off one by one and shove them down your own throat."

The owner's face went deathly pale and he ran inside, returning with the correct herb and a mortar and pestle he insisted be free of charge.

Salvarias gave Lunara instructions and she performed them well. She handed over the bowl and Salvarias drank it. "I need a bath."

"There's one in the tavern," Wilhelm said. "Let me help you."

"No, it will infect you as well," Salvarias said.

"I don't care, Salv! I can take the potion too!"

"I do care," Salvarias said, lining his voice with anger. "You must not touch me."

Varila whispered in Wilhelm's ear, and the light of his objection left. He nodded.

Forcing his legs up, Salvarias staggered down the street. He nearly fell, but caught himself on a wall. His hand was a darker gray now, as well as his entire body. He had drunk the potion too late, and there was a strong chance he might not recover. He glanced at the ground, clumps of mud and gods knew what else, but it looked inviting. Sleep ... endless ... blissful.

"Please," Lunara said.

She stood in front of him, beaming her pure smile, infusing his wicked soul with her strength. He took everything she offered and managed a step. Then another. And another. All the while he stared at her, at the moonlight imbuing her white lock with radiant light, at the blue-black shimmers of her hair fighting for attention, at her kind eyes, the strength and vulnerability in them. The city around him faded. It was just her. His light.

He did not come out from his trance until she moved from his line of sight. In front of him, a steaming tub of water waited. He must have been sick during his trek back to the inn. The front of him was covered in black bile and mud and whatever else was clotted on the street. He tossed the blanket into the fire along with his undergarment and crawled into the tub. One glance showed him it was only him and his brother in the room. The others must have given him privacy. No doubt they stood outside his door.

After cleaning off all the poison, he hauled himself out of the tub. No sooner did he hit the floor than a warm blanket and arms wrapped around him. He was carried to a new room and placed in a soft bed. It already smelled of lavender. Okulu handed over dressings, and Wilhelm wrapped Salvarias's wounds. His skin was too gray.

"I will need more of the herbs," he said. The one dose had only permitted his blood to flow again. He had taken too long to bathe, and his open wounds had given the poison too large of an opening. He should have ordered more while he was there.

"You need to fetch them," Humar said to Wilhelm. "You scared the life out of that owner, and he won't try the wrong herb again. Lunara, go with them and mix it on the way back."

"I'm not leaving him," Wilhelm muttered.

"He'll dic if you don't," Varila said. "I'll stay with him. No one will get near him while I'm here. I promise."

Wilhelm glanced at her before nodding.

"I'll come along," Okulu said. "Bastard won't fool me again."

After a gentle squeeze of Salvarias's shoulder, Wilhelm left. Salvarias resisted the urge to beg him to stay. Without his brother, endless sleep was too inviting and death still lingered at Salvarias's door.

Varila sat on the edge of the bed and smiled. It was a kind smile, a genuine warmth in her eyes he had never seen before. "Do you need anything?" she asked.

"Water," he said.

Humar paced the back of the room, hand grooming his hair constantly. Salvarias wondered how the knight had any hair left.

"We cannot delay," Salvarias said toward Humar. "We must leave in the morning."

Humar stopped his pacing to frown.

"We cannot delay," Salvarias repeated.

Slowly, the knight nodded.

Durak plopped down in a chair, whittling away at a stick. The grouchy cavrul had hid it anytime Salvarias tried to see what it was. Durak said he was making it for someone special and would not have Salvarias ruining the surprise. He assumed it was for Wilhelm or Lunara and had promised to keep it a secret, but Durak held his prize close. Salvarias wished he could see it now.

A smile lifted Durak's wrinkles. "Make it through this, lad, and me show you."

Neithelas scoffed. "The poison will kill him. Be merciful and show him."

"Shut up," Durak muttered.

"Here," Varila said.

She slipped a hand under his head and lifted him to drink. It only took a breath for the images to attack.

A figure loomed tall, same sea-blue eyes as Varila but his were colder and darker than the deepest cave. Varila was a small child, and he seemed unreasonably large, and scared Varila senseless. The man raised his hand and the image flashed to Lord Bellerum. He was squatting eye level, hazel eyes moist with tears. He was smiling as he pressed a cool cloth to her forehead. Salvarias even heard him whisper, "You're safe now. He'll never hurt you again." An aching to hear those same words directed at Salvarias pierced his chest.

Then his evil sensed his weakened state, and all else was forgotten.

The Hunters surged forward with such intensity it threw Salvarias back, freeing him from Varila's touch. His evil flung itself against his wall, chipping away pieces of stone. The Hunters clawed at his mortar, weakening it. The strain to hold up both walls seemed to split his skull. The poison once again chilled his blood, slowing its flow to dangerous levels.

Voices rose in the distance, barked orders and frantic calling. His name rang all around him, mingling with his own screamed word. "Brother" kept pouring from his lips, his hand searching, his mind begging.

A crack split across the wall blocking the Hunters. They pried at it, causing sweat to burst on his brow. His weak heart faltered.

Sssleep, my preciousss murderer. Jussst sssleep.

Darkness pressed down on him, endless darkness, endless sleep.

Desperately he reached out and shouted, "Brother!"

A hand clasped his and a dagger rammed into his skull. His sucked-in breath exploded out in a shout of pain. His heart knocked in his chest reluctantly. Strength flooded him. The crack in his wall snapped closed, and he swore he heard the Hunters howl in frustration.

Something pried open his clenched jaw, and liquid ran down his throat. He choked, but managed to swallow it.

"I'm here, Salv."

At the rumble of his brother's voice, Salvarias broke into sobs. He clawed his way into his brother's arms and curled up. Safe. He was safe.

Allowing the cruel world to fall away, he drained his brother's strength. The fight did not last long, and when he shoved away the evil, nightmares consumed him.

Chapter 24

Autumn 1018 a.r.

Lunara stood at the window and watched the rising sun battle to break the gray that seemed to veil the entire continent of Windlous. As much as she enjoyed cleansing rains, there came a point when sun was as needed as water. She longed for warmth, the old familiarity of autumn in Serinity: the spicy aroma of pumpkin and cinnamon, the earthy taste of roasted squash stew, the brilliant colors blanketing the mountain, and the joyous celebration of the Harvest. They had missed celebrating while at sea. Vuddruk was not around to remind the group to take a break from the unknown and live in song and dance.

Gray. Not even the trees were touched by autumn's gentle hand. The leaves were green one day and dead the next. They whirled around the gray city, adding just another hue of depression. She wondered if Salvarias caused it. Ever since the Stronghold, the entire world seemed to suffer his feelings of defeat and fear.

She glanced over her shoulder. Varila had fallen asleep sitting on the floor by Wilhelm's bed, holding his hand. His face had at least gained color during the night. After Salvarias had passed out, Wilhelm was close behind. He only took the time to clean up the blood running from Salvarias's nose before tumbling into bed, breathing too shallow and trembling. Even Salvarias's soft cries never woke Wilhelm.

During the long night, Salvarias had succumbed to fever. His teeth chattered together and sweat slicked his hair. He seemed to worsen with each hour.

After a light knock on the door, Humar peered in. The knight looked to have not slept either. Black ringed his eyes and his smile was not as bright as usual.

"How are you?" he asked, stepping inside.

"Can we not wait another day?" she asked. "Neither is fit for travel."

"I told the boy we'd leave. Maybe he'll change his mind."

Varila snorted, stretching her arms over her head. "He's too damn stubborn to change his mind."

Humar chuckled. "Right you are." He walked to the bed and reached for Salvarias.

"No," Lunara said, intercepting him. "Let me."

Gently, she shook Salvarias's shoulder. Heat seeped through the blankets. Salvarias's frown eased and he inhaled deeply before opening his eyes. The blackness in his eyes swirled lazily, curling around in every hue of gray. He glanced at the window and tried to speak, but his voice wouldn't come. She quickly fetched him a glass of water.

After drinking it, he rested a hand on Wilhelm's arm. "Brother."

Wilhelm's eyes fluttered open. "I'm up." He sat up seemingly too quickly since he swayed a bit. Varila steadied him. His wide eyes scanned the room and his brow furrowed. "What's going on?" He blinked a few times and wiped his eyes.

"We must leave," Salvarias said.

Wilhelm shook his head. "You look like you spent a week in Oblivion, Salv. We need to wait until you're better."

"We cannot. We must leave." Salvarias shoved himself up to sit. "I need Okulu."

Lunara went to work mixing another potion while Humar left for Okulu. Wilhelm rose from bed and began packing. He still looked a little too wide-eyed—half himself.

She'd just given Salvarias the potion when Okulu sauntered in, smiling widely, grass-green eyes lit with warmth. "About time you woke up. I thought you might've decided to try life as a bloodleder."

Salvarias leaned against the wall, closing his eyes. "I find the taste of blood ... unappealing."

Okulu plopped down on the bed in front of Salvarias, crossing his legs and resting his elbows on his knees. "Where'd our little friend go?"

"A city, small, quaint, clean. It is by a lake with woods to one side. There is a massive estate in the center while the other homes make this inn look like a shack."

Okulu frowned. "Looks like it doesn't belong in Windlous?"

Salvarias nodded slightly. "It has color. Gardens. Homes in rich woods and stone. Clean cobblestone streets. An impressively large stable."

"Lynta," Okulu said. He took a long draw from his flask. "Has he moved on yet?"

Salvarias shook his head.

"Well then." Okulu blew out a puff of air and shrugged. "Lynta it is."

In no time, Hynd was a shrinking dot behind them, and rolling hills of sickly grasses stretched before Lunara and her friends. Adok joined the group and trotted beside Salvarias, occasionally whining. The mage seemed not to notice.

"Short ride to Lynta," Okulu said after a while of silence. "Five hours if we keep a good pace."

"We must hurry," Salvarias mumbled.

Wilhelm had covered the mage in two cloaks and three blankets, but beneath all the fabric Salvarias shivered as if stuck in a snowstorm. Sweat plastered his hair to his forehead, and he swayed dangerously in his saddle. It wasn't long before he dozed undisturbed by Mithal's gait. Lunara would've doubted he could make the journey if not for the mage's stubbornness.

His gray skin continually alarmed her every time she glanced his way. It wasn't the natural ashy tone of a sick man. It was leaning more toward a light-skinned cavrul, rich gray even in its lightest hue.

She nudged Palony next to Mithal and gently lifted Salvarias's sleeve so she could see the dressing wrapped around the bite on his arm. Black liquid seeped through the white cloth, looking like someone had spilt a bottle of ink.

Wilhelm uttered a curse. "I don't know how to treat this. I can dress a stab wound, but poison is beyond me."

"He knew," Okulu said. "I'm sure it's working. He looks lighter than he did last night."

Lunara smiled her agreement at Wilhelm. "Okulu's right. The potion just needs a while to battle the poison."

Wilhelm grunted and ran a hand over his face. It shook slightly.

"Ye still look tired," Durak said, stick and knife in hand, wood shavings drifting to the tall grasses.

"I am," Wilhelm said. "He drained me faster than he ever has before."

"What does it feel like?" Neithelas asked.

Wilhelm growled deep in his throat and cast the winsire a sneer. "Go to Oblivion."

"Neithelas was just curious," Humar said. "He meant nothing by it."

Regardless, Wilhelm did not answer and the group fell back into melancholy silence.

Morning passed and the afternoon sun was still a prisoner behind a mask of clouds when they crested a hill and the city of Lynta sprang up in the distance. Indeed, it seemed quaint as the lake's banks cozied up to the city and reflected it in shimmering waters. It rose on a hill, farmlands sprinkled about outside the walls, while inside it reminded her of rings. Rows of what she assumed where shops started at the base of the hill and spiraled upward into larger homes and finally a massive estate perched at the pinnacle. Traffic wasn't bustling through its gate, and only a few farmers worked the fields outside the city. She would have called it a town but the homes were too large.

Salvarias suddenly jerked awake, taking in a sharp breath. He blinked at the city and cursed.

"What is it?" Wilhelm asked.

"He is leaving," Salvarias said. He hissed and Mithal took off at a recklessly fast pace through the hills.

"Salv!"

The rest urged their horses onward, but only Palony pulled ahead of the group. Glancing over her shoulder, she saw them falling farther and farther behind as she galloped beside the mage.

"You have to wait for the others," she yelled over the thundering hooves.

Salvarias hissed again and Mithal burst into his full gait, kicking up clods of dirt and outdistancing Lunara in breaths.

Leaning forward, Lunara pleaded to Palony, "If you can understand me, catch him."

Her mare nickered and the horse's strides grew longer, quicker, whizzing the farm fields by in a blur of browns and greens. Wind stung tears in Lunara's eyes, and the chill of it chapped her face. Even with her speed, Mithal shot ahead and entered the city.

There were no guards at the gate when she barreled through. A man was picking up a tray of spilt breads and cakes, cursing toward a street still echoing with Mithal's ringing strides.

Palony needed no guidance and traversed the city with graceful ease. All along their route, the few citizens who were out stared down the street, muttering and motioning in the direction Palony headed.

At long last her mare cleared the stable entrance and skidded to halt in the courtyard. Lunara leapt from the saddle and looked wildly around. Mithal was near an entrance leading to the stalls, white froth falling from his muzzle, coat slick with sweat, a pile of blankets at his side. Hiking up her dress, Lunara darted inside the stables. It took her eyes a breath to adjust to the dim interior, but Salvarias's soft voice guided her to the back. He stood three horse stalls from a man undoubtedly related to Wilhelm: the same man she'd seen touch Salvarias's mark.

She joined Salvarias's side, her gaze searching for the three mages supposedly traveling with Perek. No one else was there.

"It's time to give it up, boy," Perek said. "I'm doing this for us both. For Wilhelm and his father."

"What is the stone?" Salvarias asked. His voice was weak, trembling. The two cloaks clasped around him did little to hide his shaking. "What does it do?"

"Look boy, I understand you think you know what's best, and I'm fully aware the power is urging you to find the stone, but trust me when I tell you that you don't want it. It's ... Well, it's just damn evil. I've made an arrangement. In exchange for the stone, Wilhelm and Tedris will be protected. All their children will be protected. Don't you see? This is best for everyone."

"God is not one to trifle with," Salvarias said. "If he seeks the stone, it must be kept from him. You of all people know it must be guarded. It is your responsibility. And now mine."

Perek turned his back to Salvarias and began saddling a horse. "You're not changing my mind. You can't kill me because you'll never find the stone on your own. The power will eat you up into nothing unless you have it. Even the short time I've been away from it, it's been painful. You'll always need it. Once these people have it, they've sworn the power will leave us and we'll be free. I'm sorry I've done this to you. I really am. But I have to think of my family. Of Tedris's family."

"Am I not family? Am I not of Tedris's seed?" Salvarias's voice carried a hint of anger, but his emotion was only pain.

Perek shook his head. "No, you're not part of our family. Just an unfortunate kid in the wrong place at the wrong time." He glanced over his shoulder. "What got hold of you, boy? Your eyes ..."

Salvarias's sadness lanced across Lunara's heart. His voice held none of it when he said, "I will not let you give God the stone."

Perek shrugged and turned back to the task of saddling his horse. "You don't have a choice. You don't have all my powers so you can't touch it yet. And Wilhelm doesn't have his so he can't protect you. This is the way it's going to be. I'm sorry. Truly. And as much as it repulses you, you're going to let me walk out of here. You'll be too busy to stop me."

Salvarias's eyes narrowed. "What have you done?"

Perek merely smiled.

A laugh escaped Salvarias, hollow and disgusted, void of humor and mirth. "You let them win."

Perek's smile turned to a full grin, flashing his white teeth. "Like you, I can see what you see. I knew you were on my tail and gaining. Quite the determined young man you are."

"Fool!" Salvarias spat, but Lunara knew he directed the comment at himself.

"Don't be so hard on yourself," Perek said, tightening the last buckle on his saddle. "You're new to all this. I'm sorry, boy. You'll just have to follow me if you want the stone. You know the truth of it. You can't find it without me."

"Follow you?" Salvarias shook his head. "Follow you to another trap? Be fooled again? I think not."

Perek frowned and looked openly sympathetic. "You know you will. It calls you. You can't stop searching any more than you can convince yourself to stop breathing. It's got its claws in you."

A high-pitched shriek sounded from high above.

"Time's up," Perek said.

"This is not over."

Salvarias whirled around and, at the sight of Lunara, jumped. He cursed and grabbed her hand, hauling her out of the stable. His grip was tight and his palm hot and clammy. Glancing over her shoulder, she saw Perek mounting his horse and following. When they emerged, three other saddled horses where waiting. Perek took up the reins from a stableman who stared skyward.

"Good luck, boy. I don't think your fight is going to go well for you. I'm sorry. I really am."

Salvarias chose not to respond, gaze fixated above. Perek nudged his horse and soon rounded a corner and went out of sight.

"Salv!" Wilhelm's voice seemed to vibrate the entire city.

"The stables, brother," Salvarias said, still studying the sky.

Another deafening shriek cut through the air.

Salvarias inhaled a deep breath and turned to face her. "I am sick. The poison is still too strong. Should I engage whatever creature hunts me, the likelihood for us both is death. I have few spells memorized and there is a risk to new spells created without study. If I do nothing, death will be a certainty, not only for us, but this entire city."

Lunara nodded solemnly. "Do what you can."

"If by chance we survive, I will need the potion every two hours."

Lunara nodded, battling to keep her tears and fear contained. She forced out a smile. "I understand."

"I am sorry," he said, brushing her hair behind her ear.

"It's not your fault," was all she could think to say.

A gust of air and an enveloping shadow jerked Lunara's gaze skyward. Clear of the tops of surrounding buildings hung a creature from nightmares. It was as large as a two-story building, brilliantly green with leathery bat-like wings spread wide enough to cover the stable courtyard and three buildings deep in shadow. Its three-sectioned body reminded her of an ant, more shell than supple skin. Six spidery legs were spread wide, each jagged with what might as well have been hundreds of short-bladed daggers. Directly above her and Salvarias, a mucousy lime-green waterfall cascaded out from the creature's maw, sizzling and snapping at the air around it.

Lunara screamed.

Salvarias cursed, grabbed her, and flung her to the ground, his body draped over hers. Lying on her back, she watched green liquid race for them as Salvarias whispered words of magic in her ear. His voice was calm and steady, but his body shook and his muscles were tense against her.

Above them, level with the stable roof and half the size of the courtyard, a filmy white bowl materialized, reminding her of Salvarias's protection spell. It was as wide as the green stream plunging toward her, and it caught most of the liquid save for the drops sloshing out and down onto the stable courtyard.

Mithal shrieked and bolted into the stable, Palony right behind. A man screamed and flailed into view, batting at his arm as skin wept off his bone in chunks. Beside her head, a cobblestone smoked and sizzled, a drop of green eating it, and the stink was harsh, burning through her nostrils and lungs, making her throat sore and raw. A woman's muffled scream seeped out of a nearby building.

Lunara closed her eyes tightly and breathed, "Zerana help us." No bright light came to their aid.

Salvarias cried out, his back arching, face twisted in pain.

Lunara fumbled for his cloaks' clasps, managed to snag the ties loose, and tossed the cloaks off him. Acid ate a hole through the rich fabric, nibbling away at the edges.

The beast cried out again. A gust of wind plastered her hair to the cobblestones, and the shadow disappeared. Screams rose up in the distance.

Salvarias gritted his teeth and groaned out a word of magic. The bowl folded up like a pouch and shot from the city, disappearing over rooftops.

Glancing around, Lunara saw her friends had finally made it to the stables. Unfortunately, so had a horde of minotaurs. Both sides were locked in a fierce battle at the stable courtyard entrance, the groups' horses bolting for the safety of the stables. The creature was nowhere in sight.

Salvarias ripped his dagger from its sheath and ran it down his forearm, drawing a line of deep red blood. "Brother," he whispered.

Though she barely heard him, Wilhelm snapped his head around, face lined with fear.

"Unlock your inner beast, my brother," Salvarias murmured, and raised his bloody arm.

Wilhelm staggered, blinked rapidly a few times, then his face contorted first into absolute rage and then switched to a bloodthirsty grin. He roared a challenge and dove into the fray. She had little time to marvel over the blur of his swords as they slashed their way deep into the ranks of the minotaurs. Above her, the creature let out another wail, and she looked up in time to see it diving straight for her and Salvarias, blocking the sun and drenching them in shadow.

He shoved himself up with a curse and hobbled a dozen steps from her before the beast's wings snapped open and it veered to intercept him. It swept low and encased Salvarias in its legs. He cried out as blood spread across his robes, dripping down to the cobblestones in thick drops that smeared as the beast's beating wings sent gusts of wind.

Hay flew all around, and the squeals of horses mingled with a man's cry as the gale flung him against a wall. Lunara curled up, covering her head, and peered at Salvarias through her arms.

His magic reached out to her, seeking, imbuing her whole body with an ache of its plea for help. Quickly, she fed it her strength, shoving it at Salvarias in a continuous river. The magic devoured it all and Salvarias roared, *"Iche Commad Engthe!"* His voice carried a power that sent a shiver up her spine and made her feel small in its presence. He cried *"Rulose!"* and threw his arms wide.

Her mouth dropped open when the creatures legs cracked and snapped in half, orange blood leaking to the ground, and its jagged limbs ripped free from Salvarias's body. The creature's wail popped her ears, and she clamped her hands over them, crying out at her own pain. The beast's wings beat frantically, raising it level with the roof and clear of the mage.

Salvarias's eyes darkened, fists clenched at his side, skin morphing from light gray to the color of old iron. *"Ich Commad Eezia!"* he shouted.

And this time, his magic reached in and stole what it needed from her, not waiting for her offer. She didn't fight and instead opened herself to it, allowing what it sought. It drained her quickly, blurring her vision in and out, leaving her a husk of flesh.

From Salvarias's outstretched hand an orb of ice formed and then flew up toward the creature, growing with each quickened breath until it was the size of a farmhouse by the time it reached the beast. The massive orb cut straight into the center of the creature and suffused itself in the creature's body, dulling the green into an icy white as the beast curled in a ball of agony, its face frozen in a knot of pain. The impact of the ice catapulted the creature backward, sailing it over city toward the large estate looming tall at the top of the hill. She vaguely heard Okulu's strangled cry "No!"

Salvarias fell to his knees. He lifted a shaking hand, traced in the air, and a translucent blue net blossomed to life, larger than the beast itself, and flew at the creature. The net caught up and trapped the beast even as the net shot vertical. The creature's tail end clipped the top of the estate, rock burst apart, and a cloud of dust drifted into the air before the creature finally shot straight up, disappearing into the hazy clouds.

Salvarias crumpled to the ground, choking on blood spewing from his mouth. His magic's pull on her weakened.

"Hel—" Salvarias gurgled, reaching out a shaking hand toward her.

Body deprived of strength, she clawed at the cobblestones, dragging herself toward the mage. She glanced over her shoulder to see the creature plummeting back down toward the city, the net wavering in its brilliance.

"Salvarias!" Okulu shouted. "Do something!"

"Please ..." Salvarias pleaded, reaching out for her again.

His skin was darker, sweat running down his face, blood pooling under his torn body, flooding from his mouth.

"I can't," Lunara sobbed, stretching for him, begging her body to move. She had nothing left to give.

A low growl sounded behind her before Adok's jaw clamped over arm. She cried out when teeth punctured her skin, and her arm felt like it would rip off as the wolf bolted to Salvarias, dragging her along.

When close enough, he latched hold of her and cried out, *"Rulose!"* The amount of energy he used would be their death. She sensed him spiraling into a chasm of nothingness and his magic's sudden panic. The only comforting sight as darkness consumed her was the frozen creature soaring clear of the city and into the woods beyond.

Chapter 25

Autumn 1018 a.r.

Wilhelm spared a glance behind as he plunged his sword into the throat of the minotaur-like creature roaring in front of him. The feral look in its large brown eyes did not contain thought or reason; the beast wanted to spill blood and nothing else.

Behind Wilhelm, his friends were being pushed back into the courtyard, the minotaurs' numbers too great to hold. There must have been over thirty of the creatures, and none inside the city seemed interested in helping. The streets were abandoned.

He couldn't see his brother, but the glimpse of the creature sailing through the air gave him hope his brother had survived. No doubt Salvarias needed help, but Wilhelm's power was all that kept the horde from flooding the courtyard.

Okulu's voice suddenly roared out, shouting above the clashing weapons, "By order of Knight Commander Okulu Hunbred, help us!"

Wilhelm dodged a quick jab and raised his swords to block a weapon cleaving for his head. The double-headed axe was larger than any creature had the right to bear, and the force of the beast's blow nearly drove him to his knees. To his left, he saw a blade glittering in the dull light as it plunged for his exposed side. Even if he managed to hold the beast with one sword, his second would never make it in time to block the strike.

Roaring frustration, he tensed for impact and shoved with all his might. Another blade whipped into view and steered the deathblow off course. Cold steel sliced across his back, but his armor took the brunt of the blow.

Wilhelm freed one sword and rammed it into the minotaur's gut, grinning as it ate its way through thick muscle and grated against bone. The beast staggered back off Wilhelm's sword, its mouth opened in surprise.

People flooded down the street, guards raising swords overhead and citizens holding aloft brooms, crude axes, pans, and kettles as they shouted defiance. Trapped between Wilhelm and the mass of people, the minotaurs didn't stand a chance.

Wilhelm succumbed completely to his power, allowing himself careless thrusts as the beasts' attention split. He plowed through three minotaurs, taking a leg from one, a hand from another, and a head from the last. Beside him, he heard the whistle of a blade slicing air then a crunch of bone and flesh. A minotaur fell behind him, nearly taking Wilhelm down with it. He would have been dead if another blade hadn't killed the beast to his right.

People swarmed over the minotaurs like a pack of flies on dung, which was what the entrance to the stable courtyard smelled like. Shouts of men and beast alike echoed, the clash of steel and groans of the dying deafening. Wilhelm added his own voice as he cut through any limb or body covered in coarse minotaur fur. A sword kept rhythm with his, and a chuckle rose at his side.

"Brilliant!" a voice rumbled. "That's my boy!"

Blood ran in Wilhelm's eyes, sprays of it flinging through the air, seeming suspended in time. The fight had slowed for him, crawling at a speed that made him feel as if only he moved. The unknown at his back overshadowed any joy he would have reveled in. Had his brother survived? Was Salvarias battling his evil and in need of Wilhelm's strength? The longer his mind brooded, the more frantically he fought, the quicker and tighter his jabs became.

The ground turned slippery with blood and excrement, and treacherous with the fallen bodies of men, women, and minotaurs. A beast in front of him swung an axe for Wilhelm's head, but he ducked it easily. A sting on his arm made him hiss as pain blossomed and warm blood trickled down to loosen his grip on his broadsword.

Cursing, he dropped the weapon and grabbed his great sword with both hands. As he sprang up, he thrust out his elbow, driving it in the face of one minotaur, then plunged his sword into the gut of the beast in front of him. Yanking his sword free, he whirled around and planted it in the side of another minotaur, driving it deep until it grated against its spine.

Searching for his next victim, he found only people, cheering and crowding around Okulu as he felled the last beast. Wilhelm's power fled quickly, leaving him trembling with exhaustion and wincing at the burning pain in his arm. It was a deep slice, cut through enough to expose his meaty inside.

Wilhelm planted his boot on the minotaur still stuck on his great sword and shoved. The creature slid free, and then Wilhelm scooped up his broadsword. When he turned around, he was greeted by a man—a man his height and width with bright amber eyes and a crooked grin.

"Gods," the man breathed. "I never ... I'm so proud of you, son."

Wilhelm staggered back. A wave of dizziness passed over him, and his world teetered.

"Easy," a soft voice said.

He looked down to see Varila wedge herself under his arm. Blood splatters stained her face, speckling her golden hair. Her sea-blue eyes were dark with concern as her gaze flickered between him and the man standing before him.

"Tedris," the man said, extending his hand. "It's good to meet you."

Wilhelm's anger rose from a simmer to a raging boil, surprising him with how much resentment he held for the man who'd fathered him and abandoned his mother, who'd left her broke and pregnant and alone. Who'd left him to a world he didn't understand.

He knocked aside the man's hand and strode to the courtyard. The dizziness of shock faded, leaving him merely drained of strength, feeling the sting of more slices on his arms and legs.

Wilhelm's strides quickened, outpacing Humar and the others, as fear began to take hold. The entire courtyard appeared to have been gnawed on by a horde of rats. The cobblestones' former smooth surface was rough, and several holes had been burrowed to the packed soil beneath. Hay was strewn about and a few men and women were huddled together, each fussing over what looked like small burns splattered over one another. He made out Lunara, lying on the cobblestones, her hand outstretched to rest on a bloody lump of a person. Blood-matted black hair covered the face of the person lying in a pool of his own blood, Adok sitting by his side, licking a hand clean.

The sight of Salvarias's robes punched with numerous holes and the blood trickling around Lunara took Wilhelm's breath. He staggered and would have fallen if Humar hadn't caught him. Varila was already crying out Lunara's name and running for her sister.

"Gods," Neithelas said from behind.

A horrible sound left Wilhelm's throat as he bolted for his brother and fell at his side. Salvarias looked as if he'd been put in a coffin lined with short blades. None of the punctures appeared deep, but their numbers were the danger.

"Help me!" Wilhelm wept, cradling Salvarias's limp form to his chest. Gods, his brother emitted heat like an oven. Sweat streaked down his face, leaving clean lines in their wake. "Someone help me!"

"It'll be all right," Humar said, voice even and assured. "None of the wounds are deep. Look, they've stopped bleeding."

Wilhelm blinked away tears and studied his brother's wounds. Indeed, the flow on most had eased, and those jagged and torn open had begun to clot around the edges. Wilhelm pushed back his brother's hair and listened to Salvarias's breathing. It was hard to hear over the shouts of the crowd as Okulu conveyed Humar's barked orders to the people, but Wilhelm picked up on the sickly wet sounds of Salvarias's short, ragged breaths.

Varila had Lunara's head propped on her lap. "Not a mark on her," Varila said.

Wilhelm gently turned Salvarias over, examining the cuts and making sure mortal wounds were not hidden in the drying blood. A spot on Salvarias's back about the size of Wilhelm's fist looked to have been eaten, burned even, the skin raw and blistering. Just another scar to add to his mutilated body.

Humar squatted in front of Wilhelm, wearing a comforting smile that didn't reach his eyes. "Okulu's getting a wagon so we can take them both to his home." He jabbed a finger toward the towering estate in the center of town. "That, if you can believe it. It seems our friend has been holding out on us. His family knows the healer in town." Humar frowned at Salvarias. "His skin has darkened."

Wilhelm nodded numbly.

"Hopefully the healer will concoct a better remedy to fight the poison." Humar glanced over his shoulder at Tedris standing toward the back of the courtyard. "You all right?"

Wilhelm nodded. His voice had left him.

Humar unfolded a blanket and draped it over Lunara. "I didn't see anything wrong with her."

Varila nodded her agreement. "She seems unharmed."

"With the amount of magic Salvarias needed to fight that creature, I'm sure they're just tired," Humar said. He smiled kindly and patted her hand before rising to join Durak and Neithelas. They watched Okulu, who was surrounded by a group of what Wilhelm assumed where Lynta knights, all grinning broadly and clapping the merc on the back. Their armor matched Okulu's, not the knighthood of Dalnar and Loutsil, but clearly an important symbol here.

It seemed to take forever before a wagon clacked into the courtyard. Wilhelm gently lifted his brother and laid him in back on a pile of blankets. Neithelas lowered Lunara by Salvarias's side.

Tedris kicked off from the wall he'd been leaning on and came to Wilhelm's side. "If it's all right, I'd like a chance to talk. Perhaps after you patch up your brother?"

Varila snorted. "You only care for one of your sons? You haven't even looked at—"

Wilhelm grabbed her arm and Tedris's and shuffled them from the group. Turning to Varila, he said, "What you're about to hear can never be repeated, even to Lunara. If you can't handle that, walk away."

She folded her arms across her chest. "I can handle it."

Wilhelm turned to Tedris. "When you're in anyone's company you'll refer to Salvarias as your own. He can never know you're not his father."

Varila sucked in a breath.

Tedris frowned. "It's not right to lie to the boy."

"I'll decide what's best for my brother," Wilhelm growled. "If you can't agree, get out of my sight."

Tedris winced and looked at the wagon plodding up the street. "All right, son. I won't say anything."

Wilhelm grunted, wrapped an arm around Varila's shoulders, and led her after the wagon.

Okulu's home surpassed the grandeur of Varila's in Serinity by far. Wilhelm craned his neck to see the topmost tower glittering in the dull light. A thin layer of clouds parted here and there, allowing dwindling sunlight to reflect off the castle's damp stones and smooth tiled roof. It was a masterpiece of elegant craftsmanship, but likely wouldn't hold off any sort of a siege. The outer wall of the city was tall and sturdy enough, but the castle seemed more in the business of formality than practicality. It was too whimsical, too thin and curvy.

A tower off to the left side had been clipped by the creature and stones the size of wagons were scattered about, the path of their destruction evident on the home. Holes existed where they shouldn't, and a few towers had caved in where struck, confirming Wilhelm's suspicion of the castle's flimsy construction.

In the courtyard, a short man paced, hands locked behind his back. His kind face was wrinkled and weathered, drawn by something besides age. Hair had retreated to a ring, leaving the top of the man's head glistening. A tunic fit snugly around his barrel of a belly, and a sword slapped his thigh with each step.

In contrast to the short, plump man, a willowy winsire woman stood calmly in the place with the best view of the path leading to the entrance. Her hands were folded in front of her, and a wealth of strawberry-blonde hair cascaded around her slim body. Vibrant green eyes were visible at a distance, seeming enhanced by flawless olive skin. The resemblance to Okulu was unmistakable.

When the merc appeared, the man stopped pacing and rested a hand over his heart. The woman smiled and it contained all the mischief of the world.

"Can it be?" the man breathed.

The woman winked. "You look like horse dung."

Okulu glanced at his bloody armor. "So I do."

"Where have you been?" the old man said. He ran, tripping over his own feet until he fell into Okulu's arms. "We've missed you. Are you harmed? Have you been well? You look thin?"

Okulu unraveled himself from the man's embrace only to be encased in the winsire's.

"We need your hospitality and Yunfa's aid," Okulu said tightly.

"Of course, of course," the man said. He turned to the nearest servant. "Fetch Yunfa at once."

Okulu faced the group, back stiff, smile forced. "This is my father, Olivit, and my mother, Thilia. I guess we'll be staying here for a few days." He took a long pull from his flask.

Wilhelm peeled off three blankets from atop Salvarias. His brother was wet with sweat even after a cool bath, face too gray. The only two signs Salvarias lived were the occasional violent twitch of his body and the rare wheezed breath.

A crackling fire warmed the room Okulu's parents had set up. One window gifted a view of the town and woods beyond where the beast was a shattered pile of ice dissolving in its own acid. Wilhelm moved to the window and stared out at the torches speckled like stars across the landscape as citizens went to view the marvel of the dead creature. Yet again, Wilhelm's brother had saved everyone. He wondered if any would thank Salvarias once he woke.

"How is he?"

Wilhelm jumped clear of his skin. He'd been so lost in thought he hadn't heard Varila enter Salvarias's room. He shrugged and turned his gaze back out the window. "Worse. Lunara?"

"The same. Okulu said Yunfa's on his way. He should be here soon." Her warm hand slipped into his. "Tedris is outside waiting for you."

Wilhelm sighed and ran a hand over his face. "I'll talk to him."

"You don't have to," she said, turning him to face her. "You can send him away. You don't owe him anything."

Before he could respond, Varila kissed him long and deep. For that moment, nothing existed but her smell, warmth, taste, and love. It encircled him completely until he was lost in it, drowned in her care and freed from his pain and fears. Too soon she ended it. He wasn't ready and pulled her close, holding her there as he drank of her one more time, crushing her body to his. He used her care to stiffen his spine, to give him courage to talk to the man who'd abandoned him. When he felt strong enough, he reluctantly let his lips drift from hers.

"I love you," he whispered.

"I know," she whispered back. "You need anything, I'll be in Lunara's room."

Varila smiled and squeezed his hand before crossing the room and opening the door. When Tedris stepped into view, she grabbed his arm and whispered in his ear. Whatever she said made the corner of Tedris's mouth twitch with a smile he seemed to fight. Varila looked once more at Wilhelm, glared at Tedris, and closed the door.

"Quite the woman," Tedris said. "Seems she cares for you."

Wilhelm crossed his arms over his chest and turned his gaze to the dark night. "What did you want?"

Tedris positioned two chairs beside Salvarias's bed. He sat in one and motioned Wilhelm to the other. "Want me to stitch up that arm?" Tedris asked, holding up a thread and needle. "I have a knack for it."

Wilhelm glanced at his torn-open bicep, shrugged, and plopped in the chair.

"Where did you learn to fight?" Tedris asked.

"Tobin and Humar."

"Humar?"

"A Loutsil knight. A friend of Durak."

"Ah, how is that grumpy cavrul?"

"Grumpy." Wilhelm winced when the thread pinched his skin closed. He never felt it when Salvarias did it.

Tedris chuckled. "It's good to know not everything changes."

"Why are you here?"

Tedris was silent for three threads of the needle. "Perek's lost his mind."

"So I've heard."

"He intends well, but ... It must be guarded."

"What? What's Salv supposed to guard?"

Tedris shook his head. "A stone, believe it or not."

"All this for a rock?"

"It's not just any stone."

"And what's he supposed to guard it against?"

Tedris spread his free arm wide. "The world, son. Everyone and everything. Only you two can know of it. Only the Guardian can touch it. Or so we've been told."

"You never tested it? Tried to touch it?"

Tedris shuddered. "No. I know this sounds a little ... thin, but I assure you, you don't want to test this thing. When you see it, when you've been around it, you'll start to understand. I trust what my father told me. And he trusted his father. I'm sure the first Guardian and Protector knew more secrets than us, but when they passed along their task, they had very specific instructions."

Silence.

Wilhelm ground his teeth. "Which were?"

Tedris winced. "I'd hoped to speak to both you and your brother together."

"Just tell me," Wilhelm growled.

Tedris sighed audibly. "So be it, son. First, is the secret. No one can know of the stone. No one. More importantly, we can't seek knowledge about what it is. We've been told it is to be as mysterious to us as others. Second, it will recognize only the Guardian. Anyone else will perish under its will and the world will be consumed in darkness. Sounds a bit dramatic, but like I said, once you've been around it you'll start to believe it has the power to do such a thing, which is why no one can know of it. Third, the Guardian will face two wars inside him. One is the Hunters. They seek him out at all times, and no one can fight them but the Guardian himself. You can't help with those battles. The other war is with the stone's force inside the Guardian. It tries to take him over, pervert his soul, sway him toward the stone's desires."

"The evil," Wilhelm stated.

Tedris raised an eyebrow. "Yes, yes I suppose you could call it that. That's the war you will eventually help with. Fourthly, the Guardian has healing powers when it comes to the Protector."

Wilhelm smirked. "We found that one out."

"What do you mean?"

"I got disemboweled," Wilhelm said, grimacing from the memory. "Salv brought me back."

"Gods," Tedris breathed. "You nearly died?"

"I did die."

Tedris scoffed. "That's impossible. If your head is severed from your body, the Guardian can't bring you back."

"Something's different with Salv and me then, because I died. And he saved me."

Tedris bit off the string and tossed the needle on a nearby table. "Your bond must be incredibly strong. We haven't heard of that kind of power since the third Guardian and Protector. I assume he suffered much to heal you."

"He did. So that's the same?"

"Perek said it hurts, like a sharp pain in his head."

"Takes a bit more out of Salv."

Tedris nodded. "I assume your bond is different than mine and Perek's. Perhaps it is because your bloodline is closer ... tighter since you share a mother."

Wilhelm shrugged off his statement. "How do you stop taking his power?"

"I've never had a problem. Perek isn't too generous in his offering. He controls what he gives me: just enough so I can heal on my own. He can't afford to lose that much strength."

Wilhelm grunted. "That explains it. Salv gives me everything. There's no limit to it."

Tedris whistled. "Must be invigorating. I always want more, like a bad thirst, but Perek stops me."

Wilhelm's gaze rested on his brother. "Salv would give me as much as I wanted."

"Would kill him, I'd imagine."

"Almost. I've had friends around to help me stop."

A silence stretched out between them, a bottomless ravine of distance Wilhelm knew would never shrink.

At long last, Tedris spoke. "It wasn't always like this. The first Guardian and Protector had a family. So did the second. The third. The fourth. All the way up to seventh. The eighth ones had to move around, but they stayed with their families. The ninth wasn't so lucky. I'm the eleventh generation of Protectors, and I didn't meet my father until I had passed into adulthood. He took me from my home in Sundil, wrenched me from my mother's arms, dragged me out of my city. It took me a long time to forgive him."

"What's changed?"

"The strength the Guardian possesses has dwindled each time it has been transferred. Because of it, the Guardians can't fight the Hunters, and over the years it's become too dangerous for us stay with our families. To add to our ever-growing challenge, the bond between the Guardian and Protector has grown weak, which is why no Guardian for the past eight generations has been able to bring the Protector back from the dead.

"Perek needs more of my strength with each fight. I ... I think I failed him." Tedris clenched his fists. "I was so tired. He used me over and over. We both ... We just didn't have anything left to give. I woke one day, after we'd battled together, and he was gone. No note. No word. I knew then I'd lost him."

"It's hereditary," Wilhelm said. It wasn't a question. He knew, and the knowledge sank in his gut.

Tedris nodded. "You're the great-great-great, and so on, grandson of Wilhelm Firth."

"Humar told me the heir of Wilhelm Firth is destined to rule over the entire knighthood, from Loutsil all the way to Dalnar. You've never tried to claim your right? To use them to help?"

"It's an obligation we can never fulfill. We can't involve the knights in this. We can't be weighed down by responsibilities other than that damn stone, and no one's ever thought it right to put lives in danger when it's not needed. This task is for the Guardian and Protector only. The stone is all that matters. Over wife and children. That stone will become your life, and that of your brother's. There's no choice. Once you see it, you'll understand." Tedris shook his head and frowned at Salvarias. "I don't know how the boy got the mark. It enabled Perek to infect your brother with a portion of his power. When I catch my cousin, I'll make him give it all to Salvarias. I'll share my power with you, and we'll help your brother through this."

"I already have my power. I've been helping him for months."

Tedris's mouth fell open. "How? How did you obtain it?"

Wilhelm shrugged. It was obvious now what the shadowfires had infected Wilhelm with when he had battled the troll in the barbarians' arena. Clearly the shadowfires had created his brother in hopes of owning one of the Guardians, but why they would help Wilhelm, he wasn't sure. Salvarias's life must be worth more to them than withholding Wilhelm's power.

"Who's the boy's father?" Tedris asked, waving a hand at Salvarias. "What's possessed him? His eyes ..." Tedris shuddered. "I don't understand. Perek never had a child. How did he get the mark?"

"I don't trust you," Wilhelm said. "Salv doesn't know. And he can never find out. It's why I asked you to claim him as your own."

"I already told him he wasn't my son."

"Lunara said he was half out of it. He probably didn't hear you."

Tedris nodded. "I see. You're sure ignorance is best for him?"

"No. I have no idea what's best for him, but knowing what—who—created him isn't important."

Another long silence stretched before Tedris spoke in a voice thick with tears. "I'm sorry, son. I hope one day you can forgive me for leaving you and your mother. I never wanted to. I swear I would have stayed with her till the end." He looked down at his hands. "I'm happy she found someone who made her smile. Tobin seemed like a good man."

Wilhelm studied Tedris a moment before speaking. "Tobin was an amazing man and taught me about honor and fighting. He made Mother happy, and he loved Salv and me like we were his own."

Tedris nodded slightly, gaze still focused on his hands. "Then I'm in his debt when I pass to the realm of the dead."

Wilhelm scratched at his overgrown beard. He could hear his brother's argument not to judge Tedris, to look upon the situation objectively, to hear what was unsaid. Wilhelm remembered Hyde had said Tedris wanted to stay in Falar after meeting Ashra. Would Wilhelm leave Varila when Salv had the stone? It was easy to say no now. Varila was strong and she would fight by his side. But what if they had children? Would he subject his son or daughter to a life of running? To the Hunters? Sighing, he shook head. "I'm not mad at you. You thought you had to leave Mother and me to keep us safe. You were just protecting us."

"I was a fool of a young man. I shouldn't have taken advantage of Ashra's youth. But I did. And I won't apologize for it. I got an amazing son out of it. And I did love her by the night's end. I truly did."

"Thank you for telling me, Tedris."

There was a light tap on the door before Okulu entered leading an old man dressed in a tailored tunic and trews. "This is Yunfa," Okulu said.

The man smiled, showing missing teeth and adding several rows of wrinkles, and his thick, billowy beard bobbed up and down when he said, "I hear someone's sick?"

Wilhelm stood and motioned to his brother. "You can't touch him."

Yunfa's brow crinkled but he didn't protest. He hobbled over to the bed and leaned forward, looking intently at Salvarias's face. "Fever. Very high."

"He was taking a mixture of yulku, dresnn, and ginger oil to fight a poison," Wilhelm said.

"Ah, I see." Yunfa rolled his shoulders. "I think I know just the remedy!" His hands shook when he passed Wilhelm a vial of a bright-green liquid. "This will help with the fever and any poison running in his veins."

"Shouldn't you give him the same mixture he originally took?" Wilhelm asked, eyeing the bottle.

"That potion won't help with the fever." Yunfa licked his lips and his gaze darted over to Okulu then back to Wilhelm. "I'm sure Master Hunbred has vouched for my talents."

"Yunfa took care of me when I was little," Okulu said. "He's the town's favorite and only healer. Any others that have tried to set up shop here went out of business. I trust him."

Wilhelm pried open his brother's jaw and dumped the contents in his mouth. Salvarias coughed and swallowed.

"Good, good," Yunfa said. "I'll return in the morning with another potion. In the meantime, keep him covered, the fire going, and the window closed."

"Thank you," Wilhelm said.

Yunfa bowed, patted Okulu's shoulder, and left.

"Need anything?" Okulu asked. "Food?"

Wilhelm wasn't sure he could eat. His stomach was a knot of worry. He shook his head.

"I'll leave you then," Okulu said. He smiled his roguish grin at Tedris, and left the room.

A strong hand rested on Wilhelm's shoulder. "Your brother's a fighter, son. He'll pull through this. I wish I could stay, but I don't want to lose Perek's trail. Remember the rules. Salvarias needs the full power from my cousin in order to guard the stone properly, but more importantly, remember I must be there to help you. He can't gain the power without both of us to help him."

"What will happen to Salv when Perek transfers the rest of his power?"

"The whole thing is a test. It's different with every Guardian and Protector. For the Protectors, its relatively painless. Nothing but a week of switching off with my father to help Perek fight the ... *evil* you called it? Perek on the other hand." Tedris shook his head. "Gods only know what he had to endure. I can tell you it was horrible enough. He screamed unless my father or I was helping him. But with two Protectors, there were only breaths when we would switch that he was left to fight on his own. Anyway, once Perek adapted to the little bits of whatever his father gave him, he needed me and my father less. By the end of two weeks, the transition was complete. It's not always so. My father told me his great-great grandfather had a different experience. Apparently, his Guardian couldn't handle the power. He went mad. Turned into a raving lunatic. Tried to kill everyone. They had to kill him. Their fathers went out and fathered new sons, a new Guardian and Protector. They barely lived to pass along the power again."

"Salv is strong. He'll manage it."

Tedris smiled. "If he has us both. It's imperative we're all there together in the icelands, nice and safe, and we do this the right way. The power in that place helps the Guardian because they don't have to manage the Hunters and the stone's power at the same time. On top of everything, the jasner people have remedies that help ease the Guardian's pain and keep his mind strong. Without them, I don't think the new Guardians and Protectors would ever be successful.

"Perek might try to trick Salvarias into taking the stone," Tedris continued. "You need to make sure your brother doesn't. It'll call to him, and he might not be able to resist on his own." Tedris rubbed his unshaven cheek. "I hate to be so forward, son, but you and your brother need to produce an heir. I'm not sure the implications if you don't, but I'm sure you do based on your brother's birth."

Wilhelm grunted in neither agreement nor disagreement.

Tedris motioned to Wilhelm's armor and grinned. "By the way, nice armor. I might be jealous."

"You should be." Wilhelm grinned back, looking over Tedris's armor that Durak had forged. "Durak's gotten better in his old age."

Tedris laughed warmly. "I miss hearing his curses."

"Maybe sometime I could fill you in on the ones I've learned," Wilhelm said.

"I would love nothing more," Tedris said, eyes welling tears.

Wilhelm embraced his father. "Good luck and be careful."

"You too, son," Tedris said, his return embrace painfully tight. "I'm so proud of the man you've become." He cleared his throat, clapped Wilhelm on the back, and stepped away quickly. At the door, he glanced back, regret and indecision on his face, a silent plea in his eyes.

Wilhelm almost obliged and asked him to stay, to talk until all hours of the night, to tell Wilhelm all there was to know of his birth father, but Salvarias needed Perek, and therefore that was Wilhelm's priority. He merely smiled and said, "Soon."

Tedris nodded and left.

Wilhelm sank into his chair and buried his hands in his face. Nothing was solid around him. He floated in a world of mystery and danger, and his baby brother was at the heart of it.

The scent of leather and strawberries made him raise his gaze as Varila straddled him. Soft thighs slid under his hands and her warm breath washed over his lips before she kissed him. He gathered her close, relishing in her taste. When her mouth left his, she said, "I'm sorry. To see him—"

Wilhelm drowned his pain in another kiss.

Chapter 26

Autumn 1018 a.r.

Wilhelm jerked awake to a soft knock on Salvarias's door. Rubbing sleep from his eyes, Wilhelm muttered his invitation to enter.

Yunfa strolled in, two vials held in his gnarled hands. "Morning! How's our patient?"

Wilhelm rose from his chair stiff and sweating. The room was suffocatingly hot and the wood chair wasn't the most comfortable bed.

Salvarias's complexion had darkened and sweat soaked his pillow.

"Ah," Yunfa said, joining Wilhelm's side. "He's improving."

"You call that an improvement?" Wilhelm growled.

"The fever will burn away infection. The longer it stays, the longer it has to help your brother fight."

"But the infection is worse. Look at him! And you said we needed to fight the fever."

"Eyes deceive," Yunfa said, patting Wilhelm's arm. He held out the vials. "Give these to him. We'll bring the fever down slowly. Too fast and we'll harm him."

Wilhelm recognized the bright-green mixture from the day before. The next one was murky blue. He administered both to Salvarias, holding a hand over his brother's nose and mouth to get him to swallow. His brother didn't cough or stir and seemed to be a rock that occasionally breathed.

"I'll be back in the evening," Yunfa said. "I've got another concoction brewing. It'll be stronger." The old man stopped at the door. "Who is the boy?"

Wilhelm sank into his chair. "My little brother and the man who saved your city."

Yunfa slowly nodded and then quietly left.

A trail of visitors drifted in and out of Salvarias's room. Every one of them commented on his worsening state, asked Wilhelm about his father, and brought him food. He barely ate anything and merely grunted to convey his disinterest in conversation. Only Varila could pry his gaze from Salvarias, but her own worry kept her from giving comforts. Lunara had not improved.

By evening, Okulu had a new cushy chair brought in to replace the one Wilhelm had slept in the night before and added herbs to rid the room of a smell Wilhelm hadn't noticed until Okulu mentioned it. It was death, musty and stale, sour and rotted.

When Yunfa entered the room that evening, he carried three vials. Two appeared to be the same mixtures as before, but the third was a putrid orange.

"These aren't working," Wilhelm growled.

"I see, I see," Yunfa said, handing the vials to Wilhelm. "The third is more potent. It will help. I'll be back in the morning." With that, the old man left.

Wilhelm gently lifted Salvarias's head, pried apart his clenched jaw, and dumped the contents of the three vials down his throat. His brother choked on them a few times before he managed to swallow. The heat steaming off Salvarias would surely kill him, and the bed beneath his brother was soaked.

Cursing, Wilhelm removed a few blankets, alarmed to feel even the top layer damp. "Okulu!" he called.

The merc entered the room. "What is it?"

"I need fresh blankets."

"It's not right. He'll sweat himself out. We need to get water down him. And some broth."

Wilhelm nodded his agreement.

He wasn't sure how much time passed before Okulu returned with fresh bedding, water, and a bowl of broth. Wilhelm lifted his brother's limp body from the bed while a few servants brought in a fresh feather mattress and bedding.

Once all had been changed out and his brother settled, Wilhelm tried every trick to get Salvarias to drink or eat. It resulted in water and broth staining the sheets and Salvarias choking on whatever Wilhelm offered. After a few tries, he gave up and ordered everyone to leave. Alone, he took his brother's slender hand in his own and wept.

When Yunfa arrived the next morning, Wilhelm's patience had seen its end. The instant the old man entered, Wilhelm grabbed him by his tunic and raised the man to eye level.

"This isn't working," he growled. "He's getting worse."

"Y-y-yes, I know," Yunfa stammered. "I've got something that will work. I swear."

Wilhelm looked at the four vials in the man's hands. He snatched them up, dropped Yunfa unceremoniously, and gave his brother the new remedies.

"I'll b-b-be back in the evening," Yunfa said and scurried from the room.

The day progressed the same and Yunfa's evening potions were new colors and had a potent acidic stench. After the healer had left with a promise to return in the morning, Wilhelm rose from his chair, fighting to stay awake. He paced the room slowly, pausing to look out the window at torches dotting the woods where the creature had fallen. Okulu had told him that outside the castle, candles lined the streets and Lynta's denizens were praying Zerana's grace would heal Salvarias. Wilhelm bitterly wondered if they would feel the same if they saw his brother's eyes or would they recoil like everyone else? Would they spit on him when they saw his mage robes?

"You need to sleep." Wilhelm glanced over his shoulder to see Humar standing in the doorway. "Haven't seen you do so since the first night."

"He's worse. I need to be awake in case something happens." Wilhelm looked back out the window. "If he doesn't get better tonight, Yunfa and I are going to have words."

Instead of a rebuke as Wilhelm had suspected, Humar said, "I agree. Lunara ..."

Wilhelm's throat tightened. "What is it?"

"Her skin has turned the same color as Salvarias. Something's not right." A strong hand rested on Wilhelm's shoulder. "I've talked with Okulu. There's no one else around that can help us." Humar tugged Wilhelm toward the chair. "Sleep. I'll look after your brother."

Wilhelm sank into the plush cushions and was asleep before he remembered settling back.

A ray of morning light falling across his face and a soft knock woke him.

Humar was already crossing the room and opened the door. Yunfa shuffled inside, carrying one vial of black liquid.

Wilhelm glared at the old man. "Look at him! He's worse. He's not improving at all."

Yunfa nodded. "I've found something, something sure to help."

Wilhelm snatched the vial and administered it. "You better hope it does. If not, I'll make you suffer ten times more than he is."

Yunfa bowed, licked his lips, and glanced at Salvarias. "I'm sorry. Truly." He gathered his cloak about him and left the room.

Once again, Humar offered to watch over Salvarias, and Wilhelm succumbed to restless sleep, waking to the slightest noise, swimming in half-awake nightmares.

A violent eruption of rustling sheets and Humar's cry of Wilhelm's name jerked him awake. Salvarias had succumbed to seizures.

Wilhelm leapt from his chair. "Okulu!" He yanked off his belt and shoved it between his brother's clenched teeth. The merc burst into the room. "Get the healer!"

"Gods," Okulu breathed.

Before Wilhelm's eyes, Salvarias's skin darkened to the color of coal.

"Now!" Humar barked.

Okulu bolted from the room.

Wilhelm knelt by his brother. "I'm here, Salv. I'm right here."

It seemed an eternity he sat by while his brother contorted in pain, falling from seizures to convulsions and then back again, only to repeat. The stench of piss mingled with the stale rancor of sickness and Salvarias's groans of pain were like the slice of a knife across Wilhelm's heart.

When finally it ceased, Salvarias fell back to the bed, twitching occasionally, his muscles spasming.

Okulu flung open the door, face lit with fury. "Yunfa's gone! He left right after he gave Salvarias the potion."

Wilhelm was on Okulu before he knew what he was doing. The merc's tunic was balled in his fists, their faces so close Wilhelm's spittle sprayed Okulu's cheeks when he said, "Find the bastard and bring him to me!"

He flung Okulu toward the door and whirled around to Humar. "Do something!"

"We've done all we can." Humar shook his head. "I'm out of options."

A wild hope seized Wilhelm, and he glanced around the room. "Where's Adok?"

"In all the chaos, they put him in the stables. Why?"

"Watch Salv," Wilhelm growled. He marched from the room and snagged hold of the first servant he came across. "Take me to the stables."

The man took off down the hall, moving faster as Wilhelm stepped on his heels. Outside, the brisk autumn air was a shock. His breath billowed out and he mused steam was rising off his sweating body.

The stables were a short walk away and after gaining instructions from a stable boy, Wilhelm found the pen holding Adok. The wolf looked less than happy, pacing the small enclosure, teeth flashing in the sunlight, food untouched.

Wilhelm opened the cage, stepped inside, and squatted to be eye level with the wolf. "He's dying. Can you help?"

Adok shook his head, ears flattened.

"Can you find someone who can?"

Adok cocked his head to one side, eyes distant for a breath, then the wolf nodded. Wilhelm stepped aside. "Go."

Adok bolted from the pen, startling the horses and a stable boy. Screams followed the wolf like a wave in the ocean.

It was evening by the time Okulu burst into Salvarias's room, dusty and travel worn, holding the tailored collar of Yunfa's tunic in his fist.

"Bastard was fleeing," Okulu said.

Wilhelm jumped up from his chair, grabbed Yunfa, and tossed him across the room. The old man slid over a table, breaking a vase, and fell heavily to the ground. Wilhelm pounced on him and raised his fist. "What did you do to my brother?" he roared.

"They made me!" Yunfa squealed.

"Who?"

"Three mages. They gave me the potions and told me to give them to the boy."

Wilhelm hauled the old man to his feet and shoved him against the wall. "What else?"

Yunfa's gaze jerked to Okulu, apology flowing from his old eyes. "The potions were poisons, meant to kill him slowly so you couldn't follow. They said if I didn't do it, they would kill my daughter and me. I had to, Okulu. I had to!"

"Counter it!" Wilhelm ordered. "Heal him now or so help me, I'll kill your daughter myself!"

"I can't!" Yunfa wailed. "I don't know what's in the potion. If I give him the wrong herb, he'll surely die. I swear it. There's nothing I can do."

Wilhelm threw the man across the room. He crumpled in a heap at Okulu's feet.

"You bastard!" Okulu roared and kicked the old man in the ribs. "I trusted you!"

Olivit rushed into the room and held his son back. "Easy. He's a fool, but don't kill him. Make him figure it out."

Wilhelm knew the old man wouldn't discover a remedy in time. His sole hope rested in Adok. "Get out. All of you."

Okulu yanked Yunfa to his feet and shoved him out. "I'm sorry, Wilhelm. I've—"

"Get. Out."

Humar ushered the others from the room and closed the door. Wilhelm sank beside his brother's bed and lifted Salvarias's limp hand into his own. "I'm sorry, Salv. I'm so sorry."

Shouts outside Salvarias's room startled Wilhelm from his brooding. He bolted across the room, listening to people saying "You!" and "Where have you been?" and "Stay away from the boy!"

Flinging open the door, Wilhelm peered into the hall. Adok padded toward the room, Vuddruk on his heels. Any distrust Wilhelm had clung to since first meeting the old mage vanished. Time and again Vuddruk had healed Salvarias, time and again the old man had been there when Wilhelm needed him most.

He grabbed Vuddruk's arm and pulled him into the room. "You have to help me!"

"Easy, boy. Tell me what—" Vuddruk sucked in a breath when he saw Salvarias. "By Father, what happened to the boy?"

A horrible yelp left Adok as the wolf rushed to Salvarias's side.

Wilhelm filled the old man in quickly on the bloodleder attack, the battle with the flying creature, and Yunfa's poisons.

"For the love of Zerana," Vuddruk snapped. "Get some fresh air in this room. Take half those blankets off the boy. Cool cloth on the forehead." He whirled around to Humar. "Prepare a bath, not hot, not cold."

"We're not trusting you," Humar said, hand resting on the hilt of his sword. "You left us—"

"Do it!" Wilhelm ordered.

Okulu began barking orders.

"You can help him, right?" Wilhelm asked.

"That depends on the boy," Vuddruk muttered. "Your brother has stopped fighting."

Wilhelm followed Okulu to the bath, stripped off his brother's clothes, and eased him into the waters.

"How long ago did the wounds from the bloodleders cease oozing?" Vuddruk asked.

"After the first dose of whatever that old man gave him," Wilhelm muttered.

"There's nothing you can do for him, Wilhelm," Vuddruk said. "You need to rest and to be ready if he awakes. He might be subjected to an attack, and he'll need your strength. I fear most of it."

Wilhelm slowly turned his head to the old mage, blood simmering up to a boil. "Who in Oblivion are you?"

Vuddruk smiled, but it didn't reach his eyes. "Ask me and I'll walk right out of here and be on my way. I'm helping you, boy, because I hold on to a thread of hope. But it isn't strong enough for me to trust you or to betray Balance. Keep your friends away from me. Keep your questions to yourself, and we'll get your brother through this."

Wilhelm swallowed his rage, allowing his fear and helplessness to make his decision. He nodded.

Vuddruk smiled, and this time his green eyes responded in turn. "Get me the vials from the herb owner, whatever they gave him. And pull in some beds. We'll be in this room for days. The girl? Lunara?"

Wilhelm had to battle back his flood of questions. "She's bad. Fever and her skin is darkening."

Vuddruk nodded. "Go request beds and food."

Wilhelm stepped outside to find Humar, Okulu, and Durak waiting in the hall.

"We don't have a choice," he told the men. "He's our only chance to save Salv."

"Me don't trust him around the boy," Durak muttered.

"I agree," Humar said.

"I'm with Wilhelm," Okulu chimed. "We're out of options. Vuddruk has saved Salvarias before. He would have killed us a long time ago if he desired to do so."

"In case ye be forgetting," Durak growled. "The giant worm nearly ate us!"

"Nearly," Okulu said, grinning.

"The decision is mine," Wilhelm stated, standing to his full height. "We trust him." He glared at the others, daring them to challenge him.

No one did.

By the time Wilhelm pulled Salvarias from the water, it was hot and red with his brother's blood. The wounds covering Salvarias had opened.

"Don't bother dressing them," Vuddruk said. "We'll bathe him soon and they'll just open up again."

Okulu entered the washroom turned to partial bedroom and dumped a pile of vials in front of Vuddruk. "This is all he had."

Vuddruk picked up the one with black residue and sniffed it. He wrinkled his nose and when he spoke, Wilhelm barely heard him. "The poor boy."

"What is it?" Wilhelm asked.

Vuddruk looked up over the rim of the vial. "I won't lie. It's bad, but I'll come up with something." Vuddruk rose from his seat and squatted beside Salvarias. He rested his hand on Salvarias's forehead and said, "Peace, brother. Peace."

Salvarias's clenched jaw relaxed and he sobbed softly, tears spilling from his closed eyes.

Vuddruk smoothed Salvarias's hair and smiled kindly at him. "I'm sorry."

When he pulled his hand away, Salvarias moaned and his teeth snapped together, his body tensing.

"W-w-wait," Wilhelm stammered. "Help him!"

Vuddruk plopped down in his chair, looking utterly spent, face drawn, dark rings under his eyes that had not been there a breath before. "I can't do anymore today. Perhaps tomorrow." He turned to Okulu and spouted off a list of herbs. After Okulu left, the old mage motioned to a cot. "Sleep, boy. I'll wake you if needed."

Over the next few hours, Wilhelm dozed in between putting Salvarias in and out of fresh baths. It was a blur of time, and Wilhelm wasn't sure how much had passed until a beam of morning sunlight lit the room.

He rose wearily from his cot, thinking it would have been better to stay awake. A stolen hour here and there had made his head throb and deadened his limbs. Thought was sluggish and his mouth seemed stuffed with cotton.

Vuddruk knelt by Salvarias, resting a hand on his forehead, whispering over and over, "Peace, brother. Peace."

Salvarias's jaw was relaxed and tears again fell from his closed eyes. His breathing was ragged and wet sounding.

"What are you doing?" Wilhelm asked.

Vuddruk removed his hand, grimacing along with Salvarias who tensed up immediately. "Easing his pain."

"Thank you," Wilhelm said. "Thank you."

"Here," Vuddruk said. "Give this to your brother, and then it's time for another bath."

Wilhelm gently lifted his brother's head, forced his mouth open, and dumped the potion down his throat. Salvarias choked it down as Wilhelm lowered him into the bath.

"He can't take much more of this fever," Wilhelm muttered.

"True. The potion will help lower the fever and start to push out the poison from the bloodleders and Yunfa."

The day passed with more baths and more potions. The sun had been down hours when Varila burst into the room, a wide smile on her face.

"Lunara! Her fever dropped and her skin is lightening."

Wilhelm grinned at Vuddruk. "He'll be all right now, won't he?"

"Show me his wounds."

Wilhelm pulled back the blankets to reveal the bites from the bloodleders leaking black, mucousy liquid. He looked expectantly at Vuddruk.

The old man sank into his chair, running a shaking hand over his face. "It's a start, boy. We've got the poison leaving which will bring down the fever."

"Wonderful!" Wilhelm exclaimed.

Vuddruk held up a pacifying hand. "He's been in the fever's grip too long. He could be lost to it."

"What does that mean?"

"It means he might never wake up. It means if he does, he could have turned simple, mind half lost."

"Do something," Wilhelm breathed. "Help him."

"I've done all I can. The poisons, the bloodleders, pushing his magic ... he did too much. I'm sorry, boy."

"There's still a chance," Varila said, her voice hard. "There's a chance he'll pull through."

Vuddruk smiled, but it wasn't reassuring. "Of course, child. Hope is immortal."

Chapter 27

Autumn 1018 a.r.

Moonbeams and flickering light from a single candle lit the pages of the book Wilhelm read. He'd found it in his brother's pack. The edges were worn and the crease in the leather spine made the pages open to the inscription Tobin had written so long ago.

"Here," Vuddruk said, handing Wilhelm another potion. "It's time for the worst of it. We'll know the state of your brother by morning."

Wilhelm glanced at his brother tossing restlessly. His skin had lightened to an unnatural ash, which was a considerable improvement. The fever had reduced, though spasms still attacked Salvarias often.

Wilhelm administered the potion as he spoke. "What will this do?"

"It'll force your brother awake. The worst of the fever's broken, but he needs to eat if he's to get better." Vuddruk sank into a chair. "I've never been so exhausted."

Wilhelm didn't doubt it. The mage hadn't slept since he arrived. "Thank you," Wilhelm said. "For everything you're doing for him."

Vuddruk shrugged. "It goes against my better judgment."

Adok growled, flashing his teeth at the mage.

"Oh shut it," Vuddruk snapped at the wolf. "I'm entitled to my opinion. I've helped when you've asked. It doesn't mean I have to like it."

Looking at Adok, Wilhelm asked, "Does Salv know who you truly are? That you're something besides a wolf?"

Adok shook his head, scowling at Vuddruk.

"It's important he doesn't find out," Vuddruk said. "Balance is cruel, and already your brother has received more help than he should." Vuddruk curled his lip at Adok. "And she will collect, my friend. I will not give her further cause to be cruel to the boy."

Wilhelm swallowed his questions and closed his eyes. All that mattered was Salvarias's health. Wilhelm had no doubts Vuddruk would walk right out the door if asked questions.

"Must be eating you alive," Vuddruk murmured.

Wilhelm met the old man's gaze. "It is."

"Thank you, for what it's worth."

Wilhelm shrugged. "I don't have a choice. But one day, I'll get answers from you."

Vuddruk leaned his head back and closed his eyes. "The world is a game, boy. A game played by a sadistic creator. He sets the rules. He chooses His play pieces to torment, and then sits back and laughs. Questions and answers are not ours to give. They are His."

Wilhelm frowned, not understanding. "If He's so horrible, kill Him. Break the rules."

"Bah!" Vuddruk curled his lip. "You cannot kill creation. And if you break the rules, the consequences are unimaginable. You have to manipulate the rules, find loopholes. As I said, it's a game."

"And Salvarias is part of it?" Wilhelm wanted to throw up.

"The entire world is part of it. It became part of it when Nevlar created it. Nothing is safe. Nothing is hidden from Him."

Wilhelm clenched his fists. "Well my brother isn't going to play this game. I'm not going to play it."

"You say so as if you have a choice, boy. None of us do. You'll play it out of necessity. You'll play it because if you don't, the entire world will pay for your selfishness."

"If Salvarias is just a tool, why not tell him what his part is? Why not help him?"

Vuddruk sighed. "Rules. So many rules. And as I said, I'm not sure I trust your brother. He's been manipulated, turned and twisted, his mind toyed with. I shudder to think what it's like to be him."

Wilhelm's anger nearly burst free. Clenching his teeth, he snarled, "Then help me. Tell me and I can help him."

"No, I—"

Salvarias hitched violently and inky black liquid splattered on his lips.

"Turn him over!" Vuddruk barked.

Wilhelm shoved his brother on his side and what looked like oil spilt from Salvarias's lips. His brother choked up more, groaning and curling up.

"Salvarias!" Vuddruk snapped. "Come on, boy. Look at me!"

Salvarias's eyes fluttered opened. He looked first at the mage, and then focused on Wilhelm.

"Broth—" Salvarias's eyes snapped shut and he gave a whimper of pain.

"Help him!" Wilhelm pleaded.

"I can't now," Vuddruk said, his voice overflowing with joy. "That's a remarkable young man."

Salvarias retched again, spewing up black liquid. It reeked of decay and death.

Wilhelm bolted up and glared at Vuddruk. "Do something!"

"Don't you see, boy. I can't." He held up his hands, his smile broadening. "His completely healthy mind can't handle my touch."

It took a breath for it to sink in. "He's all right?"

Vuddruk laughed and clapped his hands, seeming unconcerned by another violent upheaval by Salvarias. "That boy has a fight in him, that's for certain."

Wilhelm's own smile spread as he sank to his cot beside his brother's and rested a hand on Salvarias's trembling shoulder. "I'm here, Salv. You're going to be all right."

Salvarias could not help the groan leaving his throat as he stirred awake. His entire body ached, and he would have given anything to sleep on a cloud instead of the feather mattress that might as well have been a rock with how tender his body felt. His brain was locked in a fierce battle to stay within his skull, and his stomach waged a vicious escape attempt. Salvarias only kept it under control because he was tired of throwing up and was not sure his aching body could endure the upheaval.

Even as exhausted as he was, he was dreadfully tired of sleeping. He wondered how long he had stayed locked in agony, his world nothing but pain.

With entirely too much concentration, Salvarias managed to open his eyes. Wilhelm slept in a cot beside his own.

"He's fine, boy."

Another groan left him as he moved his head to see Vuddruk. The mage stood over him, smiling kindly.

"You gave us quite a scare," Vuddruk said.

Indeed, Salvarias had been terrified himself. The pain had nearly been too much. He had almost succumbed to it, almost let it rip apart his mind so he would no longer be forced to endure it, but then came relief, a brief escape from the pain. It had lasted only a few breaths, but it gave him enough respite to fight on. Now he knew who had gifted him such bliss.

"Thank you," he rasped.

Vuddruk winked. "My pleasure. Besides, if I didn't, I have no doubts your brother would have introduced me to Oblivion."

"An unpleasant realm," Salvarias said. "I am happy to have spared you."

Vuddruk chuckled. "Thirsty?"

"Extremely." Using what strength he had, Salvarias managed to get himself sitting up, leaning on the wall for support. A gander at the room revealed Humar propped against the opposite wall of what appeared to be a washroom despite the two cots Salvarias and Wilhelm occupied. Adok jumped on his cot and licked his hand before nestling down by Salvarias's feet. The wolf's lecture started.

"Good to see you up," Humar said.

The knight looked as if he had not slept for weeks. Dark rings framed his azure eyes and his shoulders sagged forward. He had even given up his armor and wore a simple dark-green tunic and tan trews. It was a sight Salvarias was unaccustomed to seeing.

"Thank you, my friend," Salvarias said. "I am sorry."

Humar grinned. "For what, I'll never understand. You've saved the city, boy."

Salvarias accepted a glass of water from Vuddruk and drank it entirely.

"The knight refused to leave your side after your brother passed out," Vuddruk said. "I don't think he trusts me."

"As he should not," Salvarias said.

Vuddruk's smile faded. "I guess he shouldn't." The mage's gaze steadied on Salvarias, and he did not shy from the inspection. He returned it with one of his own. Eventually Vuddruk smiled. "You're a curious young man. Full of questions. A mind capable of solving them all."

Salvarias smirked. "Yet I have no answers."

"You're asking the wrong questions, boy."

"And what questions should I be asking?"

Vuddruk pursed his lips and narrowed his eyes. "And a memory to boot, eh?"

It was Salvarias's turn to narrow his eyes. "How would you know such a thing?"

"We have a mutual friend. He's been trying to get me to aid you, but I don't trust you."

"And why is that?"

"Fear, boy. You're ruled by it, and until you take ownership of your life and stop being a slave to it, I'll keep my knowledge to myself."

"Perhaps knowledge could help me overcome my fears," Salvarias whispered tightly.

"It might, or it might not. I believe it will drive you over the edge. Sorry, brother, but I'm not willing to take the risk."

"We are not brothers."

Infuriatingly, Vuddruk's smile indicated that he had all of Salvarias's answers. "I'll say it again. You've been asking the wrong questions, brother. Instead of looking outside, perhaps you should study what's inside."

"I have seen what lurks within," Salvarias hissed softly. "I have no desire to dwell on that darkness."

"Ah," Vuddruk said, holding up a finger and grinning. "One cannot have darkness without light, and light cannot be present without darkness." The mage winked and turned to Humar. "It's time I be on my way. You need to keep a better eye on the boy. I'll not be following your path anymore. I've got a new direction."

"So you were following us," Humar said, voice calm as ever.

"Perhaps it was you who was following me. Perhaps we were on the same path. Perhaps there was only one path. Regardless, now there are two." Vuddruk smiled slyly. "The world is a mystery, is it not, friend."

Humar opened the door. "Only if people make it so. Thank you for your help."

"Successful travels." Vuddruk smiled at Salvarias before leaving the room.

"That old man is a curse," Humar muttered.

"Or a gift," Salvarias said, leaning his head back and closing his eyes.

He must have dozed because when he opened his eyes, his friends and even Neithelas filled the room. Wilhelm was up, in the center of the whispered commotion, Varila wrapped in his arms, a grin taking up half his face.

Okulu broke from the cluster and sat on the cot beside Salvarias, offering a small platter of fruits and cheeses. "About time you woke up and joined the land of the living."

"I am sorry my near death inconvenienced you," Salvarias said dryly. "Are we still in Lynta?"

Okulu took a swig from his flask. "Yes. It's been a few days."

Salvarias surveyed the room, smiling inwardly when his gaze met his brother's. The washroom was too large to be that of an inn, and the cots entirely too comfortable to be boarded in meager accommodations. The small window let in the morning sunlight but only sky was visible.

"We're at my parents' estate," Okulu explained. "I'm really sorry."

Salvarias cocked his head. "For what?"

"The healer here, a man I've known since childhood, poisoned you." Okulu smiled apologetically. "The three mages traveling with whomever we're after threatened his daughter."

Salvarias picked through the food and nibbled on a few of his favorites. "Then he had no choice. Is he all right? Did my brother ..."

Okulu grinned. "Oddly, Wilhelm didn't kill him. I think he was a little distracted, what with you the color of Zeeas and all."

"I am thankful and would hope the healer is not punished."

Okulu shrugged. "My father is dealing with him."

"I would like to meet your parents and offer my gratitude."

"Now?"

Salvarias nodded, grimacing as he sat straighter. "I am anxious to move."

"I don't think you should," Okulu said, the corners of his mouth turned down. "No offense, but you look like you spent a week as Veedran's play toy."

"I feel you might be right. However, I am beyond stiff."

"Stubborn ass," Okulu muttered.

"Fake drunk," Salvarias murmured.

Okulu chuckled and hopped up, motioning to Wilhelm. "Your brother wants to commit suicide and take a stroll of the estate."

Salvarias groaned at Okulu. "I am fine, brother."

Wilhelm offered his arm and, after checking under the covers to ensure Salvarias was dressed, he used it help pull himself out of bed. When he stood straight, bones creaked and his bad leg cramped painfully. Though his entire body ached to be touched, he leaned heavily on his brother. As usual, Wilhelm supported him as if he weighed nothing. He took advantage and practically hung on his brother's arm.

"Lady Lunara?" Salvarias asked.

She stepped from behind Varila. The red dress she wore accentuated her rose red lips and dark rings under her tired eyes. Her cheeks were sunken and her color paler than normal, but otherwise she looked healthy. She smiled and her light presence in his mind beamed with warmth.

"Are you well, my lady?" he asked.

Lunara nodded. "Fine."

"My parents are probably in the library," Okulu said.

"How long is the walk?" Wilhelm asked, passing Salvarias his staff.

"Not terribly far."

As they made their way through the estate, Salvarias studied the hall and the numerous doors he and his friends passed, still clinging to Wilhelm's arm to remain upright, fighting nausea and a swimming head.

The brown stone walls were polished and well cared for, and his glimpses of rooms revealed ornately carved furniture draped in rich fabrics. On the spiral staircase, he paused to glance out the window. It was as he suspected; they were in the castle resting atop the hill.

Okulu looked away quickly when Salvarias met his gaze.

They continued down another long hallway flanked by expansive rooms set for entertaining or rooms with large meeting tables.

By the time they reached the end of the hall, Salvarias walked more or less on his own, only occasionally needing Wilhelm's support when a wave of dizziness washed over him.

They stopped at a set of double doors inlaid with iron and polished so smooth Salvarias could see his reflection. Indeed, he looked like a walking corpse.

When Okulu flung open the doors, Salvarias gasped and swayed at the sight. Rows upon rows of books climbed the walls, and the smell of leather and parchment wafted over him, gifting his mind serenity and a sense of home. His feet itched to rush to the nearest shelf, and his mind screamed at him to read, read them all!

Lunara let out a little squeal behind him and clapped her hands together. "It's wonderful, Okulu!"

The merc frowned at them and arched an eyebrow. "If you say so. Honestly, I think you two might have a small—no, make that a large—problem."

"Leave him alone," Wilhelm said.

Inside was even more wonderful. Beyond a set of open glass doors was an expansive garden. Birds chirped outside, and two massive fireplaces flanking the room quickly consumed the chilling breeze. Chairs and couches basked in the heat of the fires and were artfully placed for the best views of the gardens. He wished Lady Talura could see such a sight.

The thought startled him and he nearly tripped on a soft rug, but Wilhelm caught him.

"You all right, Salv?"

"Fine, brother. It is beautiful."

Wilhelm chuckled and ruffled Salvarias's hair. "It is."

"My dear boy!" a voice boomed. A short, round man rose from a couch, a welcoming smile plumping his rosy cheeks. "It's good to see you up." He stopped short of Salvarias and bowed. "I offer my thanks for saving our city."

Salvarias bowed, wincing when sharp pains shot up his back. "I fear your city was in danger because of me, my lord."

"Nonsense," the man said. "Kuly told me about the man that called the beast to us."

"Kuly?"

"My boy!" The man grinned at Okulu. "You've brought him home. I'm his father, Olivit, and this is my wife, Thilia."

The winsire woman was stunning and it was clear which parent Okulu took after. "My lady," Salvarias greeted, once again bowing.

"You like our library?" she asked, motioning to the books.

"Indeed, my lady. I have a love of the written word."

"Then it is yours during your stay," she said.

"You are too kind."

She winked and turned to the rest of the group. "Now he's awake, I'm sure you all are looking forward to a little break in your vigilance."

"Yes, yes," Olivit said. "Go explore our city. Abril! Abril!" he shouted.

A youth bolted into the room, bowing before fully stopping, which caused him to trip and nearly fall. Neithelas caught the young man's arm and saved him from an embarrassing blunder.

"Abril will show you all the best shops," Olivit said. "He'll give you a tour of the armory if you're interested."

"Armory?" Wilhelm asked.

"Weapons galore," Olivit said, grinning knowingly. "Looks like you could actually lift a few of them." He snapped his fingers. "Abril, give 'em the tour. Buy them whatever interests them. Feed them our best foods in the city. Our baker is known 'round the world!"

Wilhelm's stomach rumbled. "I think I'll stay here with Salv. You all go ahead."

"No," Salvarias said, giving his brother a nudge toward Varila. "I insist, brother."

"I'd like to stay," Lunara said, her eyes fixated on the garden.

Olivit chuckled. "Please, child. Be our guest."

She curtsied and left through the open glass doors.

Wilhelm leaned down and whispered in Salvarias's ear. "What if you're attacked?"

"The evil is well within my control. I promise. I am fine." Salvarias glanced at Varila and tilted his head slightly toward Wilhelm.

She grinned and strolled over, wrapped her arm with Wilhelm's, and said, "You wouldn't want to miss an armory. Olivit's offering you anything you want. After all, you took down half those minotaurs yourself."

"I promise," Salvarias said, giving his brother a gentle shove. "I am fine."

Wilhelm slowly nodded and let Varila lead him from the room. Okulu and his parents were all that remained.

"You look at these books as our daughter did," Olivit said. "She loved study."

"I was not aware Okulu had a sister," Salvarias said.

"She's dead," the merc said tersely.

"It's nice to see the flutter of robes again," Thilia said. "It's been so quiet without our children."

"She was a mage?"

"Yes," Olivit said, his gaze miles away. "Briana was your age and went to visit Hynd and apparently had not been added to the list yet. The damn Association is so negligent here the guards usually never pay any attention to the list. But the guard on duty that day was newly arrived from Dalnar." The old man stopped, blinking aside tears. "He was drunk. Hauled her off her saddle and slit her throat."

"You have my sincerest condolences," Salvarias said. "The Association is detrimental to mages being accepted in Arden. They foster and breed fear, and their practices are old and unintelligent."

Thilia smiled slightly. "Your opinion is shared by this household. We miss her magic. Always was the girl in here studying and practicing."

Olivit waddled over to an old clay pot and ran his hand over the rim. "She used to make flowers grow in this old thing. I moved each one to the garden. Now it's as empty as my home."

Thilia wiped her tears and smiled. "Enough talk. You have brought home our oldest. We have missed him dearly. You are welcome in our home anytime, dear."

"Thank you, my lady," Salvarias said with a bow.

Both bowed in return and left the room.

Okulu turned silently.

"Okulu, I am sorry."

Okulu rested his hand on the door, keeping his back to Salvarias. "I wasn't with her. I found the guard though and I killed him." He took a long swig from his flask.

Salvarias remembered the times they had approached towns and the protective stance the merc had taken.

"It's been good for me, being around magic again," Okulu continued. "I feel it's where I belong. I used to watch her all day in here, reading and making the same damn plant over and over." Okulu chuckled. "I asked her if she could make others and she said yes, but these were her favorite."

"You used to be a knight," Salvarias said.

"I was commander over the Lynta army," Okulu said softly. "After I killed him, I renounced my title but my parents begged me to keep the armor and sword. They don't blame me, but they should. I wear this crap because it reminds me everyday that I left her. I wanted to practice with my men, to wield my sword instead of watching after my baby sister, and I let her go alone."

"You punish yourself for the ignorance of others, my friend. I know none of my words could ever offer you peace, but your sister was privileged to have you for a brother. You did not fail her. You do not deserve the punishment you inflict upon yourself."

Okulu smiled and wiped his eyes with this sleeve. "Hypocrite. I know the mask of self hatred, Salvarias."

"Mask?" Salvarias murmured, turning over the notion in his head. "Hiding behind a mask is often easier than facing the cruel world, is it not?"

"I'd always thought so," Okulu said. "Until the day I stared at you and saw myself. Hiding from everything, terrified to love and lose it at the whim of some idiot. When I saw us for who we really are, I didn't want that anymore. I didn't want to rot away alone." Okulu's gaze met Salvarias's. "You're my friend. The first one I've had in a long time. Do you think it's easy for me to walk up to each city knowing a guard could easily chop off your head? I'd relive it all again. I'd lose what I'd just gained."

"You and I are not the same. You know not what you speak."

Okulu cast a wan smile. "Keep telling yourself that. Have fun with your parchment."

"Have fun with your flask," Salvarias said.

Okulu left and closed the library doors, leaving Salvarias standing alone with Adok. The wolf licked his hand and whined softly.

"Do not side with him," Salvarias scolded gently. "He does not understand."

Deeply inhaling cool, crisp air, Salvarias leaned heavily on his staff and made his way to the gardens. The sheer number of flowers blooming in autumn was shocking. Plants he had only read about were crammed together in wild chaos. Thick foliage intruded on the paths winding their way deeper into the mayhem. It was unorganized beauty, free, untamed, and breathtaking.

A warm hand slipped into his, and he looked down at Lunara smiling up at him. "Is it as you imagined?" she asked.

Salvarias entwined his fingers with hers as she led him farther along the main, graveled path. "It was you who read more of

Windlous than I," Salvarias said. "Even based on what you told me in our dreams, this far surpasses what I could imagine."

"I guess we did it."

"Did what, my lady?"

She grinned. "Remember? We always said we wanted to visit Windlous together. Our dream came true."

Salvarias smiled at the rose bush she stopped in front of. It was as it had been in their dreams: the flowers were massive, startling white, and their sweet fragrance washed over him. Sunlight split the clouds and its warmth seeped into his back.

Lunara inhaled deeply and raised her face to the sky, closing her eyes. "Finally!"

Salvarias studied the rest of the plants, noticing that one with red leaves and pink flowers dominated the space. He wondered if those were the ones Okulu's sister favored.

"Ready to head back?" Lunara asked. Her eyes lit up with excitement. "We have an entire library to explore."

Excitement stirred his blood and evoked a wide grin. "Indeed, my lady."

Salvarias jolted awake to his own soft cry. His nightmare followed him to waking hours and he groaned as the creature's barbed legs ripped from his skin. The glow of two dying fires illuminated a dark room stacked with books, and the cushy couch beneath him did little to ground him in the present. Fear clenched his throat and he whispered, "Brother?"

No rumble came from the darkness, and he frantically looked around for something familiar. His gaze rested on Lunara sleeping on a couch near his own. A book lay in her limp hands. Behind her, Sansis stood, knife gleaming in the faint light, a sick smile twisting his thin lips.

"Easy, boy." The gruff voice came from a shadowed corner.

Scrambling from the couch, Salvarias backed toward Lunara, igniting his magic and calling a spell to mind. Adok licked his hand and he finally heard the wolf telling him everything was all right.

"Easy, lad," Durak said, stepping into the light. "It just be me."

"Where am I?" Salvarias asked, wincing at his soreness and trembling legs beneath him.

"Okulu's home. Don't ye remember?"

Sinking to the nearest chair as memories rushed back to him, he said, "Forgive me."

"Nothing to forgive," Durak said, pulling up a footstool and plopping down in front of Salvarias. The cavrul glanced around the room as if ensuring they were alone. "How ye feel, lad?"

"As though that creature gnawed on me for a week before spitting me back out," Salvarias said dryly, rubbing a hand across his forehead.

Durak chuckled. "Might as well have, eh?"

"Indeed. Is everything all right? Why are you here?"

Durak shrugged. "Me made a promise."

Salvarias's confusion must have played across his features. Durak winked and handed Salvarias a piece of folded cloth.

"Lumous," he whispered, instantly comforted by the glow of his soaring sparrow. He unfolded the cloth. Resting in his palm was an intricately carved wood sparrow no larger than the tip of his thumb, suspended by a soft leather rope. The wood was warm to his touch and too detailed for words. Tears welled when he met the cavrul's gaze. "You were carving it for me."

"Aye."

Feeling unworthy of such a gift, Salvarias tied it around his neck and raised the sparrow so he could examine it once more. "It is beyond words, my friend."

"Bah." Durak waved aside the compliment. "It be nothing."

"No," Salvarias insisted. "It is truly ..." His voice choked off and words failed him.

Durak grinned. "Me glad ye like it, lad."

"You could not begin to understand how much."

Durak scowled. "Me didn't go to all that trouble for the recipient to die. Scare me like that again, and I'll give ye a wallop ye'll not soon forget."

Salvarias arched an eyebrow. "I would like to see you try, my short friend."

Durak growled deep in his throat, but a smile twitched on the corners of his mouth. "Me axe could beat that magic of yours anytime, ye flimsy stick of a boy."

Salvarias's grin emerged. "Next time you are on watch, perhaps we should put your confidence to the test."

Durak chuckled. "Aye. Ye need a good beatin' every now and again. Keep that ego of yours under control." He rose from his stool and smoothed his beard. "Me headed for sleep."

"Good night, my friend."

"Good night, lad."

Salvarias fiddled with the sparrow carving as he watched the cranky cavrul saunter from the library. After Durak left, Salvarias hauled himself up and draped a blanket over Lunara before hobbling to the opposite corner of the room. His glowing sparrow lit up the empty pot resting on a stand. He grabbed it up and stepped out into the gardens, Adok following while lecturing Salvarias on the dangers of engaging in fights with flying beasts the size of small towns.

He rested the pot in the middle of the path, scooped up some loose soil, and put it in the pot. Glancing around, he found the red-leafed plant favored in the garden, plucked a leaf, and dropped it in the pot as he chanted his spell. The leaf burrowed into the soil and a breath passed before the bush blossomed to life, red leaves cascading around the pot and pink flowers bursting to full bloom. He hoped it would ease some of the emptiness in Olivit and Thilia's hearts.

Next, he enchanted the sparrow necklace to return to him at his call, just as his staff did. When done, he hefted up the pot, carried it inside, and deposited it back on its stand. Exhausted from the small exertion, he limped to his couch, covered himself with a blanket, and fell asleep to Adok's continued lecture.

Chapter 28

Autumn 1018 a.r.

Wilhelm left the washroom, cleansed of the sweat from his morning jog through Lynta, and took the stairs two at a time, finally feeling rested and refreshed. The day was bright with the promise of a warm sun and the absence of gray clouds. Sunlight dappled the hallway to the library, sparkling dust that never seemed to land.

He inched open the library door, wincing as it squeaked, and peeked inside. His brother was sleeping on a couch, book loosely held, Adok lying on the floor in front of him, Lunara on a nearby couch.

Wilhelm slipped inside and found Okulu sitting in a dark corner, staring at a pot with a plant spilling out of it. "Did you stay the entire night?" Wilhelm asked.

Okulu inhaled deeply, seeming to come from some half-asleep trance. "I did. Stayed out of sight so he didn't know I was spying on him, as you asked."

Wilhelm ignored the merc's snippy tone. "Did Salv sleep?"

"Same as usual."

Wilhelm clapped the merc on the shoulder. "Why don't you head up for some sleep?"

"Not tired. Do you think we'll be leaving soon?"

"If I know Salv, it'll be today."

"Good," Okulu said. "I'm ready for a change of scenery."

"You've a wonderful family. I'm surprised you want to leave."

Okulu shrugged, but didn't explain further. Wilhelm went to his brother and rested a hand on Salvarias's shoulder. At least his brother's skin was back to its normal color, though a tad pale. Dark circles still rimmed his eyes. "Salv?"

Salvarias groaned, opening heavy eyelids. Wilhelm smiled. "It's morning. Can we stay here another day?"

Salvarias shook his head. "We must leave." He shoved himself up, wincing. "Okulu?"

"Right here," the merc said, squatting in front of Salvarias.

"A city near the sea," Salvarias said, gaze distant. "It is relatively clean and has a large wall surrounding it. It can be seen from a hill. There is—"

Okulu nodded. "Bren. About three days ride. What after?"

"Sea. He took another boat." Salvarias gifted a small smile to the merc. "I do not suppose you know a sea captain in Bren willing to sail with a mage."

Okulu grinned. "I know a few. I'll have the horses readied and supplies added to our packs."

"Thank you," Salvarias murmured.

Okulu took a swig from his flask as he left the room.

Wilhelm looked at his brother curiously. Salvarias rarely shared his smile. "You all right?"

His brother leaned back and closed his eyes. "I am fine."

"I'll wake the others. A little breakfast before we go?"

Salvarias nodded his head slightly. "I will meet you in the dining hall."

Wilhelm gently ruffled his brother's hair, missing the returned punch, and headed out to wake the others. Humar was already up, and after cursing Wilhelm to several impressive torments in Oblivion, Durak hauled himself out of bed. Leaving Neithelas to Humar, Wilhelm knocked on Varila's door. She mumbled something he took as an invitation and opened the door. She was curled up in her massive bed, feather-stuffed blankets pulled up to her chin, and her open window let in the cold breeze from outside.

"Want me to close that?" Wilhelm asked.

"No, I like the fresh air. I'm tired of being cooped up with sick people," she mumbled, patting the bed beside her.

"Good news then. We're leaving after breakfast." Wilhelm sat on the edge of the bed, fighting the impulse to crawl under the covers and feel her warmth.

Arms wrapped around his neck and pulled him down to her. Soft lips met his. Desire spread across him like a rampant wild fire and burned his kiss with passion. She returned his fervor and her deep moans drove him insane with want. Her shoulder was warm under his hand as he pushed the blanket down, revealing her bare skin, and her neck smelled of strawberries as his lips explored.

"We should eat," she breathed, arching her back, gifting him more skin.

"I'm fine with skipping," he murmured.

"Who said anything about skipping?"

Gods, he wanted her, and when her nails dug into his back, he nearly lost control. He stumbled off the bed, backing away until he was at the window. Gripping the edge, he inhaled several times, trying to steady his breathing, holding on for dear life or else he would cave and return to her, take what his body screamed at him to take.

"Why?" she asked. "We've both done this before."

"Until you see him for who is, I can't be with you."

"Then for all of Zerana's love, tell me! Dammit, Wilhelm. I can't know him if you two don't let me. He's bottled up inside himself and only you can see in. You keep everything about him a secret from me."

"Shadowfires," Wilhelm blurted.

"What?"

Wilhelm ran his hand over his face, wiping away sweat beading on his forehead. "Salvarias was ... made by shadowfires." He regretted his confession instantly. His chest tightened at the mere thought of Salvarias ever learning the truth. "You can't tell him. Please, you—"

Varila flung aside the blankets, snatched up a robe from the edge of the bed, and wrapped it around herself as she walked to him. "You're telling me shadowfires—the same creatures that murdered people in Falar—created your brother? I don't understand. Did your mother know? Did he just, I don't know, appear?"

"They ... they impregnated my mother."

Varila's gaze steadied on him. "Tell me everything."

Wilhelm rested a hand on his chest and looked out the window, turning his back to Varila. "I ... I can't."

He could see Salvarias's eyes now, filled with betrayal at Wilhelm's lie, overflowing with horror. Never could he cause his brother such pain. Never could his brother learn the truth. Varila's mouth ran away from her when she was upset, and it would slip. He was such a fool. "It was a mistake," he said. "I shouldn't have told you."

"Gods, what's wrong with you two? What happened that perverted your relationship into this toxic nightmare?"

"You didn't see him," Wilhelm said.

"Didn't see what?"

Wilhelm closed his eyes tightly, the memories bombarding him with more pain than he realized he harbored. "Can you imagine watching Lunara crawl away from people? Can you imagine her huddling in a corner, crying? Scared beyond what any child should ever feel? Can you imagine being helpless? Watching her cry herself to sleep at night? Watching her wake from nightmares screaming? Seeing her sick all the time? Pale and weak, thin and bruised? Can you imagine nearly losing her, watching her die? Seeing her mutilated body and knowing she lived a year in torture because you failed to protect her? Imagine it now, and then tell me what you wouldn't do to keep her safe, to keep any bit of pain from her you could. Tell me I'm being irrational."

He opened his eyes to see her standing before him, eyes soft. "You're being irrational. Even if I despised your brother, I would never hurt him."

"You have," Wilhelm said. "Words cut my brother deeper than swords. You called him a demon, Varila. You look at him with nothing but hate. I'm sorry. I'm sorry I told you. If you tell him, I'll ..."

Varila bit her lip and nodded. "He'll never hear it from me."

Wilhelm kissed her forehead and left the room. He took a moment in the hallway to collect himself. He never realized how painful those memories were, how much their childhood had shaped their relationship.

Shaking himself to rid his melancholy, he strolled through the estate and found the dining hall he'd become familiar with last night. His friends were there, except Lunara and Varila.

"I think he's on his way to Loutsil," Okulu was saying.

"Loutsil?" Humar asked sharply.

Salvarias looked up from a book and his hooded head turned toward the knight.

Okulu shifted in his seat. "Bren provides the shortest distance. If you look at a map of Arden, he's making a straight line for Loutsil."

Humar rose and started pacing the length of the table.

"Is something wrong, Humar?" Salvarias asked.

"Depends on where we go," Humar said vaguely.

"My brother and I can go alone," Salvarias offered.

Humar's eyes hardened. "No. I'm coming with you. Stop trying to get us to stay behind." His voice was harsher than what Wilhelm preferred, but a look from his brother stopped him from interjecting.

Humar mumbled a curse and then said, "I'll go pack." He strode from the room, leaving a trail of muttered words.

Wilhelm sat next to his brother. "What was that about?"

Salvarias shrugged. "We will find out soon enough." He raised his head slightly and squinted at Wilhelm. "What is wrong?"

Wilhelm grinned and ruffled his brother's hair. "Nothing, Salv."

"You are a poor liar, my dear brother."

Wilhelm feigned a grunt when a weak elbow landed in his ribs. "Ouch."

Chapter 29

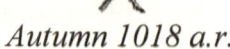

Autumn 1018 a.r.

The three day journey to Bren was blessedly uneventful. Though the holes in Salvarias's body made each movement scream pain, he had learned in Zeeas how to conceal most of his torment. His brother's worried glances were few, considering. The Hunters were easily fought, the evil well contained, and the spirit of the group surprisingly high. The only unsettling development was Varila. Salvarias caught her watching him often, her eyes narrowed, a fingernail cracking between her teeth. To say it made him uncomfortable was an understatement. He had learned to read people well, and obviously she was battling with something, something that would change her. He did not like that that something involved him.

The afternoon sun was once again in hiding when Salvarias and his group crested a hill and saw a bustling city nearly as large as Falar with docks far more impressive than Salvarias's home. Ships dotted the harbor and two main roads were heavy with traffic.

"It's the main trading post with Loutsil," Okulu explained. "Bren is our most prosperous city."

"Good," Varila grumbled. "Hopefully my bed won't have fleas."

Okulu chuckled. "I said prosperous, my lovely golden-haired warrior, not clean."

"Go to Oblivion," Varila said. "And stop calling me that!"

"You should not tease her," Neithelas said. "She deserves—"

"I don't need you defending me," Varila growled, scowling at the prince. "Let's just get on with it."

Neithelas startled in his saddle, hurt filling his eyes. "Forgive me, my lady."

Wilhelm arched an eyebrow at her but said nothing.

"You heard her," Humar said. "Lead the way, Okulu."

As they plodded down the hill, Wilhelm steered Lilly beside Okulu and engaged in a hushed conversation. Salvarias, however, knew the inflections of his brother's voice and picked up a few words.

"How are we going ... guard ... list ... bribe ... how much ... I have enough ... are you sure ... if not, I'll kill you."

Salvarias shook his head, but refrained from barging in on the conversation. Once Okulu and Wilhelm had concluded their business, the merc nudged his horse next to Mithal.

"When we get to the gate, stay in the back of the group. Let your brother and me handle it."

"Hopefully you survive," Salvarias said dryly.

"Something we can agree upon," Okulu said, and took a swig from his flask. "His temper is getting worse, you know."

Salvarias lowered his voice and said, "Have you noticed anything between him and Varila? A fight perhaps while I was ill?"

Okulu grinned. "No, but I have noticed her staring at you. Unnerving?"

"Extremely."

Okulu shrugged. "I doubt she'd kill you."

"Thank you for stating the obvious."

Okulu clucked his tongue. "I said doubt. You can never be certain about these things. She's a fiery one."

There was a long line at the gate, and Salvarias wondered if there was a point. Guards were not looking in wagons or asking where anyone had come from. Of course, they made it appear as if they did, but in the end, coins clinked with each passing person. He understood now that Okulu and Wilhelm planned to buy their way through. Perhaps it would work.

Neithelas snorted. "Despicable. Extorting these poor people."

"Indeed," Salvarias murmured.

For some reason, Neithelas had stayed in back with Salvarias, allowing the others to crowd around Wilhelm and hiss at one another on what their actions would be for each dreadful scenario they could concoct.

Neithelas cleared his throat and shifted in his saddle. "It seems you and Lady Lunara have grown close."

Salvarias tilted his head in agreement. "I consider her a dear friend."

"Nothing more?"

Salvarias's throat constricted. Swallowing hard, he said, "I approve of you, Prince Neithelas. You would make a fine husband, and it is clear you care for her. I wish nothing more than for the two of you to be united."

"She would be better off without your friendship," Neithelas said.

"That she would."

"Then deny her your company."

Salvarias sighed and turned to the prince. "We have a ... connection that runs deeper than friendship. Turning her away is something I have tried to do and failed miserably. As her friend, I have counseled her to accept your courtship and should ever you ask it, I would encourage her to be your wife. There is nothing else I can do."

Neithelas's lip curled. "You are as selfish as I always thought. You are a man that attracts danger. If truly she were your friend, you would cast her aside. As well as the rest of us."

Salvarias ground his teeth together, battling to keep his voice even and polite. "If you will recall, Prince, I have tried to do so but this entire group is bent on following me. You as well have journeyed with me under my protest. What else would you have me do?"

"Sneak away in the night. Leave us and never look back."

Salvarias's gaze drifted to his brother. "I cannot leave him yet."

"Then you doom us all," Neithelas hissed.

Their turn to pass through the gate came none too soon. Salvarias struggled to keep his breathing even as Wilhelm and Okulu conversed with the guard, laughing occasionally as coins glinted in one hand to another. The guard shot furtive glances in Salvarias's direction, and each time his expression hardened. Just as Salvarias thought his brother had failed, the guard motioned Salvarias's group through the gate.

Past the impressive wall, Bren reminded Salvarias of Falar. It teemed with variety. They passed filthy sections, and the stink of emptied chamber pots in alleys mingled with the droppings of animals in the unkempt street. Lunara raised a lock of hair to her nose, and Salvarias fought an overwhelming desire to pull her into his saddle and drown his face in her hair.

In other areas, the streets were scrubbed clean and estates sprawled out on too much land. Well-dressed men and women strolled the street, still mixes of races, all smiling and laughing as if life had no worries for them. Salvarias watched them with hidden jealousy.

"We'll stay at Seatide Inn tonight and go to the docks in the morning," Okulu announced. "This place is pricey, but the ladies deserve a bit of spoiling after three days riding."

"Speak for yourself," Varila said. "I've watched you scowl at your bedroll every night. You've grown soft, merc."

Okulu grinned wickedly at Varila. "Is it a sin to want a warm bed?"

She grunted. "Just don't blame it on the women when it's what you want too."

Okulu gave a mocking bow in his saddle. "Of course, my lov—"

"Say it and I'll rip out your tongue," Varila growled.

The Seatide Inn was as Okulu described. The walls themselves seemed to have been polished that morning, and their gray stone gleamed in the masked sunlight.

Inside, Salvarias mused that the inn solely catered to the overly wealthy, those that had servants wiping the floor after each step. Tables were oiled spotless and carved with intricate designs of sea creatures. The inn even afforded art, displaying a painting of the sea above a fireplace too perfect in its rhythmic dance. The smells from the kitchen were simply sinful, and Salvarias distinctly caught the aroma of herb bread. Not a single crumb dirtied the polished stone floor littered with warm rugs. Overall, Salvarias felt completely out of place. He was suddenly aware of how dusty the hem of his robes were, and the clod of dirt on the end of his staff had left a trail. His boots as well.

"This is nice and all," Wilhelm said, looking around with apprehension. "But I don't want to use all of Edium's money on one night's stay. I don't care how clean the bed is."

Okulu chuckled and clapped Wilhelm's shoulder. "Harriot?" he called. "Herald?"

An old, thin man came from a back room, wiping his hands on towel. When he saw Okulu, he snapped to a halt. "My boy? Is it really you?"

Okulu grinned and opened his arms. "I've missed you, Uncle."

The old man ran to Okulu, embracing him tightly, clear joy on his wrinkled face. His laugh turned into a violent cough. Salvarias absently concocted a remedy in his mind for Herald, one he would mix tonight. Once the old man's cough was under control, he smiled at them. "Please, come in. Rest those weary bones. You all look like you've traveled for days." He turned to Okulu, looking him up and down. "My, you've grown into quite the man. You look just like your mother. Oh, Kuly, tell me you visited them. Your father has simply been half a man since you left."

Okulu's bright eyes darkened and he nodded. "I did see them. Spent a few days in Lynta, as a matter of fact." He waved his hand, as if discarding the uncomfortable conversation. "We need a few rooms for the night."

"I have enough for all your friends," Herald said.

"If it's not too much trouble, I'd like to stay with my brother," Wilhelm said, motioning to Salvarias.

"And me with my sister," Varila said.

Herald glanced at Salvarias then turned to Okulu. "You travel with one? Is that wise? You took—"

Okulu nodded. "It's been good for me, Uncle."

A high-pitched squeal that nearly burst Salvarias's ears was followed by a plump woman rushing Okulu. She flew into his arms, knocking him back several steps, planting kisses over his entire face between saying, "Kuly! My boy! Look at you! Handsome as ever! Cessia's here, you know. She asks about you every time she's in town. She's even prettier than she was all those years ago. Oh, Kuly, tell me you're here to stay. Tell me you'll marry her and give me nieces and nephews. Did you—"

Okulu unwound the woman, interrupting her rushed words. "Easy, Auntie. Cessia's in town?"

"Yes, dearie. Just arrived yesterday."

Okulu grinned at Salvarias. "I think I found us a boat."

"If I remember correctly," Humar said. "Things ended ... poorly between you and Cessia."

"Oh no," Harriot exclaimed. "It was a misunderstanding. Cessia loves my Kuly."

Humar bowed, the corners of his mouth twitching a smile. "Forgive me, my lady."

Harriot rested a hand over her heart, her cheeks blotching red. "Such manners. A Loutsil knight, at that? You've been keeping good—" Her words cut off when she turned to Salvarias. "A mage!"

Salvarias bowed. "My lady. It is a pleasure to meet you."

She clapped her hands together. "Oh this is wonderful, Kuly! Is he your friend? Did he know Briana?"

Okulu stiffened at the name. "No."

Harriot seemed to notice and frowned. "Surely you don't still blame yourself?"

"My lady," Salvarias said, bowing again, hoping to distract the prying woman. "The journey has been long indeed. Is there a place we can wash before dinner?"

"Oh dear me, of course. Herald!" she shouted.

The old man, who stood behind her, winced. "Here, you old windbag."

"Well don't just stand there," she said, putting her hands on her hips. "Show our guests to their rooms."

As Herald led them to the second floor, he said, "Our rooms aren't designed for multiple guests. However, the beds are plenty big if you don't mind sharing."

"That'll be fine," Wilhelm said.

"If you're worried for the mage's safety, I can assure you, we have no crime here."

"I mean no disrespect," Wilhelm said carefully. "But I'd prefer to keep an eye on him myself."

"Of course, of course," Herald said.

The room he opened for Wilhelm and Salvarias was spacious, the bed big enough to comfortably sleep three. On one side of an expansive fireplace, a table sat near a double window with a view of the sea, and it was the first time Salvarias realized how close they were to the water. Another door led to their own private washroom.

"Satisfactory?" Herald asked.

"Quite," Wilhelm responded. "How much for the night?"

"Oh don't be absurd. Okulu's like a son to us. His father and I are brothers. Never had children of our own, so Kuly and Briana used to stay with us often when they were young. Such a good lad."

Wilhelm reached for his purse. "I can't stay here without offering you—"

"You'd insult me, boy. Your horses are being tended to and your packs will be sent up shortly. Freshen up and join us for dinner. Naarin caught a buck this morning. You like venison, don't you? Big boy like you?"

Wilhelm's crooked grin spread. "Venison so happens to be my favorite."

Herald winked. "Mine as well." He turned to Salvarias. "And you, my boy?"

"He doesn't eat meat," Wilhelm said. "Herb bread, if you have it, fruits, cheeses—"

"I have just the meal!" Herald exclaimed. "Roasted mushroom and onions fried in butter."

"Sounds wonderful," Salvarias said, bowing.

"Good, good! See you in a bit."

The old man hobbled away. Salvarias concocted another remedy for Herald's obvious joint pain.

"Nice people," Wilhelm said, walking around the room, checking corners, looking under the bed.

Salvarias watched him with mild amusement. "Indeed, brother."

Dinner was a heated journey of spices flavoring boiled, fried, and roasted vegetables, wafting scents so foreign Salvarias found himself missing the simpler foods of Lady Talura's home. The herb bread was not as warm and fluffy, the butter too sweet, the pears overripe, and the oats gummy. His tongue burned from the heavy hand of Herald's seasoning, and Salvarias drank nearly a pitcher of water himself. Neithelas droned on to Lunara about how similar the spices were to those in Meitholias. She looked half interested and seemed distracted ever since Salvarias had handed Harald the potions, along with the recipes, he had made for the old man's ailments.

Once Salvarias could no longer endure another bite, he politely excused himself and made his way up to his room. Adok was curled up by the window, nose tucked in his tail. Salvarias shivered and closed the open window, apologizing to the wolf for letting it get so cold.

A soft knock on the door was followed by Lunara asking to enter.

He opened the door for her, draping a blanket over her shoulders as she passed.

"It's so cold," she said, rubbing her arms.

"My brother must have opened the window. Is there something you needed, my lady?"

"Actually, there is."

She sat in one of the chairs and produced a piece of parchment, an ink bottle, and a quill. Apparently, she would be staying for some time. Salvarias settled into the other chair after gathering his spell book.

"I want to learn herblore," she announced, tossing her hair as if in challenge for him to deny her.

Salvarias shrugged. "Of course, my lady. Might I ask why?"

Her posture relaxed. "I've seen you hurt so many times, and I can't help. And that old man, with just a look you helped him."

"I have studied for years, my lady. It will take you the same before you are able to see ailments as I do."

"I'm a fast learner."

Salvarias opened his book and nestled comfortably into his chair. "We will have plenty of time when at sea. We will start then, if that is acceptable."

"Yes, of course." She smoothed out the parchment and began to write. "Is there anything you want me to tell my father?"

Salvarias inhaled a deep breath as he ignited his magic, reveling in its warmth and care. It was eager to study. "Please tell him we are headed to Loutsil. I intend to meet with King Lilkous and warn him of Dalnar's plague. I hope to persuade him to look within his own country for the other part of the army. Okulu has asked his father to do the same. With both countries looking for god, hopefully he can be discovered before it is too late."

"Queen."

"Pardon?"

"Loutsil's king was murdered. Their queen rules."

"So be it, the queen."

Lunara looked up at him. "Loutsil's rulers have no love for the rest of Arden. I doubt she would listen or believe you."

"I must try."

It was late when the door to Salvarias's room burst open. Wilhelm teetered in, arm draped over Varila's shoulders, eyes bloodshot and breath reeking of ale.

"Hello!" Wilhelm rumbled. He ruffled Salvarias's hair. "I wish you could drink."

Salvarias caught his brother as he toppled to the side and grunted under the weight. "And I wish you would eat less," he said, steering his brother to the bed.

"I can't help it," Wilhelm said sheepishly. "I'm always hungry."

Salvarias helped his brother sit, remove his armor and boots, and then lie back.

"It's hot," Wilhelm muttered, and then started to snore.

"He can't handle his ale," Varila said loudly.

Lunara giggled and helped support her swaying sister. "I see he can't. You, on the other hand, are functioning just fine."

"I am." Varila tugged on Lunara's white lock of hair. "I love your new look."

Salvarias crossed the room and opened the window. When he turned around, Varila stood directly in front of him, nose to nose, her eyes squinted nearly shut. "I don't understand you," she slurred. "I try, I do. But you don't let me. Why?"

"Perhaps you would like to discuss this another time, my lady," Salvarias said.

Varila snorted. An awkward moment of silence passed before tears brimmed in her eyes. "You wouldn't, would you?"

"Pardon?"

"You wouldn't hate me if I was the daughter of Sansis, would you? Or Dethal? Or even Veedran himself."

Perplexed, Salvarias glanced at Lunara for guidance. She shrugged and said, "My sister is emotional when she drinks."

Salvarias turned his gaze back to the woman in front of him and slowly spoke his answer. "We cannot choose our mother or father. It would not make sense to hate a child because of whose womb it grew in or whose seed spawned it."

Varila blew out a puff of ale-drenched breath. She spoke softly enough that Salvarias struggled to hear her. "Why did you do that to your parents' murderer? Why did you laugh?"

Salvarias regarded her for a long moment before he whispered, "Because it felt good to watch him burn as my mother did."

Varila held his gaze for what seemed like an eternity before she leaned closer and whispered in his ear, "Now that's the most honest answer I could've expected from you." She looked over her shoulder at Wilhelm. "I'm going to marry your brother," she continued. "We both know he won't unless we get along."

"Yes, my lady."

"And you want me to marry him, right?"

"I desire nothing more."

She turned back to him and leaned closer. "Then prove it. Answer me this: did your mother beat you?"

Salvarias tensed and even as he stepped back, she moved with him, light on her feet, her lips never far from his ear.

"You listen to me," she hissed. "He's not going to marry me until you trust me. Until you open up to me. You want your brother to be happy, right?"

Salvarias swallowed hard and glanced at his snoring brother. Wilhelm's happiness was all that mattered in life. "Yes."

"Good. Then for his sake, answer me. Did your mother beat you?"

Salvarias closed his eyes, battling for each tiny gulp of air. "Y-yes."

"And why didn't you tell Wilhelm?"

"She said she would take me from him."

"She never hurt Wilhelm?"

"No."

"And you were certain she never would?"

"Yes."

"She thought something was wrong with you?"

"Yes." Hot tears burned his eyes. He blinked them away.

"That's a good first step, don't you think?" Without waiting for a reply, she whirled around, careened her way to the bed, and plopped down by Wilhelm. She snuggled close to him, and pulled his arm around her. His brother stirred briefly, shifting to encase her in his arms, and both started snoring.

"Are you all right?" Lunara asked, taking his hand in hers.

He needed comfort, something to chase away his pain. As if reading his mind, she wedged herself into his embrace. "I am fine," he said.

He held her for a long moment before she gently pulled from his arms, keeping her hand locked to his. "Come, let's get some rest."

She led him from the room and into the one next door. It was the same and the bed looked entirely inviting. Lunara kicked off her boots, and he did the same. Though shame burned his cheeks, it was not enough for him decline her when she guided him into the bed. He held her close, tightly, using her intoxicating smell and softness to chase away his rotted and harsh memories.

Chapter 30

Autumn 1018 a.r.

Salvarias lazily awoke to the early rays of morning subdued by the thick drapes covering the windows. The scent of spring and the deep breathing of Lunara brought a warmth that reached the deepest parts of him. She was snuggled down in his arms and blankets, her face a serene picture of peace. He stared at her for some time, memorizing the curve of her lips, her lashes caressing her cheeks, and the strands of raven hair contrasting her pale skin. He could have spent eternity in that moment, but sensations arose not appropriate toward a friend. Reluctantly and ever so slowly, he unraveled her from his embrace. She gave a soft whimper of protest, but when he brushed her hair from her face, she quieted, a slight smile on her lips. What would it be like to wake to her every morning?

Sighing at his selfishness, he silently made his way to the washroom where he found a fresh set of his robes that had not been there the night before. Also waiting him was the puzzle box. Apparently his brother had woken in the night and checked on him. After performing his ablutions, he crept from his room, Adok in tow, and went down the stairs to the common room. Humar sat alone by the fire, a cup of tea in his hand.

Weaving between the tables, Salvarias joined Humar. The knight's blue eyes were distant, and his tea no longer steamed. If one did not know him, one would assume he was unaware of anything but the crackling fire.

"Would you like to discuss it?" Salvarias asked as he scooted a chair closer to the flames and sat down.

"No."

"You have seen me through much over this trip, my friend. There is no shame in turning back."

Humar took a sip of tea, grimaced at it, and set it aside. "I'm coming. I just ask we avoid major cities and roads. I'll speak with Okulu about finding trails."

Salvarias ignited his magic, whispered his spell, and drew his simple rune. Humar's tea let off a wisp of steam. The knight smiled at it and took a sip, settling back comfortably in his chair.

"Nice spell."

"After the icelands, I was compelled to find one to heat up food," Salvarias said. "I will try to avoid cities at all cost, but I must visit the queen in Warton."

"Whatever for?"

"To warn her of the possible threat against her lands. There is something here," Salvarias said, feeling the familiar touch of his evil spoiling the air around him. "It is not the army, but something else. Which means if the army is not here, then they must be on Loutsil. It is the largest continent, the best place to stay hidden while they grow their forces."

Humar grunted. "She won't listen to a mage. The queen is as prejudiced as the rest of Loutsil. You'll get no understanding from her."

"I must try."

"I ..." Humar ran his hand through his hair. "I can't go to Warton."

"There will be no need. I will be there less than a day, and my brother will accompany me. There will be no danger."

"Princess Falisa would be more receptive to your warning than the queen. If you're set on doing this, I recommend talking to her instead."

Salvarias nodded. "I will. Thank you."

They sat in companionable silence, both lost in their own ponderings, until the rest of the group joined them. After a heavily seasoned breakfast, they set out for the docks.

Clouds were quick to overtake the morning sun and brought about a cold wind that made the walk seem longer. The bay was relatively calm, but outside the natural indent, choppy waves crashed against the rocky peninsula. The docks were busy for so early; burly men with hands too large and grins too fierce prepared vessels for sailing, and passengers in finery and those who had probably scraped their last copper for passage waited with packs stuffed full. Gulls cawed at the commotion, dropping here and there to snatch discarded crumbs and perching atop run-down warehouses while scouting. It was a chaotic sight, but one Salvarias found oddly appropriate and comforting.

Watythm ships were a sight to behold, just as they were when he had visited Xeroth. It was like a forest, every ship different from their kin, every ship gifting something beautiful to the scene.

Even in the traffic of the dock, the woman striding for Salvarias's group was easily noticed. Her fire-red hair needed no sun to dazzle with life, and the landscape dulled in comparison to her bright aqua-blue eyes. Leather pants hugged her thighs and her creamy-white long sleeved tunic brought attention to her pale-blue skin. A belt tightened at her waist further displayed her attractive figure and called attention to a thin, feminine-looking sword slapping her thigh as her hips swayed generously. Her lithe body exuded seduction and nearly every head turned to watch her marching along. And she was mage, a very adept mage.

Okulu opened his arms as she approached, his grin ridiculously large. "Cessia! You look—"

She slapped him across the cheek. "You cheating bastard!"

Okulu caught her wrist when she went to slap him again. Instead of anger in his eyes, they shone with desire. "Now, now, you don't mean that, do you? If you recall, you were in bed with another long before I was."

"You make me sick," she spat. "Insulting my ship! Screwing some whore!"

"She wasn't a whore," Okulu said defensively. "She was a wench in that tavern on Gri Street." He deftly avoided a knee to the groin. "Come now, my little sea-kelp. You don't want to damage the goods."

"Does it still work? Or have you contracted some disease from your whoring?"

Okulu cast his devilish grin and winked. "Want to find out?" He brazenly kissed her full on the lips, holding her struggling body close.

When he pulled away, she slapped him with her free hand before willingly planting her mouth on his. The contact was long and too intimate for a public street, but neither seemed to care. Salvarias and his group shifted uneasily, looking everywhere but at the affectionate couple.

Another woman storming toward them caught Salvarias's eye. There was no mistaking the resemblance to Cessia, but this newcomer's skin was not as pure blue, and her hair and eyes were lackluster in comparison to Cessia. She was young, a few years Salvarias's senior, perhaps, but there was a youthfulness and fearlessness in her eyes that reminded him of the little girl he had killed outside of Xeroth. Then he recalled Hyde had said one of his daughters had an erthla mother. He also remembered the younger sister was quite put out with Okulu.

"Okulu?" Salvarias said.

"Mmm?" came from the merc's throat, but his lips were still occupied.

"If I remember correctly, Madam Cessia has a younger sister."

"Uhmmm," was the response.

"I also recall she was less than pleased with you."

The crowd around the younger woman parted, revealing a dagger held in her hand. This woman was a mage as well, though her powers were nothing compared to her sister and seemed highly volatile.

"I'll handle it," Varila muttered. "Though I should let her slice his throat."

She darted in the woman's path and raised a placating hand. "As much as I want that damn merc to learn humility, I don't want to see him dead. It seems your sister, against all odds, has decided to forgive him."

The woman's furious glare jumped between Varila and Okulu, but she stopped.

"At least wait until he's done and can defend himself before you try to kill him," Varila said.

The woman folded her arms over her chest. "Are you another one of his whores?"

Varila's face contorted into an expression of disgust. "Gods no! The bastard should be castrated!"

The woman smiled suddenly, a bright, delightful smile that was surprisingly contagious. "Name's Kisra."

Varila shook hands and grinned. "Varila Bellerum."

"Edium's eldest daughter?"

"The same."

Kisra clapped her hands. "Oh, I just love your father! He's so sweet! He brought me chocolate one time when he visited. I've got quite a weakness for it. He ..."

She continued on with the story, and Salvarias pondered if she would pass out from lack of air. She spoke quickly, running together words the more excited she became, and her voice rose a few octaves. She seemed to switch effortlessly from a furious woman to a giddy girl.

During the commotion, Okulu and Cessia had finally found the strength to reclaim their individual mouths and watched Kisra with nothing but affection. Okulu did not seem concerned for his life. Once the young woman finished her story—and without missing a single beat—she turned to Cessia and in a dead voice asked, "Do you want me to kill him?"

Cessia shook her head. "He has too much to make up for, and I intend to collect all that's due me."

Okulu winced. "Surely you'll allow me some rest."

Cessia snorted, completely unladylike. "I've been waiting for you."

Okulu's eyes widened in genuine surprise. "All this time?"

Cessia shrugged. "I love you."

Okulu blushed furiously and backed up, but she caught his arm before he could escape. "No," she said, casting him a wicked grin. "There's no running now."

Kisra suddenly sucked in a breath and pointed a shaking finger at Salvarias. "Sia! Do you feel that?"

Cessia turned to Salvarias and her eyes widened. "Oh gods." Both women drew swords and backed up. "We don't want any trouble. We haven't done anything wrong. The Association has no reason to be here!"

Salvarias held up his hands in surrender. "I assure you, madams, I am not with the Association." He motioned his brother back, feeling Wilhelm's tension thicken the air and hearing his sword scrape its sheath.

"Impossible," Kisra spat. "They'd never let anyone live with that much power unless he was on the council."

"My uncle knows a few members. He saw my name was put on the list. I assure you, I hold no love for the Association."

"It's true," Okulu said. "Matter of fact, they've struck his name from the list. Looks like they finally want to be rid of him."

Cessia shook her head, expression grim. "I've been struck off as well. Luckily the guards here know me. There's a few mage sympathizers that have let me continue my work."

"Which is?" Okulu asked.

"Ferrying mages from Loutsil to here. It's safer for them in Windlous, and as of late, the Association has gotten stricter in their acceptance and careless with updating the lists. It's made life even harder for our kind," she finished with a nod toward Salvarias.

Our kind struck him oddly. He knew few mages and those he did were never caring toward him.

"Is there a private place we can talk?" Okulu asked.

Cessia and Kisra sheathed their swords and motioned the group to follow them to the safety of a deserted warehouse. Once there, Cessia asked Okulu, "You're staying at your uncle's?"

"Yes, but not for long. We're looking for passage to Loutsil."

"Gods, why would you?" Kisra asked.

"We've got business there that can't be avoided," Okulu said.

"We'll take you," Cessia said. She glanced at Salvarias. "Lower your hood so I can see you." She motioned to Lunara bundled in a cloak, shivering even though they were out of the wind. "You too. I don't take people I don't know."

Lunara lowered her hood and smiled.

"Pretty one," Cessia said.

"My sister," Varila chimed.

"Ah. Your father speaks of nothing else when he visits mine." Cessia turned to Salvarias. "Your turn."

Bracing himself for their disgust, he lowed his hood and met Cessia's gaze.

"My, my," Kisra murmured. She beamed a smile. "Such a handsome man. If you want, you can stay in my cabin."

Salvarias's checks flamed hot with embarrassment, and he quickly raised his hood, listening to Okulu and Wilhelm chuckle.

Cessia grinned as well. "Five gold as long as you instruct Kisra on her magic. I don't have the patience and she's going to get someone killed if she doesn't learn. Refuse and the passage will be seven gold."

Salvarias had never instructed another person, but found the idea intriguing. He had always longed to talk with another about magic, and instructing one would grant him the opportunity. He bowed. "It would be my honor."

"When do you want to leave?" Cessia asked.

"As soon as possible," Okulu responded.

"Then we leave tonight," Kisra said, her eyes never leaving Salvarias. "I'm anxious to begin my studies."

Kisra's giggle made Salvarias decidedly uneasy.

After a lengthy goodbye to Okulu's aunt and uncle, Varila and her friends gathered their horses and made their way to the docks. Cessia's ship was smaller compared to others anchored in Bren, but the hold had been set up nicely for horses and cargo.

Once Salvarias had settled the horses, Varila climbed the ramp behind Wilhelm and met Cessia on deck. Varila was pleased to find the sailors on Cessia's ship were more behaved than those on Ingil's. It seemed they were used to seeing a pretty woman since Cessia was quite the picture of vibrant beauty. Varila mused it was part of the watythm charm. Their women and men were always so charismatic. But Neithelas still stole the title of most beautiful in their group, aside from Salvarias when his face wasn't taut with aloofness. Kisra turned some attention toward the prince, but her gaze more often than not fell to Salvarias. He seemed unaware, or if he did notice, he made a good show of disinterest. Lunara hadn't even flinched at Kisra's bold glances at the mage. Perhaps Varila's little sister wasn't prone to jealously.

"Welcome aboard," Cessia greeted. "A few announcements and then we'll be on our way. Since my sister and I are mages, there's nothing for you to worry about, Master Salvarias. Mages are treated with respect on my ship, as are women. Everyone can move about without fear. As you can see, my ship is small. I don't usually ferry groups this large, so I don't have an abundance of cabins."

Varila shivered when a gust of wind swept over the docks, stirring the feathers on the gulls and sending several squawking away. A warm arm draped over her shoulders, and Wilhelm pulled her closer, covering them both under his cloak. Gods, the man was an oven, and she snuggled closer, feeling his warmth drive away the chill.

Cessia cast Varila a wink and playful grin. "I only have three cabins. It's up to you how you'll divide them up. Two have a single bed large enough for two while the other has four small ones." Cessia pointed at Okulu. "He'll be staying with me. Any questions?" There was a collective shaking of heads. "Good. Go below and get situated."

With that, Cessia and Kisra set out across the deck, shouting orders.

Humar ran a hand through his hair, face drawn as it had been for several days. "Since the ship is safe, we could—"

"Wilhelm and I will take a room," Varila interrupted. "And Salvarias and Lunara the other. The three of you can stay in the last one."

Wilhelm raised an eyebrow at her but said nothing. Salvarias stiffened. Lunara smiled. Okulu laughed.

"If you think it best," Humar said slowly.

"Surely you cannot be serious!" Neithelas blurted. "It is completely inappropriate for an unwed man and woman to share a room alone."

Varila turned to Salvarias, fighting back a smile as his mouth dropped open. "You'll be considerate of my sister, won't you?"

"Y-yes, of course," Salvarias stammered. "But Prince Neithelas is ri—"

"Good," Varila said, cutting him off. "It's settled."

Without waiting for further arguments, she locked arms with her sister and led the way down the stairs.

Lunara leaned close and whispered, "What's this about?"

"I want time alone with Wilhelm," Varila said with a slight shrug.

"You're a horrible liar," Lunara hissed, but her smile stretched wide.

The first cabin was the one with four beds and was surprisingly spacious. The feather beds themselves were large, with fresh white linens and heavy blankets dyed dark blue. Along the wall was a dresser and, even more surprising, a vanity with a wall-mounted mirror. Durak, Humar, and Neithelas entered and began unpacking and claiming beds.

The next cabin was something Varila would have expected to find at Okulu's uncle's inn. A soft rug covered most of the floor, and the bed, dressed in the same crisp linens, was spacious enough for Wilhelm. As well as a dresser and vanity, this cabin had a two-person table bolted down, and the chairs were plushly covered in light-blue velvet.

"This will be yours," Varila said to Salvarias and Lunara.

The mage looked first at the single bed, then Lunara, and turned abruptly to Varila. "Might I have a word?"

"We'll go above deck," Varila said, handing her pack off to Wilhelm. Lunara respectfully closed the door, but Wilhelm stood in the hallway, looking as if he would follow.

"I'd like to speak to your brother alone," Varila said.

He raised an eyebrow, but didn't move.

Varila threw her hands up, rolling her eyes at him. "What do you think I'm going to do? Throw him overboard?" When he didn't move, Varila blew out an exasperated rush of air. "We all know he's not the scrawny man he's led us to believe. He can take care of himself."

Wilhelm's other eyebrow shot up.

"It is fine, brother," Salvarias said.

Wilhelm hesitated a breath before leaving for their cabin.

"Lady Varila," Salvarias began, his voice ever so slightly strained. "I must protest. Lady Lunara should—"

"Walk with me on deck," Varila ordered, hiding her smile at how well her plan was working.

Salvarias's shoulders slouched and he deposited his pack in his room before following her up on deck. The sun had finally set, allowing the first stars of dusk to sparkle at them. The ship had left the dock and headed toward the choppy waters beyond the bay. Wind whipped her cloak about, biting at her face, and gulls soared over the boat, making a cacophony of harsh squawks.

"If this is an attempt to garner favor from my brother, I can speak to him again. There is no need to involve Lady Lunara in our plans to—"

"Shut up," she snapped, reminding herself to be cautious with her words and not confess what she knew about the shadowfires. Yet the knowledge was exactly what had started opening her eyes to Salvarias.

As a child, she had watched any traveling magician and had been able to unmask their tricks. She also had no issues calling them out.

Not only that, but her father had taught her how to read people. Though not nearly as talented as Edium, she had a small knack for it. To her, Salvarias was a mystery of the ages, one she desperately wanted to unravel, a secret she wanted to unearth. She didn't trust him fully. He lied to her for reasons she could only assume. And he was good at it. If she wanted truth from him, she had to evoke his anger. It was the only time he'd been truthful, the only time his true emotions emerged.

Taking in a deep breath, she turned to face him and said, "You lie to me. Why?"

"I do not—"

"Fine, maybe not an outright lie, but you skirt my questions. You're vague. Secretive. There's something in you Humar and Okulu see, something I want to see. So why don't you tell me about yourself? What are you so scared of?"

He turned his back to her and stared over the railing.

"Why are you such a coward?" she snapped.

The air thickened, she was certain of it. It took on a cold edge.

"Do you hate me so much that you can't even be honest with a woman who's followed you halfway around Dalnar? Who's put her life and her sister's in danger for you?"

Salvarias reeled around to face her, the wind whipping his hood back to reveal his shocked yet angered expression. "Hate you? You are the only one who shows any reasonable sense when it comes to me. You see me for what I truly am. When first you laid eyes on me, you did not trust me. You have doubts over every decision I make. You feel it unreasonable I withhold information. We both know the danger everyone has been in was because of me. You knew if a man set another aflame and laughed he should not be trusted. I do not hate you. I respect you."

His voice rose, something seemed to crack within him, and a sliver of his vulnerability shone through. His voice hardened with anger. "I have withheld so many secrets that I am surely leading our group to their deaths, yet I cannot speak them because I fear giving them voice. You have known we are doomed, yet now—for some reason I cannot begin to fathom—you suddenly find it in your heart to possibly see me as Humar and Okulu see me. Why?" he demanded, and his voice turned to stone. "What has happened that you have been fooled as they have been fooled? You have a sharp mind, Lady Varila. One that can see truths, yet here you act like an imbecile! I need you to hate me!" Those words bellowed out and the shock of it seemed to shake him from his anger. He sucked in a sharp breath and blinked a few times. The light of his bare soul dimmed, and he quickly composed himself, standing straighter and calming his expression to placid indifference. He bowed slightly. "Forgive me, my lady. I ... I fear I must be tired. I do not know what came over me."

"I do," Varila said, matter-of-factly, but not coldly. "You can't keep all this bottled up forever, Salvarias. Eventually, you will break. Eventually all those pent-up emotions will explode, and gods help anyone around you when they do. You and I ..." She shook her head, looking out over the waves coming to greet them. "You and I have built up so many walls. But if mine crumble, I can crawl my way out and survive. Can you say the same?"

When he didn't respond, she continued. "Yes, I did hate you. Yes, I did see those things. But I've recently learned something that has drastically changed my mind about you. You know what I think? I think you want me to hate you because if I do, it makes it all right for you to hate yourself. But if I don't, you have to wonder why these people care for you. And you know what else I think? I think you need me to hate you because I am the only person standing between you and your true feelings for Lunara. You love her."

Salvarias's knuckles turned white as he gripped his staff. "No. You are wrong. I care for her as a friend. Nothing more."

His voice shook on the verge of breaking again. He just needed another shove. "I think you're perfect for each other. I think, as a matter of fact, when we reach Loutsil you should marry her." What in Oblivion had she just said?

Salvarias snapped straight as a board, his eyes growing wide. "You do not know what you say," he said.

"Then tell me why you hate yourself."

"I fear this conversation is heading in a direction that will benefit neither of us."

He started to walk, but she darted in his path, got in his face, made her expression contort into anger, and added fire to words. "Tell me!"

All his emotions were fading, his entire presence barreling toward that damned indifference he bathed in. She wanted to scream, shout out her frustration. She had one last ploy. It was mean, manipulative, and she knew she'd hate herself, but he left her no choice.

"You won't tell me? Fine," she snarled. "You can share a room with your brother, because if I don't know you, then there's no point in vying for his affections. I'll walk away from him. I'll tell him I'm not interested, when in fact, it'll be because of you. I'm trying to have a trusting relationship with you, but it appears we can't. So there's no hope for Wilhelm and me. We'll die alone. And it'll be your fault."

"You would not be so cruel," he said, and his voice carried too much confidence for her liking.

"Cruel?" She smirked. "No, it would simply save us both pain. Save us from a lifetime of the dance we're doing now. No, it's not cruel, it's the kindest thing I can do for him." She whirled around and made it one step before his soft voice spoke, but she couldn't hear what he said. She turned back around. "What did you say?"

"Evil," he whispered, tears filling his eyes. She'd never seen a man look more defeated, and the knowledge she'd broken him cut her. But someone needed to push Salvarias. Everyone walked around him on eggshells, and he kept to his ways because he'd never been challenged. She'd seen it before. It was how everyone had treated her after she'd been raped. Luckily, she'd pulled herself free of the chains that had bound her. No one had had the courage to do for her what she was doing for Salvarias: to crumble his facade, to make him face his fears instead of running.

What stood before her now was a man beaten down, broken by what he tormented himself with, petrified.

"I don't understand," she said, pouring care into her voice.

Tears skimmed down his cheeks, but he continued. "There is a ... force living inside me. It is the same evil plaguing Arden. It is how I can sense them, how I knew the army was not on Windlous. I am connected to it."

Varila shook her head, the idea beyond her comprehension.

"It infects me." His eyes distanced and she could no longer tell if he trembled so violently from the cold or from his words. "I feel it eating at my soul. It hungers for it. I fight it, but I am weakening." Those words caused him to shudder. "Do you know why I do not touch others?"

She stared, baffled.

"It hurts," Salvarias said simply. "My brother and your sister are the only two people who do not cause me pain. Do you know why it hurts?" His tone turned bitter and his lip curled in a sneer. "It is because of the evil. The innocent lash back at the monstrosity that is me. The more I am around your sister and others, the more I taint them. Corrupt them. Feed upon their care. Do you not see? I am a monster." He focused on her. "I took comfort that you saw what I truly am. I thought you would help protect Lady Lunara. I thought you would help keep them from me."

"Salvarias ..." Gods, what could she say to that kind of confession.

"My brother will not listen to me," Salvarias said. "No one will believe me."

"I do." It came out before she realized it, but she let her mind run away with her mouth. "I do believe something is inside you. I do believe you have every power to infect others with it. We've seen you do things I can't explain. Anyone who denies it is an idiot. I'm not. But I see the difference between what you can do and what you are trying to do. You're fighting it. You're trying to be good and do good. That's what matters. Maybe what you did to your parents' murderer is one of the few times you caved to the evil, but I see how you've looked after Lunara. I have no doubt you would never hurt her or your brother. That is what I believe."

"Then you are a fool. One day I will lose my fight, Lady Varila, and it will overtake me. And when it does, anyone in my path will perish."

They stood staring at each other, finding no words. She'd learned too much to digest. And he was too stubborn to see anything else but what he believed.

Then she realized what drove him. "It's what your mother told you, isn't it? That's why she beat you."

Salvarias winced and pressed his hand over his heart. He turned from her, reaching out to lean on the railing. "You have learned I can talk to animals, you have learned my mother sought to rid me of my evil, you have seen me murder and laugh about it, you have learned why I cannot touch another, and you have learned what resides in my soul." More tears skidded down his cheeks. "I have nothing left to confess. I have given you everything you wanted, more than even my brother knows. I beg you again, stay with your sister. Do not subject her to me."

Varila shook her head.

His jaw rippled. "Have you at least learned enough to continue your pursuit for my brother's affections?"

"Yes," she said hoarsely.

After a curt bow, he made his way belowdecks, leaving Varila with too much information to sort through. With heavy steps, she made her way to her room. Wilhelm was lying on the bed, boots kicked off, fingers laced behind his head.

"Want to tell me what that was about?" he asked.

Varila merely shook her head, not trusting herself to speak.

"This doesn't change anything." Wilhelm sat up. "I love you, but I'm not ready for our relationship to move forward."

She mutely nodded. Nor was she. Sex was the last thing on her mind.

She wholeheartedly believed Wilhelm was wrong to withhold the knowledge of the shadowfires from Salvarias. Knowing what created him could go a long way in helping him understand himself, not to mention explaining the evil he felt inside himself and why his mother had seen him as something else besides a mere child. But Varila had made Wilhelm a promise, and she wasn't ready to break it. Yet.

Chapter 31

Autumn 1018 a.r.

Salvarias emerged on deck to be greeted by the warm sun and a bone-chilling breeze. Storm clouds from the north threatened the blue skies and calm waters.

Absently, he reached for Adok, but the wolf had lazily decided to stay in bed, taking Salvarias's spot beside Lunara. He hugged his spell book close as he politely tilted his head to sailors and made his way to the starboard railing. The gulls greeted him with enthusiasm, and he graciously declined their offers to catch him fresh fish. Soon their chatter went quiet and they merely soared alongside the ship, rising and falling with the currents.

He took a few moments to converse with a dolphin, several sharks, a pod of whales, and various fish. Like watythms, sea life was full of spirit and adventure, traveling from place to place, fulfilling needs at a whim.

The ocean's song was as lulling as the trees', and he wished he could understand it. Winsire books were near impossible to obtain, and watythms never wrote anything down so learning the language of either was unattainable. Unless of course he were to ask one, but he knew no watythms nor did he find appeal in asking Neithelas. So instead, he closed his eyes and allowed it to whisper through his mind.

Last night had been a painful lesson in self-control. He had slept as far from Lunara as possible, but he desired nothing more than to hold her and sleep a dreamless sleep. He had woken her several times with his nightmares, and she offered her comforts to him each time, but he had refused. Their relationship was getting uncomfortably close.

I told you, my little murderer, the presence hissed. *It wasss a missstake to allow her ssso clossse to you. Do you not sssee her hope? Her persssistenccce clearly statesss ssshe thinksss you will love her one day. Would you? Would you taint her purity with your wickednessss?*

No, he said firmly. *She is a friend.*

Ssso you sssay. Let usss hope you can abide by your promissse to keep her sssafe. The farther from you, the sssafer ssshe will be.

Salvarias grimaced at the voice, hating it for its words. He wanted it gone. He did not want to listen to it any longer. He knew what he must do, but being reminded, being called *murderer*, wore on his nerves.

I will never leave, the presence said. *Sssomeone mussst make you sssee yoursssself for who you truly are, my preciousss murderer.*

"Good morning!"

Salvarias nearly jumped clear of his skin. His weak heart faltered, flashing spots in his vision and making him lightheaded. Grabbing the railing for support, he looked over to see Kisra striding for him. She was as lovely as yesterday, full of life and mischief, daring and fire. Her smile was wide and welcoming, whereas her eyes were older than her years, giving off an aura of innocent seduction. He looked away, bowing slightly. "My lady."

She joined him and leaned her back against the railing, propping her elbows on it. Her white tunic was covered by a thick leather coat, and her leather pants hugged every curve. Wind whipped through her hair, tossing it about like flames.

"When are you going to teach me?" she asked.

"We can begin now, if you would like." She nodded, her smile growing and reaching to spark her eyes with life. "Do you know the light spell?" he asked.

"Of course. I'm not an idiot."

"Forgive me. I did not mean to imply such."

"I know all the level-one spells."

Salvarias tilted his head in apology. "Though it is simple, let us start with the light spell. If you would be so kind as to perform it, I might better understand where to start my instruction."

Rolling her eyes, she muttered under her breath and drew the energy. He was certain she only took from him. Her words reached inside him and plucked at his strength. Dizziness warped his vision and he latched hold of the railing as his legs nearly gave out. After a quick flick of her hand, a ball of brilliant light appeared.

Blinking his vision clear, he inhaled a shaky breath and said, "You pulled from me."

"You were the closest thing. I just grabbed whatever was around."

"Much more and you would have put me in bed."

Her grin was wicked. "Maybe that's where I want you."

"My lady, you could have easily killed me."

"Ugh! You sound like Cessia." She turned to the ocean, frown on her lips. "I don't know how else to do it."

Clearly she was distraught. In need of advice, he ignited his magic.

Kisra sucked in a breath. "My gods, you have so much power! How did you do that?"

"I do not understand," he said to her.

My wizard, his magic greeted. *None others have our relationship. None allow it to rest as you do with me. It is why they aren't as powerful as us. When I am not awake, your power does not feel as strong.*

She does not speak to it?

No. Sadly, in regards to other mages, their magic flows through them like their blood. Unrecognized, used, and mistreated.

Salvarias cringed at yet another oddity from others.

Gifts, my wizard. You have gifts, not oddities. Without them, we would not be what we are. Are you so willing to trade me for normalcy?

Of course not, my dear friend. Forgive me. Is there nothing she can do to better her connection with her magic?

Perhaps if she focuses long enough she might sense it within her. I doubt she would ever converse with it. But at least she could acknowledge it, make it feel like a friend to her instead of a foe. Right now, the reason she struggles with energy is because she thinks she knows best. She is fighting with her magic, not allowing it to guide her. I beg you, help this poor women. Her magic is petrified of her.

When he turned his attention back to Kisra, she was eying him suspiciously. "Where'd you go?" she asked. "You looked like you were miles away."

"Let us start with another exercise," he said, ignoring her question. "Think of your magic as a presence inside you. It is part of you, but also separate. You must work toward the same goals together, as one."

Kisra shook her head. "Cessia said our magic wants to kill us."

"That is what mages have been led to believe. We are told to control it fully, to enslave it to our will. But we have been misguided. Magic is as frightened of us as we are of it. Yes, we must be in control, lead it, but we do not own it. We are merely the guides. The protectors of it. Only when we fight it are we in danger. For now, I want you to practice connecting with it. Sit in a room with no distractions, and clear your mind of everything but magic. Try to feel it within you. Once you have accomplished this, find me and we will proceed."

Kisra looked less than convinced but nodded. "I'll try."

As she turned, he said, "Might I bother you with a question?"

"Sure," she said, smiling a smile that suggested he was going to ask something else.

"Yesterday, when we met on the docks, you did not immediately recognize me as a mage. Why is that?"

A frown tugged down the corners of her mouth and furrowed her brow. "I don't think I understand. I mean, we can't always be looking for mages. We'd never be able to focus on anything else."

What does she mean? he asked his magic.

I haven't a clue. Perhaps ... ask her if she has to focus to find a mage.

"What is your method of discovering if a person has magic?" Salvarias asked.

Kisra looked him up and down. "You're an odd one. You knew I was a mage. So obviously you did what I did."

"Which was?"

She blew out a puff of air and placed her hands on her hips. "I thought I saw robes under your cloak so I ... reached out to check if you were a mage."

"You have to search? You do not simply feel magic in a person?"

"No mage can. You have to look for it, purposefully. You kind of ... I don't know how to describe it, but you reach out your mind and then you can feel the magic. It doesn't just come to you." Her eyes narrowed. "How do you do it?"

Embarrassed by yet another difference, he merely shrugged off her question. "Thank you, my lady."

"Yeah, sure." She looked at him again as if he were some foreign creature before leaving to join her sister at the ship's bow.

Salvarias turned his attention back to the ocean, fighting away a pang of longing. Even in magic he was different. The desire to bond with fellow mages and learn of magic together would never be fulfilled. Yes, he might be able to instruct them, but who would instruct him? His uncle? Mafarias surely had the experience, but something had always prevented Salvarias from trusting the man. From his memories, a mage had sat idly by while his mother had beat him and poured leeches on him. The figure could have been Mafarias, but after what Idolar had said about Vuddruk visiting Falar in the brothers' youth, the old mage was as likely a suspect. Perhaps it was Himiks. That mage had owned the magic shop his mother had worked in and was cruel enough to gain enjoyment from such a spectacle.

Sighing at the uncertainties in his life, Salvarias buried his face in his hands and used the ocean's song to calm his mind.

A week passed before Salvarias was set upon by a squealing Kisra. Her voice pitched an octave past pleasant, and Salvarias was appreciative of the expansive deck. If below in a cabin, he feared his ears would explode.

Her rant was one of pure joy that lit up her wide eyes and exuded enough happiness that Salvarias found himself nearly breathless with giddy curiosity. Words flew from her mouth in such short order that he only picked up on a few, but what he did indicated she had connected with her magic. He let her go on until she was gasping for air and finally quieted.

"You were able to sense your magic?" he asked.

She nodded vigorously and rasped out, "Wonderful."

"Could you speak with it?"

Her head shook back and forth, flinging her hair wildly.

"But you felt it?"

After sucking in a long breath she said, "It's wonderful! I-I feel it!" She looked out over the ocean and spread her arms wide, closing her eyes. "Just as I can feel the breeze! As I can feel the creatures in the sea. Just as I listen to the ocean's song. My magic is so warm and caring. It loves me!" A wide grin sliced across her face. "It's even protective. It wants me to be safe. I can ... feel its emotions."

It is better than we could ever hope for, his magic said. *I never thought she could sense its emotions as you sense mine. Her magic is incredibly fond of her adventurous personality. It understands it will be challenged.*

You can speak to other people's magic?

No, but I sense its emotion as she does. She will be a very accomplished mage one day. Do you feel her power? It is so much greater.

Indeed it was. It now surpassed Cessia.

Will she be able to create new spells as we do? Salvarias asked his magic.

Perhaps. Magic has knowledge and inherent instincts when it comes to spells. It would sense an incorrect usage and probably convey disapproval to her. Because she can't talk to it, I doubt it could help her as I help you. However, if she were given your list of magical words, I am sure with study they could work together to come up with new spells. This could be a new beginning for mages, my brilliant wizard. If you taught others as you have taught her, you could free us from enslavement. You could create powerful mages. You could create a partnership of loyalty and care versus fear and ignorance. You can change everything! Ha! Do you feel it? Her magic is jealous of me. It sees what we have, how much you trust me, how much I trust you. It ... it seeks your approval.

How could I offer such a thing?

I haven't a clue, my wizard.

Tentatively, Salvarias sought the power within Kisra. Reaching out his mind, he imagined a rope tied to his magic and to that of the other magic, and then he guided his thoughts—no, perhaps his soul itself—into her and found her magic easily, like finding a candle in a dark room. It flickered with delight and he startled when it spoke to him.

It is an honor to know you, Master.

Please, he stammered. *Call me Salvarias.*

Kisra's magic had a feminine tone to it, a pulse of softness, yet was lined with hard resolve and drowned in curiosity. It had a reckless abandon that made him nervous.

It gave off a feeling of shame, and he realized how open he had made himself to it.

Forgive me, it said. *I would never hurt Kisra. I have vowed to protect her.*

I am sure you will, he said gently. *Forgive me for doubting you.*

You have so much knowledge, Mast—I mean, Salvarias. How can I help her grow?

With time. For now, continue to work on your connection with her. Drawing energy is an area where she sorely lacks finesse.

Her mind is fleeting from one thing to the next. It will be difficult for me to help her, but I will try.

It is all I could ask of you. Thank you for caring for her. I feel she has a good heart.

Indeed she does.

Be well.

You as well, Salvarias.

Slowly Salvarias withdrew, realizing for the first time that he had lost his vision and had only seen the light of her magic. When he came to himself, Kisra was on her knees, wide eyes staring up at him.

"Whatever you ask of me," she breathed, "I will do. I am yours to command."

Salvarias stepped back, looking around at the people staring at them. "Please, my lady, rise. There—"

"Are you a god?"

Salvarias whipped his head around to her. "Why would you say such a thing?"

"I ... I felt you ... your true power. It's not magic. It's something else."

"Please," he said urgently. "Rise. I am not a god. I am just a man."

Using the railing, she pulled herself to her feet, wide eyes never drifting from Salvarias. "How did you do that?"

"Forgive me, my lady. I merely wanted to understand your magic and help you." Eager to move past what he had done, he said, "Let us begin your instruction."

Her demeanor toward him had changed from open to cautious, and it shone in her eyes. Biting back a pang of regret, he vowed to never attempt such a thing with another mage ever again.

Chapter 32

Autumn 1018 a.r.

Salvarias lazily watched the rippling waves of the deep blue ocean pushing against the ship. Not far off, a strip of land sliced across the horizon: Loutsil. The most dangerous continent for mages, winsires, watythms, and cavruls. Only the Bellerum sisters, Humar, and Wilhelm were safe here. It was the one place he did not want to visit, and the one place he had no choice but to wander.

For the past three weeks, Salvarias had instructed Lunara in herblore in the evenings and taught Kisra magic in the mornings. Having another to talk to about magic, he had developed a bond with Kisra. They spent hours on deck where Salvarias learned there were only a few things he could do that Kisra could not. Enchanting was one, but the other odd one was that mages other than himself could not perform more than one spell at a time. Whenever Kisra thought to do so, her magic's emotion was simply terror and refusal. Though curious why, Salvarias accepted it as is and did not seek an audience with her magic again. He could not further estrange their relationship. She still looked at him on occasion with wide eyes, filled with part fear and part adoration. He found it unsettling.

Kisra was not the only one benefitting from his instruction. Whatever Salvarias taught her, she immediately turned around and taught Cessia. The older sister's power grew daily, and Salvarias predicted it would only continue. Her magic was as clearly eager and as adventurous as its partner.

For the entire journey, Salvarias had artfully avoided Varila, though she attempted to corner him several times. He could not meet her gaze and felt exposed, naked in front of her. What was worse, his sacrifice had been for nothing. Wilhelm's demeanor toward Varila was still guarded and distant. Whatever Varila's plan had been had failed, and Salvarias chastised himself for telling her all he had told her.

"Salvarias," Humar said, striding up to the railing Salvarias leaned against. "We'll be docking in a few hours. I've been thinking of the best way to handle this, and I'm certain I shouldn't enter the city. I want to take one of the boats ashore well outside the city limits. You should come as well."

"I fear I must enter Senti or else I have no hopes of picking up Perek's trail."

"You'll need a disguise. You can't go in there wearing robes."

Salvarias nodded reluctantly. "Of course. I will borrow some of my brother's clothes."

"No, they won't fit. You can use mine. The trews might be short, but they'll fit better than your brother's. Cessia said the guards at the docks know her ship. Anyone getting off won't be questioned or stopped, so you shouldn't run into any issues. Keep your head down and as soon as you can, change back into your robes. Once you're in the city, you won't be questioned."

"As you wish," Salvarias said. He glanced at Humar. "You can stay aboard, my friend. There is no need—"

"Nope, I'm coming. I'll take the sisters, Neithelas, Durak, and Adok with me. Okulu can talk his way out of anything, and I prefer you two to have some company in case things go poorly."

"Of course."

Humar inhaled a deep breath, his gaze locked on the approaching land. "I hate Loutsil. I really hate it."

With that, he left to talk with Cessia.

Lunara joined Salvarias as she watched Humar.

"He's scared," she said.

"Indeed." Salvarias wrapped her in his cloak when she shivered. Winter was upon Loutsil and the wind had turned biting and vicious.

Before long, the companions joined Salvarias and Lunara on deck. All watched the land growing before them, eating up sky and contentment the closer to it they drew.

"We're splitting up," Humar said suddenly. "Durak, the sisters, and Neithelas will take a boat ashore with me when we clear the inlet to the bay. The brothers and Okulu will go into the city to pick up the trail. Once they have it, we'll meet north of the city."

"I don't think it wise we split up," Lunara said.

"Agreed," Varila snapped. "You're an idiot to let Salvarias wander in there with just Wilhelm and a half-breed. Loutsil barely tolerates winsires."

"We have no choice," Humar said. "Salvarias is the only one who can pick up Perek's trail, which I'll remind all of you is the reason we're here. Okulu can handle himself. This is the right choice. No arguments."

There were of course. Salvarias barely listened to them as there was no point. Humar would win in the end. Instead, he watched the passing rocky shores of the inlet leading into Senti Bay. If Windlous would have had color, it would look like Loutsil. Mainly hills and patches of forest, the landscape lacked the dismal cloud cover and misty rain of Windlous. Instead, the sun beamed off patches of early winter snow that had yet to melt. The distant trees were stark and lifeless, as were the dying grasses. The sky, however, was the most brilliant shade of blue Salvarias had ever seen. Tufts of lonely clouds marred its solidness and dappled the undulating ground with halfhearted shadows.

"It's time," Cessia called. "Much farther and we'll be running into patrols."

Goodbyes were terse and stiff, and Varila's glare threatened to set the ship aflame. Though Wilhelm grinned and winked at her often, it did not change her scowl or curses at Humar. Adok's lecture had not stopped since Salvarias had mentioned separating, and he mused it would continue long after the wolf was out of his company.

In no time, the others were ferried ashore and when the boat returned, they were once again heading toward Senti.

"You're in for a long night," Okulu commented to Wilhelm.

"That I am," his brother said. "She's been ... odd lately." Wilhelm glanced at Salvarias. "She won't tell me what you two talked about."

Salvarias shrugged. "It is for her to share, brother. It is not my place."

Inside, he screamed in frustration. For her to torment him so and then not use her knowledge to better her relationship with Wilhelm was nothing shy of manipulative.

For the remainder of the short trip to Senti, Salvarias changed into regular clothes, finding them foreign and uncomfortable, and then made ready the horses before joining Okulu on deck. The merc was staring at the approaching docks, a frown on his face.

"Is something wrong?" Salvarias asked.

"I'm not sure," Okulu said hesitantly. He pointed toward the far end of the dock and the people congregated there, voices raised in anger. "I can't see what they're yelling at, and I can't hear what they're saying. Could be trouble, could be nothing. Knowing our luck," Okulu grumbled, "it's trouble."

Salvarias guessed the same.

Okulu glanced over at Cessia and rubbed his cheek. "If her contacts have been compromised, they'll kill her on sight. I've told her we should go back, but she insists they would never turn on her. Part of the watythm charm, I guess. They think everyone is loyal."

"Perhaps she should stay aboard," Salvarias murmured. "You as well."

Okulu frowned. "Why me?"

Salvarias arched an eyebrow. "Do you think you hide your feelings for her so easily?"

The merc let out a hardy laugh. "All right, you got me. I do love my little sea-kelp, but I'm not ready to settle down yet. Winsires and watythms live long lives. We have plenty of time. And remember, there's an army out there. If we don't find it and stop it, there will be no place safe for any of us."

Docking the ship was a trial of Salvarias's patience. It seemed to take an eternity before ropes were cast and tied and the horses led down to the solid planks of the docks. Salvarias was certain the ship still rocked beneath his feet.

Wilhelm grimaced and stomped his feet. "It'll be weeks before this damn sensation goes away."

Cessia leaned over the railing and called down to them, "Go ahead. I'll join you in a moment."

"Let's get you past the guard," Okulu said to Salvarias. "There's a tavern a few streets up, and we'll rent a room, change, and you and Wilhelm can stay there while I get provisions. Anything look familiar?"

"Actually, it does," Salvarias said, studying the rows of well-kept buildings. Even the docks were clean and exuded a sense of wealth. The cobblestone streets gleamed in the sun, and the buildings looked to have been recently washed. Men and women in fine clothes strolled here and there, servants following them, some even chained.

"If you don't have enough money for your own shop and home, you're a slave," Okulu said. "Disgusting."

Wilhelm grunted an agreement. "Let's get this over with."

As they made their way to the end of the pier, Okulu's gaze fixed on the crowd surrounding a section of dock in front of a building sporting a sign reading PORT INSPECTOR. Salvarias could hear their jeering and taunts.

"What's your business?" a gruff voiced said.

Salvarias turned his attention to the guards blocking the end of the pier.

"Visiting family in Warton," Okulu said smoothly. He grinned and nodded subtly to Cessia's boat.

The guard's dark eyes followed Okulu's motion and then focused on Wilhelm and settled on Salvarias. "You know, we've heard of a mage the Association is hunting. One recently removed from the list. One said to the most powerful mage to ever walk our world. It's said he's a tall one, black hair, black eyes, and he's got a behemoth of a brother." His gaze switched between Wilhelm and Salvarias. "And here before me is a man fitting the description. And coming in on a boat known to transport condemned mages to Windlous."

The guard flicked his hand toward the crowd, and Salvarias caught a glimpse of what drew their attention. Five guards were chained to posts, whipped near death.

"Seems your safe passage has been compromised." The guard grinned and then called over his shoulder, "Bring me the slave!"

A man, beaten and abused, with a chain around his neck, was pulled forward. He wore tattered mage robes, and Salvarias's defeat rose as he sensed the slave's magic. This was the reason mages did not try to sneak into cities.

"This boy a mage?" the guard asked.

The slave's eyes widened and his mouth moved without speaking.

The guard backhanded him, sending a tooth and blood flinging from the man's mouth. "I asked you a question!"

"Yes," the man sobbed.

"Powerful?" the guard asked.

"M-m-more power than possible," the mage responded.

"We've been waiting for you and that ship to show up," the guard said, grin spreading. "Looks like it's our lucky day. Boys!" Twenty guards filed out of the crowd. "Go find me that witch and her sister!"

The presence snorted with contempt. *I have told you before, my little murderer, you put thossse in your company in conssstant danger.*

Salvarias looked over his shoulder to see Cessia and Kisra walking down the ramp. When they saw the guards, they whirled around and began shouting to the crew to cast off. They would not make it in time. Desperate, Salvarias ignited his magic, flicked out his rune, and sent a fireball to the pier. Flames snapped wood and sparks flew into the air. The crowd screamed and raised hands to cover their faces from the heat. The fire fed upon a section blocking the guards' path to Cessia and would hopefully burn long enough to provide her time to make an escape.

Horrible pain lanced through Salvarias's head and ripped down his body. Vision left him and sounds drowned out save for a horrible ringing in his ears. Shaking his head, he looked up to see he had fallen to the ground. Wilhelm was being restrained by ten men. Grimacing, Salvarias touched the lump on the side of his head. One of the guards held a club.

"Look here," Okulu said, hands raised. "I don't know these two. I just want my horses and to be on my way. Your little slave there can check me. I'm not a mage, just a man visiting family. I thought they were too, at least, that's what they told me."

The guard narrowed his eyes and slowly nodded. "I suggest you leave this city."

"Quickly, rest assured," Okulu said with a quick bow. He cast one glance over his shoulder at Cessia's ship, briefly met Salvarias's gaze, and then scurried ahead.

"Stop," Salvarias whispered to Wilhelm. His brother paused in his struggle. "Do nothing, brother. Promise me you will do nothing."

"No," Wilhelm growled.

Salvarias moved his lips, willing his voice to be for Wilhelm's ears only. "You must wait for Okulu to find Humar to help you rescue me. You cannot do this alone. You must wait."

Wilhelm's face contorted in indecision.

"There is no other option," Salvarias insisted. "Humar will need to know where I am kept, and if both of us are imprisoned, it will take him longer to come to our aid. You know you cannot fight your way through an entire city. You must trust me. I beg you, brother, trust me."

Wilhelm slowly nodded.

Salvarias looked up at the guard as he tenderly hauled himself to his feet. Warm blood dripped down his neck. "My brother poses no harm. He has done nothing against the laws of Loutsil."

The guard looked Wilhelm up and down, eyes appraising the situation. Salvarias thanked the gods they found a guard who seemed to abide by the laws, as unjust as they were.

"Release him," the guard said. To Wilhelm, he said, "If I see you around and if you cause any trouble, I'll have you arrested and flogged." He motioned to another guard. "Bring a wagon and truss up the mage."

Salvarias looked at Wilhelm again. "I will survive this, so promise me you will not interfere. Promise me."

Wilhelm swallowed hard and clenched his jaw. "Promise."

"Leave," the guard ordered Wilhelm.

His brother yanked his arms free from those holding him and snatched up Salvarias's staff. Shoving by the guards, he disappeared in the crowd.

A flatbed wagon appeared, pulled by a single horse, and the guards dragged Salvarias onto the bed of the wagon, forced him to kneel, and chained him to a single post. Closing his eyes, he prepared himself, gaining control of his fear and setting his expression. As they entered the city, he shut out the screams of hatred, the people spitting on him, the rocks thrown at him. He did not wince, did not cry out, and did not look at Wilhelm but knew his brother followed him through the crowd.

Chapter 33

Autumn 1018 a.r.

Wilhelm pushed people out of his way, grabbing rocks he saw raised toward his brother. The wealthy and slaves alike jeered and spat on Salvarias and pelted him with rotting vegetables, some slaves going as far as flinging horse dung. His brother endured it without a single cry of pain, even as blood ran down the side of his face from an artfully thrown stone.

Wilhelm cursed those he saw hurting his brother, but as he had promised Salvarias, he did nothing else. Restraining himself was nearing impossible, so when the wagon finally came to a halt outside a single-story stone building, Wilhelm let out a puff of pent-up air.

Indented into the structure was a wide, open courtyard facing the main thoroughfare. Ten marbled columns lined it, all with chains hanging down and stained with old blood. To one, a young mage was chained. He wailed constantly, begging for mercy through retching sobs. His face was black and blue and swollen, his body sagging against his restraints. The front of him was covered in filth, some of it his own.

A set of guards dragged Salvarias from the wagon to a column on the opposite side of the courtyard. By the time he had been chained, blood ran from his nose and he convulsed from lack of air. Before he passed out, the guards finished and stopped touching him. Salvarias gasped, his face shiny and pale.

Wilhelm closed his eyes, battling his rage. He'd made a promise, and he never broke a promise. All he could do was place faith in Humar and Salvarias. Salvarias would find a way to survive until Humar came to their rescue. He had to.

A sudden uneasiness raised the hairs on the back of Wilhelm's neck. He opened his eyes and standing beside him was a cloaked figure. Whomever or whatever it was clearly had ill intentions. It reeked of it.

Before he even moved, an orange hand jetted out from beneath the cloak, one insanely long fingernail heading to the back of Wilhelm's head.

He managed to get his hand to the hilt of his dagger before sharp pain stabbed the base of his neck. The crowd dissipated from his awareness, and his mind lazily floated along a calm river of memories.

"Shush now," a voice whispered. It was not Unupture, as Wilhelm had expected. This voice was smoother, hypnotic. "Relax and breathe."

Wilhelm inhaled a long, deep breath.

"Very good," the voice said. "We're going to remember now. Do not fight me."

He doubted he could if he wanted to. He felt groggy, like he'd slept too long, and his thoughts were slow to come.

Then, rising to view were memories of Salvarias. They fleeted before him, brief images from their childhood all the way to adulthood, mainly focused on times when Wilhelm would find his brother beaten from bullies. A low babble of conversations shared with his brother blended together, again centered around Salvarias's early years. For the creature to care about those years, it made Wilhelm wonder for the first time if something else hadn't happened to Salvarias on those days Tobin had dragged Wilhelm to the training yards. Perhaps Unupture, Dethal, or Sansis had snatched Salvarias from Ashra. After all, Salvarias's reactions—now that Wilhelm so clearly recalled them—seemed excessive for a mere encounter with a couple of snotty kids. Sure, the bruises were horrible, but a walloping from a kid wouldn't make another kid so utterly withdrawn, fearing adults as much as Salvarias had done. And the marks on his brother's body had changed over the years, not looking like bruises from a fist fight. Matter of fact, they looked the same as the leech marks Salvarias had had in the swamps.

As the creature sorted through Wilhelm's memories, it began to piece together assumptions, guesses, facts. It organized them in a manner Wilhelm had never thought to do. He'd always accepted Salvarias as is. Rarely did he try to understand his brother. Wilhelm would love Salvarias regardless of what he understood or didn't. But as some of the mysteries of Salvarias's personality unraveled, the reasons for his brother's withdrawal and aloofness were painfully clear.

It all made so much sense. His brother had watched their mother be raped and burned alive, all for a power she never wanted. Tobin, a man Salvarias had just accepted, was tortured and murdered simply for being in her company. As if that weren't enough, the creature focused on the times Salvarias had confessed his evil, the hopelessness in his eyes, the defeat in his voice. The evil combined with his magic made Salvarias look upon himself as a danger to those around him.

To add to Wilhelm's sinking gut, the creature found comments Wilhelm had never paid much attention to. "I cannot leave him" had switched over the months to "I cannot leave him yet." His brother was working up to roaming Arden alone. No wife, no children, no life of his own. Salvarias, in his delusional mind, thought to spare himself and any others pain. And without needing the creature to point it out, there wasn't a damn thing Wilhelm could do to stop it. One day, his brother would abandon him. All of Salvarias's tortured life had been dragging him to one inevitable end: Salvarias would die alone and afraid.

Heartache pierced straight through Wilhelm. Ever since Tobin had come into their lives, Salvarias had slowly rotted away inside, living in his dungeon of loneliness built of tears and pain. He only fought on because Wilhelm had asked him to.

"Secrets," the creature whispered, "are the evil of the world. And you and your brother bathe in them." Wilhelm winced when the pain in his neck deepened, but it quickly vanished, leaving his mind once again tranquil. "Does it anger you knowing your brother will leave you? After all you've done for him, all you've sacrificed for him. You've given up the woman you love for him, you never joined the knighthood because you did not want to leave his side. You fought Tobin when he would take you to train, despite your love of the sword. All you've given for your brother, and he cares not. You lost him years ago, Protector. He will abandon you, and there is nothing you can do to stop him. Failure is bitter, is it not?"

It was. He tasted it in his mouth, felt the hole it carved out of his heart. All his life he'd only wanted to see Salvarias happy, and all his life he'd been delusional enough to think he could accomplish such a feat. Now, he realized how futile his fight had been, how pointless.

"Your brother will die," the creature hissed. "And you will watch the life leave his eyes, helpless to stop it. Failure, oh mighty warrior, is your destiny."

Wilhelm's entire body lurched as the creature withdrew its nail. The shock and pain of coming into ownership of his own mind crumpled him to his hands and knees, vomiting and shaking, sweat dripping down his forehead to dot the cobblestones.

People around him backed away as if he had a disease. When he finally gained control of his stomach, Wilhelm couldn't remember why he'd fallen or what had made him empty his stomach. What he did remember was a lesson: a lesson he would never forget, a lesson that revealed his brother's true heart and pain. A lesson of failure.

Anger embedded itself inside Wilhelm, and when he looked up, he hated everything he saw.

Nearly an hour passed before an older man dressed in white robes with a guard escort emerged into the square. He approached the other mage and spoke quietly with the captive. Wilhelm watched the mage's face go deathly white. The white-robed man motioned to a guard who walked forward and, without so much as a word or hesitation, slit the mage's throat. There was no uproar of anger from the crowd, only cheers.

The robed man turned and walked to Salvarias. Wilhelm's heart thudded painfully. He made it one step before Salvarias shook his head. In Wilhelm's mind, his brother's soft voice said, "That will not happen to me, and you promised."

Clenching his hands into tight fists, Wilhelm stayed put.

The robed man talked with Salvarias quietly for several agonizing moments until finally the robed man seemed to get what he wanted. He motioned a few guards over and spoke to them before heading to the nearest door in the courtyard and disappearing into the building. The men he'd spoken to unchained Salvarias and took him out of sight through the same door.

Wilhelm sought the support of a nearby wall to keep from falling to his knees in relief. Closing his eyes, he focused on breathing and calming his shaking body. He stayed that way for what seemed like eternity until a hand clamped down on his arm.

He jerked away and had a dagger in his hand before he even opened his eyes. Before him, Okulu cringed and held up his hands in surrender.

"Easy," the merc said. "What happened? Where is he?"

Wilhelm pointed the tip of his dagger toward the door the guards had escorted his brother through and said, "In there. It's been," he glanced at the sky, "a few hours since you left. What in Oblivion took so long?"

"Long story," Okulu mumbled. "Winsires are not loved here. Let's go."

Okulu led Wilhelm around the corner of a nearby building and into an alley. Humar and the sisters were waiting.

"You look like crap," Varila said.

Wilhelm grunted and turned to Humar. "How do we get him out of there?"

"Dungeons," Okulu said to the knight. "It'll be impossible to get to him."

"We need to hurry," Lunara said. "His mind is weakening. Soon he'll need you, Wilhelm."

Humar ran a hand through his hair. Sweat beaded on his forehead even in the cool winter breeze. "Dammit," he muttered. "Dammit it all to Oblivion."

"Come on old friend," Okulu said, a tinge of urgency in his voice. "He doesn't have time. Do you have a plan or not? Because if you don't, I'll wind up Wilhelm here and send him charging in."

Humar shook his head. "Inside is heavily guarded. He'll never make it."

"Humar," Lunara said. "We must hurry."

The knight slung out a string of curses. "Follow me. Don't say a word."

With that, Humar strode from the alley. He walked with purpose, standing taller than normal, his steps crisp with military training. At the door leading to where Salvarias had been taken, he stopped and addressed one of the five men standing watch. "I request an audience with the judicator who passed judgment on the two mages chained here today."

"You'll have to schedule an appointment," the guard said.

Humar tossed aside his cloak to reveal his armor. "Now."

The guard scrambled to a salute and flung open the door. "Forgive me. If you'll follow me, Sir Knight."

Wilhelm was on Humar's heels, doing everything in his power not to shove the guard down the steep stairs they descended. The air grew colder and colder the farther down they climbed, heavy breaths billowing out in visible clouds. He barely paid attention to the deterioration of the bricks the farther they went. Every bend of the stairs had an indent where two guards were posted. Smells began to waft up the narrow stairwell, and none were pleasant. It was the sweet smell of blood mingling with the sour stench of rot.

"We must hurry," Lunara urged from behind.

Humar nudged the guard in the back. "Faster."

They descended a few more floors before the stairwell dumped into a receiving room of sorts. A few desks stood in the stark stone room, each housing a man robed in white. From the room, a half-dozen corridors branched off, each blocked by a heavy iron door muffling the screams coming from beyond.

The guard led them to the man Wilhelm had seen in the courtyard, the same old man who'd ordered the mage's throat slit. He did not look up from the parchment he scribbled on, but addressed the guard. "What is it?" His voice was flat and cold.

"A knight here to see you." The guard saluted Humar and left.

The judicator looked up briefly at the group and returned to writing. "What can I do for you, Sir Knight?"

"The mage you just took into custody," Humar said, "needs to be turned over to me."

The judicator stretched out a hand, still not looking at Humar. "Papers."

"I have none."

"You know the laws, Knight."

Humar stood for a moment, indecision evident on his face. He looked at Wilhelm and inhaled a deep breath before turning back to the judicator. Drawing his sword, he tossed it on the man's desk. "By order of Prince Lilkous, I command you to release the prisoner to my care."

The judicator looked at the sword, and his eyes widened as he raised his head to meet Humar's steady gaze. "Prince Humar?"

Humar's hands shook and he pressed them to his side. "By my command, release the prisoner."

Everyone in the room went down to one knee, heads bowed, except Wilhelm and his friends. They stood with mouths gaping open.

The judicator said, "You understand, my lord, that I must take you to Warton to verify your claim. It has been years and anyone could have stolen your sword."

"You doubt my word?" Humar snarled. "Or that I can defend my birthright? You think so little of my skill?"

"N-no, my prince. But the queen has given orders. I must take you to Warton."

Sweat broke out on Humar's forehead, and Wilhelm feared the knight would pass out. Seeming to gain control of himself, Humar nodded and said, "So be it, but the mage is in my custody. He is not to be harmed."

"I regret to inform you he is already under interrogation."

"Humar," Lunara said urgently.

"Take us to him now," Humar barked.

The white-robed man bolted to his feet and fumbled with a heavy key ring as he ran toward one of the iron doors. He unlocked it and sprinted to the fourth cell. He fought the keys and selected another, unlocked the cell, and stepped aside.

Filth covered the dank cell, dead rats scattered along its sides, roaches and other unsavory insects scurrying about. Salvarias's arms were stretched over his head with his wrists chained together. Two men paused in beating on Salvarias, looking at the judicator with mild surprise.

"Unlock it!" Wilhelm roared, shoving the men from Salvarias. He gently raised his brother's face, anger roaring to life as he stared at Salvarias's eyes swollen shut and blood running from his split lip. His brother's breathing was harsh and wet.

The judicator pushed aside the men and found another key and removed the shackles. Salvarias would have fell to the floor had Wilhelm not caught him. Snatching his brother's hand, he pressed their marks together. Salvarias winced and tried to pull away, but Wilhelm held firm. Only a bit of Wilhelm's strength drained before Salvarias won his fight.

"It's all right, Salv," Wilhelm whispered. "You're safe."

Salvarias's body went limp in Wilhelm's arms. He swooped his brother up and carried him from the cell, following Humar and the judicator as they made their way back to the receiving room.

"It is a four-day journey to Warton by wagon," the judicator said. "Our most skilled guards will escort you."

348

Humar nodded. "Our horses are to follow and be tended to." He jerked his head to Okulu. "He can lead you to them and two other of my companions. None of them are to be harmed."

"Of course." The judicator gave directions to a few guards who had gathered in the receiving room, all bowing their heads. "Is there anything else I can provide, my lord?"

Humar shook his head.

"It is good to have you home again," the judicator said. "Finally, Loutsil's rightful heir will be crowned King of Arden."

Chapter 34

Autumn 1018 a.r.

Humar watched Lunara clean Salvarias's face as the wagon lurched along, wheels plodding through snow and mud. The jingle of armor accompanied the thudding timed footfalls of over two hundred guards. Plush pillows covered the wagon's bed and thick blankets kept the chilly outside air at bay. They'd been on the road for less than an hour, but the day had been long and, one by one, Humar's friends were caving to sleep. Humar could not.

Escape consumed his thoughts. He needed to be free before Warton, but with over two hundred men escorting him, he knew freedom was no longer his. Soon he would be chained to the throne, the damned crown resting upon his brow as the Lilkous curse slowly drove him mad. Could he already feel it? He wiped sweat from his forehead and closed his eyes.

What choice did he have? Salvarias would have died if Humar had not revealed his identity. And now, if he tried to escape his friends would pay for his folly. He would have to go to Warton. He would have to face his mother, face what he'd done all those years ago. And his sister. Tears flooded behind his eyelids and he quickly wiped away the one that escaped. He'd left her alone and fled the day he'd killed his father. He should've taken her with him. He should've protected her. Gods only knew what she'd suffered in his absence. Their mother was no better than their father. Surely she'd made his sister's life miserable.

Sighing in defeat, Humar drifted off into a doze.

Humar fully woke as daylight peeked through the slits in the wagon's covering. By the subdued hue of yellow, it was early morning. His friends were asleep except for Salvarias. His face looked remarkably better, but blood crusted shut one eye and one corner of his mouth was swollen.

"How are you?" Humar whispered.

"I am more concerned about you," Salvarias said. "You have risked much for my safety."

Humar forced out a smile he hoped was warm. "I consider you family, my nephews. Tobin was my brother if not by blood then by heart."

Salvarias's gaze dropped to his hands, which were running over Adok's ears. The wolf might've been asleep, but Humar couldn't be certain.

"Thank you, Humar," Salvarias said softly. "I am eternally grateful for your sacrifice."

Humar took a deep breath as a bit of weight lifted from his shoulders. The brothers were worth his freedom.

"You are heir to the throne?" Salvarias asked after a moment.

"Yes."

"Why did you leave?" Salvarias asked.

"When I was fifteen, I killed my father and fled before his blood had stopped gushing."

Salvarias's eyes flickered with curiosity. "You are not an evil man. I assume your father must have been?"

Humar nodded. "He killed his brother, the king at the time. It wasn't even the worst thing he'd done."

Okulu stretched and immediately followed it with a swig from his flask. He grinned at Salvarias. "Cessia got away."

Salvarias tilted his head. "They risked much bringing us here."

Okulu grunted. "They risk it each time they help a poor mage escape this forsaken land. No offense," he said to Humar.

"None taken," Humar assured. "Believe me, I have no love for my homeland."

A shout from outside ordered a halt for breakfast, and the wagon lurched to a stop.

Wilhelm sucked in a huge breath and jolted awake, hand grabbing the hilt of his sword.

"Are you all right, brother?" Salvarias asked.

"No, I'm not all right," Wilhelm snapped.

Salvarias flinched.

The flap of the wagon opened, and a slave bowed in greeting. "Your majesty, we have prepared breakfast and a location to bathe and change."

Wilhelm charged his way out of the wagon, knocking aside Neithelas who hadn't moved in time. Humar followed and emerged into blinding sunlight. A closed tent for bathing had been erected and another open tent was set for a casual breakfast. They'd stopped by a large pond, its murky waters reflecting the sun, lazy ripples trailing the light breeze.

Wilhelm was entering the bathing tent, Salvarias not far behind.

"Let's eat first and give them a moment," Humar said to the others.

The food laid out was fit for a king, which was probably the point, but Humar found it a taunting reminder of what lay ahead and it weakened his appetite. He forced himself to eat so as not to bring down punishment on the slaves who had prepared his meal.

Wilhelm's voice roared from the bathing tent. "I'm tired of it, Salv! I could've done something!"

The conversation was one-sided as Salvarias's voice didn't carry to the group.

"Dammit!" Wilhelm stormed from the tent and walked to a nearby cluster of small trees. He beat a poor sapling to the ground.

Salvarias stood slightly back until his brother ceased and then stepped next to Wilhelm, speaking softly.

"I don't care about anybody else!" Wilhelm snapped. "You shouldn't have done that."

Humar and his friends tried to talk and fuss over the food, but it was no use.

"Do you want to die?" Wilhelm demanded. "Is that it? You care about everyone else's happiness and health besides your own."

Salvarias stood silently with his head lowered.

Wilhelm loosed his anger on a new tree then turned back to his brother. "When are you going to do it? Huh? When will you leave me?"

Salvarias's head remained downcast and his submission seemed to only anger Wilhelm further. His fists clenched and his arm made the slightest movement. Humar bolted to his feet, thinking Wilhelm would strike his brother, but instead Wilhelm jerked his head to the bathing tent.

"Get in there and clean up," Wilhelm snarled.

The mage was not gone long before he returned to Wilhelm in fresh robes. Salvarias paused next to his brother, but Wilhelm went into the tent, not saying another word. Humar's heart nearly broke when he saw Salvarias sway once Wilhelm was out of sight. The boy's hooded head turned toward the woods, and he took a faltering step.

Okulu rose swiftly and strode over to Salvarias. The merc talked for a brief moment before he managed to lure Salvarias to Humar's tent. Though the boy's head was lowered, sunlight glistened on the tears falling down his cheeks.

Humar peered out the wagon flap when the treading wheels clomped onto cobblestones. All around, familiar white buildings soared into the dusky sky, growing grander the farther Humar's procession traveled through the city of Warton.

The trip here had been nothing shy of miserable, all due to Wilhelm. The boy refused to talk to anyone, including his brother, and those who tried were cursed to Oblivion and shoved aside. He slept too much, his dreams always troubled. Salvarias had taken the turn of Wilhelm hard. Humar had not seen the boy sleep, and Salvarias's breathing had worsened, his shaking more noticeable, and his counting was no longer a whisper of hypnotic numbers, but instead a desperate sounding stream of chaos. Adok never left the boy's side, even though Salvarias seemed half aware of the wolf's presence. He'd not even touched Adok since Wilhelm's outburst, nor had the boy picked up his spell book, or any book, for that matter. It was unsettling.

The sun that had greeted them their first day refused to make another appearance. Instead, sickly clouds spat rain and had made the journey cold and damp, so despite Humar's dread and trepidation about returning to his home, he was looking forward to a warm, dry bed.

After the lengthy ride to the center of Warton, the wagon finally came to halt. Humar's heart squeezed out a rush of blood and sweat beaded his forehead. Wiping his clammy hands on his trews, he took in a deep breath and tossed aside the wagon flap.

He was surrounded by knights, all at attention, all eyes focused on some point straight ahead of them. Bracing himself, Humar leapt down from the wagon and turned to face his men. In unison, they saluted and then dropped to one knee, heads bowed, the ringing of armor echoing in the courtyard, and the *clink clink* of rain pattering down on the metal.

Swallowing down the bile rising in the back of this throat, Humar saluted in return and shouted, "Rise, Knights of Loutsil."

Armor clanged again as they rose to their feet. Most kept their gazes straight ahead, but a few of the older ones stole brief glances his way. He thought he might have recognized a few, but he had left thirty or so years ago. Time changes all, and everyone he had ever known would be strangers.

An arm linked with his and he looked down to see Lunara smiling up at him. So often during their journey he had been sure the girl would cave to her fears and return home or simply drown in the horrors they had faced. But each time she had bravely conquered her fears, each time she fought on. Could he not do the same?

"Your home is beautiful," she said.

Humar gazed up at the castle of Warton. It soared to obnoxious heights, splendid in white marble. He had often mused in his youth that the kings of Loutsil had chosen the pure stone to atone for the blood that soaked the earth it had been built upon. High up in a mountain of towers, he made out new construction projects furthering its grandeur. He saw no need for it. It only created higher taxes to those already struggling and only served to enslave more people.

The courtyard was littered with manicured lawns, topiaries, and gaudy fountains. Ornate carriages were parked off to the side. They would have been a sight to behold if not for the slaves who stood soaking wet outside them, awaiting their masters. What Lunara saw he did not. The castle was garish to him; a stain, a symbol of tyranny, of bigotry, of every flaw of humanity. He hated his home. He always had.

The double doors to the inside were thrown open, and the torches beyond silhouetted a lone figure in the threshold, outlining a dress cut in the latest fashion. It would either be his mother or sister, and he wanted to see neither.

Turning back to the knights, he shouted, "Dismissed!"

They hesitated only a blink before filing from the courtyard. No doubt they had expected some grand speech from their prince, some promise of war and blood, some rant of how he would take up the crown and bring his home even more wealth.

"We can flee," a soft voice said.

Humar glanced over his shoulder at Salvarias. "Flee? We'd never make it out, boy." He looked over the two hundred guards standing in the courtyard. "You'd have to burn down the whole damned city."

"If you were to ask it of me, I would."

Humar blinked back his shock and met the boy's steady gaze. "That's quite the gesture, but the time for flight has passed." Inhaling a deep breath, he placed his hand over Lunara's and led them both up the set of shallow stairs. The slight figure had yet to move. She stood stoic, graceful even in stillness. Behind her, torches fluttered in the breeze sneaking inside, dancing shadows along the grand foyer.

Humar feared he might pass out. His mouth was suddenly dry, his heart beating entirely too fast, and he found air hard to come by. Gods he wanted to run, just as he had done when he was fifteen. How could he face everyone after killing his father?

Lunara's arm tightened and she beamed an encouraging smile at him.

Light finally fell across the woman's face when he was a mere three steps from her. She was close to his age, her hair darker, eyes more gray than blue, but her face was one he could never forget. His sister. His beautiful little sister.

Her eyes grew wide at his approach. "Humar?" she breathed. "Is it really you?"

"Falisa," he choked.

They both rushed into each other's arms, and he held her too tightly, feeling sobs rack through her thin body.

"Zerana's grace has blessed me this day," she said. "I've missed you."

Humar did not trust himself to speak.

"We have much to discuss," she said, and then she pulled away, even though he tried to keep her in his arms. She quickly wiped her tears and said to a slave girl by her side, "Go set up my sitting room with some tea for the prince and me."

"And my friends," Humar said. "Please."

Falisa's gaze flicked over the others, and then she nodded to the girl. To the guards standing in the drizzling rain, she waved her hand

and they began filing toward the castle gate. "I've been so worried," she said to Humar, locking arms and leading him inside. "I sent spies to find you but no one ever did. Where have you been?"

"Dalnar. Mother?"

"Dead for over a month."

He felt nothing at the announcement. Nothing at all.

Falisa bit her lip and glanced behind them at his friends. "Can they be trusted?" she asked.

"Entirely," he confirmed.

"I've been ruling in her name, but without success," Falisa said. "The Avral family has thwarted every attempt I've made toward change. They've grown their wealth enough that Henry would be crowned king should the Lilkous line end. I've managed to keep him from being crowned by insisting you lived. As of now, things have followed the same path Mother set in motion."

A man stood in the foyer, near Humar's height, as broad, and donned in the armor of a knight. His blonde hair caught the light and his smile spread to a ridiculous width when he bowed to Humar.

"My prince," the man said.

Humar glanced at Falisa for guidance, and she grinned. "You don't recognize your childhood friend?"

He blinked at the man. "Marcus?"

Marcus laughed and extended a hand as he walked up. "Humar, it's good to see you, my old friend."

Humar shook his friend's hand. "And you." Glancing at Falisa's left hand, Humar chuckled when he saw the ring. "I see you finally convinced my sister to marry you."

Both Falisa and Marcus's smiles faltered.

"What?" Humar asked.

"I'm married to Henry Avral," Falisa said. "Mother arranged it."

Humar rocked back on his heels. Falisa had loved Marcus since she was three, and he her. Though Falisa had played hard to get, Humar had never doubted they would wed. But of course the marriage would not have been advantageous to the crown. Avral brought wealth and nobility, good breeding, as his mother would say. There was no room for love in the Lilkous family.

"I'm so sorry," Humar said.

Falisa shrugged. "Even if you were here, you could not have changed Mother's mind."

"No, but I could've taken the crown."

"There's still time for you to do so," Falisa said, the hope of the world in her eyes. "Come, let's retire to the sitting room and catch up."

The sitting room ended up being as tasteless as the rest of the castle. The furnishings reminded Humar of the former lord of Serinity's home. Gunder had decorated with the same unpalatable color combinations and overly ornate pieces.

When all were seated with tea and after introductions had been made, Marcus sent away the slaves and then said, "Before your mother passed, she finally did it. She quashed the rebellions and had every city under the crown's thumb. She grew an army of near fifty thousand. They lounge around the city now, hoping for orders to kill and plunder their own homeland." Marcus's gaze steadied on Humar. "She met with the council before her death and arranged an invasion of Windlous. It is set for next year."

"What!" Humar exclaimed, jumping to his feet. "Windlous? Why?"

"She wanted complete rule over Arden just as Ctol had during the Long Wars," Falisa said.

"That's absurd!" Humar said. "No one person should have that much power. Ctol was kept in check by Zerana, and when she died, the Lilkous curse turned him into a monster. She ..." He cut himself off. His mother's ambitions had surpassed his father's. Women were not allowed the crown, so the curse never infected her. Her greed was purely her own. Running a hand through his hair, he sank back to his chair.

"You look exhausted," Falisa said.

"It's been a long trip."

"I'll have quarters prepared for you and your friends," Falisa said. "This discussion can wait until tomorrow."

Humar nodded absently, his mind awash with too many thoughts.

After his sister left, Marcus said, "Henry's tried to kill her."

Humar was on his feet again. "His own wife?"

"He wants the crown, and he can't get it until she's dead. In your absence, he'd have all the rights. I've stopped two attempts myself, her cook another. He treats her poorly." Marcus rose from his chair. "I know why you left, friend. But perhaps the time has come for you to return home. It's been a long time, and the people want—need—you. They will welcome you, even after what you did." He tilted his head to the group and quietly left the room.

Palpable silence hung in the room, and Humar felt Salvarias's black eyes studying him. Feeling cold, he rose from his chair, went to a nearby window, and gazed at the sprawling city below. Lanterns bobbed here and there and light glowed through windows, but the city was quiet in the storm.

Without prompting, Humar began speaking, confessing. "My uncle was a great man. He wanted to end slavery, to accept other races, to even make life a bit easier for mages. He wanted women to be able to own shops and fight in the army. He had great plans, and he shared them with Falisa and me. He was the one who raised us, not my father or mother. Both of them were lost. Because my father was the youngest, he would never have the crown, and it made him bitter and jealous.

"When my uncle was crowned, he started to change under the influence of the curse. He no longer cared about bettering Loutsil. He fell into the same whims as the previous kings. Worse, he just didn't care. The nobility grew restless, the rebels who'd waited for him to usher in change grew impatient, and my father saw opportunity.

"I was fifteen and in a heated argument with my uncle about all he'd taught us and all he'd forsaken when my father came into the room. He took up the king's sword and killed his own brother. I held my uncle and watched him die. His last words to me were: 'Run, son. Don't take up the crown. Don't become what I've become.'"

Humar ran a hand over his eyes. "Once my uncle had passed, I searched for my father and found him laughing, bloody sword still in his hand, lounging on the throne. I walked up to him, congratulated him, told him what a great man he was for slaying a weak one. I talked to his ego until he was laughing with me and calling me his son for the first time. Then I asked to see the sword of kings. The fool gave it me and I took it." He blinked back tears. "I chopped off his head with it. Then I ran. I ran until there was no more solid ground, and then I stowed away on a boat. When we landed in Windlous, I ran again. I kept going until I found the sea, then again took a ship. When I arrived in Dalnar, I planned to run again, but an old guard found me stealing bread. He took me to his home and introduced me to his son, Tobin. He told me I was safe, and I wanted to be safe. So I stayed and told him everything. He was the only man who ever knew who I was. He helped me avoid spies and cared for me as if I were his own." Humar looked at Salvarias. "Curse or not, I'm not meant to be a king. I don't have the mind for it."

Humar never saw Wilhelm coming until a fist landed on his jaw. Merciful as the strike was, it sent Humar reeling. Though Wilhelm didn't advance, Salvarias was already up and resting a hand on Wilhelm's arm.

For the first time in days, Wilhelm spoke, his voice hoarse and filled with anger. "You have the power to change this place, to make things better for mages and you ran?"

Humar's guilt was too great for excuses, and the full weight of his actions sank him into a chair.

Wilhelm roughly grabbed Salvarias's arm, causing the boy to wince, and pulled him toward Humar. "Look at him!" Wilhelm yelled. "Look at what they did to him! People spat on him, hit him with stones, insulted him."

"Lad, let go of your brother," Durak said.

"Don't you dare tell me what to do," Wilhelm roared. "How many did you kill? You're lucky I even allow you near him."

"Brother," Salvarias started, but was cut short.

"Shut up, Salvarias," Wilhelm snarled. Salvarias flinched. Wilhelm turned his enraged gaze back on Humar and pushed Salvarias closer. "Look at him. You don't want to be king? Well, I don't want to be on this task. I want to live in Serinity. I want to be married and starting a family. I want my brother to be safe and happy. For once in our lives, I want us to be happy longer than a day." Wilhelm's voice thundered at the last sentence. "But I know what we have to do is important. Whether I am meant for this or not, I'm going to try my damnedest."

"Brother, please," Salvarias said.

"I told you to shut up," Wilhelm bellowed. "I'm tired of your damn patience and understanding. People don't give a crap about you, and you still defend them. You're always preventing me from stopping people who try to hurt you. I'm done with it, Salvarias. You hear me?" Wilhelm was merciless in his anger and drove Salvarias to his knees in front of Humar, grabbed a chunk of Salvarias's hair, and yanked his head back so light fell across his beaten face, which winced under his brother's rough handling, and silent tears spilt down the mage's bruised cheeks. "Look at him and what your country did to him," Wilhelm snapped. "How dare you run from this. From your responsibility. We've been attacked by creatures I've never heard of, constantly beaten and defeated. Yet we don't give up, you don't give up. But when given the chance to make a difference you cower away?"

A brief knock on the door was followed by a slave entering the room. "Your quarters are ready, my lord."

"I respected you," Wilhelm shouted at Humar. "I would have done anything for you. And now I find you're a coward!" Wilhelm released his brother and stormed to the slave. "Show me now!"

The slave glanced at Humar who nodded slightly, and then the man led Wilhelm from the room.

There seemed to be hours of silence before Salvarias said to the others, "Please leave us." He rose, rubbing his arm, and sat in a chair beside Humar.

When they were alone, Humar buried his face in hands and said, "I'm sorry, Salvarias. Your brother is right."

"Do not apologize, Humar. My brother sees his responsibilities clearly. Not many can think the same as him. Not even I understand what I must do."

The two sat in silence for several moments until Salvarias raised his head, eyes flat and emotionless as always, though he had not effectively wiped away his drying tears. "The task given to you was not one any fifteen-year-old boy should have to undertake."

"Excuses," Humar said. "I should've taken up the crown. I know it's the right thing to do, but ..." He ran his hand through his hair. "I wouldn't be a good king, Salvarias. I wouldn't."

Salvarias tilted his head to the side, regarding Humar for a few breaths before he said, "Walk with me and I will show you what I see, my friend."

The two lazily strolled in silence, passing several guards who gave them odd looks but didn't seem to recognize Humar. When Salvarias finally stopped, Humar realized they had made it to the throne room, deserted now at such a late hour. The ornately carved throne postured itself with arrogance and brutality. A stream of cushy blood-red fabric cut the starkness of white marble. It loomed in the room, dominating the cavernous space. The throne of kings, the throne of slavery, of indifference, of apathy. It laughed at Humar as it had done when he was fifteen. His gaze moved to the white marbled floor. He swore he could still see the red stain from his father's spilt life.

"So young," Salvarias murmured as his eyes stared past the throne.

"Pardon?"

"So young to commit murder," Salvarias said.

Humar stiffened at the mage's choice of words, the single word he had hid himself from for nearly thirty years.

"I have often wondered if it is considered murder if one slays an evil man," Salvarias continued. "I feel it is the question of our time. One death to save many—or does that one death hold our humanity?"

"Evil men hold no humanity. Those who torment others are lost."

"There is a part of me that agrees, yet another is begging for the possibility the evil man could be turned toward the light, hopeful for the man to have the opportunity to redeem himself."

"My father would never see light. He was lost."

"So you imparted justice for those he wronged?"

Humar shrugged. "Can justice ever be given to those he tormented? I saw what he did, I saw him kill in cold blood, saw him take women he chose, saw him stone mages. He cared nothing for life and only sought power and control. He didn't even need the curse to be a vile man. My mother wasn't much different."

"Then why do you blame yourself?"

"Because he was my father," Humar said. "He was my blood."

"I sympathize, my friend. What you did was as equally right as it was wrong."

"I should have stayed."

"At fifteen, you could not have understood all that surrounded you. This Avral family would have done the same to you as Falisa. Do you doubt my words?"

Humar thought of how naive he had been, how persuadable. He had been a confused youth, lost, unsure which beliefs and feelings were his own. "No. I would like to think I could have overcome them, could have stayed true to my uncle's teachings once crowned. I was so immature, so lost as to who I was. I feel I'm still searching for myself."

"Timing is everything, my friend. Events, positive and negative, shape our lives. Our decisions, right and wrong, teach us who we are."

"I would not make a good king," Humar said weakly.

"I follow you, Humar, because you are a great leader, a kind man, and always have other's interest ahead of your own. I respect and trust you because of these traits, because you are pure in your intentions. Tell me, what is different in a great king than what you display every day?"

Humar could no longer fight back his tears as he stared at the mage. The faith Salvarias put in him was immense, and it humbled Humar.

Salvarias gazed at the throne, his eyes sympathetic. "The chair is cold," he said in a trance-like state. "No warmth has filled its cushions, no love has been gifted from its seat, no equality has been spoken from its perch. I see it." Salvarias's eyes glistened with tears. "I see it as it wants to be. It pleads for compassion, for freedom from its own starkness. It mocks its own ornate carvings as they are amplified by a barren seat. It weeps the blood of the land but longs to protectively cradle its people. As with all in this world, it is starved for love. If one person, one being in this entire world would love it, it could be reborn into the light." Salvarias turned his gaze to Humar. "You can save it, my friend. You possess the warmth, the control, the compassion. You offer freedom and love for thirsty lands. You are every bit what it needs, you are every bit a king."

Salvarias looked at the chair and whispered, moving his hand in mesmerizing grace. A warm light surrounded the throne. Suddenly it looked ... lonely, afraid, and pathetic.

"You see?" Salvarias asked.

Humar blinked away tears. "Yes."

"I would follow you to the depths of Oblivion should you ask it, my king." Salvarias bowed and left the room.

Humar leaned against the wall, watching the throne with hope in his blood for the first time in a long time. But soon, the warm light faded, and a flash of cold lightning sent menacing shadows to devour the throne of Loutsil.

Chapter 35

Autumn 1018 a.r.

By the time Salvarias made it to Wilhelm's room, he had gained control over his racing emotions. Much had happened in a few short days, and it had taken its toll. Sleep had eluded him and his beaten body threatened to give up. But what hurt worst of all was the bruise forming on his arm where Wilhelm had grabbed him. Never had his brother hurt him. Even when they wrestled as children, Salvarias had walked away with no discomfort or marks to show for their roughhousing.

Salvarias stopped outside his brother's door for a long moment, preparing himself. After another deep breath, he opened the door.

Wilhelm was sitting on his bed, head in his hands. "I don't want to see anyone," he mumbled.

Salvarias closed the door behind him and crossed the room.

"I want to be alone," Wilhelm said to the floor.

Salvarias sat beside his brother.

"I told you to leave," Wilhelm said. "I mean it, get out."

Salvarias swallowed back a wave of tears and put a hand on his brother's shoulder. "What is it, brother?"

"I told you to get out of here."

Sharp pain stabbed through Salvarias's heart, and the room swam for a few breaths. Air became elusive.

Wilhelm raised his gaze to Salvarias. His brother's normally bright amber eyes were dark and lifeless. "I told you to leave. I need time alone. I give you yours, give me mine."

Salvarias blinked aside tears. "I wish you would tell me, brother."

Wilhelm shrugged from under Salvarias's hand. "You of all people know of secrets, don't you? Keeping things from me. Now you know how it feels to be on the receiving end. Now get out of here."

"Secrets? I do not understand. I—"

Wilhelm's jaw tightened and he spoke in growl. "Get out. I don't want to hear any more of your lies."

"Brother—"

Wilhelm grabbed Salvarias's arm and hauled him to the door. "I said I wanted to be alone. Now get out." Wilhelm tossed Salvarias outside the room and slammed the door closed.

Salvarias latched hold of the wall to keep from falling. Tears flooded from his swollen eyes, and his lungs constricted painfully.

I warned you of thisss day, my murderer, the presence hissed. *I warned you he would sssee you for who you truly are and hurt you, jussst as they hurt you.*

Outside, thunder boomed and lightning flashed. His mother stood in the hall, sneering at him, light glinting on her cruel eyes. Terrified to be alone in the hall, Salvarias briskly made his way to the next room and stepped inside, closing the door behind him and leaning against it. Shadows lurked all around and the large furniture seemed ready to burst to life and attack. Sansis was sharpening his knife by the window. The fire crackled and popped, sending sparks drifting up the chute. Sinking to the floor, Salvarias drew his knees close to his chest and hugged himself. Loneliness crept inside his heart and the horror of it reduced him to breaking sobs.

He flinched when something wet brushed along his hands. Adok sat in front of him, head slightly cocked to the side, ears perked forward in concern. Salvarias flung his arms around the wolf. Adok's soft words reached through the bog of Salvarias's pain, and the reassuring tone calmed him enough to gain his breath. When he looked around the room, it did not seem as frightening. Adok coaxed him up and to the fire's warmth. Salvarias had not realized how cold he had become.

"Thank you, my friend," he said to the wolf.

Choosing the chair closest to the fire, Salvarias sat and stared moodily at the dancing flames. His mind wandered through the events leading up to his brother's change, but none explained Wilhelm's behavior, and frustration overtook Salvarias's pain.

A knock on his door provided a needed distraction from his mind running in pointless circles. He crossed the room and opened the door.

Lunara stood, wearing a long-sleeved winter dress of crimson, the front modestly cut to reveal her collar bone, and her hair shone in the torchlight. Her smile and eyes beamed warmth.

"May I come in?" she asked.

Salvarias stepped aside, picked up a blanket hanging on a nearby chair, and draped it over her shoulders as she passed.

"How is he?" she said, making her way to the fire and stirring up the embers before sitting in a chair next to his.

"I wish I knew," he said, retaking his seat. "He refuses to talk to me."

"It's not like him. These past couple days he's been withdrawn."

Salvarias grunted his agreement. Though she did not speak again, he was grateful for the company. Once again the flames lulled him into reflection.

His brother had always filled a portion of Salvarias's void, of his need for acceptance and love. Ever since he could remember, he had selfishly clung to it, desperately needed it, and willingly accepted his brother's misplaced love. Now it was gone, and the hole it left was a constant ache. Defeated, Salvarias slumped in his chair and absently watched Lunara's steady breathing as she slept in peaceful dreams, despite the thunder and rain thrashing the castle.

The presence did not even bother to tell Salvarias what he already knew: for the first time in his life, he was completely alone.

When the dark clouds showed the slightest sign of morning, Salvarias left Lunara sleeping by the fireplace and headed for his brother's room. The night had been cold and sleepless yet again. Exhaustion weighed heavily on his bones, and his evil was very aware of his weakening state. It was only a matter of time before it launched a full attack.

Softly he knocked on his brother's door. He waited for a response, but when none came he nudged open the door and peered inside. It was empty. Salvarias's heart fluttered painfully. Wilhelm's swords were gone, his armor and clothes missing. There was an unfinished meal sitting on a table, and the fire had long gone out.

Salvarias stopped a passing slave and asked, "The man who stayed here, do you know where he went?" His voice sounded strained and hoarse in his own ears.

The slave bowed. "No, my lord. He left an hour or so ago, and I fear I did not see where he went. If there's nothing else?"

Salvarias shook his head, and the slave hurried down the hall while Salvarias made his way to the front entrance. His brother was training, that was all. Just training. Salvarias would find the yard and his brother would be there laughing and sparring with Humar.

When he turned a corner and entered the entrance hall, he paused and looked about. The room should have been bustling with activity, but instead a single woman stood in its center. She was neither plump nor thin, tall nor squat. Her hair was balanced between brown and blonde, and her eyes were every color imaginable. If Salvarias were to think of a definition for average, it would be her. Her smile was zealous, as if she took pleasure in what she was about to do.

He had no desire to hear her speak, to be caught in her gaze. He wanted to leave but found himself locked in place.

Her smile grew, curving up the corners of her mouth like a sickle. "Forgive me for intruding on you in such a dire time. You must know me."

Salvarias shook his head, even as the realization hit him. This was Balance. He knew it the same as he knew he had a soul. It was instinctual knowledge. She was familiar to him, an old friend and an old foe.

"I am a cruel mistress," she said. "I take pleasure in keeping the game balanced. I am proud of what I am. Unlike you who shies away from it. You know me and therefore you know I cannot lie."

Salvarias nodded. He knew as he knew what she would say would change him forever.

"I have come to tell you something," she said, eyes gleaming with anticipation. "I told your brother, though he already knew this fact and has for some time. He has hidden it from you. Whether from shame, embarrassment, pity, or some other emotion, I know not."

Salvarias's heart beat spastically. He could hardly draw air. "Please," he begged. "Do not."

She licked her lips and purred, "Shadowfires. You know of them, do you not?"

Salvarias remembered hearing the stories, remembered Wilhelm shuddering and crying silently when as children he had recalled that horrible night to Salvarias.

"Yes, you have heard the dreadful tales," she said. "The murder spree the creatures went on that cold autumn night. They are powerful creatures, creatures capable of anything. Creatures capable of fathering a child."

"No," Salvarias choked.

"They used their powers to grow your body within your mother and then caged your soul to it. You are not Ashra or Tedris's son. You are not Wilhelm's blood brother."

The room spun around him, a spiral of white marble and a smirking woman.

Raising her face toward the sky, she said, "Balance has been restored, Father."

Then she left. Walked out as if she had not just shattered Salvarias's world.

He did not know how long he stood there. At some point, he was walking. Where he did not care. He just moved. He climbed stairs, turned down hallways, climbed more stairwells, descended stairs, and turned down more halls. Lightning pulsed through small windows in the hallways and added a disorienting effect. Thunder echoed so loudly that dust drifted from the ceiling. Rain poured down, offering an ear-shattering chorus.

He looked wildly around, but no longer recognized where he was. This part of the castle had been abandoned to rats and spiders, pigeons nesting in slotted windows.

He gazed down at his slender hands. So different from his brother ... from Wilhelm. His hands blurred out of focus, and a harsh thunder clap sent Salvarias running. Nothing was clear in front of him but tunnels of darkness cleaved by shafts of sickly green light coming through old slits for windows.

He bolted up a tight winding staircase and burst into stinging rain. He was on a balcony, near the top of the highest abandoned tower, overlooking the city.

His mother was there, a sneer marring her beautiful face. "I told you. You're a monstrosity. A demon. A creature of evil. You infected me."

"Forgive me," Salvarias begged. All those years she had lived with him knowing what had fathered him, what had impregnated her, what had tainted her.

Alone, ssso alone, the presence said. *I told you he would leave you. He isss tired of caring for you, for a monstrosssity. He no longer wissshes to be usssed by you and no longer wishesss to be in danger becaussse of your ssselfish need for his love.*

Salvarias leaned far over the thick stone railing. He was so high up nothing below seemed real. Perhaps this was all a dream. Surely if he woke, he would be sitting up in bed beside Wilhelm. His brother would smile and ruffle Salvarias's hair. Shutting his eyes tightly, he whispered, "Please be a dream. I beg any god listening to make it so."

A piercing shriek jerked Salvarias back, and he opened his eyes in time to see a sparrow smash into the railing, splitting its small skull and bathing the white marble in blood and bits of bone.

A squawk followed a raven plummeting to the stone floor, crumpling in a broken heap. Flittering before Salvarias, another sparrow struggled to stay airborne. He quickly reached out and cradled the tiny bird in his hand. Its beak was working, its chest laboring for air. It hitched violently, and its dark eyes gazed at Salvarias as its mind was awash with pain.

"Please," Salvarias begged. "I did not mean to."

It isss time, my murderer, the presence said. *It isss time to end your pain, to end the pain you cause othersss. It isss time to leave all of thisss behind, to find peaccce.*

Salvarias gazed over the city and then up at the muted green clouds.

It isss time.

"It's the only way," his mother said. "Knowing the evil I spawned has died will give me the peace I deserve, the peace you've denied me."

Numbly he climbed onto the railing, balancing himself against gusts of wind.

"I am sorry," he whispered to the bird.

He paused only a moment before he leapt.

Chapter 36

Autumn 1018 a.r.

Wilhelm didn't mind the stinging rain biting his exposed flesh, and the roaring thunder didn't trump the rage surging through his every limb. Morning had just begun to think of brightening the dark sky, but showed no signs of subjugating the storm, which suited Wilhelm's mood. The roiling sky reflected the condition of his own soul.

The Loutsil knight dropping to one knee under Wilhelm's ruthless offense sputtered oaths. Three knights were already tending their minor wounds after testing their prowess against Wilhelm's, and another score were watching the current bout. He hoped the latter group would offer him the same sparring opportunities as the others. He'd taken two on at a time, and skilled as they were, he bested them with little effort. Perhaps the knights would come at him by the half dozen so as to offer him a challenge. He'd yet to find one who compared to Humar.

"I surrender!" the knight yelled. "I surrender!"

Wilhelm eased off his advance, swallowing the word *coward*. Turning to the other men, he spread his arms. "Any of you have the stones to test your skill against mine?"

A few men shook their heads, and a few others looked to be entertaining the idea. Wilhelm grinned at them and waved them on with his sword. "Don't be shy, gentlemen."

"We'll get suited up," a man yelled above a crack of thunder, his own grin fierce. "Four too many?"

"Four's not enough."

The man laughed, perhaps thinking Wilhelm meant it as a joke, and started for the weapons rack, three other knights following him.

"Might I have a word?"

Wilhelm looked over his shoulder to see Neithelas approaching, huddled in a heavy cloak.

"No," Wilhelm growled. "Go away."

"I wanted to offer my appreciation and an ear should you need to talk," he said.

"I said go away."

"I admire you," Neithelas continued. "It must be hard to see the truth and to live with the knowledge that your brother's evil has controlled you for so long."

"Go—" Wilhelm frowned. "What?"

"Your brother's wickedness," Neithelas said. "Evil is powerful. You shouldn't blame yourself for not seeing it sooner."

"What are you talking about?" Wilhelm demanded.

Neithelas tilted his head to the side, brow wrinkling in confusion. "I had assumed you had realized your folly. After the way you've treated Salvarias, I thought you finally saw the monstrosity that has been in our company."

"The way I've what?"

Varila stormed up to Wilhelm, her eyes lit with rage. "What have you done?"

He couldn't get a word out before she slapped him. His cheek stung, and he was sure her handprint was outlined on his face.

"You bastard," she continued. "You selfish fool." Shoving him back a step, her eyes burned through him. "What's happened to you? Someone's done something to you, I know it. You've been poisoned, or enchanted, or something."

"Because I've finally seen the truth?" Wilhelm shot back.

"Because you're being an ass. You'd never hurt your brother. Never. Yet you have."

"I haven't touched him."

She slapped him again, harder. "I saw how hard you grabbed him. I saw you almost hit him."

"I ..." Had he? No, no matter how furious he was, he would never hurt his brother. "I didn't ..."

"There's a mark on his neck," Neithelas said.

Varila walked behind him. Before he could turn, he heard her dagger hiss from its sheath. He whirled around just as sharp pain pricked his neck.

A headache assailed him with such force it churned his stomach. The thunder was suddenly too loud, and the dull light of morning was like staring into the sun. He clenched his teeth to keep from vomiting.

"What is that?" Neithelas asked, disgust lining his voice.

Something warm oozed down Wilhelm's neck. Reaching behind him, his finger touched thick goo and a puncture on his neck. He planted his sword in the ground and leaned on the pummel, hoping the swaying world would stop. "What in Oblivion?" he muttered, examining the sticky clear liquid on his fingers. "What ..."

Jolting awake from a nightmare following him into waking hours, Wilhelm remembered everything, remembered what the creature had done, what it sought, what it discovered. But what made him rock back on his heels was his behavior toward his baby brother. The memory of grabbing Salvarias's arm clenched Wilhelm's fists, feeling his brother's skin bruise under his hold.

He leaned to the side and vomited.

"Wilhelm?" Varila said, resting a hand on his shoulder. "Is that you?"

Never had he hurt his brother. Never. He stared at his hand, sure it would sprout horns and drip red with Salvarias's blood. "Gods help me."

A low growl spun Wilhelm around. Adok stood, eyes wild with fear, gaze locked on the clouds above. Dread settled itself in Wilhelm's gut as the sickly green sky roiled with menace and lightning slashed through the clouds.

"What have I done?" Wilhelm breathed.

Yanking his sword free, Wilhelm sprinted toward the castle, keeping up with the loping wolf and leaving Varila and Neithelas behind. His heart raced painfully, head pounding, and his legs were hardly stable beneath him as he remembered the events since the creature had planted its nail in his skull.

After barreling through a group of knights, he burst into the main entrance hall. Balance stood there, a cruel smile on her lips. "I warned you," she purred.

"Damn you," he roared. "Damn you all to Oblivion." Turning to Adok, he shouted, "Find him."

The wolf snarled at Balance before bolting ahead, clawed paws scrabbling for hold on the smooth marbled floor.

As they made their way through the maze of the castle, Wilhelm soon became lost. They ran down long-deserted halls, passing rooms covered in cobwebs, rats, and dead pigeons. The musty air had Wilhelm gasping, and the slats lining the corridors showed lightning thrashing the city below.

When Adok stopped at a narrow staircase, Wilhelm barreled ahead, eyes widening as he passed a few rats twitching in the throes of death. He barely fit, and though he took the stairs two at a time, it seemed to take him an eternity to reach the top and spill onto a balcony. Cold air chapped his face and the stinging rain hazed the balcony and swallowed the city below. Standing on the railing was Salvarias, a dead sparrow in his hands.

Wilhelm lunged as his brother sailed over the side. Power bloomed with such intensity it momentarily blinded him, his breath leaving in a rush. When his vision returned, he'd already dove over the side after his brother. Fumbling frantically, he caught Salvarias's ankle and barely managed to hook his own on the railing.

The jolt freed the bird from Salvarias's grasp, and his brother's cry contained all the sorrow of the world as he fumbled to catch it but failed. He craned his neck awkwardly until he met Wilhelm's gaze. Emotions warred on Salvarias's face; one instant fear and the next pain—gods, such horrible pain—and then finally rage.

Ignoring it all, Wilhelm harnessed the power surging within and forced it to his one hand wrapped around his brother's ankle, making sure his grip never loosened. Awkwardly, he reached back with his free hand and heaved himself up, along with his brother. When they both slid over the side, Salvarias scrambled to his feet, taking a few steps back, looking at Wilhelm as though he were a stranger.

"I'm sorry," Wilhelm huffed, using the railing to get his shaking legs under him. The power faded quickly, harshly removing his strength and making him pay for his exertions.

"Sorry?" Salvarias said. "You lied to me. All this time, you made me believe Tedris was my father. You let me believe we were brothers."

"We are," Wilhelm said. "Nothing—"

"Why?" Salvarias asked, venom dripping from his voice. "Why do you follow me? I want none of your pity. None of it!"

Wilhelm blinked in surprise. He'd not excepted such anger from his brother. Then he noticed it. Just as it had been when they'd left the swamps, his brother's eyes were dull and his voice strained. His hands shook violently, but from anger, not cold. His gaze might've set Wilhelm aflame if it was what Salvarias wanted. The evil had found a footing and was gaining ground rapidly.

Lightning jabbed down from the sky, striking the city below. If it weren't for the howling wind, Wilhelm was sure he would have heard screams. Birds fell from the sky, pelting the balcony. A few rats skittered by, making it a few feet before they squealed and flipped on their backs, thrashing wildly before stilling.

Wilhelm tore his gaze from the sight and looked at his brother. "This isn't you, Salv. You've got to fight it."

"Do not patronize me," Salvarias spat. "You treat me like a beaten dog you rescued from the streets. You care for me out of pity. Out of some false responsibility. We share no mother. No father. We are not brothers."

Lightning struck again, hitting a turret not too far away. Stone exploded, cascading down the side of the castle. The air thickened and made Wilhelm gulp painfully, never feeling as though his lungs received enough. The smell of death tainted each breath, sticking to his tongue to make him gag.

"You're ..." Wilhelm gasped in another breath. "My brother. I love you, Salv."

Salvarias swayed slightly and his eyes unfocused, lips moving in silent conversation. Just when Wilhelm thought his brother would fight, Salvarias's shook his head and snarled, "You let her. If you were truly my brother you would have known. You would have helped me. Taken me from there. Instead you left me."

"What are you talking about?"

Salvarias sprinted for the railing, but Wilhelm darted there first, blocking his brother. "I'm not letting you, Salv."

His brother's dagger whipped out. Wilhelm grabbed Salvarias's wrist a blink too late. The tip slid into Salvarias's skin. Blood spread around the knife's point, but luckily no more than inch penetrated his brother.

"Gods, Salv. Stop!"

They grappled for control over the knife. Wilhelm managed to pry his brother's left hand from the hilt and shoved his mark against his brother's. Nothing happened.

"Dammit," Wilhelm muttered. "Salv, you've got to fight. Use it!"

"I was dead when I was born, was I not? Milred did not lie."

"Salv—"

"Tell me," Salvarias demanded

"Yes, but—"

"What did you do?" Salvarias hissed. "What did you do to me?"

"I-I ... Nothing. I-I think our marks touched, but—"

"Fool," Salvarias roared. "I was supposed to die. Look at what you have done!"

Three lightning bolts fingered down from sky, striking the city.

Salvarias's struggle for the dagger intensified, surprising Wilhelm with strength he didn't know his brother was capable of. "Please, Salv," Wilhelm gasped.

The knife sank in farther.

"Help me," Wilhelm begged.

Nothing. No shadowfires. No Lunara. No Talura. No one.

Salvarias smirked. "Where is your promise now, dear brother?" His eyes deadened. "Where is your promise to save me from the evil?"

Horror ensnared Wilhelm as the once clear rain turned into watery blood, leaking between his lips, leaving behind a metallic taste. Crying out in desperation, he sought his powers, plunging to the core of himself, to the depths of his soul.

"You are a liar," Salvarias said. "Nothing but a liar. Tell me, am I the brother you longed for? Is this what you wanted when you begged for one?"

Wilhelm clenched his jaw and leaned down until he was nose to nose with his brother. "Yes."

"Even now you lie," Salvarias roared. "Look at me! I am a monstrosity. A creature. A demon from the depths of Oblivion. I must die!"

"You're my brother," Wilhelm shouted back. "Mine! And I'll tell you when you can die!"

With that, his determination took on a power of its own. A tingle lit up on his palm, and it was all he could do not to release his brother's hand and scratch at his mark. Then his surroundings vanished and he found himself in a space of nothing but red fog. It curled around his legs and those of Salvarias, and the feel of it made Wilhelm's skin crawl. There was no rain here, no wind, no storm. It was neither hot nor cold, and it was soundless, but not oppressively so. The space was not lit by a candle or sun, it was simply lit, showing him a room he recognized, his old room above the baker.

Salvarias stood in front of him, holding the knife, struggling, sneering.

Wilhelm's gaze swept over the small space and came to rest on a translucent form of Salvarias huddled in a corner, whereas the Salvarias standing in front of him was solid.

"Salv," Wilhelm called to the other Salvarias.

"No," the solid Salvarias growled. "End this. End it now."

Wilhelm ignored him and, keeping a good hold on his brother's mark and the knife, jerked Salvarias toward the corner of the room. His brother fought, but Salvarias's determination was simply no match for Wilhelm's.

"Salv," Wilhelm called again.

"No," Salvarias snarled. "This is what you face."

The wispy, translucent form of Salvarias had his hands clamped over his ears and whispered, "Help me," over and over.

"Salv," Wilhelm said.

"No!" The solid form of Salvarias struggled harder. "I am done. Done fighting. Done with all of it! Leave me in peace."

Wilhelm spoke to the other Salvarias. "You have to fight your way out of this, Salv."

"I do not want to," the solid Salvarias shouted. "I want to die! I want this to end!"

An idea formed, a dangerous one, one that could end both brothers, but one that could save Salvarias, the only thing Wilhelm could come up with.

Rounding on the solid Salvarias, Wilhelm snarled, "You'll have to kill me first." He jerked the dagger free and twisted the point around until it was leveled at his own chest.

"I hate you," Salvarias wept, squirming to turn the knife back on himself. "You lied to me."

"You can say all those hurtful things, Salv, but I know the truth. You love me. And you'd die to protect me, to save me." Wilhelm inhaled a deep breath and braced himself. "You'd also live to do the same." He shoved the dagger in his chest, using his unnatural strength to penetrate his armor. Shooting pain nearly made him pass out. "You have to fight so you can heal me."

Salvarias cried out, eyes growing wide. He jerked his hand from the dagger and stumbled back.

A hissing voice sounded around Wilhelm, seeming to come from the walls themselves. "I told you. You will kill them all sssomeday. Look at what you did, my murderer."

Wilhelm narrowed his eyes as he looked for the source of the voice. He was sure it sounded familiar.

"No," Salvarias breathed, staring at his trembling hand. Wilhelm's blood stained his fingers.

"You killed him," the voice purred. "As I sssaid you alwaysss would."

Salvarias looked at his dagger sticking from Wilhelm's chest, and his eyes lost all sanity.

"Gods," Wilhelm breathed. "Salv, you didn't kill me. Salv!"

Suddenly the solid form of Salvarias was no more. The only form in the room was his brother in the corner, staring with wide eyes up at Wilhelm. The red fog intensified in color and thickness, writhing over Salvarias. His brother flinched from it each time.

Wilhelm ripped the dagger from his chest. The jolt of pain set the room spinning and drove him to his knees, blood sputtering up from his lips.

Salvarias cried out and scrambled over to Wilhelm.

"Forgive me," Salvarias cried, reaching for Wilhelm's hand, but Wilhelm yanked it back.

"I won't let you heal me until you fight this, Salv. Make the red go away."

Salvarias looked around with wide, horror-filled eyes. "I am scared."

"I know. But I'm here. Together we can do anything, Salv. Look at me." His brother met Wilhelm's gaze. "Fight. You have to fight or else I'll die."

Salvarias's face twisted in concentration. The strain made veins on his neck pop up and snaked one up his forehead. Blood dribbled from Salvarias's nose. Tears streaked down his cheeks. He gave a soft sob, clutching his head.

The red fog flailed about, flinging itself at Salvarias, and Wilhelm swore it growled, as if it were a living being. It scared the piss right out of him.

Fighting away every flight instinct, Wilhelm offered his hand to his brother. "Let me help, but if you try to heal me, I'll pull away. Fight first, and then help me."

Salvarias hesitated, but latched hold. Strength left Wilhelm, toppling him to the floor. Salvarias fell as well. They lay facing each other, a trickle of blood falling from his brother's nose, Salvarias

376

jerking from some unseen pain. Darkness threatened to claim Wilhelm as strength sapped out of him.

At the sight of the red fog fading to black, Wilhelm smiled at his brother. "You're almost there, Salv. Just a little more."

"I am not strong enough," Salvarias whispered through tears. "I cannot fight this."

"You don't have to be. I'm strong enough for the both of us." How he did it, he didn't know. He just shoved his own strength through the mark on his hand, willing it to Salvarias.

Salvarias shuddered, then the last of the red fog fizzled out. "Forgive me," he said. "Please forgive me."

Wilhelm had no strength to respond. Darkness crowded his vision, and breathing seemed entirely too much effort. He felt like he floated far away from himself, void of any strength or physical ties.

Then power rushed into him, rich and addicting, and Wilhelm sucked in a breath and gripped Salvarias's hand tighter. His brother's power strengthened and mended Wilhelm's battered body, blinding him with blissful warmth, sweetening the air. The gray fog deepened in color, swirling like his brother's eyes.

"Wilhelm!"

It sounded like Varila called to him from underwater.

Hating himself, he watched blood pour from Salvarias's mouth. Gods, he needed to stop, but he couldn't. He wanted more. More!

Then a knife sliced across his mind. He was certain of it. He cried out, blinking at the blackness before him.

"Wilhelm!"

It was Varila, but this time she hovered right above him. Lunara was crying.

He blinked rapidly. Freezing rain pelted him and gusty wind swept over the balcony, all disorienting him with their sudden appearance. Beside him, Lunara had Salvarias's head cradled in her lap, bathed in her tears. His dagger was on the ground, lying in a pool of bloody vomit.

"What in Oblivion happened?" Varila demanded.

The exhaustion was gone, but being ripped from his connection to Salvarias left him a pounding head, enough to make him nauseous.

"How is he?" he rasped.

"F-fine, I think," Lunara said. She smoothed Salvarias's hair from his face. "Sleeping, from what I can tell. You ..." She looked up, a slight accusation in her eyes.

"Almost killed him," Wilhelm finished.

She nodded.

"Looks like he almost did the same to you," Varila said, pointing to the hole in Wilhelm's armor.

He grimaced when he sat up, wishing his spinning head would calm. "I did that to myself." Looking up at the clouds, they were still green and churning unnaturally, but the rain was clear, no longer the color of blood. The death had stopped. He ran a shaking hand over his face. "How did you find us?"

Adok came into view, his eyes large and worried as he sat by Salvarias.

Wilhelm smiled at the wolf. "Thanks." Turning to Varila he said, "We've got problems. Salvarias found out."

"What in Oblivion is wrong with you?" Varila snapped. "You've treated him like crap and then tell him when he's at his lowest? What—"

"I didn't tell him," Wilhelm muttered. "And I was attacked in Senti." He motioned to the back of his neck. "I don't know what it did to me or even what it was. Thanks, by the way, for realizing I wasn't myself."

She pursed her lips. "You were a real ass."

"I remember," Wilhelm growled. "Let's get him out of the rain and warmed up."

Navigating down the narrow staircase while carrying Salvarias was quite a feat, but Wilhelm managed it and then followed Adok through the castle. They were all silent. Wilhelm was too busy trying to figure out how he would explain everything to Salvarias. After what Salv said, he doubted his brother would believe a word Wilhelm said.

At their rooms, Humar was pacing the hallway. Upon seeing them, he let out an explosive sigh. "I've had guards searching everywhere for you. What happened?"

Wilhelm nodded to Varila to fill in the knight—prince—whatever he was—on the events while he went inside Salvarias's room. Gently laying his brother on the bed, Wilhelm stripped off his brother's soaking robes. When he laid eyes on Salvarias's scarred body, Wilhelm froze. A nasty bruise had formed on Salvarias's arm. Trembling head to foot, Wilhelm touched the contusion and found his hand was a perfect match. Bile rose in the back of his throat, and he swallowed it down.

"I'm so sorry, Salv." Resting his forehead on the edge of the bed, Wilhelm whispered, "How will you ever trust me again?"

Chapter 37

Autumn 1018 a.r.

Salvarias slowly rose from blissful darkness, and as he did, the pounding in his skull made him regret ever leaving it. He wanted nothing more than to never wake, to never face his new, lonely world. Keeping his eyes closed, he allowed his other senses to discover where he was. Beneath him was a soft bed and the weight of several blankets covered him. The light scent of lavender mingled with the crispness of a spring meadow. Soothing fingers ran through his hair, and lazy pops and cracks of a fire were the only sounds. He was in his room with Lunara.

The longer his thoughts drifted, the more he remembered of his time since hearing Balance deliver her terrible news. His evil had almost won again. If not for Wilhelm it would have. Salvarias would have decimated the entire city of Warton. Despite the fact that Wilhelm owed Salvarias nothing, his brother had come back, aided Salvarias when he needed it most. But why? Salvarias was a pathetic excuse for family, and now he thought of it, he had nothing in common with Wilhelm. Why in all the worlds had Wilhelm stayed as long as he had? And why did Wilhelm help him? Why did Wilhelm let Salvarias leach strength from him, use him? And how in all Oblivion had his brother found a way inside Salvarias's mind? The memory made him run his fingers across his mark. It was warm, but not uncomfortably so, like the coziness of a hot cup of cocoa on a cold, stormy morning. Somehow, Wilhelm had used their marks to deepen their connection. Even without opening his eyes, Salvarias knew Wilhelm was not in the room, yet he was not far. And there was an ache, a weight, in the remnants of Wilhelm's presence. Wilhelm was suffering.

Wincing against what he knew would come, Salvarias cracked open his eyelids. Light from candles and a roaring fire jammed needles in his eyes. A groan left his throat, and he closed his eyes against the harshness.

"Blow out the candles," Lunara said.

There was a creak of leather and then the smoky smell of extinguished candles filled the air. Bracing himself, he opened his eyes. The flickering fire was the only illumination, but it was still overwhelming.

"Here," Lunara whispered, passing him a few leaves of feverfew.

He chewed them with care, though the motion helped.

"Do you need anything?" Lunara asked.

"No, my lady, but thank you." His voice was weak in his own ears.

Glancing around the room proved his initial conclusion, but one surprise was Varila. She was leaning next to the window, arms folded across her chest, eyes softer than normal.

"Is my br—" He swallowed hard and forced himself to sit up. The motion almost cost him the contents of his stomach. "Is Wilhelm harmed?"

"He's ... physically fine," Varila said. "He's in his room."

Salvarias nodded and rested his back against the wall. "And mentally?"

She smiled. "I'd ask the same of you. Lunara, why don't you give me a moment alone with Salvarias?"

Lunara glanced at him and he tilted his head, squeezing her hand, which he just now noticed he clutched in his. When her touch left, he moaned and clenched his teeth to keep down the bile rising in his throat. Thoughts swam in a tornado of emotions, and it took all his concentration not to break down and weep. He had not realized how much she had shielded him from his pain.

Varila was kind enough to give him time after Lunara left to gather himself. Opening his eyes, he saw her watching him intently.

"Now you know," she said.

Salvarias smirked. "Now I know."

"It's a lot to take in."

What could he say?

"For Wilhelm, as well," she said. She must have noticed his puzzled expression. "He's drinking himself into Oblivion in the next room. Seems he thinks he hurt you and that for some idiotic reason you think he's not your brother anymore."

"He is not," Salvarias said simply.

"So the line between friends and family is so black and white to you?"

"We share no blood."

"And that's supposed to explain why you're being such an ass about the whole thing?" She shook her head. "You two share something far deeper, far more meaningful than blood."

"What? He's my Protector?" Sarcasm dripped from his words. "Is that the connection you refer to? It is his responsibility to look after me. It is an occupation for him. He has no ties to me."

"You selfish bastard. All he's done for you and you're stupid enough to think he did it out of duty? He didn't even know he was your Protector all through your childhood. How do you explain that?"

"He thought we were brothers. You forget how well I know him. He did not learn of my parentage until the barbarian desert. That was when he changed."

"And how did he change?"

Salvarias mulled over the question. Wilhelm had been different, but exactly in what ways ... "He is more protective. His temper has grown."

"I see," Varila said sharply. "So after Wilhelm finds out you're not his blood brother, he gets even more protective of you and loses his temper faster than ever when you're threatened? Of course, how blind of me. That's the true sign of a man lost to duty with no care toward his charge."

Salvarias shook his head adamantly. "There is no reason for him to care for me. I am evil. I am not like others. I'm a creature." Gods, those words hurt. "I am a creature." Whispering it again only hurt more.

Varila thrust out her jaw, working it back and forth, her eyes too intense and thoughtful for Salvarias's comfort. "Fine. I'll give you a real example of what it means to love someone who isn't your blood." She turned her gaze outside the window, and when she spoke, her voice was reluctant and carried the fine edge of one who did not want to say what they were about to say. "I was four when Edium and Talura saved me. My birth parents were the Bellerums' first servants. Edium had just come into his wealth, and Lunara was only two years old.

"My birth father was a mean drunk, and my birth mother never wanted a family. She was a whore, really. Was never faithful to my birth father. It made him mad, and he took out his anger on me when she wouldn't come home at night. When he wasn't beating me, she was ignoring me and telling me what a burden I was. I have some memories of it, nothing too horribly locked into place. But I remember the day Edium walked in on my birth father when he'd been in one of his drunken rages. Edium started wailing on him and Talura whisked me away before I saw what happened. I think Edium killed him. I never saw my birth father again, nor did I ever want to. When my birth mother came home, I heard Edium yelling at her. I never saw her again either. Edium asked me if I wanted to live with them. I told him yes, and he said I was his daughter. He said Lunara would call me sister. He said no one would know unless I wanted them to. And he held true to his word. He sold off his property and moved us to Serinity, to a town where no one knew I wasn't his. He introduced me as his daughter, and what was even more amazing was the pride and love in his voice every time he did. Talura was no different. I've never told another soul, not even Wilhelm, not even Lunara."

Salvarias shook his head. "I am sorry you had to endure that, Lady Varila."

Varila laughed lightly. "Endure it? It was the best thing I could've ever hoped for. I gained a sister I would have never had and two parents who would murder the whole world to keep me safe. A couple of bruises were well worth it. My point wasn't to garner pity from you, it was to show you blood doesn't make two people sisters. It doesn't make two people your parents."

Salvarias ran a hand across his forehead. Could it be that simple? Could Wilhelm truly care for something as horrendous as Salvarias? Could he chance the hope of it? And that was his moment of revelation. He had talked himself out of being Wilhelm's brother to spare any possible pain of Wilhelm's care lessening. To hope all could be the same between them was a risk so terrible that Salvarias feared it more than Sansis or his mother. He could not bear the pain of it.

"So, shadowfires?" Varila said, her voice light and conversational. "That's interesting, don't you think?"

Salvarias stiffened.

She rolled her eyes. "Doesn't it help? I mean, it's helped me a great deal."

"I am happy my demonic parentage has lent you some sort of peace," Salvarias said, unable to stop the dryness dripping from his words. He did not appreciate her cruelty, nor was he in the frame of mind to accept it without rebuttal.

"Listen here, you stubborn ass, this explains everything. It explains why you talk to animals, it explains the blackfire, it explains why your mother ... why she did what she did. Don't you see? You have answers now. A place to start at least."

Salvarias eyed her warily, unsure of the purpose of her newfound compassion.

Varila sighed dramatically. "Look, I didn't understand why you were the way you were. But now I do."

"I think you are missing an obvious fact, my lady. I. Am. A creature. I am not an erthla, I am not a winsire, I am not a watythm, and I am not a cavrul. I am something else."

"True," Varila said, tapping a finger to her lips. "Very true indeed." She studied him for a moment before a slow smile spread. "Come over here."

Salvarias laboriously hauled himself from bed and joined her by the window.

"I'm going to prove something to you," she said, drawing her dagger. "Hold out your arm."

Salvarias hesitated.

"I'm not going to chop it off, idiot. Hold it out."

Salvarias held out his arm, shifting his sleeve back.

Varila grinned at him. "One more scar won't hurt." She sliced the dagger over his arm, and blood beaded up. "Oh look!" she exclaimed in mock surprise. "You bleed." She ran the dagger over her arm and held it close to his, their blood mingling as it dripped to the floor. "And look! It's just like mine."

Salvarias stared at her dumbfounded.

"My point is, you're human. The shadowfires made a human and gifted him with extraordinary capabilities and cursed him with a few not so favorable abilities."

Salvarias opened his mouth, his mind blank on a reply.

She smiled assuredly. "Something horrible happened to you. Something a man should never have to endure. But evil doesn't fight itself, Salvarias. What I have seen is a man torn up internally, inside here." She tapped her head. "I will marry your brother, but right now, you need to know something. My father and mother have already adopted you. My sister cares for you deeply. And now I've decided to adopt you as my baby brother." She grinned and winked. "You can call me 'sis' if you want. But if you call me lady one more time, I'll kick your ass to Oblivion."

Salvarias turned to look out the window. "You have shown me much trust and I thank you, but I ... I cannot. That you have accepted me will ease my—Wilhelm's—concerns, and he will wed you. But I do not want any part of your family."

Varila's jaw tightened. "Whether you want it or not, you got it. You can't make us stop caring, though I imagine you'll try." As she turned to leave, she said over her shoulder, "Your brother's hurting. If you can stop your self-pity for a moment, you should go see him."

Once alone, Salvarias took time to gather himself, set his emotions, and conjure up an air of indifference. When he calmed and composed himself, he left his room and went to the next door. He paused a breath before knocking. A deep mumble sounded from beyond the door, and Salvarias took it as an invitation.

The doorknob rattled in his shaking hands as he inched open the door and peered into the dark room. Cool air drifted by him, void of the warmth of a fire, and beyond no candles burned. Only slivers of light peeked between the closed window coverings.

Salvarias stepped inside, closed the door behind him, and muttered out his spell. Two candles flickered to life, casting long shadows in the room. Wilhelm was sitting in a chair, dark rings sagging beneath his eyes, tunic stained with ale, his hair a rumpled mess. When he looked up, his features contorted in agony and he quickly rose from his chair, taking a step backward. His hands shook violently and his chest rose and fell in heavy, harsh breaths. The sight hurt Salvarias more than anything he had ever seen.

All preparation Salvarias had done was pointless. His emotions undertook a full siege upon one another. Words faltered in his throat, and none tumbling around in his mind seemed right. There was a divide between Wilhelm and him now. He saw it, like staring at each other across an ocean.

"I've ruined everything," Wilhelm croaked.

Salvarias blinked aside tears he had not known were building. Wilhelm slumped, face drawn in resignation, eyes dull with defeat.

"I was scared," Wilhelm continued. "I didn't know what the truth would do to you, but I knew it wouldn't be good. Either you would hate yourself more, which I'm sure you do, or you'd build up a wall between us, which I know you've done." Tears cascaded down his cheeks. "I could try to convince you that I love you, that you're still my brother no matter who your father is. I could plead to you for the rest of our lives, but you'll never look at me the same. I've hurt—" Wilhelm's voice choked off and a sob left him before he barreled on. "I've hurt you. Me." He raised his hands, looking at them as if he did not know they were his. "I never meant to. I was so angry that I couldn't provide the life I've wanted for you. That you'll always live alone and afraid. And there's not a damned thing I can do about it. Now I've robbed you of every positive thing you've ever clung to. I was the one who never hurt you, and now I have. I was the one who loved you unconditionally. That hasn't changed, but you think it has. So what am I left to do?" Wilhelm looked up at Salvarias, face twisted into absolute agony, wet with a shower of tears. "What am I supposed to do, Salv? Tell me and I'll make it better. I promise I'll make it better. Just tell me what to do."

Salvarias had crossed the room before he even meant to and flung his arms around Wilhelm's neck. Words failed him, for he knew not what he felt save for the love overflowing for Wilhelm, the ache in his chest knowing the suffering Wilhelm endured.

Wilhelm's return embrace was painfully tight, and his massive frame shook with uncontrolled sobs.

"It is fine, Wilhelm," Salvarias said, using the lightest voice he could muster. "I know you love me. Everything will be fine."

Wilhelm sank to his knees, dragging Salvarias with him. Through coughed sobs, Wilhelm said, "You're lying, Salv. You won't even call me brother. You look at me different. You—" He leaned back, eyes widening and voice rushing out in whisper. "It's what they want. To drive us apart. To get you alone. To make you not trust me. It's how they'll win, Salv." He licked his lips, eyes darting back and forth as if he were piecing together a puzzle in his mind. "It's why they sent the creature, why it did that to me. It wanted to drive me mad, to make me push *you* away. And then they sent Balance so you would push *me* away. Don't you see, Salv? This is what they want."

"Creature? What are you talking about?"

Wilhelm told Salvarias of the encounter in Senti and what the creature had done. "We're falling into another trap, Salv. You see it, don't you?"

There was no doubt in Wilhelm's gaze. He believed it true. And it might very well be, but that did not change the fact Wilhelm was not his brother, that Salvarias had been created by darkness.

Wilhelm cupped Salvarias's face, forcing him to meet Wilhelm's gaze. "You know when I'm lying, Salv. You've always been able to tell, right?"

Salvarias nodded.

"Then look now." Wilhelm's gaze became as certain as stone. "You are my brother. If we were blood brothers, I couldn't care for you more than I do already. After I found out, it changed nothing. Nothing."

Fresh tears welled in Salvarias's eyes as he saw the truth to Wilhelm's words. "Why? I do not understand why. I am not a good person. I have murdered—"

"You have something inside you, Salv. It's dark and ugly, but you fight it. That's what matters. Don't you see? I'm so proud of you, little brother. Not because you're the most powerful mage out there, not because you can talk to animals, not because you're the smartest man I've ever met. I'm proud of you because there's not another soul in all the worlds that has a need to do good like you have, who has a heart as big as yours, who sees beyond facades to the people behind them. You have to believe me. I swear on all I hold dear I wouldn't change a thing about you, Salv. Not one thing. I wouldn't take the evil from you, I wouldn't want your blackfire to go away, and I certainly would never wish for a different brother."

Salvarias shook his head, amazed. Wilhelm was not lying. God had tried to drive a wedge between them, and Salvarias had let it happen. Even staring at the truth, the dark shadow of knowledge still loomed in the room, and it would never be chased away. Regardless, one thing was fact, and Salvarias voiced it. "I believe you."

"Then believe me when I say this: We. Are. Brothers."

Salvarias nodded slightly.

"Say it," Wilhelm said.

Salvarias swallowed the knot in his throat. "We are brothers."

Fresh tears glistened in Wilhelm's eyes and spilled over when he smiled. "Nothing will ever change that."

Once again, Salvarias found himself in his brother's embrace, Wilhelm's arms encasing him as they had always done. The smell of oiled leather clung to his brother though he wore a white tunic instead of armor. The steady drumming of his heart and measured breathing was a reminder of safety as it has been ever since Salvarias could remember.

Wilhelm's voice rumbled in his chest when he said, "I never meant to hurt you. I'm so sorry, Salv. Can you forgive me?"

Salvarias realized Wilhelm's hand was over the bruise he had caused, resting lightly, even as his arms clenched Salvarias securely. Closing his eyes, Salvarias completely relaxed against his brother, allowing his fears and troubles to melt away, the tension in his muscles to drain from him, and trusting Wilhelm to hold him upright. As usual, his brother did. With a smile spreading, Salvarias whispered, "Always, my dear brother."

Chapter 38

Autumn 1018 a.r.

Salvarias woke in a plush bed, surrounded by blankets and crisp sheets. Light danced from a fire and illuminated Wilhelm sitting in a chair by the bed, Adok curled at his feet. He had changed and cleaned himself up. His gaze was steady and serious until he glanced at Salvarias, then his eyes brightened and a crooked grin spread.

"You fell asleep," Wilhelm said.

"I am sorry." Salvarias closed his eyes and massaged his forehead. His headache had returned, or perhaps he was merely aware of it again.

"You look like you took a stroll through Oblivion," Wilhelm said.

"I would not be surprised if I had."

"Head hurt?"

Salvarias winced at a stabbing pain behind his eyes and nodded.

"Did ... did I cause it?"

Frowning, Salvarias opened his eyes and regarded his brother. "What do you mean?"

"When I touched our marks ... What I did ..." Wilhelm shifted in his chair, as if ashamed of his actions. "I think I was in your head."

Salvarias did not want to dwell on the moment of his failure, but Wilhelm had sparked his curiosity. Thinking back, this time he remembered the pain of what his brother had done. Salvarias had been too lost to his evil at the time, but Wilhelm's invasion had consequences. Even now, Salvarias felt the touch of his brother's mind in his own, stronger than ever. Wilhelm's emotions muddled with his, lingering on his mind like a fresh burn, forever locked there, forever scarred upon him. One more thing crowding Salvarias's thoughts.

"What you did was necessary," Salvarias said honestly. "Though my pain is partly because of it, I would have lost myself if you had not done what you had done. How did you do it?"

Wilhelm shrugged. "I wasn't about to lose you, so I ... I don't know, I just did it."

Wilhelm had used some sort of power, Salvarias was sure of it. Somehow their marks were more than what Tedris had told Wilhelm. Which begged the question: If Lunara's mark linked to Zerana's grace, where did Wilhelm and Salvarias's mark link? What grace were they tapping into?

Wilhelm's eyes narrowed at Salvarias. "You and me. Nothing's changed?"

Salvarias regarded his brother. Lying to Wilhelm was something their mother had forced Salvarias to do and, over the years, he had perfected it. Though he believed his brother, there was still an ache in Salvarias's heart, a dark shadow that had not been there before. Inhaling a deep breath, he let a casual smile form on his lips. "We are good, my dear brother."

Wilhelm surprised Salvarias with a noncommittal grunt. Shrugging off whatever doubts Wilhelm might have had, his brother grinned and lightness filtered into his voice, gifting Salvarias a sense of normalcy. "Let's eat. I'm starving."

After Salvarias untangled himself from the pile of blankets, Wilhelm wrapped an arm around Salvarias's neck and led him to door, mussing his hair.

Salvarias grinned and elbowed his brother's ribs.

"Ouch."

When Wilhelm opened the door, Okulu greeted them, hand poised for a knock.

"There you two are," he said. "Humar asked to see you, Salvarias. As soon as you were up. Seems our fearless leader is about to be crowned king."

"The coronation is today?" Salvarias asked.

"Out of tradition, but yes. They are having an evening ceremony followed by a formal dinner."

"You up for it?" Wilhelm asked.

Salvarias could not imagine eating and engaging in conversation with his brain pounding from his skull.

Okulu clucked his tongue. "You look tired, but Humar said he could really use you. Seems those in attendance don't like mages and our new little king-to-be wants to make his opinion on the matter known."

"Salv can't," Wilhelm said. "Tell Humar—"

"We will go," Salvarias said.

Okulu winked at Wilhelm. "Varila and Lunara have had seamstresses pouring in and out of their rooms all day. I think you'll be in for a pleasant view tonight."

Wilhelm grinned. "Why didn't you say so from the start?"

Okulu laughed as he strolled down the hall, heading toward his room.

In the washroom, Salvarias lingered in the tub's hot waters long enough to turn his skin into the texture of a dried prune. He ate entirely too much feverfew, but he preferred a queasy stomach to a blinding headache.

When finally he forced himself from the now-cool water, he found Wilhelm staring at the bruise on Salvarias's arm.

Running a shaking hand over his face, Wilhelm smiled slightly. "You're sure you're well enough for this?"

Salvarias muttered his spell, flicked out his rune, and ran a hand over his smooth cheek, smiling at the simple spell and the time it saved. "I will be fine, brother. It is important to Humar. Have you apologized to him yet?"

Wilhelm's eyes dulled. "No, and I'm not going to. He shouldn't have run from his responsibilities."

"He was fifteen."

"And you were ten when your world was thrown into chaos."

"Yes, and I handled it so well," he said dryly. "You must be more understanding, brother."

Wilhelm's grunt ended the conversation. After both had made themselves presentable, they left the washroom to find a slave waiting for them in the hall. It was a young man, nearly as old as Wilhelm. He bowed and said, "If it pleases you both, I can lead you to the throne room. I must beg your pardon, but Prince Humar requested the wolf stay in your room."

Salvarias bowed in return. "Of course, gentleman."

The slave looked up with wide eyes. "I am not to be addressed as such, my lord."

Wilhelm clapped the man on the shoulder and grinned. "'Lord' and 'slave' are titles my brother and I don't care for. You're a man, same as me."

The slave blinked. "As you wish."

After a small argument with Adok, which Salvarias won, he followed the slave down the hall, a set of stairs, and through massive corridors. It was a maze Salvarias found delightful to count, regardless of Adok's missing presence and the odd glances the slave cast over his shoulder.

The antechamber they ended up in was cold and dim. A candle lit the small room where a single chair rested along with a two-person table. Upon the table was a drained goblet of ale—based on the smell in the room—and a half-empty pitcher.

Humar was pacing the length of the room. Without his armor, he looked naked to Salvarias, despite the tailored trews, tunic, and doublet he wore, all died in varying shades of dark blue. Upon seeing the brothers, his eyes brightened but looked a little wild.

"Thank you for coming," Humar said. His usual calm demeanor had been replaced by a man near the verge of mild panic.

"Is everything all right, my friend?" Salvarias asked.

Humar plucked at his shirt, shrugging his shoulders as if the cotton and velvet weighed more than his armor. "Fine, fine. You look tired. Are you sure you're up for this?" His gaze flickered over to Wilhelm. "The tailor didn't see you? He was supposed to fit you with new clothes."

Wilhelm looked down at his faded black trews and travel-stained white tunic. "I didn't have time to meet with him."

Humar was already waving Wilhelm's words aside. "It's no matter. I'm not expecting to make a good first impression." The knight resumed his pacing. "Falisa has coordinated this event in record time. The poor woman has been running herself ragged, but I insisted we get this over with as quickly as possible." Humar combed a hand through his hair, sticking it up. "I've run long enough. It's time to face my fate."

Wilhelm arched an eyebrow at Humar. "What about those excuses you threw at us not but a day ago?"

Humar shrugged, squirming in his clothes again. "Excuses and nothing more. I might not make the best king, but I hope to do better than what my mother did or what Henry would do should he inherit the throne."

"The Avral family will not give in so easily," Salvarias warned.

Humar's laugh was mirthless. "Of course they won't. I'm sure they'll attempt to kill me at least daily. That is, unless the Lilkous curse turns me into a blubbering idiot first."

"I beg you to allow me to examine the crown before your coronation," Salvarias said.

"We've had every specialist in every field imaginable take a look at that crown and none have been able to even sense the curse, much less end it."

Salvarias shrugged. "I am not like others."

Humar's pacing stopped and his eyes narrowed. "No, no you're not. As you wish."

"Thank you."

After giving orders to retrieve the crown to a slave waiting outside the room, Humar said, "When I'm announced, the three of us will enter together. It'll send a clear message walking with a mage."

"A dangerous one. Perhaps you should settle into your title first," Salvarias suggested. "The road ahead of you is already wrought with enemies."

"No. I'm making my stand early on. The more changes I can make before the curse takes hold the better." Humar shifted Salvarias's cloak over his shoulders so it trailed behind him, offering a clear view of his faded burgundy robes. "Stand tall, boy," Humar murmured. "Be proud of your gift. I can't have a man at my side who doesn't show a lick of confidence."

Feeling his cheeks flush with embarrassment, Salvarias straightened slightly.

"Head up," Humar said.

Clenching his teeth together, Salvarias raised his head until only his eyes were concealed in the shadow of his hood.

"I don't suppose I could persuade you to lower your hood for the night?" Humar asked.

Salvarias shook his head. "I would prefer not."

"So be it." Humar stepped back and looked both brothers up and down. "It'll do. Wilhelm, do me a favor and try to curb your temper. People won't be nice to your brother, but I swear I won't let a soul hurt him. If you go starting fights, you'll only strike terror into those already fearful of what they don't understand. You'll put your brother at a greater risk. Clear?"

Wilhelm nodded. "But if one person lays a hand on him, I'll chop it off and shove it up their ass."

"Agreed," Humar said.

An older man entered, donned in a red-velvet robe trimmed in gold, his arms locked together within the voluminous sleeves. His face was carved like old bark, and his back humped dramatically. White had overrun most of his dull blue eyes and lines around his mouth seemed made for frowning. "You wanted to see the crown?" he asked Humar.

"Yes."

Smacking his lips a few times, he conjured enough spit to say, "As you desire."

From within his sleeve, he produced a simple gold circlet. Humar clenched his fist and took a step back as if the old man held a live snake.

Salvarias stepped forward and bowed deeply. "Thank you. May I?"

After a nod from Humar, the man handed over the crown. The instant the cold metal touched Salvarias's hand, he had a strong urge to chuck it across the room. There was no curse, not anymore, but he felt the remnants of one, and it petrified him. To leave a permanent scar on the object, the curse had to have been incredibly powerful, but that was not what drove the air from his lungs. It was because it was the same taint living in his own soul, the same corruption pulsing in the black stone he so desperately needed. The implications of that familiar evil robbed Salvarias of warmth and spun the room around him. He thrust the crown back into the man's hands and stumbled backward until running into something solid. A comforting hand squeezed his shoulder.

"It's all right, Salv," Wilhelm rumbled.

He swallowed hard and rasped, "Thank you, gentleman."

Once the man left the room, Humar sank into a chair. "That bad?"

"Quite the contrary," Salvarias said, eyes unable to focus. "The curse is gone."

"Gone?" Humar rose swiftly. "What do you mean, gone?"

"I felt the faint touch of it, but it is no longer active."

"How is that possible?" Humar asked. "There's only three ways to break the curse. Sands from the city of Quind—which we lost. The claw of a griffin dipped in the blood of Zerana—which is impossible, or ..." Humar's gaze intensified on Salvarias. "Or a mortal with the power of a god."

"Also impossible," Salvarias said.

"Perhaps." Humar's eyes narrowed. "How could you feel it but no others? And if the curse is gone, what has you frightened?"

Salvarias fought down the urge to run, to flee from everything, to find a dark hole and hide in it until the last of his days. "I need time to think about what I felt," he said with more confidence than he carried. "It is ... unclear to me."

Humar eyed Salvarias. "As you wish. You're sure you're all right?"

Salvarias nodded and stood straight, forcing his fear beneath his lake of indifference. "Yes, my friend."

A soft knock was followed by a young woman entering the room. She curtsied low, cheeks red, and said, "My lord, Princess Falisa has started."

"Thank you," Humar said. When the woman left, the knight adjusted his clothes, flattened his hair, and inhaled a deep breath. "Gods help me," he murmured and then escorted them to the main room leading to the throne room. A pair of knights standing by a massive double door saluted smartly and banged their spears on the marble floor when Humar approached.

After Salvarias and Wilhelm took position on either side of Humar, the soon-to-be king nodded. From behind the doors, a bellowing voice announced Humar's arrival as the knights hauled open the doors.

Beyond, a stream of red velvet sliced from the door to the throne at the far end of the room. Those in attendance were the wealthiest of the wealthiest; their clothes alone could have fed the city for a month. They were all down on one knee, heads bowed to their future king. Lining the walkway were knights, swords raised overhead to form an arch.

Humar strode down the walkway without show or ceremony. He walked with purpose and took his strides with military crispness. Murmurs flowed in Salvarias's wake, and though the words were unclear, their tone of disapproval and shock were not.

The walk seemed to take an eternity. Despite bowed heads, Salvarias felt the eyes of near a thousand boring into his back. He desired nothing more than to pull his hood lower and fade into the shadows, but he was here for Humar and did not intend to disappoint the prince.

When they finally reached the end of the walkway, Falisa joined Wilhelm's side. The old man stood in front of the throne, gold circlet resting on a red-velvet pillow cradled in his hands.

The actual crowning was quick with only a few invocations muttered before the crown was placed on Humar's brow. Humar inhaled deeply and then turned in a half circle to face the throng. Salvarias bowed and Wilhelm followed suit. To Salvarias's surprise, Humar bowed in return. Angered whispers shot through the crowd.

"Please stand behind me until I'm done," Humar muttered under his breath.

Once Salvarias and Wilhelm had taken their spots behind their friend, Humar spoke in a clear, confident voice. "I've returned home at the direst of times. In my travels abroad, I have encountered a true darkness. Out there, beyond the safety of these walls, is an evil that threatens our lands, our homes, and our families.

"I had no intention of returning here," Humar continued. "As you all know, I slew my father when I was fifteen. I swore on that day I would never step foot into my homeland again. It was not because of fear at what I had done. It was because I hate my home." A loud murmur rose from the crowd. Humar waited until it quieted before he continued. "Loutsil is soaked in blood. It taints each and every one of you. Your hatred and pompous vanity have corrupted my home. Your slavery and bigotry have made you all insane." Humar took a step back to stand beside Salvarias. "This is a mage." Under his breath, Humar whispered, "Make a ball of fire."

Muttering out a spell and flicking his hand, Salvarias extended his palm outward, and above it a flame sputtered to life. Gasps filled the room.

"This young man has saved my life with the use of magic. This young man saved the city of Cattlar. All with magic. Yet you arrest those like him when they hold the key to your salvation." Humar waved forward a slave waiting in a dark corner. The man's face flushed as he joined Humar and bowed deeply. The king quickly made him stand straight. "You pretend you own this man. Another human being, a life. From this day forward, this man will be paid for his service to the crown. I do not own him." Humar nearly spat the words out and anger filtered into his voice. "No one does."

Heated murmurs began to rise. Humar allowed them a brief moment before he roared, "Silence." The suddenness of it made

Humar pause. After straightening his doublet, he raised his chin and said, "I am your king and I will make this a place I am proud to call home. We will show the world the true meaning of compassion. No longer will I run in fear of what Loutsil has become. I will change every damn thing about it, and the gods help any who stand in my way. I am king, and I will bring light back to Loutsil."

A few young nobles bolted to their feet, clapping enthusiastically. The rest glared at Humar.

Spreading his arms wide, Humar smiled broadly. "Let us enjoy the fine feast my beloved sister has arranged. Be merry, my country men and women, for today we dine in Zerana's grace once again."

The few nobles cheered. When none seemed ready to depart, Humar waved his hand absently, and the knights began gently nudging people toward the exit. Salvarias generated a ball of ice and fused it with the fire, causing a loud hiss of steam before both spells canceled each other.

"You made many enemies," Falisa said.

"I've always had them," Humar muttered, his eyes hardening.

After the room cleared, Humar offered his arm to his sister and led them down the walkway, Salvarias and Wilhelm following a step behind. Trailing them were ten knights, all stone-faced old veterans, but Salvarias saw a sparkle of pride in their eyes. Apparently, Humar had been busy finding those loyal to his cause.

When they arrived at the dining hall, Humar threw open the double doors without ceremony. The smells hit Salvarias first, sparking a loud grumble from Wilhelm's stomach. Gamey meats mixed with earthy stewed vegetables and heavy winter seasoning of sage and cinnamon hung thick in the air.

Stretching before Salvarias was a cavernous room, domed ceiling painted with a scene from the Long Wars: an army of gleaming Loutsil Knights charged toward Veedran's army of twisted defilements. Tall braziers circling the room warmed up the cold marble walls. Flanking the walkway paved in red velvet were rows of long tables covered in food and lit by elegant candelabra. At the end, a table faced the room with only one man standing at it. He had a handsome face and deadly smile. As Humar started down the walkway, Salvarias and Wilhelm on either side a step behind him, Falisa murmured that the man was Henry, her husband.

Once Humar arrived at the table, he ignored Henry's offered hand and turned to the crowd, accepted a mug of ale, and raised it high. "To Loutsil!"

After a less than enthusiastic response, music started, a jovial tune at odds with the mood of the room.

Wilhelm grinned at Humar. "I'd sleep with one eye open tonight. I'm pretty sure you just told your nobles they're a worthless pile of crap."

Humar's return smile was full of mischief. "Indeed I did. But if I've learned anything, it's that disclosing your expectations early on sets the tone."

"The road ahead will be difficult," Salvarias said.

Humar nodded. "Nothing worth anything is easy. At least it should give Falisa a slight reprieve. Hopefully all efforts at killing off the Lilkous line will shift to me." He headed toward his seat and kept his voice low when he said, "How much time have we lost on Perek?"

Salvarias shrugged. "I am unsure. He has not left Loutsil."

"I'll send one of my knights to you tomorrow, one I trust that knows the land well. He should be able to help track Perek's progress. As soon as you're ready, we can be on our way."

"My friend," Salvarias said gently. "You cannot leave—"

"If we don't continue to hunt this god and Perek, I won't have a kingdom to rule," Humar said. "We'll discuss it later. In the meantime, let's try to enjoy a bit of food and a lot of ale."

Wilhelm winked at Varila. "Dress?"

Varila rose from her seat and twirled for Wilhelm's pleasure. The dress she wore was cut low in the chest and fit tightly around her upper body before flowing out in a grand skirt. The light-blue fabric set off Varila's eyes and brightened her hair. She was radiant, and Salvarias marveled over how well she carried herself, seeming to transition from warrior to a lady of court with ease.

Wilhelm's gaze lingered on her figure while a grin stretched across his face. "Well now, you're a sight to behold."

"I know," she said. Turning to Salvarias, she said, "You look like crap."

Salvarias tilted his head. "I know."

A warm hand slipped into his, and he looked over to see Lunara standing at his side. Her dress was in the same fashion as Varila's except the neckline was not as revealing and the color was the deepest blue. Her hair was pulled back to display her delicate features and large eyes.

His breath caught in his throat as he bowed to her. "You look stunning, my lady."

She beamed a smile at him and led him to his seat. Humar's choice of seating had been deliberate. On his left was Princess Falisa, followed by Marcus, Okulu, and then Henry Avral. On the right of Humar was Salvarias's seat, then Lunara, Varila, Wilhelm, Durak, and Neithelas.

As dinner progressed, Salvarias found it difficult to focus on anything other than Lunara. Not even the delicious food turned his attention as she filled him in on her room's balcony overlooking the city and the grand buildings stretched before her view. If she knew her effect on him, she showed no signs, for which he was grateful. Perhaps his eyes were not nailed to her as strongly as he thought.

The few times he managed to tear his gaze from her, he was met with unfriendly stares from the tables laid out before him, and passing nobles who came to give greetings to Humar murmured curses at Salvarias. He found it more pleasurable to ignore all except Lunara.

At some point she had scooted her chair so close to his that the arms butted against one another, and she leaned near enough that she could talk softly over the dull roar of conversation in the room. He took advantage and breathed deeply of her scent and did not shy from her touch, which always was a hand resting on his arm. The painful headache he had endured all evening began to fade, and the shadow in his heart over what he had learned of himself did not seem nearly so dark. Soon he forgot the room and the people, his pain and worry. It was just them.

Though he rarely spoke, she continued talking about whatever came to mind. There were opinions he could share, but he preferred to listen to her voice. It reminded him of their dreams. She had done the same then, never seeming to care or get upset over his lack of involvement. It was odd since she was not a chatty girl. When she spoke in a group, it related to the topic on hand or their situation. Yet alone with Salvarias, she spoke of mundane things, unimportant things, and for an unknown reason, her trivial musings were more endearing than the most heartfelt conversations around him.

"My lady!"

Both Lunara and Salvarias jumped. He had been so secluded in their conversation, it appeared neither had heard Neithelas until he shouted.

"Might I have this dance?" Neithelas asked.

Salvarias glanced around the room. Dinner had ended and the throng mingled amongst themselves, and several tables had been shifted aside to allow room for dancing.

Reality came rushing back to Salvarias, and he shifted from Lunara. "You should, my lady," he said. "I need to speak with Humar." Giving her no chance to argue, he turned his back to her to find Okulu lounging in Humar's chair, one leg propped over the armrest.

The merc grinned and winked. "Seems Humar's not here," Okulu said. "Perhaps you and I could dance? Or if you're opposed, you could take Lunara yourself."

Salvarias shook his head. "You forget, I cannot dance."

"Excuses, excuses." Okulu looked over Salvarias's shoulder and clucked his tongue. "Too late. Looks like Varila dragged her out there."

Indeed, Varila was leading Lunara and Wilhelm to the dance area, Neithelas following.

"So, you two seemed occupied," Okulu said lightly.

Salvarias settled into his chair and rolled his eyes at the merc. "No women available?" He glanced at Okulu's empty cup. "Did they run out of ale?"

Okulu laughed. "I might've had more than my fair share already, and yes, there are plenty of women. In fact, several have given me directions to their beds."

"And yet you sit here with me."

Okulu shrugged. "How did you snap Wilhelm out of his cheerfulness?"

It was Salvarias's turn to shrug.

"Salvarias," Humar said, coming up from behind. "If you're up for dirty looks and snide comments, I'd like you to accompany me as I mingle."

Salvarias tilted his head to Okulu and rose from his seat. "Of course, my friend."

The first table Humar led him to was occupied by one of the young nobles who had shown approval of Humar's speech. The man was a few years Wilhelm's senior with a face entirely too feminine. He bowed deeply to Humar and shot Salvarias a nervous glance.

"My liege," the noble said. "There are many of us that are glad you have returned. Many of us agree change is needed in Loutsil." The man licked his lips and glanced at Salvarias again.

Humar's eyes lit with amusement. "Have you never met a mage?"

"No, I have not."

Humar laughed and clapped the man on the shoulder. "I've known Salvarias since he was ten. Very respectable man."

"I heard rumors there is none his equal in magic," the noble said.

"Remind me of your name again?" Humar asked.

"Jorge Breshwood, my lord, third son to Karvl."

"Ah, your father doesn't share your opinions," Humar said.

"Indeed he does not, nor my eldest brother. But the rest of my family does."

"Good, good. Now, tell me about these rumors. How and why would the Breshwood house know of one mage's skill?"

"Wunhur Avral distributed the Association of Mages' lists to the nobles. There were names crossed off the list, and we were told to watch out for those mages. If we were to come across any, we were to report it to Wunhur immediately. I'm sure he's surprised to know the most powerful mage in all the world has been traveling with you."

Salvarias bowed at the compliment. "I promise you, there is another whose skill surpasses my own. The Association surely made an error."

Jorge smiled sheepishly. "I admit, I've always wanted to meet a mage. I heard stories from Zehnia when I was young."

"Zehnia?" Humar said. The king stiffened at the name. "Avral's daughter?"

"She still fights on behalf of mages," Jorge said. "Despite her father's protests. Of course, Wunhur would never punish Zehnia. She's his most prized jewel."

"Yes," Humar murmured, eyes distant. "I remember." Seeming to shake himself out of his thoughts, Humar smiled broadly at Jorge. "What's your favorite animal?"

"An eagle ... golden eagle."

Salvarias whispered out his spell, flicked his hand, and an eagle of pure white light floated over his left shoulder, brighter than he anticipated, larger than Durak. Gasps filled the room.

"Tell me, Humar. Is the Avral family present?" Salvarias asked.

Humar's smile widened. "Why I believe they are. There." He pointed to a table filled with sour-looking men, all glaring at their new king. One particular old man stared with more hatred than Salvarias thought the world could possess.

Smiling to himself, Salvarias sent the eagle diving for the man. He scrambled in his seat but his rotund belly held him in place. The eagle dove through him, emerged on the other side, and soared to the domed ceiling.

"Rulose," Salvarias whispered and the light vanished.

"That was amazing!" Jorge exclaimed. "I thought you had to suck out life from others to create magic."

"We do not," Salvarias said. "Ill-practiced mages draw energy from living beings causing them to be tired, but the majority are trained enough."

The room had quieted to a menacing murmur, and Salvarias became aware of the aggravated stares leveled at him. The room suddenly seemed unsafe. Humar must have noticed because his hand drifted down to the pommel of his sword. As quickly as the room had turned malicious it switched back into its less violent, disgruntled state. Salvarias let out a held breath and shifted back a step. He collided with what he thought was a wall until he looked over his shoulder to see Wilhelm looming, eyes alight with warning as he glared at any still looking at Salvarias.

Instant safety wrapped around Salvarias, and he inhaled a calming breath.

"I don't like this," Wilhelm muttered to Humar.

"It'll be fine," Humar assured him. "Follow us. I think it's time to visit Wunhur."

By the time they reached Avral's table, Wunhur had calmed enough that he had been able to remove himself from his seat. He stood behind his chair, vibrant blue eyes burning with contempt and superiority

"Wunhur Avral," Humar greeted. "How have you been?"

"Wonderful. My lands are prosperous and my wealth grows." The man stuck his nose up at Humar. "Soon I may be wealthier than the king himself."

Humar laughed. "You probably already are when it comes to gold. Not much else, though."

Wunhur floundered over his words, but before he delved out a rebuttal, a striking woman Humar's age came to his side. Her dark hair was the same as her father's, but her eyes were not beady and blue but large and brown. Wrinkles creased her eyes and framed her mouth when she smiled.

"My king," she said, curtsying. "It is good you have returned."

Humar bowed deeply and kissed her offered hand. "Zehnia, your beauty has only grown."

"I certainly hope you'll pay me a visit soon," she said. "I live on Maybur Street, next to the Neeve family."

"Of course, my lady," Humar said. His gaze locked on hers as he straightened and took an at-ease stance, face a stone mask. Tension danced between them, unvoiced questions thickening the silence.

Salvarias bowed to the woman. "My lady. Humar has told me much about you."

"Did he?" She smiled at Humar. "And what did he tell you?"

Salvarias deftly drew a rose petal from his pouch, chanted his spell, and flicked out his rune. Holding the petal in his palm, he presented it to Zehnia as it morphed into a yellow rose. "He told me of your beauty and your kindness toward mages."

Her smile grew as she accepted the rose. "Did he tell you we were in love once, long ago?"

"Zehnia!" Wunhur blurted. "You can't—"

"Hush, father," she said, never taking her eyes from Humar.

"Long ago," Humar said softly.

"Yet there are things even time cannot erode," she said.

Salvarias glanced at her hands, noticing they were ringless. "You never married." He had not meant to say those words aloud.

"No, I never did." Smelling the rose, she turned her smile to Salvarias. "It's truly an honor to meet the most powerful mage alive."

Salvarias did not miss Wunhur's stiffening stance or his eyes widening at Salvarias.

"The Association has changed for the worse," she continued. "I've been fighting them, but the tide is against me. The leaders have holed up here, for some reason. I used to meet with Kilt, but he's gone missing. The mages I meet with now do not act like they want my help."

"I am familiar with Master Kilt," Salvarias said. "He was one of the three mages that allowed me to live."

Zehnia sniffed. "How cruel is our world when a person chooses if another person should live or die?"

Salvarias shrugged. "There will always be those who are persecuted. It is in people's nature to judge and hold others above the rest."

"Such a dire outlook," she said.

"It is not my wish, merely my observation and study of history. Our world is a wheel. We are destined to come full circle."

"Unless we break it."

"Then we will make a new one."

Zehnia frowned. "So young to be so callous. I do not wish to know what horrors were bestowed upon you to make you hopeless so early on in life."

Her words sank in Salvarias's gut like a brick.

"If you'll excuse me," she said, curtsying, "it's been an eventful day and I am in need of rest."

"I'll escort you home," Humar said. "If you'll allow me, my lady."

Zehnia's smile warmed the room. "It would be an honor, my king."

Locking arms, the two strolled from the room. Salvarias glanced around, but Wunhur had disappeared.

"You all right?" Wilhelm muttered, leading Salvarias back to the main table.

"I am tired."

"Lunara was getting ready to retire for the night," Wilhelm said. "Why don't you walk her to her room?"

"Of course," he said absently.

It was not until he was strolling down the hall arm in arm with Lunara that Salvarias wondered why Wilhelm had sent them off by themselves. After the harsh looks Salvarias had received, he was surprised his brother allowed him time alone with Lunara.

When they arrived at her door, she kept hold and led him inside. Much like his own room, Lunara's sported a massive bed, a sitting area, and a roaring fireplace. Unlike his, she had a balcony and private washroom.

"I wanted to show you," she said, guiding him around furniture and out the double doors opening to the balcony.

Below them, the city of Warton spread like a swarm of fireflies on a dark night. Lights flickered for miles and stars covered the sky. He had not noticed the storm had finally ended.

Lunara shifted to stand in front of him and leaned her back against his chest. "Beautiful, is it not?"

Memories of their dreams pierced through him. So often they had stood in each others arms and gazed at a wonderful sight. With all his suffering, he needed that comfort once again. Despite his warring emotions, he wrapped his arms around her and inhaled her sweet scent.

"It is, my lady." He was not speaking of the city.

Resting his cheek against her head, he closed his eyes. The relaxation of his mind and lazy thoughts enhanced his exhaustion, weakening him to the point he found himself opening his mind to her, if only slightly. The light touch of her presence filled him with peace. His own soul warmed and healed in her light. Soft fingers snuck inside the sleeves of his robes and caressed his arms circling her waist.

Succumbing completely to her, he allowed her to drive away every ounce of his pain. A burdening weight lifted off his chest, and life had sudden clarity. None of what he had learned seemed to matter. All that surrounded him was love. It came from Lunara, from his brother, from his friends. Every horrible name his mother had called him was a lie. Every dark shadow in his heart fled. The terrible cold locked in his bones melted as warmth cascaded over him.

When finally he came to himself, Lunara had turned to face him. "No more pain," she whispered. Light fingertips trailed down his cheek and across his jaw. "I can help you, if you'll just let me."

Her ice-blue eyes held him captive. To live like this forever was a dream he had never hoped to dream. To be free of pain, to feel loved, to be at peace.

He could accept this gift, could he not? He could love. He could be happy.

Heat flared up on his left hand, startling him backward. He tripped over something, lost his footing, and fell hard on his side, coming face to face with his left hand. It was covered in blackfire. He shook his hand, but the fire burned darker. Unlike his own blackfire, this one was uncomfortably warm.

"Wilhelm!" Lunara screamed.

The room around him throbbed and Lunara's frantic voice sounded entirely too deep. Shadows seemed to sway in unison, moving back and forth to some seductive tune. The need for the stone clenched around Salvarias's heart like a vice, and he groaned as the desire faded his vision.

The fire licked up his arm and he had a satisfying feeling that he had obtained what he longed for most in life. The relentless need washed away, and he exhaled sharply at the gratification blooming within him. He clenched his left hand into a fist, certain he would feel the stone there, but his hand was empty. The realization sucked out his warmth and happiness, and the emptiness brought tears to his eyes. All he had wanted was the stone, and the brief sense of fulfillment only enhanced the truth of its absence.

As suddenly as it had begun, the fire flickered out. The room fluttered in front of him. Shadows shrank back into the darkness. Emptiness cleaved through Salvarias, and he found himself curled up on the ground, all of his pain flogging him again, his mind racing with its usual images of death.

"Brother," he choked.

Thudding footfalls sounded in the room, one foot landing harder than the other. Relief washed over Salvarias and only a breath passed before familiar arms gathered him up.

"I'm here, Salv," Wilhelm said. "What happened? Are you all right?"

Salvarias sagged against Wilhelm, gasping in lungfuls of air.

"What happened?" Wilhelm asked.

"Perek. I think he found the stone."

"Here," Varila said.

A mug of water was pressed into his hands. He drank it entirely.

"I didn't think we were that far behind him," Wilhelm said.

Salvarias closed his eyes and shifted through images. Since arriving in Senti, he had not followed Perek's path. His mind had been too distraught to even bother. He had lost sight of his goal, of his purpose, but the brief fulfillment coaxed it to burn brighter.

As Salvarias played Perek's path in his mind, he said, "He rode hard after Senti. He traveled double the distance we did each day. He is well past Warton."

"He came through here?" Varila asked.

Salvarias nodded. "Days ago."

"Is the army here?" Varila asked.

"Something is in Loutsil," Salvarias confirmed. "It is not as strong as what I felt in Dalnar. But their force is only half. If they are far away, that might lessen my sense of them as well." Frowning he said, "I still believe there was something in Windlous. It could be God." Salvarias clenched his fists. "We should have spent more time there."

"Should've doesn't help," Varila said. "We'll figure it out. Wilhelm and I will go fill in Humar." Varila smiled slightly. "You look like crap. Get some sleep in case we have to travel tomorrow."

Salvarias nodded and rose to his feet with help from Wilhelm.

"You sure you're all right?" his brother asked.

Salvarias patted Wilhelm's arm. "I will be."

After Wilhelm and Varila left, Salvarias turned to Lunara. "I am sorry."

She gently took his hand and examined it. "The fire didn't burn you."

It was his left hand, so even if it had, it would have healed.

"Let me help you to your room," Lunara said.

Wedging herself under his arm, she helped him hobble to his room. The short walk drained the last of his strength. Still, when Lunara stopped by his bed, he did not sink into its comforts. Instead, he recalled her touch, the love he had swum in, the warmth that had infused his soul.

He could protect her. He could keep her from harm. Had he not done so already? Danger had surrounded them, yet she had come through it all unscathed.

"Do you need anything?" she asked.

He did need something, and it was her.

She smiled and ran her fingers through his hair. "You must rest."

Gently she pushed him to lie down. He did not know when it was that he fell asleep, but he dreamt of walking with her in Serinity, in the gardens of the estate, holding her hand as her laughter lifted through the spring air.

Chapter 39

Autumn 1018 a.r.

Wilhelm lounged in a chair by the fire, reading a book on the Long Wars to his brother. For some reason, Salvarias had requested Wilhelm do so, though he hadn't read to his brother since they were children. He wondered if Salvarias's headaches were bad enough to make his brother give up reading. During the morning hours, Salvarias had drunk three different tea mixtures and had chewed on a few leaves and sticks Wilhelm didn't recognize.

Pausing in his reading, Wilhelm glanced at Salvarias. His brother's eyes were distant, his lips moving as he counted softly. Ever since the knight had left after laying out Perek's travels, Salvarias had withdrawn into his mind, his thoughts a whirlwind in Wilhelm's. Unable to hold his tongue any longer, Wilhelm said, "What is it?"

Salvarias smiled slightly and reached down to stroke Adok's ears. "I am sorry, brother. I assume our connection has interrupted your own mind."

"I can tell you're thinking on something. Actually, on quite a few things."

"I am. Perek has not left wherever he was last night. I assume picking up the stone has weakened him."

"We could leave today, if you want."

Salvarias ran a hand across his brow. "I do not think I am fit for travel. My brain is trying to rip free of my skull."

"Is it because of what I did?"

"Perhaps a bit, but more so it is an aftereffect of Perek obtaining the stone. I fear the day when it is I who lays hands on it."

"What do you think we'll do when you finally get it?"

Salvarias shrugged a shoulder. "Flee. Find a hole to hide in. Fight the Hunters." Salvarias paused in petting Adok.

"What?" Wilhelm asked, sitting straight.

Salvarias shifted in his chair, lowering his head and avoiding eye contact with Wilhelm. "Nothing, brother."

A lie, given away by the same tells Salvarias used to have when he said bullies had beat him. Clenching his jaw, Wilhelm settled into his chair and glared at the fire. "What happened when we were young, Salv? Who used to hurt you?"

Salvarias stiffened. "I told you."

"I want the truth."

"Bullies—"

"Look me in the eye."

Salvarias shrank back, seeming to fold in upon himself. After a long moment, he met Wilhelm's gaze. "Bullies." In that one hoarsely whispered word, Wilhelm saw the lie eat at his brother.

Biting his tongue, Wilhelm turned his gaze to the fire. He could push his brother, but he hated to cause Salvarias more pain. Obviously his brother was trying to protect Wilhelm from something. But from what eluded him.

A knock on the door was followed by Humar poking his head in. "Afternoon. Might I have a word with you both?"

Salvarias motioned to another chair. "Of course, my friend."

"I've spoken with my commanders and we're working to get the army ready for whatever might await us out there." Humar plopped into a chair.

"Mages would benefit your forces," Salvarias said. "I have been working on spells that could be used alongside the knights. A few could even be cast before the battle begins to weaken the enemy." Salvarias picked up his spell book, his eyes brightening as he spoke. "I have also come up with a few herbal remedies that will lower the outbreak of disease that usually follows armies."

Humar nodded, lips pursed. "I'll meet with Zehnia and the Association later today and see if I can put a stop to the murders and request mages be sent to the army." He slid a hand through his hair, a slow smile spreading. "You know, I could create a new garrison of mages. Maybe even an elite force combining mages and knights to help with our more difficult battles. Imagine it!"

"I have," Salvarias said. "However, mages would not receive a warm welcome in any army, despite their benefits."

"I'll assign men to protect them," Humar said. "Once the others see their benefit, I don't think they'll be as feared."

"Perhaps."

"Would you train them?" Humar asked. "I could possibly have a group ready tomorrow. I'd be forever in your debt."

"I do not know what I could teach a veteran mage, but I will certainly meet with them."

"Good."

"I have had a vision," Salvarias said.

"The last one came true," Humar noted.

"Partly. You and Okulu did not die. In this one, an army attacks Warton tomorrow. The city burns. We all die."

Humar pursed his lips. "I don't believe it."

Salvarias shrugged. "Neither do I. It is too grand. If they had that kind of force, they would have attacked us days ago."

"Why send this vision then?"

"I have no clue, my friend. I sincerely think they are toying with me."

"Regardless, I'll add security to the outer wall and close the gates early," Humar said. "If by chance they do attack, I'll be sure we're ready. And where's Perek?"

"He has not left, though when he does I do not think I will pursue him with such vigor."

"What do you mean?" Humar's eyes lit with understanding. "Good, good. Follow him closely, but not in an effort to catch him. Keep on his heels, have him lead us to god."

A faint smile touched Salvarias's lips. "Perhaps it is time we become the fishermen instead of the fish."

"I couldn't agree more." Humar rose from his seat and turned to Wilhelm. "I was going down to the yard to pass along some training to my men. I was hoping you would join me."

"It'd be my pleasure," Wilhelm said.

After strapping on his armor and swords, Wilhelm followed Humar out to the training yards. Snow had been cleared, leaving the ground muddy and cold. Sun shone brightly through a wispy trail of clouds and did nothing to warm a breeze coming in from the north.

Humar introduced Wilhelm and began speaking of the enemy while Wilhelm studied the throng before him. The knights were polished and stood at attention, helmets tucked under one arm. He recognized a few men from his brief bout the day after he had arrived in Warton. A couple still sported bruises and looked at him with a mixture of fear and respect.

It hit him then that these were his men, not Humar's. Knights in Loutsil were part of the Knight Council, even if they had attempted to branch off. Wilhelm was the supposed leader of the knights across all of Arden. However, the weight of responsibility was not one he could shoulder, not until this business with the stone had been resolved. And once it had, was it even his place to organize such a group? He had no leadership or battle experience. Humar had always praised Wilhelm in his fighting prowess and had often schooled him on battlefield tactics, also giving praise for Wilhelm's choices there. Even so, he was certain he was not, nor ever would be, the right choice to lead the knights. Better to keep the knowledge between himself and Salvarias and leave things as they were.

For the rest of the morning, Wilhelm sparred with Humar, going through his usual single-sword practice at a painstakingly slow pace so as to allow those watching to easily observe Wilhelm and Humar's movements.

By midafternoon, Humar divided up the knights into groups based on skill level. While he worked closely with the less-adept knights, he sent Wilhelm to train the few elite.

Wilhelm was in the middle of a short bout when a familiar, seductive voice sounded behind him.

"I'd like to give that a try."

He backed off from his opponent and looked over his shoulder. Varila stood, dressed in her armor, hands on her hips, a slight smile playing on her lips. Murmurs rose from the knights as they looked at her with a mixture of arousal and disapproval. After all, women in Loutsil were not allowed to be soldiers, much less knights. Sadly, she could shame half the men in front of him, yet was still denied her rightful place among the best. If ever he were to take over the knights, that'd be the first rule he would change.

He bowed to her and winked. "Are you sure you're up for a beating so close to bed?"

Varila laughed. "You've yet to try your skill against mine."

"No, no I haven't." He looked her up and down. Despite the cold, her tan thighs peeked between her boots and armored skirt. "But who wouldn't want to watch a specimen of perfection attempt to beat me?"

She walked up to him, hips swaying generously, a provocative smile stealing away a heartbeat. "Don't try to soften me up, dear."

Unable to resist, he bent down and kissed her, only to feel the sharp point of her sword pressing into the side of his armor.

"Men are so easily distracted," she purred.

The knights at his back chuckled.

"That was a one-time slip up," Wilhelm protested, grin growing.

"Well then, let's get started."

The bout began and ended as quickly as it started. Usually when they were fighting, he had no time to properly watch her. He knew she was talented, gifted even. Not only was that a truth, but never before had he been confronted straight on by her toned arms swinging her sword, or by her skirt hiking up with each lunge. The sight was distracting, and he barely parried two strikes before her sword tip pressed to his chest.

"Shame," she said. "I hoped my future husband would last longer. Is a short bout what I have to look forward to on our wedding night? Or would you like to show me what a real man is capable of?"

Wilhelm swung his leg under hers, knocking her off her feet, but caught her before she fell into the mud. He kissed her passionately. When finally he pulled his lips from hers, he grinned. "I would love to."

He took his stance as she took hers. Though he tried to remain focused, her features, her movements, and her confidence mesmerized him. Their short parry ended when she charged him, knocking him down, and straddled him. Cold metal pressed against his throat.

"Such a shame, love," she said breathlessly, lips hovering above his. "I thought you might be getting better."

He grabbed her wrist, pulled the knife from her hands, gripped her legs, and wrestled her onto her back. Pinning her arms, he kissed her even as her legs squeezed his waist, making it difficult to breath. "Perhaps you should punish me for my laziness," he suggested.

He winced when something pinched his side, just below his armor. Glancing down, the tip of a muddy dagger was stuck through his tunic, poking his skin enough to draw a dab of blood.

"Where did that come from?" he mumbled.

Varila smiled. "Perhaps later I'll let you to search me, and you can discover all sorts of hidden weapons."

Wilhelm grimaced at the instant arousal she caused, and her knowing smile only embarrassed him more.

"Need a moment, dear?" she asked, mischief in her eyes.

"You'll pay for that," he whispered.

She laughed lightly. "Promise?"

Grinding his teeth, he closed his eyes and gained control of his desire. "Promise."

He took his time rising and then offered her his hand. Most knights were polite enough to cover their smirks under a hand, but some laughed openly. The sight of Wilhelm and Varila covered in mud probably added to their amusement.

"You see, sirs," Humar said from behind. "Women are more than decoration. They can fight as well as, or better than, most men. And they don't mind getting a little dirty."

"She wasn't strong enough to toss him off her," a knight said.

"No," Humar agreed. "Just smart enough to stick a knife in his side. That'll be all for today. We'll pick back up tomorrow."

After the crowd dispersed, Humar turned a smile to Varila. "Well done." To Wilhelm he said, "Tell Salvarias I'll have a group of mages here tomorrow morning. I've set aside the northern yard for them to use. Guards I trust will be posted to protect them."

Wilhelm nodded. "If he's up for it. He doesn't seem well lately."

"I checked on him before I came down," Varila said. "I brought him soup from the kitchens and slipped him an old sleeping tea my mother used to give me. It knocked him out rather quickly, and I had Lunara stay with him. She should help him get some sleep."

Wilhelm arched an eyebrow at her. "I didn't ask you to check on him."

Her eyes flared dangerously. "I didn't know I needed your permission to look in on my—on Salvarias."

His other eyebrow rose. "Your what?"

"Nothing. Can we go? I'm freezing."

"I hadn't planned on returning yet." He looked up at the clear sky. "It's a nice day for a run."

Varila rolled her eyes and locked arms with Humar. "Just take a bath when you get back."

"One other thing," Humar said. "I've asked Zehnia to marry me. The ceremony is tomorrow night so the castle will be busy."

Wilhelm didn't bother to hide his surprise. "You're moving things along fast."

"I don't have the luxury of time. We could leave any day, and I need things in order here. Zehnia I trust as much as Falisa. The two can adequately run the kingdom in my absence. And with an Avral as queen, I hope Wunhur will not be so focused on killing my sister."

"What about love?" Varila said shortly. "You just marry the woman because it suits your purpose."

"Love has no place in the Lilkous line," Humar said. "Yet I managed to find it. I've loved Zehnia since I could first speak the word. We grew up together and leaving her was the hardest thing I've ever done. For an unknown reason, even after I had killed my father and fled, her feelings for me haven't changed. We both know a quick marriage is best."

"And she doesn't care you'll be leaving again?" Varila asked.

"She does, but understands. It's what is best for Loutsil."

"I see. Well, let's get you back so you can help her plan it."

With that, Varila left with the king.

Wilhelm glanced around at the empty training grounds and then down at his muddy armor. Shrugging off the sight of himself, he took off through the castle grounds.

As usual, the run helped clear his mind, and soon he thought of nothing but keeping his breathing regular. And Varila. She'd checked on Salvarias, and he had to admit he'd seen a change in her demeanor toward Salv. Her glances were not hateful but instead lingering, as if she were trying to decide or discover something. The fact she left Lunara alone with Salvarias time and again proved she trusted his brother, which was more than he had hoped. Perhaps all she'd learned about Salvarias had opened her eyes to his suffering.

After his run, Wilhelm bathed, turning his armor over to a servant for polishing, and then checked in on his brother. Salvarias still slept, Lunara sitting on the bed beside him, playing with a lock of his hair, Adok curled up at the foot of the bed.

Once certain his brother and Lunara were settled for the night, he headed toward his room.

As he approached his door, he frowned at the thin stream of light coming from beneath. He hadn't asked a fire be started. He hadn't belted on his swords yet, so he shifted them for easy access into one hand and slipped into his room.

A few candles burned and an open window offset the otherwise sweltering heat of the fireplace roaring with life. On the table was a platter of roasted meats, vegetables, and a full pitcher of what he assumed was ale. Laid out seductively on his bed was Varila. She wore a simple, thin robe, clearly naked beneath it. A shoulder and thigh were bared for his viewing, both kissed by the light.

The sight froze him.

A lush smile formed on her lips. "You just going to stand there?"

His body and mind refused to operate. Only his eyes drank her in.

"Well, well. The mighty Wilhelm Laybryth at a loss for words?" Slowly she rose from the bed, moving with what he assumed was purposeful erotic grace. "Paralyzed by a woman?" she continued, her voice dropping to something close to sin. "All the stories I heard and here you are, reduced to a staring idiot."

Still, he couldn't move. His body ached for her, but his mind reined in his desires with reason. He loved her. He wanted to marry her. To do things right, for once. To honor her. To honor her family.

She prowled over to him, her eyes alight with promises of fulfilling every intimate dream he had ever dreamt. Pressing lightly against him, she rose on her toes, making their lips nearly meet, and whispered, "We're done with games."

A loud clatter startled him and he realized he'd dropped his swords. Warm fingers slid under his shirt. The room throbbed with his need, and his breath caught in his throat. Gripping her arms, he whirled her around, pinning her to the door, his lips so close to hers he could feel the moisture of her breath.

"I want to marry you," he breathed. "But I'll do it right. I'll ask your father. And I'll wait until we're married."

"You think you're doing that for me?" she said. "I don't need my father's permission, and I certainly don't need to say I love you in front of others for it to be true. I want this." Her gaze lowered to his lips. "And I always get what I want."

The shift was slight, but the pressure of her body against his ended any argument. The building need for her drove him to lose control over the gentleness he normally sought to give a woman. He kissed her with all his pent-up passion, and her return kiss was painfully needy, causing him to wince when she bit his lip. Nails digging into his skin drove him mad.

Cloth tore as she ripped off his shirt, his trews following with a small struggle. They fought each other for dominance, the room their battlefield, the furniture tools for their passion. Her cries were muffled by his mouth, and his groans were animalistic in his own

416

ears. There were times he was pinned to the floor, her body draped over his, her teeth softly biting his chest. How she had managed to get him there, he couldn't remember, but he took control, grabbing her hair and sitting up as his lips found her neck, her breasts. Then he was on the bed, though he didn't remember how he got there either, and she was straddling him, her brow furrowed with desire as she slid on to him.

His hands dug into her thighs, and a short cry left him as satisfying pleasure coursed through his every fiber. Sitting up, he held her tighter, moving with her, balling her wealth of hair in his fist while his other hand pulled her closer, their lips nearly touching, the heat of her labored breath bathing him in ecstasy.

He hauled her over the edge, taking her whimpers of pleasure in his ear as if they were the word of all that was holy. He followed her, his own moan joining hers, his hands bruising her leg as her nails drew blood on his back.

They sat in the same position, panting in each other's ear, holding each other tightly long after it ended. When the fires of their passion died, he wrapped her tenderly in his arms. Her caress was soft over his slick shoulders.

"I'm sorry," he breathed.

There was a smile in her voice when she said, "I think I owe you the apology. You're the one bleeding."

Nestling his face in the crook of her neck, he inhaled the smell of her sweat and strawberries. "I rather enjoyed that part."

Her throaty laugh sent a pulse of new desire through him. "I love you," he said. Leaning back, he gazed into her eyes as he pushed back her hair. "Marry me?"

Her soft lips pressed against his, a gentle kiss that made the world fall away. "The first chance I get," she said, and kissed him again.

Chapter 40

Autumn 1018 a.r.

Lunara hurried along the path to the training yards, cursing the cold that had set into her fingers and toes. By the time she caught sight of Durak and Salvarias, Salvarias had already left the cavrul's side and headed toward the four mages awaiting his instruction.

Snow covered the training yard except for a cleared portion where a table and chairs had been set up with a stack of parchment in front of each seat. Quills, ink, and sand littered the table.

Durak waved Lunara over to a sprawling oak where he'd laid out a blanket and basket of food. As she walked to him, she watched the four mages bow to Salvarias as he approached, all folding their arms in the sleeves of their robes.

"It is a pleasure to meet you all," Salvarias said, bowing to them. "I am Salvarias Laybryth."

One man raised his head, golden hair glistened in the sunlight, and his smile wrinkled his aged face. "Bertim Hykrit," the man said.

Another man with black hair and a pale, smooth face introduced himself as Devar Gumkal. Lunara would have thought him younger, but his voice betrayed his youthful appearance.

"Fedlor Vesdril," another said, his billowy gray beard bobbing as he spoke.

"Gilra Hundsil," a woman said. She lowered her hood, revealing a strikingly beautiful, round face framed by chestnut hair. She couldn't have been older than Varila.

The group sat around the table and Salvarias began talking, his voice too soft to reach Lunara as she joined Durak. The old cavrul whittled away at a stick, his gaze resting more on Salvarias than the knife in his hand.

"I'm surprised to find you here, Durak," she said. "You've never been fond of magic."

"Aye. But me be changing my mind of late."

As time passed, Lunara watched Gilra lean close to Salvarias, elbow on the table, chin perched on her hand, eyes intent, and a lazy smile on her lips. He seemed oblivious to her lingering gazes, though

Lunara doubted he missed them, just as he had not missed Kisra's. The man was simply not interested.

As the day passed, Salvarias allowed for few breaks, and during those he did, Gilra occupied his time, despite his gaze drifting to Lunara. She smiled at him, and though she couldn't see his face, she felt the warmth of his stare. His lingering glances her direction seemed to irritate Gilra, and Lunara was the recipient of many dark glares from the young woman. Gilra must have assumed he was with Lunara.

By midafternoon, Salvarias ended the lesson, bowing to each mage as they filed from the training area, each escorted by three guards. Salvarias walked over to her and Durak and offered her his hand.

"Why did you come?" he asked as he helped her to her feet. "It is freezing out here."

She shrugged. "I wanted some fresh air."

Wrapping his cloak about them both, he put his arm around her shoulders and led the way back toward the castle.

"So they can help with the army?" Durak asked.

"I hope so," Salvarias said. "Lady Gilra has potential if she focuses on the relationship with her magic."

"I'm surprised the older ones haven't figured it out yet," Durak said. "You mentioned they get better with age."

"Indeed," Salvarias said. "The power of their spells grow, but knowledge is lacking in all mages. So much is available for us to learn. I fear what I told you before was correct."

Durak grunted. "At least you're setting things straight."

"I hope so," Salvarias said.

"Faith, boy," Durak muttered. "Ye lack it."

"I have not seen much to move me," Salvarias said.

"I have and it came from you, ye thick-skulled idiot," Durak snapped. "If ye want faith, look in the mirror."

"At least I can see in one," Salvarias quipped.

"Now listen here, boy," Durak roared. "I could beat your skinny ass to Oblivion if me chose."

"I am not sure your arms would reach, dear friend." Salvarias grinned at Durak.

Durak drew his axe, "Right now. We'll see who wins."

419

Salvarias whispered out words of magic and an ice shard floated at Durak's chest. "I have continued to beat you, friend. When will you learn?"

"Ye cheated." Durak sheathed his axe and the ice shard sank to the ground. "One day, boy, I'll win."

"My natural death does not count," Salvarias said with a frown.

Durak chuckled. "Aye, it doesn't."

When they reached the castle, Lunara split off from the men and made her way to her room. Tonight Humar would wed, and Lunara was scheduled for yet another dress fitting.

The seamstress was waiting for her when she arrived. The fitting progressed quickly, and after adding a few pins, the woman took the dress away for stitching.

Lunara lingered in a hot bath to drive off the chill of the day before drying and dressing in one of her summer dresses from Dalnar. Just as she was about to begin the task of brushing her hair, a soft knock sounded on her door.

"Who is it?" she asked.

"Salvarias."

Bounding over to the door, she flung it open, snatched up his hand, and led him inside. His slightly damp hair had just begun to curl in its usual subtle waves. With his hood thrown back, she saw his dark gaze scan the room before settling on her.

Holding up her brush, she said, "I think it's about time to take you up on one of my wagers."

Salvarias gifted her a small smile. "As my lady wishes. I believe we are down to one."

She made her way to the vanity and sat down, regarding him in the reflection of the mirror. "Yes. A walk."

He ran the brush through her hair, gently pulling it through tangles. "We walked together today."

She smiled at him. "But I didn't ask. You did so of your own free will."

Salvarias's met her gaze in the mirror, and the corner of his mouth turned up in smile. "So I did."

He continued to brush her hair in silence, his usual stern expression melting into a look of content, and his tense stance relaxed.

When she reluctantly thanked him and held up her hand for the brush, she was surprised to see him hesitate.

"Would you mind starting a fire?" she asked. "The air is chilly."

"Of course, my lady."

Watching him in the mirror as he coaxed a flame to life, she found it odd he visited her without a cause. Curiosity brimming, she joined him by the fire. "Why did you come?" she asked.

He didn't respond, but his gaze drifted to her lips. When he raised his hand, she saw it shaking before it disappeared in her hair, his gaze shifting to watch it fall between his fingers.

"Why did you come to the training yard today?" he asked.

"I ..." Gods, should she say the truth? Would it drive him away or bring him closer? She bit her lip in indecision.

His gaze slid back to her mouth, and her heart nearly leapt from her chest when his thumb glided across her jaw.

"Why?" he asked.

"I wanted to be with you."

A ridge formed between his eyebrows.

"Why did you come here?" she asked again.

The ridge deepened and he whispered, "I do not know."

"Liar," she breathed.

His gaze met hers, intense, confused, scared.

She slid her hands up his chest. "At least tell yourself the truth," she said.

Desire drowned out all other emotion in his eyes. Leaning forward, he slid his hand underneath her hair, his long fingers caressing the back of her neck, erupting waves of gooseflesh over her arms. His other hand rested on the small of her back, pressing her closer, closing any distance between them. Tilting her head up, she offered her lips, begging him with her eyes. He paused close enough that she smelled the earthy scent of his breath, felt its heat and wetness on her mouth.

When he didn't draw nearer, she ran her hands up into his hair, giving him the gentlest tug toward her.

His eyes closed and his lips parted.

A knock on the door froze his mouth a mere hair's width from hers.

"My lady?"

It was the voice of the seamstress.

Salvarias opened his eyes. For a breath, she thought he would still kiss her, but the door burst open and the seamstress bustled inside.

"I-I'm sorry," the woman stammered. "I did not mean ... I thought you were gone ..."

Salvarias blinked as if waking from a dream and stepped back. "Forgive me. You must get ready."

After tilting his head to the seamstress, he left the room.

Lunara managed to steer her swaying self into the nearest chair as the seamstress continued to apologize. It took Lunara a moment before she found her voice and assured the woman it was fine and accepted her help to dress. When the seamstress offered to put up Lunara's hair, she absently agreed, her mind still locked in her moment with Salvarias. She had come so close so many times to breaking his walls. She was sure if he kissed her in his own time, of his own accord, his wall would crumble and she would be his.

After her hair was done, she stepped from the room, surprised to see the mage waiting. He stared at her a moment then held out his arm. Smiling, she locked arms with him and walked closely to the grand hall.

"You are beautiful," he said.

"Thank you," she said, a blush heating her cheeks.

The wedding was held in the formal ballroom elaborately decorated. Flowers cascaded from pillars lining the mirrored walls. Candle-lit chandeliers cast romantic lighting upon the altar at one end of the room, raised on a dais so all could see. Among the fashionably dressed, Salvarias's hooded, cloaked form stood out, despite its rich fabric.

The ceremony might as well have lasted an eternity. Unaccustomed to such lengthy traditions, she found herself bored and uncomfortable. Salvarias stepped behind her, taking her hand in his as he gently pulled her back so she could lean heavily against him.

"We'll all be dead by the time this damn ceremony ends," Okulu muttered.

"Or sober," Salvarias whispered.

"Blasphemy," Okulu hissed. "Such horrors should never be mentioned."

"Winsire weddings are much more efficient," Neithelas said. "We spend our time celebrating the union, not performing the union itself."

"That's one thing I can agree upon," Okulu said.

"Shut up, children," Durak growled. "Show some respect to ye elders."

"The ancient one has spoken," Okulu drawled. "We must cease or else he'll cleave us in two with one of his curses."

Durak kicked Okulu's shin, causing the merc to give a yelp of pain. The throng of people turned to face them. Lunara's cheeks burned hot with embarrassment.

Humar glanced over, rolled his eyes at Okulu, and then turned back to his wife. No one spoke again.

After five more eternities crawled by, the ceremony ended. On a high balcony, music began, flowing down to create the perfect volume in the room. The mood was chipper, considering the changes Loutsil had experienced in a mere few days. Nobles mingled easily, laughter rising as more ale and wine made its way around the room. Dancing soon started and Varila was quick to drag Wilhelm out.

Lunara should have known it wouldn't be long before Neithelas approached her. Over the trek across Loutsil, he had kept his distance from her, giving her hope that he had finally accepted they would never be together. That hope was squelched when he joined her side, standing close while discussing the wedding traditions of the winsires. As usual when he visited her, Salvarias melted away, seeming to give Neithelas courage to stand closer to her.

He smelled different, a bitter, musty smell that stung her nose. They talked for several moments before he asked her to dance. She surprised herself when she agreed. Taking her hand, he escorted her to center of the room.

Halfway through the song, her head swam in a bog, but she laughed as Neithelas twirled her around. As invigorating as the dance was, she was thankful when the next tune slowed, allowing her to steady her suddenly trembling legs. Neithelas was kind enough to hold her close, helping her remain upright.

"I want to escort you to your room," Neithelas whispered in her ear. "Say yes."

Her mouth formed the word *yes* before her mind even had a chance to consider his request. As he led her to the exit, she noticed

Wilhelm, Varila, and Salvarias were nowhere in sight. Okulu remained at a table with Durak, the two drinking a pitcher of ale together.

"Where are the others?" she breathed, stumbling along in Neithelas arms.

"They retired for the evening," he said.

"I haven't seen much of you," she said. Was she slurring her words?

"I met a winsire at Humar's coronation that has made quite a name for himself, despite prejudices against our kind. It's been ... refreshing to immerse myself in winsire traditions again. I feel reconnected to my people. It is time I return to what is right, what is needed to ensure happiness for those I love."

Was there something threatening in his voice, or was it her imagination?

When she opened the door to her room, he followed her in. Surprising herself again, she did not argue.

"You have a lovely view," Neithelas said. "Show me."

She was compelled to obey and led him to her balcony. A cool breeze swept over her warm body as she pushed open the doors. Arms circled her waist, but they felt foreign, as if a stranger held her instead of Salvarias. Then she remembered she was with Neithelas.

His hand moved up her side, gliding with gentle pressure until he reached her neck and moved her hair to one side. A part of her wanted to be touched, to feel needed, to be desired. She tilted her head to the side as his lips moved over her neck. His hand slid down her side, her thigh, his fingers pressing into her skin. When he turned her to face him, she wanted to see black eyes, but instead met violet eyes.

"I love you," Neithelas breathed. "I have loved you from the moment I first saw you. Allow me to take you as my wife. I swear I will worship you. I will save you from the darkness feeding on you. I will protect you from all the horror of this world. Marry me. Say yes."

Compelled, she spoke the quietest "Yes." Marriage, to live in happiness, encased in his love, in his smile. Yet the man before her was not the image her mind conjured. Battling for one solid thought, she reached out to Salvarias and said, *Help me.* Why she did, she didn't know. She wanted Neithelas, didn't she?

Lifting her onto the balcony railing, his hand glided up her thigh, raising her dress above her knees. Warm breath washed over her face as he slid between her legs, pulling her against him.

"Say you love me," he commanded.

"I ..." She swallowed, but her throat and tongue continued without her mind's approval. "I love you."

Tears filled his eyes, a smile splitting across his face. "I knew you did. I knew in my heart you couldn't love him." He laughed lightly, joyous tears streaming down his face. "You've made me the happiest man in the entire world, Lunara."

He bent down to her, his lips converging on hers, and her mind screamed out in protest even as her lips parted to accept him.

The door to the room flew open, and Neithelas jumped back, whirling around at the intruder.

"You!" Neithelas spat. "You cannot leave her in peace, can you? You cannot accept that she loves me!"

Salvarias's eyes were lit with fury as he strode to the balcony, shoved the winsire away, and lifted Lunara from the ledge.

"How dare you," Salvarias hissed at Neithelas.

"Your jealousy shows, mage," Neithelas said. "She has agreed to marry me."

"Because you drugged her," Salvarias snapped. "Do you not remember our conversation in the caves of the Cattlar Mountains? I had hoped you listened when I said it was wrong of the winsire men to use the oil. It does nothing but manipulate the mind."

"That's not true! It has helped her see her true desires, what resides within her heart. As soon as I wore it, she was freed from your dark spell. She told me she loves me."

"Fool!" Salvarias snarled. "Your men are selfish in their wants. Has it ever entered your dim-witted skull the woman is simply not interested?"

"The woman accepts the man once her inhibitions are lowered. The oil merely helps," Neithelas said, raising his head proudly. "I would not expect a creature of evil to understand the ways of the winsires."

"Normally, I would agree with your statement, Neithelas, but now you are the creature of evil. How many marriages are happy in Meitholias? How many women cry in the night when their husbands force themselves upon them?"

"That's not true!" Neithelas roared.

The calming scent of lavender and the distance from Neithelas helped clear the musty smell from Lunara's nose. Her mind groped for solid footing, suddenly feeling as if she floated out at sea, unprotected, exposed.

"Why are only men permitted the oil?" Salvarias pressed. "Why are the trees guarded from women? You are a blind fool! You never question your traditions!"

"They've been in place for a thousand years!"

"That does not make them right!" Salvarias yelled back. "I see you are a good man, Neithelas, but you cling to the past. You are Prince of the Winsires. Open your eyes and move your people forward!"

"The traditions are in place to help our people! To help those we love," Neithelas said. "It is time you release your hold on her."

"You do not believe me? Then hear for yourself." Salvarias's fists clenched and he turned to Lunara. "Do you love him?"

Lunara pressed a hand to her temple, trying to stop the room from swaying. "No," she mumbled.

"Do you want to marry him?" Salvarias asked.

Oh gods! She had said *yes*. Grabbing the railing, she clamped a hand over her mouth in an attempt to squelch her rising stomach. When certain she was in control, she raised a furious gaze to Neithelas. "What did you do to me?"

"He drugged you," Salvarias said.

"You would do that to me?" she breathed, staring at the man she thought she knew. Then she remembered how close he had been, his hands on her, him pressed between her legs. She'd never felt so vulnerable in her entire life. "How could you!" she yelled through a building sob. "I trusted you!"

"The oil ... You agreed ... I would never force myself upon you." Neithelas dropped to all fours, face deathly white. "I never knew. I swear to you, Lunara, I never knew. Please forgive me!"

"Get out!" Lunara yelled.

"I swear I did not know!" Neithelas sobbed. "Please forgive me!"

"I never want to see you again!" Lunara wept.

"Leave, Neithelas," Salvarias said, lifting Lunara in his arms. "Save your apologies for when her mind has cleared."

She clung to the mage, burying her face in his chest, sobbing at the thought of what might have happened. She heard Neithelas's choked apology the entire way across her room until the door closed. Salvarias lowered her to bed, removed her shoes, and fetched a glass of water. She realized how parched she was. She drank two glasses and then crawled under the covers.

"How are you feeling?" Salvarias asked.

Now that he asked, she realized she was exhausted. "Tired," she mumbled, her eyelids drooping. "Thank you."

His soft hands brushed aside her hair. "You must not remain angry with him. He is ignorant and naive because of his love for his people and their beliefs. Because of his love for you. He will see with time that the winsires must rid themselves of archaic practices."

"I never want to see him again," Lunara said, holding back another wave of tears.

"You may feel different in the morning," Salvarias said. "Sense his true emotions and you will know, though misguided, his intentions were pure and done out of love."

"How can you say that after what he did?" Lunara said.

"Because I understand. I do not condone," he said quickly. "But I understand his intent. Neithelas is a good man who is confused, lost, and trying to learn of a world he has been sheltered from his entire life. You know as well as I that his heart is pure."

Lunara closed her eyes. "I hate him."

"Your heart is not capable of hate, my lady. Wait until the morning." His fingers ran through her hair, and she slept.

She woke in the night and fetched herself another glass of water, wincing at her pounding head and churning stomach. Wrapping herself in a blanket, she opened the doors to her balcony and stared at the sleeping city.

Rubbing her arms, she tried to drive away the memory of his hands, her unnatural need for him, and her inability to control the situation. He'd violated her trust. Yet Salvarias's words kept ringing in her mind. Neithelas was a good man with a kind heart, and yes, he was confused. She sensed it in him several times—a lost man after truths.

Sighing, she stepped back into her room and froze. A shadow had moved. She swore she'd seen the darkness shift. An uneasy feeling crawled up her spine. She was being watched. Before she cried out, Gilra parted from the shadows, and shock lodged a knot in Lunara's throat.

"The Association has some questions," Gilra said.

A man stepped into the moonlight to her right. Scars ran down the side of his face, partly covered by his long, wheat-colored hair.

Lunara opened her mouth to scream, and the world suddenly went dark.

Chapter 41

Autumn 1018 a.r.

Lunara woke to a throbbing head and an uncomfortable wooden chair. A single candle resting on a nearby table grappled with the darkness of the room. Pillars supported the ceiling, not the usual white marble of Warton, but old, earthy brown stone. Moss crept here and there, thriving in the damp air. Shadows clung to the area beyond the pillars, but she didn't need to see to know something was there. She smelled it: rotting meat, sweat. Evil.

A man's voice rose from the darkness. "Hello, my lady."

She swore she'd heard the voice before, but couldn't place it.

"I apologize for the manner in which you were collected," he continued politely. "Most unfortunate my help was not more gentle. I'm sure this is frightening, but I will not harm you if you answer my questions."

"Where am I?" Lunara asked.

"A meeting place for the Association of Mages. We have reports of your many travels with the young mage, Salvarias."

Lunara bit her tongue and held her head high, trying to convey that complying with their wishes was the last thing she intended to do.

"Did you know the Association was started in Loutsil shortly after the gods left?" the man said. "It began here with the heir of King Ctol Lilkous. The man despised mages and began murdering any he found. A group of wizened mages approached him and offered to start an order to protect the general populace. The king agreed and thus the Association and her laws were formed."

Lunara reached out her mind to Salvarias, but he was caught in a horrible nightmare. He would not wake easily.

"It's all for the greater good, you see," the man continued. "And as such, we only hope to help the young mage in your company. We have just a handful of questions and then you can be on your way, my lady.

"It has come to our attention Salvarias Laybryth knew of mages on board a ship when docking in Loutsil. Do you know who these mages were? Again, we do not want harm to come to the boy, but we must find these rogue mages. For the greater good of course."

Still Lunara remained quiet and desperately tried to wake Salvarias. No doubt the intent of the room was malicious, despite their assurances. And where had she heard that voice?

The voice sighed. "You will stay here as long as needed until you provide answers. We are the ones who uphold the laws of the Association and will ensure its success. Though we will protect the boy, we must correct his ... lack of enforcement in regards to our laws."

"You're lying," Lunara said defiantly. "You can tell me all you want about your intentions, but I know what lurks in your heart."

"Then let us quit the charade," the man said, dropping his light tone. It was then she recognized him. Henry, Falisa's husband.

Another voice came from the darkness, harsh and cold. Wunhur. "I want to know the boy's routines. I want to know when he is alone. Will you tell us willingly?"

They had no intention of ever letting her leave this place. She would die here. Filling her voice full of all the strength she could muster, she said, "Of course not." Surprisingly, her words came out strong and defiant, despite her stomach knotting.

"Your stay here will not be pleasant," Wunhur said. "We've tried to be cordial. You've given us no choice."

Salvarias's mind finally stirred awake. With her first plea, she sensed his building worry, and the instant she filled him in on her captors, his anger burned in her own blood. She smiled at the shadows. "I give you one chance to let me go. Do so and you will live. I swear it on the name of my father." She waited until the men stopped laughing before she continued. "Harm me in any way and you will die this night. That I promise you. No pleading will save you. No king. No queen. Not even I could stop him. Hurt me and he will kill you all."

Wunhur bolted from the shadows and rushed to stand in front of her, spit flying from his lips when he shouted, "We'll rid the world of mages, whore, and any who befriend them." He pinched her chin roughly. "Do you know why we chose you out of all his companions?" His voice dropped to a whisper. "Because you're the weak one, girl. We'll beat the answers out of you. Rip off your fingers. Pull off arms and legs until nothing is left. Do you understand me, girl? Talk now and I'll spare you."

Lunara smiled. "He's definitely going to kill you." She'd kept her connection open during the man's rant, and Salvarias's anger had boiled over. "The first one to die will be the first one that hurts me. Release me and I'll stop him from coming down here and burning you all to Oblivion."

The man struck her hard enough to send her flying from her chair. Tears welled in her eyes from the sting, and when she ran her tongue along her lip, she tasted her own blood.

"Such an innocent," another voice said from shadows. It was deep, too deep to be human, too raspy to come from the throat of a man. "She will break, Avral."

Henry emerged from the shadows and alongside him stood a creature of nightmares. Where its body peeked clear of its green cloak, she saw rust-colored lumps and shriveled bulges of jaundice yellow and spoiled pea green. Eyes of red coals glowed beneath the shadow of its hood. When it folded its hands in front of it, she made out tendrils of intestines, knobs of withered muscles, and other body parts she couldn't identify, all writhing against one other, disappearing inside the creature only to emerge in a new location. Leaning to the side, she retched.

"You see," it said. "She is just a girl. Young. Shy. Helpless. Pain is a stranger to her, an idea, a word. She has never laid eyes on true evil, on absolute darkness. It will not take long." It turned to Henry who, despite his early bravado, cowered from the thing. "Take her and do with her as you please. Be imaginative."

Henry grabbed a chunk of her hair and dragged her from the room, down a maze of hallways lined with thick wood doors behind which people pleaded for death. The stink of excrement and blood hung thick in the air.

He tossed her into a pitch-black room. "You will tell me what I want to know. The sooner you confess, the more of your body will remain whole."

She remained silent.

Stinging pain flared on her cheek, sprawling her on the floor. She pressed a hand to her face, hating to hear a whimper escape her throat.

"Tell me of the mage. Everything you know."

Another blow struck her right cheek, then another to her left, and a final one to her right. Sobs left her, bloody spit hung from her swelling lip, and her brain rocked against her skull.

Hot breath washed over her face as Henry grabbed her hair, yanking her head back. A soft hand slid along her jaw.

"He will not find you," Henry said. "He will search for years and never find this place. Save yourself more pain. How do we get to him?"

Willing her strength to subdue her sobs, she croaked, "I will never tell you."

A foot planted in her stomach, and air whooshed from her lungs. She coughed, nearly caving to panic when air evaded her. Another kick landed in her ribs. She curled up, gasping, tasting blood. Darkness pressed in at the edges of her vision, but she clung to consciousness, recalling to Salvarias all she'd seen, focusing her mind on every detail she remembered.

The man straddled her and clutched her hair in his fists. "Tell me, whore!"

He slammed her head into the stone floor. Sound drowned out and her connection with Salvarias slipped away into the torrent of pain. She barely heard the man ranting about the defilement of mages and the need to rid them from the lands. He spoke of their power as his fists struck her, his fingers dug into her arms, and he tossed her about the room.

Wunhur called from beyond. "Is she talking?"

"Not yet," Henry snarled, his breathing harsh. Metal hissed against leather. "Soon though."

"If she doesn't give you answers, kill her. We can't have her talking to the king."

"I know," Henry snapped.

"I'm going back to visit Zehnia. Better I be seen tonight than go missing."

"Of course, Father," Henry said.

Footsteps faded and then a light flickered on. Lunara squinted through her left eye, the one not swollen shut. A candle burned steadily and showed her the line of bloody drool falling from her cut lip. She coughed up blood.

Henry knelt beside her, holding a dagger in his hand. "Last chance before we start to lose fingers."

Even if Lunara wanted to talk, which she didn't, she wouldn't have possessed the strength.

Cold steel rested on the upper digit of her pinky. "Tell us how to get to him."

She spit up blood. She watched in a half dream-like trance as the dagger sliced open her skin and struck bone. He sawed, and it took a moment for the pain to register, but when it did, she screamed.

Salvarias burst through the front door of the abandoned estate, Wilhelm and Adok on his heels. The home was musty and cold. Moonbeams lanced through uncovered windows, giving monstrous forms to the furnishings draped in white linens.

"Dammit," Wilhelm uttered. "Do you want me to get Humar?"

This was the third house Salvarias had invaded. Lunara's images were spotty, and he was merely going off the architecture she had shown him. He cursed himself for not waiting for Humar's search party. Then Adok stated there was a faint scent of her.

"No," he said, marching inside. "Adok, find another entrance that leads underground."

Salvarias searched alongside Wilhelm and the wolf, worry gnawing a hole in his gut. He had lost her connection.

Adok growled from one of the back rooms. As Salvarias set off for it, Lunara's pain slammed into him. He staggered from the sensation, and only his sheer terror shoved aside the debilitating effects her emotions had on his mind. Forcing himself to move, he made it to the back room, only aware once there that Wilhelm had held him steady.

Adok was near a bookcase. Salvarias grabbed books and yanked them from the shelves. Wilhelm joined him. One such purge and stone groaned. They stepped back as a slab of wall to their left parted to reveal a creature standing at the top of a steep staircase. One glance at its lumpy, multihued rotting body and Salvarias knew it was one of the Four. Standing half a head taller than Wilhelm, Remnant's frame took up the entire entry to the staircase.

It turned its gleaming eyes to Salvarias. "Truly, Veedran smiles on me this night."

Adok growled low, shifting to stand in front of Salvarias, and backed up, forcing Salvarias to retreat. Wilhelm stepped forward.

"Ah," Remnant purred. "The Protector. You and I have a score to settle. You killed a brother of mine."

Wilhelm drew his swords and grinned. "Marrow was a weak bastard. He went screaming just as you will."

A deep rumble sounded from Remnant's throat, some sort of laugh that sent chills up Salvarias's spine. "I agree. Marrow was the weakest of us. I am not."

Slowly, Salvarias snuck his hand in the sleeve of his robe and gripped the hilt of his dagger. Somewhere below, Lunara screamed.

"Salv," Wilhelm said, stepping back to allow Remnant to enter the room. The two circled each other slowly, eyes never venturing from the other's. "Go below and get Lunara."

"Brother, I—"

"No arguments," Wilhelm said. "Go."

Salvarias slid his dagger free and ran it down his hand, squeezed to let the blood bubble up, and then held it aloft as he edged toward the door. He waited until Wilhelm's line of sight gave a clear view of the blood running down Salvarias's hand.

"Unlock your inner beast, brother."

Breath rushed out of Wilhelm and he swayed as though struck. When it passed, his eyes darkened and his grin switched to one that would haunt Salvarias's nightmares. Muscles bulged and flexed beneath Wilhelm's skin, seeming to expand under some invisible building force.

Remnant hissed and took a step back.

"Go," Wilhelm snarled, sparing a sideways glance at Salvarias. "Go with him, Adok."

A scream from Lunara urged Salvarias down the stairs dangerously fast, making him use his staff to save him from a few near falls.

He ended up in a hallway, doors lining both sides. Lunara's next scream guided him past five rooms before he stopped in front of the sixth. He never remembered casting the spell, but the door was simply not there anymore. In its place was a pile of metal and wood deteriorated to the consistency of sand.

Inside, Lunara lay on the ground, the tip of her pinky and ring finger sawed off, blood falling from her lips, trickling down her forehead, eye swollen shut, bruises covering her face, and her breath was raspy and wet. Her good eye met his and a heart-rending whimper of relief left her.

He turned his gaze to Henry holding a dagger, the blood of the woman Salvarias loved dripping from its blade.

His anger did not stem from pain, it did not stem from touching a murderer, it grew from the very heart of Salvarias. He shook with it, and when the beast burst forth from his lake, he embraced it like an old friend. Henry screamed and stumbled back.

"You're an abomination!" Henry wailed.

Salvarias smiled. "Allow me to show you the truth of your words."

Amidst the man's frantic screams, Salvarias latched hold of Henry's throat and lifted him eye level. Knowing what to expect made the pain no different. The murders were brutal, the victims all mages, tortured for reasons outside of their control. Henry's mind was righteous in his actions, no shame or guilt. He did what he did for the greater good. But Salvarias had a gift, and he used it. He showed Henry the suffering he had inflicted, showed how helpless mages were, how scared they were when he tormented them, how much innocent life he had stolen from the world, how many lights flickered out by his hand.

By the time Salvarias finished, Henry was weeping and begging for forgiveness.

"Forgiveness is forgetfulness," Salvarias hissed. He spread his fire over Henry, burning him slowly, smiling at the former Prince of Loutsil's screams. When the man's life slipped away, Salvarias stood at the towering gates of Oblivion. One touch and the doors flung open, the fog eager and expectant.

"Know her light," Salvarias said to Henry. "Know of her virtue and pure heart. Understand her sister's pain if she were to perish. Her parents' pain. Understand the pain the world would suffer at the loss of something so beautiful. But most of all, understand my pain."

He shoved the man through the doors. Henry's scream pierced the air as the black fog enveloped him. Intense satisfaction blossomed in Salvarias at feeling the fog carry out his order and hearing Henry sob in misery too profound for words. Salvarias grinned and gave the gleeful chuckle rising in his throat freedom.

Chapter 42

Autumn 1018 a.r.

Wilhelm and Remnant stalked each other, circling and appraising. He knew he couldn't spend long learning his foe's movements: what it favored, how it shuffled its feet, how it responded to strikes. Salvarias was alone in a place where evil casually walked the halls. The gods only knew what else lurked in the darkness below. If one of the Four had bothered itself to be here, perhaps the red-robed man was here too. Wilhelm needed to end this fight. Quickly.

"Do you still think the boy is himself? The same boy you grew up with?" Remnant asked conversationally. "Do you have any idea how much we've twisted him, toyed with his mind, steered him toward our cause? Do you think you can still save him?"

"Is the red-robed man here?" Wilhelm asked. "I'd like a word with him."

Remnant laughed, a horrid sound like a tortured roll of thunder. "You people know nothing, do you? 'Red-robed man'? Honestly, that is what you call him?"

"Give me a name, then," Wilhelm snarled.

"I believe ignorance will play to our side." Remnant drew a sword ridiculously long. Blood rusted the metal and a yellow substance budded up along the blade. Even so, Wilhelm had no doubts the weapon could slice him in half. "I will give you one chance, Protector. Walk away and leave your brother to me."

Wilhelm smirked. "Marrow offered me the same thing. Want to know what I said?"

Remnant's smile was a braid of twisted tendons. "Do tell."

Wilhelm lunged, driving his blades straight for the center of Remnant's chest, the same place the red pustule inside Marrow had lived. His blades sank deep, ripping through body parts. It did nothing.

Bile rose in Wilhelm's throat as putrid yellow vines of intestines wrapped around his blades, pulling them in deeper, yanking him closer. He had no choice but to relinquish his swords or be stuck within striking range.

Hissing a curse, Wilhelm spun away as air whistled a near inch from his head. He smelled the blade, like rotted eggs and rust. Sweeping low, he snatched his mother's dagger from his boot and jabbed it up at Remnant's stomach. It dodged aside, teetering ever so slightly off balance as it tried to recover from its swing and that of Wilhelm's. He took advantage, stepped forward, and stabbed wildly. Quick thrusts, one after another. It sounded like he stabbed too-wet meat, causing sucking and squishing noises that made him want to vomit.

Before Remnant countered, Wilhelm leapt back, clear of any rebuttal. Remnant stood straight, taking the break to yank Wilhelm's swords free and toss them aside, out of reach. The frenzied wounds Wilhelm had inflicted had done nothing. It was like trying to kill a carcass. Worst of all, Remnant wasn't built the same as Marrow. Whatever gave it life did not reside in its chest. Something else fueled the creature.

"You will lose," Remnant said. "After I kill you, I will go below and take your brother. I will torment him until nothing is left but a drooling fool." Its red eyes burned brighter. "He will be ours."

And that was the answer. Wilhelm grinned. "You should never contemplate the rewards of victory until you have conquered the field."

He rushed for his discarded swords, hearing Remnant's feet pounding after him. It was faster. A mountain might as well have landed on his back. He hit the ground hard, face flat, air rushing from his lungs, lights flashing in his vision, blood filling his mouth. Mushy hands rolled him on his back. Remnant straddled him and raised a fist. Wilhelm punched its face while searching with his other hand for his sword. His fingertips grazed over cold metal.

Remnant's return punch along Wilhelm's jaw nearly stole his consciousness. Everything spun. A wool drum beat in his ears. The room vibrated.

Stretching himself painfully, he roared out his frustration and grabbed the blade of his sword. Metal cut the mark on his palm in half, the rush of blood making his hold slippery. Afraid to lose his grip, he clamped his hand tighter, growling out in pain as the blade dug in. Luckily he'd grabbed his great sword. The long guard was a weapon in and of itself. He swung it up, using the guard as a blade. It sunk deep into Remnant's eye. The creature staggered to its feet, grabbing its eye, shrieking like a tortured cat.

With a sickening wet sound, Wilhelm pulled the blade free of his palm, biting back a groan of pain. Exhausted and head pounding terribly, he lurched to his feet, snatching up his broadsword as he did.

"My brother is mine," Wilhelm said, walking with determined steps toward Remnant. "Sansis can't have him. God can't have him. And you can't have him."

Plunging his strength into his left arm, he drove his broadsword into Remnant's other eye. His blade sank up to the hilt, bursting open the eye and causing it to pour out whatever red acid gave the creature life.

Remnant fell back, sliding off Wilhelm's sword, its wail sending a chill up his spine. It collapsed into a gruesome pile of human body parts, the impact on the marble floor launching bits of the repulsive creature across the room. The horrible stench of it hit Wilhelm like an angry wave.

With the danger gone, his power imploded, leaving him so weak he wanted nothing more than to crumple to the floor and curl up. He spat blood from his mouth and sheathed his swords. Glancing at his right hand, he was surprised to see it in one piece. He'd figured his hand would've been cut in two, hanging on by a flap of skin.

Inhaling a deep breath, he pushed aside his exhaustion and plunged down the stairs after his brother.

Salvarias knew what would happen if he dropped the corpse and released his rage. With all the wickedness still surrounding him, he clung desperately to his anger, fueling it with the screams resonating through the underground chamber. Vengeance had not been satiated for this place, and he still had work to do.

Gritting his teeth, he dropped Henry. Blackfire continued to burn, infusing Salvarias with its need to kill. And he would oblige.

When he turned from the corpse, he saw Lunara encased in Wilhelm's arms, sobbing softly into Wilhelm's chest. Blood ran down Wilhelm's face, and Salvarias doubted his brother even noticed the shallow slice on his side. He swayed on his feet, eyes focusing in and out, sweat plastering his hair to his forehead.

"Take her from here," Salvarias said through clenched teeth.

"Salv, I think I should stay with you," Wilhelm said.

"Please do as I ask."

Wilhelm nodded and headed down the hall. Salvarias stepped out of the room and waved his hand. Doors exploded into dust and startled screams erupted. Men burst from the rooms, holding bloody knives and devices Salvarias recognized from his days with Sansis.

"What in Nevlar's fury!" a man cried. "What is that?"

Salvarias smiled. "Oblivion."

By the time Wilhelm had climbed the stairs leading up from the torture rooms below, Lunara had stopped crying.

"No," she said in a feeble voice. "We can't leave."

"You need a healer," Wilhelm muttered.

"I have no strength to argue," she said. "He will need me."

Cursing under his breath, he carried her to a nearby couch and gently lowered her. "You're hurt bad," he said, wincing at her blue face and bloodied hand.

"I'll be fine." She pressed an arm over her ribs, tears welling but held in. "You don't look well yourself."

Wilhelm pulled up a chair and plopped down. Screams started below, all filled with such horror it made Wilhelm shudder.

The door to the estate burst open and ten knights piled inside, immediately followed by Humar, Varila, and Okulu. The group was a rumpled mess, all woken in the middle of the night, hastily throwing themselves together.

When Varila's gaze found her sister, blood drained from her face. She shot across the room and knelt by Lunara.

"Gods," Varila choked.

"I'm fine," Lunara said, forcing a smile. It opened up a cut on her lip.

One of the knights went to her side with a healing kit. He began working on binding her hand.

"You found this place quickly," Wilhelm noted.

"Lilly found us." Humar glanced at Lunara, Wilhelm, and then the opened door where a fresh scream erupted.

"Salv's below with Adok," Wilhelm said. "There's a few more bad guys he's taking care of."

Okulu's friendly smile faded. "You left him down there? Alone?"

Humar had started for the stairs, so Wilhelm raised his voice. "He was mad. Very, very mad. I suggest we stay clear until he's done."

The king stopped and motioned back his knights. He knew what Salvarias could do when angry.

"I hope he burns every last one of those bastards," Varila growled, peeling pieces of crusted hair from Lunara's forehead.

Wilhelm snorted. "Convenient when it serves your purpose, isn't it?"

She turned a cold glare on him. "Yes, yes it is. They deserve it."

"Any other time you'd look at him like he was a monster," Wilhelm shot back.

Varila's jaw rippled. "That was before. I don't look at him like that anymore. And you know it."

Wilhelm bit his tongue. She hadn't, and yes he did know. Exhausted, he leaned his head back and closed his eyes. "Sorry."

"Let's get you out of here," Varila said to Lunara over another violent scream from below.

"No," Lunara said. "No arguing with me either. I won't leave until Salvarias is done."

"It was Henry," Wilhelm said to Humar. "Salv killed him."

"I never knew the Avrals would stoop so low."

"Killing a nobleman ..." Wilhelm let the unasked question hang in the air.

Humar waved it aside. "I'll deal with it. Nothing will happen to your brother."

"Thanks," Wilhelm said.

They sat through more victims of Salvarias's rage, each voice raised in a different octave of terror. Soon, the smell of burnt flesh wafted up, burdening the air of the enclosed space. One of the knights was sick. Others began breaking windows.

To listen to someone screaming, no matter how well deserved, seemed to tamper with time. It crawled by, moving slower than the moon passing overhead.

And then it was over. All was silent, eerily so, an unnatural feeling after listening so long to the cries of the damned.

"Hurry," Lunara said urgently, reaching her arms toward Wilhelm. "Take me to him."

He lifted her carefully, grimacing against her soft groans. As smoothly as he could, he navigated down the stairs, keeping his breathing shallow, but still the taint of burnt flesh filled his mouth.

"Faster," Lunara said.

Salvarias cried out and Wilhelm bolted. Bodies were strewn down the hallway, charred beyond recognition, lined up as if waiting their turn. He knew that'd been the case, and he shivered at the thought. Following the wake of bodies led him to an open room. Then everything moved as if the world was stuck in quicksand.

In the center of the circular, pillar-lined room, Salvarias knelt, dagger gripped in both hands, driving the blade straight for his heart. Adok had already leapt to intercept the strike. The blade plunged into the wolf, sinking up to the hilt. Adok yelped and collapsed to the floor. Seemingly unaware, Salvarias yanked his dagger free.

Wilhelm bolted toward his brother. His shout lodged in his throat and came out as an indecipherable gurgle. Dumping Lunara from his arms, he dove for Salvarias. Barely in time, Wilhelm snagged his brother's arm, his momentum slamming them both backward to hard stone. Salvarias grunted and immediately struggled to stab himself again.

"Stop!" Wilhelm gasped, his own wounds making him weak against Salvarias's strength. Wrestling a heart-stopping breath, Wilhelm managed to rip the dagger from his brother's hand and tossed it away.

One punch from Salvarias and a twist from Wilhelm brought them both face to face with Adok. The wolf lay silent, eyes focused on Salvarias, chest rising haltingly. Salvarias instantly stopped fighting and sucked in a breath, eyes opening wide, somehow distant and seeing, haunted and insane. Crying out, he scrambled to the wolf and balled Adok's fur in his hands. "Help me! Someone help me!" He didn't seem to notice anyone in the room.

Okulu dropped on the other side of the wolf, wide eyes focused on Salvarias.

"Help me!" Salvarias screamed.

Prying Salvarias's blood-soaked fingers from Adok, Wilhelm wrapped his arms around his brother's chest and hauled Salvarias back. "Get the wolf out of here," Wilhelm said to Okulu.

Salvarias screamed and stretched his arms toward the wolf, struggling to reach it. "I did not mean to! I did not mean to!"

Okulu seemed unable to rip his stunned gaze from Salvarias.

"The wolf, Okulu! Now!" Wilhelm barked.

Okulu jerked himself out of his shock and with a grunt and groan dragged the wolf toward a group of gaping knights.

Something snapped in Salvarias when the wolf went out of sight. He stiffened, eyes focusing somewhere far away, then he raised his blood-soaked hands in front of him. "What have I done?" he croaked. Frantically, he wiped Adok's blood on his robes, breath coming in sharp intakes. "I cannot get it off! Help me!"

Lunara sat in front of him. Fumbling in the pouch tied around Salvarias's waist, she withdrew a stained cloth.

"I'm here," she whispered. Gently, she took one of Salvarias's hands and ran the cloth over it.

"I did not mean to," he choked. "Help me."

"You have to let me, Salvarias," she said, bending to catch his eye. "You have to let me in."

For the first time, Salvarias's eyes focused on reality, on Lunara. Something unspoken passed between them, and whatever transpired reduced Salvarias to soft sobs. He gathered Lunara in his arms and whispered, "Make it go away. Please make it go away."

Wilhelm stood on shaking legs, backed up from the two, and looked around the room. The path Okulu had dragged Adok along was marked by smears of blood. Humar stood beside Varila, both gaping at Salvarias. When Wilhelm joined them, no one spoke. What could they say? He didn't understand exactly what had happened. Salvarias's eyes had not dulled as they normally did when controlled by evil. If Wilhelm had to say, he would guess it was a brief moment of insanity. It was not a comforting possibility. He could kill creatures that threatened Salvarias, he could help his brother fight the evil, and he didn't care if the Hunters won every fight. He'd kill whatever they sent. But this ... this was something he couldn't protect his baby brother from. And the words from Remnant now resonated through Wilhelm's mind: "Do you have any idea how much we've twisted him, toyed with his mind, steered him toward our cause? Do you think you can still save him?"

Not for the first time, Wilhelm doubted he could save his brother. Failure seemed to be his destiny.

Chapter 43

Autumn 1018 a.r.

It had been a full day and Wilhelm had not left Salvarias's side. It was for two main reasons. First and foremost, Wilhelm simply didn't trust Salvarias alone, didn't trust his brother wouldn't try to stab himself again. The second was Wilhelm's sheer concern. Ever since arriving in his room, Salvarias had crawled into his bed with Adok—who'd been deposited there after the healers had tended to the wolf's wound—and never moved except to perform his ablutions. None knew if Adok would survive. Wilhelm doubted it. The wolf hadn't stirred.

The only noise in the room was the occasional crackle of the constant fire Wilhelm kept alive, the shallow breathing of Adok, and the clicking of the puzzle box, which Salvarias had yet to put down.

Wilhelm regarded his right hand for the hundredth time. The gash he'd made on his palm when he'd picked up his sword was gone. Simply gone. No scar. No soreness. And he had full range of motion. His mark had healed perfectly. Yet another mystery.

A knock on the door made Wilhelm growl as he crossed the room. He'd left instructions not to be disturbed. Salvarias needed time alone, time to recover, time to accept what had happened to Adok.

He opened the door, scowling. Varila, Humar, and Zehnia stood together, whispering amongst themselves.

"What is it?" Wilhelm said tersely.

"Just wanted to fill you in," Humar said.

Reluctant but curious, Wilhelm stood aside and allowed them in, but kept them by the door.

"He killed sixteen people," Humar whispered. "Two of them were prisoners."

Wilhelm frowned. Killing the torturers made sense, but not those imprisoned. Snorting, he realized he just didn't care. Salvarias had his reasons, of that Wilhelm harbored no doubts. He'd not start questioning his brother now.

"I'm going to dismantle the Association and start a new order," Zehnia said. "One that will help mages, not persecute them. I'd love to discuss my ideas with your brother."

"Later," Wilhelm said.

"Of course," she said. "We captured my father."

Salvarias lifted his head. "I would like to be there when you question him."

Humar frowned. "You look like Oblivion chewed on you for a few days, boy. Perhaps it's better you rest."

"I have questions pertaining to 'god,'" Salvarias said. "I must hear his answers myself."

Humar pursed his lips.

"I don't think it wise," Zehnia whispered. "The girl was a traveling companion, a friend. He might hurt my father."

"I trust the boy," Humar said. Raising his voice, he said to Salvarias, "If you think it best. We were heading there now."

Salvarias checked on Adok before joining them at the door. His expression was calm. Too calm. It set Wilhelm's nerves on edge.

"Perek has left," Salvarias said, voice soft and lulling as always.

Humar sighed. "Horrible timing."

"Not necessarily," Salvarias said. "He is backtracking. Though likely he will avoid Warton, I think he is heading to Senti and will take a ship to Windlous. Which leads me to believe what I felt in Windlous was god. He separated from his army."

"Why would he do such a thing?"

Salvarias shrugged. "A question for the ages."

"If Perek is heading to Windlous, I'll send word to Senti to ready the ships. When you're ready, we'll leave."

"It should be soon," Salvarias said. "Within a day or two. Travel will be slow due to," he glanced over his shoulder, "the injuries within our group."

Humar slid a hand through his hair, sticking it up higher. "So be it. One thing at a time, though. Let's deal with Avral."

"A word alone?" Varila asked Salvarias.

She and Salvarias headed down the hall toward the dungeons, heads together in soft conversation.

"I wouldn't trust him," Wilhelm said to Humar. "He's pissed. He's not himself. Gods only know what he's capable of. And honestly, Wunhur deserves it." Glancing at Zehnia he said, "No offense, my lady."

"My father might deserve to be executed," she acquiesced, "but he's still my father."

Wilhelm scratched at his beard. "Keep an eye on him."

"Has he been to see Lunara?" Humar asked. "She's asking for him."

"No. I don't think he will anytime soon. Guilt is all he's feeling."

"It wasn't his fault," Zehnia said.

"She was taken because of him. What happened to her wasn't his fault, but that's how he'll see it," Wilhelm said.

The creature in Senti had given Wilhelm valuable insight into his brother's self-hatred. Something like this would eat at Salvarias, and his brother wasn't one to forgive himself.

Salvarias entered the prison cell behind Humar, leaving Zehnia just outside. The room was dank, small, and windowless. Cold made a home here. The stones were stained with old piss and gods only knew what else. Salvarias had a brief, debilitating memory of his time in Zeeas. In the dark and cold. In the lonely and empty. Closing his eyes, he willed away the rat eating his leg, the roaches and other unsavory things crawling over him, the cold blade of Sansis's knife sinking into him. He choked down a building whimper. It was not real. It was not real.

"You think I'll talk with that creature in my presence?" Wunhur snarled.

The nobleman's voice lifted Salvarias from his nightmare. It had been short lived; Humar had yet to fully clear the way for Salvarias. Wunhur sat against one wall, hands shackled apart from one another at chest level. He had recently soiled himself. The room stunk of it.

Closing the door behind them, Humar shrugged at Wunhur and said, "If you don't, I'll leave this room and let him do what he wants to you. The girl you took is a dear friend of his."

Wunhur spat on the hem of Salvarias's robes. "Go to Oblivion."

Humar lifted one shoulder in a halfhearted shrug. "You've attempted to kill my sister and take the throne. Why shouldn't I let the torturers have you?"

"You won't do anything," Wunhur sneered. "My daughter won't allow it."

"Let's see how she feels about it." Humar opened the cell door. "My queen."

Zehnia stepped inside. Her eyes were dead. "Yes, my king?"

"Your father here thinks you are concerned for his health."

Zehnia arched an eyebrow. "Does he?" She turned to Wunhur. "You've blood on your hands, Father. You've killed innocents. No, I care not what happens to you." She bowed to Salvarias and then Humar. "Do with him as you please, my king. He is no blood of mine."

"Wretched girl!" Wunhur snapped. "You whore!"

Humar moved catlike and struck Wunhur with a gauntlet-clad fist. Blood dribbled from the man's split lip and real fear shone in his eyes. Humar rarely lost his temper. "Do not speak that way to my wife," Humar barked. "To your queen!"

"Goodbye, Father." Zehnia left the room.

The man's former cockiness receded. Licking blood from his lip, he turned a new eye to Humar, a calculating one, one looking for a way out. It did not take the man long to conclude there was no escaping his fate unless he cooperated. Slouching against his bindings, he said, "What do you want to know, my liege?"

"Everything," Humar said evenly.

Most of the man's confessions were those of attempting to kill the princess. His others were of how he took over the Association and employed mages to help carry out his endeavors to rid Arden of every last mage. Salvarias listened in numb detachment. He knew most of it. He also knew he would kill Wunhur before leaving this cell. Though Zehnia's performance was brilliant, she truly did not want harm to come to her father. Humar would oblige the queen. Salvarias would not. This was the man who had ordered men to hurt Lunara; Salvarias's light, his dearest friend, and the one person in all of Arden who deserved none of the pain she suffered.

Varila had wanted to kill Wunhur herself, but Salvarias had refused her. She would not have blood on her hands. Salvarias swam in it on a daily basis. One more life would not matter. He could lie to himself and say he was going to kill Wunhur for Varila, but truth be told, he was going to do it for himself. He wanted the man dead. It was simple, barbaric, sickening, and exactly what an abomination such as himself would do. He wondered if his father would be proud. Perhaps a shadowfire was here, watching him, smiling in approval. He shuddered at the thought.

As the man droned on, a part caught Salvarias's attention.

"Repeat that," he said, surprised by how calm and steady his voice sounded.

"Edran was the one who supplied men that boosted my own forces. He—"

"No, describe him again," Salvarias said.

"Tall, your height actually." Wunhur's eyes narrowed. "Matter of fact, his features were like yours. Black hair, cruel black eyes. No whites, just pools of black. He wore the oddest choice of red robes. He swore he wasn't a mage, but—"

"Was anyone with him?"

"Two men armored in black. Never did see their faces."

"How do you get in touch with Edran?" Salvarias asked.

"I don't. New men appear every month to replenish any I lost. They're paid enough up front to employ them for the next fifteen years."

"Why would 'god' want to get rid of mages?" Humar asked.

Though Salvarias doubted the king was expecting an answer, he delivered one anyway. "Because if any army were to employ mages, their forces would be near unstoppable."

"With fourteen spells?" Humar said. "I doubt it."

Salvarias shrugged. "You have seen me perform outside the fourteen, my friend. There could be countless spells created. I just need to devise them and publish them. I suspicion Mafarias and Vuddruk could come up with new spells as well."

Humar ran a hand through his hair. "True, I've seen you do remarkable things, and I think I see your point. Our little 'god' is getting smart."

"God is weak in strategy or else Arden would have already been consumed in flames. He is using the Four."

Humar frowned and turned back to Wunhur. "Why would a mage help them? Gilra was the one who took Lunara. You would think a mage wouldn't help."

"Some powerful mages needed to be fought and could only be bested by another mage. We bought them with the promise of safety. With protection from the guards."

"And you would stay true to your promise?" Humar asked.

Wunhur snorted. "No. As soon as the powerful ones were dead, I planned to kill every single mage."

"Anything else?" Humar asked Wunhur.

The man shook his head. "I've told you all I know."

Humar nodded. "I believe you."

The king rapped on the door and it opened. The instant Humar passed through it, Salvarias hissed out his spell and flicked his hand. The door slammed closed and remained so.

"Salvarias!" Humar banged his fists on the door. "Don't do this, boy!"

"Please!" Zehnia begged.

Salvarias drew his dagger.

"What are you doing?" Wunhur shouted, "Humar, help me! Zehnia!"

"They cannot help you," Salvarias said. Tossing his hood back, he squatted eye level with the man. Wunhur shuddered and looked away. "No, look at me."

Wunhur slowly turned his head.

"I will share something with you I have never voiced aloud," Salvarias said. "I love her, and no one will hurt her and live."

He raked his dagger across the man's throat. He watched the man's eyes widen and blood gurgle up from the slice, forming bubbles that dribbled down his neck. Chains rattled as Wunhur tried to reach his throat, to stop his life from draining away. His feet scraped against the stone as the throes of death held him in their thrall.

Then it was quiet.

Ah, you murder again, my pet, the presence hissed. *Yet ssstill you deny there isss an abomination alive inssside you.*

Salvarias wiped his dagger clean, rose, flicked his hand, and opened the door. He brushed by Humar and did not feel guilt even when Zehnia cried out in grief.

Lunara gingerly hobbled her way about her room, waving aside her sister's insistence that she should be resting. She wanted to move, to prepare herself for travel. It was only a matter of time before Salvarias would be ready to leave, and she refused to slow down the group or, worse, be left behind.

Movement was agony. Her side hurt. Her face hurt. Her insides hurt. Her hand hurt. About the only thing that didn't hurt were her feet. Henry hadn't had time to cut off her toes. No doubt if Salvarias had taken any longer that would have been Henry's next torment.

Despite the horror she'd experienced, what resounded in her mind was the fact that, no matter what Henry had done, she hadn't disclosed anything. She'd kept silent about Salvarias. Somewhere deep inside herself she'd found a pit of strength and defiance. There was no reason not to be proud. Clinging to it made the pain bearable, made it easier to get out of bed.

"Is Salvarias in his room?" Lunara asked Varila. He had not been to see her, though she knew why, and she also knew she'd have to be the one to make the first move. Despite his attempts to block her from his mind, guilt was an ever-present weight. No doubt he was drowning in it.

"He's with Humar. They've gone to question Wunhur," Varila said.

Her sister's voice was a bit too dead for Lunara's comfort, but Varila hadn't spoken much since Lunara's rescue.

A knock on the door sprang alive her hope. Perhaps Salvarias had changed his mind. Smoothing her hair, she prayed to Zerana's grace that she didn't look as bad as she felt.

Varila opened the door. It was Neithelas. His eyes were puffy red, and he looked as if he hadn't slept for days.

"I would like to visit with Lady Lunara," he said.

"Go to Oblivion," Varila growled.

"It's fine, Varila." Lunara smiled assuredly when her sister scowled at her. "Neithelas will be on his best behavior."

She meant it as assurance for her sister, but the prince winced.

Varila muttered a few curses and left the room. She didn't close the door, and Neithelas made no attempt to do so himself. He stepped inside and walked half across the room. He bowed.

"My lady, I will beg all my days for your forgiveness. I—"

"I know, Neithelas," she interrupted. Her experience had made her feel pity for others instead of anger. Emotions could lead all astray, including Henry, Wunhur, and poor Neithelas. The heart was complicated and confusing. "Your emotions turned you down a path you knew wasn't right. We've all made mistakes. I forgive you, but our courtship is over."

Neithelas flinched. "As my lady desires. I will bother you no more." He turned to leave.

"You are my friend," she said. "If you are willing to accept that, give me time and these wounds between us will heal."

"I do not deserve your friendship," he said, his back toward her. "But I would be honored to receive it considering what I have done." She heard the tears in his voice, and she hated that she caused anyone such suffering, misguided or not. "And rest assured, my lady, I will burn every tree that produces the oil. Never will I allow it to hurt another. Never."

"Thank you," she said.

He tilted his head and swiftly left.

Lunara continued circling her room, all the while ignoring Varila's continued hovering.

On one such pass, she caught sight of Salvarias gliding by her open door to his across the hall. As quickly as she could, she made her way to the door.

As he opened his, she said, "Hello."

With his back still to her, he said, "My lady. You should be resting."

"Is it done?" Varila asked.

"It is," Salvarias responded, and entered his room. His door clicked closed.

"Is what done?" Lunara asked Varila.

Her sister shrugged. "Nothing you need to worry about."

"What happened?" Lunara insisted.

"It doesn't matter. Do as he says and rest."

Humar stormed up the hall with five knights and Wilhelm. The king pointed at Salvarias's door and addressed the knights. "Not one single noble is allowed in there. Not one. Only his brother, the Bellerum women, Okulu, or Durak. No one else, you hear me? Especially the queen."

The soldiers saluted smartly and lined up by Salvarias's door.

"He'll be safe?" Wilhelm asked.

"I'm trying my damnedest, Wilhelm," Humar said. "I can convince Zehnia in time. She wasn't close with him, but that doesn't ease her grief. We leave the day after tomorrow. I'll have wagons readied for Lunara and the wolf. I don't care where we go, but the sooner I can get him out of the city, the safer he'll be. I just have to get Marcus up to speed on what needs to be done in my absence."

"Thanks," Wilhelm said. "I appreciate what you're doing."

Humar sighed and ran his hand through his hair. "I don't blame the boy. I wanted to do it myself, but murdering a noble is an executable offense. My only hope is to convince the other nobles that he did so on my order. I've got to go."

Humar marched down the hallway and called over his shoulder to the knights. "If that boy leaves the room, you follow him. Don't stop him, but you dare leave him alone and I'll have your heads."

The king went out of sight.

Lunara turned widening eyes to Varila. "You knew?"

Her sister shrugged.

Horror snaked up Lunara's spine as she looked to Wilhelm. He didn't seem fond of what had happened, but he didn't say as much.

Lurching across the hall, she knocked on Salvarias's door.

"I prefer to be alone," Salvarias called.

Ignoring him, Lunara walked into the room and closed the door on Wilhelm.

Salvarias stood by the window, staring out at the churning green clouds spitting down fitful rain. She hadn't remembered seeing them when she'd passed her balcony.

When he glanced up, she saw the trail of tears on his cheeks before he turned to look back out the window, wiping his face with the sleeve of his robes. His hand shook badly.

"I prefer to be alone," he said again.

Using the furniture to help support her, she crossed the room and stood by his side. He wouldn't meet her eyes.

"You killed him?" she breathed.

Jaw clenched, he inhaled a deep breath. When he met her gaze, it was guarded, as if bracing himself for her anger ... or rejection. "Yes. I slit his throat while he was shackled—helpless—to a wall." His voice was a challenge, tinged with satisfaction. He assumed she would withdraw her friendship. It was written clearly on his face, no matter how hard he tried to hide it.

"Why?" she asked. "You've only killed those who would harm others. He was in prison. He would have had no other opportunities. Why?"

"It does not matter."

"It matters to me. Tell me."

"No."

"Yes."

"He hurt you," he snapped. He exhaled heavily and lowered his head.

He loved her. With those three words, he might as well have confessed it. Of all she wanted to tell him, to blurt out at the top of every mountain, her lips formed two weak words. "Thank you."

He raised his gaze to hers, slight shock breaking his emotionless mask. "I ... I do not ... I killed him. In cold blood. I killed a defenseless man. Surely you, of all people, could not still care for me."

She wedged herself between the window and him and wrapped her arms around his neck. "Thank you."

"I stabbed Adok," he said, desperation to convince her how evil he was clearly conveyed in his tone. "I have likely killed him. You cannot—"

Pressing a finger to his lips, she said, "Shhh. It's going to be all right."

Tears brimmed in his eyes. "Hate me. I beg of you. Hate me."

Cupping his face in her hands, she whispered, "Never."

Right before her eyes, he broke, his pain tearing down his usual stern gaze. He shook with sobs as he folded her in his arms.

"Forgive me," he cried softly. "Please forgive me."

Words would never convince him what had happened wasn't his fault. Instead, she kissed his cheek and filled his presence with thoughts of sunshine and meadows.

Chapter 44

Autumn 1018 a.r.

Salvarias sat in the light of his sparrow, studying the myriad of spells his magic and he had concocted over the long trips at sea. It was the middle of the night, but sleep eluded him. With his anger spent, nothing guarded his conscience. A part of him was at peace with it. Another part was not.

My wizard, his magic said. *Your mind is awash with thought. You are not focusing.*

"Sorry."

No need to apologize. Perhaps if we came up with a new spell, your mind would not be so apt to wander.

"I was thinking of attempting to create a portal."

Most excellent!

A soft whine clenched Salvarias's heart. Rising from his chair, he turned to his bed to see Adok watching him, grinning.

The lecture started immediately. It was not a lecture of what a horrible person Salvarias was, nor was it about his carelessness, his self-hatred, or his lost mind. Nowhere in Adok's tone was there any malice toward Salvarias. The lecture was as it always was. It was about Salvarias finding trouble, how he should be more careful of those that sought to hurt him. Tears burned Salvarias's eyes. He fell to his knees, burying his face in his hands. How could the wolf still care for him? Why?

A slick tongue licked his hand. Overwhelming guilt, joy, hate, and love broke Salvarias to violent sobs. When he had enough air, he merely begged for forgiveness, in his mind and aloud.

Adok wedged himself into Salvarias's embrace and repeated all was forgiven.

Once Salvarias calmed, he unhinged his fingers from Adok's fur. "You should be resting," he said, frowning at the distance the wolf had crossed from the bed to where Salvarias knelt. "You are not yet healed."

Adok grinned and said he felt fine.

Gingerly, Salvarias unwound the wolf's dressing. The wound had closed nicely, looking as if it were months old, not mere days.

Such a wound should not have healed so quickly. Something about the wolf was not right. Even as fear started to bubble, even as he started to shrink back from the wolf, he lost his train of thought. The wound was no longer interesting, just simply healed as it should have been.

Smiling, Salvarias stroked the wolf's ear. "I am grateful you are well."

Adok licked Salvarias's face before continuing his lecture. A soft knock stopped the wolf.

"Salvarias?" Humar called.

After wiping his tears and collecting himself, Salvarias said, "Enter."

The king strolled in wearing a plain royal blue tunic and black trews. His face was haggard and his hair stood up from the times he must have ran his hand through it. "How are you?" Humar asked.

"I am sorry, my friend. I have caused you much grief. I understand if—"

Humar waved his hand. "It's fine, boy. There's a part of me that's relieved. Getting things done might be a bit easier. When I met with the nobles and told them I had sanctioned Wunhur's execution, they looked about ready to piss themselves. I think they'll be much more cooperative." He glanced at Adok, frowned, then smiled. "I see our friend is up and about."

"Yes, remarkably healed," Salvarias commented.

Humar rubbed his cheek, the corners of his mouth dropping. "Healed already?"

"It is as it should be," Salvarias said.

Humar shook himself and shrugged. "Odd, but yes, it's as it should be." Clearing his throat, he motioned toward the hall. "Take a walk with me."

Salvarias set aside his spell book, grabbed his aspen branch, and followed Humar, with Adok and a guard of twenty Loutsil knights trailing behind him.

"You are not sleeping," Salvarias said.

Humar snorted. "Look who's talking. I saw the light from under your door for most of the night. You look exhausted."

Salvarias smiled slightly. "Look who is talking."

Humar chuckled. "Things have been a little hectic for you of late. You've helped me out immensely and since we're leaving tomorrow, I wanted to give you a little gift."

"My dear friend, I have burdened you with more problems than solutions."

"Not so, Salvarias, not so at all."

They walked in comfortable silence down long hallways, a few flights of stairs, and three more corridors until they were well beneath the castle. Chilling as it was, torches flickered along the last hallway they wandered, driving away shadows. It smelled old, like wet dirt and mossy stone.

At the end of the hallway stood a thick, iron-decorated double door. A lock hung around the handles, old and probably easily picked by the most unskilled thief.

Grinning, Humar winked and threw open the doors.

Enclosed oil lanterns lit up a library easily reaching three stories. The musty smell of leather and aging parchment washed over Salvarias, and he breathed it in. Several tables were strewn with books and dust.

"It is ..." Salvarias smiled at Humar. "It is beautiful."

"It's yours."

Salvarias's mouth dropped open. "My friend, I could not accept such a gift."

Humar walked inside, spreading his arms wide. "You can do more with these books than anyone else. I loved this place when I was younger. I spent hours reading every war book I could find. I wrote one myself on fighting techniques. I'm sure it's in here somewhere." Humar ran a finger along a table and wiped away a few years of dust. "It's the king's library. Has the some rarest books in all of Arden."

"I ..." Salvarias laughed with sheer delight and entered the room, squinting at the longest stretch of bookcases he had ever seen. "I will never leave here."

"You'll have to leave in the morning. Figured you might want to browse a bit and take a few with you." Humar dropped a massive book on a table. Dust flew up and Salvarias covered his nose. "Sorry," Humar murmured. "This is a catalog of everything we have. I'll come get you when we're ready to leave." Dropping the key on the table, Humar added, "I've got the only other key. You'll have privacy whenever you want it."

Salvarias sat down at the table and opened the catalog. "Thank you, my friend."

The king marched out of the room and, beyond the closing doors, ordered the knights to stand guard.

Salvarias glanced around the room, wishing Lunara could see it. Returning his attention to his task, he scanned the catalog. He knew what he wanted, but the sheer number of books took time to sift through.

His eyes hurt by the time he found it: a book discussing the goddess and the link she had granted to a handful of her children. Navigating the expansive library took nearly as much time as it had to find the book's location. When he gently pulled it from the shelves, he held his breath, thinking it might fall apart. It was old, in poor condition, but he had never seen one like it before. Taming his desire to read it instantly, he returned to the catalog and found every book he could on Wilhelm and Travard Firth.

By the end of his search, he only had six books. He feared they would not be enough to gain the knowledge he needed. While Wilhelm's father had told him that the stone's purpose—what it was—should remain a secret, Salvarias disagreed with every fiber in his body. Knowledge was power. Without it, they were walking blind around an erupting volcano. The time for ignorance was at an end.

He also knew that after he had the stone, he would leave his brother. He would search for answers on his own, he would ensure his brother married Varila, and with Salvarias's absence, Lunara would be safe, guarded against those who sought to do her harm because of him. The company of friends was at an end. He needed to move forward alone, less burdened, with less need to be so guarded. No doubt it would be difficult, but once he had answers, perhaps he could rid himself of the evil within. Perhaps he could be happy.

The presence laughed. *Sssome hopesss are merely dreamsss, my little murderer.*

Chapter 45

Winter 1018 a.r.

Salvarias stood at the bow of the ship, watching Windlous loom into view. A steady, freezing drizzle fell from darkening storm clouds chasing them ashore. Despite the chill outdoors, Salvarias had spent most of the journey on deck, as usual when out to sea. To think of missing some wondrous sight was enough to fight off the cold. Furthermore, Wilhelm had not left Salvarias's side, and his brother's warmth made the chapping wind bearable.

The trip had been remarkably uneventful. Then again, there was nothing Salvarias needed to fear. Near an entire fleet had escorted the king from Senti to Windlous. The enslaved watythm sailors had been freed upon Humar's arrival at the docks in Senti, and a watythm was promoted to captain on each ship. The erthla captains had been given ridiculous sums of money to step down from their posts and find other employment. No doubt they would never have to work another day in their lives. Apparently, Loutsil was wealthier than Salvarias had guessed. With the watythms' freedom came fierce loyalty to the king. All in Salvarias's company were treated with respect and their every whim fulfilled. Peace gifted Salvarias a strong mind, strong enough to easily battle the evil and the Hunters.

The restful ocean seemed to speed up Lunara's recovery. Her bruising was only a painful memory for Salvarias, but her missing fingers drove a knife into his heart every time he saw them. What hurt even more was the fact Lunara seemed unbothered by her mutilation. To see her so strong in the face of such torture made what Henry had done all the more heinous. Never should one so innocent and caring have to reach into that deep well of strength and experience firsthand what humanity was truly capable of performing. The last of her naiveté had fled. He had watched it slowly burning away, leaving her eyes duller than when they had first met. And it was all his fault.

"Where's Perek?" Wilhelm asked.

Salvarias inhaled a deep breath, closed his eyes, and focused on the images. "He left Bren already. He is a day ahead of us, but his travel is slow. The weight of the stone is bearing down on him. Without Tedris, his fights are arduous."

"You've been handling yours well."

"I have." Salvarias motioned around him. "There is an army protecting us."

"Your headaches?"

Salvarias smiled slightly, but it was not one of amusement, more of wry acceptance. "Ever present. But I have learned to ignore them."

"None of your remedies have helped?"

"No, brother." He had been tempted to try the concoction the jasner had supplied, but one of the herbs was a mystery. Milred would know of it. She had spent much time in Windlous before she joined her mother in Falar, but until he had answers, he would not take an untested remedy. Healing herbs were not to be handled lightly, and several could be deadly if combined with his breathing treatment.

Wilhelm wrapped an arm around Salvarias's neck. "Once we get this god, we can finally go home."

"Home?" Salvarias elbowed his brother's ribs, smiling at Wilhelm's feigned pain. "And where is our home, brother? We have no money of our own. I could work for Milred again, but—"

"No, you won't. She turned you over to them, Salv. You won't go near her."

"She had no choice."

"People always have a choice. Besides, Falar won't be our home. Serinity will."

Salvarias smiled at the thought of the Bellerum estate, of the wonderful meals, the library, Lady Talura and Lord Bellerum welcoming them. That was Wilhelm's fate, however. Not Salvarias's. His smile faded. "Of course, brother. Have you finally overcome your daftness and decided to marry Varila?"

"I have," Wilhelm said. "And you and I will live at the Bellerum estate. We'll be happy there. Safe."

The longing in Wilhelm's voice cut deep. Ever since their parents were murdered, safety had been a dream Wilhelm had sought for them both. It was attainable for Wilhelm, but Salvarias had no hopes of living in the same dream. It was not his usual pessimistic views that made this thought a fact, it was simply how his life would be. He knew it just as he knew who Balance was upon first meeting her. An instinctual knowledge, one that saddened him, but one he was beginning to accept.

Salvarias's companions emerged on deck, all huddled in thick cloaks. Neithelas immediately separated himself from the group. Ever since Humar's wedding night, the prince had been a recluse. A part of Salvarias wanted to march over to the winsire and slit his throat for what he had done to Lunara. However, a rational side had taken over and wanted to offer Neithelas words of comfort. He could empathize with the prince on guilt. Salvarias could even imagine how difficult Neithelas's journey had been. Matter of fact, he doubted few realized how difficult. To be raised in a world where beliefs were the center of one's being, to grow up with those beliefs molding one's life, one's decisions, one's character, and then to be thrust into a world that revealed some of those beliefs to be deceitful and hurtful, to have those revelations shatter every foundation one stood upon. In a way, Neithelas suffered far more than Salvarias.

"I'm not bringing a lot of men," Humar said. "Maybe a dozen knights."

"A wise decision. We must travel swiftly."

Humar followed Salvarias's gaze. "I'll talk with him."

"He is alone in all this."

Wilhelm growled deep in his throat. "Bastard."

"Do not judge so quickly, brother. His entire world is crumbling beneath him."

"And yours did too," Wilhelm said. "I don't see you going out and drugging women to get what you want."

"No," Salvarias said softly, tearing his gaze from the prince. "I merely murder people with unholy blackfire and haul their souls to Oblivion to endure endless torment."

Wilhelm muttered out a curse, but did not respond.

"How far should we stay behind Perek?" Humar asked.

"I prefer a few hours. I will be able to sense when he is getting close to god. It is then we must intercept Perek. Under no circumstances can he give the stone to god."

"That's some tricky timing," Humar pointed out.

"Indeed."

"I'll see to it."

Salvarias tilted his head gratefully. "I am sure you will, my dear friend."

Travel from Bren was set upon with grueling efficiency. The ten knights were experts at building and breaking down quick camps, meals were nothing but flavorless nourishment, and rest was a few hours at night and a few midday.

Salvarias's formerly strong mind weakened with every passing hour. The only time he had slept soundly was the brief respite in Lynta. By the time they passed Hynd, the entire group displayed signs of weariness, even Wilhelm. Regardless, they pressed on and were rewarded for their diligence. Salvarias guessed they were no more than four hours behind Perek.

Of course Perek knew they were close. After all, he saw Salvarias's surroundings just as Salvarias saw Perek's. And so it was that they entered the Evil Enchanted Forest in the late afternoon hours on a particularly chilly winter day. Apparently Perek believed the woods would hinder Salvarias's group. However, the forest had no favorites and soon Perek's pace was slowed.

Okulu navigated the woods cautiously, avoiding the Dead Wood by miles as Perek had done. Snow could not breach the canopy of trees and instead turned to freezing rain, muddying the ground.

Zerana's grace had bombarded Salvarias ever since they had entered the woods, feeling as though a troll constantly thumped his entire body with its club. That and maintaining a solid link to Perek's images molded Salvarias's headache into a new torture device. Upon the first two hours in the woods, he had been sick twice. What little light fought its way through the thick clouds might as well have been the sun. The continuous clanking of armor was louder than a strike of a blacksmith's hammer. Every step was agony. When they would walk to rest the horses, his bad leg crumpled beneath him often and only his staff kept him upright. It was one such near fall that evoked a colorful curse from Durak.

"We need to rest," Durak snapped at Humar. "The boy's exhausted."

"I am fine," Salvarias said through teeth clenched in pain.

"Shut up," Durak growled. "Ye be too stubborn to see ye own limits."

"I agree, Durak," Humar said, shoving a low branch out of his way. "But I also agree with Salvarias. We can't let Perek get away."

"Ye both be fools," Durak said. "Stubborn idiots! Dull-witted bast—"

"I think we get the idea," Humar said dryly.

The sun had mercifully decided to begin its nightly decent when the images of Perek erupted into chaos. What little Salvarias unraveled painted a terrifying picture.

Along the journey, Perek had lost to the Hunters several times, but the mages had easily bested the minor forces sent. This time, when the Hunters attacked, a new form was there. A man loomed in front of Perek, amber eyes set with determination. Tedris. Several flashes showed the two fighting a horde of minotaurs as they argued. All the while, Tedris artfully controlled the battle, slowly separating Perek from the mages.

"Salvarias!"

Something shook him, but he ignored it, focused only on Perek.

The flashes of the fight soon switched to wild flight. Perek ran alongside Tedris, both escaping the battle, leaving the mages to be butchered by a horde of creatures.

"Salvarias!"

Allowing his own surroundings to surface, Salvarias found himself held upright by Wilhelm, his brother's bright amber eyes full of concern.

"What is it?"

"We must help them," Salvarias breathed, still reeling from what he saw. "Your father has Perek and they are fleeing from the mages and Hunters. Together."

"Nevlar's anger," Humar cursed. "He actually got through to Perek?"

"They cannot outrun them," Salvarias said, wobbling over to Mithal. "Perek is too weak."

"Mount up!" Humar ordered. To Salvarias he said, "Circle us around the skirmish. We'll catch up to them hopefully before the mages or Hunters. Then we can make a stand together."

They set off again, Salvarias pleading with the horses to move as swiftly as possible. He led them wide, giving the battle area wide birth, and followed Perek's path in parallel as best he could.

Over the next few hours, the images he received from Perek were heart-stopping. Several times the two had to stop so Tedris could aid Perek in his fight of the evil. As often, Tedris's exhaustion slowed them enough that Salvarias thought capture was inevitable. To make their travel even slower, the formerly mild storm burgeoned to violent life and devoured the last few rays of the setting sun, pitching them into darkness and calling forth howling winds and sheets of sharp rain.

Eventually, Salvarias led his group back toward the path of Tedris and Perek. However, once sure he was on their trajectory, nothing looked familiar. Reining in Mithal, he whispered, *"Lumous,"* and his sparrow flickered dimly to life. He scanned frantically around for something he recognized: a tree, a rock, a puddle, animal tracks. Anything.

"What is it?" Humar asked.

"I lost them," Salvarias said. He spun Mithal around, searching, cursing his stupidity.

"Did we get past them?" Varila asked, shielding her eyes. "They would have been tired from the fight. We're not."

Salvarias glanced back. She had a point. He could have pulled ahead.

A shout rang out behind them, whipped around by the wind, making it seem to come from several points.

"Adok, help me," Salvarias pleaded, despite knowing the wolf could not pick up a scent in the storm.

Adok raised his noise, ears flattened. Just as Salvarias nearly caved to panic, the wolf bounded off.

"No way he can smell them in this wind," Varila shouted.

Salvarias paid her no mind. Urging Mithal, he followed the wolf.

Angry lightning lanced across the sky, causing shadows to leap at Salvarias. Thunder soon joined the ringing of swords.

A deep cry at his side made Salvarias look back. Wilhelm had doubled over in his saddle, eyes shut tight, fists curled against his chest.

"Brother!" Fear rattled Salvarias's heart as he swung off Mithal and bolted to Lilly.

Wilhelm folded over more, and as Salvarias came to his brother's side, he heard how laboriously Wilhelm breathed.

Wilhelm jerked and his eyes rolled back in his head, his entire body going limp. The massive man slid sideways, and Salvarias's efforts to ease his brother's fall were nearly pointless. Wilhelm's weight knocked Salvarias to the ground.

Then he felt it. Power. Gods, such power. It crept across the ground in a visible stream of black fog. Panic stole Salvarias's breath as it burrowed its way inside Wilhelm's chest.

"Help me!" he cried, igniting his magic.

It means him no harm, his magic said. *It is the same power he has now. It will not hurt him.*

The end of the stream came into view and it circled around Wilhelm, encasing him in soft gray fog. As it danced there, Salvarias had the distinct feeling it watched him. Suddenly, it churned in chaotic swirls, then plunged into Wilhelm. He hitched violently, his eyelids fluttered, and then he stilled. The fog was gone.

"Brother," Salvarias said. Hesitantly, he placed a hand on Wilhelm's arm and gently shook him. "Brother."

Wilhelm sucked in a massive breath, shuddered, and opened his eyes. Moaning, he curled up, hugging his chest.

"Brother," Salvarias said. Tears he had not realized he had shed mixed with the rain streaming down his face.

"I'm all right," Wilhelm groaned. "Just give me a moment."

Weight lifted off Salvarias's heart, flashing spots in his visions. He blinked them aside and looked around. All his friends had circled them, and opposite Salvarias was Varila. Her chest rose in shaky breaths, but her hands were steady and her eyes fierce.

"What in the Oblivion was that?" she asked.

Salvarias glanced at where the fog had come from. The same place he imagined Tedris and Perek. All his thoughts came to one horrible conclusion. He could not find strength to voice it.

Slowly, Wilhelm sat up. His breathing was steady, his hands as well, but his eyes betrayed his fear. He had come to the same thought.

Grunting, he pushed himself up, hauling Salvarias to his feet. Wilhelm swayed and leaned a bit of weight on Salvarias.

"Brother, please stay behind."

"I'm fine," Wilhelm said. Inhaling a deep breath, he turned a crooked grin to Salvarias. "That was ... intense."

Despite himself, Salvarias smiled. "You nearly stopped my heart."

Wilhelm ruffled Salvarias's soaked hair and cocked his head to the side, listening. Salvarias did the same. The fight was close. Closer than he would have liked.

"He might not be dead," Wilhelm said, hopeless hope in his voice.

What could Salvarias say? Both knew any sort of agreement would be a lie.

Wilhelm nodded, a frown stealing his smile. "Let's get this over with." Drawing his sword, he charged ahead.

Leaving the bulky horses behind, the group took up the charge. A flash of lightning lit up the battle when they were nearly upon it. A huge body lay at the feet of Perek who clutched his side with one hand, the other using his sword to block merciless blows by a beast taller than Wilhelm. Blond fur covered its stocky body, and from its gnarled fingers claws longer than Salvarias's entire hand bent in an ugly curve. The beast's elongated jaw looked like a crocodile, sporting more teeth than a shark.

Wilhelm roared a challenge and leapt forward, but it was too late. The beast flicked aside Perek's sword, bent sideways, and clamped his torso in its jaw. He dropped his sword and cried out as blood gushed into the beast's mouth.

Wilhelm slid his great sword into the creature's side. It wailed, mouth opening enough to let Perek tumble out. The creature had no chance for a counter. Wilhelm plunged his broadsword into the beast's skull. It blinked its yellow eyes, shock frozen on its reptilian face, then it crumpled to the ground, twitching as its body died.

Wilhelm knelt beside the still form of his father.

"I'm sorry," Perek gasped, clutching his torn-up stomach.

Salvarias sank to his knees beside Perek as the others rushed around them, enclosing them in a circle of protection.

"I should have listened to him," Perek continued.

Wilhelm bowed his head over Tedris's decapitated body and said nothing. Perek turned his watery gaze to Salvarias.

"Forgive me. I've doomed you both."

"Where is the stone?" Salvarias asked.

Perek reached beneath his tunic and drew out a small leather pouch tied around his neck.

"No," Wilhelm said. "You can't touch it, Salv."

"I was such a fool," Perek said. "Wilhelm's right. Your only option is to leave it. Let them find me and take it."

Salvarias knew once god had the stone Arden would be no more. He was certain of it. "Tell me how to protect it."

"You can't. You won't survive it with only one Protector."

"What can I expect when I take it?"

"Death," Perek growled.

"I will do this, with or without your help."

Perek coughed. Red bubbled up on his lips. He did not have much time left. "You can only touch it with your left hand. Your mark protects you from it. After you touch it, the battle you face will be the hardest thing you've ever done. Even with two Protectors. I'm telling you, you won't survive it. It'll make you go mad." Perek choked up blood, swallowed it, and then continued. "If anyone else touches it, they'll die. I saw it happen once, when I set it down. A thief tried to take it. He blew up. Tiny bits of him all over the place. That's why I keep it around my neck." He turned to Wilhelm. "Forgive me. I loved your father. I truly did."

"Wilhelm!" Humar called.

Okulu pointed his sword to the right. "Minotaurs. Lots of them. More of those other creatures, too."

Wilhelm drew his swords, stepping into the circle. "Stay behind us, Salv."

Salvarias glanced down at Perek. He had passed on. His eyes were dull, mouth hanging open, blood washing away in the rain.

Salvarias braced himself, waiting for the power that would come like Tedris's had to his brother. But nothing happened. His gaze drifted to the stone. Slowly, he reached out for it.

Adok growled, shaking his head, warning Salvarias it was too dangerous.

Indecision warred within Salvarias. All his life he had known he had a task. This was it. To guard this stone. And he knew if god were to obtain it, life on Arden would end. All those he loved would die. Salvarias was the only one who could protect it. He glanced up at Lunara, then his brother. For them, he could be strong enough. For them, he could win whatever battle was to come.

Gritting his teeth, he reached out and yanked the pouch from Perek's neck. A tingle shot up his arm as a pulse of pain slammed into him like one giant fist had struck him wholly, knocking him backward.

Then it was over. All the pain was gone. His headache was gone. The longing sensation always eating at him was gone. He felt ... whole. Strong. Rested. At peace.

"What have you done?" Wilhelm breathed.

Salvarias looked up to see his brother standing over him.

"I am fine," Salvarias said. "I ... I feel better than I have my entire life." Gripping the pouch tight, he rose to his feet.

"Dammit!" Okulu cursed. "We can't fight all these, Humar."

The horde rushing them had to be over fifty strong. The mages were nowhere in sight.

Humar turned to Wilhelm. "Get your brother out of here. We'll delay them."

"No, we can help," Salvarias said.

"Take the girl with you," Humar commanded.

Wilhelm met Varila's gaze. She nodded.

"No, brother," Salvarias pleaded. "We must stay."

Wilhelm's jaw rippled as he sheathed his great sword, grabbed Salvarias's arm, and hauled him back toward the horses. Salvarias twisted in his brother's hold.

"They will die!" Salvarias said.

"Don't fight me," Wilhelm muttered.

"We can help them!" Lunara shouted over the rain, barely keeping up with Wilhelm. "You can't leave my sister!"

"They are our friends, brother. We can be victorious if we remain together."

Wilhelm suddenly stopped, his eyes squinting as he stared ahead of them. Salvarias ceased his struggles, focusing where Wilhelm's gaze fell. It was a puddle, deep certainly, but nothing—

"Bloodleders," Salvarias hissed.

Even as he voiced it, the puddle began to bubble, rising inch by inch, building upon itself as it sprouted limbs and a featureless head. Wilhelm's heavy hand rested on Salvarias's shoulder.

"Keep her safe and behind me," Wilhelm muttered.

Three more puddles began to boil up. Holding his hand out in front of him, Salvarias whispered his spell, flicked out his rune, and let a faint smile touch his lips as three spheres of ice hovered over his hand.

"Three," Wilhelm said, grin growing. "That's impressive, Salv."

"We fight together, brother." He looked up at Wilhelm. "Together."

Wilhelm's grin widened. "All right, Salv. Together it is."

Just as the first creature took a step, Salvarias sent his ice straight toward the creatures. One orb struck the standing bloodleder, crystallizing it into a soft pink hue. The other two spheres froze two of the new creatures twisting into existence. Wilhelm took two massive steps, flicked his sword, and shattered the first bloodleder. With a sharp crack, chunks of ice flew all around.

Wilhelm kicked the half-risen second bloodleder while swinging his sword wide on the third. The two creatures fractured apart, falling into a heap of shards.

The last one had taken form and leapt at Wilhelm. He artfully avoided it, managing a slice across the bloodleder's back. The beast whirled around, seeming to reappraise its foe.

From behind them and over a snap of thunder, Salvarias heard Humar's voice. Looking back, Salvarias's friends and four knights were sprinting toward them, followed by a pack of blond-furred creatures.

"Run!" Humar yelled.

Cursing, Salvarias stepped in front of Lunara, trusting his brother to keep the bloodleder at her back occupied.

"Down!" he ordered. He whispered out his spell as his friends dove to the ground. Tracing his rune, he shouted, *"Rulose!"* Energy surged from his body into the rune and ignited a blade of wind at waist level.

The spell was far more effective than he could have ever hoped. The might and precision of it sliced the first row of creatures in half at the waist. The second and third row were flung back with enough force to crush any creature unfortunate enough to collide with a tree or rock. Those remaining were slammed to the ground. It helped thin the horde. Perhaps twenty creatures were left. Manageable if Wilhelm's powers were ignited.

Salvarias whipped out his dagger and ran it over his hand, harshly enough so the flow of blood was immediate.

"Brother!"

Wilhelm spared the quickest glance, but it was enough. He sucked in a breath, staggered for its duration, then his eyes dulled and that cruel smile formed. Muscles bulged and squirmed under his skin, stretching it taut enough to appear painful. His movements became blurred and the bloodleder was soon nothing but drops of blood splattered across the forest. The rain washed off any on Wilhelm's skin, saving him from infection.

Just as Salvarias was about to revel in his spell's effectiveness and his brother's powers, Lunara screamed. Her wide eyes focused over Salvarias's shoulder. When he turned, he was greeted by a chest full of fur and the stink of rotting meat. Before he even processed what was happening, he found himself flung over the shoulder of a creature, pinned artfully, held too tightly to move his arms. Twisting his wrist, he managed to free his hand, but as he started his rune, a clawed paw grabbed his wrist and snapped it. Salvarias cried out, feeling bone puncture through skin. The world went white and soundless. It was over in a few breaths, and as his mind cleared from pain, he made out a short figure in pursuit.

Durak shouted out a curse at the creature, axe held aloft and ready. Though the cavrul's short legs would have allowed the creature to outdistance him, it was Durak's limber form that had him keeping pace as he dodged easily between clustered trees.

Regardless, he neither gained nor fell farther behind. One would tire, and Salvarias suspicioned it would be Durak. The old cavrul must have concluded the same. With a colorful curse, Durak drew his carving knife, squinted one eye closed, and sent the blade sailing toward the creature. It struck the creature in the left calf.

An ear-shattering roar rang in Salvarias's head as the world spun around him. Landing hard on his back pushed air from his lungs. Sharp pain shot up his left side. Then the creature's weight slammed into him, pinning him to the ground. Spots blotted out his surroundings. Gasping, air refused him.

Just as darkness was about to pounce, he sucked in sweet air. Gulping it eagerly, he blinked several times to clear his vision. The creature's massive form blocked Durak from view, but by the dominating stance of the beast, the cavrul was not winning.

Groaning, Salvarias rolled his body on its side, gasped more air, and drew his dagger, clutching it tightly in his right hand. He avoided looking at his left wrist, but shuddered at feeling it swaying back and forth. Staggering to his feet, he teetered toward the creature.

It swiped one arm and Durak grunted, fell to the ground, and disappeared as the creature lunged on top of him. The moist sound of tearing flesh stuttered Salvarias's heart. He slipped in the mud, fell forward, and luckily landed on the creature's back. Using all his strength, he rammed his dagger into the creature's neck. Spoiled green blood spurted up, a river of it covering Salvarias's hand. The beast reared back, tossing Salvarias off it. Pressing a paw to the wound, it rounded on him, claws raised, dripping bright red blood clotted with chunks of gray flesh. It made it one step before its eyes rolled back in its head and it collapsed.

Digging his fist into the mud, Salvarias used it to drag his body to Durak. The old cavrul lay on his back, hands clutching his torn-open chest.

"Durak," Salvarias whispered, gaze sweeping over the cavrul's body. There was nothing Salvarias could do. Nothing.

"There, there, lad," Durak croaked.

"I am so sorry," Salvarias wept.

"It's not ye fault." Durak winced as he shifted. A trickle of blood fell from the corner of his mouth. "Me sorry I wasn't kinder to ye. Ye were a good boy, always polite and respectful."

Salvarias yanked off his cloak and covered his friend. "You cannot leave me," he choked. "Please, do not leave me."

Durak's lips quivered out a smile. "Ye saved me, boy. Me never told ye how much, but ye kindness saved me."

What have you done? the presence hissed. *What have you done to your friend?*

"Be strong, son. Ye must be strong, now." Durak's dark eyes lost focus.

"No!" Salvarias grabbed Durak, shaking him. "You cannot leave me! You cannot!"

Images blossomed in his mind, blocking out the rain, the cold, the blood of his friend seeping into ground. The first he saw was of Durak's family, his son and daughter, his young wife, but soon they were replaced by images of death. Of horrible murder. Of innocent life being snatched away in the night.

The cruelty of it burned hot in Salvarias's soul. Anger bubbled the surface of his lake. Death after death burgeoned his horror until his anger morphed into rage. With a sharp cry of fury, blackfire burst to life, covering him in warmth, thickening a desperate thirst for vengeance.

"No," Durak rasped.

Salvarias's hands were clamped over the cavrul's throat. Durak beat his fists against Salvarias's arms, but the cavrul's attempt lacked any strength.

The dead hissed in Salvarias's ear, demanding their vengeance. Blackfire licked down his arms, bathing his hands, and then ate its way over Durak. The stench of burning flesh filled Salvarias with peace, and Durak's anguished cries were sweet music. With euphoric release, he poured the tortured souls' horror and pain back into Durak, forcing the old cavrul to relive all he had done, to understand what he had taken from the world, from parents, from lovers, from children. He watched the light fade from Durak's eyes, felt the old man's body twitching in the last throes of death, and Salvarias smiled as satisfaction quenched his thirst.

In a blink, he stood before the towering doors of Oblivion. Hands reached through the foggy walls. Faces protruded here and there as the damned tried to escape their prison. Screams echoed across the plain, and Salvarias closed his eyes, inhaling the torment as if it were the sweetest flower.

Gray fog curled around Salvarias, embracing him, filling him with a sense of love. He lived wholly in that moment, feeling at home, feeling as though this was where he belonged.

When he finally opened his eyes, he heard Durak crying. The cavrul's soft pleas tainted Salvarias's happiness. Glancing down, he saw Durak kneeling, face buried in his hands. The sight sent a knife straight through Salvarias's heart. He turned widened eyes upon Oblivion's doors.

"No," Salvarias choked. "I will not do this. He does not deserve to be here."

The fog spoke, its voice deep and logical. "He killed innocents."

"He regrets his actions. He realizes what he did was wrong."

"Just because a person acknowledges their mistakes does not make them forgivable. The pain each person suffered as he hacked them apart does not change. The families he left without sons, daughters, wives, husbands, fathers, and mothers are not made whole by his regret."

Salvarias looked down at Durak. "He is my friend. You cannot ask me to do this."

"If every person simply asked for forgiveness and all their horrible deeds were wiped clean, then Oblivion would not exist. All are sorry when forced to fully understand their own cruelty, their own dark souls. Durak chose to murder. He must live with his choices. Touch the door," the fog ordered.

"No," Salvarias said. "He is my friend."

"You have no friends. Your task is to sentence."

"I refuse," Salvarias said.

"Dethal begged for forgiveness, but you showed him none."

"He was not truly sorry."

"Ah, but he was," the fog said. "I taste his sorrow now. I listen to him beg for my mercy, for the mercy of those he killed. He weeps his apologies to them, and he is sincere."

Salvarias reached out and touched the doors. They yawned open.

"Force him in," the fog commanded.

"Please, lad," Durak choked, clutching at Salvarias's robes. "Don't send me there, son."

The images, the pain and fear each mage had felt as Durak killed them intensified, consuming Salvarias's entire being. Then he was shown a mother weeping over her dead son. A father holding his daughter's butchered body. A husband wailing at his wife's fresh grave.

"What if they were your children?" the fog asked. "Your wife, your husband ... your brother. Would you be so sympathetic?"

The pain of each loved one stabbed Salvarias, embedding itself in his soul. The potency of their suffering drove Salvarias to loud sobs. So much loss, so much pain.

"Please lad," Durak wept.

With a furious shout, Salvarias grabbed Durak, hauled him up, and shoved him through the doors of Oblivion. Durak screamed as the doors thudded closed.

The finality of it, of what he had done, smothered his anger. He had just condemned a dear friend to an eternity of torment.

"Forgive me!" Salvarias cried.

It was too late. Before him was a shriveled, blackened corpse. Salvarias unclenched his shaking hands from Durak's neck, raising them in front of him. Charred skin stuck to fingers. His left wrist had snapped into place, leaving an already healing hole where the bone had protruded as the only evidence of his injury.

What have you done, my murderer? the presence said in his mind. *What have you done to your friend?*

Salvarias fell backward, scrabbling from Durak until his back hit a tree. "No-no-no," he repeated.

You killed him. A friend. You burned him alive, my murderer. You burned him alive!

"No!" Salvarias screamed, covering his ears with his hands. "I did not mean to! I did not mean to!"

I know, my pet. I know your sssuffering. My poor, poor pet. I do not hate you. But they *will. Flee. Flee!*

Salvarias bolted to his feet and managed a few steps before his bad leg gave out beneath him. Thunder boomed and lightning flashed. Dead insects covered the ground. Plants withered into nothing. Trees creaked and groaned in the wind, stripped of life. The stink of death was all around him.

Imagining his staff, he grabbed it when it appeared in front of him and used it to gain his footing. The staff sank into the mud, but helped him run. He had to stop at one point to allow his churning stomach victory.

Your brother isss coming! the presence cried. *Fassster! You mussst run fassster!*

Salvarias forced his beaten body to move even as he fumbled for his dagger. Sobs left him as he realized he had left it in the creature's neck.

Twigs snapped behind him and Wilhelm's voice rose above the thunder, calling to Salvarias to stop. He ignored it, wretched cries leaving his throat as he cursed his weak leg.

Then Adok was in front of him, hackles raised, teeth bared. The wolf said justice had been served, that what Salvarias had done was right.

His bad leg tweaked painfully when he tried to dodge around the wolf. Falling face first in the mud, he lay there for a breath, weeping, feeling utterly hopeless, utterly hateful of himself.

"Salv!"

"No," he sobbed, using the word to give himself strength. He could not look at his brother, at those who had trusted him and called him friend. At her.

Slipping and crawling, he finally got to his feet. No sooner did he take a step than massive arms wrapped around his chest.

"It's all right, Salv," Wilhelm said. "I'm here. It's all right."

"No!" Salvarias shouted, twisting and contorting in a futile attempt to escape. "Let me go! Let me go!"

"Never, Salv. Never."

Those words crushed Salvarias to the ground. He wanted to dissolve in the rain, to bleed into the soil, to be a faint memory to those who knew him. Curling up, he hugged himself.

"I cannot," he sobbed. "I cannot do this anymore!"

"You didn't mean it," Wilhelm said softly, holding Salvarias tightly, hiding him in a place no one ever found him, a place no one ever hurt him. "I know, Salv. You didn't mean it."

Curling up smaller, he tucked himself away from it all. He refused the presence in his mind voice, he refused to listen to Wilhelm's comforts, and he refused to acknowledge the cruel world around him. Here, he disappeared, sank beneath his lake. Here, he searched for the hand that would take him from his pain, that would send him someplace so dark no light could ever reach him, someplace no one could ever find him. He begged for it to help him, but it did not come.

Chapter 46

Winter 1018 a.r.

Salvarias was not sure when the dead had assailed his mind or when she had come to help him. As his mind fully returned, he realized he was encased in Wilhelm's arms, and Lunara was kneeling in front of him, a cloth in her hands which she had used to clean away the blood of all the innocent mages he had killed.

Rain had soaked him through. The stench of death was all around him. The storm still raged. He refused to look at her. Whether she regarded him with fondness or with hate, neither would matter.

Resting a hand over his heart, he folded up tighter, aching at the hole Durak's death had created. Loss tore at him like a rabid animal, shredding his heart into pieces. More than anything he wanted to hear Durak's curses, wanted to see the cavrul whittling away at a stick, wanted to see his stern frown. Salvarias's grief manifested itself as physical pain, an ache all over, an unending chasm of emptiness where once there had been joy.

"Leave us," Wilhelm said.

Mud sloshed and her footsteps faded in the rain. Wilhelm sat in silence, his arms tight, his breathing measured, the smell of wet metal and leather pungent. Salvarias dreaded what his brother would say more than he used to dread his days alone with their mother.

He will leave you, the presence said. *We can only hope he doesss ssso that we may ssspare him your evil.*

When Wilhelm spoke, his voice was a soft rumble; strong, truthful, and full of love. "You're my baby brother. Nothing will change that. Nothing will change how much I care for you. Do you understand?"

Salvarias nodded, hating every word his brother spoke.

"Do you believe me?"

He nodded again.

"We're going to be all right. I promise. But we have to join up with the others."

"Do not make me," Salvarias whispered. "I cannot face them, brother. I ... I killed him."

"He would have died anyway, Salv. The creature tore him up."

"I burned him." Tears welled at the memory. "He pleaded with me to stop, but I did not."

Wilhelm tapped Salvarias's chin. Blinking his eyes clear, he raised his gaze to his brother's.

"You didn't mean it, Salv. I know, and that's all that matters. You and me. To Oblivion with the others if they don't understand. But we need their protection. I'm hurt."

Salvarias yanked back from Wilhelm, gaze sweeping over his brother. A large gash on Wilhelm's side leaked blood.

Thrusting out his hand, Salvarias said, "Let me help you."

"It'll heal on its own, but I'm not going to be able to keep us safe like this. We need their help for now. No one will say anything to you. I promise. And if they have a problem with ... with what happened, then we'll leave as soon as I'm ready. But ..." Wilhelm bent to keep Salvarias's gaze. "But if they don't change, we're staying with them."

Swallowing the lump in his throat, he nodded. It would not matter. He would find a way to leave, leave them all. He needed no one. No one.

You finally have my ressspect, little murderer, the presence hissed. *We will leave them and they will be free to live their livesss in peaccce, to be free of your evil.*

"Let's go," Wilhelm said, rising to his feet and hauling Salvarias to his.

Feeling sick with each step, they made their way through the woods to the spot Salvarias had killed Durak. The cavrul's body had been covered and strapped to a horse, as well as Tedris and Perek. All his companions were there. Grief etched on their faces as they readied the horses, crunching dead insects beneath their boots.

Neithelas's glance at Salvarias held murderous intentions, which was expected and welcomed. Salvarias hoped the prince would find the strength to loose an arrow in Salvarias's heart, but the winsire did no such thing. Instead, he spat on the ground and returned to his task of tightening the straps of his saddle.

Humar's gaze was void of the anger, hatred, and disgust that Salvarias had hoped to see. Worse, it was filled with disappointment.

Varila offered a small smile. It lacked its usual warmth, something forced but not felt.

Okulu openly stared. His gaze held no emotion, only calculation as it had when they first met. He had not decided upon hate or forgiveness.

Lunara's smile was bright as sunshine, but tears still trailed down her cheeks.

"Instructions, my liege?" a knight asked.

"You've got the stone?" Humar asked Salvarias.

He nodded.

"Lynta," Humar said to the knight. "We need rest, and Olivit will help arrange the bodies' transport to Dalnar." He turned an even gaze at Salvarias. "That is, if that's all right with you?"

He nodded.

Humar motioned at Wilhelm. "Patch your brother up and then we'll head out. Lunara, take care of the others."

Salvarias's gaze drifted back to the bundled body of his friend. A strong hand rested on his shoulder and squeezed softly. It did not erase or ease the memory of what he had done. It did not bring back his friend.

They rode a few hours in uncomfortable silence, the knights setting a slow pace for the wounded. When they stopped for a short rest, Salvarias slipped from the group and found a quiet place to sit. He stared at the rain beating into the soaked ground and listened to the steady drum of it, ignoring Adok's attempt at comfort. At least the wind had let up.

A sharp snap of a twig jerked Salvarias alert, calling a spell to his lips. Okulu stepped from behind a tree. He had a dagger in his hand, flipping it handle over blade.

"I would prefer to be alone," Salvarias said.

Okulu shrugged. "And I prefer your company. Wanna argue or let me join you?"

"I killed him."

Okulu pursed his lips, eyes narrowing. "You did. Burned him alive, from what I could tell."

"And then I tossed him into Oblivion to suffer an eternity of torment." Salvarias raised his gaze to Okulu, anger festering. Why had the merc come to torture him? Why could they not let him be?

Or better yet, why could one not scrounge up an ounce of bravery and drive a stake through Salvarias's heart?

"Oblivion, you say?" Okulu raised his eyebrows. "That must be an unpleasant place to visit. Is it hot? I always imagined it full of fire and little demons running around poking people."

Salvarias opened his mouth, closed it, and tried to get his mind to muddle through what Okulu had just said.

"No?" the merc continued. "No fire then?" He sighed. "I guess that's for the better. I'd like my eternity to be cold."

"You are not destined for Oblivion," Salvarias said.

"Shame. I thought when I murdered the man who killed my sister I'd won myself admittance."

"You killed a killer," Salvarias said. "Oblivion is reserved for those who torment the innocent."

"Ah." Okulu grinned. "Then when I die, we'll still get to have these lovely chats."

Salvarias shook his head, dumbfounded and angry. "I killed your friend. I killed an inno—"

"He was your friend too. And he was far from innocent. Matter of fact, all the people you've killed had blood on their hands. Lots of blood." Okulu's smile faded as he sat beside Salvarias. He spread his arm wide, as if motioning to some unseen expanse. "Lives are like oceans. When it's looked upon, some simply see blue sky and waves. But there is life below the waves and stars beyond the sky. And you, my friend. Well, you see yourself as those poor souls see the ocean. You see only what you want, and not what lies beneath and above." Okulu winked. "People tend to look at me the same. They see a man too handsome and charismatic to be possible. They don't see how smart I am."

Salvarias rested his head in his hands, allowing Okulu's company to lighten him as it always did. "I wish you would hate me, my friend."

"I know you do, Salvarias. I know you do."

When the forest edge came into view, Salvarias resisted the urge to run for the meadow sprawling beyond. Zerana's grace would cease once they cleared the trees, and the rolling hills stretching before them would allow faster travel. His body was near collapsing, and his mind near breaking. The sooner they arrived in Serinity, the sooner his brother could marry, and the sooner Salvarias would be free to leave.

"Still nothing with the stone?" Wilhelm asked.

Salvarias touched the pouch hanging round his neck, tucked beneath his robes. "Nothing."

"I don't understand," Wilhelm muttered. "After everything Perek and Tedris said, you'd think something would have happened."

"Perhaps it is because of Zerana's grace," Salvarias said, absently puzzling it out. "We were supposed to make the transition in the icelands because of it. Though, in the forest, it is ten times stronger."

"Then why did you have to fight the Hunters?"

"I am not sure. Perhaps Zerana's grace is different here." Salvarias frowned. Indeed, it was different. Grief ridden instead of joyous. Angry instead of peaceful.

"But ..." Wilhelm rubbed his growing beard. "If the power is helping you, that means we should stay in the forest."

No sooner had Salvarias determined Wilhelm was correct then they passed the last of the trees. Zerana's ending grace lifted off his body, enough that he felt sure he would float into the air. The fresh scent of winter rinsed away the rotten decay of the forest he had breathed for days. He inhaled deeply of it, letting it cleanse the smell of Durak's flesh. Closing his eyes, he allowed that moment to consume him.

Then in a rush, it was gone. What replaced it was utter and absolute agony. Every injury he had ever suffered raked across his body as if it were happening again. His brain thumped violently in his skull, vibrating everything around him. His weak lungs seemed to shrink even more, and his damaged heart faltered to practically nothing, then beat like a galloping horse's hooves, only to nearly stop again.

"Run!" Wilhelm roared.

Doubling over, Salvarias barely managed a glance behind. Speeding for him was a river of tangible red and black fog, each fighting one another to reach Salvarias first. He never had time to even convey this thought to Mithal.

Both fogs hit him simultaneously. They launched him out of his saddle, flinging him to the ground. His cry lodged in his throat as they plunged inside him like two barbed knives, ripping him apart from the inside out. Voices shouted all around, nothing coherent above his own internal screaming.

Rolling on his side, he hugged himself, feeling warm blood flooding his mouth, running out his ears, streaming from his nose, and leaking out his eyes.

Wilhelm's strength slammed into him, and he gulped it like water for a man stranded too long in the desert. Desperately he tried to shield his soul, his mind, his body—everything—but the powers were too strong. They tossed aside his efforts as if he was nothing but the weak and frail child he had been so many years ago.

He drained more strength, clawing at it with sheer fear, even as Wilhelm shoveled it into Salvarias as fast as he consumed it. Despite their efforts, they failed.

Utter terror gripped Salvarias. The evil would win. He would be lost to it. All his fights for his entire life had been pointless.

Then, as if by a command of someone snapping their fingers, it all stopped.

Pain, light, and warmth abandoned him until he lived in nothing but the deepest darkness, colder than any place he had ever been. There was no sound. But something dwelled here. And it petrified him.

"No," a voice hissed. "Fear me not." A soft red glow formed in front of Salvarias, lighting a thin hand reaching for him. "Give yourssself to me and I will end your pain. Accccept and I will grant your brother peaccce and joy. Deny me and I will ssshow you true sssuffering."

Somewhere far, far off in the darkness, Salvarias faintly heard his brother say, "Please, Salv, for me. You have to fight it."

Taking a step back, Salvarias shook his head at the hand. "You cannot have me. My soul is my own."

Darkness slowly eroded away the light as the voice said, "Ssso be it. When you are ready, call for me and I will come. Until then ..."

The light blinked out, and then came pain. Gods, such pain.

———✦———

Wilhelm plucked up his brother and ran back to the forest. Salvarias jerked in his arms, eyes wide and staring at nothing, silent tears mingling with blood running from his eyes. The sight nearly sent Wilhelm into shock. His mind wanted to shut down, forget all he'd just seen, forget the heart-wrenching screams coming from his baby brother.

Wilhelm's exhaustion made the short sprint to the woods seem like miles. When he passed the first tree, Salvarias's twitching erupted into violent seizures. Blood flowed from his nose and ears, spattering his lips with his gurgled screams.

Jumping back a step, Wilhelm left the forest. Salvarias calmed instantly to his former violent jerks and soft groans. Cradling his brother tight, Wilhelm whispered, "What do I do, Salv? Tell me how to help."

Salvarias hitched, but nothing more.

"What in all of Oblivion was that?" Varila snapped.

Wilhelm turned to Lunara. "What's wrong with him?"

"I don't know," she said, tears falling freely. "I can't sense anything. Not even pain. Fear. Nothing. He's completely shut off from me."

"Can you help him?"

"I don't think it wise I try. If he is battling, my touch will do more harm than good."

Wilhelm looked to Humar. "What do we do now?"

"We need to get to Lynta," Humar said. "You're not going to last much longer, and I doubt your brother is going to be able to fight off whatever force seeks him. We'll be attacked out here. We need safety."

"Can you make it?" Okulu asked Wilhelm.

Salvarias had stopped draining Wilhelm's strength rapidly, but he could feel his brother touching upon it, taking it so slowly Wilhelm almost didn't notice. Regardless, he knew he wouldn't last a whole day. "Probably not."

"We'll ride hard," Okulu said. "Get as far as we can."

Wilhelm mounted Lilly and situated his brother in front of him. He kept his mark pressed against Salvarias's and continually whispered to his brother, hoping beyond all hope that Salvarias could hear him.

Chapter 47

Winter 1018 a.r.

Time was meaningless as Salvarias wandered landscapes defying all he had ever seen. Forests with trees shooting so high he could not see their tops. Deserts where the sun was blood red, and at night, three moons hovered in the sky. He walked the bottoms of oceans, breathing water as if it were air. Each place he roamed, new horrors were visited upon him. Creatures existed that no words had been created to describe. Each inflicted new wounds on his battered body, leaving behind rivers of his own blood. In some fights he would lose limbs or pieces of his insides, would cave to darkness as he pleaded for death. Then he would wake whole, in a new place with a new terror gripping his heart, new fear at what he would have to face next.

All that kept him going was the faint voice of his brother, always out of reach, always calling to him. Pain had nearly made him go mad, and he instead chose to forget everything in life—friends, family, everything—other than Wilhelm and the strength not to beg the skeletal hand to end Salvarias's suffering.

Finally, after roaming for days, years—he could not tell—in one of the new worlds where boundless hills of sand birthed giant redwoods and the sun baked Salvarias's skin dry, Wilhelm's voice grew stronger, closer. Using his remaining arm, Salvarias dragged himself across scorching sands, tongue swollen from lack of water, lips cracked and bleeding. Blood clotted the sand in the trail he left behind from the gash on his stomach. The occasional chunk of some organ slipped free, shriveling instantly in the heat, looking like black stones against the tan sand. He cried, though no tears shed. He begged for help, though no sound left his throat.

When he crested one hill, he was greeted by dull amber eyes ringed by thick black. Tears welled and skimmed down Wilhelm's face. They were lying beside each other.

"You're all right," Wilhelm said. "I'm ... here." His eyes closed and his tense face went slack.

Tears fled from Salvarias's once-dry eyes, spit and blood filled his mouth and leaked between his lips, his formerly missing arm hung loosely at his side, and the cut on his stomach had closed. His head shook with pain, his body tensed with it, jerking as the last of the sensations faded, a new exhaustion seeming to pull his body into the ground.

Blinking away tears, he gazed up at churning green clouds, flinching as rain bathed his face. Off in the distance, a new creature cawed.

"No," he groaned. Feeling like he was fighting quicksand, he raised his shaking hand and shoved Wilhelm. "Brother, we must fight."

Something was coming. He heard a squishing noise by his head.

"Drink," a soft voice said.

Poison, no doubt. Wherever they were, they needed to flee before the creatures ate them alive. Wilhelm, however, had fallen into a deep sleep.

Spitting up bloody drool, Salvarias propped his weak body up on his elbow. People stood around him, faces bruised, looking disheveled and menacing. One with light olive skin squatted beside Salvarias.

Moaning from the effort, Salvarias grabbed his dagger and rammed it at the man who dodged it easily. The man wrestled the dagger from Salvarias's hand.

"Easy," the man said. His grass-green eyes were warm, but no doubt it was a ruse. Soon he would butcher Salvarias and Wilhelm. "We're almost to Lynta. You need to eat."

A woman knelt on his other side. Her raven hair was slicked to her head, eyes red and puffy. She smiled as sweet as sunshine, but Salvarias did not trust her either. Nothing good lived where he lived.

Using more strength than it should have taken, Salvarias shoved her away. Coughing a spell, he flicked out his rune. An ice shard appeared. The effort it took for the small spell drained the last of his energy. Even as he sent the shard for the man at his side, darkness pounced upon him.

He blinked and opened his eyes. His body was whole and his energy restored as it always was when he ended up in a new world. It was night. A blue moon hung in the dark sky. Prickly tall cacti surrounded him, poking at ferns sprouting from white soil. None of it mattered. Finally he had found his brother.

Smiling, he looked to the side. Wilhelm was gone. Bolting up, Salvarias scoured the hillside, but once again, he was alone.

"Brother!" Salvarias shouted. "Help me!"

No one came and, for the first time, his brother's voice did not call to him. All was deadly silent.

"I have been kind to you," the voice behind the thin hand said. "But you have angered me. And now ..." The voice chuckled. "Now you are unprotected. Now I am free. Tell me, my preciousss little pet, do you think you know pain? Do you think you are ssstrong?" A hand reached out to him, surrounded by red light. "Accept my offer."

Weeping, Salvarias hugged himself, backing away.

"Then let usss sssee which one of usss winsss, my little pet."

The cacti turned to him, suddenly not plants but creatures with murder in their red eyes. Thousands upon thousands of needles shot straight inside Salvarias. He screamed, blinded by a pain that went beyond physical, beyond mental.

He wanted nothing more than to accept the hand, to beg for it all to stop. But with mad desperation he clung to one thought: Wilhelm would save him. All Salvarias had to do was fight until his brother came and whisked him away somewhere safe, somewhere free of pain. Wilhelm had promised him that, and his brother never broke a promise.

Humar cried out and fell away from Salvarias. Tendrils of red fog shot up from the boy's body, climbing into the sky. Salvarias arched and screamed past blood gurgling up from his throat, trickling out his ears, nose, and eyes. The tendrils stopped, wavering like a forest of majestic trees, then plunged downward, spiraling with the speed of a diving hawk. They stabbed through Salvarias and then whipped around him in a cocoon of vines, making an audible *snap* as they enveloped the boy completely.

Lunara rushed to Salvarias, ignoring Varila's shouted warning. The girl never reached his side. A foot away, a tendril shot out and hit her hard across her stomach, sending her flying a few feet away. Neithelas ran to her side. Aside from a scorch mark on her dress where the fog had touched her, she appeared fine.

Okulu stumbled over to Wilhelm, hand pressed to his side where Salvarias's ice shard had sliced his skin open, deep, but mendable. Only Okulu's quick dodge had saved him.

"Wilhelm!" Okulu shook the boy, but Wilhelm seemed to have been drained of strength. He did not wake.

Humar scanned the hills. They were maybe an hour or so from Lynta and its protection. Turning to one of his knights, he said, "Ride to Lynta. Get Olivit Hunbred to send a wagon, healers, and an escort. Tell him I have his son with me. We need help."

The knight saluted, mounted, and rode hard out of sight.

Snatching up a small rock by his foot, Humar tossed it lightly at the fog. It passed through, thumping when it hit Salvarias.

Okulu reached out a tentative hand and rested it on Salvarias. Nothing happened to Okulu, but the entire cocoon twitched and dismantled into a mass of snake-like forms. They writhed in and out of Salvarias, causing the boy to twitch and jerk violently. They parted enough that Humar caught a glimpse of the boy's face. Salvarias's eyes were open, darting around, seeing something Humar could not. The spouting blood had turned to a tiny stream trickling out the corner of Salvarias's mouth.

Varila, upon seeing the fog benevolent toward Okulu, dropped beside Salvarias. She raked her hands at the fog, but they passed through as if it wasn't solid. "I can't get it off," she growled.

Okulu tried again, followed by Humar, and then Neithelas, but none could grab hold of it.

"What do we do?" Varila asked. "We can't just leave him like this."

Humar ran a hand through his hair. "There's nothing we can do. Our only option is to get him to Lynta." His gaze swept over the hills again. "Before something comes to kill us all."

Humar and Okulu leaned against the wall by the door inside Salvarias's room. They'd been in Lynta for a day, Okulu's family all too willing to help.

Salvarias had awoken three times, and on each one he had attempted to kill someone, screaming the entire time for Wilhelm who had yet to wake. They'd been forced to bind Salvarias's hands and fingers, preventing further spells. It might have saved their lives, but the past two times Salvarias had woke, the ties pitched him into violent panic. To Humar's relief, it never lasted long before the boy lost his hold on reality.

"I wish there was something we could do," Okulu growled. "I've never felt so helpless."

"He tried to kill you."

Okulu shook his head. "He tried to kill something he saw, someone perhaps, but not me. He didn't recognize me."

Humar grunted, unconvinced. Ever since Salvarias had burned Durak alive, Humar had a difficult time mustering up trust in the boy, much less looking at him.

"Tsk-tsk," Okulu said. "You're going to regret how cold you've been toward him."

"Am I?" Humar said, allowing his anger to deepen his voice. "We've seen this side of Salvarias before. It disgusted me then. I chose to ignore it, turn a blind eye, but he did it to a dear friend."

"A dear friend that was a murderer," Okulu said.

Humar curled his lip. "The boy is evil."

"No one walking this world is free of evil, my friend. What we call 'good' is merely the nicest level of evil."

"Lunara is."

Okulu smiled at the young woman sitting beside Salvarias. "In our eyes, yes. You and I have seen the deepest pits of evil. We consider the upper levels she and those like her live in saintly. Those levels are puppies and butterflies compared to what we've seen ... what we've done. But ask her and I bet she'd tell you she's done something wrong, something evil. Evil is relative."

"And that justifies what Salvarias did?"

The door opened and Wilhelm stepped inside, Varila wedged under one arm to support his swaying body. His cheeks were sunken, eyes rimmed with black, skin too pale. He looked sick, like a man close to death.

"You should be—"

"What in Veedran's defilement!" Wilhelm cursed, eyes widening as he looked at his brother.

The red fog still swarmed over Salvarias, sinking into his skin only to emerge again. His eyes were open—always open—twitching this way and that, and his body spasmed constantly. The trickles of blood had yet to cease.

"We don't know what it is," Humar explained, following Wilhelm across the room. "We can touch it, except for Lunara, but we can't grab hold of it."

Lunara bolted over to Wilhelm, grabbed his hand, and pulled him toward the bed. "You have to help him!" she pleaded. "He's in so much pain!"

"Why haven't you?" Wilhelm snarled. "You're—"

"I can't," Lunara cried. "The fog won't let me near him."

Cursing again, Wilhelm released Varila, wobbled one step, and collapsed to his knees by the bed. The small walk broke sweat on Wilhelm's forehead, and his chest rose in violent breaths. With help from Varila, Wilhelm managed to haul himself up to sit on the edge of the bed.

Looking Salvarias up and down, Wilhelm's jaw rippled. "Why is he tied up?"

"He nearly killed Okulu," Humar explained. "It's like he doesn't recognize us."

Wilhelm inhaled a deep breath, then touched the fog. The screech it made popped Humar's ears. He clamped his hands over his ears, as did everyone.

Grimacing, Wilhelm reached through the fog and pressed his right palm to Salvarias's left. The fog wailed and wailed, the writhing mass flopping around like a dying fish, until finally it dove inside Salvarias, its shriek echoing in the stone room.

The boy's voice belted out in a mid scream, as if it had started ages ago. His eyes snapped shut, shedding a fountain of tears. When his scream trailed off, it was replaced by loud sobs.

"Salv," Wilhelm said, voice already shaking with exhaustion. "You have to fight, little brother. I can't ..." He shuddered, his body sagging. "Salv ... I can't ..." His eyes began to close. "You have to fight."

"Help me," Salvarias wept. "Do not leave me, brother."

Wilhelm's eyes fluttered, then rolled back in his head. His body slid off the bed, thudding in a twist of arms and legs.

Salvarias cried, "Do not leave me!"

The red fog burst to life. It rammed in and out of Salvarias, so violently it shook the entire bed. Blood began to flow from the boy's nose, eyes again locked open, gaze darting about.

"No!" Lunara pleaded. She rushed to Wilhelm's side and shook him, but he was unresponsive.

"The gods help us," Okulu breathed.

Humar ran a hand through his hair. "What gods there might have been have abandoned the boy. Demons own him now."

Chapter 48

Winter 1018 a.r.

Varila stood beside Okulu, both staring down at Salvarias. It had been twenty-six days since they'd arrived in Lynta. During that time, Wilhelm had woken every other day and gave all his strength to Salvarias. It was the only time the red fog disappeared. The only time Salvarias closed his eyes. One such session had just passed.

"Wilhelm's going to die," Okulu said softly.

Varila bit the inside of her cheek, refusing the tears threatening to cloud her eyes. Okulu was right. Her soon-to-be husband was thin, weak, his mind not right when he woke. Several times they thought his body had finally given up.

"Salvarias will go mad," Okulu continued.

The first signs had already started. When he woke, he didn't recognize his own brother. He screamed and screamed, eyes wild with fear, spitting up bloody drool, losing control of his bowels. His body had wasted to nothing. They barely got broth and water down him. And what they did he rarely kept down. They'd moved him into a washroom, forgoing a bed in place of a wood plank they could easily wash.

It was a harrowing thing to witness. To see one so smart, so collected, collapse into a blubbering mess made one realize how precious one's sanity was.

"And your sister as well," Okulu said.

Lunara had only left Salvarias's side to perform her ablutions. She slept on a cot they'd moved into the room, seemingly oblivious to the stench. One would not have guessed whatever Salvarias endured was not affecting her. Her eyes were sunken as well, she slept little, and she barely ate. Varila wondered if she looked as bad as her sister.

"What do you suggest?" Varila asked. "Humar hasn't come up with anything. We've had about every healer in Windlous look at him. We've sent notes to their uncle."

Okulu glanced around the room as if to be sure they were alone. "I want to drug Wilhelm."

Varila frowned at the merc. "Drug him with what?"

489

"A sleeping concoction. Something that will keep him under for days." He licked his lips. "A week."

"Sounds dangerous. And messy."

"It isn't dangerous, but messy is something we've gotten use to dealing with."

"And the point of it?"

"Right now, he can't stay awake long enough to help Salvarias," Okulu said. "He's too weak. If we get him rested up, he might be able to do what he hasn't been able to so far."

Varila pursed her lips. "You're sure it won't hurt Wilhelm in any way?"

"Yes, it's completely safe. You can confirm it with Lunara. Remember, Salvarias taught her about herblore."

"Then what's got you afraid?"

Okulu laughed lightly. "Wilhelm's reaction when he finds out what we've done. He hasn't let himself recover, and when he finds out we've taken that decision from him, angry won't begin to describe his rage."

"But if it helps Salvarias ..." She left the comment open.

"Hopefully he'll realize that before he kills us."

"What did Humar think?"

"He thought it was a bad idea. He said during that time, whatever the fog is might kill Salvarias. He thinks what Wilhelm's doing is all that's keeping Salvarias alive."

"Humar will know what we've done."

"On the contrary." Okulu's smile faded. "Your father's sent word. Arthias is dead. Humar's going to have his hands full helping Neithelas cope with his brother's death, not to mention giving him pointers on being a king."

"Neithelas is next in line," Varila murmured. "Poor bastard. He's had a rough go of it."

Okulu shrugged. "It's his own making."

Varila inhaled a deep breath. "All right. Let's give it a try. After all, can it be any worse?"

"Yes," Okulu said softly. "I believe it can."

He screamed until his voice gave out and blood seeped up from his raw throat. The cloud of pain receded enough for him to make out his surroundings. He was in a stark washroom. Beneath him, a hard wood plank bruised his bony body. The stench of an overused chamber pot made him nauseous. Hot tears burned down his cheeks, harshly contrasted against how cold he felt. When he tried to move, he found his hands bound, wrists rubbed raw and bleeding. Even more alarming, he had no memories. He did not know who he was, his name even.

A man sat at his side, tall, ridiculously large-framed, but thin, sickly looking. The man smiled, and it made him feel safe.

"Salv," the man said. "I'm here."

His gaze darted over to an olive-tinged man with grass-green eyes, grin roguish and full of mischief. Two women stood at his side, gorgeous, sinfully so.

The man turned to the olive-skinned one and asked, "How long have I been at it?"

"An hour. How much longer can you make it?"

"Not much. I'm tired."

"Wh-where am I?" he asked. Fear clogged his throat. "Wh-who am I?"

The man frowned, his square features tightening with concern. "You're safe. Your name is Salvarias. I'm your brother, Wilhelm."

Swallowing hard, Salvarias shook his head. "I-I do not remember."

He jerked violently when a voice hissed in his mind, *They will hurt you. You mussst kill them.*

The woman with raven hair smiled, and it made him think of meadows and sun, warmth and peace. Something inside his mind—no, inside his soul—stirred with her smile. "Don't be afraid," she said. "I want to help you, to make your pain go away. Will you let me?"

He shook his head, shrinking from her. All he remembered was he needed the pain. The pain meant he was good. If he gave up the pain, he would be evil. A monster. The thin hand would see to it. "N-no," he stammered.

He cried out when an enormous black wolf padded up beside the man named Wilhelm.

The man looked at the wolf. "Suggestions?"

491

The wolf growled, cocked his head to the side, then nudged the man's tunic. Brow furrowing, Wilhelm reached inside his tunic and withdrew a small box. The sight of it captured Salvarias wholly. The room faded, the people faded, the vicious wolf faded. All he saw was the carved box made of more tiny cubes. He stretched against his bindings for it, whimpering in a sudden need, a need that was painful. Pain. Blessed pain.

His hands were abruptly freed and he snatched up the device. It was warm, familiar. From far off, he heard the rumble of one word: bear. That word made him sob. It meant something to him. Something incredibly important. Safety. Love. Through tear-blurred vision, image after image appeared, showing the box moving and twisting, dancing into new shapes, beautiful shapes. His fingers moved swiftly, elegantly.

As the first piece clicked into place, it all came back in a flood. Sobs left him as he whirled the box faster, drinking in memory after memory. Soon he could not see past his tears, but it mattered not. The puzzle box moved by instinct alone, and his memories continued to pour into him until all were retrieved.

The puzzle box fell from his hands, and he bolted into Wilhelm's arms. "Help me!" he wept. "Please help me!"

"I'm trying, Salv, but you have to fight this. I'm not strong enough."

Wilhelm's voice was weak, and his body shook violently. Soon, his brother would have no strength left, and Salvarias would be alone again. Alone and in pain.

"No!" he screeched, gripping tightly to his brother. "Do not leave me!"

"I don't want to, Salv. We need another way, something else that can help you."

A voice barged into his mind, forcing away all other thought. It was deep, strong, caring. *Magic,* it said. *Use your magic.*

Salvarias's gaze focused on Adok. The wolf stared at him intently. The voice had been Adok's, but behind it lived a power Salvarias had never heard before. Scrabbling backward, he fell hard from the wood plank. Wilhelm never let go of Salvarias's left hand, but fear gave Salvarias unnatural strength. He crawled backward, dragging Wilhelm with him.

The wolf wasn't a wolf. He saw something alive behind the wolf's golden eyes, something powerful, something familiar. What he once thought was a normal wolf was suddenly dangerous, a liar.

"Get away from me!" Salvarias shouted at it. "Get away!"

No, Adok barked. *You* will *listen to me, son. Listen!* The wolf's voice bounced around in Salvarias's skull, ridding him of will. *Use your magic! Stop blocking it!*

He did not know how he had done so, but his magic was far from his reach, tucked away somewhere deep within his mind. Regardless of its distance, Salvarias had no choice but to obey the wolf, to recklessly swim around in his insanity.

Once he reached that dark place his magic lived, it took concentration to ignite it, like trying to walk after being bedridden for years. He felt clumsy, his hold on his magic wobbly and volatile.

My wizard, you are in danger, his magic said. *Not only from what you fight, but from me. You must solidify our connection. You must focus on me or else my power will rip your mind apart.*

Salvarias shut his eyes tightly, thinking of his magic, of its warmth and care.

"Salv," Wilhelm said, his voice fading. "I can't ..." Wilhelm's hand loosened. "I can't ..." A thud sounded beside Salvarias.

A few more heartbeats passed before the connection to his magic popped into alignment. Warmth and confidence flooded him, easing his pain, his fears.

Very good, my dear friend, his magic said. *Release your brother, or else you will kill him.*

Salvarias had not realized he was still draining Wilhelm, sucking the life out of him. With a short cry, he jerked his hand free. The instant their marks separated, red pulsed in Salvarias's vision. Aches began to throb all over his body. Blood and bile filled his mouth.

No, his magic said, voice deadly and flat, speaking to someone else beside Salvarias. *He is mine, and he is under my protection. You cannot have him.*

Blinding sapphire light burst in Salvarias's vision. It imbued him with astounding strength and clarity, boundless confidence. Warmth. Friendship. Safety. Comfort. He breathed it in, the familiarity of it, the trust he placed in it.

Salvarias's eyes snapped open. Reaching through the ocean of red fog surrounding him was a thin hand plunged into his chest, clamped around his soul. It had been there ever since they had left the forest, manipulating him, violating him in a way that made him ashamed and ... furious. Gritting his teeth, he grabbed its wrist.

"My soul is my own!" he shouted.

His magic joined his fight. He might as well have tried to pull a sword with the weight of a mountain from his chest. The red fog itself became an enemy, forming cruel fists covered in blades. It pounded on Salvarias, ripping apart his flesh.

Through the jolts of pain, he cried, "Help me!" and thought of blackfire. It sparked to life, bathing over him, its own anger joining his. With blackfire's help, the hand's grip had the strength of a butterfly. With one pull, it yanked free of Salvarias.

He exhaled sharply, a cry of utter relief leaving his lips. A rush of black fog tore into the red fog like a starved predator devouring its prey. Warmth seeped into Salvarias's bones, the pain ebbed to a horrible memory, one his body still thought real. He spasmed with its lasting effects, tears falling freely.

Rest, my wizard, his magic said, its voice weary. *I will protect you while you sleep.*

An exhaustion Salvarias had never known sank into his bones. His head felt like the anvil at Durak's forge, being pounded on by what must have been a troll. The pain of it all emptied his stomach, but before he even stopped retching, he allowed a black blanket of darkness to encase him.

Varila lounged in the washroom in the same chair she had sat in for the past two days. Wilhelm lay in a cot by Salvarias, both sleeping as soundly as the dead. On the other side of Salvarias, Lunara slept in a third cot, hand holding Salvarias's tightly as it had for two days. Adok was curled up at Salvarias's feet.

The past month would forever be locked in Varila's memory, but the events two days ago would haunt her nightmares. Wilhelm had died. After helping Salvarias, his body had just given out. Bruises still marred Wilhelm's chest from Okulu pounding on it to get the man's heart beating. Luckily, the merc had succeeded. Over the past two days, Wilhelm had woken once, and only long enough to check on Salvarias and take a piss.

A soft moan jerked her head up. Wilhelm's eyes were slowly opening. Quietly, she moved to sit on the edge of his cot. When he looked at her, his eyes were bright with alertness and his breathing steady and strong.

"About damn time," she said.

Wincing, he ran a hand over his chest. "What in Oblivion happened to me?"

"You died," Varila said, lightening her voice. "Okulu had to beat on you to get your heart started."

"I think he enjoyed it a bit too much," Wilhelm growled. Groaning, he managed to sit up with barely any help from Varila. Looking Salvarias up and down, he frowned, squinting.

"Blue light," Varila noted. It still pulsed ever so slightly around Salvarias.

Wilhelm rested a hand on Salvarias's chest, and once it rose with a small breath, he slouched and whispered, "Well done, little brother."

"Want to walk around a bit?" Varila asked.

Wilhelm ran a hand through his sweat-crusted hair, wrinkling his nose at the stench coming from him. "I'd like a bath."

"Lunara woke up not too long ago," Varila said. "She'll sleep through it."

Once she asked a servant for fresh bathwater and a privacy divider, word of Wilhelm's recovery had spread. He received a train of visitors, each one seeming to irritate him. Glancing at Salvarias, she understood. Wilhelm feared the commotion would wake his brother, and after being awake for a month, Salvarias needed as much sleep as he desired. Still, she didn't think an earthquake would wake the mage. He'd not moved since he'd passed out two days ago.

Nevertheless, Wilhelm did, so Varila exerted her control over the room, sending everyone away with threats and curses. When it was just the four of them, Wilhelm offered his gratitude, stripped, and crawled into the tub filled with lukewarm water. He didn't seem to mind.

"Tell me what happened," Wilhelm said. "I don't remember anything after I gave him the puzzle box."

Varila shuddered at remembering the puzzle box whirling around in Salvarias's palm. He hadn't even manipulated the pieces. They'd moved on their own, twisting and turning, clicking into place.

Clearing her throat, she said, "After Adok approached Salvarias, that blue light shot out from him, the same one you see now, only it was as bright as the sun. It was ... beautiful, actually. Then his blackfire came to life. I saw ..." She swallowed hard, fighting back a shudder. "I saw the red fog trying to leave him, but the blue light and blackfire kept it inside him. He went into convulsions when you died. Almost bit off his tongue." She blinked aside tears. "He kept screaming. Over and over, like something was eating him alive. Then it all stopped and he passed out."

"I'm sorry," he said.

Tears broke free. Angry at her weakness, she busied herself with laying out fresh clothes for Wilhelm and then leaned against the wall beside Lunara's cot. Water sloshed as he rose from the tub.

When he emerged from behind the divider, he was dressed in an unbelted white tunic and his normal black trews. They were too big for him, now. She'd not realized how much weight and muscle he had lost. Plopping down in the chair, he gazed at Salvarias.

"Do you hate him?" Wilhelm asked. "Because of what he did to Durak?"

She'd spent a lot of time contemplating that same question. She might have, but after seeing what the red fog had done, she doubted Salvarias's ownership of himself.

"No, I don't hate him."

Wilhelm's shoulders dropped and he exhaled a held breath. "And the others?"

"Humar's having a hard time with it, as is Neithelas. Okulu and Lunara are not."

"I almost lost him." Tears welled in his eyes. "I ... I can't lose him, Varila. I'm nothing without him."

Making her way around the cots, she straddled Wilhelm, lifting his gaze to hers. "I know," she said. "He can't lose you either. That's why he fought his way back to us. He's stronger than you give him credit for."

Warm, rough hands caressed her lower thighs. "Thank you for taking care of him."

Her heart stuttered at his touch. She'd missed his presence desperately, his smile, his smell.

A true smile touched her lips when she said, "He's my little brother, too."

He blinked at her, emotions sprinting through his eyes so fast she wasn't sure what she saw. Then his lips were upon hers, hands gliding her up thighs, him hardening between her legs. She returned his kiss with fervor, matching his longing.

Bolting up from the chair, he kept hold of her as he made his way to the door, her legs wrapped securely around his waist to help his trembling arms. He fumbled briefly for the door handle, stepped out of the room, and quietly closed the door behind him, all the while deepening his kiss. She pulled up for air and breathed out, "Two doors down," before succumbing to him once again.

He slipped into her room, slammed the door shut, and shoved her back against it. He took her like that: against the rough wood door, his hot breath on her neck, quickening with each thrust, his deep moans mingling with her soft cries of utter ecstasy.

Chapter 49

Winter 1018 a.r.

Wilhelm sat in the washroom, staring at his sleeping brother. It'd been a week since Wilhelm had awoken, and still Salvarias had yet to stir, to move, to twitch. Life was only the slight, rare rise of his chest and the faintest of life beat showing in his neck. He'd thinned to a skeleton, eyes sunken, rimmed by black, face gaunt and too pale. Blood trickling from his nose and ears had stopped a few days ago. Wilhelm took it as a good sign. He had to.

Tearing his gaze from his brother, he regarded the wolf. Adok paced the room, an occasional growl rumbling like distant thunder. As the days had passed, the wolf became increasingly annoyed, nipping at anyone other than Lunara and Wilhelm.

"I want to talk to you," Wilhelm said.

Adok paused midstep and turned his golden eyes to Wilhelm.

"Did you help him?" Wilhelm asked.

The wolf shook his head.

"You knew the puzzle box would help. What is it?"

Adok rolled his eyes.

Grinding his teeth, Wilhelm said, "Can't you talk to me like you talk to him? These yes-and-no questions will get me nowhere."

Adok shook his head.

Sighing, Wilhelm leaned back in his chair and regarded the wolf. "Did you make the puzzle box?"

Adok teetered his head back and forth.

"Whatever you are, you're inhabiting the wolf, right?"

Adok nodded.

"So what you were before, you made it?"

A nod.

"Was it made for him?"

No.

"But it helps him?"

Yes.

"Vuddruk said we're playthings to something out there. I assume it's a god?"

Adok tilted his head side to side.

"Something bigger?"

A nod.

"And it makes rules?"

Yes.

Wilhelm blew out a puff of air. "This is ridiculous." The wolf agreed. "Will Salv be all right?"

Adok turned sad eyes to Salvarias and shrugged.

"Are you a god?" Wilhelm asked, fear making his voice come out in a hoarse whisper.

Adok didn't look at him, didn't answer, which was answer enough.

"If the wolf dies, will you die?"

Adok shook his head.

"Do we even stand a chance against the ... thing trying to take over Arden?"

Adok lowered his head, shoulders stiffening. After a few heartbeats, the wolf shrugged.

The washroom door swung open and Varila sauntered in. She'd left her hair down, its mass catching the candlelight and brightening the room. Smiling at him, she took her usual seat by Lunara.

He watched her openly, admiring her seductive wink and her tan skin peeking between her boots and armored skirt.

"I wish this room had a window," Varila complained.

"What time is it?" Wilhelm asked.

"Morning. Okulu said he'd bring you breakfast."

Wilhelm's stomach growled in excitement. Luckily, he was packing on his weight with ease.

Lunara stirred awake, her hand still clamped to Salvarias's. The sight made Wilhelm smile.

He left the room while she washed and ended up eating his breakfast in the hall with Okulu. After Lunara was done, he rejoined the sisters, helped bath Salvarias, and then picked up a book. He didn't have the love of books Salvarias had, but he'd read since he could remember, and it gave his idle mind something to do. Varila sat behind Lunara on the cot, brushing her hair, both giggling and whispering.

Lunara's light laugh cut off suddenly. Peering over the top of his book, Wilhelm saw her gaze focused on Salvarias.

"What is it?" Varila asked.

"I ..." Lunara frowned. "I guess it was nothing. I thought his hand moved."

Wilhelm set aside the book and stared at Salvarias. "He's breathing faster."

Lunara shifted to face Salvarias and gently ran a hand through his wet hair. Behind closed lids, his brother's eyes started to move.

"He's waking up," Wilhelm breathed, heart racing, his joy springing to life.

Lunara groaned and pressed fingertips to her temple. "Gods, my head."

Salvarias jerked, and his eyes slowly opened. His gaze never quite focused as he hitched. Moaning, he rolled on his side and vomited.

Wilhelm rushed to Salvarias. "Salv?"

His brother's lips moved and Wilhelm had lean close to hear him. "H ... hel ... p."

Fear swatted away Wilhelm's joy. Taking Salvarias's left hand in his right, he pressed their marks together. Nothing happened. Glancing over his brother, he tilted his head to Lunara. "Let go of him."

When her touch left, Salvarias whimpered, eyes squeezing shut, and he threw up again. A tiny bit of Wilhelm's strength left him before Salvarias's hand went limp. Tears fell from his brother's eyes, and a drop of blood inched down his upper lip from his nose.

"What is it?" Wilhelm asked.

Salvarias curled up, dry heaved, but he'd barely eaten for the past month and nothing else came up. When he choked down a breath of air, he said, "My h ... head."

"It's unbearable," Lunara confirmed.

"Mix him something," Wilhelm demanded.

Lunara's face paled. "I don't have anything that could help this." She pressed her hand over her mouth, sweat beading her forehead.

"My ..." Salvarias exhaled sharply. "Spell book."

Without being asked, Varila hopped up and sprinted from the room. Salvarias tried to be sick, but only gagged, whimpers leaving him in a steady stream. Lunara paled with every breath.

Varila rushed back inside the room and deposited Salvarias's spell book in Wilhelm's lap. "I've got it," he said.

"Parch ..."

Lunara ran to the chamber pot and heaved.

"Parchment ..." Salvarias croaked.

Wilhelm shook the book, and a scrap of parchment fell out. He glanced at it, recognizing one herb. Once Lunara had emptied her stomach, he showed it to her.

She read it twice before nodding. "Get me his herb pouch and a kettle of hot water. It's a tea mixture."

"Is it safe?"

Lunara shrugged. "I don't recognize one of the herbs, but he wants to try it."

Varila darted out and returned quickly with Salvarias's herb pouch. "A servant is bringing in the kettle."

Lunara rummaged through the pouch, pulling out vials of liquids and leaves folded delicately in scraps of cloth. By the time the kettle had arrived, Lunara's hands shook violently. Even so, she managed to make the mixture and dumped it into the kettle. During that time, Salvarias had completely folded up, sobbing softly, a steady trickle of blood falling from his nose.

"Drink it," Varila told her sister.

"It's not my pain," Lunara said. She paused, pressing her fingers over her lips. After swallowing a few times, she said, "Mine won't end until his does."

Cursing his clumsy hands and the delicate cup, Wilhelm poured the tea, squatted beside his brother, and said, "It's ready, Salv."

His brother grabbed the cup and drained it before Wilhelm could even warn that the mixture was hot. Salvarias thrust the tea cup back to Wilhelm. "More," he wept.

It took three cups before Lunara recovered. Her cheeks were flushed, face still glistening, but her eyes held no pain. Taking the cup from Wilhelm, she helped Salvarias drink two more servings. Finally, by the last, his tense body relaxed into its normal curl. He breathed deeply, eyes closed, fists clenching and unclenching the blankets covering him. Silent tears trickled down his face.

"Why don't you give us some time alone," Wilhelm said to the sisters. "Let everyone know Salv is awake and all right, but no visitors."

Varila nodded and guided her protesting sister from the room. After they left, Salvarias opened his eyes. They were alert, focused, and carried more pain than the world could bear.

Forcing a grin, Wilhelm sat beside his brother, gathered him up in his arms, and whispered, "I'm proud of you, little brother."

Salvarias folded up, shoulders shaking with silent sobs. "I am losing myself, brother. Eventually I will fail."

Wilhelm stared up at the ceiling, tightening his arms. "As long as I'm here, it'll never get you."

"I want it gone," Salvarias said, his once silent tears breaking to loud sobs. "I want to be whole. I want Durak to be alive." He choked in a breath of air. "I am not strong enough. I-I cannot do this!" His voice rose, his sobs turning into a desperate plea. "Make it stop! I just want it all to stop!"

Thunder shook the home and echoed in the room. Rain drummed outside.

Wilhelm shut his eyes against his own tears, against the sharp pain in his heart, against his desire to do nothing more than ease his brother's burden. Rocking Salvarias gently, he said, "I know, Salv. And I promise, we'll find out what to do with the stone. We'll find out how to get rid of it. And I swear on all I hold dear that you're strong enough to beat it. I promise you that's the truth." Salvarias's cries softened and he sucked in a few steady breaths. Wilhelm filled his voice with conviction. "You're my baby brother, and you can do anything."

Varila gazed up at the sickly green clouds churning over the sleepy city of Lynta. The courtyard of Okulu's home was quiet, all keeping to the cover of nearby buildings, or huddled inside where fireplaces waged a losing battle against the cold. The streets were beginning to show the first signs of flooding, and the lake itself was rising to alarming levels. The rain had not stopped since Durak's death.

"It's so cold," Lunara said, drawing her cloak about her, huddling closer to the estate entrance and its cover.

"It is," Varila agreed. "But I've been itching for some fresh air."

"Me too," Lunara said. "It's been a long month."

"Soon we'll be home. Humar said we'll be leaving for Dalnar in the morning." Motioning to the clouds, Varila said, "Shouldn't this have stopped? Salvarias is awake, has been for a full day. He's eating, he stopped getting sick. He's sleeping. So why is the storm still here?"

Lunara rested her head on Varila's shoulder. "Salvarias is in pain. Guilt and grief own him wholly."

"Can't you do anything?"

"I wish," Lunara said. "I've tried to talk with him, but I doubt he even hears me."

"Wilhelm hasn't had luck either."

"I know." Lunara looked up at the sky, eyes dark and sad. "And the world will suffer as much as Salvarias."

"You really think he has that kind of control over Arden?"

"I do." A light smile touched Lunara's lips. "When he is happy, the world brightens. Like a weight is lifted from the air. Like a veil is pulled away from the sun. When he smiles, the world smiles with him. And when he grieves, the world grieves with him."

Varila couldn't deny it. She'd experienced the same sensations. "What could make a man have that kind of power?"

"A man?" Lunara laughed lightly. "Salvarias is no man."

Varila arched an eyebrow at her sister. "I never thought you would call him a monster."

"I never would. He's not a monster. Not even close."

"Then what?"

"I haven't figured it out yet. But there've been moments I've felt his power. It's more than magic, more than the blackfire he uses. I don't think he can feel it. And if he could, he'd probably be frightened of it. But ..."

When she didn't continue, Varila nudged her. "But what?"

"He shouldn't be. It's ..." Lunara closed her eyes, face relaxing to an expression of adoration. "It's beautiful, Varila. The most beautiful thing I've ever felt."

Chapter 50

Spring 1019 a.r.

Salvarias stood on deck of the ship, watching his hometown of Falar loom into view. The stone was warm in his hand, resting comfortably in his palm. Over the near month voyage from Windlous, Salvarias had spent a great deal of time studying the stone. He felt sorry for the previous Guardians, those who did not have the benefit of magic. Understanding power, Salvarias had been able to divide the forces within the stone. One wanted to destroy him while the other sought to help him. Uncovering their intentions let him tap into the stone's inner strength, its need to remain in the Guardian's possession. The other side of the power continually tried to manipulate him, tried to show him what horrors would be inflicted on those he loved should he not drop the stone into the ocean. Between the benevolent power in the stone and his own magic, they were able to keep reality stable. He knew the scenes of his friends' torture and death were nothing more than threats. He also knew if he were to cave to those threats, the suffering his friends would truly endure would be beyond what the stone had shown him. Sadly, the stone's strength could not help battle away his mother or Sansis at his side. Those two haunted him in his waking hours, but he had learned to tell himself they were not real. He did not wince when Sansis cut him with a knife anymore. He did not feel pain as he once did. His mother beat him, but her strikes lacked the conviction she used to show him. So he lived with his two nightmares constantly.

When he was not studying the stone's powers, he was enchanting it. His magic had been adamant they could do more to protect it, to hide it, and days of pouring over his spell book had achieved something spectacular. The stone was invisible. Completely. Both by feel and sight. No one could see it but Salvarias. No one could touch it but him. For the first time in the stone's life, it was hidden, safe. To help tame its potency, he had even enchanted a power-dampening spell. Those who could sense power would not sense the stone's. He used the spell on himself, subduing the sense of his power to that of an experienced mage, but one not as advanced as he truely was. Anyone meeting him would not attempt him harm, but likewise he would not attract unwanted attention. Because he could not sense his own power, he had done exactly as his magic instructed. It granted him a level of relaxation he doubted any Guardian had achieved before, which in turn gave him more of his mind to focus on controlling his own evil and fighting off the Hunters. Not once had he used Wilhelm, and for the first time since touching Perek, Salvarias had the upper hand in the battle for his soul. The tea mixture helped as well, calming his headache to manageable, although he required two cups a day. He was quickly running out of herbs, especially his mystery herb.

Of course, all he had done had one end goal: to leave his brother. Soon, he would set off on his own. It was a liberating feeling. No longer would he have to worry about hurting those around him.

Salvarias pocketed the stone and raised his hands in front of his face, turning them over, staring at their alienness. He had always hated his hands, and now the sight of them made him want to vomit. So clearly he could recall the feel of Durak's throat collapsing in his hands, of the old cavrul's skin melting to Salvarias's. Shuddering, he hugged himself, hiding away the horrid sight, battling back the memory.

Durak's death was a burden weighing more heavily than any of his responsibilities, and the memory of it could never be forgotten. He hated himself, and any time he looked in a mirror, it cracked from his pure emotion. How it did so, he did not understand. Nor did he care. Monsters, after all, were mysteries of the world.

He pulled his hood lower as the ship glided into Falar's harbor. Rain from the unhealthy green clouds had yet to stop since Durak's death. Salvarias knew he caused the storm, a result of his evil tainting the very world, but he had not been able to stop it, nor had Wilhelm's encouraging words. Though going off alone was certainly the right thing to do, Salvarias feared he would regret not having Wilhelm by his side to not only protect him, but to offer comfort when Salvarias needed.

You trussst me, do you not? the presence said. *You trussst me to sssave thossse you love?*

Salvarias closed his eyes, battling away the sudden onset of tears. The presence had spoken to him nearly nonstop since leaving Lynta, reminding Salvarias of the times it tried to warn him, of all it had done to save his friends. For his entire life, he had ignored its advice in that matter, and it had been Durak that had paid the price.

"Yes," he said. "I trust you."

You will not be alone, my little pet. I will love you; I will protect you from yourssself.

Hot tears fell down Salvarias's cheeks, mingling with the cold rain. "I know, my friend."

Wilhelm stopped Salvarias on the docks and adjusted his brother's cloak, concealing as much of the burgundy mage robes as possible. Salvarias stood despondent as usual, staring at the sprawling city of Falar. The docks were busy despite the rain. Sailors cursed and drank aboard surrounding ships, and merchants hauled stuffed wagons into the bustling streets.

Wrapping an arm around Salvarias's shoulders, Wilhelm led his brother after Humar.

"We'll split up," Humar said. "Wilhelm and Salvarias will come with me. The rest of you get supplies and settle the horses."

Adok whined, nuzzling Salvarias's hand. His brother patted the wolf's head absently, eyes still distant, head lowered.

As they walked down Market Street, Wilhelm inhaled the rotten odors that had always clung to the city. He couldn't help but smile at their familiarity. Some guards recognized him, but Wilhelm kept his hellos short, promising to catch up at a later date.

As they approached Mildred's shop, Salvarias looked up and his sudden stop made Wilhelm take a second gander at the store. The windows and door were boarded.

Waving to the nearest guard, Wilhelm asked, "Where's Milred?"

The guard sighed, shaking his head. "Sad day. It happened weeks ago. We found her in the shop tortured to death. I've never seen so much blood. The things they did to her ..."

Wilhelm tightened his arm, feeling Salvarias's entire weight sag under his hold. His brother's face was paler than snow, his eyes wide and brimmed with tears.

Nodding a goodbye, Wilhelm hurried his brother along, nearly carrying him until Salvarias's legs worked again.

"It wasn't your fault," Wilhelm said.

Salvarias's response was a roll of thunder, the sky flashing pulses of violent lightning.

Of course Humar's destination was Durak's smithy. Cursing under his breath, Wilhelm stopped a few shops down. "Go without us," he growled to Humar.

"Durak left something for you both in his shop," Humar said.

"It is fine," Salvarias said.

Muttering out a few more curses, Wilhelm followed Humar, holding tighter to his brother.

In the time they had been gone, the smithy had not changed save for the boards blocking windows from being broken and a new guard posted at the door whom Durak had hired to watch over his shop while away. A pang of loss ripped through Wilhelm at the sight of the cold forge. A few homeless men and women had taken shelter under the covered area. No one told them to leave.

Humar waved a hello to the guard, produced a key, unlocked the living quarters, and led the brothers inside. The darkness quickly vanished when Salvarias's sparrow bloomed to life. The home was unchanged save for a new layer of dust.

"He left the smithy to a cousin from Cattlar," Humar said, disappearing into Durak's room. There was a thud, and then the king returned. "But his fortune he left for you two. The old bastard had more money than Edium. I've already arranged for it to be transferred to Serinity. Edium will teach you both how to manage that large of an inheritance."

Salvarias didn't respond to the news, but Wilhelm knew his brother cared no more for the money than Wilhelm did.

Humar handed Wilhelm a dagger, obviously made by Durak's skillful hand. The carving in the fuller was a battle scene, small and detailed, where creatures of evil fell under the swords of Zerana's Army of Light. The handle had similar carvings. It was masterful piece, one that should be displayed, but its sturdiness was made for fighting.

"He crafted that for his son long ago," Humar said. "He thought it appropriate for you to have it."

Wilhelm accepted it, unable to form words, swallowing back his tears.

To Salvarias, Humar offered a book. It was written in the cavrul tongue, but Salvarias had learned to read the language years ago.

"This was his wife's most-prized book on herblore."

Salvarias gently took the book, hugged it closed, and said, "Thank you." With that, he slipped from Wilhelm's embrace and left the home.

"Guilt is—" Humar started, but Wilhelm cut him off.

"Durak was his friend, you ass. Didn't you see them sneak off together at night?"

Humar frowned, shaking his head.

Wilhelm looked down at the king, lip curling. "Salvarias took watch with Durak. They'd talk for hours. Salv loved Durak, and if you don't think what he did to the old man is eating him alive, then you never knew my brother. Never."

Wilhelm turned on his heel and marched out of the home. He found Salvarias outside, standing by the forge, rain soaking him. Inhaling a deep breath, Wilhelm went to his brother and folded him in a tight embrace.

"I'm so sorry, Salv."

His brother said nothing, but his shoulders began to shake and the softest whimper reached Wilhelm's ears.

Talura hummed her favorite tune, her needle weaving in and out of the slate-blue fabric, its steady pace taming her worry. Papers shuffled softly, Edium's quill scribbling away communications to the other cities. The war waged alongside the winsires had taken its toll. Arthias's death had been a devastating blow. The king and queen of the winsires were both on their deathbeds, and Talura assumed they only hung on to maintain their line until Neithelas arrived to take his rightful place. She pitied the young prince all he would face upon his return. His whole family would die, and he would be left to rule a kingdom he had not seen for over a year.

The single reason Edium's army had been successful was due to Mafarias. He joined with Edium midcampaign, and from what she heard, the spells he unleashed devastated entire hordes of creatures. Regardless, Edium still looked upon the mage with open hostility. Trust was not something her husband gave away. Even with Edium's cold welcome, Mafarias had insisted on staying with them until the boys returned.

Edium dropped his quill and flexed his fingers. "Damn cold," he muttered.

Spring had been lazy in driving away winter's lasting effects. The air was unseasonably cold, the breeze from the ocean gusty and angry. Clouds were always about, threatening a downpour, sometimes delivering. Today they had turned an unhealthy green hue, heaving like churning curdled milk. The rain they spat was viciously cold and sharp, more a weapon than the usual nurturing spring showers.

Edium took a sip of tea, grabbed his cane, and hauled himself up. It pained Talura to watch him hobble about. The gash across his thigh was healing slowly and twice had succumbed to infection. The healer had feared he'd lose it more than once. The cost of war, the healer had said.

After Edium stirred the fire, he plopped down in the closest chair. "It's got to be soon," he said, flicking her a quick smile.

Talura responded in kind. Humar's curt letters had estimated their return at any day. What little he had conveyed made her heart heavy. All the suffering her children had endured over the long winter was too much for anyone to handle, much less ones so young.

"It's not right," Edium said softly, barely loud enough for her to hear. "What they've been through."

"Mmm," she said, keeping her needle rhythmic.

"What do you make of what Salvarias did to Durak?"

Her needle wavered.

"The boy's never been ... normal," Edium continued. "Something's wrong with—"

"There's nothing wrong with him," she said, immediately aware how harsh her voice had been. Clearing her throat, she shot her husband a bland smile. "He's unique, dear. With unique problems. Unique gifts. We cannot begin to understand him. All we can do is offer our support and love. The young man needs it and we will give it freely."

She truly believed her words. Varila had confided in Talura via a letter she'd received a week ago. Of course Talura had shared the information with Edium. Her husband had seemed to take it all in stride, but now the moment was upon them, his uncertainties were showing.

For Talura, she had boiled it down as her daughter had done: Salvarias was fighting against whatever had fathered him. He wanted to be a good man. And he was a good man. A good man who sometimes did bad things, things he obviously regretted, things that ate him alive.

Edium saw a young man born of contradictions; he saw ugly cruelty blended with unparalleled compassion. Her husband could not understand the conflict raging inside Salvarias as she could. Edium was a man of black and white, good and evil. A person was one or the other. But the world was not so clear, and people were far from such simple confines.

A knock was followed by Brice saying, "They're here."

Talura and Edium shared a surprised look before both rushed from the room. Mafarias was with Brice, eyes sparkling with excitement. He bowed to them both.

"Most welcoming news, is it not?" he asked.

Ignoring him, Edium asked Brice, "How do they look?"

Brice grimaced. "Older. Sad."

When they left the estate and entered the courtyard, Talura took stock of everyone. They were soaked, shivering, and, as Brice had warned, older. Humar's mousy brown hair had lightened around his temples, probably streaked with gray only noticeable in bright sunlight. Neithelas stood aside from the group, withdrawn, his face long, his shoulders heavy. Okulu's roguish grin spread quickly in greeting, but it was his eyes that were duller than they had been a season ago. Wilhelm's smile was one of relief, as if he had just stepped foot in a place where nothing could ever harm him. Varila, standing by his side, shared the same smile. Lunara flew into Edium's arms before Talura got a look at her daughter's face, but by her white-knuckled grip, Lunara had truly suffered. Her hand was still bound in light dressing around the stumps of her two missing fingers. Anger bubbled up in Talura, and she forcibly withdrew her gaze before allowing it to consume her. If Neithelas was withdrawn, Salvarias might as well have not been there at all. His shoulders were folded forward, seeming to give him a shrinking presence. His usually lowered head now faced directly down, his chin almost touching his chest.

"I've missed you both," Lunara said, flying into Talura's arms.

"And we you," she responded. "You're freezing."

"The rains haven't stopped since ..." Lunara pulled away. Her smile lacked any conviction. Sorrow had mantled itself upon her, muting her once happy eyes.

Greetings were made, Mafarias spending extra time embracing Wilhelm. After all had said their hellos, Edium said, "Inside. Let's get out of this rain."

Talura waited for them to pass and fell in line by Salvarias, who followed last.

"It's good to have you home," Talura said.

Salvarias cringed from her and did not respond.

"The trip must have been arduous," she said. Still nothing. Inside, she stopped, folding her arms under her breasts. "Salvarias."

He stopped as well, back toward her, head lowered.

"I know what happened with Durak. Humar told us." No response. "It doesn't change my care toward you," she said gently. "If you should choose to unburden yourself, I'm here to listen, son."

The last word shook through him like an earthquake. Regardless, he did not acknowledge her.

"Your room is ready, as it always will be," she said. "I've missed you."

Instead of following the others, he turned right and headed to the stairs leading to his room. Adok padded behind the young man, casting her one of the saddest glances she'd ever seen from an animal.

She joined the others in the dining hall, all crowding around the fire.

Edium was saying, "You have the support of Serinity, my liege."

Humar waved a hand as if batting away a fly. "Just call me Humar, Edium. You're a good friend. Nothing's changed that."

"No," Edium said. He wrapped an arm around Varila's shoulders, pulled her close, and kissed her forehead. "But you are my king. We can't ignore that."

Humar ran a hand through his wet hair. "I've delivered the boy to you. I'm relying on your entire army to keep him safe. He has something, something very important. He needs protection, and no doubt many forces will try to get a hold of him."

"I'll protect him with my life," Edium said. He grinned at Wilhelm. "I heard you asked for my daughter's hand."

Wilhelm shifted a step back. "I would have asked your permission first, Edium, but—"

Her husband clapped Wilhelm on the shoulder. "Nonsense, boy. Varila makes her own decisions. I'd have had to ask her if you asked me first." He winked.

Wilhelm smiled. It lacked any real warmth. "Thanks."

"When should we have the wedding?" Edium asked. "Looks like you could all use some cheer. We could start the preparations."

"Oh no," Varila said, holding up her hand. "We don't want a big ceremony. Just our closest friends and family."

"Even so," Wilhelm said, "We need to wait until we get settled. Salv and I have a lot to discuss before—"

"They should wed tomorrow," Salvarias said from behind.

All eyes turned to the young man. He'd changed into dry clothes, his head slightly lowered to shield his eyes from view. His voice was light, but Talura knew it to be a ruse.

"Tomorrow?" Wilhelm said. "Salv, I think we need to talk about what's next. What you need to do."

Salvarias shrugged. "I have the stone. I have enchanted it to protect it and myself. I have not needed your strength for near a month. I am well in control, brother. Life must move on. There is no reason for you not to wed Varila."

Talura took note he had not said *Lady Varila*. Had he truly let her oldest in?

"But you said we'd have to hide," Wilhelm persisted. "Run."

"I was wrong, brother." He stepped forward and held out three vials of bright-green liquid to Edium. "For your wound, my lord. It will cure the infection and promote healing."

"Just Edium, son."

"You're sure?" Mafarias asked. "I don't think it's safe here. I can feel it."

Salvarias stiffened, raising his head ever so slightly to regard Mafarias. "Do you, Mafarias?"

The mage shifted his feet, glancing from Wilhelm to Salvarias. "I ... Well, I feel something ... a power."

"I see," Salvarias said. He bowed to the group. "If you will excuse me, I am tired from the journey." He looked at Wilhelm. "Tomorrow, brother."

With that, he quietly glided from the room.

512

"That was ..." Humar started.

"Weird," Okulu finished. "He's up to something."

Varila narrowed her eyes at Wilhelm. "What do you think?"

The young man leaned on a wall, rested his head against it, and closed his eyes. A few heartbeats passed before he inhaled deeply and cast Varila a crooked grin. "Guess you won't have time to wiggle your way out of this."

She grinned back. "Guess I won't."

"Tomorrow it is," Edium said.

Talura glanced at her youngest. Lunara's face was drawn in a frown, her gaze locked to where Salvarias had stood. Indeed, something wasn't right.

Chapter 51

Spring 1019 a.r.

Salvarias gazed across the table at Mafarias, half aware of the conversation the mage was having with Wilhelm. Poking at his breakfast of cooked oats, Salvarias recalled Mafarias's words from yesterday and Salvarias's own conversation with his magic. His magic had been certain no one should be able to feel the stone's power. That meant either Salvarias had failed, which he doubted, or Mafarias knew more than he should.

A hand resting on Salvarias's shoulder jolted him from his thoughts. "Salv?" Wilhelm said.

"My apologies," Salvarias said. "My mind must have wandered."

"I was saying," Mafarias said, "I don't think it right Wilhelm straps himself down to a wife, a family. Though you've trusted me with little information, dragging the Bellerums into this task doesn't sound wise."

"Thank you for your input, Uncle," Salvarias said, adding heat to the word *uncle*. "If you will excuse me, I would like to study."

"Want to go for a walk through the gardens instead?" Wilhelm asked.

"Of course, brother."

Without another word to their uncle, they left the dining hall and meandered through the estate in comfortable silence until finding their way outside. Salvarias had spent most of the previous evening trying to dispel the storm he had created. He would be damned if his brother married under such dreary weather. Though he had managed to get the rain to cease, the sky was still an ugly green.

They walked the garden in light conversation, Wilhelm's arm around Salvarias's shoulders. The simple gesture had always gifted him a lightness to his step, easing the burden of breathing and walking on his broken leg. Now it felt as if Wilhelm held Salvarias up, staining the once comforting feeling with his own weakness.

When the conversation lulled, Wilhelm tapped Salvarias's chin with one hand while the other pushed down the hood of Salvarias's robes. "There's something I want to tell you," Wilhelm said, voice low and serious.

Perhapsss he will finally voiccce his disgussst of you, the presence said.

"You are the most important thing in my life," Wilhelm said. "Above anyone. Even Varila. Nothing will ever change that. Do you understand me?"

Salvarias went to lower his head, but Wilhelm held Salvarias's chin, keeping his gaze locked on his brother.

"It's important you know that to be true," Wilhelm said. "You're my life, Salv. And not even a wife and children will change that."

"Brother—"

Wilhelm held up a hand. "No, don't tell me how wrong that is. I already know. It still doesn't change anything." He bent lower to hold Salvarias's gaze. "Do you believe me?"

Salvarias swallowed past the growing lump in his throat. "I do."

"I love you, little brother."

"I love you too, brother. More than anything, I want you to be happy."

Ruffling Salvarias's hair, Wilhelm said, "I am, Salv. I promise I am."

It was late in the afternoon hours when a group of servants gathered up Wilhelm and ushered him inside to be fitted for his wedding attire. Salvarias remained in the gardens, finding his favorite bench overlooking the ocean, and chatted with Adok.

It felt good to be here. Though Salvarias hated to admit it, this felt like home. A place of love and safety. Warmth. Here he did not feel so cold, so secluded from the world, so ... monstrous. Here he felt half human.

"Hello, boy," Lord Bellerum said from behind.

Salvarias clenched his jaw. He had been able to avoid Lady Talura and Lord Bellerum ever since his arrival. Shoving himself to his feet, Salvarias bowed. "My lord."

"Will you ever just call me Edium?"

"No, my lord."

Lord Bellerum sighed heavily, plopped down on the bench, and motioned Salvarias to do the same.

Gritting his teeth, Salvarias sat.

"Rain finally stopped," Lord Bellerum said.

"So it did. Is that what we are to discuss? The weather?"

"You know what I find interesting?" the lord said. "You have an abundance of politeness when it comes to others, no matter how they treat you, but several times you've been curt with me. I wonder why that is?"

"Perhaps it is because you refuse to leave me be." Though Lord Bellerum raised a good question.

Lord Bellerum chuckled. "True. I don't like this recluse side of you. My wife might tolerate it, as well as the others, but I think you need to be forced out of that shell you live in."

"You are not my father," Salvarias said darkly.

"No, no I'm not." Lord Bellerum turned his face skyward, smiling as if staring at the sun. "You don't have a father, do you? You have a donor."

Salvarias's entire body tensed.

"Yes, I learned the truth," Edium said lightly. "Shadowfires, huh? Must be ... difficult carrying around such knowledge. Oh, and what you did to Durak?" He shook his head. "Horrible, really. I admit, when I learned about it, I wasn't sure how I felt. It's a lot to take in. But then I saw you ..." The lord turned a steady gaze on Salvarias. "I saw you in that courtyard, and you know what I wanted to do?"

"Have me hanged in the gallows? Quartered, perhaps?" Salvarias said. "I wel—"

"I wanted to tell you what a remarkable man you are. I wanted to tell you that everything would be all right, that I was here, and I would protect you. I wanted to tell you I love you, son."

Salvarias bolted up from his seat.

"Sit down," Lord Bellerum commanded.

As with Lady Talura, his voice was heavy with parental control, that tone that made children obey. Salvarias sat.

"I would have done exactly as I wanted," Lord Bellerum continued, his voice once again light. "But Talura told me not to push you. To give you time. Well, I think that's a load of horse crap. The more we handle you like fragile glass, the thinner you'll become. I saw it in you just now. You need to be knocked upside the head with love, boy. You need to be bombarded by it until it beats you into submission, until you have no choice but to face the facts.

You're loved. My entire family loves you. Including Lunara, though hers is a different kind of love. Which brings me to my point. If you chose to, I give my permission for you to court her."

Salvarias rounded on the man, breathing hard and irregular, heart pounding loud in his own ears. "You are a fool," he growled. "To offer up something as pure as her to something as dark as me. And you are a bigger fool to think that at any point in my life I will accept your love. I do not need it. I do not want it."

He rose from his seat and made it a step before Lord Bellerum said, "What did Tobin do to you, boy? What did your mother do to you?"

Salvarias's steps faltered, a sharp pain at the memories burning tears in his eyes and gouging out his heart. "Go to Oblivion," he whispered, and left the gardens.

To Salvarias, the wedding was perfect. Only a group of twenty gathered in the gardens. He recognized his companions and Commander Brice, but the rest were strangers to him. Varila greeted them as if they were family.

She was stunning in a simple dress of white, her hair down, her smile beautiful. Wilhelm was also donned in wedding attire, the white doublet fitted to his large frame, his once overgrown beard expertly trimmed, crooked grin containing more happiness than Salvarias could have ever hoped.

The ceremony was conducted by the King of Arden and was blissfully short and poetic. Salvarias had never known Humar to be so well spoken, so lyrical. It had brought a tear to everyone's eye.

After it was done, Wilhelm was whisked away into the welcoming arms of the Bellerum family and their friends. His laugh boomed out several times, sparking Salvarias's smile to life.

Discreetly, Salvarias made his way from the crowd to the gardens overlooking the sea. Waves thundered lazily against the cliff, adding their own music to that of the trees. Closing his eyes, he listened, allowing it to imbue him with warmth and beauty.

"I get to officially call you baby brother," Varila said from behind.

Salvarias glanced over his shoulder. She was alone, smiling at him.

"So you can," he said.

She came to his side and asked, "What are you up to? I know you're planning something."

Salvarias turned fully to face her, allowing light to fall across his eyes. "My brother is happy, is he not?"

"Very."

"Then I am as well. As long as he is happy and safe, my happiness will surpass his. Do you believe me?"

"Yes." Her eyes narrowed. "What's this about?"

No matter what his mind concocted to confuse his emotions, he was certain of one thing. He smiled and with all his love he voiced it. "I love you, sister."

Her mouth dropped open, worked a bit, then a smile split across her face. "I love you too, baby brother."

"My brother ... is my life."

"I know," she said, her smile fading.

"Promise you will keep him happy?"

"I will."

Salvarias looked back over the ocean, drinking in the sight for what might be the last time. Once he had every detail firmly in place, he planted a quick kiss on Varila's cheek. "Thank you, sister."

Without waiting for a reply, he walked with determined purpose from the gardens toward his room. Adok nuzzled his hand.

"Stay with my brother," Salvarias said. "Keep watch over him tonight, my dearest friend."

Adok whined disapproval but bounded away.

What you are doing isss right, the presence said. *It isss hard, but it isss the only way to keep them sssafe, though it isss you who mussst sssacrificccce your happinessss. Truly, you are brave.*

Salvarias slipped into his room unnoticed, flicked his hand, and several candles burst to life. He jumped when Lunara emerged from the shadows.

"My lady," he said, bowing. "You left the party early."

"As did you." Her eyes flicked to the side, showing him she knew of his pack and its provisions. "Going somewhere?"

He had anticipated her interference. Gliding across the room to her, he snuck a hand in the pouch tied about his waist, searching for what he needed. "Perhaps. You should join the others."

She planted her feet firmly, hands clenched in tight fists at her sides, jaw set with determination. She was stunning. "I know you're up to something."

"As does your sister, and I assume everyone else." He stopped in front of her, amused and touched at the same time. "Do you think you can stop me?"

Her defiance faltered, her eyes darting to the side, mouth turning down in a frown. She recovered quickly. "I'll try, if I have to."

Sighing, he clenched his spell component in one hand and with his free one he reached out and touched her hair. He always marveled at its silkiness, how each strand weaved around his fingers. The candlelight played off the blue, purple, and green hues of black, creating a rainbow of color. It had always mesmerized him, and now was no different.

Her soft hand slid along his cheek. "Take me with you," she said.

Taking her hand in his, he pulled it back and studied it. Her fingers were long, slender, but her hand was small in his.

"I love you," she said.

Her words ripped through him like a tornado, devastating everything in its path, upturning all his emotions. Something pure loved him, something of light found a way to care for something of darkness.

In that moment, he wanted to kiss her and tell her he would never leave her, that he would protect her. The words were forming on his tongue when the white bandages around her missing fingers caught the light. He could not protect her, and the acknowledgment hurt more than anything he had ever suffered.

Pushing everything below his lake of indifference, he raised his gaze to hers. Lying was pointless. "I have loved you for years," he said. "But you must understand, though I love you more than my heart can bear, I cannot be with you." He whispered his spell and placed the owl feather in her hand. He caught her as she fell instantly asleep.

When Wilhelm woke in the late morning hours, he never remembered feeling so happy. His new wife lay in his arms, snoring softly, her tangled hair tickling his face. An entire city guard watched diligently over his brother's safety. They had a family, a home, something they'd not had since Salvarias was ten years old.

Closing his eyes, he inhaled deeply and let it out slowly, and with it, all his worries. Things would be better now. With protection and stability, he could finally focus completely on helping his brother overcome his fears. Soon, Salvarias would be laughing, married to Lunara, with children of his own. Wilhelm would see to it. It was a promise he made to himself.

A loud *bang* on his door was followed by Lunara yelling his name. Her tone sent a chill straight through him. Bolting from bed, he hopped into a pair of trews as he crossed the room. He flung open the door. Lunara's dress was rumpled along with her hair. It looked like she had just woken up.

"What is it?" he asked.

"He left!" Lunara cried.

Wilhelm shook his head, taking a step backward. "He wouldn't," he breathed. "He wouldn't leave me."

Even as he said it, he recognized the lie and the desperation behind it.

"He cast some spell on me," Lunara continued, seeming to toss aside his statement. "I woke up and he was gone. All his things. Adok's missing as well as Okulu."

Wilhelm shoved past her. He wasn't sure where his feet were taking him. People flocked around him, words buzzing like a beehive. He didn't hear anything above his own hammering heart.

His brother had left him. Alone.

Already a hole was forming in Wilhelm's heart, carved out painfully with a spoon, dull and horribly final.

He found himself in the stables grabbing Lilly's mane, trying to hoist himself up on her bare back. Hands were pulling on him, voices ringing all around. A wave of dizziness washed over him, twisting and turning horses and faces until he was overcome with it all. Air was as elusive as a fleeing hummingbird. His vision blackened.

His brother had left him. Willingly. Purposefully.

Through the cacophony of voices, a few words reached his ears: "He left you a note."

Wilhelm forced himself to breath deeply, sharply sucking in air. Blinking back his vision, he saw parchment clutched in Lunara's hand. He took it, shaking violently enough that Varila helped break the seal and unroll it. Inside, his brother's perfect handwriting flowed across the page.

My Dearest Brother,

You must know I love you. My entire life you have watched over me, gifted me everything I needed. Now it is time for you to have what you need. Varila, the Bellerum family, the knighthood, are all things that you deserve, that you should embrace. You can make a change in Arden. You can help mages. With Durak's money, you can build the knighthood to what it was supposed to be. It is your destiny. One I wish you to pursue with all the dedication you have shown for me.

I must find answers to my questions. I must find myself. To do so, I need to be on my own. I <u>want</u> to be on my own.

Please know you will never find me should you try. All you will accomplish is a delay in taking your rightful place. I have shown you my own strength, how I have contained the evil, how I have mastered the Hunters. You have nothing to fear. I will be safe on my own. I will be happy.

I beg you, let me go.

Salvarias

Rage exploded. His vision went red with it. His roar was one of sheer fury. He unleashed it all on whatever was around him.

When spent, he found the stables in disarray. Wooden stalls had been torn apart. Hay was everywhere. The remains of barrels littered the floor. All the horses had fled. His knuckles were bloody and raw.

"Wilhelm," Mafarias called.

Edium and Mafarias peered in from outside.

"It's your fault," Wilhelm panted. "You pushed him, Edium. You prodded until you broke him." His voice crescendoed with each word. "And you!" He pointed at Mafarias. "He's scared of you. Always has been. You tell him all the time he has to leave everyone. And now he has! He's out there alone! Unprotected!"

Varila stepped into view, cast Mafarias a sneer, and turned a steady gaze to Wilhelm. "None of that matters now. We have to find him. Where would he go?"

Wilhelm clenched his fists. "I don't know."

"It'd be a place he felt safe," Talura said, emerging from behind Varila. "A place accepting of mages."

"Windlous," Lunara said.

"I assume he won't talk to you?" Varila asked her sister.

Lunara shook her head. "He's blocked me out completely. I can only sense he's alive."

"Father," Varila said, her tone crisp and businesslike. "Gather a small guard. We leave for Falar." When no one moved, she clapped her hands. "Now, people!"

Everyone dispersed except for Varila. She walked up to Wilhelm, staring him dead in the eyes. "We *will* find him. And we *will* bring him home."

Something inside Wilhelm cracked and tears blurred his wife, but her arms were strong around his waist, holding him up when all he wanted to do was crumble to the ground.

Chapter 52

Spring 1019 a.r.

Salvarias reined in Mithal outside the bustling gate of Falar. The past five days of travel had been arduous, not only for himself but for Mithal as well. The horse was near exhaustion, but promise of a month's rest seemed to give Mithal unnatural endurance.

"Let us try to enter the city unnoticed, my friend," Salvarias murmured to Mithal.

The horse nickered out an agreement and fell in line with a wagon train. Covering as much of his robes as possible, Salvarias lowered his hood and tried to blend in with the crowd. He nearly made it through before a familiar voice called his name. Cursing under his breath, Salvarias lifted his head and regarded Sir Idolar.

"Salvarias," Idolar said again. His gaze surveyed the wagons. "Where's Wilhelm? You two are never apart."

Salvarias shoved away the sharp pang of guilt and said, "He is married to Varila Bellerum and living in Serinity."

"That's wonderful!" Idolar said. "Still doesn't explain why he isn't with you."

"I have been seeking a gift for his wedding," Salvarias said, surprised at how easily the lie came to him. "It has taken me many months to find it, but now I know where it is, I would prefer to surprise him. I would appreciate it if you told him I went to Hadrium should he come asking for me."

Idolar smiled. "Of course. I'll send him that way. He'll figure it out sooner or later, though."

"Later I hope. Thank you again, Sir Idolar."

"Anytime, Salvarias. Be sure to find lodgings early. There are reports of a large storm between here and Windlous. It should catch us in another day or so, and the inns will fill up quickly."

"Are ships sailing?"

Idolar shook his head. "None of the smart ones. You're crossing the sea for this present?"

Salvarias shrugged. "My destination is part of the secret. Thank you for the news." Salvarias bowed in his saddle and entered his former home.

After stabling Mithal, Salvarias headed to the docks, hood pulled low, thick cloak hiding his robes. When he arrived, he looked for Captain Ingil. He found him fighting another man and waited patiently for him to finish. After kicking some teeth out of the younger sailor and breaking the man's arm, Ingil muttered colorful curses and pushed through the crowd.

"Gentleman Ingil?" Salvarias called as the man passed.

His eyes grew wide with recognition. "I remember you! You saved my ship."

Salvarias bowed slightly. "Yes. I was hoping to purchase fair to Windlous for my horse and myself."

Ingil frowned. "There's a storm out there and no one is sailing."

"It is imperative I leave at once."

Ingil's gaze swept over Salvarias's shoulder. "Where's that brother of yours? Seemed might protective of you last time ye sailed with us."

"Married," Salvarias said evenly. "I travel alone."

Ingil nodded. "All right. Three gold and we'll leave before dinnertime." Ingil grinned. "Hopefully we survive the seas. Springs storms are not to be trifled with."

"I trust your expertise," Salvarias said. "If my brother does happen to show, I offer five additional silver if you deny seeing me."

"Ten," Ingil countered.

Salvarias counted the funds. "Two gold now, one upon arriving in Windlous."

Ingil spit in his hand and held it out. Salvarias tilted his head politely. "I trust you, Ingil." He dropped an extra silver onto the man's palm and went off to find a quiet place on the docks to enjoy an apple and read a book.

He found himself suddenly questioning his course. Wilhelm would certainly come looking for him. His brother was a determined man. Varila would not be able to stop Wilhelm.

Remember, my little pet, the presence said. *You run to protect him. Yesss, he will follow. But when he cannot find you he will return home. He will ssstart his life. He might be sssad in the beginning, but with you gone he will realizzze all he hasss missed in life. He will finally be free of your burden.*

Salvarias inhaled a deep breath. The presence was right. Alone, Wilhelm would find happiness. Alone, Salvarias would find answers. It was best for everyone.

Indeed, my pet. You're finally thinking of othersss besssidesss yoursssself.

Wilhelm and his friends reached Falar late in the evening. Traffic had died down and guards lounged lazily against Falar's walls.

As Wilhelm approached the gate, Idolar stepped out of the guardhouse, smiling. "Wilhelm! Edium!"

"My brother's gone missing," Wilhelm said, gaze locked beyond the gate to the busy streets. "Have you seen him?"

Idolar's smile faltered. "He stopped by here on his way to Hadrium."

"Hadrium?" Wilhelm asked, surprised.

"Congratulations on your marriage."

Wilhelm grunted his thanks and nudged his horse forward but Idolar caught the reins.

"You don't look like a happy man. For one recently married, you seem less than pleased," Idolar said.

"My brother is in danger. I'm not happy."

Idolar bit his lip and his gaze swept toward the city. "Danger?"

Wilhelm stifled a growl. "He told you to lie to us, didn't he?"

Idolar nodded.

"How many days ago?" Wilhelm asked.

"It was just this morning. I haven't seen him leave the city. He still must be inside. Do you want me to gather the guard and start a search?"

"Yes," Edium said. "The boy must be found."

Idolar inclined his head to Edium. "As you say. I ..." He looked apologetically at Wilhelm. "I would have kept an eye on him if I knew. He seemed fine."

Wilhelm exhaled heavily, allowing the words to lift a small burden from his shoulders.

"Have you seen a half-winsire or the black wolf that stayed with Wilhelm?" Edium asked.

"The wolf, no, but then again, he could have snuck in. A half-breed did pass through here this morning. Matter of fact, he was waiting outside when the gates opened. He looked travel-worn and his horse died shortly after he arrived. Pushed the beast to death."

"Okulu must have caught up," Edium said. "He'll detain Salvarias."

Varila shook her head. "He's Salvarias's friend. He'll go with him, not tell him to stay."

"She's right," Humar confirmed.

"I think he means to take a ship," Idolar supplied. "He was asking if any were sailing."

Wilhelm's heart lurched. Dropping Lilly's reins, he bolted through the gate, shoving his way through the evening crowd as he sprinted toward the docks.

Salvarias glanced around the docks, searching for familiar faces. When certain it was clear, he left cover and strode straight to the ramp leading up to Ingil's ship. He made it a few steps up the ramp before something grabbed the hem of his robes. Looking down, large golden eyes glared at him. The wolf's lecture started immediately.

"You cannot come," Salvarias said. He handed Mithal off to a sailor and then walked down the ramp, Adok following. At the bottom, Salvarias knelt level with the wolf. "I need you to protect Lunara and look after my brother. You cannot go where I go."

He rose, but Adok stubbornly refused to be left behind.

"I am sorry, my dear friend," Salvarias said. He chanted his spell, flicked out his rune, and walked up the ramp. His tears built as Adok howled against the spell holding him in place.

Once aboard, he motioned for Ingil to cast off. Adok's howl turned to horrible whines, as if he had been wounded. Salvarias could not bear the sight and closed his eyes.

It seemed an eternity before the ship slowly pulled away from the dock. As it did, Salvarias released his spell. Adok paced the edge of the dock, whining, looking first to the water and then the ship.

"Do not—"

Before Salvarias finished, the wolf jumped into the freezing ocean. Panic nearly stole Salvarias's breath. He called to Ingil, hearing fear in his shrill voice. Nets were tossed overboard, sailors shouting to one another as they tried to coordinate their efforts. Salvarias paced, staying out of the sailors' way, worry gnawing at his gut.

When the wolf was dumped on deck, Salvarias rushed to the beast and flung his arms around Adok's neck. "You fool!" he scolded, draping his cloak around the shivering wolf.

"Actually," a familiar voice said from behind. "You're both fools."

Salvarias slowly looked over his shoulder. He tried not to smile, but one snuck out. "What does that make you?"

Okulu grinned and winked. "The smart one."

Wilhelm watched the ship shrink on the horizon, the setting sun silhouetting it. His anger festered like an infection, seeping in so deep it flowed with his blood.

Whirling around, he glared at the docks and sailors. "I need a captain that can sail now! I'll pay!" he roared. All eyes focused on him, but none spoke. "Cowards! One sailed. Will no others follow?"

A tall, lean watythm stepped forward. "The storm has worsened. Ingil is a fool."

"Ten gold to the captain who will take me," Wilhelm said.

Heads shook.

Edium held up a heavy purse. "Twenty gold."

Watythms glanced at one another, but it was the lean man who raised his hand first. "I'll need time to prepare."

"We have horses," Edium said. "There are seven of us. How soon?"

"A day. We leave early tomorrow."

"Why not now?" Wilhelm snapped.

"I need time to gather supplies," the man said. "Our journey will be an extra week because I'll have to sail around the storm."

"Will Ingil?" Edium asked.

"Ha! That old fool will sail right through it. I'll not do the same. No amount of money could make me."

Wilhelm growled and turned his back on the affair, gazing at the speck of the ship taking away his brother.

Chapter 53

Spring 1019 a.r.

Varila hastened after Wilhelm, trailing in his wake as he shoved people aside. They'd just arrived in Windlous at the city of Bellend, and Wilhelm had disembarked without a word or care for their horses. The others were busy tidying up business with the ship captain, which left Lunara and Varila alone with her husband.

Over the trip at sea, Wilhelm had deteriorated into a mess of man. He was unkempt, cold and brooding, and refused to engage in conversation with anyone, including his own wife. So far, married life was not what Varila had expected. Then again, if it were Lunara that had run away, she wouldn't have acted any differently.

When they entered the Hanged Man, the tavern was the same as Varila remembered. Tables and chairs wobbled and the stench was enough to turn off any appetite.

Wilhelm's gaze combed over the common room until resting on a man behind the bar. He cringed from Wilhelm's cold stare.

Varila stepped in front of her husband and made her way over to the barman. "Greetings," she said.

He licked his lips and tore his gaze from Wilhelm. "My lady. By chance, is that Wilhelm Laybryth?"

"What if it is?"

"I've a message for him from a man named Okulu," he said.

She didn't need to motion Wilhelm over. He'd heard.

"What is it?" he asked as he approached the barman.

"He said to tell you they left for Alt not but six days ago. He said he would try to delay your brother, but you'd better hurry."

Wilhelm narrowed his eyes. "That's it?"

The barman nodded vigorously. "I swear on my mamma's life."

Wilhelm turned to leave, but Varila stepped in his path. "I know you want to head to Alt right now, but we need to gather supplies. It'll do us no good if we starve to death on our way there. And it's almost night. We won't make it far before we'll have to stop. Okulu will stall Salvarias."

Wilhelm ground his teeth, but voiced no argument.

KEEPERS OF ARDEN

They booked rooms at the inn and partook of the congealed stew offered for dinner. Wilhelm ate little, his gaze distant and sullen. Varila didn't wait long before she led him up to their private room. As he did every night, he curled up on a bed, not bothering to remove his armor, and slept.

She snuggled next to him, missing his arms and warmth, his presence. What lay beside her was not the same man she married a month ago.

No sooner did sleep call to her than Wilhelm thrashed wildly, soft whimpers fluttering from his throat. Shaking his arm, she called his name.

"Salv!" he cried, sitting straight up, eyes popping open. His breath came in sharp gasps as his gaze darted around the room.

"Easy," she said.

He ran a shaking hand over his face and plopped backward. For the first time since Salvarias ran away, Wilhelm looked at her, really looked at her.

"I can't do this," he breathed. "I can't live without him. I love you. I do. But he's my life."

"I know," she said. Jealousy had no home in her heart.

Wilhelm closed his eyes. "I'm so sorry. I wish ..."

"Shhh." She rested a fingertip on his lips. "I knew it before we married. I accepted it as who you are. And I would love you less if you were any different."

"I don't deserve you," he said.

"Who does?" she said playfully. Turning her tone serious, she said, "You can't go on like this. We will find him, and when we do, what will he say? How guilty will he feel when he looks at you?"

He was still for a moment, then he exhaled slowly. "I'm sorry. I'm so sorry. Forgive me?"

"Give me a reason," she purred.

He did. Twice.

Chapter 54

Spring 1019 a.r.

Salvarias tossed yet another useless book on the table. They had arrived in Gilrin late last night, and as exhausted as Salvarias was from the journey from Alt, he could not sleep once the sun brightened the rolling green clouds. The inn Okulu had chosen was clean, the room spacious for the two of them and Adok, but Salvarias's frustration chipped away any joy he might have had for the comfortable bed.

He glanced at Okulu sprawled out on the second bed, snoring softly. Adok slept soundly, feet twitching from a dream. Salvarias already knew the location of the bookstore, thanks to the tour Okulu had given last night. He could let his friend sleep and find what he needed on his own.

Slipping from the room, he made his way out of the quiet tavern and into the sleepy city streets. He did not bother hiding his mage robes. There were few people out, and in all his travels through Windlous, no one had spat on him.

Passing an alley, he caught sight of orange robes. He only cast a cursory glance in the direction. Sansis stood in shadows, eyes tracking Salvarias. He reminded himself it was not real and kept his breathing calm and steady. Despite his efforts, his heart still ached.

When Salvarias arrived at the bookstore, the owner had just opened his doors. The man was an erthla mixed with octril, his skin more scales than flesh, one arm containing two forearms. He was old, white hair cut short, face clean-shaven.

"Welcome," he said, ushering Salvarias inside. "Chilly morning, isn't it?"

Salvarias bowed. "Indeed, gentleman."

"What brings you out so early?"

"I am looking for any books you might have on the goddess Zerana."

The man's eyes sparkled. "You've come to the right place, my dear boy. I have a few." He listed off five books Salvarias had already read. When told as much, the old man's eyes narrowed. "You're a student of learning, aren't you, lad?"

"I am."

"You speak and read cavrul?"

"I do."

The man grinned. "Smart boy, eh? I have one book I, uh, borrowed from a merchant traveling to Cattlar. It's an old one, this book. It's a written copy in cavrul of a book found ages ago and since lost to us. It's not for sale, but if you'd like, I can set you up in the back room. You can read it there." The man looked up sheepishly. "I hold a fascination with Zerana, or else I would sell it to you."

"I would be eternally grateful just to read it," Salvarias said.

He followed the man down a short hall and into a reading room. A table and chair situated by a window took up most of the space, leaving only a small walkway to the outside garden. The man lit a few candles and retrieved a wooden box from a wall mounted shelf. He pulled out a book wrapped in cloth.

"Here it is, young man." He placed it on the table and patted the chair. "Stay as long as you like."

"Again, thank you for your kindness."

"Bah, it's rare to find one so young interested in learning. It's my pleasure to help."

After the man left, Salvarias seated himself, fingers itching to touch the book. A shadow moved across the light streaming in from a window. Salvarias glanced up. Sansis stood, gazing inside. Sighing, Salvarias turned his attention back to the book.

Most of it was a recount of a woman's life. She had survived the Retribution and had left Cattlar with her newborn and husband, who met his fate shortly thereafter. Frustration at yet another failed attempt to find Lunara answers nearly made him toss the book aside, but he continued. The last page paid him extensively for his persistence.

~ ~ ~

A darkness is creeping across our world. It sits in my stomach like a bad meal. And here we are, fragile, as new as we are old. Only now has the ground stopped trembling, only now have the mountains ceased spitting death, only now have the oceans calmed. Nevlar's Retribution has finally ended, but what festers in our land I fear will be our end.

She cries in my dreams: my mother, my sister, my creator, my goddess. She is held captive in a desolate land, alone and afraid, trapped in hungry darkness. I must find Her. I must save Her.

I fear we have all been fooled, none more than my beloved father. Nevlar's anger was too great to see truths. And now, his children must pay the price.

My baby and I are the last of our kind. I am alone in my mission. I will likely die. My goddess is too weak to protect me. She wants me to hide, but I will not. I love Her too much to leave Her to such a dark end. No, I will find Her, I will save Her, and then She will save us. I must believe this or all is for not.

I will entrust my baby to a friend, and I pray to see my daughter again. I hope she lives long enough to have children of her own, to pass along her gift and mark, to keep hope alive. If I should perish, it falls to her to find our goddess and save Arden. Such a weight for a child to carry. My poor baby girl. The last cleric of Zerana.

~ ~ ~

He sat back in his chair, eyes wide and mind stumbling to process all those two pages had gifted him. A click made him jump. Sansis glided into the room. Salvarias ignored him, turning his attention back to the pages.

"Hello," Sansis whispered.

Again, Salvarias paid the image no attention.

"Ah, do you think I'm not real, my son? Do you think I was killed in the desert?"

The image had tried this ploy before. During Salvarias's time in Zeeas, it had become clear that Sansis had grown infatuated with Salvarias, thinking of him as a son, carving him up with what Sansis referred to as love. Salvarias had no illusions that the man had died in the forsaken barbarian desert. But Sansis could not be standing here now. He could not have found him. Regardless of willing it to be true, Salvarias shifted in his seat. He smelled old skin.

"Truly I am blessed this day," Sansis said. "For the first time, you left your friend's side."

Salvarias told his body to stay still, but when Sansis drew a knife, Salvarias cringed. Closing his eyes, he repeated it was not real. The last thing he needed was his evil to surface, or for the Hunters to attack him. He had to remain in control.

White-hot pain shot up Salvarias's side. He exhaled sharply, doubling over. Pressing a hand to his side, he found warm blood matting his robes. The image had not caused him pain since he had mastered his hallucinations.

Sansis rammed the knife in three more times, quick like.

"You see," Sansis whispered in Salvarias's ear. "I never left you, son. I never abandoned you. I knew all I had to do was wait. I knew one day you would be alone. And here you are. I have so much planned for you. So much."

The room blurred in and out. Sweat trickled down Salvarias's forehead even as cold ran through him. He lurched from his seat and immediately fell to the floor. Sansis stuck the knife in Salvarias's lower back, causing him to give the softest cry. A tingle shot up his spine. When it passed, Salvarias could not feel his legs.

"There, there," Sansis whispered. "We don't want any attention."

Salvarias's vision pulsed, his head feeling as if it floated up and up, detached from his numb body.

"Yes," Sansis hissed. "Sleep, my son. When you wake, we can pick up where we left off."

Salvarias whimpered for his brother, and then haunting darkness claimed him.

Wilhelm burst into the tavern, gaze sweeping over the occupied tables and the shadows where the fireplace light could not penetrate. They'd missed Okulu and Salvarias in Alt by five days. Now, here in Gilrin, he swore if they hadn't caught up he was going to lose his mind.

"Wilhelm!" Okulu called.

The merc was bolting down the stairs two at a time. Okulu's wild eyes nearly stopped Wilhelm's heart. Something had happened.

"He disappeared," Okulu blurted, crossing the room to join Wilhelm. "He left five mornings ago while I was sleeping. I ..." Okulu shook his head. "I shouldn't have told him where the bookstore was. If I'd made him wait, I would've been there. But I didn't think he'd go off on his own. Things were going well. He never left my side the whole time. I swear it!"

"You have no idea where he went?" Edium asked.

"No, but I asked the bookstore owner. He said Salvarias was reading in the back room. When the old man went to check later in the afternoon, Salvarias was gone and there was ... blood. A lot of blood."

Wilhelm glanced at Lunara. She'd grown paler over the past few days.

"I've been asking around, but no one has seen him," Okulu said. "The wolf was gone too, but the bookstore owner never saw him."

Motioning to Lunara, Wilhelm asked, "Can you find him?"

"Perhaps, with time," she said.

Time wasn't something they had.

"You can," Lunara said.

Wilhelm narrowed his eyes. "What do you mean?"

"Your relationship with him has changed," she said. "I've seen it. You two can speak to each other across a forest. You hear him. This bond you two share has grown. Certainly, if you try, you can find him."

She wasn't wrong. When Wilhelm had used their marks to get inside Salvarias's mind, it had muddled their thoughts together for weeks. Perhaps he could tap into that feeling again.

Closing his eyes, he thought of his brother. It took him several long moments before he realized his feet were twitching to move. Walking from the tavern, he relinquished control of his legs to some inner part of himself. As he strode down the street, a new feeling blossomed in his chest, as if someone had tied a rope around his heart and pulled it in the same direction his feet wanted to move.

"Okulu!" a voice squeaked.

Wilhelm looked over his shoulder at a young octril boy running up to the merc. The others had apparently followed Wilhelm.

"What have you found?" Okulu asked, tossing a coin at the boy.

"A wagon left the city five days ago," the boy said between gasping breaths. "One of my friends swore he saw blood on the back."

"Where did it go?" Edium asked.

The boy pointed in the direction Wilhelm had been walking. "Out that gate. An old man in orange robes drove it."

Wilhelm's heart dropped to the ground. Cursing, he bolted for Lilly.

Chapter 55

Spring 1019 a.r.

Salvarias gazed absently at blood steadily dripping from his fingers. The thin thread binding his fingers against drawing runes had cut through his skin over the time he had been Sansis's prisoner. His wrists were raw from the shackles stained brown by old blood. Pain should have owned him, but some part of Salvarias's mind had taken him far away until pain was a distant sensation, like soreness from a long day plowing fields. The hole in his side had stopped bleeding excessively, blood crusted over the nubs of his two newly missing fingers—his right hand, so there was no chance they would grow back—and the only evidence of his many disembowelments was a new scar and the constant vomiting he no longer paid mind to.

A part of him was aware of his stench, of how he was covered in his own filth. Sansis did not seem bothered by the smell or mess. He hummed a lullaby, eyes alight with madness. The sight chilled Salvarias every time.

Sansis sighed heavily from his seat upon a stool at Salvarias's side. "You must cave to me eventually. It would be easier for both of us if you accepted your fate. No one will come to save you. Not your brother. The girl. The king. The merc. None of them." Sansis frowned. "Well, maybe your grandfather, though he would not do so out of the kindness of his heart. Matter of fact, we should hope your grandfather doesn't find you."

Salvarias's gaze flicked over to Sansis.

The old man smiled, showing yellow teeth. "You did not guess yet, son? Think, boy. Think. Who around you could be your grandfather? Who cared for Ashra as a daughter? Who visited you?"

Salvarias's eyes widened with realization.

"Yes," Sansis purred. "Mafarias tried to play both sides, but now he's been forced to choose. They found out all the little help he's given you. Did you know the reason he stayed with Ashra was to ensure she didn't kill you? And before he left, he urged her to help you. He sent the men to kill Ashra so her abuse would stop, against all God wanted. He even secretly ended Humar's contract, allowing the knight to return to Falar upon your parents' death so you both would not be alone. He did all this even as he worked alongside us. He was one who betrayed Wilhelm when your brother was looking for you at Zeeas. He was the one who set up portals in the Cattlar mountains so we could infiltrate the city through the caves." Sansis smoothed Salvarias's hair. "How does his betrayal feel, my son? It hurts, does it not? I would never betray you as he did. I would never run off with a woman as your brother did. I would never put you in danger like Humar has done. I would never abandon you as Durak did."

When Salvarias remained quiet, Sansis sighed and rose from his stool. "I'll be gone a little while. I have to go find you some food."

The mention of food pushed bile up Salvarias's throat. He had no strength to bother with it. It streamed out the sides of his mouth, hot and acidic, until he choked on it.

"There, there," Sansis said, his lips pulled back in a caring smile. He kissed Salvarias's forehead. "Just rest, son."

The old man went out of sight, and the door creaked opened, then squeaked closed. Salvarias closed his eyes. He might have cried. He might have begged for his brother. He might have cursed his grandfather. He was not sure what he did. His body was no longer his own. Sansis's vile power had molested him, touched him in ways that would always haunt him, that drove his mind to the brink of insanity. All that mattered was that Salvarias fought, just as he had promised his brother he would. He did not cave to the evil. He did not cave to the Hunters, though he had lost several battles. Sansis was a man that could not be killed, so despite his age he had bested every creature sent to kill them. Salvarias wondered if the man enjoyed it. There was a disturbing gleam in Sansis's eyes after a fight. The few wretched creatures that survived the initial encounter went squealing into death under Sansis's knife. The old man did not heal them as he healed Salvarias. He let them bleed out, carved them up like Durak used to carve sticks.

Salvarias was not sure how long he lay there, staring at his dripping blood, mind numb and aware at the same time. A loud crash jerked his gaze toward the sitting room. Glass splattered the ground, and crouched in the middle of the room was a massive wolf, golden gaze sweeping over the room.

Tears blurred his vision and a pathetic rasp issued from his lips. "Help me."

Adok padded into the room, glanced at Salvarias's bindings, and went to work on the thread tying together the fingers of his left hand. Once the wolf had chewed through it, Salvarias flexed his fingers, crying out as he did. Gods, the pain.

Adok burst into urgent commands. Sansis was coming back.

Groaning from the effort, Salvarias choked out a spell and fumbled a rune. The stiffness of his drawing made the energy burn like a too-hot bath, but it worked. The metal shackles thudded to the wood floor.

Salvarias rolled himself off the table he had been strapped to, landing in a coil of agony. Temporarily blinded by all the sharp jolts of fire-hot pain, he suddenly realized he had more wounds than what he initially thought. It did not matter though, so he pushed away the awareness of them, not allowing his eyes to obtain facts.

Adok pawed at another door, whining. Using furniture in the room, Salvarias dragged himself across the floor, slowly gaining strength. Fear played a major role in his ability to crawl on his hands and knees. By the time he reached the door, he used the knob to help pull himself to his feet. One blurry image of his staff and it appeared in front of him. He latched hold and staggered outside into the freezing rain. Opening his mouth, he let it wash out the rancid taste and coat his throat in the sweetest sensation he could remember.

Adok whined again, padding in circles and urging Salvarias to the woods. He managed small steps, using his staff to replace his broken foot.

Time passed slowly, agonizingly so. The rain never stopped, but Salvarias did not care. He welcomed it and the cleansing it provided. He was naked, though he hardly cared about that either. All his focus was on following Adok.

Night blended into day and night again. At one point, his body gave out. He lay in mud, curled up and hugging himself, shivering despite Adok's body draped over his. Pain started to push into his awareness. Headaches were the first to start. They pulsed his vision and strained his mind until he sobbed openly, unable to keep anything in. Fighting his evil became harder, the Hunters impossible.

He must have passed out at some point. He woke to Adok's barked warning. There were five octrils running for him, curved knives held aloft, crying out in victory. One spell killed them before they made it within stabbing range. Forcing himself up, he followed Adok again, walking half awake, focusing on his evil.

It was evening when Adok growled again. Whatever hunted them rammed into Salvarias, taking him to ground and pinning him there. The stench of wet fur assailed him. Adok leapt on the creature, his momentum knocking the beast off Salvarias. As Adok ripped into the beast's jugular, another one fell on Salvarias, all claws and teeth. He fought as best he could, but his body was simply too weak.

A vicious growl from Adok was followed by a flash of white teeth, then the creature on Salvarias stiffened and fell away.

Again, Salvarias forced himself to his feet and walked. He shuffled onward, not knowing if it was day or if the moon imbued the clouds with light. The storm made everything dark. Made shadows come to life.

Before long, they were attacked again. Vaguely he realized these beasts had swords, jagged and cruel-looking weapons made for tearing. Gathering up energy, he sent ice shards at the three charging him. They screeched inhumanly when they fell and died. Another five of the same shaggy creatures were sprinting for him and Adok. The wolf let out a horrible growl full of defiance and anger, and then rushed to meet the charge. Leaping on the creature in the lead, Adok tore into the beast's throat, sending up a spray of red. As the beast fell backward, two other creatures rammed swords into Adok. The wolf howled, a horrible wail of rage and pain.

Salvarias choked out a *no* as he stiffly drew his rune. Five fire shards sailed for the creatures. Three went down, but a fourth still sprinted for Salvarias. Weeping in desperation, he raised his hand to draw a rune, but it was too late. The jagged sword slashed down. Salvarias dodged and it saved his life, if barely. The blade tore across his side, flaying his skin. Staggering aside, he turned to find the sword swiping for him again. He raised his arm and cried out when the metal bit into his flesh. Bright blood gushed up. Pain from the first wound throbbed, his vision bouncing with each sporadic beat of his heart.

The creature yanked the sword free, raised it again, and brought it down with a roar. Salvarias fell out of the way, shouted a spell, jerked out a rune, and sent an ice sword straight through the creature's chest.

The beast looked down at the ice-blue blade, gurgled something unintelligible, and toppled over.

Blackness pulsed on the edge of Salvarias's vision, movement was sheer agony, but he crawled over to the motionless form of Adok.

Two wounds had shredded open the wolf's stomach.

"No," Salvarias wept, balling his fists in the wolf's thick fur. "You cannot leave me."

Adok looked at him with sad golden eyes, but the tone of the wolf's voice was comforting and calm, telling Salvarias to fight on, that one day they would meet again.

"No," Salvarias cried, burying his face in Adok's neck. "I cannot go on without you. You must get up! Get up!"

Adok's tongue slid along Salvarias's hand and stopped suddenly. The wolf's eyes glazed over, mouth hanging open. The last breath wheezed out of Adok.

"No!" Salvarias shouted, shaking the wolf. "No!"

A wisp of black fog bled from Adok's mouth. Salvarias was not interested in what it might mean. It did not matter. He did not care what it would do to him. All that lived in his mind was grief.

Through watery eyes, Salvarias watched it caress his mark, sending a warm tingle through his whole body, easing his pain. Folding in upon himself, he wept. He wept until he could not weep anymore. Then he slept deeply, dreaming of warmth and love, for that was what watched out for him. It was what kept the shadows at bay and the Hunters locked away. It battled his evil. It held him securely, keeping him safe and secret. At one point, it whispered into the darkness of Salvarias's mind and Lunara appeared. She sat by his side and smiled at him. He shifted to rest his head in her lap. Soft fingers ran through his hair, and no longer did he sleep in comforting darkness. He slept in a meadow of sunshine and warmth, blooming with love and hope.

When he woke, he was lying in pool of Adok's cold blood. The wolf's face was relaxed, peaceful even. A blanket of black fog covered Salvarias, but it faded every heartbeat he was awake until he was not sure if it had been real.

What have you done? the presence asked.

For the first time in Salvarias's life, the presence felt ... wrong, as though it was a violation, an unwanted disease.

Ignoring it, Salvarias shoved himself to his feet and walked. He did not walk aimlessly. He walked toward his brother. He was certain of it. And as each foot moved, he came to a realization. He did not want to be alone. He needed Wilhelm. Not for his brother's strength or protection, but for Wilhelm's love. He needed Lunara. Not for the sleep she granted him or the strength, but for her compassion and love.

"I ..." Inhaling a deep breath, Salvarias whispered, "I do not want to be alone."

The walls blocking Lunara crumbled, and her strength rushed into him like a flash flood. Her joy and loved infused itself into his soul, his body.

"Help me," he wept. "I do not want to be alone." His voice rose in a harsh shout, one he filled with all his emptiness, his loneliness. "I do not want to be alone!" Hugging himself, he fell to his knees. "Forgive me," he begged her. "Forgive me, but I love you."

He would never deserve her, but he wanted her, needed her. He hated himself for it, but he choked out his love again, opening himself so she could see how deeply his feelings dwelled, how wholly she owned his heart.

Joy fused with his pain. Her own love roared to life in his mind, in his heart, in his very soul. Then he heard her beckoning to him.

Weeping, he forced his battered body up. He dared not look at his wounds for fear they would spiral him into panic. All he needed to do was walk. One foot in front of the other. And so he did.

He did it for what felt like years, decades. All the while, he begged for his brother. At one point he was attacked again. He paid no mind to what slashed and clawed at him. He cast spell upon spell until the sharp pains stopped. Then he walked more.

It was late in the night when he came to from a stupor. The rain had stopped at one point. Moonlight battled a layer of fading clouds. An owl voiced its eternal question. A wolf howled somewhere.

With Salvarias's next step, his body finally gave out and he tumbled to the ground.

Lunara fed him a surge of strength, but it was no use. His body simply would not move. Glancing down, blood covered him. Some slashes and holes were crusted, others still dribbled blood. Coughing, he tasted it on his tongue and realized he had for some time. Four wounds were fatal, beyond any healer's gift.

He would die. He knew it as he knew the moon was beautiful tonight. He knew it as he knew Lunara would survive. He knew it as he knew his brother would not.

Hot tears fell down his cheeks. Lunara's grief was overwhelming, so much so that he was forced to erect a wall between them. He told her he loved her before he did.

Lying on crunchy pine needles, he stared at the canopy of trees, listening to their soft song, and he smiled. For one moment, he had lived in absolute love. For one moment, he had more than he had ever dreamt of having. It was worth all his years of suffering. That one moment.

A snapping branch drew his attention to the forest. His vision was failing, but what he made out was massive. Happiness drained away, replaced by fear. Blackness of the night surrounded him, and hungry shadows reached for him. He did not want to die in darkness.

"Lumous." He would die in the light.

Chapter 56

Spring 1019 a.r.

Wilhelm bolted through the forest, leaping over fallen trees, feet lighter than they should have been. No hidden rocks or ferns tripped him, no creatures hunted him. The night seemed to melt away for him, gifting safety, blessing his task. He couldn't explain it. Nor would he question it.

He saw a lump on the ground ahead of him. Then his brother's sparrow of light bloomed into existence. A cry of utter relief left Wilhelm's lips until he saw the state of his brother.

Salvarias was red head to toe. All of his skin was flayed open. Blood stained his too pale lips and pooled around him. His arm and foot bent at impossible angles.

Salvarias reached out his good arm and wept, "Brother!"

Wilhelm slid to a stop and fell to his knees. Ignoring his brother's wounds, he swept Salvarias up in a tight embrace. "I'm here, Salv. You're safe. I've got you."

"Forgive me," Salvarias choked. He coughed, his whole body rattling like a broken wooden doll. "Please forgive me."

"There's nothing to forgive, Salv."

"I love you," Salvarias said, tension draining from him. He smiled, curling up against Wilhelm as he done since they were children. There was no pain in his eyes when he met Wilhelm's. Only love and peace. The smile spread up to Salvarias's eyes, brightening the dark night, warming the chilly air, filling Wilhelm with unexplainable happiness. "I fought," Salvarias said. "Just as I promised I would."

Wilhelm smoothed his brother's hair. "I know, Salv. You did great, little brother."

Salvarias hitched, eyes losing focus. "Brother?" His hands groped Wilhelm.

"I'm here, Salv," Wilhelm said, gathering his brother closer, hiding him from the cruel world. "I've got you. You're safe."

Salvarias relaxed again. "My brother."

Those words contained all the love they normally did. Wilhelm rested his cheek on top of Salvarias's head. He swore he could still smell lavender.

"I love you, Salv."

His brother sagged, and a long breath wheezed out of him.

Wilhelm buried his face in Salvarias's crusty hair, and rocked him. "You can't leave me, Salv. You can't leave me."

His brother did not respond, and Wilhelm's world went dark and cold.

Lunara screamed, hugging herself, doubled over in overwhelming grief. Salvarias's presence weakened, but his love for her never waivered. It grew with every rapid heartbeat.

"Lunara!" Varila cried.

Hands wrapped around Lunara's arms and shook her. Nothing could distract her from Salvarias. She stayed focused on him as long as she could, but he began to fade. The warmth of his life always within her, his soul and presence, blinked out. And with it, her own heart stuttered to a halt. The world went black. Through the darkness, a voice called to her, the same voice from her dreams.

"No, my child. It is not time. There is much left for you do. Live, Lunara. Live and help him. Only he can find me."

White light flared. Air sucked into her chest and she gagged on it. A dark forest blossomed in front of her. Varila was crying. Okulu's wide eyes were filling with tears.

Lunara cared about nothing as she curled up and wept. A cavernous pit formed where once there had been love and joy, where the man she loved had once lived.

Chapter 57

Spring 1019 a.r.

Varila followed the procession through the white city of Warton. People lined the streets, though she doubted they knew what the world had just lost. Brice and her mother were on either side of Lunara. Brice's hand rested on Lunara's back, ready to catch her should her steps falter again.

Okulu, Humar, Wilhelm, and Edium carried Salvarias's litter. Wilhelm moved in silence as he had done since he had carried Salvarias's mutilated body back to their camp in Windlous. His eyes were dull and dark, a storm of rage thrashing behind his gaze.

In the litter, she could see Salvarias outlined through the sheer white curtains. Death seemed too respectful of her little brother to maim him anymore. Decay had not touched Salvarias. Cleaned and clothed, he looked as beautiful as he always had been when resting peacefully.

The hunters Humar had sent had found the wolf's corpse. Death had not been so kind to Adok. The wolf had been shipped to Serinity where her father said he'd bury Adok in the gardens. She thought it fitting as so often Salvarias had walked there with his friend.

When they entered the crypt, Varila shivered. Torches sputtered life into the darkness, illuminating a long, straight staircase that took them well under the castle. The masses paying their respects or merely gawking were kept out. Only a small group accompanied them below.

At the bottom, a hallway lined with doors stretched out before them.

Humar led the way past near fifty doors before he stopped in front of one. On it was engraved:

SALVARIAS LAYBRYTH
SPRING 1000 – SUMMER 1019
BELOVED BROTHER AND FRIEND.
MAY HIS LIGHT FOREVER SHINE IN OUR HEARTS.

Within the room, raised on a dais, was a stone tomb. The top was carved with the likeness of Salvarias, done by Mafarias who stood at its side, shedding his own tears.

Together, the four men lowered the litter. Wilhelm reached inside and picked up the limp form of Salvarias. Lunara sobbed and Okulu's shoulders began to shake.

Varila's husband lowered his brother into the tomb, resting the mage on a bed of blankets, the sides lined with white roses per Lunara's request. Wilhelm slipped a pouch under the pillow supporting Salvarias's head. Varila caught a scent of lavender.

No words were spoken. For a man like Salvarias, few would be adequate. They stood in silence, each experiencing their own grief.

It was not long before Wilhelm left. Varila went to the edge of the tomb and gently smoothed Salvarias's hair. Blinking aside tears, she leaned over, kissed his forehead, and whispered, "I love you, little brother. Rest peacefully. One day we'll see each other again."

After giving Lunara a hug, Varila set off to find her husband. She found him in their room, hefting a pack over his shoulder.

"Where are you going?" she asked.

"To kill Sansis," Wilhelm growled.

"I'll come with you," she said, moving toward her pack.

"No," Wilhelm said quietly, his voice shaking with rage. "He left because of you. I lost everything because of you. You're not my wife and you're not part of my life anymore. Go find another man." He turned to leave.

"You can't walk out on me," Varila snapped. "This wasn't my fault and you know it."

Wilhelm opened the door.

"I'm pregnant," Varila blurted.

Wilhelm paused. Turning his head slightly, he said, "It'd be best if the baby didn't know its father. Goodbye, Varila."

Her tears blurred him as he walked out the door. Resting a hand over her belly, she sank to the nearest chair. She wasn't surprised, just disappointed. She'd known the first time she'd seen Wilhelm look at Salvarias that her husband would die if Salvarias did. And so he had.

The Laybryth brothers were no more, and Arden was doomed.

Author Note

Thank you for taking time to read my story. I hope you found it enjoyable. If you have questions, comments, or would just like to talk, you can reach me through my website (booksbylkevans.com), or send me an email at booksbylkevans@gmail.com.

www.ingramcontent.com/pod-product-compliance
Lightning Source LLC
Chambersburg PA
CBHW031022030726
47497CB00004B/966